Doctor Dolittle

VOL. 2

The Complete Collection

READ ALL OF DOCTOR DOLITTLE'S ADVENTURES!

Doctor Dolittle
The Complete Collection, Vol. 1
The Voyages of Doctor Dolittle
The Story of Doctor Dolittle
Doctor Dolittle's Post Office

Doctor Dolittle
The Complete Collection, Vol. 2
Doctor Dolittle's Circus
Doctor Dolittle's Caravan
Doctor Dolittle and the Green Canary

Doctor Dolittle
The Complete Collection, Vol. 3
Doctor Dolittle's Zoo
Doctor Dolittle's Puddleby Adventures
Doctor Dolittle's Garden

Doctor Dolittle
The Complete Collection, Vol. 4
Doctor Dolittle in the Moon
Doctor Dolittle's Return
Doctor Dolittle and the Secret Lake
Gub-Gub's Book

DOCTOR DOLITTLE

VOL. 2

The COMPLETE COLLECTION

Doctor Dolittle's Circus ∗ *Doctor Dolittle's Caravan*
Doctor Dolittle and the Green Canary

HUGH LOFTING

Aladdin

NEW YORK LONDON TORONTO SYDNEY NEW DELHI

This book is a work of fiction. Any references to historical events, real people, or real places are used fictitiously. Other names, characters, places, and events are products of the author's imagination, and any resemblance to actual events or places or persons, living or dead, is entirely coincidental.

ALADDIN
An imprint of Simon & Schuster Children's Publishing Division
1230 Avenue of the Americas, New York, New York 10020
First Aladdin edition November 2019

Cover designed by Karin Paprocki
Interior designed by Mike Rosamilia
The text of this book was set in Oneleigh Pro.
Manufactured in the United States of America 1020 FFG
4 6 8 10 9 7 5 3
Library of Congress Control Number 2018959981
ISBN 978-1-5344-4894-0 (hc)
ISBN 978-1-5344-4893-3 (pbk)
ISBN 978-1-5344-4895-7 (eBook)
These titles were previously published individually with slightly different text and art.

CONTENTS

DOCTOR
DOLITTLE'S
CIRCUS
TOLD AND ILLUSTRATED BY
HUGH LOFTING

Contents

PART FOUR

PART FIVE

PART ONE

THE FIRST CHAPTER

The Fireside Circle

THIS IS THE STORY OF THAT PART OF DOCTOR Dolittle's adventures that came about through his joining and traveling with a circus. He had not planned in the beginning to follow this life for any considerable time. His intention had only been to take the Pushmi-Pullyu out on show long enough to make sufficient money to pay the sailor back for the boat which had been borrowed and wrecked.

But a remark Too-Too had made was true: it was not so hard for John Dolittle to become rich—for indeed he was easily satisfied where money was concerned—but it was a very different matter for him to *remain* rich. Dab-Dab used to say that during the years she had known him he had, to her knowledge, been quite well off five or six times; but that the more money he had, the sooner you could expect him to be poor again.

Dab-Dab's idea of a fortune was not of course very large. But certainly during his experience with the circus the Doctor repeatedly had enough money in his pockets to be considered well-to-do;

and, as regular as clockwork, by the end of the week or the month he would be penniless again.

Well, the point from which we are beginning, then, is where the Dolittle party (Jip the dog, Dab-Dab the duck, Too-Too the owl, Gub-Gub the pig, the Pushmi-Pullyu, and the white mouse) had returned at last to the little house in Puddleby-on-the-Marsh after their long journey from Africa. It was a large family to find food for. And the Doctor, without a penny in his pockets, had been a good deal worried over how he was going to feed it, even during the short time they would be here before arrangements were made to join a circus. However, the thoughtful Dab-Dab had made them carry up from the pirates' ship such supplies as remained in the larder after the voyage was done. These, she said, should last the household—with economy—for a day or two at least.

The animals' delight had at first, on getting back home, banished every care or thought of the morrow from the minds of all—except Dab-Dab. That good housekeeper had gone straight to the kitchen and set about the cleaning of pots and the cooking of food. The rest of them, the Doctor included, had gone out into the garden to re-explore all the well-known spots. And they were still roaming and poking around every nook and corner of their beloved home when they were suddenly summoned to luncheon by Dab-Dab's dinner bell—a frying pan beaten with a spoon. At this there was a grand rush for the back door. And they all came trundling in from the garden, gabbling with delight at the prospect of taking a meal again in the dear old kitchen where they had in times past spent so many jolly hours together.

"It will be cold enough for a fire tonight," said Jip as they took their places at the table. "This September wind has a chilly snap in it. Will you tell us a story after supper, Doctor? It's a long time since we sat around the hearth in a ring."

"Or read to us out of your animal storybooks," said Gub-Gub, "the one about the Fox who tried to steal the King's goose."

"Well, maybe," said the Doctor. "We'll see. We'll see. What delicious sardines these are that the pirates had! From Bordeaux, by the taste of them. There's no mistaking real French sardines."

At this moment the Doctor was called away to see a patient in the surgery—a weasel who had broken a claw. And he was no sooner done with that when a rooster with a sore throat turned up from a neighboring farm. He was so hoarse, he said, he could only

"He could only crow in a whisper."

crow in a whisper, and nobody on his farm woke up in the morning. Then two pheasants arrived to show him a scrawny chick that had never been able to peck properly since it was born.

For, although the people in Puddleby had not yet learned of the Doctor's arrival, news of his coming had already spread among the animals, and the birds. And all that afternoon he was kept busy bandaging, advising, and giving medicine, while a huge motley crowd of creatures waited patiently outside the surgery door.

"Ah me!—just like old times," sighed Dab-Dab. "No peace. Patients clamoring to see him morning, noon, and night."

Jip had been right: by the time darkness came that night it was very chilly. Wood enough was found in the cellar to start a jolly fire in the big chimney. Round this the animals gathered after supper and pestered the Doctor for a story or a chapter from one of his books.

"But look here," said he. "What about the circus? If we're going to make money to pay the sailor back, we've got to be thinking of that. We haven't even found a circus to go with yet. I wonder what's the best way to set about it. They travel all over the place, you know. Let me see: Who could I ask?"

"Sh!" said Too-Too. "Wasn't that the front door bell ringing?"

"Strange!" said the Doctor, getting up from his chair "Callers already?"

"Perhaps it's the old lady with rheumatism," said the white mouse as the Doctor walked out into the hall. "Maybe she didn't find her Oxenthorpe doctor was so very good after all."

After John Dolittle had lit the candles in the hall he opened the front door. And there, standing on the threshold, was the Cat's-Meat-Man.

"Why, it's Matthew Mugg!"

"Why, it's Matthew Mugg, as I'm alive!" he cried. "Come in, Matthew, come in. But how did you know I was here?"

"I felt it in my bones, Doctor," said the Cat's-Meat-Man, stumping into the hall. "Only this morning I says to my wife, 'Theodosia,' I says, 'something tells me the Doctor's got back. And I'm going up to his house tonight to take a look.'"

"Well, I'm glad to see you," said John Dolittle. "Let's go into the kitchen where it's warm."

Although he said he had only come on the chance of finding the Doctor, the Cat's-Meat-Man had brought presents with him:

a knuckle bone off a shoulder of mutton for Jip; a piece of cheese for the white mouse; a turnip for Gub-Gub, and a pot of flowering geraniums for the Doctor. When the visitor was comfortably seated in the armchair before the fire, John Dolittle handed him the tobacco jar from the mantelpiece and told him to fill his pipe.

"I got your letter about the sparrow," said Matthew. "He found you all right, I s'pose."

"Yes, and he was very useful to me. He left the ship when we were off the Devon coast. He was anxious to get back to London."

"Are you home for a long stay now?"

"Well—yes and no," said the Doctor. "I'd like nothing better than to enjoy a few quiet months here and get my garden to rights. It's in a shocking mess. But unfortunately I've got to make some money first."

"Humph," said Matthew, puffing on his pipe. "Meself, I've bin trying to do that all my life—Never was very good at it. But I've got twenty-five shillings saved up, if that would help you."

"It's very kind of you, Matthew, very. The fact is I—er—I need a whole lot of money. I've got to pay back some debts. But listen: I have a strange kind of new animal—a Pushmi-Pullyu. He has two heads. The monkeys in Africa presented him to me after I had cured an epidemic for them. Their idea was that I should travel with him in a circus—on show, you know. Would you like to see him?"

"I surely would," said the Cat's-Meat-Man. "Sounds like something very new."

"He's out in the garden," said the Doctor. "Don't stare at him too hard. He isn't used to it yet. Gets frightfully embarrassed. Let's take a bucket of water with us and just pretend we've brought him a drink."

When Matthew came back into the kitchen with the Doctor he was all smiles and enthusiasm.

"Why, John Dolittle," said he, "you'll make your fortune—sure as you're alive! There's never bin anything seen like that since the world began. And anyway, I always thought you ought to go into the circus business—you, the only man living that knows animal language. When are you going to start?"

"That's just the point. Perhaps you can help me. I'd want to be sure it was a nice circus I was going with—people I would like, you understand."

Matthew Mugg bent forward and tapped the Doctor on the knee with the stem of his pipe.

"I know the very concern you want," said he. "Right now over at Grimbledon there's the nicest little circus you ever saw. Grimbledon Fair's on this week and they'll be there till Saturday. Me and Theodosia saw 'em the first day they was on. It isn't a large circus, but it's a good one—select like. What do you say if I take you over there tomorrow and you have a chat with the ringmaster?"

"Why, that would be splendid," said the Doctor. "But in the meantime don't say anything to anyone about the idea at all. We must keep the Pushmi-Pullyu a secret till he is actually put on show before the public."

THE SECOND CHAPTER

The Doctor Meets a Friend—and a Relative

NOW, MATTHEW MUGG WAS A PECULIAR MAN. He loved trying new jobs—which was one reason, perhaps, that he never made much money. But his attempts to get into some new kind of work usually ended in his coming back to selling cat's meat and rat-catching for farmers and millers around Puddleby.

Matthew had already tried to get a job with the circus at Grimbledon Fair and been refused. But now that he found the Doctor was going into the business—and with such a wonderful exhibition as a Pushmi-Pullyu—his hopes rose again. And as he went home that night he already in imagination saw himself in partnership with his beloved Doctor, running the biggest circus on earth.

The next day he called at the little house early. After Dab-Dab had made them up some sardine sandwiches to take with them for lunch, they set out.

It was a long walk from Puddleby to Grimbledon. But after the Doctor and the Cat's-Meat-Man had been trudging down the road awhile, they heard the sound of hooves behind them. They turned round and there was a farmer coming toward them in a trap. Seeing the two travelers upon the road, the farmer was going to offer them a ride, but his wife did not like the ragged looks of the Cat's-Meat-Man, and she forbade her husband to stop for them.

"What d'yer think of that for Christian charity?" said the Cat's-Meat-Man as the cart went spinning by them. "Sit comfortable in their seats and leave us to walk! That's Isidore Stiles, the biggest potato-grower in these parts. I often catches rats for him. And his wife, the snobby old scarecrow! Did yer see that look she gave me? A rat-catcher ain't good enough company for her!"

"But look," said the Doctor. "They're stopping and turning the trap around."

Now this farmer's horse knew the Doctor very well both by sight and reputation. And as he had trotted by he had recognized the little man tramping along the road as none other than the famous John Dolittle. Delighted to find that his friend had returned to these parts, the horse had then turned around of his own accord and was now trotting back—in spite of his driver's pulling—to greet the Doctor and inquire for his health.

"Where are you going?" asked the horse as he came up.

"We're going to Grimbledon Fair," said the Doctor.

"So are we," said the horse. "Why don't you get into the back of the trap beside the old woman?"

"They haven't invited me," said the Doctor. "See, your farmer is trying to turn you around again toward Grimbledon. Better not anger him. Run along. Don't bother about us. We'll be all right."

Very unwillingly the horse finally obeyed the driver, turned about and set off once more for the fair. But he hadn't gone more than half a mile before he said to himself, "It's a shame the great man should have to walk, while these bumpkins ride. I'm hanged if I'll leave him behind!"

Then he pretended to shy at something in the road, swung the trap around again suddenly and raced back toward the Doctor at full gallop. The farmer's wife screamed and her husband threw all his weight on the reins. But the horse took not the slightest notice. Reaching the Doctor he started rearing and bucking and carrying on like a wild colt.

"Get into the trap, Doctor," he whispered. "Get in, or I'll spill these clowns into the ditch."

The Doctor, fearing an accident, took hold of the horse's bridle and patted him on the nose. Instantly he became as calm and gentle as a lamb.

"Your horse is a little restive, sir," said the Doctor to the farmer. "Would you let me drive him for a spell? I am a veterinary surgeon."

"Why, certainly," said the farmer. "I thought I knew something about horses meself. But I can't do a thing with him this morning."

Then, as the Doctor climbed up and took the reins, the Cat's-Meat-Man got in behind and, chuckling with delight, sat beside the indignant wife.

"Nice day, Mrs. Stiles," said Matthew Mugg. "How are the rats in the barn?"

They reached the Grimbledon about the middle of the morning. The town was very full and busy and holidayfied. In the cattle-market fine cows, prize pigs, fat sheep, and pedigreed draft horses with ribbons in their manes filled the pens.

"The Doctor took hold of the bridle."

Through the good-natured crowds that thronged the streets, the Doctor and Matthew made their way patiently toward the enclosure where the circus was. The Doctor began to get worried that he might be asked to pay to go in, because he hadn't a single penny in his pockets. But at the entrance to the circus they found a high platform erected, with some curtains at the back. It was like a small outdoor theater. On this platform a man with an enormous black mustache was standing. From time to time various showily-dressed persons made their appearance through the curtains, and the big man introduced them to the gaping crowd and told of the wonders they could perform. Whatever they were, be it clowns, acrobats, or snake charmers, he always said they were the greatest in the world. The crowd was tremendously impressed; and every once in a while people in ones and twos would make their way through the throng, pay their money at the little gate, and pass into the circus enclosure.

"There you are," the Cat's-Meat-Man whispered in the Doctor's ear. "Didn't I tell yer it was a good show? Look! People going in by the hundreds."

"Is that big man the manager?" asked the Doctor.

"Yes, that's him. That's Blossom himself—Alexander Blossom. He's the man we've come to see."

The Doctor began to squirm his way forward through the people, with Matthew following behind. Finally he reached the front and started making signs to the big man on the platform above to show that he wanted to speak to him. But Mr. Blossom was so busy bellowing about the wonders of his show that the Doctor—a small man in a big crowd—could not attract his attention.

"Get up on the platform," said Matthew. "Climb up and talk to him."

So the Doctor clambered up one corner of the stage and then suddenly got frightfully embarrassed to find himself facing so large a gathering of people. However, once there, he plucked up his courage and, tapping the shouting showman on the arm, he said:

"Excuse me."

Mr. Blossom stopped roaring about the "Greatest Show on Earth" and gazed down at the little round man who had suddenly appeared beside him.

"Er—er—" the Doctor began.

Then there was a silence. The people began to titter.

Blossom, like most showmen, was never at a loss for words and seldom missed an opportunity of being funny at somebody else's expense. And while John Dolittle was still wondering how to begin, the manager suddenly turned to the crowd again and, waving his arm toward the Doctor, shouted:

"And this, Ladies and Gentlemen, is the original Humpty-Dumpty—the one what gave the king's men so much trouble. Pay your money and come in! Walk up and see 'im fall off the wall!"

At that the crowd roared with laughter and the poor Doctor got more embarrassed than ever.

"Talk to him, Doctor, *talk* to him!" called the Cat's-Meat-Man from down below.

Soon, when the laughter had subsided, the Doctor made another attempt. He had just opened his mouth when a single piercing cry rang from amid the crowd—*"John!"*

The Doctor turned and gazed over the heads of the people to see who was calling him by name. And there on the outskirts of the throng he saw a woman waving violently to him with a green parasol.

"Who is it?" said the Cat's-Meat-Man.

"Heaven preserve us!" groaned the Doctor, shamefacedly climbing down off the stage. "What'll we do now? Matthew—*it's Sarah!*"

THE THIRD CHAPTER

Business Arrangements

"WELL, WELL, SARAH!" SAID JOHN DOLITTLE when he had finally made his way to her. "My, how well and plump you're looking!"

"I'm nothing of the sort, John," said Sarah severely. "Will you please tell me what you mean by gallivanting around on that platform like a clown? Wasn't it enough for you to throw away the best practice in the West Country for the sake of pet mice and frogs and things? Have you no pride? What are you doing up there?"

"I was thinking of going into the circus business," said the Doctor.

Sarah gasped and put her hand to her head as thought about to swoon. Then a long, lean man in parson's clothes who was standing behind her came and took her by the arm.

"What is it, my dear?" said he.

"Launcelot," said Sarah weakly, "this is my brother, John Dolittle. John, this is the Reverend Launcelot Dingle, rector of Grimbledon, my husband. But John, you can't be serious. Go into the circus business! How disgraceful! You must be joking—and who is this person?" she added as Matthew Mugg shuffled up and joined the party.

"This is Matthew Mugg," said the Doctor. "You remember him of course?"

"Ugh!—the rat-catcher," said Sarah, closing her eyes in horror.

"Not at all. He's a meat merchant," said the Doctor. "Mr. Mugg, the Reverend Launcelot Dingle." And the Doctor introduced his ragged, greasy friend as if he had been a king. "He's my most prominent patient," he added.

"But listen, John," said Sarah, "if you do go into this mad business, promise me you'll do it under some other name. Think what it would mean to our position here if it got known that the rector's brother-in-law was a common showman!"

The Doctor thought a moment. Then he smiled.

"All right, Sarah, I'll use some other name. But I can't help it if someone recognizes me, can I?"

After they had bidden farewell to Sarah, the Doctor and Matthew again sought out the manager. They found him counting money at the gate, and this time were able to talk to him at their ease.

John Dolittle described the wonderful animal that he had at home and said he wanted to join the circus with him. Alexander Blossom admitted he would like to see the creature, and told the Doctor to bring him here. But John Dolittle said it would be better and easier if the manager came to Puddleby to look at him.

This was agreed upon. And after they had explained to Blossom how to get to the little house on the Oxenthorpe Road, they set out for home again, very pleased with their success so far.

"If you do go with Blossom's Circus," Matthew asked, as they tramped along the road chewing sardine sandwiches, "will you take me with you, Doctor? I'd come in real handy, taking care of the caravan, feeding and cleaning and the likes o' that."

"You're very welcome to come, Matthew," said the Doctor. "But what about your own business?"

"Oh, that," said Matthew, biting viciously into another sandwich. "There ain't no money in that. Besides, it's so tame, handing out bits of meat on skewers to overfed poodles! There's no—no what d'y' call it?"—(he waved his sandwich toward the sky)—"no adventure in it. I'm naturally venturesome—reckless like—always was, from my

"He waved his sandwich toward the sky."

cradle up. Now the circus: that's the real life! That's a man's job."

"But how about your wife?" asked the Doctor.

"Theodosia? Oh, she'd come along. She's venturesome, like me. She could mend the clothes and do odd jobs. What do you think?"

"What do I think?" asked the Doctor, who was staring down at the road as he walked. "I was thinking of Sarah."

"Strange gent, that what she married, ain't he," said Matthew, "the Reverend Dangle?"

"Dingle," the Doctor corrected. "Yes. He's venturesome too. It's a funny world—Poor dear Sarah!—Poor old Dingle!—Well, well."

Late that night, when the Grimbledon Fair had closed, Mr. Blossom, the ringmaster, came to the Doctor's house in Puddleby.

After he had been shown by the light of a lantern the Pushmi-Pullyu grazing on the lawn, he came back into the library with the Doctor and said:

"How much do you want for that animal?"

"No, no, he's not for sale," said the Doctor.

"Oh, come now," said the manager. "You don't want him. Anyone could see you're not a regular showman. I'll give you twenty pounds for him."

"No," said the Doctor.

"Thirty pounds," said Blossom.

Still the Doctor refused.

"Forty pounds—fifty pounds," said the manager. Then he went up and up, offering prices that made the Cat's-Meat-Man, who was listening, open his eyes wider and wider with wonder.

"It's no use," said the Doctor at last. "You must either take me with the animal into your circus or leave him where he is. I have promised that I myself will see he is properly treated."

"What do you mean?" asked the showman. "Ain't he your property? Who did you promise?"

"He's his own property," said the Doctor. "He came here to oblige me. It was to himself, the Pushmi-Pullyu, that I gave my promise."

"What! Are you crazy?" asked the showman.

Matthew Mugg was going to explain to Blossom that the Doctor could speak animals' language. But John Dolittle motioned to him to be silent.

"And so you see," he went on, "you must either take me *and* the animal or neither."

Then Blossom said no, he wouldn't agree to that arrangement. And to Matthew's great disappointment and grief, he took his hat and left.

But he had expected the Doctor to change his mind and give in. And he hadn't been gone more than ten minutes before he rang the doorbell and said that he had come back to talk it over.

Well, the upshot of it was that the showman finally consented to all the Doctor asked. The Pushmi-Pullyu and his party were to be provided with a new wagon all to themselves and, although traveling as part of the circus, were to be entirely free and independent. The money made was to be divided equally between the Doctor and the manager. Whenever the Pushmi-Pullyu wanted a day off he was to have it, and whatever kind of food he asked for was to be provided by Blossom.

When all the arrangements had been gone into, the man said he would send the caravan here the next day, and prepared to go.

"By the way," he said, pausing at the front door. "What's your name?"

The Doctor was just about to tell him, when he remembered Sarah's request.

"Oh, well, call me John Smith," said he.

"All right, Mr. Smith," said the showman. "Have your party ready by eleven in the morning. Good night."

"Good night," said the Doctor.

As soon as the door had closed Dab-Dab, Gub-Gub, Jip, Too-Too, and the white mouse, who had been hiding and listening in various corners of the house, all came out into the hall and started chattering at the top of their voices.

"Hooray!" grunted Gub-Gub. "Hooray for the circus!"

"My," said Matthew to the Doctor, "you're not such a bad

"Hooray for the circus!"

businessman after all! You got Blossom to give in to everything. He wasn't going to let the chance slip. Did you see how quickly he came back when he thought the deal was off? I'll bet he expects to make a lot of money out of us."

"Poor old home," sighed Dab-Dab, affectionately dusting off the hat rack. "To leave it again so soon!"

"Hooray!" yelled Gub-Gub, trying to stand on his hind legs and balance the Doctor's hat on his nose—"Hooray for the circus!—Tomorrow!—*Whee!*"

THE FOURTH CHAPTER

The Doctor Is Discovered

VERY EARLY THE NEXT MORNING DAB-DAB had the whole house astir. She said breakfast must be eaten and the table cleared before seven, if everything was to be ready for their departure by eleven.

As a matter of fact, the diligent housekeeper had the house closed and everybody waiting outside on the front steps hours before the wagon arrived. But the Doctor, for one, was still kept busy. For up to the last minute animal patients were still coming in from all parts of the countryside, with various ailments to be cured.

At last Jip, who had been out scouting, came rushing back to the party gathered in the garden.

"The wagon's coming," he panted. "All red and yellow—it's just around the bend."

Then everybody got excited and began grabbing their parcels. Gub-Gub's luggage was a bundle of turnips; and just as he was hurrying down the steps to the road the string broke and the round, white vegetables went rolling all over the place.

"Waiting on the front steps"

The wagon, when it finally came in sight, was certainly a thing of beauty. It was made like a gypsy caravan, with windows and a door and a chimney. It was very colorfully painted and quite new.

Not so the horse; he was quite old. The Doctor said that never had he seen an animal so worn out and weary. He got into conversation with him and found out that he had been working in the circus for thirty-five years. He was very sick of it he said. His name was Beppo. The Doctor decided he would tell Blossom that it was high time Beppo should be pensioned off and allowed to live in peace.

In spite of the newness of the van, Dab-Dab swept it out before she put the packages in it. She had the Doctor's bedding tied up in a sheet, like a bundle of clothes for the laundry. And she was most careful that this should not get dirty.

When the animals and the baggage were all in, the Doctor got terribly afraid that the load would be too much for the old horse to pull. And he wanted to push behind, to help. But Beppo said he could manage it all right. However, the Doctor would not add to the weight by getting in himself. And when the door was shut and the window curtains drawn, so no one could see the Pushmi-Pullyu on the way, they set out for Grimbledon, with the man who had brought the wagon driving and the Doctor and the Cat's-Meat-Man walking behind.

On the way through Puddleby marketplace the driver stopped to get something at a shop. And while the caravan waited outside, a crowd gathered about the wagon, wanting to know where it was going and what was inside. Matthew Mugg, his chest now swelling with pride, was dying to tell them, but the Doctor wouldn't let him make any speeches.

They reached the Grimbledon Fairgrounds about two o'clock in the afternoon and entered the circus enclosure by a back gate. Inside they found the great Blossom himself, waiting to welcome them.

He seemed quite surprised, on the van's being opened, to find the odd collection of creatures the Doctor had brought with him—he was particularly astonished at the pig. However, he was so delighted to have the Pushmi-Pullyu that he didn't mind.

He at once led them to what he called their stand—which, he said, he had had built for them that very morning. This the Doctor found to be similar to the place where he had first spoken with Blossom. It was a platform raised three feet from the ground so that the board-and-canvas room on the top of it could be seen. It had steps up to it, and a little way back from the front edge of the platform curtains covered the entrance to the room, so no one could see inside unless they paid to go in.

Across the front of it was a sign:

THE PUSHMI-PULLYU!
COME AND SEE THE MARVELOUS
TWO-HEADED ANIMAL
FROM THE JUNGLES OF AFRICA!
ADMISSION SIXPENCE

The red-and-yellow wagon (in which the Doctor's party, with the exception of the Pushmi-Pullyu, were to live) was backed behind the "stand." And Dab-Dab immediately set about making up beds and arranging the inside so it would be homelike.

Blossom wanted to have the Pushmi-Pullyu put on show at once, but the Doctor refused. He said any wild animal would need to rest after the journey from Puddleby. And he wished the timid beast to get used to the noisy bustle of circus life before he was stared at by a crowd of holidaymakers.

Blossom was disappointed, but he had to give in. Then, to the animals' delight, he offered to show the Doctor around the circus and introduce him to the various performers. So after the Pushmi-Pullyu had been moved to his new home in the stand and the Doctor had seen that he was provided with hay and water and bedding, the Puddleby party started out to make a tour of the circus under the guidance of the great Alexander Blossom, ringmaster.

The main show took place only twice a day (at two in the afternoon and at six thirty at night), in a big tent in the middle of the enclosure. But all around this there were smaller tents and stands, most of which you had to pay extra to get into. They contained all manner of wonders: shooting galleries; guessing games; bearded ladies; merry-go-rounds; strong men, snake charmers; a menagerie and many more.

Blossom took the Doctor and his friends to the menagerie first. It was a dingy third-rate sort of collection. Most of the animals seemed dirty and unhappy. The Doctor was so saddened he was all for having an argument with Blossom over it. But the Cat's-Meat-Man whispered in his ear:

"Don't be starting trouble right away, Doctor. Wait a while. After the boss sees how valuable you are with performing animals you'll be able to do what you like with him. If you kick up a fuss now we'll maybe lose our job. Then you won't be able to do anything."

This struck John Dolittle as good advice. And he contented himself for the present with whispering to the animals through the bars of their cages that later he hoped to do something for them.

Just as they had entered, a dirty man was taking around a group of country folk to show them the collection. Stopping before a cage where a small furry animal was imprisoned, the man called out:

"And this, ladies and gents, is the famous Hurri-Gurri, from the forests of Patagonia. 'E 'angs from the trees by 'is tail. Pass on to the next cage."

The Doctor, followed by Gub-Gub, went over and looked in at "the famous Hurri-Gurri."

"Why," said he, "that's nothing but a common opossum from America. One of the marsupials."

"One of the marsupials"

"How do you know it's a Ma Soupial, Doctor?" asked Gub-Gub. "She hasn't any children with her. Perhaps, it's a Pa Soupial."

"And this," roared the man, standing before the next cage, "is the largest elephant in captivity."

"Almost the smallest one I ever saw," murmured the Doctor.

Then Mr. Blossom suggested that they go on to the next show, Princess Fatima the snake charmer. And he led the way out of the close, evil-smelling menagerie into the open air. As the Doctor passed down the line of cages he hung his head, frowning unhappily. For the various animals, recognizing the great John Dolittle, were all making signs to him to stop and talk with them.

When they entered the snake charmer's tent there were no other visitors there for the moment but themselves. On the small stage they beheld Princess Fatima, powdering her large nose and swearing to herself in cockney. Beside her chair was a big shallow box full of snakes. Matthew Mugg peeped into it, gasped with horror, and then started to run from the tent.

"It's all right, Matthew," the Doctor called out. "Don't be alarmed, they're quite harmless."

"What d'yer mean, harmless?" snorted Princess Fatima, glaring at the Doctor. "They're king cobras, from India—the deadliest snakes livin'."

"They're nothing of the sort," said the Doctor.

"They're American blacksnakes—nonpoisonous." And he tickled one under the chin.

"Leave them snakes alone!" yelled Fatima, rising from her chair. "Or I'll knock yer bloomin' 'ead orf."

At this moment Blossom interfered and introduced the ruffled princess to Mr. Smith.

The conversation that followed (Fatima was still too angry to take much part in it) was interrupted by the arrival of some people who had come to see the snake charmer perform. Blossom led the Doctor's party off into a corner, whispering:

"She's marvelous, Smith. One of the best turns I've got. Just you watch her."

Behind the curtains at the back somebody started beating a drum and playing a pipe. Then Fatima rose, lifted two snakes out of the box, and wound them around her neck and arms.

"Will ze ladies and ze gentlemen step a little closair," she cooed softly to her audience. "Zen zay can see bettair—zo!"

"What's she talking like that for?" Gub-Gub whispered to the Doctor.

"Sh! I suppose she thinks she's speaking with a Middle Eastern accent," said John Dolittle.

"Sounds to me like a hot-potato accent," muttered Gub-Gub. "Isn't she fat and wobbly!"

Noticing that the Doctor did not seem favorably impressed, the circus master led them out to see the other sideshows.

Crossing over to the strong man's booth, Gub-Gub caught sight of the Punch-and-Judy show, which was going on at that moment. The play had just reached that point where Toby the dog bites Mr. Punch on the nose. Gub-Gub was fascinated. They could hardly drag him away from it. Indeed, throughout the whole time they spent with the circus, this was his chief delight. He never missed a single performance—and, although the play was always the same and he got to know every word by heart, he never grew tired of it.

At the next booth a large audience was gathered and people were gasping in wonder as the strong man lifted enormous weights in the air. There was no fake about this show. And John Dolittle, deeply interested, joined in the clapping and the gasping.

The strong man was an honest-looking fellow with tremendous muscles. The Doctor took a liking to him right away. One of his tricks was to lie on the stage on his back and lift an enormous dumb-bell with his feet till his legs were sticking right up in the air. It needed balance as well as strength, because if the dumbbell should fall the wrong way, the man would certainly be injured. Today when he had finally brought his legs into an upright position and the crowd was whispering in admiration, suddenly there was a loud crack. One of the boards of the stage had given way. Instantly, down came the big dumbbell right across the man's chest.

The crowd screamed and Blossom jumped up on the platform. It took two men's strength to lift the dumbbell off the strong man's body. But even then he did not arise. He lay motionless, his eyes closed, his face a deathly white.

"Get a doctor," Blossom shouted to the Cat's-Meat-Man. "Hurry! He's hurt hisself—unconscious. A doctor, quick!"

But John Dolittle was already on the stage, standing over the ringmaster, who knelt beside the injured man.

"Get out of the way and let me examine him," he said quietly.

"What can you do? He's hurt bad. Look, his breathing's gone strange. We've got to get a doctor."

"I am a doctor," said John Dolittle. "Matthew, run to the van and get my black bag."

"You a doctor!" said Blossom, getting up off his knees. "Thought you called yourself *Mr. Smith*."

"Of course he's a doctor," came a voice out of the crowd. "There wur a time when he wur the best known doctor in the West Country. I know un. Dolittle's his name—John Dolittle, of Puddleby-on-the-Marsh."

THE FIFTH CHAPTER

The Doctor Is Discouraged

THE DOCTOR FOUND THAT TWO OF THE strong man's ribs had been broken by the dumbbell. However, he prophesied that with so powerful a constitution, the patient should recover quickly. The injured man was put to bed in his own caravan and until he was well again, the Doctor visited him four times a day and Matthew slept in his wagon to nurse him.

The strong man (his show name was Hercules) was very thankful to John Dolittle and became greatly attached to him—and very useful sometimes, as you will see later on.

So the Doctor felt, when he went to bed that first night of his circus career, that if he had made an enemy in Fatima the snake charmer, he had gained a friend in Hercules, the strong man.

Of course, now that he had been recognized as the odd physician of Puddleby-on-the-Marsh, there was no longer any sense in his trying to conceal who he was. And very soon he became known among the circus folk as just "the Doctor"—or "the Doc." On the very high recommendation of Hercules, he was constantly called upon for the cure of small ailments by everyone, from the bearded lady to the clown.

The next day, the Pushmi-Pullyu was put on show for the first time. He was very popular. A two-headed animal had never before been seen in a circus and the people thronged up to pay their money and have a look at him. At first he nearly died of embarrassment and shyness, and he was forever hiding one of his heads under the straw so as not to have to meet the gaze of all those staring eyes. Then the people wouldn't believe he had more than one head. So the Doctor asked him if he would be so good as to keep both of them in view.

"You need not look at the people," he said. "But just let them see that you really have two heads. You can turn your back on the audience—both ends."

But some of the silly people, even when they could see the two heads plainly, kept saying that one must be faked. And they would prod the poor, timid animal with sticks to see if part of him was stuffed. While two farmers were doing this one day the Pushmi-Pullyu got annoyed, and bringing both his heads up sharply at the same time, he jabbed the two inquirers in the legs. Then they knew for sure that he was real and alive all over.

As soon as the Cat's-Meat-Man could be spared from nursing Hercules (he turned the job over to his wife), the Doctor put him on guard inside the stall to see that the animal was not molested by visitors. The poor creature had a terrible time those first days. But when Jip told him how much money was being taken in, he determined to stick it out for John Dolittle's sake. And after a little while, although his opinion of the human race sank very low, he got sort of used to the silly, gaping faces of his audiences and gazed back at them—from both his heads—with fearless superiority and the scorn that they deserved.

During show hours the Doctor used to sit in a chair on the front platform, taking the sixpences and smiling on the people as they went in—for all the world as though every one of them were old friends visiting his home. And in fact he did in this way remeet many folks who had known him in years gone by, including the old lady with rheumatism, Squire Jenkyns, and neighbors from Puddleby.

Poor Dab-Dab was busier than ever now. For in addition to the housekeeping duties, she always had to keep one eye on the Doctor; and many were the scoldings she gave him because he would let the children in for nothing when she wasn't looking.

At the end of each day Blossom, the manager, came to divide up the money. And Too-Too, the mathematician, was always there when the adding was done, to see that the Doctor got his proper share.

Although the Pushmi-Pullyu was so popular, the Doctor saw very early in his new career that it would take quite a time to earn sufficient money to pay the sailor back for the boat—let alone to make enough for himself and his family to live on besides.

He was rather sorry about this; for there were a lot of things in the circus business that he did not like and he was anxious to leave it. While his own show was a perfectly honest affair, there were many features of the circus that were faked; and the Doctor, who always hated fake of any kind, had an uncomfortable feeling that he was part of an establishment not strictly honest. Most of the gambling games were arranged so that those who played them were bound to lose their money.

But the thing that worried the Doctor most was the condition

"Too-Too was always there."

of the animals. Their life, he felt, was in most cases an unhappy one. At the end of his first day with the circus, after the crowds had gone home and all was quiet in the enclosure, he had gone back into the menagerie and talked to the animals there. They nearly all had complaints to make: their cages were not kept properly clean; they did not get enough exercise or room enough; with some the food served was not the kind they liked.

The Doctor heard them all and was so indignant he sought out the ringmaster in his private caravan right away and told him plainly all the things he thought ought to be changed.

Blossom listened patiently until he had finished and then he laughed.

"Why, Doc," said he, "if I was to do all the things you want me to, I might as well leave the business! I'd be ruined. What, pension off the horses? Send the Hurri-Gurri back to his home? Keep the men cleaning out the cages all day? Buy special foods? Have the animals took out for walks every day, like a young lady's academy? Man, you must be crazy! Now, look here: You don't know anything about this game—nothing, see? I've given in to you in all you asked. I'm letting you run your part of the show your own way. But I'm going to run the rest of it my way. Understand? I don't want no interference. It's bad enough to have the strong man on the sick list. I ain't going to go broke just to please your Sunday school ideas. And that's flat."

Sad at heart, the Doctor left the manager's quarters and made his way across to his own caravan. On the steps of his wagon, he found the Cat's-Meat-Man smoking his evening pipe. Close by, Beppo, the old horse, was cropping the scrubby grass of the enclosure by the light of the moon.

"Nice night," said Matthew. "You look kind of worried, Doctor. Anything wrong?"

"Yes," said John Dolittle, sitting down miserably on the steps beside him. "Everything's wrong. I've just been talking to Blossom about improving conditions in the menagerie. He won't do a single thing I ask. I think I'll leave the circus."

"Oh, come now," said Matthew. "Why, you ain't hardly begun, Doctor! Blossom doesn't know yet that you can talk animal language even! Circuses don't have to be bad. *You* could run one that would be a new kind; clean, honest, special—one that everybody in the world would come to see. But you got to get money first. Don't give up so easy."

"No, it's no use, Matthew. I'm doing no good here and I can't stay and see animals unhappy. I never should have gone into the business."

At this moment the old horse, Beppo, hearing his friend's voice, drew near and pushed his muzzle affectionately into the Doctor's ear.

"Hulloa," said John Dolittle. "Beppo, I'm afraid I can be of no help to you. I'm sorry—but I am going to leave the circus."

"But, Doctor," said the old horse, "you're our one hope. Why, only today I heard the elephant and the Talking Horse—the cob who performs in the big show—they were saying how glad they were that you had come. Be patient. You can't change everything in a minute. If you go, then we'll never get anything we want. But we know that if you stay, before long you will be running the whole show the way it should be run. We're not worried as long as you're with us. Only stay. And mark my words, the day will come when the new circus, 'The Dolittle Circus,' will be the greatest on earth."

For a moment the Doctor was silent. And Matthew, who had not understood the conversation with the horse, waited impatiently for him to speak.

At last he arose and turned to go into the caravan.

"Well," said the Cat's-Meat-Man anxiously, "are you going to stay?"

"Yes, Matthew," said the Doctor. "It seems I've got to. Good night."

At the end of that week the Grimbledon Fair was over and the circus had to move on to the next town. It was a big job, this packing up a large show for a long journey by road. And all day Sunday the enclosure was a very busy place. Men ran around everywhere shouting orders. The big tent and the little tents were pulled down and rolled up. The stands were taken apart and piled into wagons. The large space that had looked so cheerful was quickly changed into a drab, untidy mess. It was all very new to the Doctor's pets; and though Dab-Dab joined in the general hustle of packing, the rest of them enjoyed the excitement and the newness of it to no end.

One thing that amused them very much was the change in the appearance of the performers when they got out of their circus dress to travel. Gub-Gub was very confused, because he couldn't recognize anybody anymore. The clown took the white paint off his face. Princess Fatima laid aside her gorgeous garments and appeared like a respectable charwoman ready for a holiday. And the Bearded Lady took off her beard, folded it up, and packed it in a trunk.

Then in a long procession of caravans the circus set out upon the road. The next town to be visited was fifty miles off. This journey could not, of course, be covered in a single day, going at a walk. The nights were to be spent camping out by the roadside or in whatever convenient clear spaces could be found. So, beside the new amusement of seeing the country by day from a home on wheels, the animals had the thrill of spending the nights camping, wherever darkness found them. Jip got lots of fun chasing the rats out of the ditches along the road and often going off across a meadow on the scent of a fox. The slowness of the circus's pace gave him time for all sorts of small adventures; and he could always catch up. But Gub-Gub's chief delight was guessing where they would spend the night.

This part of the life, the halting for sleep, seemed to be

"On the scent of a fox"

enjoyed by all. When the kettle was put on to boil over the roadside fire, everyone cheered up and got talkative. Jip's two friends, the clown's dog and Toby, the Punch-and-Judy dog, always came around as soon as the procession stopped for the night, and joined the Doctor's party. They, too, seemed to be much in favor of John Dolittle's taking charge of the show or running a circus of his own. And when they weren't amusing the family circle with wonderful stories of a show dog's life, they kept telling the Doctor that a real Dolittle Circus would, to their way of thinking, be a perfect institution.

John Dolittle had always said that there were just as many

different characters and types among dogs as there were among people—in fact, more. He had written a book to prove this. He called it *Dog Psychology*. Most metaphysicians had pooh-poohed it, saying that no one but a harebrain would write on such a subject. But this was only to hide the fact that they couldn't understand it.

Certainly these two, Swizzle, the clown's dog, and Toby, the Punch-and-Judy dog, had very different personalities. Swizzle (to look at, he was nothing but a common mongrel) had a great sense of humor. He made a joke out of everything. This may have been partly on account of his profession—helping a clown make people laugh. But it was also part of his philosophy. He told both the Doctor and Jip more than once that when he was still a puppy he had decided that nothing in this world was worth taking seriously. He was a great artist, nevertheless, and could always see the most difficult jokes—even when they were made at his own expense.

It was Swizzle's sense of humor that gave the Doctor the idea for the first comic papers printed for animals—when later he founded the Rat-and-Mouse Club. They were called *Cellar Life* and *Basement Humor* and were intended to bring light entertainment to those who live in dark places.

Toby, the other, was as different from his friend Swizzle as it is possible to be. He was a small dog, a dwarf white poodle. And he took himself and life quite seriously. The most noticeable thing about his character was his determination to get everything that he thought he ought to get. Yet he was not selfish, not at all. The Doctor always said that this shrewd, businesslike quality was to be found in most little dogs—who had to make up for their small

"Toby and Swizzle"

size by an extra share of cheek. The very first time Toby came visiting to John Dolittle's caravan he got on the Doctor's bed and made himself comfortable. Dab-Dab, highly scandalized, tried to put him off. But he wouldn't move. He said the Doctor didn't seem to mind and he was the owner of the bed. And from that time on he always occupied this place in the caravan's evening circle when he came to visit. He had won a special privilege for himself by sheer cheek. He was always demanding privileges, and he usually got them.

But there was one thing in which Toby and Swizzle were alike; and that was the pride they took in their personal friendship with John Dolittle, whom they considered the greatest man on earth.

One night, on the first trip between towns, the procession had stopped by the side of the road as usual. There was a nice old-fashioned farm quite near and Gub-Gub had gone off to see if there were any pigs in the stye. Otherwise the Doctor's family circle was complete. And soon after the kettle had been put on to boil, along came Toby and Swizzle. The night was cool; so instead of making a fire outside, Dab-Dab was using the stove in the caravan, and everybody was sitting around it chatting.

"Have you heard the news, Doctor?" said Toby, jumping up on the bed.

"No," said John Dolittle. "What is it?"

"At the next town—Ashby, you know, quite a large place—we are to pick up Sophie."

"Who in the world is Sophie?" asked the Doctor, getting out his slippers from behind the stove.

"She left us before you joined," said Swizzle. "Sophie's the performing seal—balances balls on her nose and does tricks in the water. She fell sick and Blossom had to leave her behind about a month ago. She's all right now, though, and her keeper is meeting us at Ashby so she can join us again. She's rather a sentimental sort of girl, is Sophie. But she's a good sport, and I'm sure you will like her."

The circus reached Ashby about nine o'clock on a Wednesday evening. It was to open to the public the first thing the following morning. So all through that night, by the light of flares, the men were busy hoisting tents, setting up booths, and spreading tanbark. Even after the Pushmi-Pullyu's stand was put together and the

Doctor's family retired to rest, no one got any sleep; for the ground still shook with the hammers driving pegs; and the air was full of shouts and the spirits of work, till the dusk of dawn crept over the roofs of Ashby and showed the city of canvas that had been built in a night.

John Dolittle decided, as he climbed wearily from his sleepless bed, that circus life took a lot of getting used to. After breakfast, leaving Matthew in charge of his stand, he set out to make the acquaintance of the performing seal.

"Climbed wearily from his sleepless bed"

The Sixth Chapter

Sophie, from Alaska

SOPHIE'S KEEPER, LIKE THE REST OF THE showmen, had by this time got his part of the circus in readiness to open to the public. The seal was accustomed to perform in the big tent twice a day, following the Pinto Brothers (trapeze acrobats) and the Talking Horse. But during the rest of the day she was a sideshow like the Pushmi-Pullyu. Here in an enclosed tank she dived after fish for the amusement of anyone who paid threepence to come and see her.

This morning—it was still quite early—Sophie's keeper was eating his breakfast outside on the steps when the Doctor entered the stand. Inside, a tank about twelve feet across had been let into the ground; and around it was a platform with a railing where visitors stood to watch the performance. Sophie, a fine five-foot Alaskan seal, with sleek skin and intelligent eyes, was wallowing moodily in the water of the tank. When the Doctor spoke to her in her own language, and she realized who her visitor was, she burst into a flood of tears.

"What is the matter?" asked John Dolittle.

The seal, still weeping, did not answer.

"Calm yourself," said the Doctor. "Don't be hysterical. Tell me, are you still sick? I understood you had recovered."

"Oh yes, I got over that," said Sophie through her tears. "It was only an upset stomach. They *will* feed us this stale fish, you know."

"Then what's the matter?" asked the Doctor. "Why are you crying?"

"I was weeping for joy," said Sophie. "I was just thinking as you came in that the only person in the world who could help me in my trouble was John Dolittle. Of course, I had heard all about you through the Post Office and the *Arctic Monthly*. In fact, I had written to you. It was I who contributed those articles on underwater swimming—you remember?—The *Alaskan Wiggle*, you know—double overhand stroke. It was printed in the August edition of your magazine. We were awfully sorry when you had to give up the *Arctic Monthly*. It was tremendously popular among the seals."

"But what was this trouble you were speaking of?" asked the Doctor.

"Oh yes," said Sophie, bursting into tears again. "That just shows you how glad I am; I had forgotten all about it for the moment. You know, when you first came in I thought you were an ordinary visitor. But the very first word of sealish that you spoke—and Alaskan sealish at that—I knew who you were; John Dolittle, the one man in the world I wanted to see! It was too much, I—"

"Come, come!" said the Doctor. "Don't break down again. Tell me what your trouble is."

"Well," said Sophie, "it's this: While I—"

At that moment there was a noise outside, the rattling of a bucket.

"Sh! It's the keeper coming," whispered the Doctor quickly. "Just carry on with your tricks. I'm not letting them know I can talk to the animals."

When the keeper entered to swab the floor, Sophie was frisking and diving for an audience of one: a little fat man with a battered high hat on the back of his head. The keeper just glanced at him, before setting to work, and decided that he was quite an ordinary person, nobody in particular at all.

As soon as the man had finished his mopping and disappeared again, Sophie continued:

"You know," said the seal, "when I fell sick we were performing at Hatley-on-Sea, and I and my keeper—Higgins is his name—stayed there two weeks while the circus went on without us. Now, there's a zoo at Hatley—only a small one—near the esplanade. They have artificial ponds there with seals and otters in them. Well, Higgins got talking to the keeper of these seals one day, and told him about my being sick. And they decided I needed company. So they put me in the pond with the other seals till I should recover. Among them there was an older one who came from the same part of the Bering Strait as I did. He gave me some very bad news about my husband. It seems that ever since I was captured, he has been unhappy and refused to eat. He used to be leader of the herd. But after I was taken away he had worried and grown thin, and finally another seal was elected leader in his place. Now he isn't expected to live." (Quietly Sophie began to weep again.) "I can quite understand it. We were devoted to each other. And although he was so big and strong and no other seal in the herd ever dared to argue with him, without me, well, he was just lost, you know—a mere baby. He relied on me for everything. And now—I don't know what's happening to him. It's just terrible—terrible!"

"Well, wait a minute," said the Doctor. "Don't cry. What do you think ought to be done?"

"I ought to go to him," said Sophie, raising herself in the water and spreading out her flippers. "I ought to be by his side. He is the proper leader of the herd and he needs me. I hoped I might escape at Hatley, but not a chance did I get."

"I ought to go to him."

"Humph!" muttered the Doctor. "It's an awful long way to the Bering Strait. How on earth would you get there?"

"That's just what I wanted to see you about," said Sophie. "Overland, of course, my rate of travel is very slow. If I could only have got away at Hatley I'd have been all right. Because, of course," she added with a powerful swish of her tail that slopped half the water out of the tank, "once I reached the sea I'd be up to Alaska in no time."

"Ah yes," the Doctor agreed, as he shook the water out of his boots. "I see you are a powerful swimmer. How far are we from the coast here?"

"About a hundred miles," said Sophie. "Oh dear! Poor Slushy! My poor, poor Slushy!"

"Poor who?" asked the Doctor.

"Slushy," said the seal. "That's my husband's name. He relied on me in everything, poor, simple Slushy. What shall I do? What *shall* I do?"

"Well, now listen," said John Dolittle. "This is no easy matter, to smuggle you to the sea. I don't say it's impossible. But it needs thinking out. Perhaps I can get you free some other way—openly. In the meantime I'll send word up to your husband by bird messenger and tell him to stop worrying, because you are all right. And the same messenger can bring us back news of how he is getting on. Now, cheer up. Here come some people to see you perform."

A schoolmistress with a band of children entered, accompanied by Higgins, the keeper. As they came in a little fat man went out, smiling to himself. Soon the children were laughing with delight at the antics of the big animal in the tank. And Higgins decided that Sophie must now be feeling entirely recovered, for he had never seen her so sprightly or so full of good spirits before.

THE SEVENTH CHAPTER

The Messenger from the North

LATE THAT NIGHT THE DOCTOR TOOK TOO-TOO with him and went to visit the seal again. "Now, Sophie," said he when they had reached the side of the tank, "this owl is a friend of mine, and I want you to describe to him just where in Alaska your husband can be found. Then we'll send him off to the seashore, and he will hand on your message to the gulls who are going northwestward. Let me introduce you: Sophie, this is Too-Too, one of the cleverest birds I know. He is particularly good at mathematics."

The owl sat on the rail while Sophie told him exactly how Slushy could be reached and reeled off a long and loving message for her husband. When she had ended he said:

"I think I'll make for Bristol, Doctor. It is about the nearest coast town. There are always plenty of gulls to be found in the harbor. I'll get one to take this and pass it on to its destination."

"Very good, Too-Too," said the Doctor. "But we want to hurry it all we can. If you can find some seabird who is willing to take it the whole way as a special favor to me, it would be better."

"All right," said Too-Too, preparing to depart. "Leave the window of the caravan open, so I can get in. I don't suppose I shall be back much before two in the morning. So long!"

Then the Doctor returned to his wagon and rewrote the last part of his new book, which was called *Animal Nation*. Sophie had given him a lot of helpful hints on good swimming style, which made it necessary for him to add three more chapters.

He got so interested in this he did not notice how the time was passing till, somewhere between two and three in the morning, he suddenly found Too-Too standing on the table before him.

"Doctor," said he, speaking low so he would not wake the animals. "You could never guess whom I met. You remember the gull who brought you the warning about Cape Stephen Light? Well, I ran into him in Bristol Harbor. I hadn't seen him since the good old houseboat days. But I recognized him at once. I told him I was hunting for someone to take a message up to Alaska; and when he heard it was you who sent me, he said he would attend to it himself with pleasure. He doesn't expect to be back under five days, though—at best.

"Splendid, Too-Too, splendid!" said the Doctor.

"I am returning to Bristol Friday," said the owl, "and if he isn't back then, I'll wait till he comes."

The following morning John Dolittle told Sophie that her message had been sent on; and she was very pleased. For the present there was nothing further to be done but to wait for the gull's return.

On Thursday (a day before the time Too-Too had planned to return to Bristol) the Doctor's whole party was seated round the table in the caravan listening to a story from Toby, the Punch-and-Judy dog. Just as Toby paused breathless at the most exciting parts, there came a gentle tapping on the window.

"Booh!" said Gub-Gub—"How spookish!" And he crawled under the bed.

John Dolittle rose, drew back the curtains, and opened the window. On the sill stood the gull who months before had brought him another message by night when he lived in the houseboat post office. Now, weather-beaten and weary, he looked more dead than alive. Gently the Doctor lifted him from the windowsill, and set

"He crawled under the bed."

him down on the table. Then they all drew near, staring at him in silence, waiting for the exhausted bird to speak.

"John Dolittle," said the gull at last, "I didn't wait for Too-Too to meet me in Bristol, because I thought you ought to know at once. The seal herd to which Sophie and her husband belonged are in a bad way—very bad. And it has all come about because Sophie was taken away and her husband Slushy lost the leadership. Winter has set in up there early this year—and my, such a winter! Blizzards, mountainous snowdrifts, the seas frozen months ahead of the usual time. I nearly died of the cold myself—and you know we gulls can stand awful low temperatures. Well, leadership for the seal herds is tremendously important in bad weather. They're not much different from sheep—same as all animals that travel and live in packs. And without a big, strong boss to lead them to the open fishing and the protected wintering places, they're just lost, that's all—helpless. Now it seems that ever since Slushy started to mope, they've had one leader after another—and none of them any good. Arguments and little revolutions going on in the herd all the while. And in the meantime, the walruses and sea lions are driving them out of all the best fishing and the seal hunters are killing them right and left. No seal herd can last long against the fur hunters up there if they haven't got a good leader with wits enough to keep them out of danger. Slushy was the best they ever had, as strong as an ox. Now all he does is lie on an iceberg, mooning and weeping because his favorite wife's been taken away. He's got hundreds more, just as good-looking, but the only one he wants is Sophie, and there you are. The herd's just going to pieces. In the days of Slushy's leadership, they tell me it was the finest seal herd in the Arctic Circle. Now, most likely, with this extra bad winter setting in, it'll be wiped right out."

For fully a minute after the gull finished his long speech silence reigned in the caravan.

Finally John Dolittle said:

"Toby, does Sophie belong to Blossom or to Higgins?"

"To Higgins, Doctor," said the little dog. "He does something the same as you do; in return for letting the seal perform in the big ring, Higgins gets his stand in the circus free, and pockets whatever money he makes on her as a sideshow."

"Well, that *isn't* the same as me at all," said the Doctor. "The big difference is that the Pushmi-Pullyu is here of his own accord and Sophie is kept against her will. It is a perfect scandal that hunters can go up to the Arctic and capture any animals they like, breaking up families and upsetting herd government and community life in this way—a crying shame! Toby, how much does a seal cost?"

"They vary in price, Doctor," said Toby. "But I heard Sophie say that when Higgins bought her in Liverpool from the men who had caught her, he paid twenty pounds for her. She had been trained on the ship to do tricks before she landed."

"How much have we got in the money box, Too-Too?" asked the Doctor.

"All of last week's gate money," said the owl, "except one shilling and threepence. The threepence you spent to get your hair cut and the shilling went to celery for Gub-Gub."

"Well, what does that bring the total to?"

Too-Too, the mathematician, cocked his head on one side and closed his left eye—as he always did when calculating.

"Two pounds, seven shillings," he murmured, "minus one shilling and threepence leaves—er—leaves—two pounds five shillings and ninepence, cash in hand, net."

"Good Lord!" groaned the Doctor, "barely enough to buy a tenth of Sophie! I wonder if there's anyone I could borrow from. That's the only good thing about being a people's doctor. When I had a practice I could borrow from my patients."

"If I remember rightly," muttered Dab-Dab, "it was more often your patients that borrowed from you."

"Blossom wouldn't let you buy her even if you had the money," said Swizzle. "Higgins is under contract—made a promise—to travel with the circus for a year."

"Very well, then," said the Doctor. "There's only one thing to be done. That seal doesn't belong to those men, anyhow. She's a free citizen of the Arctic Circle. And if she wants to go back there, back she shall go. Sophie must escape."

Before his pets went to bed that night, the Doctor made them promise that for the present they would say nothing to the seal about the bad news the gull had brought. It would only worry her, he told them. And until he had helped her to get safely to the sea, there was no need for her to know.

Then, until the early hours of the morning, he sat up with Matthew making plans for Sophie's flight. At first the Cat's-Meat-Man was very much against the idea.

"Why, Doctor," said he, "you'll get arrested if you're caught. Helping that seal escape from her owner! They'll call it stealing."

"I don't care that much," said the Doctor, snapping his fingers. "Let them call it what they like. Let them arrest me—if they catch me. If the case is taken to the courts, at least I'll get a chance to say a word for the rights of wild animals."

"They won't listen to you, Doctor," said Matthew. "They'll say you're a sentimental crank. Higgins would win easy. Rights of property and all that. I see your point, but the judge wouldn't. He'd tell you to pay Higgins his twenty pounds for a lost seal. And if you couldn't, you'd go to jail."

"I don't care," the Doctor repeated. "But listen, Matthew: I wouldn't want you to get mixed up in it if you don't think it's right. I shall have to use deception if I'm to be successful. And I should be very sorry to get you into trouble. If you would prefer to stay clear of it, say so now. But for my part, my mind is made up: Sophie is going to Alaska even if I have to go to jail—that will be nothing new. I've been in jail before."

"So have I," said the Cat's-Meat-Man. Was you ever in Cardiff Jail? By Jingo, that's a rotten one! The worst I was ever in."

"No," said the Doctor. "I've only been in African jails—as yet. They're bad enough. But let us get back to the point. Would you sooner not help me in this? It's against the law—I know—even if I think the law is wrong. Understand, I shan't be the least offended if you have conscientious objections to aiding and abetting me. Eh?"

"Conscientious objections, me eye!" said the Cat's-Meat-Man, opening the window and spitting accurately out into the night. "O' course I'll help you, Doctor. That old sour-faced Higgins ain't got no right to that seal. She's a free creature of the seas. If he paid twenty pounds for her, more fool him. What you say goes, Doctor. Ain't we kind of partners in this here circus business? I think it's a good kind of a lark meself. Didn't I tell you I was venturesome? Lor' bless us! I done worse things than help a performin' seal to elope. Why, that time I was telling you of, when I was jailed in Cardiff—do you know what it was for?"

"No, I have no idea," said the Doctor. "Some slight error, I have no doubt. Now let us—"

"It was no slight error," said Matthew, "I—"

"Well, never mind it now," said John Dolittle quickly. "We all make mistakes, you know." ("It was no mistake, neither," muttered Matthew as the Doctor hurried on.) "If you are quite sure that you will have no regrets about going into this—er—matter with me, let us consider ways and means. It will be necessary, I think, in order to avoid getting Blossom suspicious, for me to leave the circus for a few days. I will say I have business to attend to—which is quite true, even if I don't attend to it. But it would look very odd if I and Sophie disappeared the same night. So I will go first, leaving you in charge of my show. Then a day—or better, two days—later, Sophie will disappear."

"Also on business," put in Matthew, chuckling. "You mean you'll leave me the job of letting her out of her tank after you're gone?"

"Yes, if you don't mind," said the Doctor.

"It'll give me great pleasure," said the Cat's-Meat-Man.

"Splendid!" said the Doctor. "I'll arrange beforehand with Sophie where she is to meet me, once she's clear of the circus. And then—"

"And then your job will begin in earnest," laughed Matthew Mugg.

PART TWO

The First Chapter

Planning the Escape

ALTHOUGH THE PLANS FOR SOPHIE'S ESCAPE were of course kept a strict secret from any of the people in Blossom's establishment, the animals of the circus soon got to know of them through Jip, Toby, and Swizzle. And for days before the flight took place it was the one subject of conversation in the menagerie, in the stables, and in the Doctor's caravan.

When John Dolittle returned from telling Blossom that he was about to leave the circus on business for a few days, he found his own animals seated about the table in the wagon talking in whispers.

"Well, Doctor," said Matthew, who was sitting on the steps, "did you speak to the boss?"

"Yes," said the Doctor. "I told him. It's all right. I'm leaving tonight. I felt frightfully guilty and underhanded. I do wish I could do this openly."

"You'd stand a fat chance of succeeding, if you did!" said Matthew. "I don't feel guilty none."

"Listen, Doctor," said Jip. "All the circus animals are tremendously interested in your scheme. They've asked if there's anything they can do to help. When is Sophie going to get away?"

"The day after tomorrow," said John Dolittle. "Matthew, here, will undo the door of her stand just after closing time. But listen, Matthew: you'll have to be awfully careful no one sees you tinkering with the lock. If we *should* get caught we would indeed be in a bad fix then. Tinkering with locks makes it a felony instead of a misdemeanor, or something like that. Do be careful, won't you?"

"You can rely on me, Doctor," said the Cat's-Meat-Man, proudly puffing out his chest. "I've got a way of me own with locks, I have. No force, sort of persuasion like."

"Get clear out of the way as soon as you have let her free," said the Doctor, "so you won't be connected with it at all. Dear me, how like a low-down conspiracy it sounds!"

"Sounds like lots of fun to me," said Matthew.

"To me too," said Jip.

"It'll be the best trick that's been done in this show for a long while," put in Swizzle. "Ladies and Gentlemen: John Dolittle, the world-famous conjurer, will now make a live seal disappear from the stage before your eyes. Abracadabra, Mumble-and-Jabberer, Hoop la—Hey Presto!—*Gone*."

And Swizzle stood on his hind legs and bowed to an imaginary audience behind the stove.

"Well," said the Doctor, "even though it sounds underhanded, I don't feel I'm doing anything wrong—myself. They've no right to keep Sophie in this slavery. How would you and I like it," he asked of Matthew, "to be made to dive for fish into a tub of dirty water for the amusement of loafers?"

"Swizzle bowed to an imaginary audience."

"Rotten!" said Matthew. "I never did care for fish—nor water, neither. But look here, have you arranged with Sophie where she's to meet you?"

"Yes," said John Dolittle. "As soon as she gets clear of the circus enclosure—and don't forget we are relying on you to leave the back gate open as well as Sophie's own door—as soon as she's out of the fence, she is to cross the road where she will find an empty house. Alongside of that there is a small, dark passage, and in that passage I will be waiting for her. My goodness, I do hope everything goes right! It's so dreadfully important for her—and for all those seals in Alaska, too."

"And what are you going to do then," asked Matthew, "when she's got as far as the passage?"

"Well, it's no use trying to plan too far as to detail. My general idea is to make for the Bristol Channel. That's about our shortest cut to the sea from here. Once there, she's all right. But it's nearly a hundred miles as the crow flies; and as we'll have to keep concealed most of the way, I'm not expecting an easy journey. However, there's no sense in meeting your troubles halfway. I've no doubt we shall get along all right once she's safely away from the circus."

Many of the Doctor's pets wanted to accompany him on his coming adventure. Jip tried especially hard to be taken. But in spite of his great desire to have the assistance of his friends, John Dolittle felt that he would arouse less suspicion if he left his entire family with the circus just as it was.

So that night after a final talk with Sophie he set out alone—on business. He took with him most of what money he had, leaving a little with Matthew to pay for the small needs of his establishment while he was away. His "business" as a matter of fact did not take him farther than the next town—which journey he made by a stagecoach. In those days, you see, although there were railways, to be sure, they were as yet very scarce. And most of the cross-country traveling between the smaller towns was still done in the old-fashioned way.

On his arrival at the next town he took a room in an inn and remained there the whole time. Two nights later he returned to Ashby after dark and, entering the town from the far side, made his way through unfrequented streets till he reached the passage that was to be his meeting place with Sophie.

"Made his way through unfrequented streets"

Now all his pets, though they had not been given any particular parts to play in the plot of Sophie's escape, were determined to do anything they could to help things on their own account—which, as you will see, turned out to be a good deal. And as they waited for the arrival of the appointed hour their excitement (which Gub-Gub, for one, worked hard to conceal) grew every minute.

About ten o'clock, when the circus was beginning to close up, Too-Too stationed himself on the top of the menagerie where he could see everything that went on. He had arranged with the elephant and the animals of the collection to start a rumpus in the menagerie on a given signal—to attract, if necessary, the attention of the circus men away from the escaping seal. Gub-Gub gave himself the job of watching Blossom, and he took up a post underneath the ringmaster's private caravan.

There was a full moon, and even after the circus lamps were put out there was still a good deal of light. The Doctor would have postponed the escape on this account until later, but he realized that the state of affairs among the Alaskan seals made it necessary for Sophie to get away as soon as possible.

Well, about an hour after Blossom had locked up the fence gates and retired to his caravan, Matthew slipped away from the Pushmi-Pullyu's stand and sauntered off across the enclosure. Jip, also pretending he was doing nothing in particular, followed him at a short distance. Everyone seemed to be abed and not a soul did Matthew meet till he came to the gate the Doctor had spoken of. Making sure that no one saw him, the Cat's-Meat-Man quickly undid the latch and set the gate ajar. Then he strolled away toward Sophie's stand while Jip remained to watch the gate.

He hadn't been gone more than a minute when along came the circus watchman with a lantern. He closed the gate, and, to Jip's horror, locked it with a key. Jip, still pretending he was just sniffing round the fence after rats, waited till the man had disappeared again. Then raced off toward Sophie's stand to find Matthew.

Now, things had not turned out for the Cat's-Meat-Man as easy as he had expected. On approaching the seal's tank house, he had seen from a distance the figure of Higgins sitting on the steps smoking and looking at the moon. Matthew therefore withdrew into the shadow of a tent and waited till the seal's keeper should go away to bed.

Higgins, he knew, slept in a wagon close to Blossom's on the other side of the enclosure. But while he watched and waited, instead of Higgins going away, another figure, the watchman, joined the man on the steps, sat down, and started chatting. Presently Jip, smelling out Matthew behind the tent, came up and tried frantically to make him understand that the gate he had opened had been closed again and locked.

Jip had very little success in trying to make the Cat's-Meat-Man understand him, and for nearly an hour Matthew stayed in the shadow waiting for the two figures on the steps of Sophie's stand to move away and leave the coast clear for him to let the seal free. In the meantime John Dolittle, in his narrow, dark passage outside the circus enclosure, wondered what the delay was and tried to read his watch by the dim light of the moon.

Finally Matthew decided that the two men were never going to bed. So, swearing under his breath, he crept away from the shadow of the tent and set off to seek Theodosia, his wife.

On arrival at his own wagon he found her darning socks by the light of the candle.

"*Pst!*—Theodosia," he whispered through the window. "Listen."

"Good Lord!" gasped Mrs. Mugg, dropping her needlework. "What a fright you gave me, Matthew! Is it all right? Has the seal got away?"

"No, it's all wrong. Higgins and the watchman are sitting on the steps talking. I can't get near the door while they're there. Go up and draw 'em off for me, will yer? Tell 'em a tent's blown down or something—anything to get 'em away. They're going to sit there all night if something ain't done."

"All right," said Theodosia. "Wait till I get my shawl. I'll bring them over here for some cocoa."

Then the helpful Mrs. Mugg went off and invited Higgins and the watchman to come to her husband's wagon for a little party. Matthew would be along to join them presently, she said.

As soon as the coast was clear the Cat's-Meat-Man sped up the steps of the seal's stand and in a minute his nimble fingers had the door unlocked. Just inside lay Sophie, all ready to start out upon her long journey. With a grunt of thanks she waddled forth into the moonlight, slid down the steps, and set off clumsily toward the gate.

Once more Jip tried his hardest to make Matthew understand that something was wrong. But the Cat's-Meat-Man merely took

"His nimble fingers soon had the door unlocked."

the dog's signals of distress for joy and marched off to join his wife's cocoa party, feeling that his share of the night's work had been well done.

In the meantime Sophie had waddled her way laboriously to the gate and found it locked.

Jip had then gone all around the fence, trying to find a hole big enough for her to get through. But he met with no success. Poor Sophie had escaped the captivity of her tank only to find herself still a prisoner within the circus enclosure.

Everything that had happened up to this had been carefully watched by a little round bird perched on the roof of the menagerie. Too-Too, the listener, the night seer, the mathematician, was more than usually wide-awake. And presently, while Jip was still nosing round the fence trying to find Sophie a way out, he heard the whir of wings over his head and an owl alighted by his side.

"For heaven's sake, Jip," whispered Too-Too, "keep your head. The game will be up if you don't. You're doing no good by running round like that. Get Sophie into hiding—push her under the flap of a tent or something. Look at her, lying out in the moonlight there as though this were Greenland! If anyone should come along and see her we're lost. Hide her until Matthew sees what has happened to the gate. Hurry—I see someone coming."

As Too-Too flew back to his place on the menagerie roof, Jip rushed off to Sophie and in a few hurried words explained the situation to her.

"Come over here," he said. "Get under the skirt of this tent. So—Gosh! Only just in time! There's the light of a lantern moving. Now lie perfectly still and wait till I come and tell you."

And in his small, dark passage beyond the circus fence

John Dolittle once more looked at his watch and muttered:

"What *can* have happened? Will she never come?"

It was not many minutes after Matthew had joined the cocoa party in his own wagon that the watchman rose from the table and said he ought to be getting along on his rounds. The Cat's-Meat-Man, anxious to give Sophie as much time as possible to get away, tried to persuade him to stay.

"Oh, stop and have another cup of cocoa!" said he. "This is a quiet town. Nobody's going to break in. Fill your pipe and let's chat awhile."

"No," said the watchman, "thank ye. I'd like to, but I mustn't. Blossom give me strict orders to keep movin' the whole night. If he was to come and not find me on the job I'd catch it hot."

And in spite of everything Matthew could do to keep him, the watchman took his lamp and left.

Higgins, however, remained. And while the Cat's-Meat-Man and his wife talked pleasantly to him of politics and the weather, they expected any moment to hear a shout outside warning the circus that Sophie had escaped.

But the watchman, when he found the stand open and empty, did not begin by shouting. He came running back to Matthew's wagon.

"Higgins," he yelled, "your seal's gone!"

"Gone!" cried Higgins.

"Gone!" said Matthew. "Can't be possible!"

"I tell you she 'as," said the watchman. "'Er door's open and she ain't there."

"Good heavens!" cried Higgins, springing up. "I could swear I locked the door as usual. But if the gates in the fence was all closed, she can't be far away. We can soon find 'er again. Come on!"

And he ran out of the wagon—with Matthew and Theodosia, pretending to be greatly disturbed, close at his heels.

"I'll go take another look at the gates," said the watchman. "I'm sure they're all right. But I'll make double certain anyway."

Then Higgins, Matthew, and Theodosia raced off for the seal's stand.

"The door's open, sure enough," said Matthew as they came up to it. "'Ow very peculiar!"

"Let's go inside," said Higgins. "Maybe she's hiding at the bottom of the tank."

Then all three of them went in and by the light of matches peered down into the dark water.

Meanwhile the watchman turned up again.

"The gates are all right," he said. "Closed and locked, every one of them."

Then at last Matthew knew something had gone wrong. And while Higgins and the watchman were examining the water with the lamp, he whispered something to his wife, slipped out and ran for the gate, hoping Theodosia would keep the other two at the stand long enough for his purpose.

As a matter of fact she played her part very well, did Mrs. Mugg. Presently Higgins said:

"There ain't nothing under the water. Sophie's not here. Let's go outside and look for her."

Then just as the two men turned to leave Theodosia cried, "What's that?"

"What's what?" said Higgins turning back.

"That—down there," said Mrs. Mugg, pointing into the dirty water. "I thought I saw something move. Bring the lantern nearer."

The watchman crouched over the edge of the tank; and Higgins, beside him, screwed up his eyes to see better.

"I don't see nothing," said the keeper.

"Oh! Oh! I'm feeling faint!" cried Mrs. Mugg. "Help me. I'm going to fall in!"

And Theodosia, a heavy woman, swayed and suddenly crumpled up on top of the two crouching men.

Then, *splash! splash!*—in fell, not Theodosia, but Higgins and the watchman—lamp and all.

"Oh! Oh! I'm feeling faint!"

THE SECOND CHAPTER

"Animals' Night" at the Circus

THE WHITE MOUSE WAS THE ONLY ONE OF the Doctor's pets that witnessed that scene in Sophie's tank-house when Mrs. Mugg pushed the two men into the water by-accident-on-purpose. And for weeks afterward he used to entertain the Dolittle family circle with his description of Mr. Higgins, the seal keeper, diving for fish and coming up for air.

That was one of the busiest and jolliest nights the circus ever had—from the animals' point of view; and the two men falling in the water and yelling for help was the beginning of a grand and noble racket that lasted for a good half hour and finally woke every soul in Ashby out of his sleep.

First of all, Blossom, hearing cries of alarm, came rushing out of his caravan. At the foot of the steps a pig appeared from nowhere, rushed between his legs, and brought him down on his nose. Throughout the whole proceedings Gub-Gub never let Blossom get very far without popping out from behind something and upsetting him.

"A small pig tripped him up."

Next Fatima the snake charmer ran from her boudoir with a candle in one hand and a hammer in the other. She hadn't gone two steps before a mysterious duck flew over her head and with one sweep of its wing blew the candle out. Fatima ran back, relit the candle, and tried again to go to the rescue. But the same thing happened. Dab-Dab kept Fatima almost as busy as Gub-Gub kept Blossom.

Then Mrs. Blossom, hastily donning a dressing gown, appeared upon the scene. She was met by the old horse Beppo, who had a habit of asking people for sugar. She tried to get by him and Beppo made politely to get out of her way. But in doing so he trod on her corns so badly that she went howling back to bed again and did not reappear.

But although the animals managed by various tricks to keep many people occupied, they could not attend to all the circus folk; and before long the watchman and Higgins, yelling murder in the tank, had attracted a whole lot of tent riggers and other showmen to Sophie's stand.

In the meantime, Matthew Mugg had reopened the gate in the fence. But when he looked around for Sophie she was nowhere to be seen. Jip and Too-Too, as a matter of fact, were the only ones who really knew where she was. Jip, however, with all this crowd of men rushing around the seal's stand near the gate, was afraid to give Sophie the word to leave her hiding place. More of Blossom's men kept arriving and adding to the throng. Several lanterns were lit and brought onto the scene. Everybody was shouting, one half asking what the matter was, the other half telling them. Mr. Blossom, after being thrown down in the mud by Gub-Gub for the sixth time, was hitting everyone he met and bellowing like a mad bull. The hubbub and confusion were awful.

At last Higgins and the watchman were fished out of their bathtub, and highly perfumed with kerosene and fish, they joined the hunt.

Everyone was sure that Sophie must be somewhere near—which was quite true: the tent, under the skirt of which she was lying, was only thirty feet from her stand. But the gate by which she was to pass out was also quite near.

While Jip was wondering when the men would move away so he could let her go, Higgins cried out that he had found a track in the soft earth. Then a dozen lanterns were brought forward, and the men started to follow the trail that Sophie had left behind on the way to her hiding place.

Luckily, with so many feet crossing and recrossing the same part of the enclosure, the flipper marks were not easy to make out. Nevertheless, even with Matthew doing his best to lead them off on a wrong scent, the trackers steadily moved in the right direction—toward the tent where poor Sophie, the devoted wife, lay in hiding with a beating heart.

John Dolittle, waiting impatiently in his little passage, had heard the noise of shouting from the circus. He knew that meant Sophie had gotten out from her stand. But as minute after minute went by and still she did not come to the meeting place, the Doctor's uneasiness increased a hundredfold.

But his anxiety was no worse than Jip's. Closer and closer the trackers came toward the spot where he had hidden the seal. The poor dog was in despair.

However, he had forgotten Too-Too the mathematician. From his lookout on the menagerie roof, away off on the far side of the enclosure, the little owl was still surveying the battlefield with a general's eye. He was only waiting till he was sure that all the circus folk had left their beds to join the hunt and that there were no more to come. When he played his masterstroke of strategy he did not want any extra interference from unexpected quarters.

Suddenly he flew down to a ventilator in the menagerie wall and hooted softly. Instantly there began within the most terrible pandemonium that was ever heard. The lion roared, the opossum shrieked, the yak bellowed, the hyena howled, the elephant trumpeted and stamped his floor into kindling wood. It was the grand climax to the animals' conspiracy.

"He stamped his floor into kindling wood."

On the other side of the enclosure the trackers and hunters stood still and listened.

"What in thunder's that?" asked Blossom.

"Coming from the menagerie, ain't it?" said one of the men. "Sounds like the elephant's broke loose."

"I know," said another. "*It's Sophie.* She's got into the menagerie and scared the elephant."

"That's it," said Blossom. "Lord, and us huntin' for 'er over here! To the menagerie!" And he grabbed up a lantern and started to run.

"To the menagerie!" yelled the crowd. And in a moment, to Jip's delight, they were all gone, rushing away to the other side of the enclosure.

All but one. Matthew Mugg, hanging back, pretending to do up his shoelace, saw Jip flash across to a small tent and disappear under the skirt.

"Now," said Jip. "Run, Sophie!—Swim! Fly! Anything! Get out of the gate!"

Hopping and flopping, Sophie covered the ground as best she could while Jip yelped to her to hurry and Matthew held the gate open. At last the seal waddled out onto the road and the Cat's-Meat-Man saw her cross it and disappear into the passage alongside the deserted house. He closed the gate again, and stamped out her tracks at the foot of it. Then he leaned against it mopping his brow.

"Holy smoke!" he sighed. "And I told the Doctor I done worse things than help a seal escape! If I ever—"

A knock sounded on the gate at his back. With shaking hands he opened it once more; and there stood a policeman, his little bull's-eye lantern shining at his belt. Matthew's heart almost stopped beating. He had no love for policemen.

"I ain't done nothing!" he began. "I—"

"What's all the row about?" asked the constable. "You've got the whole town woke up. Lion broke loose or something?"

Matthew heaved a sigh of relief.

"No," he said. "Just a little trouble with the elephant. Got his leg caught in a rope and pulled a tent over. We 'ave 'im straightened out now. Nothing to worry about."

"Oh, is that all?" said the policeman. "Folks was going around asking if the end of the world was come. Good night!"

"Good night, constable!" Matthew closed the gate for the third time. "And give my love to all the little constables," he added under his breath as he set off for the menagerie.

And so at last John Dolittle, waiting, anxious and impatient, in the dark passage alongside the empty house, heard to his delight the sound of a peculiar footstep. A flipper-step, it should more properly be called; for the noise of Sophie traveling over a brick pavement was a curious mix between someone slapping the ground with a wet rag and a sack of potatoes being yanked along a floor.

"Is that you, Sophie?" he whispered.

"Yes," said the seal, hitching herself forward to where the Doctor stood.

"Thank goodness! What in the world kept you so long?"

"Oh, there was some mix-up with the gates," said Sophie. "But hadn't we better be getting out of the town? It doesn't seem to me very safe here."

"There's no chance of that for the present," said the Doctor. "The noise they made in the circus has woken everybody. We dare not try and get through the streets now. I just saw a policeman pass across the end of the passage there—luckily for us, just after you popped into it."

"But then what are we going to do?"

"We'll have to stay here for the present. It would be madness to try and run for it now."

"Well, but suppose they come searching in here. We couldn't—"

At that moment two persons with lanterns stopped at the end of the passage, talked a moment, and moved away.

"Quite so," whispered the Doctor. "This isn't safe either. We must find a better place."

Now, on one side of this alleyway there was a high stone wall and on the other a high brick wall. The brick wall enclosed the back garden belonging to the deserted house.

"If we could only get into that old empty house," murmured the Doctor. "We'd be safe to stay there as long as we wished—till this excitement among the townsfolk dies down. Can you think of any way you could get over that wall?"

The seal measured the height with her eye.

"Eight feet," she murmured. "I could do it with a ladder. I've been trained to walk up ladders. I do it in the circus, you know. Perhaps—"

"Sh!" whispered the Doctor. "There's the policeman's lantern again. Ah, thank goodness, he's passed on! Listen, there's just a chance I may find an orchard ladder in the garden. Now you wait here, lie flat, and wait till I come back."

Then John Dolittle, a very active man in spite of his round figure, drew back and took a running jump at the wall. His fingers caught the top of it; he hauled himself up, threw one leg over, and dropped lightly down into a flower bed on the other side. At the bottom of the garden he saw in the moonlight what he guessed to be a toolshed. Slipping up to the door, he opened it and went in.

Inside his groping hands touched and rattled some empty flowerpots. But he could find no ladder. He found a grass mower, a lawn roller, rakes and tools of every kind, but no ladder. And there seemed little hope of finding one in the dark. So he carefully closed the door, hung his coat over the dirty little cobwebby window, in order that no light should be seen from the outside, and struck a match.

And there, sure enough, hanging against the wall right above his head, was an orchard ladder just the right length. In a moment he had blown out the match, opened the door, and was marching down the garden with the ladder on his shoulder.

Standing it in a firm place, he scaled up and sat astride the wall. Next he pulled the ladder up after him, changed it across to the other side, and lowered the foot end into the passage.

Then John Dolittle, perched astride the top of the wall (looking exactly like Humpty Dumpty), whispered down into the dark passage below him:

"Now climb up, Sophie. I'll keep this end steady. And when

"He lowered the ladder into the garden."

you reach the top get onto the wall beside me till I change the ladder over to the garden side. Don't get flustered now. Easy does it."

It was a good thing that Sophie was so well trained in balancing. Never in the circus had she performed a better trick than she did that night. It was a feat that even a person might well be proud of. But she knew that her freedom, the happiness of her husband, depended on her steadiness. And, though she was in constant fear that any minute someone might come down the passage and discover them, it gave her a real thrill to turn the tables on her captors by using the skill they had taught her in this last grand performance to escape them.

Firmly, rung by rung, she began hoisting her heavy body upward. The ladder, fortunately, was longer than the height of the wall. Thus the Doctor had been able to set it at an easier, flattish slope, instead of straight upright. With the seal's weight it sagged dangerously; and the Doctor on the wall prayed that it would prove strong enough. Being an orchard ladder, for tree pruning, it got very narrow at the top. And it was here, where there was hardly room enough for a seal's two front flappers to take hold, that the ticklish part of the feat came in. Then, from this awkward situation Sophie had to shift her clumsy bulk onto the wall, which was no more than twelve inches wide, while the Doctor changed the ladder.

But in the circus Sophie had been trained to balance herself on small spaces, as well as to climb ladders. And after the Doctor had helped her by leaning down and hoisting her up by the slack of her sealskin jacket, she wiggled herself along the top of the wall beside him and kept her balance as easily as though it were nothing at all.

Then, while Sophie gave a fine imitation of a statue in the moonlight, the Doctor hauled the ladder up after her, swung it over—knocking his own high hat off in the process—and lowered it into the garden once more.

Coming down, Sophie did another of her show tricks: she laid herself across the ladder and slid to the bottom. It was quicker than climbing. And it was lucky she did slide. For the Doctor had hardly lowered the ladder to the lawn when they heard voices in the passage they had left. They had only just got into the garden in time.

"Thank goodness for that!" said the Doctor when the sound of footsteps had died away. "A narrow squeak, Sophie! Well, we're safe for the present, anyway. Nobody would dream of looking for you here. Oh, I say, you're lying on the carnations. Come over here onto the gravel. Now, shall we sleep in the toolshed or the house?"

"This seems good enough to me," said Sophie, wallowing into the long grass of the lawn. "Let's sleep outdoors."

"No, that will never do," said the Doctor. "Look at all the houses around. If we stay in the garden, people could see us out of the top windows when daylight came. Let's sleep in the toolshed. I love the smell of toolsheds—and then we won't have to break open any doors."

"Nor climb any stairs," said Sophie, humping along toward the shed. "I do hate stairs. Ladders I can manage; but stairs are the mischief."

Inside the toolshed they found by the dim light of the moon several old sacks and large quantities of bass-grass. Out of these materials they made themselves two quite comfortable beds.

"My, but it's good to be free!" said Sophie, stretching out her great, silky length. "Are you sleepy, Doctor? I couldn't stay awake another moment if you paid me."

"Well, go to sleep, then," said the Doctor. "I'm going to take a stroll in the garden before turning in."

THE THIRD CHAPTER

In the Deserted Garden

THE DOCTOR, ALWAYS FASCINATED BY ANY kind of a garden, lit his pipe and strolled out of the toolshed into the moonlight.

The neglected appearance of the beds and lawns of this deserted property reminded him of his own beautiful home in Puddleby. There were weeds everywhere. John Dolittle could not abide weeds in flower beds. He pulled one or two away from the roots of a rose tree. Farther along he found them thicker still, nearly smothering a very fine lavender bush.

"Dear me!" he said, tiptoeing back to the shed for a hoe and a basket. "What a shame to neglect a fine place like this!"

And before long he was weeding away by moonlight like a Trojan—just as though the garden were his own and no danger threatened him within a thousand miles.

"After all," he muttered to himself as he piled the basket high with dandelions, "we are occupying the place—and rent-free at that. This is the least I can do for the landlord."

After he had finished the weeding he would have gotten the mower and cut the lawn—except he was afraid the noise might wake the neighbors.

And when, a week later, the owner of the property rented the place to his aunt, that good lady entirely puzzled her nephew by writing to congratulate him on the way he had had his garden kept!

The Doctor, going back to bed after a hard night's work, suddenly discovered that he was hungry. Remembering the apple trees he had noticed behind a wisteria arbor, he turned back. But no fruit could he find. It had all been gathered or taken by marauding boys. Knowing that he would not be able to move about the garden after daylight came, he then started hunting for vegetables. But in this he had no better luck. So, with the prospect of a foodless day before him tomorrow, he finally went to bed.

In the morning the first thing Sophie said when she woke up was:

"My! I've been dreaming about the dear old sea all night. It's given me a wonderful appetite. Is there anything to eat around, Doctor?"

"I'm afraid not," said John Dolittle. "We'll have to go without breakfast—and lunch, too, I fear. I dare not to try to get out of here by daylight. As soon as it gets dark, though, I may be able to go by myself and bring you some kippers or something from a shop. But I hope that late tonight they'll have given up hunting for you and that we can both make for the open country and get on our way to the sea."

Well, Sophie was very brave and made the best of it. But, as the day wore on they both got ravenously hungry. Somewhere near one o'clock in the afternoon, Sophie, suddenly said:

"Sh! Did you hear that?"

"No," said the Doctor, who was looking for onions in a corner of the shed. "What was it?"

"It's a dog barking in the passage—the other side of the garden wall. Come out from under the bench and you'll hear it. Goodness! I do hope they're not hunting me with dogs now. The game's up if they do."

The Doctor crawled out from under a potting table, came to the door and listened. A low, cautious bark reached his ears from over the wall.

"Good Heavens!" he muttered. "That's Jip's voice. I wonder what he wants."

Not far from the shed there was a thick, branchy pear tree standing close to the wall. Making sure no one saw him from the windows of houses overlooking the garden, the Doctor sped across and got behind the tree.

"What is it, Jip?" he called. "Is anything wrong?"

"Let me in," Jip whispered back. "I can't get over the wall."

"How can I?" said the Doctor. "There's no door and I'm afraid the neighbors may see me if I move out in the open."

"Get a rope and tie a basket on the end," whispered Jip. "Then throw it over the wall behind the tree and I'll get in it. When I bark, pull on the rope and haul me up. Hurry! I don't want to be seen around this passage."

Then the Doctor crept back to the toolshed, found a planting line, and tied the garden basket on the end of it.

Returning to the cover of the tree, he threw the basket over the wall, but kept the end of the line in his hand.

Presently a bark sounded from the passage and he started

hauling in the rope. When the basket reached the top of the wall on the other side, Jip's head appeared.

"Keep the rope tight, but tie it to the tree," he whispered. "Then spread your coat out like an apron. I want you to catch some things."

The Doctor did as he was told. And Jip threw down to him the contents of the basket: four ham sandwiches, a bottle of milk, two herrings, a razor, a piece of soap, and a newspaper. Then he threw the empty basket onto the lawn.

"Now catch me," said Jip. "Hold your coat real tight. Ready? One, two, three!"

"My goodness!" said the Doctor, as the dog took the flying dive and landed neatly in the coat. "You could perform in the circus yourself."

"I may take it up some day," said Jip carelessly. "Whereabouts in this place have you been living? In the cellar?"

"No. Over there in the toolshed," whispered the Doctor. "Let's slip across quietly and quickly."

A minute later they were safe in the toolshed, Sophie was gulping a herring, and the Doctor was chewing hungrily on a ham sandwich.

"You're a marvel, Jip," said he with his mouth full. "But how did you know we were here—and in need of food? Both of us were just starving."

"Well," said Jip, throwing the seal another herring, "after Sophie got out of the gate the excitement still went on inside the circus. Blossom and his men hunted around all night. Then we decided, from the people's heads popping out of the windows, that the town, too, was pretty much disturbed by the rumpus. Too-Too was awfully worried.

"The dog took the flying dive."

"'I do hope,' he kept saying, 'that the Doctor has not tried to get out into the country. He'll surely be caught if he has. The thing for him to do for the present is to hide.'

"So all night long we sat up expecting any minute to see you and Sophie dragged back into the circus. Well, morning came and still you hadn't been captured—and, as far as I know, nobody suspects that you, Doctor, have had anything to do with it. But the circus folk were still searching even when daylight came, and Too-Too kept fussing and worrying. So I said to him:

"'I'll soon tell you if the Doctor is still in Ashby or not.'

"And I went off on a tour of inspection. It was a damp

morning and a good one for smelling. I made a circular trip right round the outside of the town. I knew that if you had left it by any means except flying I could pick up your scent. But nowhere did I cross the Dolittle trail. So I went back to Too-Too and I said:

"'The Doctor hasn't left Ashby yet—unless he went by balloon.'

"'Good,' says Too-Too. 'Then he's safe in hiding someplace. He's got wits, has the Doctor—in some things. Now, nose him out—and come back and tell me where he is. In the meantime I'll have some food got ready for him. Both he and the seal will be hungry. They've neither of them had a thing probably since noon yesterday, and they'll certainly have to stay where they are till late tonight.'

"So then I went smelling around *inside* the town and picked up your incoming trail from where the coach stops. And it led me first, as I expected, by roundabout side streets to the dark passage. But from there, to my surprise, it didn't go on—just stopped dead. Sophie's didn't go on any farther either. Well, I knew you couldn't have crept down a rat hole or flown up in the air; and for a couple of minutes I was absolutely fogged. Then, suddenly, I got a whiff of tobacco smoke coming over the wall—I know the brand you smoke—and I was certain you were in the garden. But, if you ask me, I should say that both of you are pretty fine jumpers."

The Doctor laughed as he started on a second sandwich, and even Sophie, wiping her fishy whiskers with the back of her flipper, smiled broadly.

"We didn't jump the wall, Jip," said John Dolittle. "We used that ladder over there. But how did you get this food here without being seen?"

"Sophie smiled."

"It wasn't easy," said Jip, "not by any means. Too-Too and Dab-Dab made up the sandwiches, and we got Sophie's herrings from Higgins's fish pail. The milk was delivered at our wagon by the usual dairyman. Then Too-Too said you'd surely like to see a newspaper—to pass the time—if you had to stay here all day; and I chose *The Morning Gazette*, which is the one we had often seen you reading. Then the white mouse said not to forget your razor and soap, because you hated to go without shaving. And we put *them* in. But all this stuff together weighted quite a lot—too much for me to carry in one trip. So I made two, hiding the first load behind an ash barrel in the passage till I could fetch the second. On the first journey I got stopped by an old woman—you see, I had the things rolled up in the newspaper, so they wouldn't look so noticeable. 'Oh my,' said the old lady, 'look at the nice doggie carrying the newspaper for his master! Come here, clever doggie!'

"Well, I gave her the slip and got away all right. And then on the second trip I met some more idiots—dog idiots. They caught the scent of the herrings I was carrying for Sophie and started following me in droves. I ran all round the town trying to get away from them and nearly lost the luggage more than once. Finally I put my package down and fought the whole bunch of them. No, it wasn't an easy job."

"Goodness!" said the Doctor, finishing his last sandwich and opening the milk. "It's wonderful to have such friends. I'm awfully glad you thought of the razor. I'm getting terribly bristly around the chin. Oh, but I haven't any water."

"You must use milk," said Jip. "Steady! Don't drink it all. We thought of that, too, you see."

"Humph," said the Doctor, setting down the half-empty bottle. "That's an idea. I never shaved with milk before. Ought to be splendid for the complexion. You don't drink it, Sophie, do you? No. Oh well, now we're all fixed up."

And he took off his collar and began to shave.

After he had finished, Jip said:

"Well, I must be leaving, Doctor. I promised them at the caravan I'd come and let them know how everything was going with you as soon as I could. If you don't succeed in getting away tonight I'll be back again the same time tomorrow, with some more grub. The townsfolk have pretty much calmed down. But Higgins and

Blossom haven't given up the hunt yet, by any means. So you will be careful, won't you? You're all safe and snug here. Better stay two days—or even three more, if necessary, rather than run for it too soon and get caught."

"All right, Jip," said the Doctor. "We'll be careful. Thank you ever so much for coming. Remember me to everyone."

"Me too," said Sophie.

"And tell Too-Too and the rest we are ever so grateful for their help," the Doctor added as he opened the door of the shed.

Then they slipped across to the pear tree again. And after he had climbed into the branches of it, the Doctor put Jip inside the basket, over the wall, and let him down on the string into the passage.

Nothing further of excitement happened for some hours. And though from time to time they heard the voices of people hunting for them in the passage and the streets around, a pleasant afternoon was spent by the two fugitives, the Doctor reading the paper and Sophie lolling thoughtfully on her bed.

After darkness began to fall, John Dolittle could no longer see to read; so he and Sophie took to chattering over plans in low tones.

"Do you think we'll be able to get away tonight, Doctor?" asked Sophie. "Surely they'll have given up hunting me by then, won't they?"

"I hope so," said the Doctor. "As soon as it's dark I'll go out into the garden and see if I hear anything. I know how anxious you are to be getting along on your trip. But try and be patient."

About half an hour later the Doctor took the ladder, and mounting near the top of the garden wall, he listened long and carefully.

When he came back to Sophie in the toolshed he was shaking his head.

"There are still an awful lot of people moving about in the streets," he said. "But whether they are circus men hunting you, or just ordinary townsfolk walking abroad, I can't make out. We'd better wait a while longer, I think."

"Oh, dear!" sighed Sophie. "Are we never going to get farther than this garden? Poor Slushy! I'm so worried."

And she began to weep softly in the darkness of the shed.

After another hour had gone by the Doctor went out again. This time, just as he was about to climb the ladder, he heard Jip whispering to him on the other side of the wall.

"Doctor, are you there?"

"Yes, what is it?"

"Listen! Higgins and the boss have gone off somewhere with a wagon. Blossom just came and told Matthew to take on some extra jobs with the circus because he wouldn't be back for a while. Too-Too thinks it's a grand chance for you to make a dash for it and get out of the town. Start in an hour, when the circus is in full swing and the men are all busy. Have you got that?"

"Yes, I heard you. Thank you, Jip. All right. We'll leave in an hour." And the Doctor looked at his watch. "Which way did Blossom go?"

"East—toward Grimbledon. Swizzle followed them out a ways and came back and told us. You make for the West. Turn to the left at the end of this passage and then double to the left again at the next corner. It's a dark bystreet and it leads you out onto the Dunwich Road. Once you reach that you'll be all right. There aren't many houses on it and you'll be in the open country in no time. I'm leaving some more sandwiches here in the passage for you. Pick them up on your way out. Can you hear me?"

"Yes, I understand," whispered the Doctor. Then he ran back to the shed with the good news.

Poor Sophie, when she heard they were to leave that night, stood up on her tail and clapped her flippers with joy.

"Now listen," said the Doctor. "If we meet anyone on the street—and we are pretty sure to—you lie down by the wall and pretend you're a sack I'm carrying—that I'm taking a rest, you see. Try and look as much like a sack as you can. Understand?"

"All right," said Sophie. "I'm frightfully excited. See how my flippers are fluttering."

Well, the Doctor kept an eye on his watch; and long before the hour had passed, he and Sophie were waiting at the foot of the ladder ready and impatient.

Finally, after looking at the time once more, the Doctor whispered:

"All right, I think we can start now. Let me go first, so I can steady the ladder for you, the way I did before."

But alas, for poor Sophie's hopes! Just as the Doctor was halfway up, the noise of distant barking, deep voiced and angry, broke out.

John Dolittle paused on the ladder, frowning. The barking, many dogs baying together, drew nearer.

"What's that?" said Sophie in a tremulous whisper from below. "That's not Jip or any of our dogs."

"No," said the Doctor, climbing down slowly. "There's no mistaking that sound. Sophie, something's gone wrong. That's the baying of bloodhounds—bloodhounds on a scent. And they're coming this way!"

"John Dolittle paused."

THE FOURTH CHAPTER

The Leader of the Bloodhounds

JIP, AFTER HIS LAST CONVERSATION WITH the Doctor over the garden wall, returned to the caravan and his friends, feeling comfortably sure that now everything would go all right.

He and Too-Too were chatting under the table while Dab-Dab was dusting the furniture, when suddenly in rushed Toby, all out of breath.

"Jip," he cried. "The worst has happened! They've got bloodhounds. That's what Blossom and Higgins went off for. There's a man who raises them, it seems, in the next village. They're bringing 'em here in a wagon—six of 'em. I spotted them just as they entered the town over the toll bridge. I ran behind and tried to speak to the dogs. But with the rattle of the wagon wheels they couldn't hear me. If they put those hounds on Sophie's trail she's as good as caught already."

"Confound them!" muttered Jip. "Where are they now, Toby?"

"I don't know. When I left them they were crossing the

marketplace, on their way here at the trot. I raced ahead to let you know as quick as I could."

"All right," said Jip, springing up. "Come with me."

And he dashed out into the night.

"They'll try and pick up the trail from the seal's stand," said Jip as the two dogs ran on together across the enclosure. "Perhaps we can meet them there."

But at the stand there were no bloodhounds.

Jip put his nose to the ground and sniffed just once.

"Drat the luck!" he whispered. "They've been here already and gone off on the trail. Listen, there they are, baying now. Come on! Let's race for the passage. We may be in time yet."

And away he sped like a white arrow toward the gate, while poor little Toby, left far behind, with his flappy ears trailing in the wind, put on his best speed to keep up.

Dashing into the passage, Jip found it simply full of men and dogs and lanterns. Blossom was there, and Higgins and the man who owned the hounds. While the men talked and waved the lamps, the hounds, six great, droopy-jowled beasts, with long ears and bloodshot eyes, sniffed the ground and ran hither and thither about the alley, trying to find where the trail led out. Every once in a while they would lift their noses, open their big mouths, and send a deep-voiced howl rolling toward the moon.

By this time other dogs in the neighborhood were answering their back from every backyard. Jip ran into the crowded passage, pretending to join in the hunt for scent. Picking out the biggest bloodhound, who, he guessed, was the leader, he got alongside of him. Then, still keeping his eyes and nose to the ground, he whispered in dog language:

"Get your duffers out of here. This is the Doctor's business—John Dolittle's."

The bloodhound paused and eyed Jip haughtily.

"Who are you, mongrel?" he said. "We've been set to run down a seal. Stop trying to fool us. John Dolittle is away on a voyage."

"He's nothing of the kind," muttered Jip. "He's on the other side of that wall—not six feet away from us. He is trying to get this seal down to the sea, so she can escape these men with the lanterns—if you idiots will only get out of the way."

"I don't believe you," said the leader. "The last I heard of the Doctor he was traveling in Africa. We must do our duty."

"Duffer! Numbskull!" growled Jip, losing his temper entirely. "I'm telling you the truth. For two pins I'd pull your long ears. You must have been asleep in your kennel the last two years. The Doctor's been back in England over a month. He's traveling with the circus now."

But the leader of the bloodhounds, like many highly trained specialists, was (in everything outside his own profession) very obstinate and a bit stupid. He just simply would not believe that the Doctor wasn't still abroad. In all his famous record as a tracker he had never failed to run down his quarry, once he took up a scent. He had a big reputation and was proud of it. He wasn't going to be misled by every whippersnapper of a dog who came along with an idle tale—no, not he.

Poor Jip was in despair. He saw that the hounds were now sniffing at the wall over which Sophie had climbed. He knew that these great beasts would never leave this neighborhood while the seal was near and her fishy scent so strong all about. It was only a matter of time before Blossom and Higgins would guess that she was in hiding beyond the wall and would have the old house and garden searched.

While he was still arguing an idea came to Jip. He left the knot of bloodhounds and nosed his way carelessly down to the bottom of the passage. The air was now simply full of barks and yelps from dogs of every kind. Jip threw back his head and pretended to join in the chorus. But the message he shouted was directed over the wall to the Doctor:

"These idiots won't believe me. For heaven's sake, tell 'em you're here—*Woof! Woof! WOO—!*"

And then still another doggish voice, coming from the garden, added to the general noise of the night. And this is what it barked:

"It is I, John Dolittle. Won't you please go away? *Wow! Woof! Wow-ow!*"

At the sound of that voice—to Blossom and Higgins no different from any of the other yelps that filled the air—the noses of all six bloodhounds left the ground and twelve long ears cocked up, motionless and listening.

"By ginger!" muttered the leader. "It is he! It's the great man himself."

"What did I tell you?" whispered Jip, shuffling toward him. "Now lead these men off toward the south—out of the town, quick—and don't stop running till morning."

Then the dog trainer saw his prize leader suddenly double round and head out of the passage. To his delight, the others followed his example.

"All right, Mr. Blossom," he yelled, waving his lantern. "They've got the scent again. Come on, follow 'em, follow 'em! They're going fast. Stick to 'em! Run!"

Tumbling over one another to keep up, the three men hurried after the hounds; and Jip, to help the excitement in the right direction, joined the chase, barking for all he was worth.

"They've turned down the street to the south," shouted the owner. "We'll get your seal now, never fear. Ah, they're good dogs! Once they take the scent they never go wrong. Come on, Mr. Blossom. Don't let 'em get too far away."

And in a flash the little dark passage, which a moment before was full and crowded, was left empty in the moonlight.

Poor Sophie, weeping hysterically on the lawn, with the Doctor trying to comfort her, suddenly saw the figure of an owl pop up onto the garden wall.

"Doctor! Doctor!"

"Yes, Too-Too. What is it?"

"Now's your chance! The whole town's joined the hunt. Get your ladder. Hurry!"

And two minutes later, while the hounds, in full cry, led Blossom and Higgins on a grand steeplechase over hill and dale to the southward, the Doctor led Sophie quietly out of Ashby by the Dunwich Road, toward the westward and the sea.

Long afterward, when Sophie's mysterious escape from her circus career had become ancient history, John Dolittle often told his pets that if he had only known at the beginning what kind of a job it was to move a seal secretly over a hundred miles of dry land, he doubted very much if he would have had the courage to undertake it.

The second half of his adventures with Sophie, in which none of his own animals took part, came, indeed, to be a favorite tale with the Dolittle fireside circle for many, many years—particularly one chap-

"A steeplechase over hill and dale"

ter. And whenever the animals were feeding in need of a cheerful yarn, they always pestered the Doctor to retell them the part of his elopement with the seal, which Gub-Gub called "the Grantchester Coach." But we are going ahead of our story.

When Sophie and John Dolittle had traveled down the Dunwich Road as far as where the houses of Ashby ended and the fields of the country began, they both heaved a sigh of relief. What they had been most afraid of while still in the streets was being met by a policeman. The Doctor guessed that Higgins had probably applied to the police station and offered a reward for the return of his lost property. If he had, of course, all the town constables would be very much on the lookout for stray seals.

As they now plodded along the road between hedgerows, the Doctor could tell from Sophie's heavy breathing and very slow pace that even this bit of land travel had already wearied the poor beast. Yet he dared not halt upon the highway.

Spying a copse over in some lonely farming lands to his left, he decided that it would make a good, snug place in which to take a rest. He therefore turned off the road, found a hole in the hedge for Sophie to crawl through, and led her along a ditch that ran up toward the copse.

"He found a hole for Sophie to crawl through."

Arriving at the little clump of trees and brambles, they found it excellent cover and crawled in. It was the kind of place where no one would be likely to come in a month of Sundays—except perhaps stray sportsmen after rabbits, or children berry picking.

"Well," said the Doctor, as Sophie flopped down, panting within the protection of dense hawthorns and furze, "so far, so good."

"My," said Sophie, "but I'm winded! Seals weren't meant for this kind of thing, Doctor. How far do you reckon we've come?"

"About a mile and a half, I should say."

"Good Lord! Is that all? And it's nearly a hundred to the sea! I tell you what I think we ought to do, Doctor; let's make for a river. Rivers always flow to the sea. I can travel in water as fast as a horse can run. But much more of this highroad walking will wear holes in the sole of my stomach. A river's the thing we've got to make for."

"Yes, I think you're right, Sophie. But where to find one? That's the point. If we were anywhere near Puddleby now I could tell you at once. But I don't know a thing about the geography of these parts. I ought to have remembered to bring a map with me. I don't want to be asking people—not yet, anyway. Because I'm still supposed to be miles away from here, attending to business."

"Well, ask some animal, then," said Sophie.

"Of course!" cried the Doctor. "Why didn't I think of that before? Now, what kind of a beast could best give us the information we want?"

"Oh, any sort of water creature will do."

"I know; we'll ask an otter. Otters are about your nearest relatives in England, Sophie. They travel and hunt in fresh water very much the way you do in salt. Now, you stay here and take a good rest and I'll go off and find one."

It was about one o'clock in the morning when the Doctor returned to the copse. The noise he made entering woke Sophie out of a sound sleep.

With him he had brought a rather unusual animal. In odd, curving, graceful leaps this creature kept bounding up out of the high bracken that carpeted the copse to get a good look at Sophie. He seemed somewhat afraid of her, but very interested.

"Isn't she large, Doctor!" the new creature whispered. "Did you say she was related to us?"

"In a way, yes. Though, strictly speaking, she is a *pinniped*, while your people are *musteloids*."

"Oh, well, I'm glad of it. She is so clumsy. And look, she hasn't any hind legs—just sort of stubby things. Are you sure she won't bite?"

Finally, the otter was persuaded that Sophie was harmless, and, drawing close, he talked pleasantly with this other furred fisherman from foreign parts.

"Now," said the Doctor, "as I have told you, we are anxious to get down to the sea by the quickest and quietest way possible. And Sophie thinks that the best thing is to make for some stream."

"Humph!" said the otter. "She's quite right, of course. But you've come to a pretty poor place for waterways. The only reason I stay in this neighborhood is because there are no otter hounds here. I live and do my fishing in a few ponds. They're not much good, but at least I'm not hunted by the packs. There are no decent rivers in these parts—certainly none that *she* could swim in to the sea."

"Well, where do you recommend us to go, then?" asked the Doctor.

"I really don't know," said the otter. "You see, I travel so little myself. I was born in this district. And my mother always told me that this was the only safe place left in England for otters to live. And so I've stayed here—my whole life."

"Well, could you get us some fish, then?" asked Sophie. "I'm famished."

"Oh, surely," said the otter. "Do you eat carp?"

"I'd eat anything just now," said Sophie.

"All right. Wait a minute till I go down to my pond," said the otter, and he turned around and bounded out of the copse.

In less than ten minutes he was back again with a huge brown carp in his mouth. This Sophie disposed of in a couple of gulps.

"Why don't you ask the wild ducks, Doctor?" said the otter. "They travel, following the waterways up and down to the sea, feeding. And they always go by the quietest streams, where they won't meet people. They could tell you."

"Yes, I think you're right," said John Dolittle. "But where can I get hold of any?"

"Oh, that's easy. They're always flying by night. Just go up on a hill some place and listen. When you hear them passing overhead, call 'em."

So, leaving Sophie and her freshwater cousin chatting quietly in the copse, the Doctor climbed up a ridge till he came to a high field, from where he could see the moonlit sky all around him. And after a minute or two he heard, a long way off, a faint quacking and honking—wild ducks on the wing. Presently, high above his head, he could make out a V-shaped cluster of little dots, heading seaward.

Putting his two hands to his mouth like a trumpet, he sent a call hurtling upward. The cluster paused, broke up, and started flying round in circles, coming downward—cautiously—all the time.

Presently in the copse, Sophie and the otter stopped chatting and listened tensely to the sound of approaching footsteps.

Then the figure of John Dolittle stepped into the hiding place, with a lovely green and blue duck tucked comfortably under each arm.

"Well," said the ducks, after the Doctor had explained the situation to them and asked their advice, "the nearest river, big enough to be of any use to a seal, is the Kippet. Unfortunately, there are no brooks or anything leading into it from here. To reach the valley of Kippet River, you'll have to cross about forty miles of land."

"Humph!" said the Doctor. "That sounds bad."

"Very bad," sighed Sophie wearily. "Poor Slushy! Such a time I'm taking to get to him. What kind of land is this that we've got to cross?"

"It varies a good deal," said the ducks. "Some of it's hilly; some of it's flat; part of it standing crops; part of it heath. It's very mixed traveling."

"Dear me!" groaned Sophie.

"Yes," said the ducks, "it would be easier, as far as the river, if you went by road."

"But don't you see," said the Doctor, "I'm afraid of being met and stopped? That's why we left the Dunwich Road. There are too many people who've heard of our escape round these parts."

"But," said the ducks, "you wouldn't have to go back onto the Dunwich Road. Listen; if you follow that hedge on westward, it will lead you down onto another road, the old Roman road from Igglesby to Grantchester. Coaches use it, going north and south. You're not likely to meet Ashby folks on that. Well, if you go along

"'Yes,' said the ducks."

that road for about forty miles north you'll come to the Kippet River. The highway crosses it at Talbot's Bridge—just before you enter the town of Grantchester."

"It sounds simple for a good walker," said the Doctor. "But for Sophie it's another matter. Still, I suppose it's the best. Follow the Grantchester Road north as far as Talbot's Bridge, and there take to the river, the Kippet—is that it?"

"That's right," said the ducks. "You can't go wrong, once you reach the road. After you take it to the stream you'd better make some more inquiries of other waterfowl, because, although the

Kippet will lead you to the sea, there are places on it where you must be careful."

"Very good," said the Doctor. "You have been most kind. I thank you."

Then the ducks flew off about their business and John Dolittle looked at his watch.

"It's now two o'clock in the morning," said he. "We have three hours more before daylight comes. Would you prefer, Sophie, to stay here and rest till tomorrow evening, or shall we push on and get as far as we can before dawn?"

"Oh, let's push on," said Sophie.

"All right," said the Doctor, "come along."

While they were making their way along the hedge toward the road, the little otter went off and got Sophie a large meal of fresh fish, to help strengthen her for her hard trip. About a mile below, at the end of a long field, he showed them a hole through another hedge, told them the road was just on the other side of it, and bade them farewell.

Crawling through, they came out upon a fine highway that stretched away into the night on either hand, wide and well paved.

With a sigh of resignation from Sophie, they turned to the right and set off northward.

THE FIFTH CHAPTER

The Passengers from Penchurch

"OH DEAR! OH DEAR!" SAID SOPHIE, AFTER they had traveled for about an hour. This road is just as hard and knobby and scrapy as the other one. How far have we come now?"

"About another mile," said the Doctor.

Sophie began to weep big tears into the white dust of the road.

"Always 'about another mile'! I'm afraid I'm being a dreadful nuisance to you, Doctor."

"Oh, not at all," said John Dolittle. "Don't be downhearted. We'll do it yet. It'll be easy going once we reach the river."

"Yes, but we are still thirty-nine miles from that," said Sophie. "And I'm *so* worn out."

The Doctor looked down at her and saw that, indeed, she was in a very exhausted state. There was nothing for it but to halt again.

"Come over here," he said, "off the road. Now, lie down in this ditch, where you won't be seen, and take a rest."

Poor Sophie did as she was told, and the Doctor sat down upon a milestone, thinking hard. Although he was doing his best to cheer Sophie along, it was beginning to look, at this rate, as though they could never get as far as the river.

While he was pondering drearily over the difficulties of the situation, Sophie suddenly said:

"What's that noise?"

The Doctor looked up and listened.

"Wagon wheels," he said. "You're quite safe where you are. Just keep still till it passes. You'll never be seen in the ditch."

The rumbling noise drew nearer, and presently, round a bend in the road, a light came in sight. Soon the Doctor could see that it was a closed carriage of some kind. As it drew level with him the driver stopped his horses and called out:

"Are you waiting for the coach?"

"Er—er," the Doctor stammered. "Oh, are you the coach?"

"We're one of 'em," said the man.

"Where do you go to?" asked the Doctor.

"We are the local," said the driver. "Penchurch to Anglethorpe. D'yer want to get in?"

While he hesitated over an answer, a wild idea came into the Doctor's head.

"Have you got many passengers?" he asked.

"No, only two—man and his wife—and they're asleep. Plenty o' room inside."

The carriage, lit within by a lamp that shone dimly through drawn curtains, had stopped a little beyond the Doctor's milestone. The driver, from where he sat, could see neither Sophie's hiding place, nor the back door of his own coach.

"Are your passengers from these parts?" asked the Doctor, lowering his voice.

"No, we come from Penchurch, I told you. What more would you like to know? If you want to get in, hurry! Can't stay talking all night."

"All right," said the Doctor. "Wait just a second till I get my luggage."

"Want any help?"

"No, no, no! Stay where you are. I can manage."

Then the Doctor slipped behind the end of the coach and opened the door. A man and a woman, with their heads sunk upon their chests, were dozing in the far corner. Leaving the door open, the Doctor ran to the ditch, put his arms around Sophie, and lifted her huge weight bodily in his arms.

"We'll cover part of the ground this way, anyhow," he whispered as he carried her to the coach. "Keep as still and quiet as you can. I'm going to stow you under the seat."

For entering the carriage, whose floor stood high above the level of the road, there were two little iron steps hung below the doorsill. As the Doctor looked in the second time, the passengers were still apparently sleeping. But in trying to mount the steps with his tremendous burden, he stumbled noisily. The woman in the corner woke up and raised her head. The Doctor, Sophie's flippers still clinging about his neck, stared, speechless.

"John!"

It was Sarah.

Mrs. Dingle fainted with a shriek into her husband's arms. The horses bolted. The Doctor lost his balance entirely. And the

"He carried her to the coach."

coach rattled off into the night, leaving him seated in the road, with Sophie on his lap.

"Heigh-ho!" he sighed, picking himself up wearily. "Of course, it would be Sarah! It might have been anyone else in the world, but it *had* to be Sarah. Well, well!"

"But what did you mean to do?" asked Sophie. "You could never have got me under the seat. There wasn't room there to hide a dog."

"Oh, well, I just acted on the spur of the moment," said the Doctor. "I might have got you a few miles on your journey—if

I hadn't stumbled and woken Sarah. Bother it! But, you know, Sophie, I think that the coach idea is our best scheme, anyhow. Only we must arrange it a little differently; we must lay our plans with care. In one way it was a good thing it was Sarah. If it had been anyone else who had seen me carrying a seal they might have talked and set people on our track. But Sarah and her husband are ashamed of my being in the circus business and they won't say anything, we may be sure.

"Now listen: over in the east the sky is growing gray—look. It's no use our trying to get farther today. So we'll hide you in those woods down there, and then I'll go on alone to the next village and find out a few things."

So they moved along the highway a short distance to where some pleasant woods bordered the road.

Entering the cover of these preserves, they found a nice place for Sophie to lie hidden. Then, when he had made her comfortable, the Doctor set out down the road just as the cocks in the nearby farms began crowing their first greeting to the morning sun.

After a walk of about two miles he came to a village with a pretty little ivy-covered inn, called "The Three Huntsmen." Going in he ordered breakfast. He had not had anything to eat since he had left the deserted garden. A very old waiter served him some bacon and eggs in the taproom.

As soon as the Doctor had eaten, he began chatting to the waiter. He found out a whole lot of things about the coaches that ran up and down the Grantchester Road—what the different ones were like to look at, at what hour they were to be expected, which of them were usually crowded, and much more.

Then he left the inn and walked down the street till he came to the few shops the village had. One of these was a general clothier's and haberdasher's. The Doctor entered and asked the price of a lady's cloak that was hanging in the window.

"Fifteen shillings and sixpence," said the woman in charge of the shop. "Is your wife tall?"

"My wife?" asked the Doctor, entirely bewildered. "Oh, ah, yes, of course. Well—er—I want it long, anyway. And I'll take a bonnet, too."

"Is she fair or dark?" asked the woman.

"Er—she's sort of medium," said the Doctor.

"There's a nice one here, with red poppies on it," said the woman. "How would she like that?"

"No, that's too showy," said the Doctor.

"Well, they do say them flowery ones is right fashionable up to London just now. How would this do?"

And the woman brought forward a large, plain, black bonnet. "This is very genteel. I wear this kind myself."

"Yes, I'll take that one," said the Doctor. "And now I want a lady's veil—a heavy one, please."

"Oh, mourning in the family?"

"Er—not exactly. But I want it pretty thick—a traveling veil."

Then the woman added a veil to the Doctor's purchases. And with a large parcel under his arm, he presently left the shop. Next, he went to a grocery and bought some dried herrings for Sophie—the only kind of fish he could obtain in the village. And about noon he started back down the road.

"Sophie," said John Dolittle, when he reached the seal's hiding place in the woods. "I have a whole lot of information for you, some food and some clothes."

"How would this do?"

"Some clothes!" said Sophie. "What would I do with clothes?"

"Wear them," said the Doctor. "You've got to be a lady—for a while, anyhow."

"Great heavens!" grunted Sophie, wiping her whiskers with the back of her flipper. "What for?"

"So as you can travel by coach," said the Doctor.

"But I can't walk upright," cried Sophie, "like a lady."

"I know. But you can sit upright—like a sick lady. You'll have to be a little lame. Any walking there is to be done, I'll carry you."

"But what about my face? It isn't the right shape."

"We'll cover that up with a veil." said the Doctor. "And your hat will disguise the rest of your head. Now, eat this fish I've brought you and then we will rehearse dressing you up. I hear that the Grantchester coach passes by here about eight o'clock—that is, the night one does; and we'll take that, because it's less crowded. Now, it's about a four hours' ride to Talbot's Bridge. During all that time you'll have to sit up on your tail and keep still. Do you think you can manage that?"

"I'll try," said Sophie.

"Perhaps you'll have a chance to lie down for a spell if we have the carriage to ourselves part of the way. Much will depend upon how crowded the coach is. It makes three stops between here and Talbot's Bridge. But being a night coach, I don't suppose it will take on many passengers—if we're lucky. Now, let me try these clothes on you and we'll see how you look."

Then the Doctor dressed up Sophie, the performing seal, like a lady. He seated her on a log, put the bonnet on her head, the veil across her face and the cloak over the rest of her.

After he had gotten her into a human sitting position on the log, it was surprising how natural she looked. In the deep hood of the bonnet her long nose was entirely concealed; and with the veil hung over the front of it, her head looked extraordinarily like a woman's.

"You must be careful to keep your whiskers inside," he said. "That's very important. The cloak is quite long, you see—comes right down to the ground—and while you are seated and it's kept closed in the front it will look quite all right in a dim light. You can keep it drawn together with your flippers. Now, you look just as though you had your hands folded in your lap—that's the idea,

"He put the veil across her face."

splendid! So long as you can stay that way no one would take you for anything but a lady passenger. Oh, look out! Don't wiggle your head or the bonnet will fall off. Wait till I tie the ribbons under your chin."

"How am I supposed to breathe?" asked Sophie, blowing out the veil in front like a balloon.

"Don't do that," said the Doctor. "You're not swimming or coming up for air. You'll get used to it after a while."

"I can't keep very steady this way, Doctor. I'm sitting on the back of my spine, you know. It's an awfully hard position for balancing—much worse than walking on a ladder. What if I should slip down onto the floor of the coach?"

"The seat will be wider than this log and more comfortable. Besides, I'll try to get you into a corner and I'll sit close beside you—so you'll be sort of wedged in. If you feel yourself slipping, just whisper to me and I'll hitch you up into a safer position. You look splendid—really, you do."

After a little more practice and rehearsing, the Doctor felt that Sophie could now pass as a lady passenger. And when evening came it found him by the edge of the road, with a heavily-veiled woman seated at his side, waiting for the Grantchester coach.

THE SIXTH CHAPTER

The Granchester Coach

AFTER THEY HAD WAITED ABOUT A QUARTER of an hour, Sophie said:

"I hear wheels, Doctor. And look, there are the lights, far down the road."

"Yes," said John Dolittle. "But it isn't the coach we want. That's the Twinborough Express—a green light and a white light. The one we want has two white lights in front. Step back a little farther into the shadow of the hedge. Try not to walk on your cloak. You mustn't get it muddy."

A little while after the Twinborough Express had rattled by, along came another.

"Ah!" said the Doctor. "This is ours, the Grantchester coach. Now sit up by the side of the road here and keep perfectly still till I signal the driver. Then I'll lift you in, and let's hope we find a corner seat empty. Is your bonnet on tight?"

"Yes," said Sophie. "But the veil is tickling my nose most awfully. I do hope I don't sneeze."

"So do I," said the Doctor, remembering the cowlike bellow that seals make when they sneeze.

Then John Dolittle stepped out into the middle of the road and stopped the coach. Inside he found three passengers—two men at the far end and an old lady near the door. To his delight, the corner seat opposite the old lady was empty.

Leaving the door open, he ran back and got Sophie and carried her to the coach. The two men at the far end were talking earnestly together about politics. They took little notice as the lame woman was lifted in and made comfortable in the corner seat. But as the Doctor closed the door and sat beside his companion, he noticed that the old lady opposite was very interested in his invalid.

The coach started off, and the Doctor, after making sure that Sophie's feet were not showing below the long cape, got out a newspaper from his pocket. Although the light from the oil lamp overhead was too dim to read by, he spread out the paper before his face and pretended to be deeply absorbed in it.

Presently the old lady leaned forward and tapped Sophie on the knee.

"Excuse me, my dear," she began in a kindly voice.

"Oh, er"—said the Doctor, looking up quickly. "She doesn't talk—er—that is, not any English."

"Has she got far to go?" asked the old lady.

"To Alaska," said the Doctor, forgetting himself, "er—that is, eventually. This journey we're only going to Grantchester."

Wishing people would mind their own business, the Doctor plunged again into his paper as though his life depended on his reading every word.

"'Excuse me, my dear,' she began."

But the kindly passenger was not easily put off. After a moment she leaned forward once more and tapped the Doctor on the knee.

"Is it rheumatics?" she asked in a whisper, nodding toward Sophie. "I noticed that you had to carry her in, poor dear!"

"Er, not exactly," stammered the Doctor. "Her legs are too short. Can't walk. Can't walk a step. Been that way all her life."

"Dear me!" sighed the old lady. "How sad; how very sad!"

"I'm slipping," whispered Sophie behind her veil. "In a minute I'm going to slide onto the floor."

While the Doctor was putting away his newspaper and getting ready to hitch Sophie up higher, the old lady spoke again.

"What a nice sealskin coat she's wearing!"

Sophie's knee was sticking out through the cloak.

"Yes. She has to be kept warm," said the Doctor, busily wrapping his invalid up. "Most important."

"She'll be your daughter, I suppose?" asked the old lady.

But this time Sophie spoke for herself. A deep roar suddenly shook the carriage. The tickling of the veil had finally made her sneeze. The Doctor was now standing up, but before he could catch her she had slid down onto the floor between his feet.

"She's in pain, poor thing," said the old lady. "Wait till I get out my smelling bottle. She's fainted. I often do it myself, traveling. And this coach does smell something horrible—fishylike."

Luckily for the Doctor, the old lady then busied herself hunting in her handbag. He was therefore able, while lifting the seal back onto the seat, to place himself in between Sophie and the two men, who were now also showing interest in her.

"Here you are," said the old lady, handing out a silver smelling bottle. "Lift up her veil and hold it under her nose."

"No thank you," said the Doctor quickly. "All she needs is rest. She's very tired. We'll prop her up snugly in the corner, like this. Now, let's not talk, and probably she'll soon drop off to sleep."

Finally the poor Doctor got the little old lady to mind her own business and keep quiet. And for about an hour and a half the coach continued on its way without anything further happening. But it was quite clear that the men at the other end were puzzled and curious about his invalid. They kept glancing in her direction and talking together in whispers in a way that made him very uneasy.

Presently the coach stopped at a village to change horses. The driver appeared at the door and told the passengers that if they wished to have supper at the inn (in whose yard they had halted), they had half an hour to do so before they went on.

The two men left the coach, eyeing Sophie and the Doctor as they passed on their way out; and soon the old lady followed their example. The driver had now also disappeared, and John Dolittle and his companion had the coach to themselves.

"Listen, Sophie," the Doctor whispered. "I'm getting uneasy about those two men. I'm afraid they suspect that you are not what you pretend to be. You stay here now, while I go in and find out if they're traveling any farther with us."

Then he strolled into the inn. In the passage he met a serving maid and asked the way to the dining room. She showed him an open door with a screen before it a little way down the passage.

"Supper will be served in a minute," she said. "Just walk in and sit down."

"Thank you," said the Doctor. "By the way, do you happen to know who those two men were who came in off the coach just now?"

"Yes, sir," said the maid. "One of them's the County Constable and the other's Mr. Tuttle, the mayor of Penchurch."

"Thank you," said the Doctor, and passed on.

Reaching the screen door, he hesitated a moment before entering the dining room. And presently, he heard the voices of the two men seated at a table within on the other side of the screen.

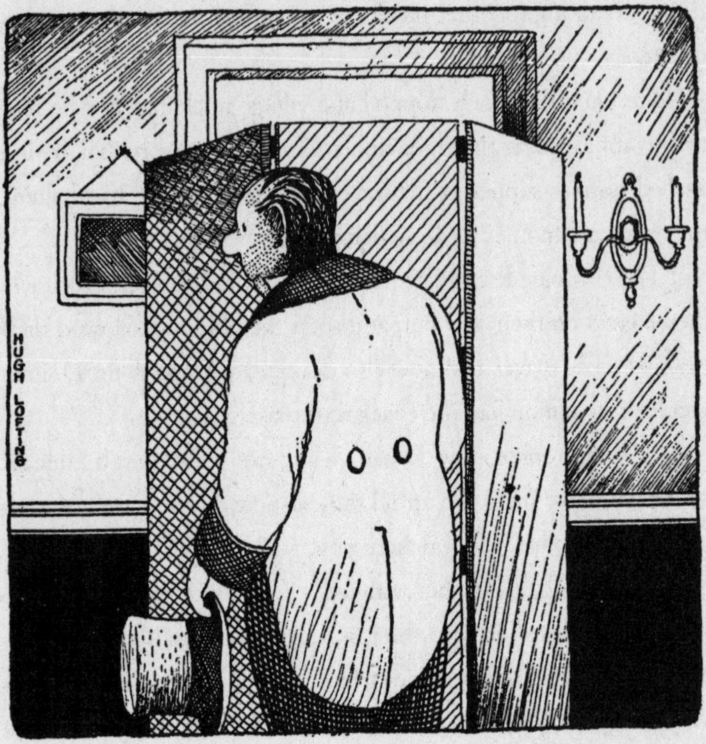

"He heard the voices of two men at a table within."

"I tell you," said one in a low tone, "there's not the least doubt. They're highwaymen, as sure as you're alive. It's an old trick, disguising as a woman. Did you notice the thick veil? As likely as not it's that rogue, Robert Finch himself. He robbed the Twinborough Express only last month."

"I shouldn't wonder," said the other. "And the short, thick villain will be Joe Gresham, his partner. Now, I'll tell you what we'll do—after supper let's go back and take our seats as though we suspected nothing. Their plan, no doubt, is to wait till the coach is full and has reached a lonely part of the road. Then they'll hold up the passengers—money or your life!—and get away before the alarm can be raised. Have you got your traveling pistols?"

"Yes."

"All right, give me one. Now, when I nudge you—you tear off the man's veil and hold a pistol to his head. I'll take care of the shorter one. Then we'll turn the coach about, drive back, and lodge them in the village jail. Understand?"

While the Doctor was still listening, the maid came down the passage again with a tray full of dishes, and touched him on the back.

"Go in, sir," she said, "and sit down. I'm just going to serve supper."

"No thank you," said the Doctor. "I'm not really hungry. I think I'll go out into the air again."

Luckily, on reaching the yard, he found it deserted. The horses had been taken out of the shafts and put into the stable. The new ones had not yet been hitched up to the coach. The Doctor sped across the yard and opened the door.

"Sophie," he whispered, "come out of that. They think we're highwaymen in disguise. Let's get away—quick—while the coast is clear."

Hoisting the seal's huge weight in his arms, the Doctor staggered out of the yard with her. On account of the lateness of the hour there was no one in the road. All was still and quiet but for the rattle of dishes from the inn kitchen and the noise of watching from the stables.

"Now," said he, putting her down, "we haven't far to go. See, this place is the last in the village. Once we reach those fields and get beyond the hedge we should be all right. I'll go ahead and find a place to get through, and you follow along as quick as you can.

Give me your cloak and bonnet—that's it. Now you can travel better."

A few minutes later they were safe behind a high hedge, resting in the long grass of a meadow.

"My!" sighed Sophie, stretching herself out. "It's good to be rid of that wretched cloak and veil. I don't like being a lady a bit."

"That was a narrow escape," said the Doctor. "It's a good thing I went in and overheard those men talking. If we had gone on with them in the coach we'd have been caught for sure."

"Aren't you afraid they'll come hunting for us?" asked Sophie.

"Oh, maybe. But they'll never look for us here. They take us for highwaymen, you see. And by the time they discover our escape they'll probably think we've gone miles. We'll wait here till the coach passes and then we needn't worry."

"Well," said Sophie, "even if we are safe it doesn't seem to me we are much better off than we were before."

"But we're this much farther on our way," said the Doctor. "Have patience. We'll do it yet."

"How far have we come now?" asked Sophie.

"That village was Shottlake," said the Doctor. "We've only got eighteen miles more to go to reach Talbot's Bridge."

"Well, but how are we going to travel? I can't walk it, Doctor; I simply can't—not eighteen miles."

"S-h-h! Don't speak so loud," whispered John Dolittle. "They may be snooping around somewhere, looking for us. We'll find a way—don't worry. And, once we reach the river, the worst will be over. We must first wait till the coach goes by, though, before we can stir."

"Poor Slushy!" murmured the Sophie, looking up at the

moon. "I wonder how he's getting on . . . will you try to take another coach, Doctor?"

"No. I think we'd better not. They may leave word at the inn and drivers will be on the lookout for a woman of your description."

"Well, I hope they don't find us here," said Sophie. "It doesn't seem to me we're very well concealed. Good heavens! Listen—a footstep!"

The place where they lay was the corner of a pasture field. Besides the hedge that hid them from the road there was another, on their right, dividing their field from the next. Behind this they now heard a heavy footstep passing up and down.

"Keep still, Sophie!" whispered the Doctor. "Don't move an inch."

Presently the top branches of the hedge began to sway and the crackling of twigs reached their ears.

"Doctor," said Sophie in a frightened whisper, "they've discovered us. There's someone trying to get through the hedge!"

For a moment or two the Doctor was undecided whether to keep still or to run for it. He thought at first that if it was someone out looking for them he might not know exactly where they were, anyway, and would, perhaps, if they kept quiet, go to some other part of the hedge easier to pass through.

But the crackling of branches grew louder—only a few feet away from them. Whoever it was, he seemed determined to enter the field at that place. So, with a whispered word to Sophie, the Doctor sprang up and started off, running across the meadow, with the poor seal flopping along at his side.

On and on they went. Behind them they heard a crash as the hedge gave away, and then heavy footsteps beating the ground in pursuit.

From the sound the pursuer, whoever he was, was gaining on them. And presently the Doctor, fearing that as highwaymen they might be fired upon without warning, turned to look back.

And there, lumbering along behind them, was an old, old plow horse!

"It's all right, Sophie," panted the Doctor, halting. "It isn't a man at all. We've had our run for nothing. Good lord, but I'm blown!"

The horse, seeing them stop, slowed down to a walk, and came ambling toward them in the moonlight. He seemed very decrepit and feeble; and when he came up, Sophie saw with great astonishment that he was wearing spectacles.

"Heavens!" cried the Doctor. "It's my old friend from Puddleby. Why didn't you call to me instead of chasing us across the country? We expected you to shoot us in the back any minute."

"Is that John Dolittle's voice I hear?" asked the old horse, peering close into the Doctor's face.

"Yes," said the Doctor. "Can't you see me?"

"Only very mistily," said the plow horse. "My sight's been getting awful bad the last few months. I saw fine for quite a while after you gave me the spectacles. Then I got sold to another farmer, and I left Puddleby to come here. One day I fell on my nose while plowing, and after I got up my spectacles didn't seem to work right at all. I've been almost blind ever since."

"Let me take your glasses off and look at them," said the Doctor. "Perhaps you need your prescription changed."

Then John Dolittle took the spectacles off the old horse and, holding them up to the moon, peered through them, turning them this way and that.

"John Dolittle peered through them."

"Why, good gracious!" he cried. "You've got the lenses all twisted. No wonder you couldn't see! That right glass I gave you is quite a strong one. Most important to have them in proper adjustment. I'll soon set them right for you."

"I did take them to the blacksmith who does my shoes," said the old horse, as the Doctor started screwing the glasses around in the frames. "But he only hammered the rims and made them worse then ever. Since I was brought to Shottlake I couldn't come to you about them and, of course, our local vet doesn't understand horse's glasses."

"There, now," said the Doctor, putting the spectacles back on his old friend's nose. "I've fixed them tight, so they can't turn. I think you'll find them all right now."

"Oh my, yes," said the old horse, a broad smile spreading over his face as he looked through them. "I can see you as plain as day. Goodness! How natural you look—big nose, high hat and all! The sight of you does me good. Why, I can see the blades of grass by moonlight! You've no idea what an inconvenience it is to be short-sighted, if you're a horse. You spend most of your grazing time spitting out the wild garlic that you chew by accident. . . . My, oh, my! You're the only animal doctor there ever was!"

PART THREE

THE FIRST CHAPTER

The Highwayman's Double

"IS HE A DECENT FELLOW, THIS FARMER YOU'RE working for now?" asked the Doctor, seating himself in the grass of the meadow.

"Oh yes," said the old horse. "He means well. But I haven't done much work this year. He's got a younger team for plowing. I'm sort of pensioned off—only do odd jobs. You see, I'm getting pretty old—thirty-nine, you know."

"Are you, indeed?" said the Doctor. "You don't look it—nothing like it. Thirty-nine! Well, well! Yes, to be sure, now I recollect. You had your thirty-sixth birthday the same week I got you your spectacles. You remember the garden party we gave for you—in the kitchen garden—when Gub-Gub overate himself with ripe peaches?"

"Very well, I do. Ah, those were the days! Good, old Puddleby! But what's this animal you have with you," asked the plow horse as Sophie moved restlessly in the grass, "a badger?"

"No, that's a seal. Let me introduce you: this is Sophie, from

Alaska. We're escaping from the circus. She has to go back to her country on urgent business, and I'm helping her get to the sea."

"Sh!" said Sophie. "Look, Doctor, there's the coach going by."

"Thank goodness for that!" murmured John Dolittle as the lights disappeared down the road.

"You know," said he, turning to the old horse again, "we've had a hard time getting even this far. Sophie has to keep concealed, and she can't walk much. We are making for the Kippet River, at Talbot's Bridge. We came by coach up to Shottlake, but we had to leave it. We were just wondering how we could continue our journey, when you scared the life out of us behind that hedge."

"You want to get to Talbot's Bridge?" said the old horse. "Well, that should be easy. Listen; you see that barn up on the skyline? Well, there's an old wagon in it. There's no harness, but there's plenty of ropes. Let's run up there and you can hitch me between the shafts, put your seal in the wagon, and we'll go."

"But you'll get into trouble," said the Doctor, "taking your farmer's wagon off like that."

"My farmer will never know," said the old horse, grinning behind his spectacles. "You leave the gate on the latch as we go out and I'll bring the wagon back and put it where we found it."

"But how will you get out of your harness alone?"

"That's easy. If you knot the ropes the way I tell you, I can undo them with my teeth. I won't be able to take you the whole way, because I couldn't get back in time to put the wagon up before daylight comes. But I've got a friend about nine miles down the Grantchester Road, on the Redhill Farm. He gets put out to graze nights, like me. He'll take you the rest of the way. It'll be easy for him to get back to his place before anyone's about."

"Old friend," said the Doctor, "you have a great head. Let's hurry and get on our way."

Then they climbed the hill to the barn. Inside they found an old wagon. The Doctor dragged it out. Then, getting down some ropes that hung coiled against the wall, he rigged up a kind of harness, with the help of an old collar that he found thrown in the manger. And when the plow horse had set himself between the shafts, John Dolittle hitched him up, being careful to make all the knots exactly the way he was told.

Then he lifted Sophie into the wagon and they started off down the meadow toward the gate.

"He rigged up a kind of harness."

As they were going out the Doctor said:

"But suppose anyone should meet me driving a wagon in a high hat? Wouldn't it seem sort of suspicious? Oh, look: there's a scarecrow in the next field. I'll borrow his hat."

"Bring the whole scarecrow with you," the old horse called after him as the Doctor started off. "I'll need something as a dummy driver when I'm coming back. Folks would stop me if they thought I was straying around the country without a driver."

"All right," said the Doctor, and he ran off.

In a few minutes he came marching back with the scarecrow on his shoulder. Then he set the gate on the latch, so the old horse

"Came marching back with the scarecrow on his shoulder"

could push it open on his return, threw the scarecrow up into the wagon and climbed in himself.

Next, he took the scarecrow's tattered hat and put it on his own head, in place of his high one. Then he got into the driver's seat, lifted the rope reins in his hands, called "Gee-up!" to his old friend between the shafts, and they started off.

"You better keep your cloak and bonnet ready to slip on, Sophie," said he. "Somebody might ask for a ride. And if we are compelled to give anyone a lift, you'll have to be a lady again."

"I'd sooner be almost anything in the world than a lady," sighed Sophie, remembering the tickling veil. "But I'll do it if you say so."

Thus, driving his own farm-wagon coach, with a scarecrow and a seal for passengers, John Dolittle successfully completed the next stage in his strange journey. They passed very few people, and no one asked for a ride. They had one anxious moment, however, when a gentleman armed with pistols in his saddle-holsters galloped up on a very fine horse and asked if they had seen anything of a man and a veiled woman along the road.

The Doctor, sitting on top of Sophie, leaned on the side of his wagon, with his scarecrow hat pulled well down over his eyes.

"I saw a couple getting into a field a few miles back," he said, trying to talk like a countryman. "But I reckon they be a long ways from there by now."

"That'll be they, sure enough," said the man, putting spurs to his horse. "Finch and Gresham the highwaymen. They boarded the coach below Shottlake. But they got away before we could arrest them. Never mind, we'll get 'em yet. Good night!"

And he galloped off down the road.

"Poor Mr. Finch!" said the Doctor, as the old horse moved on. "I'm afraid we are not improving his reputation for him."

"It's a good thing I got you away from Shottlake," said the old horse. "I reckon that fellow will set the whole country busy hunting for you now."

"Their hunting won't do us any harm back at Shottlake," said the Doctor. "Good thing if they're kept busy. But I hope you don't get into trouble on your return to the farm."

"No, I don't suppose so," said the old horse. "Even if I'm seen, they'll never guess how I got hitched up. Don't bother about me. I'll manage."

A little farther on the plow horse stopped.

"This is Redhill Farm on the right," said he. "Wait till I call Joe."

Then he went close to the hedge beside the road and neighed softly. Presently there was a scampering of hooves and his friend, a much younger horse, poked his head over the hawthorns.

"I've got John Dolittle here," whispered the plow horse. "He wants to get to Talbot's Bridge in a hurry. Can you take him?"

"Why, certainly," said the other.

"You'll have to use a wagon of your own," said the plow horse. "I must get mine back to the barn before my farmer wakes up. Got a cart or something anywhere about the place?"

"Yes, there's a trap up in the yard. It'll be faster than a wagon. Come over this side of the hedge, Doctor, and I'll show you where it is."

Then, hurrying lest daylight overtake them, they made the exchange. Madame Sophie was transferred from a farm wagon to a smart trap. The old plow horse, after an affectionate farewell from the Doctor, started back with his own wagon, driven by his scarecrow propped up on the front seat. At the same time John Dolittle and Sophie were carried at a good, swift pace in the opposite direction, toward the Kippet River.

It was not until some time afterward, when the Doctor revisited his old friend—in a way you will hear of later on—that he learned the story of that return journey which the plow horse made alone. About halfway back to his farm he met the gentleman with the pistols again, still galloping up and down the Grantchester Road, looking for Robert Finch, the highwayman. Recognizing the wagon and the driver whom he had met before, the rider stopped and asked some more questions. The driver of the wagon

"The horseman pulled the hat off the driver's face."

didn't answer. The man repeated his questions. Still the driver sat motionless in his seat, saying not a word. Growing at last somewhat suspicious, the horseman leaned forward in his saddle and pulled the hat off the driver's face.

The face was made of straw and rags!

The horseman, seeing he had been fooled, felt sure that the man who drove the wagon the first time he met it must have been the real highwayman, and that this scarecrow driver was just another of Finch's clever dodges to put the police on the wrong scent. Another wild story was added to the list of Finch's wonderful pranks—in one night he had passed himself off as a woman and as a scarecrow!

Then, to mix things up still more, that same day at two o'clock in the morning the real Robert Finch held up and robbed the Ipswich coach, more than a hundred miles away. And how he got across England to do it in that short time is still one of the great mysteries in the history of highway robbery. John Dolittle had been quite right when he said that they were adding to Finch's reputation!

On arriving at his own farm, the old horse found everyone in a great state of excitement. People were rushing wildly up and down the fields with lanterns. The scarecrow had been missed—so had the old wagon, so had the old horse. The farm laborers were following the wheel tracks across the meadow. As soon as the plow horse reached the gate he was surrounded by a mob with lamps and guns, all guessing and advising and chattering at once. But his owner, thinking he had been stolen and harnessed by the highwayman, did not blame him for the adventure. And for long afterward he was visited in his pasture and pointed out by the village gossips as the horse who had been driven by Finch's scarecrow double.

In the meantime the Doctor and Sophie, in their trap, were spanking along the road in the direction of Talbot's Bridge. And, although the horseman (he was the County Constable's Assistant) galloped after them as hard as he could, he never overtook them, with the good start they had gained.

On reaching the river, the Doctor lifted Sophie out of the trap and dropped her over the bridge and into the stream. Telling the Redhill horse to go back to his farm by a different way, lest he be met by the man again, John Dolittle leapt off the parapet of the bridge onto the bank. Then, while he ran along the stream beside her, Sophie, with gurgles of delight, plunged and darted through the river, catching all the fish she wanted on the way.

THE SECOND CHAPTER

To the Sea by River

AS THEY HAD EXPECTED, JOHN DOLITTLE and Sophie now found that the worst part of their troublesome traveling was over. For one thing, the constant anxiety of being seen worried them no longer. If they met anyone on the banks of the stream, Sophie just ducked underwater till the danger was past, while the Doctor pretended he was fishing, with a willow wand for rod and a piece of string for line.

They still had a long way to go. The journey north to Talbot's Bridge, you see, had not brought them any nearer to the coast.

The countryside through which the Kippet flowed was changeful scenery, but always beautiful and pleasant. Sometimes it was flat, sedgy meadowland, where the banks were boggy; sometimes the streams run through little forests and the shores were overhung with alders; and sometimes it passed close by a farm with fords, where cattle drunk. At these places the travelers would either wait till nightfall, lest they be seen, or if the depth of the river permitted, Sophie would do her swimming underwater while the Doctor would go around by the roads and meet her farther down.

While the going was, for the most part, easy for a seal, it was by no means always simple for the Doctor. The hundreds of hedges he had to get through, the walls he had to climb, the bogs he had to cross, made his part of the journey a hard and slow one. Sophie had to slacken her pace constantly and do a lot of loitering and waiting in order that he might keep up with her.

"Look here, Doctor," said she, about the middle of the second day when John Dolittle was resting on the bank, "it doesn't seem to me there is really any need for you to come farther. This going is so easy for me I can do the rest of the journey by myself, can't I?"

"I think not," said the Doctor, lying back and gazing up at the willows over his head. "We don't know yet what sort of difficult places the river may run you into before it reaches the sea. We had better consult some other waterfowl, as the ducks said we should, before we go farther."

Just at that moment a pair of fine bitterns flew down into the stream not far away and started feeding. The Doctor called them and they came up at once to his side.

"Would you please tell us," said John Dolittle, "how much farther the river runs before it reaches the sea?"

"Counting all the bends and wiggles," said the bitterns, "about sixty miles."

"Dear me!" said the Doctor. "Then we are barely halfway yet. What kind of country does it pass through? This seal wishes to swim all the way to the coast, and we must avoid having people see her on the way."

"Well," said the birds, "you will have plain sailing for another ten miles yet. But after that there are several places pretty dangerous for a seal to travel. The first one is Hobbs's Mill. It's a water mill, you understand, and the stream is dammed up with a high dam, a weir, and a big waterwheel. She'll have to leave the water at Hobbs's Mill and join it again below."

"All right," said the Doctor, "we can do that, I imagine. Then what's the next trouble?"

"The next is a town. It isn't a large one, but it has machinery buildings in it on the riverbank. And the river is made to run into pipes to turn these machines, and if your seal went floating down the pipes she'd get all mixed up in the machinery."

"I understand," said the Doctor. "Then we'll have to go around the town by land—after dark."

"Go around to the *right*," said the bitterns, "to the northward. On the other side the machinery-men's houses spread out a long way.

"After that you'll be all right till you get very nearly to the sea. But there you will meet with another town—a port. Your seal can't possibly swim through that town because the river flows over many little waterfalls and rapids right where the houses and bridges are thickest. So as soon as you come in sight of the port you had better leave the stream again, and make for the seashore at some lonely place to the north of it. You won't have far to go, but you'll have to do some stiff climbing, for the coast thereabouts is all high cliffs. If you get safely past the port without being caught, your troubles will be over."

"Well, thank you very much," said the Doctor. "This knowledge will be most helpful to us. Now, I think we had better be getting on our way."

Then after wishing John Dolittle good luck, the bitterns went back to their feeding, and the Doctor proceeded along the bank with Sophie swimming in the river. They reached Hobbs's Mill just as evening was coming on. As soon as the Doctor had explored around the buildings to see that all was quiet and nobody abroad, Sophie got out of the stream and hobbled across a couple of meadows and joined the river below the millrace on the other side. There they waited till the moon rose, and soon, with sufficient light for the Doctor to see his way along the shore, they went on again.

"They reached Hobbs's Mill just as evening was coming on."

Coming in sight of the machinery town of which the bitterns had spoken, John Dolittle left Sophie with orders to duck underwater if anyone should pass that way, and went forward into the town to explore and get some food for himself.

Although most of the shops were shut at this hour, he managed to buy some sandwiches and fruit at a hotel. In making these purchases he noticed that his supply of money was getting very low. Indeed, he had only just enough to pay for what he had bought. However, never having bothered much about money, this did not disturb him. And after spending his last twopence to get his boots cleaned—they were frightfully muddy from all this boggy walking—he proceeded to explore a way for Sophie to come around the town by land.

The journey she would have to make on foot proved to be quite a long one. But the Doctor found a way over a chain of ponds, waterlogged meadows, and a little brook that ran into the Kippet about two miles the other side of the town.

By the time he returned to Sophie the night was nearly passed, and they had to hurry to reach the river again before daylight came.

With Sophie safely back in the stream, John Dolittle decided he had better take a little sleep before going on. Sophie, too, was pretty weary, in spite of her anxiety to push on with all possible speed. So, asking a little moorhen who had her nest in the bank of the stream to mount guard and wake them on the approach of danger, they both took a nap—Sophie sleeping in the water, with her head poked out onto a stump, and the Doctor propped against a willow tree on the shore.

The sun was high in the heavens when he awoke to find the moorhen plucking at his sleeve.

"There's a farmer driving a team across the meadow," whispered the little bird. "He'll come right by here. He might not take any notice of you, but Sophie he couldn't miss. Get her to stick her head under the water. She's snoring like a foghorn, and I can't wake her up."

After the Doctor had made Sophie disappear beneath the water, and the danger of discovery was past, they started off once more and traveled all day and the following night toward the sea.

Gradually the landscape changed to a kind of scenery that, so far, they had not met with on their journey. The country, open turfy downs where sheep grazed, got rollier and hillier. And finally, on the evening of the next day, they saw the lights of the seaport town twinkling in the distance. The land on either side of it sloped upward to cliffs overlooking the Bristol Channel.

A little farther down the stream, roads ran on either side of the river, presumably going into the town. Along these, every once in a while, coaches and carriages passed them on their way to the port.

Feeling that it would be unwise to go farther by water, they now left the stream for the last time and hit out across the countryside.

The Doctor made Sophie keep her bonnet on, and he had her cloak ready to throw over her at any minute, because there were many roads to cross, and farmhouses to pass upon the way.

About a mile had to be covered before they would reach the top of the long slope and come in sight of the sea beyond the cliffs. Picking out a line that would miss most of the barns on the downs, they proceeded steadily and slowly forward. On this upland country they met with many stone walls. And, though they were low enough for the Doctor to jump, they were too much for Sophie to manage, and the Doctor had to lift her over.

She did not complain, but the uphill going was telling on her terribly. And when at last they came to a level stretch at the top, and the wind from the Channel beat in their faces, Sophie was absolutely exhausted and unable to walk another step.

The distance now remaining to the edge of the cliffs was not more than a hundred yards. Hearing the voices of people singing in a house nearby, the Doctor began to fear that they might yet be discovered—even with the end of their long trip in sight. So, with poor Sophie in a state of utter collapse, he decided there was nothing for it but to carry her the remainder of the journey.

As he put the cloak about her he saw the door of the house open and two men come out. Hurriedly he caught the seal up in his arms and staggered with her toward the edge of the cliffs.

"Oh," cried Sophie when they had gone a few yards, "look, the sea! How fresh and nice it sparkles in the moonlight. The sea, the sea at last!"

"Yes, this is the end of your troubles, Sophie," the Doctor panted as he stumbled forward. "Give my regards to the herd when you reach Alaska."

At the edge, John Dolittle looked straight downward to where the deep salt water swirled and eddied far below.

"Good-bye, Sophie," he said with what breath he had left. "Good-bye, and good luck!"

Then, with a last tremendous effort, he threw Sophie over the cliff into the Bristol Channel.

Turning and twisting in the air, the seal sped downward—her cloak and bonnet, torn off her by the rushing air, floating more slowly behind. And as she landed in the water the Doctor saw the white foam break over her and the noise of a splash gently reached his ears.

"He threw Sophie into the Bristol Channel."

"Well," he said, mopping his brow with a handkerchief, "thank goodness for that! We did it, after all. I can tell Matthew that Sophie reached the sea and I *didn't* go to jail."

Then a cold shiver ran down his spine. A heavy hand had grasped his shoulder from behind.

THE THIRD CHAPTER

Sir William Peabody, J. P.

JOHN DOLITTLE, TURNING ABOUT SLOWLY, found a large man grasping his collar. He wore some kind of a sailorlike uniform.

"Who are you?" asked the Doctor.

"Coast guard," said the man.

"What do you want? Let go of my coat."

"You're arrested."

"What for?"

"Murder."

While the Doctor was still trying to recover from his astonishment, he saw more people coming across the downs from the lonely house that he had noticed earlier. When they came close he saw they were two men and a woman.

"Have you got him, Tom?"

"Yes. Caught 'im right in the act."

"What was it?"

"A woman," said the coastguardsman. "I grabbed him just as

he threw her over the cliff. Jim, you run down to the station and get the boats out. You may be in time to save her yet. But I doubt it. I'll take him along to the jail. You come on down there or send me word, if you find anything."

"It'll be his wife," said the woman, peering at the Doctor in awe and horror. "Murdered his wife! You Bluebeard! Maybe he's a Turk, Tom—from Constant-what-d'yer-call-it."

"No, 'e ain't no Turk," said the coast guard. "'E talks English."

The woman gazed over the edge of the cliff with a shudder. "I wonder if they'll find 'er. Seems to me almost as though I could see something floating on the water down there. Poor creature! Well,

"You Bluebeard!"

that's the end of her troubles. Maybe she's better off than she was, married to him, the brute!"

"It wasn't my wife," said the Doctor sullenly.

"Who was it, then?" asked the coastguardsman. "It was some woman—'cause I seen you carrying her in your arms."

To this the Doctor decided, after a moment of thought, to say nothing. Now that he was arrested he would probably have to admit in the end that it was Sophie he had thrown into the sea. But until he was compelled in court to tell the whole story, it seemed wiser to keep silence.

"Who was it?" the man repeated.

Still the Doctor said nothing.

"It was his wife, all right," said the woman. "He has a wicked eye. I'll bet he has five or six wives stowed away somewhere—waiting for their doom, poor things."

"Well, he don't have to answer," said the coastguardsman. "It's my duty to warn you," he said very grandly, turning to the Doctor, "that anything you say may be used in evidence against you. Now let's go down to the courthouse."

Fortunately for the Doctor, it was by this time well on into the early hours of the morning. And when after crossing the downs they finally made their way into the town they found the streets deserted. The woman had not accompanied them. And the Doctor and his coastguardsman reached the courthouse without meeting a single soul.

Just as they were about to enter the police station next door, Jim, the other coastguardsman, ran up and joined his companion with Sophie's wet cloak on his arm and her bonnet in his hand.

"We couldn't find the body, Tom," said he, "but these clothes was floating at the foot of the cliff. I've left Jerry Bulkley in the boat still searching. I brought these down to you 'cause I thought you might want 'em."

"Yes, they'll be needed in evidence," said the other, taking the things from him. "Better go back and carry on with the search. I'll come and join you as soon as I've got the prisoner locked up."

Then the poor Doctor was taken into the police station; and after his name and various particulars about him were written down in a big book, he was placed in a little stone cell with some bread and water and left to his meditations.

As the noise of the clanging door and rattling bolts died away, John Dolittle noticed the gray light of dawn creeping in at a little barred window at his elbow.

"Heigh-ho!" he sighed, gazing round the bare stone walls. "Jail again! I congratulated myself too soon. I wonder if Matthew was ever in *this* prison."

Where the morning sun fell in a patch upon the wall he noticed some letters and signs scratched in the stone by former prisoners. He crossed the cell and examined them. Among them he found a very badly made "M. M."

"Yes," he said, "Matthew's been here, too. Seems proud of it. Well, well, it's a funny world."

Picking up the loaf that had been provided for him, he broke it in half and ate a couple of mouthfuls. He was very hungry.

"What good bread!" he murmured. "Quite fresh. I must ask the jailer where he gets it. The bed isn't bad either," he added, punching the mattress. "I think I'll take a nap. Haven't had a decent sleep in I don't know how long."

Then he took his coat off, rolled it up for a pillow and lay down.

"He found a very badly made 'M. M.'"

And when, about ten o'clock in the morning, the superintendent of police entered with a tall white-haired gentleman, they found the prisoner stretched on his cot snoring loudly.

"Humph!" murmured the old gentleman in a low voice. "He doesn't look very dangerous, does he, Superintendent?"

"Ah," said the other, shaking his head, "it only shows you, Sir William, what a life of crime will do. Fancy being able to sleep like that after throwing his poor wife into the sea!"

"Well, leave us alone for a little while," said the older man. "Come back in about a quarter of an hour. And, by the way, you need not mention my visit here to anyone—not for the present."

"Very good, Sir William," said the superintendent. And he went out, locking the door behind him.

Then the white-haired old gentleman went over to the cot and stood looking down a moment into the Doctor's peaceful face.

Presently he shook the sleeper gently by the shoulder.

"Dolittle," he said. "Here—John, wake up!"

Slowly the Doctor opened his eyes and raised himself on his elbow.

"Where am I?" he said drowsily. "Oh yes, of course, in jail."

Then he stared at the man who stood beside him. And at last a smile spread over his face.

"Heavens above! It's Sir William Peabody," said he. "Well, well, William! What on earth brings you here?"

"I might still more reasonably ask you how *you* come to be here," said the visitor.

"My goodness!" murmured the Doctor. "It must be fifteen years since I've seen you. Let me see: the last time was when we both got pretty angry—you remember?—arguing for and against fox hunting. Have you given it up yet?"

"No," said Sir William. "I still hunt two days a week. That's all I can manage now with my court duties and other things. They made me a Justice of Peace about five years ago."

"Well, it ought to be stopped," said the Doctor with great earnestness, "altogether. You can say what you like, but the fox is not given a square deal. One fox against dozens of dogs! Besides, why should he be hunted? A fox has his rights, the same as you and I have. It's absurd: a lot of grown men on horses, with packs of hounds roaring across the countryside after one poor little wild animal."

The old gentleman sat down on the bed beside the Doctor, threw back his head and laughed.

"Same old Dolittle," he chuckled. "Did anyone ever see the like? In jail, charged with murder, the first thing he does when I come to see him is try and open a discussion about fox hunting. Ever since I've known you, John—even when you were a scrubby little boy at school studying beetles under a magnifying glass—you've been the same. Listen: I haven't come here to argue about the rights of foxes. As I told you, I'm a J. P. You're due to appear before me for examination in about an hour. What I want to hear is your version of this charge that is brought against you. You are accused of murdering your wife. I happened to notice your name on the police book. From what I remember of you, I can well understand your killing any woman who was mad enough to marry you. But the part I don't believe is that you ever had a wife. What's it all about? They tell me you were seen throwing a woman into the sea."

"It wasn't a woman," said the Doctor.

"What was it, then?"

The Doctor looked down at his boots and fidgeted like a schoolboy caught doing something wrong.

"It was a seal," he said at last, "a circus seal dressed up as a woman. She wasn't treated properly by her keepers. And she wanted to escape, to get back to Alaska and her own people. So I helped her. I had the very dickens of a time bringing her across country all the way from Ashby. I had to disguise her as a woman so we could travel without arousing suspicion. And the circus folk were out after me. Then, just as I got her here to the coast and was throwing her into the sea so she could swim back to her native waters, one of your coastguardsmen saw me and put me under arrest. What are you laughing about?"

Sir William Peabody, who had been trying to suppress a smile throughout the Doctor's story, was now doubled up with merriment.

"As soon as they said it was your wife," he gurgled when he had partly recovered, "I knew there was something fishy about it. And there was, all right! You do smell terribly."

"Seals have to smell of fish," said the Doctor in an annoyed tone. "And I was compelled to carry her part of the way."

"You'll never grow up, John," said Sir William, shaking his head and wiping the tears of laughter from his eyes. "Now tell me: How far back on this trip of yours were you and the lady you eloped with seen? Because although we can certainly get you out of the charge of wife murder, it may not be so easy to clear you on the charge of stealing a seal. Were you followed down here, do you think?"

"Oh, no. We were not bothered by the circus folk after we got away from Ashby. Then at Shottlake we got taken for highwaymen and caused a little sensation when we traveled by coach. But after that nobody suspected anything till—till—"

"Till you threw your lady-love over the cliff," Sir William put in. "Did anyone see you being brought in here?"

"No," said the Doctor. "No one down here knows anything about it except the three coastguardsmen and a woman—the wife of one of them, I suppose. The streets were quite empty when I was brought to the jail."

"Oh, well," said Sir William, "I think we can manage it. You'll have to stay here till I can get the charge withdrawn. Then get away from this part of the country as quick as you can."

"But what about the coast guard folk?" asked the Doctor. "Are they still hunting for the body?"

"No, they've given it up now," said Sir William. "They brought back your victim's cloak and bonnet. That was all they could find. We'll say you were just throwing some old clothes into the sea—which is partly true. When I explain matters to them they won't talk—and even if they do, it isn't likely their gossip will ever reach your circus people. But listen, Dolittle: Do me a favor and don't bring any more menageries down here to throw over our cliffs, will you? It would get hard to explain if you made a habit of it. Besides, you'll spoil the circus business. Now, you stay here till I've fixed things up officially; and as soon as they let you out, get away from this district. Understand?"

"All right," said the Doctor. "Thank you. But listen, Will, about that fox hunting. Supposing you were in the fox's—"

"No," said Sir William, rising. "I refuse to reopen the argument now, John. I hear the superintendent coming back. We have too many foxes in this country. They need to be kept down."

"Quite a nice prison you have here, Will," said the Doctor as the superintendent opened the door. "Thanks for calling."

When Sir William and the superintendent had disappeared, the Doctor fell to walking up and down his cell for exercise. He began to wonder how things were getting on with his household in his absence. And he was still thinking over the animals' idea of a reformed circus when, about half an hour later, a police sergeant appeared at the door, extraordinarily polite and gracious.

"The superintendent presents his compliments, Doctor," he

said, "and apologizes for the mistake that was made. But it was not our department's fault. It was the coast guard's who made the arrest. Very stupid of them, very. The charge is now withdrawn, sir, and you are free to go whenever you wish."

"Thank you," said the Doctor. "I think I'll go now. It's a nice prison you have here—almost the best I was ever in. Tell the superintendent he needn't apologize. I've had a most refreshing sleep—so well ventilated. It would make a splendid place for writing—undisturbed and airy. But unfortunately I have matters to attend to and must leave right away. Good day to you."

"Good day, sir," said the sergeant. "You'll find the exit at the end of the passage."

At the front door of the police station the Doctor paused.

"My goodness!" he muttered. "I haven't any money to pay the coach back to Ashby. I wonder if Sir William would lend me a guinea."

And he turned back. But at the superintendent's office he was told that the Justice of Peace had gone off hunting for the day and wouldn't be back till tomorrow morning.

Once more he set out to leave the station. But at the door he paused again.

"I might as well take the rest of my loaf with me," he murmured. "It belongs to me after all—and I'll need it if I'm to get to Ashby without a penny in my pockets."

And he hurried back to his cell.

He found a policeman putting the place in order.

"Excuse me," said the Doctor. "Don't let me disturb your sweeping. I just came back for something I left behind me. Ah, there it is—my loaf! Thank you. Excellent bread you have here."

And after enquiring at the superintendent's office on the way out for the name of the baker who supplied the police station, John Dolittle sallied forth to freedom with half a loaf under his arm.

"Excellent bread you have here."

THE FOURTH CHAPTER

Nightshade the Vixen

PENNILESS BUT HAPPY, THE DOCTOR WALKED through the seaport town till he reached the market-place in the center. At this point three big highways met: one from the north, one from the south, and one from the east.

After admiring the town hall—it was a very beautiful and ancient building—the Doctor was about to set off along the road to the eastward. But he had not gone more than a pace or two before he paused, thinking. It occurred to him that it would be wiser if he found some other way to return to Ashby than that by which he had come.

He therefore changed his direction and swung off along the road to the south, intending to work his way back round to Ashby by some route where he would run no risk of meeting the people who had seen him in the coach or the Shottlake inn.

It was a pleasant morning. The sun was shining, sparrows chirping; and he felt as he strutted down the road with his loaf of bread under his arm that in such weather it was a pleasure to be alive.

Before long he had left the last houses of the town behind and found himself in the open country. About noon he came to a crossroads where a signpost, pointing down a very pretty little country lane, read, "To Appledyke, ten miles."

"That looks like a nice road," said the Doctor to himself. "And it runs in the right direction for me. I like the sound of Appledyke, too."

So, although he was not very far yet from the seaport town that he had left, he struck off eastward along the country lane to Appledyke.

"He came to a crossroads."

Soon he decided it was lunchtime and looked about him for a brook where he might get a drink of clean water to wash down his dry bread meal. Over to his right he saw a place where the land dipped downward into a hollow filled with trees and bushes.

"I'll bet there's a brook down there," the Doctor murmured. "It is certainly most delightful country, this."

Then he climbed over a stile and set off across the meadows that led down into the hollow.

He found his brook, all right; and the banks of it, shaded by the trees, formed the most charming picnicking ground anyone could wish for. After he had taken a drink, the Doctor sank down with a grateful sigh on the grass at the foot of a spreading oak, took out his loaf, and began to eat.

Presently he saw a starling hopping around near him, and he threw him some crumbs. While the bird was eating them the Doctor noticed that one of his wings seemed strange, and on examining it he found that the feathers were all stuck together with tar. The tar had hardened and the wing would not spread open the way it should. John Dolittle soon put it right and the bird flew off about his business. After his lunch, the Doctor felt that before continuing on his journey he would like to rest a while in this pleasant spot. So he leaned back against the trunk of the oak tree and soon he fell asleep to the music of the murmuring brook.

When he awoke he found four foxes, a vixen with three cubs, sitting patiently beside him waiting till he should finish his nap.

"Good afternoon," said the vixen. "My name is Nightshade. Of course, I've heard a lot about you. But I had no idea you were in the district. I've often thought of coming all the way to Puddleby to see you. I'm awfully glad I didn't miss you on this visit. A starling told me you were here."

"Well," said the Doctor, sitting up, "I'm glad to see you. What can I do for you?"

"One of these children of mine"—the vixen pointed toward her three round little cubs who were gazing at the famous Doctor in great awe—"one of the children has something wrong with his front paws. I wish you would take a look at him."

"Certainly," said the Doctor. "Come here, young fellow."

"He has never been able to run properly," said the mother as John Dolittle took the cub on his lap and examined him. "It has nearly cost us all our lives, his slow pace, when the dogs have been after us. The others can run beautifully. Can you tell me what's the matter with him?"

"Why, of course," said the Doctor, who now had the cub upside down on his knees with its four big paws waving in the air. "It's a case of flat feet. That's all. The muscles of the pads are weak. He can get no grip of the ground without good pad muscles. You'll have to exercise him morning and night. Make him rise on his toes like this: One, two! One, two! One, two!"

And the Doctor stood up and gave a demonstration of the exercise, which in a person strengthens the arches of the feet and in a fox develops the muscles of the paw pads.

"If you make him do that twenty or thirty times every morning and every night, I think you'll soon find his speed will get better," said the Doctor.

"Thank you very much," said the vixen. "I have the greatest difficulty making my children do anything regularly. Now you hear what the Doctor says, Dandelion: every morning and every night,

"It's a case of flat feet."

thirty times, up on your toes as high as you can go. I don't want any flat-footed cubs in my family. We've always been—great heavens! Listen!"

The mother fox had stopped speaking, the beautiful brush of her tail straight and quivering, her nose outstretched, pitiful terror staring from her wide-open eyes. And in the little silence that followed, from over the rising ground way off to the northeastward, came the dread sound that makes every fox's heart stand still.

"*The horn!*" she whispered through chattering teeth. "They're out! It's th—th—the huntsman's horn!"

As he looked at the trembling creature, John Dolittle was reminded of the occasion that had made him an enemy of fox hunting for life—when he had met an old fox one evening lying half dead with exhaustion under a tangle of blackberries.

As the horn rang out again, the poor vixen began running around her cubs like a crazy thing.

"Oh, what *shall* I do?" she moaned. "The children! If it wasn't for them I could perhaps give the dogs the slip. Oh, why did I bring them out in daylight to see you? I suppose I was afraid you might be gone if I waited till after dark. Now I've left our scent behind us, all the way from Broad Meadows, as plain as the nose on your face. And I've come right into the wind. What a fool I was! What shall I do? What shall I do?"

As the horn sounded the third time, louder and nearer, joined by the yelping of hounds in full cry, the little cubs scuttled to their mother and cowered under her.

A very firm look came into the Doctor's face.

"What pack is this?" he asked. "Do you know the name of it?"

"It's probably the Ditcham—their kennels are just the other side of Hallam's Acre. It might be the Wiltborough, over from Buckley Downs—they sometimes hunt this way. But most likely it's the Ditcham—the best pack in these parts. They were after me last week. But my sister crossed my trail just below Fenton Ridge and they went after her—and got her. There's the horn again! Oh, what a fool I was to bring these children out in daylight!"

"Don't worry, Nightshade," said the Doctor. "Even if it's the Ditcham and the Wiltborough together, they're not going to get you today—nor your children, either. Let the cubs get into my pockets—come on, hop in, young fellows. Now you,

Nightshade, come inside the breast of my coat. That's the way—move toward the back. You can stick your feet and your brush into the tail-pocket. And when I've buttoned it up like this—see?—you will be completely covered. Can you breathe all right back there?"

"Yes, I can breathe," said the vixen. "But it won't do us much good to be out of sight. The hounds can smell us—that's the way they run us down—with their noses."

"Yes, I know," said the Doctor. "But the men can't smell you. I can deal with the dogs all right. But you mustn't be seen by the men. Keep as still as a stone, all four of you—don't move or try to run for it, whatever happens."

And then John Dolittle, with his coat bulging with foxes in all directions, stood in a little clearing in the wooded hollow and awaited the oncoming of the Ditcham Hunt in full cry.

The mingled noises of the dogs, men, horns, and horses grew louder. And soon, peeping through the crossing branches of his cover, the Doctor saw the first hounds come in view at the top of the ridge. For a moment the leaders paused and sniffed the wind. Then in a beeline for the bottom of the hollow they came on down, stretched at full speed. Over the ridge and after them came the rest of the pack; and close behind the dogs rode the men, in red coats on fine, swift horses.

Ahead of most of the huntsmen galloped one man, old, lean, and white-haired—Sir William Peabody, the Master of the Foxhounds. Halfway down the slope he turned in his saddle and called to a man on a gray mare close behind him.

"Jones, they're making for the spinney. Don't let the leaders break into it before we've got it surrounded. Watch Galloway; he's yards ahead. Mind, he doesn't put the fox out the other side—watch Galloway!"

Then the man on the gray mare spurted ahead, cracking a long whip and calling, "Galloway! Here, Galloway!"

As the Doctor peered through the foliage he saw that the leading hound was now quite close. But, wonderfully trained to the huntsmen's command, Galloway suddenly slackened his pace within a few yards of the trees and remained, yelping and barking, for the others to come up.

Over the ridge more riders came pouring—fat parsons on stocky cobs, country squires on hacks, ladies on elegant, dainty thoroughbreds—all the gentry of the neighborhood.

"My goodness!" murmured the Doctor. "Was there ever anything so childish? All this fuss for a poor little fox!"

As the hounds, under the guidance of the men with long whips, spread, yelping, around all sides of the spinney, the people called and shouted to one another and the noise was tremendous.

"We'll get him," bellowed a fat farmer on a pony. "Hounds have gone all around now and scent don't go on. It's a killing, sure. Wait till Jones lets 'em into spinney. We'll get him!"

"Oh no you won't," the Doctor muttered, the firm look coming back into his face. "Not today, my fat friend—not today."

The dogs, impatient and eager, sniffed and ran hither and thither, waiting for permission to enter the little patch of woods and finish the hunt.

Suddenly a command was given and instantly they leapt the underbrush from all sides.

John Dolittle was standing in his clearing, with his hands over his pockets, trying to look all ways at once at the moment when the hounds broke in. But he had not known from which direction the vixen had entered and left her scent behind. And suddenly, before he knew it, four heavy dogs had leapt on his back, and he went down on the ground, simply smothered under a tangled pile of yelping, fighting foxhounds.

Kicking and punching in all directions, the Doctor struggled to his feet.

"Get away!" he said in dog language. "Lead the hunt somewhere else. This fox is mine."

The hounds, spoken to in their own tongue, now had no doubt as to who the little man was that they had knocked down.

"I'm awfully sorry, Doctor," said Galloway, a fine, deep-chested dog with a tan patch over one eye. "We had no idea it was you. We jumped on you from behind, you know. Why didn't you call to us while we were outside?"

"How could I?" said the Doctor irritably, pushing away a dog who was sniffing at his pocket. "How could I—with you fools making all that din? Look out, here come the huntsmen. Don't let them see you smelling around me. Get the pack out of here, Galloway, quick."

"All right, Doctor. But it smells to me as though you had more than one fox in your pockets," said Galloway.

"I've got a whole family," said the Doctor. "And I mean to keep them, too."

"Can't you let us have even one of them, Doctor?" asked the hound. "They're sneaky little things. They eat rabbits and chickens, you know."

"No," said the Doctor, "I can't. They have to get food for themselves. You have food given you. Go away—and hurry about it."

At that moment Sir William Peabody came up.

"Great heavens! Dolittle!" he exclaimed. "Haven't you left these parts yet? Did you see the fox? Hounds headed right down into this hollow."

"I wouldn't tell you, Will, if I had seen him," said the Doctor. "You know what I think of fox hunting."

"Funny thing!" muttered Sir William as he watched the dogs lurching about among the brush uncertainly. "They can't have lost the scent, surely. They came down here as firm as you like. Curious!—oh, heavens! I know what it is: they've followed your rotten fish smell—the seal! Good Lord!"

At that moment a cry came from the huntsmen that the hounds had found another scent and were going off to the south. Sir William, who had dismounted, ran for his horse.

"Hang you, Dolittle!" he shouted. "You've led the hounds astray. I should have kept you in jail."

The few dogs remaining within the spinney were now melting away like shadows. One of the fox cubs stirred in the Doctor's pocket. Sir William had already mounted his horse outside.

"Goodness, I forgot again!" muttered the Doctor. "I must get that guinea. I say, Will!"

Then John Dolittle, his pockets full of foxes, ran out of the spinney after the Master of the Hunt.

"Listen, Will!" he called. "Would you lend me a guinea? I haven't any money to get to Ashby with."

Sir William turned in his saddle and drew rein.

"I'll lend you five guineas—or ten—John," said the magistrate, "if you'll only get out of this district and stop putting my hounds on false scents. Here you are."

"Sir William turned and drew rein."

"Thanks, Will," said the Doctor, taking the money and dropping it in his pocket on top of one of the cubs. "I'll send it back to you by mail."

Then he stood there by the edge of the spinney and watched the huntsmen, hallooing and galloping, disappear over the skyline southward.

"What a childish sport!" he murmured. "I can't understand what they see in it. Really, I can't. Grown men rushing about the landscape on horseback, caterwauling and blowing tin horns—all after one poor little wild animal! Perfectly childish!"

The Fifth Chapter

"The Dolittle Safety Packet"

RETURNING TO THE SIDE OF THE BROOK within the shelter of the trees, the Doctor took the foxes out of his pocket and set them on the ground.

"Well," said the vixen, "I had often heard that you were a great man, John Dolittle, but I never realized till now what a truly marvelous person you are. I don't know how to thank you. I'm all overcome—Dandelion, get away from that water!"

"There is no need for thanks," said the Doctor. "To tell you the truth, I got quite a thrill myself out of diddling old Will Peabody—even if I did borrow money off him. I've been trying to get him to give up fox hunting for years. He thinks that the hounds followed my scent down by mistake."

"Ah, they're not easily fooled, those dogs," said the vixen. "Galloway—that big beast who did all the talking—he's a terror. Nose as sharp as a needle. It's a poor lookout for any fox whose scent he crosses."

"But you've been hunted before and got away, haven't you?"

asked the Doctor. "They don't always run the quarry down."

"That's quite true," said the vixen. "But we only escape by luck when weather conditions or some odd chance is in our favor. The wind, of course, is a terribly important thing. If the hounds pick up our scent on the wind and begin the hunt upwind, as we call it, there's hardly any chance of our getting away—except when the countryside has plenty of cover and we've got enough of a head start to come around and get behind them, where their scent blows toward us, instead of ours toward them. But the countryside is usually too open to give us a chance to do that without being seen."

"Humph!" said the Doctor. "I understand."

"Then sometimes," the vixen went on, "the wind will change when the hunt's in full cry. But such luck is a rare thing. Still, I remember one time when it saved my life. It was October, dampish weather—the kind the huntsmen like. There was a gentle breeze blowing. I was crossing over some meadows close to Thorpe Farm when I heard them. As soon as I got their direction I saw I was on the bad side of the wind, and, out in flat, uncovered country, I was going to have a fiend of a run for it if I was to get away. I knew the neighborhood real well, and I said to myself as I let out at full gallop, 'Topham Willows. It's my only chance.'

"Now, Topham Willows was a big, dense patch of old neglected preserves about fifteen miles away to the west. It was the nearest decent cover there was. But a long, long stretch of bare fields and downs lay between me and it. However, if I reached it, I knew I'd be all right, because it was brambly, tangled and thick, no men or horses could enter it and it was too big to be surrounded by the pack.

"Well, I went away for all I was worth, hoping to lengthen my start on them at the outset. The hounds sighted me at once. And a 'View, hullo-o-a!' went up from the riders. Then the whole hunt came after me like the Devil on horseback. After that it was one long, steady, pounding, cruel run for fifteen miles. The only screens that lay this side of Topham Willows were a few low stone walls. And no fox would be fool enough to try and take cover behind them. I just leapt them on the run, and each time my brush topped the walls, another 'View, hullo-o-a!' broke from the hunt.

"About three miles this side of the Willows I got a sort of cramp in my heart. My eyes went strange and I couldn't see straight. Then I stumbled over a stone. I got up and staggered on. Topham Willows was in sight, but my speed was going. I had opened the run with a pace too fast."

Nightshade, the vixen, paused in her story a moment, her ears laid back, her dainty mouth slightly open, her eyes staring fixedly. She looked as though she saw that dreadful day all over again, that long terrible chase, at the end of which, with a safe refuge in sight, she felt her strength giving out as the dogs of Death drew close upon her heels.

Presently in a low voice, she went on:

"It looked like the finish of me. The hounds were gaining—and with lots of breath left. And then!—suddenly the wind changed!

"'Gosh!' I thought to myself, 'if I only had a ditch or hedge handy now! I'd give them the slip yet! But of course in the open, in full view like that, scent didn't matter so much. I stumbled on. Then suddenly I noticed a ridge over to my left. On top of it were a few bracken patches—small, but quite a number of them, dotted about here and there. I changed direction, left the beeline on the Willows and made for the ridge. I still had a short lead on the dogs. I shot into the bracken, and for the first time in fourteen miles I was out of view from my enemies. Then I ran from patch to patch, leaving my scent all over the place. Next I raced off down the other side of the ridge, found a ditch leading toward the Willows, popped into it and doubled back in my old direction.

"By that time my pace was little better than a crawl, but as I'd expected, as soon as I was out of sight, the changing wind had got the dogs all confused. Peeping out of my ditch as I staggered along it toward the Willows, I saw them rushing from patch to patch among the bracken on top of the ridge. If the wind had been still blowing off me toward them, some of them would certainly have hit my trail down to the ditch, where the scent was hottest, and cut me off from the cover I was making for.

"But that short halt, while they fooled around among the bracken, trying to refind the scent, gave me time to reach the cover I had come so far to find. And as I crept, blown and dead beaten, into the tangle of Topham Willows, I flung myself down to rest and thanked my lucky stars for the wind that changed—just in time to save my life."

"Well, well," said the Doctor, as the vixen ended her story, "that's very interesting. From what you say, I suppose that if one could only deal with the hounds' sense of smell it would always be easy for you to get away from them, eh?"

"Oh, of course," said the vixen. "In nearly all hunting country a fox could find enough cover to keep out of the reach of the dogs if it wasn't for their horribly keen noses. We nearly always hear them, or see them, a good way off—long before they see us. If you could only put the hounds on the wrong scent, the fox could get away every time."

"I see," said the Doctor. "Well, now I have an idea. Supposing a fox was made to smell like something else, instead of a fox—some strong smell that dogs don't like—no pack of hounds would follow such a trail, would it?"

"No, I shouldn't think so—so long as they didn't know it was a fox that was carrying it. And, even then, maybe they wouldn't follow it if it was a smell they hated enough."

"That's just what I mean. Such a thing would be a scent-blind. It would—if we could only get it sufficiently powerful—entirely cover up your natural scent. Now, look here," said the Doctor, pulling a thick black wallet out of his pocket, full of neat little bottles. "This is a pocket medicine case. Some of these medicines have a strong, pungent smell. I'll let you sniff one or two. . . . Try this."

The Doctor pulled the stopper from one of the tiny bottles and held it to the vixen's nose. She started back after one sniff.

"My gracious!" she barked. "What a powerful odor. What's the name of it?"

"That's spirits of camphor," said the Doctor. "Now, try another. This is eucalyptus. Smell."

The vixen put her nose to the second bottle. And this time she sprang back three feet with a yelp.

"Great heavens! It gets in your eyes! That's worse—and stronger yet. Cork it up, Doctor, quick!" she cried, rubbing her nose with her front paws. "It makes me weep tears."

"All right," said the Doctor. "But listen: both these medicines, although they are so strong, are quite harmless—so long as you don't drink them. People use them for colds in the head and other things. That shows you. Now, do you suppose a dog would keep away from a smell like that?"

"I should say he would," Nightshade snorted. "He'd run a mile

"This is eucalyptus. Smell!"

from it. Any dog who got a whiff of that wouldn't be able to smell straight for the rest of the day. Dogs have to be more particular about their noses—especially hunting dogs."

"Fine!" said the Doctor. "Now look: when this little bottle is corked tightly and rolled in a handkerchief, no odor remains about it at all. See, you can take it in your mouth and carry it. Try—just to be sure that it's all right."

Gingerly the vixen took the rolled handkerchief, with the little bottle inside, in her mouth.

"You see?" said the Doctor, taking it back from her. "It's quite harmless and you can smell nothing while it is like that. But supposing you were to place the handkerchief on the ground and drop a heavy stone on top of it: the glass bottle inside would be broken, the medicine would run out and soak into the handkerchief, and the smell would be very strong. You understand me so far?"

"Quite," said the vixen, "quite—Dandelion, stop playing with my tail. How can I attend to what the Doctor's saying? Go over to that tree and do your exercises."

"And then," John Dolittle went on, "if you were to lie down on the wet handkerchief and roll in it, you too would smell very

"Dandelion, stop playing with my tail."

strong—of the medicine. After that, I think we could safely say that no hounds would follow you. For one thing, they wouldn't know what it was when they crossed your trail; and for another, as you say, it is so strong that they'd run a mile to get away from it."

"They certainly would," said the vixen.

"Very well. Now, I'll give you one of these bottles. Which will you have? Would you prefer to smell of camphor or eucalyptus?"

"They're both pretty bad," said Nightshade. "Could you spare the two of them?"

"Certainly," said the Doctor.

"Thank you. Have you got two handkerchiefs as well?"

"Yes. Here they are—a red one and a blue one."

"That's splendid," said the vixen. "Then I can make the cubs smell of camphor and myself of eucal—euca—"

"Eucalyptus," said the Doctor.

"It's a pretty name," said the vixen. "I'll call my other son that. I never could think of a nice name for him—Dandelion, Garlic, and Eucalyptus."

"The three sons of Nightshade," added the Doctor, watching the round cubs gamboling over the roots of an oak. "Very pretty—has almost a Roman, a classic sound. But listen: you must be very careful how you wrap the handkerchiefs around the bottles. If you don't do it properly you might get yourself cut by the broken glass inside. Make sure that the wrapping is thick and paddy. I've got a piece of string in my pocket. Perhaps I'd better wrap the bottles myself and tie them up for you."

Then John Dolittle fixed up the bottles in the proper manner and handed over his new invention, the fox's safety packets, to Nightshade the vixen.

"Now, remember," he said, "to carry them always with you, and as soon as you hear the hounds, smash them with a stone and get the medicine well soaked into your back. Then I think you'll be safe from any dogs—even from Galloway."

Well, John Dolittle, after the vixen and her family had thanked him many times for his kind services, left them with their new scent-destroyers and continued on his journey toward Ashby.

But he little guessed, as he made his way out of the hollow—and Nightshade, with her family, trotted off to their lair—what an important effect this new idea of his was to have.

That very evening, on their way homeward, the vixen and her cubs were scented by the hounds who were returning to that part of the country after a fruitless afternoon's search for foxes.

As soon as she realized that the dogs were on her trail, Nightshade put her packages on the ground and kicked stones against them. Instantly the air was filled with powerful medicinal odors.

In spite of the fact that the smell made her eyes run tears, the vixen rolled in one, while she made the cubs soak themselves in the other.

Then, reeking like a chemist's shop, choking and gasping to get away from their own smell, the four of them raced off across a wide pasture toward home. The hounds, to the leeward, seeing them in the open, cut across from a field the other side of a hedge, hoping to head them off before they reached the bushes at the foot of the pasture.

For the hounds this was easy, because Nightshade, with the flat-footed Dandelion to look after, couldn't put out her full speed.

On came the dogs, with the famous Galloway in the lead.

The huntsmen, seeing the chances of a kill after a dull day's sport, cheered and put spurs to their horses.

But in spite of the wind's being the wrong way, the leading dogs suddenly stopped within about five paces of their quarry.

"What's the matter with Galloway, Jones?" Sir William shouted to the man on the gray mare. "Look, he's sitting down, *watching the foxes run away!*"

Then suddenly the fitful evening wind swung to the eastward and blew a gust back toward the hunt. The pack, like one dog, turned tail and scattered, terrified, out of the pasture. Even the horses pricked up their ears and snorted through their noses.

"My heavens, what a stench!" cried Sir William. "Some chemical or other. What is it, Jones?"

But the man on the gray mare was galloping across the countryside, trying to get his pack together, cursing and cracking his long whip.

Peacefully and undisturbed, Nightshade reached her lair that night and put her cubs to bed. As she did so she kept murmuring to herself: "He's a great man—a very great man."

But the next day, when she went out to get food for her family, she met another fox. This neighbor, as soon as he smelled her, didn't even say good morning, but also ran, as if she were the plague.

Then she found her new odor something of an inconvenience as well as a blessing. None of her relatives would come near her, and she and her camphory-eucalyptus cubs were not allowed in any other foxes' lairs. But after a while it got around in fox society that Nightshade could go where she liked without ever being hunted by dogs. Then John Dolittle began to get requests by mysterious animal messengers for more eucalyptus. And he sent hundreds

"Cursing and cracking his long whip"

of little bottles, rolled in handkerchiefs, to that part of the world. Before long, every single fox in the neighborhood was supplied with, and always carried, his "Dolittle Safety Packet" when he went abroad in the hunting season.

In the end the result was that the famous Ditcham pack went out of existence.

"It's no use," Sir William said, "we can't hunt foxes in this district unless we can breed and train a pack of eucalyptus hounds. And I'll bet my last penny it's Dolittle's doing. He always said he'd like to stop the sport altogether. And, by George! so far as this county is concerned, he's done it!"

PART FOUR

The First Chapter

Back to the Circus

AND NOW, WITH MONEY IN HIS POCKET TO pay for a ride, John Dolittle set about finding a coach that would carry him back in the direction of Ashby.

At the village of Appledyke his little country lane led him onto a bigger highway running north and south. Making inquiries of the village blacksmith, he found that coaches plied this road and that he could expect one to pass in about half an hour. So, after buying some toffee at the one small shop that Appledyke could boast of, the Doctor settled down to wait, munching his sweets to pass the time.

About four o'clock in the afternoon a coach came along and took him to the next large town. From there he caught a night coach going east; and in the early hours of the following morning he was back within ten miles of Ashby again.

The remainder of the journey he thought he had better do on foot for safety's sake. So after he had a shave and a breakfast and a rest at an inn, he set out to walk the short remaining distance.

He had not gone more than about a mile before he came upon some gypsies camped by the side of the road. One old woman among them hailed him, offering to tell his fortune. The Doctor didn't want his fortune told but stopped to chat. In the course of conversation he mentioned Blossom's Circus. The gypsies then told him that it was no longer at Ashby, but had left for the next town.

On his asking for the right road to take to reach the next town, the gypsies told him that a man with a wagon, who was on his way to join Blossom's Circus, had passed them only half an hour ago. If he hurried on, they said, he might easily overtake him, as his horse was a slow walker.

The way from here to the town where the circus would next perform was rather a complicated cross-country journey; and the Doctor thought it would be much easier if he had someone with him who knew the way. He therefore thanked the gypsies and hastened on to try and catch the man who was bound, like himself, for Blossom's Circus.

By making inquiries of the wayfarers along the road, the Doctor was able to follow the route the man had taken. And about noon he came up with him halted at the roadside taking his lunch.

His wagon was very peculiar. All four sides of it were covered with signs. "Use Doctor Brown's Ointment," "Have Your Teeth Pulled by Doctor Brown," "Doctor Brown's Syrup Cures All Liver Complaints," "Doctor Brown's Pills" do this, "Doctor Brown's Liniment" does that, etc.

After reading all the advertisements with much medical interest, John Dolittle went up to the fat man who was eating bread and cheese by the roadside.

"Am I addressing Dr. Brown himself?"

"Pardon me!" said he politely. "Am I addressing Doctor Brown himself?"

"That's me," said the man with his mouth full. "What can I do for you? Want a tooth pulled?"

"No," said the Doctor. "But I understand you are going to join Blossom's Circus. Is that so?"

"Yes. I'm meeting it at Stowbury. Why?"

"Well, I was on my way to the same destination," said the Doctor. "I thought, perhaps, I might accompany you—if you have no objection."

Doctor Brown said he had no objection, and after he had finished his lunch he invited John Dolittle into his wagon while he got ready to hitch up. The inside of the wagon seemed to be principally used for making the medicines that were advertised on the outside. And the most important things in their preparation were, as far as the Doctor could see, lard and salad oil. Brown himself seemed a vulgar sort of person—not in the least like a real doctor. And presently John Dolittle began asking him questions about where he had gotten his medical degree; at what hospital he had learned dentistry, etc. Brown didn't like this at all and seemed rather annoyed at the Doctor's cross-examination.

Finally John Dolittle came to the conclusion that the man was most likely nothing but a quack selling fake medicines. He decided he would sooner go on alone. So, without waiting for Brown, he set off down the road ahead of him on foot.

The way the Doctor first knew that he was nearing the circus was by hearing Jip's bark in the distance. The sound was joined by two other barks. And presently, rounding a bend in the highway, he found Jip, Toby, and Swizzle all yapping about the foot of a tree, up which they had chased a black cat. Still farther down the road he saw the tail end of the wagon train winding on its way.

As soon as he came in view the dogs forgot all about the cat and came racing down the road.

"Doctor! Doctor!" yelped Jip. "How did everything go off? Did Sophie get away?"

Then the three of them jumped all over him, and he had to answer a hundred questions at once. From beginning to end he told the story of his adventurous journey to the sea. And when a little later he overtook the circus train and reached his own wagon,

"All yapping about the foot of a tree"

he had to tell it all over again for the benefit of the rest of his delighted family.

Dab-Dab hustled around and prepared a meal right away—a sort of tea-and-supper-combined arrangement; and she kept the rest of the household busy pulling out the bed linen to be aired, so that the Doctor should have dry sheets to sleep in.

Then Matthew Mugg got wind of his great friend's arrival, and he came and joined the party, and the story had to be told a third time.

"It was a great piece of work, Doctor," said he, "couldn't have gone better. Blossom never got the least suspicious that you was in on it at all."

"What's happened to Higgins?" asked the Doctor.

"Oh, 'e's doing honest work now. Took a stable-man's job in Ashby. Good thing, too! 'E's no loss to the circus business anyhow."

"Has Blossom put on any extra turn to take Sophie's place?" asked the Doctor.

"No," said Matthew. "We were short 'anded for a bit. But Hercules the strong man is back on the job now and the show's as good as ever."

"And we've made lots of money with our part of it, Doctor," cried Too-Too. "How much do you think the Pushmi-Pullyu took in last week?"

"I've no idea."

"Twelve pounds nine shillings and sixpence!"

"Great heavens!" cried the Doctor. "That's enormous—twelve pounds a week! That's more than I ever made in the best days of my practice. Why, we'll soon be able to retire at that rate!"

"What do you mean, retire, Doctor?" asked Toby, pushing his head up onto the Doctor's knee.

"Well, we hadn't meant to stay in the business for good, you know," said John Dolittle. "I have work of my own to look after in Puddleby—and—and—oh, heaps of things to attend to."

"I see," said Toby sadly. "I thought you were going to stay with us for quite a while."

"But how about the Dolittle Circus, Doctor?" asked Swizzle. "Aren't you going to try that idea—the reformed show we talked about?"

"It's a great notion, Doctor," Jip put in. "All the animals are crazy about the scheme. They've been working out the details of their own part of the performance."

"And what about our theater, Doctor—'The Animals' Own Theater'?" Gub-Gub put in. "I've written a play for it since you've been gone. It's called *The Bad Tomato*. I do the comic fat lady's part. I know my lines by heart already."

"And what about the house in Puddleby? That's what I'd like to know?" said Dab-Dab, angrily brushing the crumbs off the table. "All you animals ever think of is having a good time. You never think of the Doctor and what he wants. You never think of the house going to ruin back there and the garden turning into a jungle. The Doctor has his own work and his own home and his own life to attend to."

A little silence followed the housekeeper's furious outburst, and Toby and Swizzle rather shamefacedly retired under the table.

"Well," said the Doctor at last, "there is something in what Dab-Dab says. I do think as soon as the Pushmi-Pullyu has made enough to pay back the sailor for his boat—and a little to spare—we ought to think about leaving the business."

"Oh dear!" sighed Toby. "The Dolittle Circus would have been such a wonderful show!"

"Heigh-ho!" said Gub-Gub. "And I would have been simply splendid as a fat lady. I always thought I ought to have been a comic actor."

"Huh!" snorted Dab-Dab. "Last week you said you ought to have been a greengrocer."

"Well," said Gub-Gub. "I could be both—a comic greengrocer. Why not?"

That same night Blossom's Circus entered the town of Stowbury. And, as usual, before dawn the next morning the tents had been set up and everything got in readiness for showing.

As soon as the news of the Doctor's arrival got about, Mr. Blossom came to see him. And from all appearance John Dolittle decided that no suspicions had been aroused in the mind of the ringmaster by his "business" trip.

Another caller at the Doctor's stand that morning was Hercules the strong man. Hercules had never forgotten the kind attention shown him at the time of his accident, and he was glad to find that his friend had returned. His pleasant chat was cut short, however, when he suddenly discovered that it was time for him to give his first performance. The Doctor accompanied him back to his stand.

While returning across the circus enclosure the Doctor noticed, as he passed the tent of Fatima the snake charmer, a strong odor of chloroform. Fearing an accident might have happened, he went inside and found that Fatima was out at the moment. Within the tent the smell was stronger, and it seemed to be coming from the snake box. The Doctor looked into the box and found the six snakes in an almost unconscious state from the drug. One of them still had sense enough left to tell the Doctor, in answer to his questions, that Fatima always dosed them with chloroform on hot days, when they were too lively, in order to make them easier to handle for her performance. They hated it, the snake said, because it gave them headaches.

On this pleasant, sunny morning the Doctor had forgotten for a moment the wretched condition of many of the animals, which had so often sickened him of the whole circus business. This piece of senseless cruelty threw him into a boiling rage and he hurried off at once to look for Blossom.

He found him in the big tent, and Fatima with him. The Doctor

"They hated it, the snake said."

firmly demanded that the custom of chloroforming the snakes be forbidden. Blossom merely smiled and pretended to be busy with other matters, while Fatima hurled a lot of vulgar language at the Doctor's head.

Discouraged and sad, John Dolittle left the tent, intending to return to his own wagon. The gates were now open and the crowds were coming in thick and fast. The Doctor was wondering how American blacksnakes would manage in the English climate if he contrived their escape, when he noticed a throng of visitor's collecting about a platform down at the other end of the enclosure.

At this moment Matthew came up and joined him, and together they started toward the platform. On this the Doctor now saw his acquaintance, Doctor Brown, delivering a lecture about the wonders of his pills and ointments, which could cure in one dose all the ailments known to mankind.

"What arrangement has this fellow with Blossom?" the Doctor asked of Matthew.

"Oh, he pays him a percentage," said the Cat's-Meat-Man. "Blossom gets so much on all he takes in. He's going on with us to the next three towns, I hear. Doing a good trade, ain't he?"

Indeed, Doctor Brown was very busy. Country folk, after listening to his noisy medical lectures, were buying his wares right and left.

"Go and get me a pot of that ointment, will you, Matthew?" said the Doctor. "Here's some money—and get me a box of the pills as well."

"All right," said Matthew with a grin. "But I don't reckon you'll find them much good."

The Cat's-Meat-Man returned with the purchases and the Doctor took them to his wagon. There he opened them, smelled them, examined them and tested them with chemicals from his little black bag.

"Rubbish and bunkum!" he cried when he had ended. "This is just highway robbery. Why did I ever go into this rotten show business? Matthew, get me a stepladder."

The Cat's-Meat-Man went out, disappeared behind some tents, and presently returned with the stepladder.

"Thank you," said the Doctor, putting it on his shoulder and marching off toward the platform. There was a dangerous light in his eyes.

"What are you going to do, Doctor?" asked Matthew, hurrying after him.

"I'm going to give a medical lecture myself," said the Doctor. "Those people are not going to pay their money for quack rubbish if I can help it."

Jip, who was sitting at the door of his wagon, suddenly pricked up his ears and sprang to his feet.

"Toby," he called over his shoulder, "the Doctor's going over to the patent medicine man's platform. He's got a stepladder. He looks awfully mad about something. There's going to be a fight, I fancy. Get Swizzle and let's go and see the fun."

John Dolittle on reaching the crowd at Brown's lecture stand set up his stepladder right opposite to the speaker, and Matthew Mugg cleared a space around it so the audience shouldn't knock it over while the Doctor climbed it.

At the moment of his arrival, Brown was holding up in his left hand a pot of ointment.

"This preparation which I 'old in my 'and, ladies and gentlemen," he bawled, "is the greatest remedy in the world for sciatica, lumbago, neuralgia, ague, and gout. It 'as been hendorsed by all the leadin' physicians. It is the same what is used by the royal family of Belgium and the Shah of Persia. One application of this marvelous remedy will—"

At this point another voice, still more powerful, interrupted the lecture. The people all turned around, and there behind them, perched on a stepladder stood a little round man with a battered high hat on his head.

"Ladies and gentlemen," said the Doctor, "what this man is telling you is not true. His ointment contains nothing but lard mixed with a little perfume. His pills are no good either. I do not recommend you buy any."

For a moment there was a dead silence. While Doctor Brown was trying to think up something to say, the voice of a woman, Fatima the snake charmer, was heard from the edge of the crowd.

"Don't you listen to him," she yelled, pointing a fat finger at John Dolittle. "He's nothing but a showman. He doesn't know anything about medicines. Push 'im orf 'is ladder."

"Just a minute," said the Doctor, addressing the crowd again. "It is true that I am in the show business—for the moment. But I am a medical graduate of the University of Durham. I am prepared to stand by what I have said. These preparations that this man is trying to sell you are worthless. Also I have grave doubts about his education in dentistry and I do not advise any of you to have your tooth touched by him."

The crowd now began to get restless. Several people had already purchased Brown's wares and these could now be seen making their way to the platform and demanding their money back. Brown refused it and tried to make another address to his audience in answer to the Doctor's statements.

"Listen," yelled John Dolittle from his ladder. "I challenge this man to produce a medical degree or credentials of any kind to prove that he is a qualified doctor or dentist. He is a quack."

"You're a fake yourself," yelled Brown. "I'll have the law on you for libel."

"Push 'im down!" howled Fatima. "Mob 'im!"

But the people did not seem inclined to follow her orders. Presently the Doctor was recognized by one of his old patients among the audience—just as he had been in the case of the strong man's accident some weeks before. A little old lady suddenly waved an umbrella above the crowd.

"That's John Dolittle," she shouted, "who cured my son Joe of whooping cough back in Puddleby ten years ago. Like to die he was. He's a real doctor—none better in the West Country. T'other's a quack. Ye be fools if ye turn a deaf ear to what John Dolittle tells ye."

Then other voices were heard here and there among the crowd. The general restlessness increased. More people struggled forward to Brown's platform to bring back the wares they had bought. A growing murmur arose.

"Mob 'im! Knock 'im down!" yelled Fatima, trying to make herself heard.

Doctor Brown thrust aside two men who had climbed up onto his stand for their money, came to the edge of the platform and opened his mouth to begin another medical lecture.

But a large, well-aimed turnip suddenly sailed across the heads of the audience and hit him squarely in the face. The mobbing had begun—but it wasn't directed against John Dolittle. Soon carrots, potatoes, stones, all manner of missiles, were flying through the air.

"Grab 'im!" yelled the crowd. "He's a crook."

And the next moment the whole audience surged toward the platform yelling and shaking their fists.

The Second Chapter

The Patent Medicine Riots

JOHN DOLITTLE HIMSELF GREW A LITTLE alarmed as he saw what an ugly mood the crowd was now beginning to show. When he had first mounted his ladder and interrupted the quack doctor's lecture he had meant to do no more than warn the people against buying fake medicines. But as he watched the throng swarm over the platform, wrecking and smashing it on the way, he began to fear for Brown's safety.

When the riot was at its height the police arrived. Even they had considerable difficulty in calming the crowd. They had to use their clubs to make them listen at all. There were many broken heads and bloody noses. Finally the police saw that their only chance of restoring order would be to clear the circus enclosure together.

This was done—in spite of the people's objection that they had only just come in and wanted their admission money back before they left. Then the circus was ordered by the police to remain closed until further instructions.

It was not long before the further instructions were forthcoming. Much indignation had been aroused throughout the respectable town of Stowbury over the whole affair. And the mayor sent word to Blossom about noon that he and the aldermen would be obliged to him if he would pack up his circus and take it out of their town immediately.

Brown had escaped and gotten away across country long before this. But that wasn't the end of the affair so far as John Dolittle was concerned. Blossom, already annoyed, became so furious when the mayor's order was brought that everybody thought he was going to have a fit. Fatima had been railing against the Doctor to Blossom all morning; and on hearing the last bit of news, which meant considerable loss, he got very red in the face.

Many of the showmen were with him when the policeman delivered the order. On them too Fatima had been working, trying to arouse bad feeling against the Doctor.

"Blast it!" yelled Blossom, rising to his feet and reaching for a thick walking stick that stood behind his wagon door. "I'll teach him to get my circus closed up! Come on, some of you fellows!"

With waving fists Fatima and four or five of the showmen standing near followed the ringmaster as he marched off toward the Doctor's stand.

Both Jip and Matthew had also been hanging around Blossom's wagon. They too now departed, Jip running ahead to warn the Doctor and the Cat's-Meat-Man going off in a wholly different direction.

On their way to the Doctor's wagon Blossom and his party of vengeance were joined by several tent riggers and others. By the time they arrived at his door they numbered a good dozen. To their surprise the Doctor came out to meet them.

"Good afternoon," said John Dolittle politely. "What can I do for you?"

Blossom tried to speak, but his anger was too much for him—nothing more than spluttering gurgles came from his throat.

"You've done enough for us already," shouted one of the men.

"We're going to do for you now," screamed Fatima.

"You've got the show turned out of the town," growled a third. "One of the best places on the road. You've cost us a week's pay."

"You've been doing your best to put my show on the blink," snarled Blossom, finding his voice at last, "ever since you've been with us. But, by Jiminy, you've gone too far this time!"

Without further words the group of angry men, led by the ring-master, rushed upon the Doctor and he went down under a football scrum of kicking feet and punching fists.

Poor Jip did his best to drag them off. But it was little help he could give against twelve such enemies. He couldn't see the Doctor at all. He was beginning to wonder where Matthew was when he saw the Cat's-Meat-Man running toward the fight from the other side of the enclosure. And beside him ran an enormous man in pink tights.

On reaching the scrum the big man began pulling off the show-men by their feet or hair and tossing them aside as though they were wisps of straw.

Finally Hercules the strong man—for it was he—had thinned the fight down to two, Blossom and the Doctor. These still rolled upon the ground trying to throttle each other. With a hand the size of a leg of mutton, Hercules, grasped the ringmaster by the neck and shook him like a rat.

"If you don't be'ave yourself, Alexander," he said quietly, "I'll slap your face and knock your brains out."

"I'll slap your face."

There was a little silence while the rest of the showmen picked themselves up from the grass.

"Now," said Hercules, still grasping Blossom by the collar, "what's this all about? What are you all settin' on the Doc for? Ought to be ashamed—a good dozen of yer—and him the littlest of all!"

"He went and told the people that Brown's ointment wasn't no good," said Fatima. "Got 'em all worked up, asking for their money back. Called him a fake in front of the audience—and 'im the biggest fake that ever walked himself."

"You're a nice one to talk about fakes," said Hercules. "Didn't

I see you painting bands on your poor harmless snakes last week—to make 'em look like real deadly ones? This man's a good doctor. He couldn't 'ave mended my busted ribs for me if he wasn't."

"He's got the show turned out of the town," growled one of the men. "We had our thirty-mile trip from Ashby for nothing—and another forty miles ahead of us before we take in a penny. That's what your precious *Doctor* has done for you!"

"He's not going any further with my show," spluttered Blossom. "I've taken about all I'm going to stand from him."

He wriggled himself out of the strong man's grasp and advancing toward the Doctor shook a finger in his face.

"You're fired," he yelled. "Understand? You leave my show today—now."

"Very well," said the Doctor quietly. And he turned away toward the door of his wagon.

"Just a minute," Hercules called after him. "Do you want to go, Doctor?"

John Dolittle paused and turned back.

"Well, Hercules," he said doubtfully, "it's rather hard to answer the question."

"What he *wants* 'as got nothing to do with it," said Fatima. "The boss 'as fired 'im. That settles it. 'E's got to go."

As the Doctor looked into the jeering eyes of this woman that hated him, he thought of the snakes who were in her care. Then he thought of several other circus animals whose condition he had hoped to improve—of Beppo, the old wagon horse who should have been pensioned off years ago. And while he hesitated, Swizzle pushed his damp nose up into his hand and Toby plucked at the tail of his coat.

"No, Hercules," he said at last. "All things considered, I do not want to go. But if I'm sent away there's nothing I can do about it, is there?"

"No," said the strong man. "But there's something others can do about it. Look here," he said, spinning Blossom around by the shoulder and shaking an enormous fist under his nose. "This man's an honest man. Brown was a crook. If the Doctor goes, I go too. And if I go, my nephews, the trapeze acrobats, will come with me. And I've a notion that Hop the clown will join us. Now how about it?"

Mr. Alexander Blossom, proprietor of "The Greatest Show on Earth," hesitated, chewing his mustache in dismay and perplexity. With Sophie the seal gone, deserted by the strong man, the trapeze brothers, his best clown, and the Pushmi-Pullyu, his circus would be sadly reduced. While he pondered, Fatima's face was a study. If looks could have killed, both Hercules and the Doctor would have died that day twice over.

"Well," said the ringmaster at last in quite a different voice, "let's talk this over, friendlylike. There's no end for hard feelings—and no sense in breaking up the show just because we've come a cropper in one town."

"If I stay," said the Doctor, "I insist that no more fake medicines be sold while I am with you."

"Huh!" snorted Fatima. "See what he's goin' to do? 'E's beginnin' again. 'E's goin' to tell you how to run your show."

"Also," said the Doctor, "I shall require that this woman no longer have the handling of snakes or any other animals. If you want to keep me, she must go. I will buy her snakes from her myself."

Well, in spite of Fatima's screaming indignation, matters were at last arranged peaceably. But that night, when Too-Too was sitting

"He's bought six fat snakes with it!"

on the steps of the wagon listening to a brother owl who was hooting to him from the town cemetery, Dab-Dab came out and joined him, with tears in her eyes.

"I don't know what we'll ever do with the Doctor," she said wearily. "Really I don't. He has taken every penny we had in the money box—the whole twelve pounds nine shillings and sixpence that we had saved up to go back to Puddleby with. And what do you think he has gone and spent it on? He's bought six fat snakes with it!" (Dab-Dab burst into a renewed flood of tears.) "And he—he—has put them in my flour bin to keep till—till he can get a proper bed for them!"

The Third Chapter

Nino

AFTER THE DEPARTURE OF FATIMA THE snake charmer, John Dolittle liked the life of the circus a good deal better. It had mostly been the thought that he was not doing anything to help the animals that had made him so often speak against it. But now that he had sent Sophie back to her husband, freed the snakes from a life of slavery and chloroform, and forbidden the selling of quack medicines, he began to feel that his presence here was doing good.

And then Blossom, ever since the medical lecture riot, had shown him a great deal more respect. The ringmaster had always known that he had a good thing in the Pushmi-Pullyu. And if it had not been for his blind rage on being turned out of the town by the mayor, and for Fatima's eternal nagging against the Doctor, he would never have dreamed of trying to get rid of him at all.

John Dolittle's own popularity with the circus people themselves was in the end improved greatly by the incident at Stowbury. In spite of the fact that she had successfully turned many of the showmen against the Doctor, Fatima herself had always been disliked by almost everyone. And when it became known that the Doctor had brought about her departure, he was very soon forgiven for the loss caused by the circus being ordered out of the town.

However, his real power and influence with the show people did not properly begin until the day that the Talking Horse fell sick.

The circus had moved on to a town called Bridgeton, a large manufacturing center, where good business was expected by Blossom. The animals and clowns and bareback riders and the rest had made their usual procession through the streets; big bills were posted all over the place, and when the enclosure was opened to the public, great throngs of people had crowded up to the gates. It looked like one of the best weeks the circus had ever known.

At two o'clock the show at the big tent (for which an extra sixpence was charged) was to begin. Outside the entrance a large sign was set up showing the program: "Mademoiselle Firefly, the Bareback Rider; the Pinto Brothers, Daring Trapeze Artists; Hercules, the Strongest Man on Earth; Hop, the Side-Splitting Clown, and His Comedy Wonder-Dog, Swizzle; Jojo, the Dancing Elephant," and (in large letters) "NINO, the World-Famous Talking Horse."

Now, this Nino was just an ordinary, cream-colored cob who had been trained to answer signals. Blossom had bought him from a Frenchman; and with him he had bought the secret of his so-called talking. In his act he didn't talk at all, really. All he did was stamp his hoof or wag his head a certain number of times to give answers to the questions Blossom asked him in the ring.

"How many do three and four make, Nino?" Blossom would say. Then Nino would stamp the floor seven times. And if the answer was yes, he would nod his head up and down, and if it was

"They had made their usual procession through the streets."

no, he would shake it from side to side. Of course, he didn't know what was being asked of him at all, as a matter of fact. And the way he knew what answers to give was from the signals that Blossom made to him secretly. When he wanted Nino to say yes, the ringmaster would scratch his left ears; when he wanted him to answer no, he would fold his arms and so on. The secret of all these signals Blossom kept jealously to himself. But, of course, the Doctor knew all about them because Nino had told him how the whole performance was carried on.

Now, in advertising the circus, Blossom always put Nino, the World-Famous Talking Horse, before all the other turns in importance. It was a popular performance and the children loved shouting questions down to the little plump cob and seeing him answer with his feet or his head.

Well, on the circus's first day in Bridgeton, a little before the show in the big tent was to begin, the Doctor and the ringmaster were in the clown's dressing room talking. Suddenly, in rushed the head stableman in a great state of excitement.

"Mr. Blossom," he cried. "Nino's sick! Layin' in his stall with 'is eyes closed. The show's due to begin in fifteen minutes and I can't do nothing with 'im—can't even get 'im on his feet."

With a hearty curse Blossom rushed out and tore away in the direction of the stables, while the Doctor followed him on the run.

When they got to Nino's stall, Blossom and the Doctor found the horse in a bad state. His breathing was fast and heavy. With difficulty he was made to stand up on his feet, but for walking even a few steps he seemed far too shaky and weak.

"Darn the luck!" muttered the manager. "If he can't perform it will ruin the whole week's showing. We've posted him as the star turn. The crowd will want to know about it if they don't see him."

"You'll have to make a speech and explain," said the Doctor. "That horse has a bad fever. I doubt if he can leave his stall today."

"Good heavens, man, we'll have to!" cried Blossom. "We'll likely have the audience asking for its money back if he don't appear. We can't have any more riots like—"

At that moment a boy came up.

"Five minutes to two, Mr. Blossom. Pierce wants to know if you are all ready."

"Hang it!" said the manager. "I can't take the ring for the first turn. I must get Nino fixed up before I can come on."

"We ain't got nobody else, sir," said the boy. "Robinson 'asn't got back yet."

"Lord, what a day!" groaned the manager. "Well, the show can't open without a ringmaster, that's sure. And I can't leave Nino yet. I don't know what—"

"Excuse me, governor," said a voice behind him. And turning, Blossom looked into the crossed eyes of Matthew Mugg.

"Couldn't I take your place, boss?" said the Cat's-Meat-Man, "I know your whole line of talk by heart. I could introduce the turns—same as you—and nobody know the difference."

"Well," said Blossom looking him up and down, "you're about the scrubbiest ringmaster I ever see'd. But beggars can't be choosers. Come with me—quick—and I'll give you these clothes."

Then, while the Doctor turned his attention to Nino, Blossom and Matthew made off on the run for the dressing rooms. There, with the aid of Theodosia (who put a large swift pleat in Blossom's riding breeches) and a little rouge and a false mustache from the clown's makeup box, Mr. Mugg was transformed from a Cat's-Meat-Man into a ringmaster. The ambition of his life was realized at last. And as he swaggered into the ring and looked up at the sea of faces around him, his chest swelled with dignity; while Theodosia, watching him through a slit in the tent flap, glowed with wifely pride and prayed that the pleat in his riding breeches would hold till the show was over.

In the meantime, from an examination of Nino, the Doctor became certain that there was no hope of his recovering in time to perform that day. He went and got some large pills from his black bag and gave him two. Presently Blossom, now dressed in a jersey and flannel pants, joined him.

"You can't have this horse perform today, Mr. Blossom," said the Doctor, "nor for a week, probably, at least."

"Well," said the ringmaster, throwing up his hands in despair, "we're just ruined—that's all—ruined! That row up in Stowbury got into the papers, and now if we have another frost here, we're done for. And if Nino don't go on, the crowd's going to ask for their money back, sure as you're alive. He's the star turn. We might manage if we had another act to put on in his place, but I haven't a blessed thing for an extra. And it was a short program, anyhow. We're ruined. Darn it, I never saw such a run of rotten luck!"

Poor Blossom seemed genuinely crestfallen. While the Doctor

"You can't have this horse perform today."

looked at him thoughtfully, a horse in the stall next to Nino's neighed softly. It was Beppo, the veteran wagon horse. A smile came into the Doctor's face.

"Look here, Mr. Blossom," said he quietly. "I think I can help you out of this trouble, but if I do you've got to promise me a few things. I know a good deal more about animals than you suppose I do. I've given up the best part of my life to studying them. You advertised that Nino understood you and could answer any questions you put to him. You and I know that's not so, don't we? The trick was done by a system of signals. But it took the public in. Now I'm going to tell you a secret of my own, which I don't boast about because nobody would believe me if I did. I can talk to horses in their own language and understand them when they talk back to me."

Blossom was staring down moodily at the floor while the Doctor spoke. But at the last words he gazed up at John Dolittle, frowning.

"Are you crazy?" he said, "or didn't I hear straight? Talk to animals in their own language! Look 'ere: I've been in show business thirty-seven years, knocked around with animals ever since I was a nipper. And I know there ain't no such thing as a man talking with a horse in horse language. You got a cheek to tell me a yarn like that—me, Alexander Blossom!"

The Fourth Chapter

Another Talking Horse

"I AM NOT TELLING YOU A YARN," SAID THE DOCTOR quietly. "I am telling you the truth. But I can see that you will not believe me till I prove it to you."

"You bet I won't," sneered Blossom.

"Well, there are five horses in this stable, aren't there?" asked the Doctor. "And none of them can see me here where I stand, can they? Now if you will ask me to put some question to any one of them I will endeavor to give you his answer."

"Oh, you're crazy!" said Blossom. "I ain't got time to fool with you."

"All right," said the Doctor. "My intention was to help, as I told you. But, of course, if you don't want my assistance, then that ends the matter."

He shrugged his shoulders and turned away. The noise of clapping sounded from the big tent.

"Ask Beppo," said Blossom, "what's the number of the stall he's in."

Beppo's was the second from the end. On his door was marked a large "2" in white paint.

"Do you wish to have him tell me the answer in horse language?" asked the Doctor, "or shall I have him tap the number?"

"Have him tap the partition with his foot, Professor," sneered Blossom. "I don't know no horse grammar; and I couldn't tell, t'other way, whether you are faking or not."

"Very good," said the Doctor. And from where he stood, quite invisible to Beppo, he made some snuffy breathing noises—rather as though he had a cold in his head. Immediately two taps sounded from stall number 2.

Blossom's eyebrows went up in surprise. But almost immediately he shrugged his shoulders.

"Pshaw! Could easily 'ave been an accident. Maybe he just fell against the partition. Ask 'im—er—ask 'im 'ow many buttons I 'ave on my waistcoat—the one your cross-eyed assistant is wearing in the ring now."

"All right," said the Doctor. And he made some more snuffly noises, ending with a gentle whinny.

But this time, unintentionally, he did not include Beppo's name in his message. Now, all five horses in that stable knew Blossom's waistcoat very well, of course. And each one thought the question was being asked of him. Suddenly from every stall six sharp raps rang out, and even poor Nino, lying in the straw with eyes closed, stretched out a hind leg and weakly kicked his door six times. Mr. Blossom's eyes looked as though they were going to pop out of his head.

"Now," said the Doctor smiling, "in case you should think that that was accidental too, I will ask Beppo to pull down the rag you see there hanging on his partition and to throw it up in the air."

In response to a few more words of horse language the rag, whose end hung over the top of the partition, suddenly disappeared. The Doctor had not moved. Blossom ran down the stable to look inside stall number 2. There he found the aged wagon horse tossing the rag up in the air and catching it—rather like a schoolgirl playing with a handkerchief.

"Now do you believe me?" asked the Doctor.

"Believe you!" cried Blossom. "I believe you're the Devil's younger brother. Just the same, you're the man I want, all right. Come on down to the dressing room and let's put some togs on you."

"Just a minute," said the Doctor. "What do you mean to do?"

"Dress you up," said Blossom, "of course. You're going to do a turn for us, ain't yer? Why, you could take any cab horse and make a Nino of him. You said you was going to help me?"

"Yes," answered John Dolittle slowly, "and I will—after, as I told you, you have promised me a few things. I am willing to make Beppo provide your ring with a talking horse on certain condition. Nino's act doesn't come on till the end of the show. We have a half hour to talk this over in."

"There's no need," cried Blossom, all excited. "I'll promise you any bloomin' things. Why, if you can talk animals' language, we'll make a fortune in a season! Lor' bless us! I never believed you could do it. You ought to 'ave joined show business years ago. You'd 'ave bin a rich man by now—instead of a broken-down country doctor. Come on over and we'll pick you out some nifty togs. Can't go on in them baggy trousers; people 'ud think you'd never bin on a horse in your life."

Blossom and the Doctor left the stable and made their way across to the dressing rooms where out of some of the well-traveled trunks the ringmaster began pulling costume after costume and piling them on the floor. While he was going through the gaudy clothes, the Doctor laid down the conditions under which he would give the performance.

"Now, Mr. Blossom," said he, "ever since I have been with your circus I have noticed certain things that were distasteful to my ideas of honest business and the humanitarian treatment of animals. Some of these I have brought to your attention, and in almost all cases you refused to listen to me."

"Why, Doctor," said Mr. Blossom, yanking a pair of red

"Why, Doctor, how can you say such a thing?"

Persian trousers out of a trunk, "how can you say such a thing? Didn't I get rid of Brown and Fatima because you objected to 'em?"

"You parted with them because you had to," said the Doctor, "not to oblige me. I have felt very uneasy about being part of a show, which I did not consider strictly honest. It would take a long time to go into all the details. For the present, the bargain I am going to strike with you is this: Beppo, the horse I will use for the talking act, is far too old to work. He has been in service now thirty-five years. I want him, as a reward for this help that he will give you, to be pensioned off for the remainder of his days, made comfortable, and given the kind of life he likes."

"I agree. Now how would this do?"

Blossom held up a cavalier's jerkin against the Doctor's chest. "No—too small. You ain't very high from the ground, but you're full-sized around the middle, all right."

"The other thing I want you to do," the Doctor went on, as Blossom turned back to the trunk for another costume, "is to put your menagerie in proper order. The cages are not cleaned often enough; some of the animals have not sufficient space for their needs, and many of them never get the kinds of food they like best."

"All right, Doc, we'll do anything in reason. I'll let you draw up a set of rules for the menagerie-keeper and you can see that he toes the line. 'Ow would you like to be a Western cowboy?"

"I wouldn't," said the Doctor. "They are inconsiderate to their cattle. And I don't approve of that silly business of flapping a hat in a horse's eyes to make him buck. Then, for the rest, I shall from time to time expect you to make many minor reforms for the animals' comfort. I shall expect you to treat my suggestions reasonably and cooperate with me for their welfare. What do you say?"

"I say it's a go, Doc," said Blossom. "We ain't begun yet. If you stay with my outfit for a year—with your gift of talking to animals—why!—I'll make every other circus look like a two-penny peepshow. Oh, my! 'Ere's the very thing—a cavalry uniform—Twenty-first Huzzars. Just your size. Medals and all! Suits your complexion, too."

This time Blossom held a bright scarlet tunic over the Doctor's bosom and beamed on him with delight.

"Ever seen anything so nifty!" he chuckled. "My word! I tell yer—we'll make this town sit up! Could you get these things on your feet?"

"Oh, I dare say," said the Doctor, taking a gaudy pair of military riding boots from the ringmaster and sitting down to unlace his own. At that moment the door opened and a stable boy came in.

"Joe, you're just in time," said Blossom. "Run over to the stables and give Beppo a rubdown with the currycomb. He's going to do an act."

"Beppo!" cried the boy incredulously.

"That's what I said, block'ead!" shouted Blossom. "And put the green 'alter with the white rosettes on 'im—and braid 'is tail with a red ribbon. Hop about it!"

As the lad disappeared, the clown with Swizzle entered for a short rest between acts. The Doctor, in smart regimental breeches and top boots, was now buttoning up the scarlet tunic about his chin.

"'Ow's my cross-eyed understudy doing?" asked Blossom.

"Governor, he's a wonder!" said Hop, sinking into a chair. "A born ringmaster. You never heard such a voice. He's got a gift of the gab, all right. Ready with a joke if anybody slips; cracking quips with the audience—I tell you, governor, you've got to look to your laurels if you leave him with the ladies for long. Who's the military gentleman? My hat, it's the Doctor! What's he going to do?"

At this moment another lad ran in.

"Only ten minutes before the last act goes on, Mr. Blossom," he cried.

"All right," said Blossom. "We can do it. Here's your sword-belt, Doctor. How's the crowd, Frank?"

"Great!" said the boy. "Pleased as punch! They brought the whole grammar school down at the last minute. And the Soldier's and Sailors' Home is coming tonight. People standing two deep in the aisles. It's the biggest business we've played to this year."

The Fifth Chapter

The Star Turn Gives a Great Performance

TREMENDOUS EXCITEMENT NOW PREVAILED behind the scenes in Blossom's "Mammoth Circus." As the clown, Hop, opened the dressing room door to go back into the ring, mingled cheers and hand-clapping, the noise of a big audience's applause, reached the ears of John Dolittle and the manager.

"Listen, Hop," said Blossom, "pass the word to Mugg as you go back in that Nino is going to play anyway—in substitute—and the Doc here is doing the part of the trainer. Mugg can give 'em the introduction patter just the same. Tell 'im to lay it on thick. It's going to be the greatest little turn we ever showed—better than Nino at his best."

"All right, governor," said the clown, grinning through his paint. "But I wish you had picked a better-looking horse."

At the last moment one of the Doctor's shoulder straps was found to be loose. Only two minutes now remained before his act was due. Someone flew off and found Theodosia, and with frantic

"Listen, Hop."

haste she put it right with a needle and thread. Then, complete in his wonderful uniform, the Doctor ran out of the dressing room to join his partner, Beppo, whose bridle was being held at the entrance to the big tent by the boy, Frank.

Poor Beppo did not look nearly as smart as the Doctor. Years of neglect and haphazard grooming could not be remedied by one currycombing. His coat was long and dingy-looking, his mane straggly and unkempt. In spite of the smart, green-and-white headstall and the red ribbon in his plaited tail, he looked what he was: an old, old servant who had done his work faithfully for many, many years and got little credit or thanks for it.

"Oh, I say, Beppo!" the Doctor murmured in his ear as he took the bridle from Frank. "Anyone would think you were going to a funeral. Brace up! Draw your head back, high. That's it. Now blow out your nostrils—ah, much better!"

"You know, Doctor," said Beppo, "you mightn't believe it, but I come from a very good family. My mother used to trace her pedigree way back to the battle-charger that Julius Caesar used—the one he always rode when he reviewed the Prætorian Guard. My mother was very proud of it. She took first prizes, she did. But when the heavy battle-chargers went out of fashion, all the big military horses got put to draft work. That's how we came down in the world. Oughtn't we to rehearse this act a bit first? I've no idea of what I'm expected to do."

"No, we haven't time now," said John Dolittle. "We are liable to be called on any minute. But we'll manage. Just do everything I tell you—and put in an extras you think of yourself. Look out, you're drooping your head again. Remember your Roman ancestor. Chin up—that's the way. Arch your neck. Make your eyes flash. Look as though you were carrying an emperor who owned the earth. Fine! That's the style! Now you look great."

Within the big canvas theater, Mr. Matthew Mugg, ringmaster for a day, was still covering himself with glory, bossing "The Greatest Show on Earth" with creditable skill and introducing the performers with much oratory and unusual grammar. He was having the time of his life and making the most of it.

In between the turns of the Pinto Brothers and the strong man, he saw Hop return into the ring and recommence his arms, which always so delighted the children. As the clown did a somersault past the ringmaster's nose, Matthew heard him whisper:

"The boss is putting on another talking horse with the Doctor playing the trainer. He wants you to introduce him the same as Nino."

"Right you are," Matthew whispered back. "I've got the idea."

And when Jojo, the dancing elephant, had bowed himself out amid a storm of applause, the ringmaster stepped to the entrance flap and himself led forward the next, the star turn.

For a moment old Beppo, accompanied by a short, stout man in cavalry uniform, seemed a little scared to find a sea of faces staring down at him.

Motioning to the strange-looking performers to remain by the edge of the ring a moment, Matthew advanced into the center. With a lordly wave of the hand he silenced the wheezy band that was still finishing Jojo's last dance. And in the quiet that followed he looked up at the audience and filled his lungs for his last and most impressive speech.

"Ladies and gentlemen," roared Ringmaster Mugg, "we 'ave now harrived at the last and most himportant act in our long and helegant program. You 'ave all 'eard, I'm sure, of Nino—Nino, the World-Famous Talking Horse, and his gallant owner, the dashing Cossack cavalry officer, Captain Nicholas Pufftupski. There they are, ladies and gentlemen; you see them before you in the flesh. Kings and queens have traveled miles to witness their act. Only two months ago, when we are playing in Monte Carlo, we 'ad to turn away the prime minister of England because we 'adn't got a seat for 'im in the 'ouse.

"Nino, ladies and gentlemen, is very old. He came originally from the back steps of Siberia. His present owner, Major Pufftupski, bought 'im from the wandering Tartar tribes. Since then 'e 'as been through fifteen wars—which accounts for his wore-out appearance. This is the self-same 'orse what Colonel Pufftupski rode when, single 'anded 'e drove Napoleon out of Moscow and saved Russia from fallin' under the hiron 'eel of Bonaparte. And the center one of them three medals you see 'anging on the Brigadier's chest is the one the Czar gave 'im as a reward for 'is brave hact."

"Oh, stop his nonsense, Matthew," whispered the Doctor coming up to him, dreadfully embarrassed. "There's no need to—"

But the eloquent ringmaster hurried on with thunderous voice:

"So much, ladies and gentlemen, for the military career of this remarkable 'orse and 'is brave owner. General Pufftupski is a modest man and he forbids me to tell you about 'is other medals what was given 'im by the king of Sweden and the empress of China. I now pass on to the hextraordinary hintelligence of the animal you see before you. On 'is way back from chasing Napoleon out of Russia, Count Pufftupski was took prisoner—and 'is 'orse, the famous Nino, with 'im. During their himprisonment they became very hintimate. So much so that at the end of the two years, while they was captives of the French, Nino and 'is owner could talk to one another freely—the same as you and I might do. If you don't believe what I say you can prove it for yourselves. All you 'ave to do is to ask any question of Nino through his owner and it will be answered—if it 'as an answer. The field marshal talks all languages except Japanese. If any Japanese ladies or gentlemen in the audience wants to ask questions, they'll 'ave to turn 'em into some other language first. Marshal Pufftupski will open 'is performance with this marvelous 'orse with a few tricks just to show you what they can do. Ladies and gentlemen, I 'ave great pleasure in introducing to you the Archduke Nicholas Pufftupski, Commander-in-Chief of the Russian Army, and 'is battle-charger, the one and only, world-famous NINO."

As the band played a few opening chords, the Doctor and Beppo stepped forward to the center of the ring and bowed. A tremendous burst of applause came from the people.

It was a strange performance, the only one of its kind ever given to a circus audience. The Doctor, when he entered the ring, had no definite idea of what he was going to do—neither had Beppo. But the old, old veteran knew that the performance was going to win him comfort and freedom from work for the rest of his days.

"The Commander-in-Chief of the Russian Army"

Every once in a while during the course of the act he would forget his noble ancestry and slump back into his usual weary, worn-out appearance. But on the whole, as Hop said afterward, he made a much better-looking show horse than anyone had expected; and so far as the audience was concerned, his success surpassed anything Blossom had ever exhibited.

After doing a few tricks Colonel Pufftupski turned to the people and offered (in remarkably good English) to make the horse do anything they asked. Immediately a little boy in the front row cried out:

"Tell him to come over here and take my hat off."

The Doctor made a sign or two and Beppo went straight to the boy, lifted the cap from his head and put it into his hand. Then numberless questions were shouted by the audience, and to every one Beppo gave an answer—sometimes by tapping the floor, sometimes by shaking his head, and sometimes by word of mouth, which the Doctor translated. The people enjoyed it so much that Blossom, watching through a slit outside, thought they'd never be done. And when at last the gallant Pufftupski led his horse out of the ring, the audience clapped and cheered and called to him again and again to come back and receive their applause.

The news of the wonderful success of the circus's first performance in Bridgeton, mostly brought about by the marvelous Talking Horse, quickly spread through the town. And long before the evening show was due, people were lined up outside the big tent, four deep, waiting patiently to make sure of seats; while the rest of the enclosure and all the sideshows were packed and thronged so tight that you could hardly move through the crowds.

The Sixth Chapter

Beppo the Great

THE MONEY, OVER THE SPENDING OF WHICH poor Dab-Dab had so worried, was soon replaced in the Dolittle savings box. The addition of six snakes to the Doctor's household was not an expensive one in upkeep—even though the good housekeeper continued to plead and argue with John Dolittle for the ousting of what she called the messy, squirmy creatures. But during the days at Bridgeton the throngs that crowded into the enclosure left so many sixpences at the booth of the "Two-headed animal from the jungles of Africa" that soon Too-Too prophesied the record takings of the Ashby week would be easily beaten.

"I estimate, Doctor," said he, putting his mathematical head on one side and closing his left eye, "that in six days we should easily make sixteen pounds—and that's not allowing for any extra business on the market day or Saturday."

"And most of that you can put down to the Doctor's act with

Beppo," said Jip. "If it wasn't for that turn, and the talk it has made, the crowds wouldn't be half so big."

Finding what a success John Dolittle's performance was making, Blossom came to him after the first showing and begged him to keep it up for the whole of the week that the circus stayed at Bridgeton.

"Well, but look here," said John Dolittle, "I've promised Beppo that he would be pensioned off for obliging you in your emergency. I don't know how soon Nino will be able to work again; but I did not say anything to Beppo about acting all week. I supposed you would put something else in our place as soon as you had time to look around."

"Good Lord, Doctor!" said Blossom. "I couldn't find anything to take the place of your act if I looked around for a year. There's never been anything like it since the circus was invented. The news of it has gone all over the town—and a good ways outside of it, too. They say folks are coming all the way from Whittlethorpe to see your turn. Listen, can't you ask Beppo to oblige us? It ain't heavy work for 'im. Tell 'im we'll give 'im anything 'e likes—asparagus for breakfast and a feather bed to sleep in—if 'e only says the word. My outfit, with the sideshows and all, is taking in pretty near fifty pounds a day now. Never saw such business! If this keeps up we shan't 'ave to stay in the game long before we're all on easy street."

There was something of contempt in the Doctor's face as he looked at Blossom and paused a moment before answering.

"Oh yes," he said rather sadly, "you're willing enough to treat your poor old servant well now, aren't you? Now that he is bringing you in money. For years and years he has worked for you and never even got his coat brushed in return—just enough hay and oats to keep him going. Now you'll give anything in the world. Money! Bah! It's a curse."

"Well," said Blossom, "I'm helping to make up for it now, ain't I? It ain't 'eavy work, answering questions and doin' tricks. You go and talk to 'im, Doctor. Lord bless me! Don't it sound strange?—me asking you to go and talk to 'im—and twenty-four hours ago I didn't know there ever was such a thing as talking to 'orses!"

"Except with a whip," said John Dolittle. "I wish I could put you in his place and make you work thirty-five years for Beppo in return for hay and water and a lot of beating and neglect. All right, I'll put your request before him and see what he says. But remember, his decision is to be final. If he refuses to give one single performance more I shall hold you to your promise—a comfortable home for him and a good pasture to graze in for the rest of his life. And I almost hope he'll say no."

The Doctor turned on his heel and, leaving the ringmaster's wagon, set off toward the stables.

"Poor old Beppo!" he murmured. "His ancestor carried Julius Caesar in military reviews—heard the legions cheer the conqueror of the world who sat astride his back! Poor old Beppo!"

When he entered the stables he found the wagon horse gazing out of the window of his stall at the pleasant fields that lay beyond the circus enclosure.

"Is that you, John Dolittle?" said he, as the Doctor opened the door. "Have you come to take me away?"

"Beppo," said John Dolittle, putting his hand on the veteran's gaunt and bony back, "it seems you are now a great man—I mean, a great horse."

"How's that, Doctor? I don't understand."

"You've become famous, Beppo. This is a funny world. And we humans, I often think, are the funniest animals in it. Mr. Blossom has just found out, after you have been in his service for thirty-five years, how valuable and intelligent you are."

"In what way valuable?"

"Because you talk, Beppo."

"But I've always talked."

"Yes, I know. But Mr. Blossom and the world *didn't* know until I proved it to them in the circus ring. You have made a great sensation, Beppo, just on the eve of your retirement. Now they don't want you to retire. They want you to continue being wonderful—just talking, the way you've always done."

"It sounds crazy, doesn't it, Doctor?"

"Perfectly. But you have suddenly become so valuable to Blossom that he will give you asparagus for breakfast, a valet to brush your coat and another to curl your mane if you'll only stay and act for him for the rest of the week."

"Humph! That's what it means to be famous, does it? I'd sooner be turned out into a nice big field."

"Well, Beppo, you are to suit yourself—at last, after thirty-five years of suiting other people. I've told Blossom I'm going to hold him to his bargain. If you don't want to do it, say so. You shall retire today if you wish."

"What would you advise me to do, Doctor?"

"There is this about it," said John Dolittle. "If you give Blossom what he wants now, we may be able to get you what you want—that is, more exactly what you want—later. You see, he has no farm of his own to put you on; he would have to get a farmer to graze you and take care of you for him. And besides, he will probably be better disposed toward me and some plans I have for the other animals."

"All right, Doctor," said Beppo. "Then that settles it. I'll do it."

There was no happier man in the world than Alexander Blossom when John Dolittle came and told him that Beppo had consented to act all the week. He at once got handbills printed and had them sent to the neighboring towns and given away in the streets. These told the public that the World-Famous Talking Horse was to be seen at Bridgeton for only four remaining days, and that those who did not miss the chance of a lifetime had better hurry up and come to "Blossom's Mammoth Circus."

"He had handbills given away in the streets."

The Doctor was caused considerable embarrassment during the special parades through the streets, which were arranged for Beppo by having himself pointed out as the Archduke Pufftupski, the famous horse's owner and trainer. For this absurd title, which Matthew had bestowed on the Doctor, the manager insisted on his sticking to.

Tuesday, Wednesday, and Thursday of that week were each record-breakers for Blossom's box office. For the first time in his life the ringmaster had to turn people away from the gates of his circus. The crowding of the enclosure reached a point where he was afraid to let any more in. The police of Bridgeton had to lend him nearly their whole force to keep the throngs in order and to see that no accidents happened in the crush.

Nothing succeeds like success. It was only necessary to have the news go through the town that people were being turned away, to make twice the number clamor for admission. "Bridgeton Week" came to be spoken of among the show folk for a long time afterward as the outstanding period in the circus's whole career.

THE SEVENTH CHAPTER

The Perfect Pasture

IN THE MEANTIME, JOHN DOLITTLE WAS MAKING Blossom fulfill the other parts of his bargain. It was not long after the circus had opened at Bridgeton that the elephant sent Jip for the Doctor because he was suffering from an acute attack of rheumatism—brought on by living in an exceedingly damp and dirty stable.

The poor creature was in considerable pain. The Doctor, after examining, prescribed massage. Blossom was sent for and ordered to buy a barrel of a special, costly balm. A few weeks before, of course, the ringmaster would have flatly refused to go to such an expense for his animal's comfort. But now, with John Dolittle bringing him in the biggest business that his show had ever seen, he was ready to do almost anything to please him. The balm was sent for right away, and then the Doctor demanded six strong men to help him.

Massaging an elephant is no light work. A large audience gathered in the menagerie to watch the six men and the Doctor

"Massaging the elephant"

crawling over the elephant's body, rubbing and pummeling the ointment into his hide till the sweat ran from their foreheads.

Then the Doctor ordered a new stable built for the big creature, with a special kind of wooden floor with drainage under it and a lot of other up-to-date features. And, although this work was also expensive, carpenters were brought in and it was completed in three hours. The result was that the elephant got well in a very short time.

The Doctor also drew up rules for the menagerie-keeper that improved the condition of all the other animals. And in spite of the fact that the keeper grumbled a good deal about "running a zoo like a beauty parlor," Blossom made him understand that he would be discharged immediately if the Doctor's new regulations were not strictly obeyed.

Poor Nino was still pretty sick. He was getting better, but his recovery was dreadfully slow. The Doctor visited him twice a day. But Blossom now realized that the cob's act, which had always been done under his own guidance, could never take the place of the far finer performance of Beppo and the Doctor. Beppo, his age and appearance notwithstanding, was a much cleverer horse than Nino.

Well, the week wore on toward its end. John Dolittle had made arrangements with Blossom that after the last performance on Saturday, he and Beppo were to leave and go away to a certain farmer who had agreed to keep the old horse in good grazing for the remainder of his days. He was to have all the oats he wanted and white radishes (a delicacy that Beppo was particularly fond of) twice a week. The Doctor and Beppo were going to inspect this farm, and if they didn't like it, another one to their satisfaction was to be found.

The last performance was over; the big tent was being pulled down and the Doctor and Beppo were all ready for their departure. The old horse's luggage consisted of a blanket (a new one the Doctor had made Blossom buy as a farewell present), which he wore. The Doctor's luggage was his little black bag and a small bundle, which was also carried on Beppo's back. John Dolittle was standing at the gate, his hand on Beppo's bridle waiting for Matthew, who had run back to the wagon to get some sandwiches that Dab-Dab was preparing.

Presently he saw Blossom hurrying across the enclosure in a great state of excitement. A little way behind walked a short, very smartly dressed man.

"Listen, Doc," panted the ringmaster coming up, "I've just had the biggest offer I ever got in my life. That toff coming along is the proprietor of the Manchester Amphitheater. He wants my outfit to show in his theater—one of the biggest in the country—week after next. And 'e especially wants Beppo. What do you think he guarantees us? A hundred pounds a day! And maybe more if—"

"No!" the Doctor interrupted firmly, holding up his hand. "Beppo may not have many more years to live, but what he has he's going to spend in comfort. Tell that to your manager. Beppo retires—today—from the circus business for good."

And without waiting for his sandwiches, he led the old horse out of the enclosure and hurried down the road.

Beppo and John Dolittle had not gone very far before they were overtaken by Too-Too.

"Doctor," said the owl, "I came after you to let you know about the money."

"Too-Too," John Dolittle replied, "at the present moment the subject of money is more than usually distasteful to me. Beppo and I are trying to get away from the very smell of it."

"But just think what you can *do* with money, Doctor," said Too-Too.

"Yes, that's the trouble with the beastly stuff. It's the power of it that makes it such a curse."

"Dab-Dab asked me," Too-Too went on, "to come and let you know how much the Pushmi-Pullyu had made this week at Bridgeton, because she thought perhaps you might think of retiring to Puddleby when you heard. I only just got it figured out—deducting Blossom's share and the bills we owe the tradespeople. It was a big piece of arithmetic, I can tell you. My estimate was way off. Instead of sixteen pounds, we made twenty-six pounds thirteen shillings and tenpence, clear profit."

"Humph," murmured the Doctor. "It's a large amount, but not enough for us to retire on, Too-Too. Still, it would go quite a long way toward it. Tell Dab-Dab to keep it safely for me and we will talk over the matter when I get back. I am returning tomorrow, you know. Good-bye—and thank you very much for bringing me the news."

Now, the Doctor had in his pocket the address of the farmer to whom they were going. Imagine his surprise on reading his destination to find that it was the same farm as the one where his old friend, the plow horse, lived!

There were hearty greetings, a good deal of astonishment, and much joy at the meeting. The old plow horse, beaming through his green spectacles, was introduced to Beppo and Beppo was introduced to him. It was curious that although the Doctor had known the plow horse for so long, he had never heard his name. And it was only on introducing the two old horses to each other that he learned it for the first time. It was Toggle.

"You know," said the plow horse, "I am tremendously glad to see you both, but I am a little sorry, for Beppo's sake, that it was to this farm that Blossom sent him. The farmer himself is a very decent follow, but this pasture I have here leaves a good deal to be desired."

"But we don't *have* to stay here," said the Doctor. "I told Blossom that if it did not meet with Blossom's approval he must find another. In what way is this place unsuitable? Is the grass bad?"

"No," said Toggle, "the grass is all right—a little rank in August if there's much rain, but it's sweet enough most of the year. But the meadow slopes the wrong way. You see, this hillside is fac-

"The old plow horse was introduced to Beppo."

ing northeast. It's only in midsummer that you get any sun. It stays behind the hill the rest of the year. Then the prevailing wind is a cold northeaster that blows across the meadow, and there's little protection from it—excepts along that hedge over there, and one soon eats up that bit of grass."

"Well, tell me," said the Doctor, turning to Beppo, "what, for you, would be the ideal, the most attractive place for an old horses' home?"

"The place I've always dreamed of," said Beppo, gazing across the landscape with a wistful look in his old eyes, "is like this—part of it is sloping and part of it is flat. Slopes are such a nice change: the grass is nearer to your nose, and the flats are restful to get back to after the slopes. Then it has trees, big spreading trees with fat trunks—the kind horses love to stand under and think—after a hearty meal. It has a copse where herbs and wild roots grow, the sorts we love to nibble for a change—especially the wild mint, which is soothing to the stomach when you've eaten too much. It has good water—not a muddy, little pond, but a decent brook where the water is always sparkling and clear. In a hollow it has a nice old shelter with a dry floor and a mossy, tiled roof that doesn't let the rain in. The pasture varies: some places are firm, croppy turf; others are deep, luscious, long hay-grass with buttercups and fragrant wild flowers mixed in it. At the top of the hilly part you can get a view of the sunsets to the west and the south. And on the summit there is a good firm post to scratch your neck on. I love to watch the sun go down as I scratch my neck of an evening. The whole place is protected from snappy dogs and worrisome people with good fences. It is quiet. It is peaceful. And that, John Dolittle, is the place where I would spend my old age."

"Humph!" murmured the Doctor when Beppo had ended. "Your description sounds delightful—almost like the place where I'd wish to spend my own old age—though I suppose I'd want a little more furniture than a scratching post. Toggle, do you know of a pasture such as this that Beppo speaks of?"

"I do, indeed, Doctor," said Toggle. "Come with me and I'll show you."

Then the plow horse led them over the brow of the hill and down the other side a way. Here, facing the sunny south, they looked over a farm gate into the loveliest meadow you ever saw. It was almost as if some fairy had made old Beppo's wish come true, for it was the retreat he had described in every detail: there was the clump of great elm trees; there was the copse and the sparkling brook; there was the snug shelter in the hollow; and on the summit of the slope, against the red glow of the setting sun, stood the post for Beppo to scratch his neck on.

"This is it, Doctor," said Beppo quietly. "This is the spot—just as I had always planned it. No horse could ask for any better place to pass his old age."

"They looked over a farm gate."

"It's wonderful," said the Doctor, himself entirely captivated by the beauty of the scene. "It has character, that meadow. Does this land belong to your farmer, Toggle?"

"No," said the plow horse. "I've often tried to break in here and graze. And I did get through the hedge, once or twice, but the owner always chased me out again. It belongs to a farmer who lives in the little house with the red roof down there."

"I see," said the Doctor. "I wonder how much a piece of ground like that would cost."

"Not very much, I shouldn't think," said Toggle. "Although it is large, the farmer has never raised anything but hay on it."

"But, Doctor," said Beppo, "why buy it? I thought you said Blossom was going to pay for my pensioning off."

"Yes," said the Doctor. "But he has only agreed to pay for your board and lodging. I've always had an idea I'd like to start a Home for Retired Cab and Wagon Horses. And this place is such an ideal one for aged horses that I thought, if I could, I'd buy it. Then we would form 'The Retired Cab and Wagon Horses' Association' and you could keep the place for your own for good."

"What a marvelous idea!" cried both horses together.

"But have you got enough money, Doctor?" asked Beppo. "Jip often told me that you were as poor as a church mouse."

"That is so—more or less," the Doctor agreed. "Money with me has always been a most uncertain thing. But, as you heard Too-Too come and tell me shortly after we had left the circus, I am now some twenty-six pounds to the good. I owe a sailor a lot of money for a boat, but his need is not so urgent as your own—I sent a bird to find out, so I know. I can make some more money later on to pay him with. Of course, twenty-six pounds is not enough to buy a piece of land that big, outright. But perhaps the farmer will let me pay so much down and the rest by installments every year. If he will, it becomes yours right away and nobody can take it away from you—unless I fail in my payments. Now, you two wait here and I'll go and see him about it."

Leaving the two horses by the gate, the Doctor set off across country for the little red-roofed house that Toggle had pointed out.

THE EIGHTH CHAPTER

The Retired Cab and Wagon Horses' Association

NOW, THE FARMER WHO OWNED THE LAND was, at the moment when John Dolittle knocked upon his door, sitting at his parlor table talking to Toggle's farmer. He was sorely in need of twenty pounds to buy seed potatoes with. But Toggle's farmer, with many apologies, had been compelled to refuse him because he himself was very short of money at this time. It was this conversation that the Doctor's call interrupted.

The farmer was very hospitable and invited John Dolittle to come in and sit down at the table with his other guest. Mugs of fragrant cider were brought in by the host's wife. Then the Doctor described the piece of ground that Toggle had shown him and asked if it was for sale. And as it was one that the farmer seldom used, he immediately said yes, it was. For how much, the Doctor asked. For one hundred and twenty pounds, the farmer told him.

"Well," said the Doctor. "I only have twenty-six pounds at present. Suppose I gave you that down and promised to pay the rest

"John Dolittle knocked upon his door."

in twenty-pound installments every six months: Would you let me have it?"

The farmer, seeing a chance of getting his seed potatoes, was going to agree at once, but the other, Toggle's farmer, broke into the conversation.

"What be you going to use the land for, stranger?" he asked. "You ain't thinkin' of puttin' up no glue factory, I hope."

"Oh no," said the Doctor. "I want to make it into a rest farm for old horses—just a grazing ground. Practically nothing will be altered."

The two farmers thought the stranger must be crazy. But, as he and the plan he proposed seemed harmless enough, they readily gave in.

"By the way," said the Doctor, still speaking to Toggle's owner, "you have a friend of mine at your farm, a plow horse; he wears spectacles that I gave him years ago when he lived in Puddleby."

"Oh aye," said the farmer. "I know 'un—Toggle. A strange beast, that. 'E wouldn't be parted from them specs for anything. What about 'im?"

"He is too old to work, isn't he?" said the Doctor. "You let him graze now most of the time, I understand. He wishes to use this same pasture with the horse I have brought today. Will you let him?"

"That I will," said the farmer. "But how come you to know all this about my cattle?"

"Oh, well," said the Doctor, looking sort of embarrassed, "I have ways of my own knowing what horses want. I'm a naturalist."

"Sounds like you was an *unnaturalist* to me," said the farmer, winking at his neighbor.

After a little discussion on how the first money would be sent, the bargain was closed and the Doctor was told that now, so long as his part of the arrangement was fulfilled, the land belonged to him.

"Not to me," he said as he rose and bade the farmers farewell. "The land belongs to the Association. I am turning it over to the horses themselves."

Having inquired of his host where he could find a carpenter, the Doctor left. And when, a half hour later, the two farmers walked across the field together, they saw the strange naturalist and the carpenter busily putting up a large signboard in the middle of the pasture. On it was written in big letters:

REST FARM

THIS LAND IS THE PROPERTY OF THE
RETIRED CAB AND WAGON HORSES'
ASSOCIATION. TRESPASSERS AND
VICIOUS DOGS WILL BE KICKED.

BY ORDER,
(Signed, on behalf of the Committee.)
BEPPO, President.
TOGGLE, Vice-President.

NOTE—MEMBERSHIP FREE
FOR ADMISSION APPLY AT THE GATE

Well, after seeing the first two members of "The Association" enter into possession of their new quarters, John Dolittle bade Beppo and Toggle farewell and set off on his return journey.

As he passed down the road he looked back many times to watch the two old veterans prancing around their beautiful new home. The sight warmed his heart and he smiled as he hurried on.

"I'm not sure," he murmured to himself, "but I think that is almost the best job I ever did. Poor creatures! They are happy at last, growing young again after a life of hard work. I must establish some more institutions like that. I've one or two in mind. The Rat and Mouse Club, for instance. I'd like to see that started. Of course, I shall get in a frightful row over this from Dab-Dab when she finds out that I've spent all the money again. Oh well, it's worth it. I'll send some London cab horses down to join them as soon as I get to the city again. Humph!"—(the Doctor paused and looked back)—"There they are—at it still—Beppo rolling down the hill and Toggle splashing through the brook. Great heavens! I forgot all about the radishes. Why didn't Beppo remind me?"

He hurried back. On the way he met a lad playing in the road. Questioning him, he found he was the son of the farmer who had sold the land.

"Would you like to earn a shilling a week?" asked the Doctor.

"I'd like to earn a shilling a month," said the boy. "I want to save up and buy some skates for next winter. I've only got ninepence so far."

"Do you know how to grow radishes?"

"Would you like to earn a shilling a week?"

"Yes," answered the boy. "That's easy. They're about the only thing I can grow."

"Very good," said John Dolittle. "Now, you see that meadow where the horses are—and the shelter at the bottom? Well, I've just bought that land from your father. It's to be a home for horses. If you'll plant me a radish bed behind the shelter, the white kind, you know, I'll pay you a shilling a week for keeping it in order. Are you willing?"

"I should say I am, sir!" cried the boy.

"All right. Here's your first shilling—and here's a penny to buy a packet of seed with. I appoint you head gardener to the Rest Farm. You're now on the payroll of the Retired Cab and Wagon Horses' Association. Make the radish bed fairly big, because I may be sending down some more horses later. When the radishes are ripe, you make them up into bunches and hand them out to the members twice a week. And don't forget to plant new seed every so often, to keep up the supply. Understand?"

"Yes, sir."

"Now give me your Christian name," said the Doctor, "and I'll send you your wages every week. And if you should have to leave your job—to go away or anything—get your father to write me a letter. He knows how to reach me."

The boy, pleased as punch with his good luck, gave the Doctor his name, took his money, and ran off to get a spade and fork and start his new work.

"Well, so that's that," the Doctor murmured as he hurried on toward Bridgeton. "Now, I must try to think out a way to break the news gently to Dab-Dab that our money box is emptied again."

The Rest Farm, which the Doctor established that day, continued to flourish and grow for many years. And another worry was added to the many that harassed Dab-Dab, the careful housekeeper. For not only had the Doctor bound himself to send the farmer twenty pounds every six months, but he further reduced the Dolittle fortunes by buying, every once in a while, some specially old and weary horse that he would meet on the streets. He bought them from cab drivers, from rag-and-bone men, from all sorts of people. Poor Dab-Dab used to be terrified when she saw a gypsy wagon come in sight on the road. For their horses were always particularly thin and scrawny-looking, and it was almost certain that the Doctor would try to buy the poor creatures from men who were much better skilled than he in shrewd bargaining.

All these old waifs and wrecks of horses the Doctor would send down to the Rest Farm to be made free members of the Association. Beppo's and Toggle's partnership grew into quite a family circle of old cronies—horses from all walks of life. And many were the interesting tales of bygone days told beneath the big trees of an evening or around the post on top of the hill. Here the old fellows would stand in line, waiting to scratch their necks, watching the beauty of the peaceful landscape grow dim in the red glow of the setting sun.

And still the membership list grew longer and longer. The boy who kept the radish garden sent a letter to the Doctor, saying he had had to enlarge the bed and needed help. He had a school friend, he wrote, who was also saving up to buy skates. Would the Doctor employ him, too?

The Doctor did; and the payroll of the Association advanced to two shillings a week. John Dolittle paid a visit to the farm after it had been going for about three months. On consulting with the committee (five of the oldest veterans), he found that money was required for repairing fences and keeping the ditches clear beneath the hedges. Some of the members needed their hooves trimmed (they didn't bother to wear shoes, of course). So he arranged with the lad he had first appointed as gardener to extend the radish bed considerably, in order that quite a large crop of vegetables could be grown—more than was needed for the members.

The lad had a good head for business and this was done; and two more friends of his were employed for the extra work. Then the money that was made by selling the vegetables was used to form a "Fencing and Farriers' Fund" to hire hedgers and ditchers and

"'What's the use?' cried Too-Too."

blacksmiths every so often to keep the fences in repair and to trim the members' hooves.

Paying the extra boys, of course, took still more from the Dolittle money box—and added still more to the worries of Dab-Dab the housekeeper.

"What's the use?" cried Too-Too one evening when they were discussing accounts. "What's the use of my doing all this double-entry bookkeeping, making my head fairly ache with arithmetic? It doesn't do any good to calculate how much the Doctor has—or to estimate how much he's going to have. No matter what it is, he spends it all!"

PART FIVE

The First Chapter

Mr. Bellamy of Manchester

BY GETTING A LIFT ON THE ROAD IN A FAST TRAP that overtook him, John Dolittle reached the circus late that night instead of early the following morning, as he had expected. And the first thing that Matthew Mugg said to him as he entered the wagon was:

"Blossom told me he wanted to see you as soon as you got in. That toff from Manchester is still with him."

Thereupon the Doctor immediately left his own wagon and set out for that of the ringmaster. Jip asked if he could come along, and the Doctor said yes.

The circus was now all packed up and ready for departure early tomorrow morning. As John Dolittle approached Blossom's caravan he saw a light in the window. It was very late—after midnight.

Within he found the ringmaster sitting at the little table with the smartly dressed man whom he had seen earlier in the day.

"Good evening, Doctor," said the ringmaster. "This gentleman is Mr. Frederick Bellamy, proprietor and manager of the Manchester Amphitheater. He has something 'e'd like to say to you."

The Doctor shook hands with Mr. Bellamy, who at once leaned back in his chair, put his thumbs in the armholes of his white waistcoat, and began:

"I have delayed my return to Manchester, Doctor Dolittle—in spite of urgent and pressing business—in order to discuss with you an engagement that I had offered to Mr. Blossom this afternoon. I witnessed your act with the Talking Horse and was greatly interested in it. Mr. Blossom tells me that he tried to get you to consent to take part in his show's performance in my theater, but that you refused—took the horse away to put him grazing."

The Doctor nodded, and Mr. Bellamy went on:

"I then supposed that the deal was off, because—I don't mind telling you—without your turn, I would not be interested in this circus. But Mr. Blossom has persuaded me to remain and talk with you myself. He assured me that the intelligence of the performance was not in that particular horse, but in your own unusual powers with animals—that you could give as good a show with any horse. He tells me, though I confess I can hardly believe it, that you can actually communicate with animals in their own language. Is that so?"

"Well," said the Doctor, looking uncomfortable, "I'm sorry that Mr. Blossom told you this. I don't claim it, or talk of it, myself, because I find that people don't usually believe me. But—yes, it is true. With most animals I can converse freely."

"Indeed," said Mr. Bellamy. "Most extraordinary! That being the case, we had thought that perhaps you would be willing to do us an act with some other animal, or animals, in place of the horse that you have just taken away. My idea is to make it something more elaborate—to have it form the bigger, more important part of Mr. Blossom's show. It is something quite new, this gift of yours. And, properly put on, it ought to make a great sensation. Of course, you understand, it would be well paid for—very, I might say. Would you consider it?"

"I haven't any other turn worked out at the moment," said the Doctor. "I am somewhat new to this business. My idea of shows with animals is that they must always be done with the consent and willing cooperation of the animals themselves."

"Oh, quite, quite," said Mr. Bellamy. "It is very late now. Suppose you think it over until tomorrow. I cannot catch the coach tonight. And if you consider it, let me know in the morning, eh?"

As the Doctor made his way back to his own wagon, Jip, who had listened to the conversation with great interest, trotted by his side.

"Doctor," said he, "this seems to me a grand chance for us to do our play—just your own family—me, Too-Too, Gub-Gub, Toby, Swizzle, and perhaps the white mouse. You know, you said you would let us try it sometime—'The Animals' Theater.' You write a comic play for us—Gub-Gub's is no good—sort of vegetable knockabout. You write a play of your own—for animals—something high-class. And we'll act it. I'm sure it will make a great sensation in Manchester. It's a big city. And we'll have a real intelligence audience."

In spite of the lateness of the hour, John Dolittle found, when he went back to his own wagon, that all his pets were sitting up waiting to see him and to hear the story of his day's doings.

Jip immediately told them of the interview with the Manchester manager and his own idea of providing an act by getting up an animal play. This was greeted with tremendous enthusiasm and applause from everyone, down to the white mouse.

"Hooray!" gurgled Gub-Gub. "At last I'm to be an actor.

And just think, I shall make my first appearance in *Manchester*!"

"Don't go so fast," said the Doctor. "We don't know yet that there will be a play. It may not be possible. It doesn't follow because a play amuses you that it will amuse your audience."

Then began a heated argument among the animals about plots for plays—about what kind of things amused people.

"Let's do *Cinderella*," cried the white mouse. "Everybody knows that, and then I can be one of the mice that the witch turned into footmen."

"Let's do *Little Red Riding Hood*," said Swizzle. "Then I can play the wolf."

The discussion became so general and interesting that the Doctor thought this would be a good time to break the news to Dab-Dab that he had spent the twenty-six pounds.

This he did. And the evening was spoiled for the housekeeper.

"Doctor, Doctor!" she sighed, shaking her head. "What *shall* I do with you? You're not to be trusted with money—really, you're not. Oh dear, we'll never get back to Puddleby, I suppose."

But the others, wrapped up in their new interest, brushed the matter aside as though it were nothing.

"Oh," said Gub-Gub airily, "we'll soon make some more. What is money? Poof! Look here, Doctor, why don't we do *Beauty and the Beast*? Then I can act the part of the Beauty."

"Great heavens!" cried Jip. "What an idea! No; listen, Doctor: you write the play yourself—because you know what will interest people."

"Why don't you let the Doctor go to bed?" asked Dab-Dab angrily. "He has had a long day. And it's time you were all asleep yourselves."

"My gracious!" said the Doctor, looking at his watch. "Do you know what time it is? It is two o'clock in the morning. . . . Go to bed, all of you."

"Oh, we're traveling tomorrow, Doctor," said Gub-Gub. "It doesn't matter what time we get up. Let us stay a little longer. We have to settle on what play we are going to give."

"No you don't," said Dab-Dab, "not tonight. The Doctor's tired."

"No, I'm not tired," said John Dolittle.

"Well, it's bad for them to stay up late. There's nothing like early bed as a habit."

"Yes, I suppose so," said the Doctor. "But myself, I don't like getting into habits, you know."

"Well I do," said Dab-Dab, "when they're good ones. I like regular people."

"Do you, Dab-Dab? That's why you're such an excellent housekeeper. There are two kinds of people: those who like habits and those who don't. They both have their good qualities."

"You know, Doctor," Gub-Gub put in, "me—I always divide people into the pickle-eaters and the plain-feeders—those who like chutneys and sauces on their food and those who like everything plain."

"It's the same idea, Gub-Gub," the Doctor laughed. "Those that like change in their lives and those that like sameness. Your chutney-eaters are the change-lovers and your plain-fooders are the er—housekeepers. Myself, I hope to grow more adaptable as I grow older."

"What's 'adaptable,' Doctor?" asked Gub-Gub.

"It would take too long to explain now. Go to bed. We'll talk about the play in the morning."

The Second Chapter

Animal Plays

WHEN THE DOLITTLE HOUSEHOLD awoke next morning they found that the wagon was moving. This was nothing new for them. It only meant that the circus had gotten underway very early while they were still asleep—as it often did in moving from town to town. It was a part of the life, this, that Gub-Gub greatly enjoyed—waking in the morning and looking out the window to see what kind of new scene lay around their moving home.

Gub-Gub used to boast that this showed he was a born traveler, that he loved change, like the Doctor. As a matter of fact, he was really by nature much more like Dab-Dab; for no one loved regular habits, especially regular meals, more than he. It was just that this life provided a continuous and safe sort of adventure for him. He liked excitement, but comfortable excitement, without hardship or danger.

Matthew Mugg came in while the family was still at breakfast.

"It was a part of the life Gub-Gub greatly enjoyed."

"Doctor," said he, "that Mr. Bellamy is still with the outfit. Said he might as well come along with us, as we was going the same way as him. But, if you ask me, I reckon the real reason is because he's afraid he may lose sight of you. He's just crazy to get you to do a turn at his theater—don't care nothin' about the rest of Blossom's show. But he's willin' to pay any amount to get you to give a performance of your own with animals."

"Well," said the Doctor, "it isn't as easy as it sounds, Matthew. My own pets here are anxious to do a play. I wrote a sort of comedy last night after they had gone to bed. But, of course, it will have to be rehearsed over and over before it is in shape for him to see it. The animals must know their parts properly. You might go forward and tell him, will you, that I will try to rehearse it while we are traveling, and that I will let him see it tomorrow, if we are far enough on with it."

"All right," said Matthew, and he stepped out of the back of the moving wagon and ran forward to overtake the ringmaster's caravan with his message.

Doctor Dolittle had, as you know, written plays before for animals—dozens of them. I have told you of his very famous little book called *One-Act Plays for Penguins*. He had also written longer dramas for monkeys and others. But all these had been intended for audiences of animals and were written in animal languages. The penguin plays were (and are still, so far as I know) performed during the long winter nights in the open-air theaters of the Antarctic, where the vast audience of quaint birds sit around on the rocks in solemn groups, clapping their flipperlike wings when anything said by the actors strikes them as particularly sensible.

The plays for monkeys were of a much lighter kind. They preferred comedies and farces to the more serious and thoughtful dramas that the penguins liked. The monkey plays were enacted in clear places in the jungle, and the audience sat in the trees all about. The seats in the boughs right over the stage were the most expensive in the monkey theaters. And a family box, which consisted of a whole branch of a tree, cost as much as a hundred nuts. There was a special rule that families occupying these places should not throw their nutshells or banana peels down onto the performers' heads.

So you see, John Dolittle was quite experienced as a playwright for animals. But the thing needed by Mr. Bellamy, which was to be shown to an audience of people, had to be different, because people don't understand animal languages. And after much thought the Doctor decided to do away with language altogether. The whole play was to be action. And he called it *The Puddleby Pantomime.*

The rehearsals for the pantomime were greatly enjoyed by everyone except Dab-Dab. The poor housekeeper, who had herself a part to play in it, was continually stopping the performance to shout at someone about upsetting the furniture or breaking the teacups or pulling down the curtains.

The inside of the wagon was very close quarters, as you can easily imagine, for acting a play. Added to this, the caravan was moving all the time; and whenever the horse who was pulling it went around a curve or a sharp bend in the road, everybody on the stages sat down on the floor, and a squawk from Dab-Dab would show that some new piece of damage had been done to her home. But the rest of the animals got almost as much fun out of the accidents in rehearsal as they did out of the play itself.

The pantomime was just like the old-fashioned Harlequinade. Toby played the part of Harlequin, Dab-Dab was Columbine, Gub-Gub was Pantaloon, Swizzle was the policeman, and Jip was Pierrot. The dance by Harlequin, Columbine, and Pierrot caused a lot of merriment, because whenever the dancers were on the tips of their toes, that was certain to be the time when the wagon would give an extra bad lurch and throw the dancers under the bed.

Swizzle, as the policeman, was always arresting poor Pierrot (Jip) and anybody else he met. For a club he used a cucumber—until he broke it in half over Pantaloon (Gub-Gub), whom he was supposed to chase all around the wagon for stealing the string of sausages. Then the prisoner took the policeman's club away from him and ate it. And the Doctor decided to put that idea into the real show and to use a cucumber in Manchester.

Coming on and off the "stage" was very difficult, because the performers had to go out the door and stand on the narrow steps while the wagon was still going. Gub-Gub, in his part of the comic Pantaloon, had a hard time. He had to make many entrances and many exits—bounding in and out with the red-hot poker or the string of sausages. And in spite of the Doctor's warning him repeatedly to go out carefully, he always forgot that the wagon was moving, and, making his flying exit, he almost invariably fell out of the wagon, upside down, into the road. Then the rehearsal would have to be stopped while Mr. Pantaloon picked himself up and ran after his moving theater to get on the stage again.

The piece was gone through four or five times during that morning while the circus was traveling on to the next town. And when the train of wagons halted for the night, the Doctor sent word to Mr. Bellamy that, although the act was still very imperfect and no customers ready yet, he could come and see if it would do.

Then the pantomime was performed again, this time on the solid ground by the side of the road, before an audience of Mr. Bellamy, Blossom, Matthew Mugg, and the strong man. On this stage, that stood still instead of lurching from side to side, the piece went much better; and, although Pantaloon got a bit mixed up and popped on and off the stage many times too often, the audience clapped loud and long when it was over and declared it one of the most amusing shows they had ever seen.

"Perfectly splendid!" cried Mr. Bellamy. "It's just the thing we want. With a little more rehearsing and proper clothes, that

"The pantomine was performed by the side of the road."

should make a great hit. Nobody can say this act it not enjoyed by the animals that take part in it. Now, I'm going on to Manchester this evening. And after Mr. Blossom has played his week in Little Plimpton, he'll bring you on to my theater to open the beginning of the following week. Monday the seventeenth. In the meantime, I'll do some advertising. And I think we can promise you an audience worth playing to."

The circus's week at Little Plimpton was chiefly occupied by the Dolittle household in preparing and rehearsing *The Puddleby Pantomime* for its showing in Manchester. As for the Pushmi-Pullyu, the useful Matthew Mugg took entire charge of his stand, leaving the Doctor free to take care of the play.

Day after day the act was gone through until everyone knew his part perfectly and there seemed no possible chance of a mistake. The Doctor wanted the whole performance to be done by the animals, without himself or any person appearing on the stage from beginning to end. During the rehearsals, accidents and odd things happened that gave the Doctor ideas, many of which he put into the play itself, as he had done with the cucumber. Then, too, several of the actors thought up comic notions of their own while the show was being tried out. And if they were good enough John Dolittle put them into the pantomime. For these reasons the act toward the end of rehearsals was much longer and quite a little different from what it had been when shown to Mr. Bellamy. It was much better, too. Gub-Gub thought it so comical that often in the middle of it he would get a giggling fit over his own funniness and be so doubled up with mirth that he couldn't go on with his part.

Theodosia Mugg was very busy during these days, making the costumes. Fitting suits of clothes to animals is not easy. Gub-Gub gave the most trouble. At the first dress rehearsal he came on with his suit upside down, and his wig back-to-front. He had his hind legs through the sleeves of the coat, wearing them as pants. His makeup, too, gave a lot of extra work to the stage manager. Mr. Pantaloon liked the taste of grease paint and he would keep licking his chops during the performance. So of course the rouge on his cheeks very soon got smeared all around his mouth and made him look as though he had been eating bread and jam.

But Pantaloon's greatest trial was his trousers. When at last they did make him understand how his suit was to be worn, he at first fastened his trousers to a belt. But his stomach was so round and smooth his belt would keep slipping off it. And at the first few dress rehearsals, whenever he ran onto the stage (always chased by the policeman, of course), as often as not he would lose his pants on the way and arrive on the stage wearing only a coat and a wig. Then Theodosia made a special pair of suspenders for him to keep his pants up with, and the Doctor always inspected his dressing himself.

A similar accident happened frequently at the beginning to Dab-Dab, who acted the part of Columbine. Theodosia had made her a very cunning little ballet skirt of stiff pink net. But the first

"He would arrive on the stage wearing only a coat and a wig."

time she wore it, the dainty web-footed toe-dancer, doing an especially high kick in her dance with Harlequin, kicked her skirt right over her partner's head. The excitement was added to considerably when Pantaloon, who had just rushed in, picked up the skirt, and put it on himself in place of the pants he had lost, as usual, in his hurried entrance.

So as you can easily imagine, Stage Manager Dolittle and Theodosia, the mistress of the wardrobe, had their hands pretty full. Acting as people was hard enough for the animals by itself; but acting in clothes that they were not accustomed to wearing was a tremendous job, when only a week could be taken for rehearsing. Many times the Doctor was in despair over the costuming part of it. However, Theodosia worked out a lot of very cunning dodges, by means of secret buttons, hooks, elastics and tapes, to hold the clothes and hats and wigs in place. Then by making the actors wear their costumes all day long, the Doctor finally got his performers so they could move and run and dance in clothes as easily as they could without them.

THE THIRD CHAPTER

The Poster and the Statue

THE DAY THE CIRCUS MOVED TO MANCHESTER was a great one for the Dolittle household. None of the animals except Jip had been in a really large city before. On the way there Gub-Gub was constantly at the window of the caravan, watching the road and shouting out word over his shoulder to the others when anything new or wonderful came in sight.

Mr. Bellamy's show place was situated on the edge of the city. It was a big amusement park, with all sorts of sideshows of its own and a large theater building in the center. Prizefights, wrestling matches, brass band contests and all manner of entertainments were held in a large open-air place behind the theater. It was oval in shape and had seats banked up high all around it. This was what had given it its name, the amphitheater, because it was like the great open-air theaters of the Romans.

To Mr. Bellamy's amusement park the citizens of Manchester came out in thousands when they were in need of recreation—

especially Saturday afternoons and in the evenings. At night the whole place was lit up with strings of little lights, and very bright and pretty it looked.

The park was so big that Blossom's "Mammoth Circus" could fit into one corner of it and not be seen. The ringmaster was greatly impressed.

"Lor' bless me," he said to the Doctor, "this is the way to run the show business all right—on a grand scale. Bellamy must be rolling in money. Why, the theater building alone could hold three times as many people as we can fit into our big tent!"

Blossom's Circus party, feeling dreadfully small and unimportant in such a huge concern, were guided to a place where they could halt and settle down. Shortly after the horses were stabled, and the great Mr. Bellamy himself turned up. The first thing he inquired for was the *Puddleby Pantomime* troupe.

"As for the rest of your show," he said to Blossom, "I'll leave you this corner of the grounds, and you can set up and do what business you can on your own. We get the bigger crowds after five o'clock in the evening and all Saturday afternoon—when we usually run a prizefight over in the arena. But Doctor Dolittle's company I am going to take care of separately. Of course, I'll pay the money through you, as I told you, and you divide it in whatever way you two arrange. But from now on he and his animals are under my management, you understand, and are not to be interfered with by anybody else. That's what we agreed on, isn't it?"

Then while Blossom and his men got their own sideshows set up, the Dolittle household and its wagon were taken off to another part of the grounds—close to the theater—and given a space within a high fence, where they could settle down in comfort.

Here they found a few other tents and caravans, the homes of various special performers taking part in the daily, or rather nightly, show that was given in the theater. Dancers they were, tightrope walkers, singers and what not.

After the beds were made up and the Dolittle wagon put in order, the Doctor suggested a walk through the city. Jip and Gub-Gub at once asked if they could come, and the Doctor consented. Dab-Dab thought she ought to remain behind and finish unpacking and get food cooked for supper.

Then when the Doctor had been over to make sure that

"He set out to see the sights of Manchester."

Matthew Mugg had got the Pushmi-Pullyu comfortably settled, he set out, accompanied by Gub-Gub and Jip, to see the sights of Manchester.

To reach the city proper they had to walk about half a mile through districts of ordinary houses and gardens surrounding the big town.

Of course, John Dolittle and Jip, having been in London more than once, knew what a regular city looked like. But Gub-Gub, when they entered the thronged streets, teeming with traffic, bordered by grand shops and buildings, was greatly impressed.

"What a lot of people!" he murmured, his eyes nearly popping out of his head. "And just look at the cabs! I didn't know there were so many in the world—following one another down the street like a parade. And such splendid vegetable shops! Did you *ever* see such enormous tomatoes! Oh, I like this place. It's much bigger than Puddleby, isn't it? Yes, I like this town."

They came to an open place, a big square with especially fine stone buildings on all sides of it. Gub-Gub wanted to know all about each of them, and the Doctor had to explain what a bank was, and a corn exchange and a municipal hall, and many more.

"And what's that?" asked Gub-Gub, pointing to the middle of the square.

"That's a statue," said the Doctor.

It was a very grand monument of a man on horseback. And Gub-Gub asked who he was.

"That's General Slade," said the Doctor.

"But why do they put a statue up to him?"

"Because he was a famous man," answered the Doctor. "He fought in India—against the French."

They passed out of this square and a little farther on entered another, a smaller one, with no statue in it. As they were crossing it Gub-Gub suddenly stopped dead.

"Great heavens, Doctor!" he cried. "Look!"

At the far side of the square, on a hoarding, was an enormous poster—a picture of a pig dressed as Pantaloon, holding a string of sausages.

"Why, it's *me*, Doctor!" said Gub-Gub, hurrying toward it.

And sure enough, written across the top in large letters was: "The Puddleby Pantomime. *A Mystery. Come and see the Unique Harlequinade. Bellamy's Amphitheater. Next Monday.*"

The manger had been as good as his word. He had had an artist make pictures of the characters in the Doctor's play and posted them all over the city.

They couldn't get Gub-Gub away from it. The idea of coming into this big town and finding his own pictures on the walls and himself a famous actor already, entirely fascinated him.

"Perhaps they'll put up a statue of me next," he said, "like the general. Look, there's room for one here. They haven't got any in this square."

As they went through the streets they found more pictures of their show—some of Dab-Dab, poised on her toes in a ballet skirt; some of Swizzle, with a policeman's helmet on his head. But whenever they passed one of Pantaloon, they had the hardest work dragging Gub-Gub away. He would have sat in front of it all night if they had let him, admiring himself as a famous actor.

"I really think you ought to speak to the mayor about my statue, Doctor," said he, as he sauntered homeward with his nose carried high in the air. "Perhaps they'll want to move the general into a smaller square and put me in the larger one."

On the morning of Monday, the day when the Pantomime was to make its first appearance before the public, there was a dress rehearsal of it and the rest of the show to be given in the theater. This was what is known as a variety show. There were a number of different acts, dancers, singers, jugglers, and so forth. They came onto the stage in turn and went through their performance, with the orchestra playing the proper music for each one.

At the sides of the stage there were little frames, and at the beginning of each act footmen in livery came out and pushed big cards into them. These cards had the name of the new act on them, and were displayed in this way so that the audience could read what was coming. The Doctor suggested that with *The Puddleby Pantomime* the card-changing should be done by animals instead of footmen. Mr. Bellamy thought it was a splendid idea. And while the Doctor was wondering what animals he could get, Too-Too suggested that he be given the job.

"But we need two," said the Doctor. "You see how the footmen do it—like soldiers. They march out with the cards in their hand—just as though they were drilling, go to each side of the stage—pull the old card out and stick the new one in."

"That's all right, Doctor," said Too-Too. "I can soon get another owl and we'll make a better pair than those footmen. You wait till I take a hunt around the country outside the city."

Too-Too flew off, and before half an hour had passed he was back again with another owl who was the dead image of himself, and the exact same size. Then stools were placed on the corners of

"Footmen came out and pushed big cards into them."

the stage, so that the little birds could reach the frames and the owl footmen were drilled in their parts.

Even the musicians in the orchestra, accustomed to seeing wonderful things done on the stage, were astonished when Too-Too and his brother owl appeared from behind the curtains. They were really much smarter at the job than the footmen in velvet. Like two clockwork figures, they hopped onto the stools, changed the cards, bowed to the imaginary audience, and retired.

"My!" said the bass fiddler to the trombone player. "Did you ever see the like? You'd think they'd been working in a variety hall all their lives!"

Then the Doctor, who was himself quite a musician, discussed with the conductor what kind of music should be played while the pantomime was going on.

"I want something lively," said John Dolittle, "but very, very soft—pianissimo the whole time."

"All right," said the conductor. "I'll play you the thing we do for the tightrope walkers—sort of tense."

Then he tapped his desk with his baton to make the orchestra get ready, and played a few opening bars. It was exciting, trembly music, played very, very quietly. It made you think of fairies fluttering across lawns in the moonlight.

"That's splendid," said the Doctor, as the conductor stopped. "Now, when Columbine begins to dance, I want the minuet from *Don Juan*—because that's the tune she has always practiced to. And every time Pantaloon falls down, have the percussion give the bass drum a good bang, please."

Then *The Puddleby Pantomime* was gone through on a real stage, with a real orchestra and real scenery—the last dress rehearsal. Gub-Gub found the glare of the footlights dazzling and confusing. But he and all the actors had by this time done the piece so often that they could have played it in their sleep. And the show went with a dash from beginning to end, without a single accident or slip.

When it was over Mr. Bellamy said:

"Just one thing more: when the audience is here, your actors will be called out before the curtain. You'll have to show them how to take the call."

Then the performers were rehearsed in bowing. The five of

them trooped on again, hand in hand, bowed to the empty theater, and trooped off.

In the course of their eventful lives the animals of Doctor Dolittle's household had had many exciting times. But I doubt if anything ever happened to them that they remembered longer or spoke of afterward more often than their first appearance before the public in the famous *Puddleby Pantomime*.

I say famous because it did, in fact, become very famous. Not only was it reported in the newspapers of Manchester as a sensational success, but it was written up in those magazines devoted to stagecraft and theatrical news, as something entirely new to show business. Lots of acts with animals dressed as people had been done before, of course—some very good. But in all of them the performers never knew just why they did the things they did, nor the meaning of most of their act. Whereas the Doctor, being able to converse with his actors in their own language, had produced a play that was entirely perfect, down to the smallest detail. For instance, he had spent days in showing Toby how to wink one eye, and still longer in getting Pantaloon to throw back his head and laugh like a person. Gub-Gub used to practice it in front of a mirror by the hour. Pigs have their own way of laughing, of course, which most people don't know of; and that is just as well, because sometimes they find humans very amusing. But to have animals laughing and frowning and smiling at the right places in a play—perfectly natural and exactly the way people would do it—was something that had never been seen on the stage before.

Good weather and Mr. Bellamy's advertising had brought a large crowd out to the amusement park Monday evening. Long before the show was due to start, the theater was beginning to fill.

"Gub-Gub used to practice it by the hour."

Of the Dolittle troupe, waiting their turn behind the scene, no one was more anxious than the Doctor himself. None of his animals, with the exception of Swizzle, had ever performed before a real audience before. And it did not follow that because they had acted all right with only Mr. Bellamy and a few others looking on, they would be just as good when facing a packed theater.

As he heard the first few notes of the orchestra tuning up their instruments, the Doctor peeped through the curtain into the audience. He could see nothing but faces. There did not seem to be room to get another in anywhere, but still the people crowded up to the big entrances at the end of the long hall, trying to find standing room in the aisles—or even outside of the doorways, where, on tiptoe, they could still get a glimpse of the stage.

"Doctor," whispered Dab-Dab, who was also peeping, "this at last ought to make us rich. Blossom said that Mr. Bellamy had promised him one hundred pounds a day—and more, if the audiences were larger than a certain number. It would be impossible for it to be bigger than this. You couldn't get a fly into that theater, it's so packed. What are they stamping and whistling for?"

"That's because the show is late in beginning," said the Doctor, looking at his watch. "They're impatient. Oh, look out! Let's get off the stage. They're going to pull the curtain up. See, there's the singing couple in the wings, ready to do the first act. Come on, hurry! Where's Gub-Gub got to? I'm so afraid that wig of his will slip out of place—oh, here he is. Thank goodness, it's all right—and his pants, too. Now, all of you stay here and keep together. Our show goes on as soon as this act is over. Stop licking your face, Gub-Gub, for heaven's sake! I won't have time to make you up again."

THE FOURTH CHAPTER

Fame, Fortune— and Rain

STAGE MANAGER DOLITTLE'S ANXIETY ABOUT his company's behavior before a real audience turned out to be unnecessary. The lights and the music and the enormous crowd, instead of scaring the animals, had the effect of making them act better. The Doctor said afterward that they had never done as well in rehearsal.

As for the audience, from the moment the curtain went up they were simply spellbound. At the beginning many people would not believe that the actors were animals. They whispered to one another that it must be a troupe of boys or dwarfs, with masks on their faces. But there could be no disguising the two little owls who had opened the show by marching out like soldiers with the announcement cards. And as the pantomime proceeded, even the most unbelieving of the audience could see that no human actors, no matter how well trained and disguised, could move and look like this.

At first Gub-Gub was an easy favorite. His grimaces and

antics made the audience rock with laughter. But when Dab-Dab came on, opinion was divided. Her dance with Toby and Jip simply brought down the house, as the saying goes. She captivated everybody. And it was really marvelous, considering how ungainly she usually was in her movements, to see with what grace she did the minuet. The people clapped, stamped the floor, yelled "Encore!" and just wouldn't let the show go on till she had done her dance a second time.

Then a lady in the front row threw a bunch of violets onto the stage. Dab-Dab had never had flowers thrown at her before and didn't know what to make of it. But Swizzle, an old actor, understood. Springing forward, he picked up the bouquet and handed it with a flourish to Columbine.

"Bow!" whispered the Doctor from the wings in duck language. "Bow to the audience—to the lady who threw the bouquet!"

And Dab-Dab curtsied like a regular ballerina.

When the curtain came down at the end and the music of the orchestra blared out loud, the applause was deafening. The company trooped on hand in hand and bowed again and again. And still the audience called them back. Then the Doctor made them take the calls separately. Gub-Gub did antics and made faces; Swizzle took off his helmet and bowed; Toby sprang into the air with harlequinish agility; Jip struck tragic Pierrot-like attitudes, and Dab-Dab once more brought down the house by pirouetting across the stage on her toes, flipping kisses to the audience with the tips of her wings.

More bouquets were thrown to Columbine and a bunch of carrots to Pantaloon—which he started eating before he left the stage.

Mr. Bellamy said he had never seen such enthusiasm in the

"Dab-Dab curtsied like a regular ballerina."

theater since he had owned it. And he immediately asked Blossom if he would be willing to renew the engagement for a second week.

When the other turns were over and the audience left the theater, Gub-Gub went out into the hall to look at the stage from the seats. There he found many programs scattered around the floor. He asked the Doctor what they were. And he was delighted when he was shown his own name printed there as playing the part of Pantaloon.

"Humph!" said he, folding it carefully. "I must keep this. I think I'll put it in my menu album."

"Don't you mean your stamp album?" asked the Doctor.

"No," said Gub-Gub. "I gave up collecting stamps some time ago. I collect menus now. They're much better fun to look at."

The Dolittle household, now that they were encamped near the theater, did not see so much of their old friends of the circus. Nevertheless, the Doctor frequently went across the amusement park to see how Matthew and the Pushmi-Pullyu were getting on. And Hop the clown, Hercules, and the Pintos often visited the theater to see the pantomime and to make tea at the Dolittle wagon.

The extraordinary success of the Doctor's play continued throughout the week—the crowds growing greater, if anything, with each performance. It became necessary to secure seats a long way in advance if you wanted to see the show, a thing that had only happened once before at the amphitheater when a world-famous violinist had played there.

Wealthy gentlemen and elegant ladies called at the Doctor's little wagon almost every evening to congratulate him and to see and pet his marvelous animal actors. Gub-Gub got frightfully conceited and put on no end of temperamental airs, often refusing to see his admirers if they called during the hour he was accustomed to take for his nap.

"Famous artists have to be very careful of themselves," he said. "I am only at home to callers between ten and twelve in the morning. You better have that printed in the newspapers, Doctor."

One lady brought an autograph album for him to sign, and with the Doctor's help, he put a very clumsy "G. G." in it for her and the picture of a parsnip, which, he said, was his family crest.

Dab-Dab, although she had become just as famous, was much more easily interviewed by visitors. Immediately after each performance she could be seen bustling about her household duties in the wagon, often still wearing her ballet skirt while she made beds or fried potatoes.

"That pig makes me tired," she said. "What's the use of our putting on airs? None of us would be famous if it hadn't been for the Doctor. Any animal could do what we do if they had him to teach them. By the way, Doctor," she added, spreading the tablecloth for supper, "have you been to see Blossom about the money?"

"No," said the Doctor. "Why bother yet? The first week is hardly over. And I understand the pantomime is to run a second one. No, I haven't seen Blossom in—let me see—not in three days."

"Well, you ought to. You should go and get your share of the money every night."

"Why? Blossom is a trustworthy man."

"Is he?" said Dab-Dab, putting the salt shakers on the table. "Well, I wouldn't trust him further than I could see him. If you take my advice, you'll get your money each night. There must be a lot owing to you, especially since they put the pantomime on twice a day instead of only in the evening."

"Oh, that's all right, Dab-Dab," said the Doctor. "Don't worry. Blossom will bring me the money as soon as he has his accounts straightened out."

The housekeeper during the next few days frequently asked John Dolittle to see about this matter, but he never would. And even after the first week was over and the second nearly so, Blossom had not come forward with the Doctor's share, nor, indeed, was he often seen by any member of the Dolittle household. The Pushmi-Pullyu had also done well with his sideshows, and, as the money made by this was quite sufficient for living expenses, the easygoing Doctor, as usual, refused to worry.

Toward the end of the second week the fame of *The Puddleby Pantomime* had become so great and so many people had called to interview the Doctor and his company that it was decided to hold an "at home" and to invite the public to tea.

Then for a whole morning the good housekeeper was more than usually busy. Over two hundred printed cards of invitation had been sent out. Mrs. Mugg was called in to help. A large number of small tables were set about the wagon; the inside of the caravan was decorated with flowers; lots of tea and cakes were prepared and at four o'clock on Saturday afternoon the gates of the little enclosure beside the theater were thrown open to visitors.

All the animals, some of them dressed in their pantomime costumes, then acted as hosts and sat around at the tables, sipping tea with the elegant ladies and gentlemen who were anxious to meet them. It was a farewell party, for the next day the whole of Blossom's Circus was to leave. The mayor of the city came and the mayoress and a number of newspaper reporters, who made sketches in their notebooks of Hostess Dab-Dab pouring tea and Gub-Gub handing around cakes.

The next day, after one of the most successful visits of its career, the circus packed up and moved out of Manchester.

The town they went to was a small one, some twelve miles to the northeast. Rain began to fall as the wagons arrived at the show ground, and the work of setting up was very disagreeable for everyone. For, besides the wretched, steady drizzle, the dirt underfoot soon got worked up into mud with the constant tramping of feet.

The rain continued the next day, and the next. This, of course,

"Gub-Gub handing around cakes"

was a terrible thing for the circus business, because nobody came to see the show.

"Well, never mind," said the Doctor, as his family sat down to breakfast on the third rainy morning. "We made plenty of money in Manchester. That should tide us over a bad spell easily."

"Yes, but you haven't got that money yet, remember," said Dab-Dab. "Though goodness knows I've told you often enough to ask Blossom for it."

"I saw him this morning," said John Dolittle, "just before I came in to breakfast. It's quite all right. He says it was such a large amount he was afraid to keep it on him or in his wagon. So he put it in a bank in Manchester."

"Well, why didn't he take it out of the bank when he left," asked Dab-Dab, "and give you half of it?"

"It was a Sunday," said the Doctor. "And, of course, the banks were closed."

"But what does he mean to do about it, then?" asked the housekeeper. "He isn't going to leave it there, is he?"

"He's going back today to fetch it. He was just starting off on horseback when I spoke to him. I didn't envy him his ride in the rain."

Now, running a circus is an expensive thing. The animals have to be fed, the workmen and performers have to be paid, and there are a whole lot of other expenses for which money must be handed out hourly. So that during these rainy days, when no people came and the enclosure stood wet and empty instead of making money, "The Mammoth Circus" was losing it every day—every hour, in fact.

Just as the Doctor finished speaking, the menagerie-keeper, with his coat collar turned up against the rain, poked his head in at the door.

"Seen the boss anywhere around?" he asked.

"Mr. Blossom has gone into Manchester," said John Dolittle. "He expects to be back about two in the afternoon, he told me."

"Humph!" said the man. "That's a nuisance."

"Why?" asked the Doctor. "Is there anything I can do for you?"

"I want money for rice and hay—for the menagerie," said the keeper. "The boss said he'd give me some this morning. The corn dealer's brought the feed. 'E won't leave it unless he gets his money. And my animals need the stuff bad."

"Oh, I suppose it slipped Mr. Blossom's mind," said the Doctor. "I'll pay the bill for you and get it from him when he returns. How much is it?"

"Thirty shillings," said the keeper. "Two bales of hay and fifty pounds of rice."

"All right," said the Doctor. "Too-Too, give me the money box."

"There you are! There you are!" Dab-Dab broke in, her feathers all ruffled up with anger. "Instead of getting the money from Blossom that he owes you, you are paying his bills for him! The animals' feed isn't your concern. What's the use? What's the use? Blossom getting richer and you getting poorer; that's you, all over."

"The animals must be fed," said the Doctor, taking the money from the box and giving it to the keeper. "I'll get it back, Dab-Dab. Don't worry!"

The rain grew heavier and heavier all that morning. This was the circus's fourth day in this town. Hardly a penny had been taken in at the gates since the tents had been set up.

The Doctor, ever since his performance with Beppo at Bridgeton, had been looked upon by the show folk with an almost superstitious respect. Any man, they felt, who could talk the language of animals must know more about them than a mere ringmaster like Blossom. The Doctor had little by little made great changes throughout the management of the whole concern—though there still remained a tremendous lot that he wished to alter. Many of the performers had for some time considered him as the most important man in the circus, and Blossom as just a figurehead.

The menagerie-keeper had hardly left before another man turned up wanting money for some other of the daily expenses of the show. And throughout that morning people kept coming to the

Doctor with tales that Blossom had promised them payment at a certain time. The result, of course, was that before long the Dolittle money box (which had been quite well filled by the Pushmi-Pullyu's exhibition the last two weeks) was empty once more.

Two o'clock in the afternoon came—three o'clock—and still Mr. Blossom hadn't returned.

"Oh, he must have been delayed," said the Doctor to Dab-Dab, who was getting more anxious and more angry every minute. "He'll be here soon. He's honest. I'm sure of that. Don't worry."

At half past three, Jip, who had been out nosing around in the rain, suddenly rushed in.

"Doctor!" he cried. "Come over to Blossom's wagon. I think there's something wrong."

"Why, Jip? What's the matter?" said the Doctor, reaching for his hat.

"Mrs. Blossom isn't there," said Jip. "At first I thought the door was locked. But I pushed it, and it wasn't. There's nobody in it. His trunk is gone—and nearly everything else, too. Come over and look. There's something strange about this."

THE FIFTH CHAPTER

Mr. Blossom's Mysterious Disappearance

JIP'S WORDS BROUGHT A PUZZLED FROWN onto the Doctor's face. Slowly he put on his hat and followed the dog out into the rain.

On reaching Blossom's wagon he found everything as Jip had described it. There was no one within. Every article of value had been taken away. A few torn papers lay scattered on the floor. In the inner room, Mrs. Blossom's private boudoir, the same situation met the Doctor's eyes. The whole place looked as though those who lived there had left in a hurry, to be gone a long time.

While John Dolittle was still gazing confusedly around him, someone touched him on the shoulder from behind. It was Matthew Mugg.

"Looks kind of bad, don't it?" he said. "Blossom didn't have to take his trunk and all to go and get his money out of the bank. If you was to ask me, I've a kind of a notion that we ain't goin' to see our good, kind manager no more. Eh?"

"Well, Matthew," said the Doctor, "we mustn't jump to

conclusions. He said he'd be back. He may have been delayed. As to his trunk and things, they're his own. He has a right to do what he wants with them. It would be wrong to pass any judgments until we have more evidence than that.

"Humph!" muttered the Cat's-Meat-Man. "O' course, you always did hate to think anybody crooked. Still, I think you can say good-bye to the money you earned in Manchester."

"We haven't any proof, Matthew," said the Doctor. "And listen: if what you suspect is true, it's going to be a very serious matter for all the people in the circus. Please don't say anything of your suspicions for the present, will you? There is no need to get the show folk excited until we really know. Now, will you please saddle up a horse quietly and go into Manchester for me? See Mr. Bellamy and ask him if he knows anything of what has become of Blossom. Get back here and bring me word as soon as you can, will you?"

"All right," said Matthew, turning to go. "But I don't think Mr. Bellamy'll know any more of where our manager's gone than what you do. 'E's probably on 'is way to the Continent by now."

Jip, after listening to this conversation, slipped away and joined the other animals in the Doctor's own wagon.

"Fellows," he said, shaking the wet out of himself, "Alexander Blossom has skedaddled."

"Good heavens!" cried Too-Too. "With the money?"

"Yes, with the money—drat him!" growled Jip. "And there was enough coming to the Doctor to keep us in comfort for the rest of our days."

"I knew it!" groaned Dab-Dab, throwing out her wings in despair. "I told the Doctor not to trust him. I guessed him to be a fishy customer from the start. Now he's wallowing in luxury while we scrape and pinch to pay the bills he left behind."

"Oh, what does it matter?" cried Gub-Gub. "So much the better if he's gone. Now we'll have a real circus—The Dolittle Circus—which the animals have always hoped for. Good riddance to Blossom—the crook! I'm glad he's gone."

"What you *don't* know," said Dab-Dab, turning on the pig severely, "would fill a library. How is the Doctor to run a circus without a penny in his pocket? How is he going to pay wages—ground rent? How is he going to feed the animals and himself? It costs pounds and pounds a day to keep a circus going, you pudding, you! And look at the rain—coming down as though it never meant to stop! And the whole show just standing here and not a soul coming to see it! And wagonloads of animals eating up pounds of money a day! And the payroll of dozens of men mounting higher every minute. '*Glad* he's gone!' . . . you . . . you sausage!"

After Matthew had gone, the Doctor remained within the shelter of Blossom's deserted wagon, thoughtfully watching the rain splatter into the muddy puddles outside. Presently he sat down on an old packing case and lit his pipe. From time to time he took out his watch and looked at it, frowning.

After half an hour had gone by he saw Hercules, dressed in ordinary clothes, approaching across the enclosure. He was running to avoid the rain. Reaching the wagon, he sprang within, and then shook his wet overcoat outside the doorway.

"I hear the boss has skipped," he said. "Is it true?"

"I have no idea," said the Doctor. "He is late in returning from Manchester. But something may have detained him."

"Well, I hope he comes soon," said Hercules. "He owes me a week's wages. And I need it."

The strong man sat down and he and the Doctor fell to chatting about weather and weather signs.

Not many minutes later along came Hop the clown, with his dog, Swizzle. Evil news travels fast. He, too, had heard a rumor that Blossom had deserted the circus. The Doctor tried again to excuse the ringmaster, and insisted that he not be suspected till proof was obtained.

Then, rather awkwardly and without much interest, the conversation continued about the weather.

Next, the Pinto Brothers, trapeze artists, arrived with mackintoshes thrown over their gawdy tights. They also wanted to know where Blossom was, and why they hadn't received the pay which they had been promised would be given them this morning.

The Doctor, growing more and more distressed, hoping Blossom would turn up any minute, began to find it hard to keep the talk on any other subject but the mysterious disappearance of the manager.

At last the foreman of the tent riggers joined the circle.

"It looks rummy to me," he said when he had been told all there was to be told. "I got three children and a wife to keep. 'Ow are they going to live if I don't get no wages? My missus ain't got enough food in the wagon for another meal."

"Yes," said one of the Pinto Brothers. "And we got a new baby in my family. If Blossom's running off with the money, we ought to let the police know."

"But we have no proof he is running off," said the Doctor. "He may arrive any minute."

"The Pinto Brothers arrived."

"And he may not, Doctor," Hercules put in. "If he is up to no good, by the time you get your proof he'll be in China, maybe—where nobody can get at him. It's nearly six now. The Pintos are right. What are we standing around here for, guessing and wondering? At least we ought to send somebody into Manchester to find out what we can."

"I have sent somebody in," said the Doctor. "Matthew Mugg, my assistant, has gone."

"Humph!" said one of the acrobats. "So you got kind of suspicious yourself, Doctor, eh? What time did you send him?"

The Doctor looked at his watch again.

"About four hours ago," said he.

"Time to get there and back," grunted Hercules. "'E couldn't find no trace of 'im, I'll warrant. Boys, it looks to me like we was ditched, all right. . . . Lord! I wish I had 'im here. I'd make Mr. Blossom look like the last rose of summer."

And the strong man's hamlike hands went through the action of twisting the top off something.

"But 'e's left an awful lot of property behind," said the tent-rigger. "I don't yet understand what made 'im skip at this stage of the game."

"What 'e left behind—besides unpaid bills," said Hercules, "ain't nothing compared with what 'e took with 'im. 'Eaven only knows what 'e got from Bellamy for the Doctor's show—biggest takings this outfit ever saw. And all 'e give us was excuses—kept puttin' off payin' us for some fake reason or other—for three weeks back. I reckon 'e 'ad it in 'is mind to clear out all the time—'ad it planned as soon as 'e saw a big haul in sight."

"Well, what are we going to do?" asked Hop.

"Yes, that's the question," said the Pintos. "What are we going to do now?"

"We got to find another manager," said Hercules. "Someone to take over the outfit and get us out of this hole."

The Sixth Chapter

The Doctor Becomes Manager of the Circus

IT WAS CURIOUS TO SEE HOW, AS SOON AS THE strong man spoke of a new manager, all the eyes of the little crowd gathered in the wagon turned upon John Dolittle.

"Doctor," said Hercules, "it looks to me like you've got to be the new boss. And if anybody was to ask me. I'll say you'd make a pretty good one. How about it, boys?"

"Aye! Aye!" they all cried. "The Doc's the man."

"That being the case," said Hercules, "in the name of the staff of the Greatest Show on Earth, I present you, Doctor, with the circus of the late lamented Alexander Blossom. From now on, with us, your word is law."

"But—good heavens!" the Doctor stammered. "I don't know anything about circus management, and besides, I—"

"Oh yes you do," Hercules broke in. "Wasn't it your act with Beppo that made the big week at Bridgeton? And wasn't it you what got the circus brought to Manchester? Why, bless me, you can talk to the bloomin' animals! We ain't worried. Meself, I've a kind

"But I don't know anything about circus management."

of an idea we'll make more money under you than ever we made—or lost—under Blossom. You go ahead and manage."

"Yes," said Hop. "That's right, Doctor. Lord only knows what's going to happen to us if you don't. We're in the soup—dead broke. And you're the one to pull us out."

For a full minute the Doctor did not answer—just sat, thinking, on his packing case. At last he looked around at the miserable waiting group and said:

"Very well. I had not intended going into this business for long when I started. But I certainly can't get out of it now—not only on your account, but on account of my own animals and my responsibility to them. For I, too, am—er—dead broke. If you want me to manage for you, I'll try it. But I'm going to do it a little differently from Blossom's way. I'm going to run the circus on a cooperative basis—that is, instead of wages, we will all take our share of the money made, after expenses are paid. That means that when business is bad you will get very little—may even have to pay a little; and when business is good you will do well. Also, I claim the right to dismiss anyone from the circus without notice at any moment."

"That's the idea!" said Hercules. "That's the way a circus should be run—everybody partners in the business, but one man boss."

"But listen," said the Doctor. "For the beginning it's going to be hard work and very little money. We haven't got a cent in hand, and until the rain stops we shan't make a penny. What's worse, we will probably run into debt for a while—supposing, even, that we can get anybody to give us supplies on credit. Are you willing?"

"You bet we are!" . . . "We're with you, Doc!" . . . "Nobody's going to grumble!" . . . "You're the right boss!" they cried. And immediately the appearance of the whole crowd had changed from miserable gloom to hopeful smiles and enthusiasm.

In the midst of this arrived Matthew Mugg, with Mr. Bellamy himself.

"I'm terribly sorry to hear of this," said Mr. Bellamy, addressing the Doctor. "I gave that scoundrel Blossom two thousand pounds. He has cleared out with the whole lot, it seems—even left tradespeople unpaid in the city. It was their coming to me that first told me of his crookedness; and then your Mr. Mugg arrived. I've put the police on Blossom's trail, but I don't think there's the least chance of their catching him. You had better come back to

Manchester, and I will give you space at the amphitheater park until you have made enough to carry on."

"Hooray!" yelled Hop. "And, look, the rain has stopped! Our luck has changed. Hooray for the Dolittle Circus."

"Pardon me!" said a small, polite voice from the door. "Is Doctor Dolittle here?"

Everyone turned; and there stood a small man in the entrance. Behind him the sun was now shining brightly.

"I am John Dolittle," said the Doctor.

"How do you do," said the little man. "I have been sent on a special mission by a firm of theatrical producers. I am instructed to make you an offer. They wish you to bring your troupe to London next month—if you have not been already booked."

"Hah!" cried Hercules. "What did I tell you, boys? First minute he's manager he gets an offer from Manchester and another from London. Three cheers for the Doctor!"

It was a day of great rejoicing for both the animals and the people of the circus when the Doctor took over the management. As soon as the news got around, the enclosure tent-riggers, stable boys, performers—everybody, in fact, who was part of the establishment—came to the Doctor to congratulate him and to say how glad they were to be under his direction. With the stopping of the rain a general cheerfulness and hustle began. And the very first thing done was the taking down of the "Blossom's Mammoth Circus" sign over the main entrance and erecting in its place the "Dolittle Circus"—a more modest title, but one that was to become far greater and better known than Blossom's had ever been.

Mr. Bellamy was very kind. Realizing that the Doctor and everyone had been left practically penniless, he offered to help

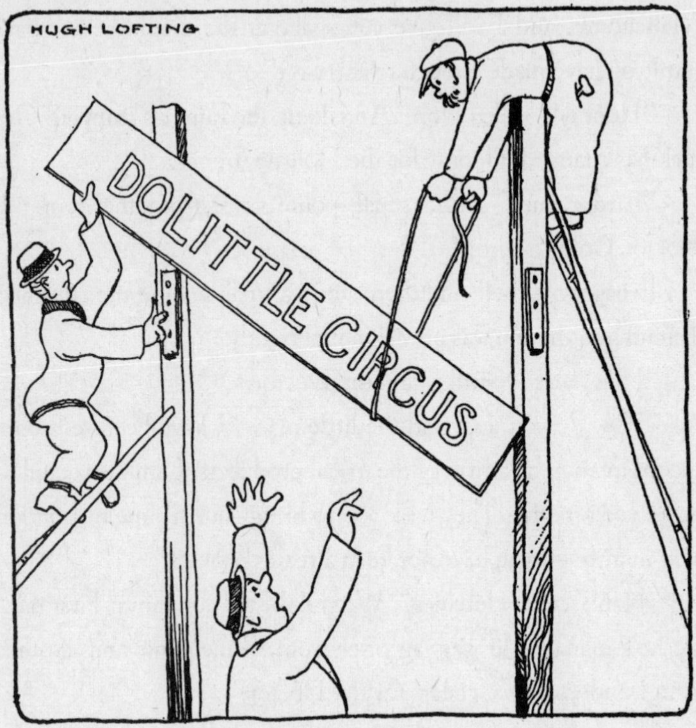

"Putting up the new sign"

the new management with loans of money or in any other way he could. However, John Dolittle was most anxious to avoid getting the circus further into debt than it already was, and all he asked of Mr. Bellamy was to visit some of the tradespeople of this town with him and ask them to give him credit, to trust him for a while. Mr. Bellamy was, of course, very well known for miles and miles around Manchester. And the local corn-dealer, grocer, butcher and the rest were perfectly willing, when he asked them, to give the Doctor provisions and to wait for their money till the circus had made enough to pay its bills.

For the same reason, to avoid getting into debt, the Doctor

decided not to move back to Manchester, but to keep the show where it was for the present. And with better weather the attendance soon began to be quite considerable. Mr. Bellamy's arrival and his visit to the tradespeople of the town were a good advertisement for the Dolittle Circus. Another advertisement better still was, curiously enough, Blossom's theft and disappearance. No sooner had it become known in Manchester that the ringmaster had run away with a large sum of money than the newspapers took it up and wrote long stories of how the famous *Puddleby Pantomime* players had been robbed and left stranded in a small town twelve miles from the city. The story was reprinted in country papers. And suddenly the people of this same small town woke up to the fact that they had the cast of *Puddleby Pantomime* in their midst and hadn't noticed it (on account of the rain) till they read of it in the papers.

Then, of course, everybody began talking of the robbery and everybody wanted to go and see the pantomime and the Doctor and the famous animal actors who had made such a sensation in Manchester. And then the whole town was tramping in at the gates of the Dolittle Circus.

As I have said, it was not a large town, but for the three days the business was good enough to enable the Doctor to pay all the bills off and to buy more provisions on which to keep going. There was even a little over to pay everybody a small—very small—amount of wages.

Too-Too, the expert accountant, was busier now than he had ever been. For not only did he keep record of how much the Pushmi-Pullyu made, but he kept the books for the whole circus. This, with the Doctor's new "cooperative" arrangement, was no easy task. Strict account of all money paid out to tradespeople had to be carefully entered, and the profits left divided among all the people of the circus in proportion to the amount of work they did. For instance, some of the tent-riggers and wagon-drivers who really only worked one or two days a week did not get so large a share as the sideshow performers who were at work all the week. But everyone got more when business was good, and less when it was bad.

Although nearly the whole staff were glad to have the Doctor's management and willingly stayed on with the circus even in the distressful conditions under which the new management began, there were, nevertheless, one or two malcontents who wanted large wages right away before the debts and bills were paid. These, as a matter of fact, were people that the Doctor was glad to part with anyway. And as soon as he could raise the money to pay them off, he sent them about their business. The Dolittle Circus began, in consequence, somewhat smaller than the Blossom Circus ended, but it began along strictly honest lines and with every man and animal in it united, hopeful, and contented under the new management.

THE SEVENTH CHAPTER

Matthew Mugg, Assistant Manager

ANOTHER MEMBER OF THE STAFF, BESIDES Too-Too, the accountant, to be more than usually occupied in the first days of the Dolittle Circus was Dab-Dab, the housekeeper.

"You know," said she to Too-Too and Jip one night, "all this looks very nice—and I certainly don't want to be a killjoy—but I wish we had someone else besides the Doctor to take care of the business end of things. He is fine where working out of new animal shows is concerned. As a stage manager no one could be better. But I know what's going to happen: all the other partners, Hercules and Hop and the Pintos and the rest, are going to get rich; and the Doctor is going to stay poor. Why, only last night he was talking about sending the opossum back to Virginia. He wants to climb trees, it seems—in the moonlight—and we haven't got the right kind of trees or moonlight here. I told him the moon in England is just as good as it is in Virginia. But he says it isn't—not green enough. Heaven only knows how much his ticket to America would cost. Yet I'm certain that as soon as the Doctor has the price of it he'll send him. He spoke of the lion and the leopard, too—says the big hunting animals should never be kept in confinement. I do wish we had some other man as well—somebody with good business sense—who could keep an eye on the Doctor's schemes."

"I quite agree with you," said Jip. "But I have great hopes of Matthew Mugg, myself. He isn't nearly such a fool as he looks."

"He's a very kind fellow," Swizzle put in. "Almost every time he meets me or Toby he pulls a bone or something out of his pocket and gives it to us."

"Oh yes," said Jip. "That used to be his profession—Cat's-Meat-Man, you know. He has a good heart. And I think, Dab-Dab, you'll find he has a pretty good business head, too. It was he who arranged the next three towns we're going to. The Doctor didn't know how to book the circus ahead or where to go next or anything about touring a circus around the country. He consulted Matthew. And Mugg went off at once to the next town and found out when the fair week was usually held and arranged for fodder supply and renting a show ground and everything. And he's just crazy about the circus business. I've often heard him boasting to people along the road that he's the partner of John Dolittle, M. D.—the famous showman. He knows how to advertise, too—and that's important in this game. It was Matthew who got the Doctor to have those big posters printed. I hear they're already stuck up in every street in Tilmouth, our next town. Yes, I'm quite hopeful about Matthew. He's a good man."

The Dolittle Circus was an entirely new kind of circus. Now that he had the control of things in his own hands, the Doctor proceeded to bring about the reforms and changes that he had so often wished for in the days of Blossom's management.

It was, as Jip had said, a good thing that Matthew was there to keep an eye on the Doctor. Otherwise he would most likely have begun by letting his new ideas run away with him. Certainly the average circus-going public had never seen anything like his show before. For one thing, John Dolittle insisted on the strictest politeness from all attendants. For another, he would allow no form of misrepresentation, as he called it. Ordinarily, circus folk had often been accustomed to say that their shows were "the greatest on earth," that their animals were "the only ones in captivity"—or something similarly extravagant and exaggerated.

This the Doctor would not permit. He said he wanted everything advertised just as it was, in order that the public should not be misled or cheated into paying to see something that they didn't see. To this, at the beginning, Matthew Mugg objected. He said you could never get a good crowd unless you "played it up big." But he soon found that the Doctor was right. When the people got to realize that whatever was promised in the Dolittle advertisements would be actually provided, the new circus earned a reputation for honesty that brought people in a way that nothing else would.

Another thing that worried Matthew in the first days of the Doctor's management was his insistence on providing tea, free, for the public.

"Why, Doctor," he said, "you'll be ruined! You can't serve tea for thousands of people without charging them for it. This ain't a hotel—or a Widows' and Orphans' Home!

"Matthew," said the Doctor, "the people who come to visit my show are, in a way, my guests. Some of them come long distances—with babies to carry. Afternoon tea is a nice custom. I hate to go without it myself. It won't cost so much when we buy the tea and sugar by the hundredweight. Theodosia can make it."

So afternoon tea for all visitors became an institution. And shortly after, another one was added: that of free packets of peppermints for the children. And what the Doctor prophesied came true. In one town where the Dolittle Circus crossed paths with another, a much bigger show, the Doctor's circus did twice the business that the other one did, because the people knew that they'd be given tea and treated honestly and politely.

"Free packets of peppermints for the children"

The Eighth Chapter

The Dolittle Circus

IT WAS SIX WEEKS BEFORE THE SHOW WAS DUE to appear in London. The first town to be visited on the way there was Tilmouth. And it was here that the Doctor once more got put in prison—but only for one night. This is how it came about.

The animals, as I have said, were, if anything even more pleased to exchange Blossom for the Doctor as a boss than were the human performers. And one of the first things that John Dolittle did, as soon as a little extra money was made, was to go round and ask all the animals if they had any complaints to make. Of course there were plenty. To begin with, nearly every creature in the menagerie wanted his den repainted. So the Doctor had all the cages done over, each in the colors that its owner preferred.

Not long after the Doctor had had the menagerie done up, he received another complaint. This, indeed, was one that he had often heard before. The lion and the leopard were weary of confinement.

They longed to get out of their narrow cages and stretch their legs in freedom.

"Well, you know," said John Dolittle, "myself, I don't approve of keeping you shut up at all. If I had my way I'd ship you back to Africa and let you go free in the jungle. But the trouble is the money. However, as soon as I get enough together I will attend to it."

"If we could only get out a few minutes each day," said the lion, looking wistfully over the Doctor's shoulder toward the rolling hills of the countryside, "it wouldn't be so bad."

"No," said the leopard, "that would make life bearable. Oh, I'm sick of the four walls of this wretched box!"

The tone of the leopard's voice was so pathetic and the lion's face so sad the Doctor felt that something just had to be done right away.

"Look here," he said, "if I let you out for a run every evening, would you promise me something?"

"Anything," said the two together.

"Would you come back at the end of half an hour? Honestly?"

"We would."

"And would you promise solemnly not to eat any people?"

"On our word of honor."

"All right," said the Doctor. "Then every evening after the show is over I'll open your cages and you can run free for half an hour."

So this, too, like the afternoon tea and the children's peppermints, became a custom of the Dolittle Circus. The menagerie animals were put upon their honor and allowed to run free every evening provided they came back of their own accord. It worked surprisingly well for quite a while. The show people soon realized that the animals were acting up to their promise and could be trusted not to molest anyone. And even Theodosia got used to the idea of meeting a lion or a leopard roaming through the enclosure after dark on his way back to his den when his evening run was over.

"It is quite proper," said the Doctor. "I don't know why I didn't think of it before. They work all day, the same as we do, being in the show. They deserve a little freedom and playtime at night."

Of course the animals, when they went beyond the circus fence, were careful to keep out of the way of people because they didn't want to scare them—and people didn't interest them anyway. They were, in fact, heartily sick of them, having them gazing and staring in at the cages all day. But one evening when the circus had moved to a new town, a rather serious thing happened. Matthew came rushing to the Doctor's wagon about ten o'clock and said:

"Governor, the lion hasn't come back! I went round to lock up just now and found the cage empty. And it's more than an hour since I let him out."

"Good heavens!" cried the Doctor, jumping up and dashing off toward the menagerie with Matthew at his heels. "I wonder what's wrong. He certainly wouldn't have run away after giving me his promise. I hope no accident has happened to him."

On reaching the menagerie, the Doctor went to the leopard's cage and asked him if he knew where the lion was.

"I think he must have got lost, Doctor," said the leopard. "We started out together and went for a stroll across that moor to the east. But it was new country to us. We came to a stream and couldn't get across. He went upstream and I went down, looking for a shallow place where we could get over to the other side. I had no luck. The stream got wider and deeper the farther I went along the bank. Then I heard the church clock strike and I realized it was time to be getting back. I expected to find the lion here when I got home. But he wasn't."

"You didn't meet any people?" the Doctor asked.

"Not a soul," said the leopard. "I passed a farm but I went round it to avoid scaring anyone. He'll find his way back. Don't worry."

The Doctor stayed up all that night waiting for the lion to return. He even went out into the country and hunted along the stream that the leopard had spoken of. But no trace of the missing animal could he found.

Morning came, and still no lion. And the Doctor was very worried. However, the opening of the circus kept his mind occupied. The people came thronging in and good business claimed everyone's attention.

At teatime, as was his custom, John Dolittle acted as host to his visitors and Theodosia was kept busy running back and forth waiting on the many little tables crowded with holidaymakers in their Sunday clothes.

Suddenly, just as the Doctor was passing among the tables to offer a lady a dish of cakes, he spied Mr. Lion strolling into the circus through the main gate. At the moment, everybody was busy eating and drinking, and the Doctor hoped that the lion, who was quietly making for the menagerie, would reach his den before he was seen by the guests. But, alas! a party, a farmer and his family, coming out of the sideshow, ran right into the lion before he got to the menagerie door. There was a scream from the farmer's wife, who grabbed her children and ran. The farmer threw his walking stick at the lion and also ran. Then for a couple of minutes pandemonium reigned. Women shrieked, tables were overturned, and finally some stupid person in the crowd fired a gun. The poor lion, thoroughly frightened, turned about and ran for his life.

The excitement now partly died down, but the people were far too upset to stay and enjoy the circus any further, and very soon they all went home and the enclosure was deserted.

So Mr. Lion, after his brief reappearance, was again missing; and the Doctor feared that now, terrified at his reception, he would be harder to find than ever.

John Dolittle was arranging search parties to go out and hunt when two policemen came to the circus and put him under arrest. He was charged, they told him, with keeping wild animals at large and endangering the public. Furthermore, the lion, it seemed, had broken into a chicken yard and eaten all the chickens. As the Doctor was marched through the town to the jail, the owner of the chickens followed him, calling him names and telling him how much he owed him.

The Doctor spent the night in prison. But in the meantime, the lion had taken refuge in the cellar of a bakery, and neither the baker nor anybody else dared go down to him. Everybody in the house was scared to go to bed. Messages were sent to the circus to send someone to take the lion away. But the wily Matthew Mugg, although he knew the lion was easily handled by those who knew him, told the people that the Doctor was the only one who dared go near him and they better hurry up and let him out of jail if they wanted the lion taken away.

So early the next morning they came and set the Doctor free. Then he went down into the cellar and talked to the lion.

"I'm fearfully sorry, Doctor," said he, "but I lost my way out on that moor. I wandered around all over the place. And it wasn't until the next day that I found my own tracks and made my way back to the circus. I tried to slip into the menagerie without being seen. But when that fool started firing a gun I got scared and ran for it."

"But the chickens?" said the Doctor. "I thought you promised me not to molest anything when you were out?"

"I only promised not to eat people," said the lion. "I had to eat something. I was starved to death after wandering around that moor all night. How much are they charging you for the chicken?"

"One pound ten shillings and sixpence," said the Doctor. "Eleven at half a crown apiece."

"It's highway robbery," said the lion. "They were the toughest old things I ever tasted. And anyway, I only ate nine."

"He led the lion home."

"Well, in future," said the Doctor, "I think I had better accompany you on your walks."

Then he led the lion home. And the terrified townsfolk watched through the cracks of doors as the dread animal strolled down the street at John Dolittle's heels as meek and quiet as a lamb.

And now that the Doctor could give the animals the kind of consideration he wished, he really enjoyed the life himself a good deal. And poor Dab-Dab began to feel that her chance of getting him away from it, back to his own life at Puddleby, grew dimmer and more distant every day.

John Dolittle's chief occupation in his spare time was, as I have told you, thinking out new and interesting animal shows. And in doing this he always kept the children particularly in mind as an audience, and designed his plays and entertainments more for them than for the grown-ups. The success of the Talking Horse and *The Puddleby Pantomime* showed him that his knowledge of animal languages could be put to great use here. The snakes that he had bought from Fatima, for example, were later trained by him to give a little show of their own. Instead of a snake charmer's tent with a foolish woman in it, pretending to be something that she wasn't, the Dolittle Circus had a sideshow where the snakes gave their own performance, entirely unaided by any person. To the tune of a music box they danced a very peculiar but graceful sort of dance. It was something like a mixture between a quadrille and a game of cat's cradle. On a little stage of their own they glided about on their tails in time to the music, bowing to their partners, doing the grand chain, looping into knots with one another, drilling like soldiers, and doing a hundred fascinating things that people had never seen snakes do before.

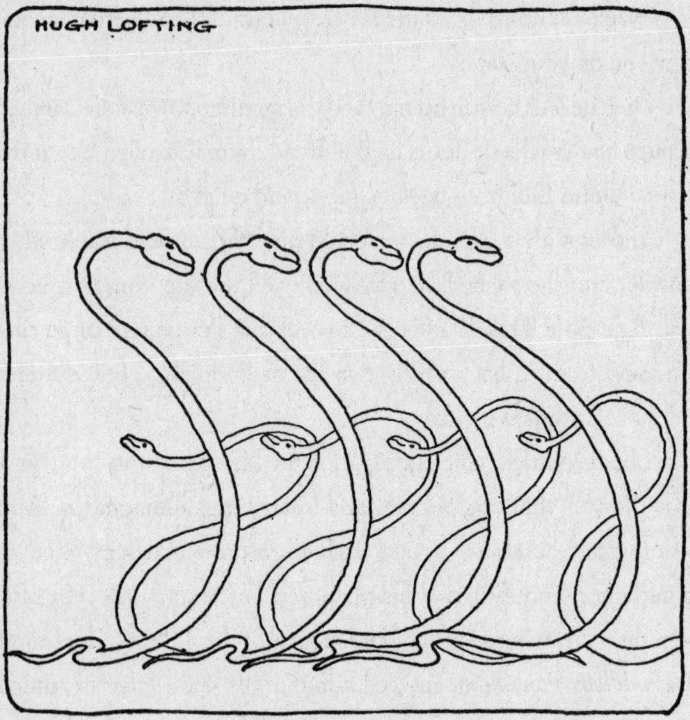

"The Snakes' Quadrille"

Indeed, as time went on, the Dolittle Circus's animal sideshows were almost without exception run independently by the animals themselves. There were a great number of them and each one was descriptive of that particular animal's special quality. The snakes' entertainment, for instance, was designed to show off their gracefulness; for, in John Dolittle's opinion, the snake was the most graceful creature in the world. The elephant, on the other hand, did feats of strength, instead of silly balancing tricks for which he wasn't suited.

"You don't want people in an animal performance," the Doctor said to Matthew one day. "Hercules and Hop and the acrobats, they're different. Those are shows, given by people, where the human performers are the whole thing. But what's the sense in seeing a stupid man in uniform driving a lion through hoops with a whip? People seem to think that animals have no ideas to express. If they're left to themselves they can give much better shows on their own, once they're told what kind of things amuse a human audience—especially in the funny shows. The animal sense of humor is far superior to the human. But people are too stupid to see the funniness of things that animals do to amuse one another. And in most cases I have to bring them down to our level—to have them make their style of jokes rather—er—crude and broad. Otherwise people mightn't understand them at all."

And so, you see, the Dolittle Circus was indeed quite different from any other. The Doctor's kind and hospitable treatment of all who came to see his show made it more like a sort of family gathering than a strictly business matter.

There were no rules, or hardly any. And if little boys wanted to see "behind the scenes," or to go into the elephant's stall and pet him, they were personally conducted wherever they wished to go. This alone gave the circus a quality quite individual. And whenever the wagon train moved on its way, the children would follow it for miles along the road and for weeks after would talk of nothing but when it would come back again to visit their town. For children everywhere were beginning to regard the Dolittle Circus as something peculiarly their own.

The End

[illegible]

The End

DOCTOR DOLITTLE'S

CARAVAN

WRITTEN AND ILLUSTRATED BY

HUGH LOFTING

Contents

PART ONE

The First Chapter

The Animal Shop

THIS BOOK OF THE MEMOIRS OF DOCTOR Dolittle has been called the *Caravan* because it is in part a continuation of the *Circus* and the adventures that he met within his career as a showman. Moreover, on his arrival in London, the headquarters of the Dolittle household became the Doctor's caravan on Greenheath (just outside the city), where his surgery and animal clinic continued their good work. And this too made that name for the book seem proper and in place.

It will be remembered that shortly after John Dolittle was elected as the new manager of the circus he had received a special invitation from some theater owners in London to come and put on a show for them. And while he was still taking the circus to small towns and working to get enough cash in hand to put the circus on its feet again, he was continually trying to think up some good and original shows to put on in London.

He was most anxious that his company's first appearance in the big city should be a success. The staff of the Dolittle Circus now consisted of Matthew Mugg, assistant manager; Hercules, the strong man; the Pinto Brothers, trapeze artists; Hop the clown; Henry Crockett, the Punch-and-Judy man; Theodosia Mugg, mistress of the wardrobes; and Fred, a new menagerie-keeper whom the Doctor had recently hired. Then of course there were the animals: the lion, the leopard, and the elephant—the big animals that constituted the important part of the menagerie; several smaller beasts, such as the opossum (known as the "Hurri-Gurri"); the Pushmi-Pullyu; the snakes; the Doctor's own animal household (Jip the dog, Gub-Gub the pig, Too-Too the owl, Dab-Dab the duck, and the white mouse); and a few other oddments.

It was not a large company. And for this John Dolittle was grateful. In the hard days that followed Blossom's heartless desertion, it was difficult enough to earn sufficient money to buy food for even these. But they were all, without exception, extremely sportsmanlike when things went badly. On the Doctor's new plan (the "cooperative system," as he called it) all the staff shared in the profits instead of getting wages. Often when business was poor, this had meant no salary at all, nothing but three meals a day. Yet there were no desertions and no grumbling. Everyone felt sure that sooner or later John Dolittle would steer the company's ship into prosperous waters, and they stuck to him through thick and thin. And the day came when their confidence was justified.

The way the Doctor finally hit upon an idea for an unusual show for London was rather curious. Like many important things, it began from a small chance happening.

One evening, when the show had moved to a moderate-sized market town, the Doctor went for a walk with Matthew Mugg and Jip. They had been busy all day getting the circus set up and

"They sat down to drink a glass of ale."

the Doctor had not yet had an opportunity to see the town. After going through the main streets, they came to an inn that had tables and chairs set outside before the door. It was a warm evening and the Doctor and Matthew sat down at the inn tables to drink a glass of ale.

While they were resting and watching the quiet life of the town, the song of a bird reached their ears. It was extraordinarily beautiful, at times tremendously powerful, at others soft and low and mysterious—but always changing. The singer, whoever he was, never repeated himself.

The Doctor had written books on birdsongs and he was interested.

"Do you hear that, Matthew?" he asked.

"Great, ain't it?" said the Cat's-Meat-Man. "Must be a nightingale—up on them big elms by the church there."

"No," said the Doctor, "that's no nightingale. That's a canary. He is singing scraps of a nightingale's song which he has picked up—and parts of many others, too. But he has a canary's voice, for all that. Listen: now he's imitating a thrush."

They sat a while longer and the bird ran through a wonderful range of imitations.

"You know, Matthew," said the Doctor, "I think I'd like to have a canary in the wagon. They're awfully good company. I've never bought one because I hate to see birds in cages. But with those who are born in captivity, I suppose it's really all right. Let's go down the street and see if we can get a glimpse of this songster."

So after the Doctor had paid for the ale, they left the tables and walked along toward the church. But before they reached it they saw there were several shops to pass. Presently the Doctor stopped.

"Look, Matthew," said he. "One of those shops is an animal shop. That's where the canary is. I hate animal shops; the poor creatures usually look so neglected. The proprietors always keep too many—more than they can look after properly. And they usually smell so stuffy and close—the shops, I mean. I never go into them now. I don't even pass one if I can help it."

"Why?" asked Matthew.

"Well," said the Doctor, "ever since I became sort of known among the animals, the poor beasts all talk to me as soon as I go in, begging me to buy them—birds and rabbits and guinea pigs and everything. I think I'll turn back and go around another way, so I won't have to pass the window."

But just as the Doctor was about to return toward the inn, the beautiful voice of the song bird burst out again and he hesitated.

"He's marvelous," said John Dolittle, "simply superb!"

"Why not hurry by with just one eye open?" said Matthew. "Maybe you could spot the bird without stopping."

"All right," said the Doctor. And putting on a brisk pace, he strode toward the shop. In passing it he just gave one glance in at the window and hurried on.

"Well," asked Matthew, as the Doctor paused on the other side. "Did you see which bird it was?"

"Yes," said John Dolittle. "It's that green canary near the door, the one in the small wooden cage, marked three shillings. Listen, Matthew, go in and buy him for me. I can afford that much, I think. I dare not go myself. Everything in the place will clamor at me at once. I have an idea those white rabbits recognized me already. You go for me. . . . Don't forget—the green canary in the wooden cage near the door, marked three shillings. Here's the money."

So Matthew Mugg went into the store with the three shillings, while the Doctor waited outside the window of the shop next door.

The Cat's-Meat-Man wasn't gone very long—and when he returned he had no canary with him.

"You made a mistake, Doctor," said he. "The bird you spoke of is a hen and they don't sing. The one we heard is a bright yellow male, right outside the shop. They want two pounds ten for him. He's a prize bird, they say, and the best singer they ever had."

"How extraordinary!" said the Doctor. "Are you sure?"

And, forgetting for the moment all about his intention of not being seen by the animals in the shop, he moved up to the window and pointed again to the green canary.

"The Doctor waited outside the window of the shop next door."

"That's the bird I meant," he said. "Did you ask about that one? Oh, Lord! Now I've done it. She has recognized me."

The green canary near the door end of the window, seeing the famous Doctor pointing to her, evidently expected him to buy her. She was already making signs to him through the glass and jumping about her cage with joy.

The Doctor, quite unable to afford two pounds ten for the other bird, was beginning to move away. But the expression in the little green canary's face as she realized he didn't mean to buy her after all was pitiful to see.

John Dolittle had not walked with Matthew more than a hundred yards down the street before he stopped again.

"It's no use," said he. "I'll have to buy her, I suppose—even if she can't sing. That's always the way if I go near an animal shop. I always have to buy the most wretched and most useless thing they have there. Go back and get her."

Once more the Cat's-Meat-Man went into the shop and presently returned with a small cage covered over with brown paper.

"We must hurry, Matthew," said the Doctor. "It's nearly teatime and Theodosia always finds it hard to attend to it without our help."

On reaching the circus the Doctor was immediately called away on important business connected with the show. He asked Matthew to take the canary to the wagon, and he was himself occupied with one thing and another until suppertime.

And even when he finally returned to his wagon, his mind was so taken up with the things of the day that he had forgotten for the moment all about the canary he had bought. He sank wearily into a chair as he entered, and Too-Too, the owl who kept the circus's accounts, immediately engaged him in a financial conversation.

But the dull discussion of money and figures had hardly begun before the Doctor's attention was distracted by a very agreeable sound. It was the voice of a bird warbling ever so softly.

"Great heavens!" the Doctor whispered. "Where's that coming from?"

The sound grew and grew—the most beautiful singing that John Dolittle had ever heard, even superior to that which he had listened to outside the inn. To ordinary ears it would have been wonderful enough, but to the Doctor, who understood canary language and could follow the words of the song being sung, it was an experience to be remembered.

It was a long poem, telling of many things—of many lands and many loves, of little adventures and great adventures, and the melody, now sad, now happy—now fierce, now soft, was more wonderful than the finest nightingale singing at his best.

"Where is it coming from?" the Doctor repeated, completely mystified.

"From that covered cage up on the shelf," said Too-Too.

"Great heavens!" the Doctor cried. "The bird I bought this afternoon!"

He sprang up and tore the wrapping paper aside. The song ceased. The little green canary peered out at him through the torn hole.

"I thought you were a hen," said the Doctor.

"So I am," said the bird.

"But you sing!"

"Well, why not?"

"But hen canaries don't sing."

The little green bird laughed a long, trilling, condescending sort of laugh.

"That old story—it's so amusing!" she said. "It was invented by the cocks, you know—the conceited males. The hens have by far the better voices. But the males don't like us to sing. They peck us if we do. Some years ago a movement was started—'Singing for Women,' it was called. Some of us hens got together to assert our rights. But there were an awful lot of old-fashioned ones who still thought it was unmaidenly to sing. They said that a hen's place was on the nest—that singing was for men only. So the movement failed. That's why people still believe that hens *can't* sing."

"But you didn't sing in the shop?" said the Doctor.

"Neither would you—in *that* shop," said the canary. "The smell of the place was enough to choke you."

"Well, why did you sing now?"

"She laughed a long, trilling, condescending laugh."

"Because I realized, after the man you sent came in a second time, that you had wanted to buy that foolish yellow male who had been bawling out of tune all afternoon. I knew, of course, that you only sent the man back to get me out of kindness. So I thought I'd like to repay you by showing you what we women can do in the musical line."

"Marvelous!" said the Doctor. "You certainly make that other fellow sound like a second-rate singer. You are a contralto, I see."

"A mezzo-contralto," the canary corrected. "But I can go right up through the highest soprano range when I want to."

"What is your name?" asked the Doctor.

"Pippinella," the bird replied.

"What was that you were singing just now?"

"I was singing you the story of my life."

"But it was in verse."

"Yes, I made it into poetry—just to amuse myself. We cage birds have a lot of spare time on our hands, when there are no eggs to sit on or young ones to feed."

"Humph!" said the Doctor. "You are a great artist—a poet and a singer."

"And a musician!" said the canary quietly. "The composition is entirely my own. You noticed I used none of the ordinary birdsongs—except the love song of the greenfinch at the part where I am telling of my faithless husband running off to America and leaving me weeping by the shore."

Dab-Dab at this moment came in to announce that supper was ready, but to Gub-Gub the pig's disgust, the Doctor brushed everything aside in the excitement of a new interest. Diving into an old portfolio, he brought out a blank musical manuscript book in which he sometimes wrote down pieces for the flute, his own favorite instrument.

"Excuse me," he said to the canary, "but would you mind starting the story of your life all over again? It interests me immensely."

"Certainly," said the little bird. "Have my drinking trough filled with water, will you please? It got emptied with the shaking coming here. I like to moisten my throat occasionally when I am singing long songs."

"Of course, of course!" said the Doctor, falling over Gub-Gub in his haste to provide the singer with what she wanted. "There! Now, would you mind singing very slowly? Because I want to take down the musical notation and the time is a little complicated. Also, I notice you change the key quite often. The words I won't bother with for the present, because I couldn't write both at once. I will ask you to give me them again, if you will, later. All right. I'm ready whenever you are."

The Second Chapter

The White Persian

THEN THE DOCTOR SAT DOWN AND WROTE page after page of music while the green canary sang him the story of her life. It was a long song, lasting at least half an hour. And during the course of it Gub-Gub interrupted more than once with his pathetic—

"But, Doctor, the supper's getting cold!"

When she had finished, John Dolittle carefully put away the book he had been writing in, thanked the canary, and prepared to have supper.

"Would you care to come out of your cage and join us?" he asked.

"Have you any cats?"

"No," said the Doctor. "I don't keep any cats in the wagon."

"Oh, all right," said the canary, "then if you'll open my door I'll come out."

"But you could easily get away from a cat, couldn't you," asked Jip, "with wings to fly?"

"I could if I was expecting it or knew where it was," said the canary, flying down onto the table and picking up a crumb beside the Doctor's plate. "Cats are most dangerous when you can't see them. They are the only really skillful hunters."

"Huh!" grunted Jip. "Dogs are pretty good, you know."

"Excuse me," said the canary, "but dogs are mere duffers when compared with cats in the hunting game—I'm sorry to hurt your feelings, but *duffers* is the only word I can use. You are all very fine at following and tracking—even better than cats at that. But for getting your quarry by the use of your wits—well, there! Did you ever see a dog sit and watch a hole in the ground for hours and hours on end, silent and still as a stone—waiting, waiting for some wretched little mouse or other creature to come out? Did you ever know a dog with the patience to do that? No. Your dog, when he finds a hole, barks and yelps and scratches at it—and of course the rat, or whatever it is, doesn't dream of coming out. No, speaking as a bird, I'd sooner be shut in a roomful of dogs than have a single cat in the house."

"Did you ever have any unpleasant experience with them?" asked the Doctor.

"Myself, no," said the canary. "But that was solely because of someone else's experience with one. It taught me a lesson. I lived once in the same house with a parrot. One day the woman who owned us got a fine, silky white Persian. She was a lovely creature—to look at. The old parrot said to me the morning the cat came, 'She looks a decent sort.'

"'Pol,' said I, 'cats are cats. Don't trust her—never trust a cat.'"

"I wonder if that's what makes them the way they are," said the Doctor, "the fact that no one ever trusts them. It's a terrible strain on anybody's character."

"Fiddlesticks!" said the canary. "Our woman trusted this cat—even left her in the room with us at night. My cage was hung high up on a chain, so I wasn't afraid of her reaching in to me with her claws. But poor old Pol, one of the most decent old cronies that ever sat on a perch, he had no cage at all—just one of those fool stands they make for parrots—a crossbar perch and a long chain on his ankle. He wouldn't believe that this sweet creature in white was dangerous, until one day she tried to climb up the pole of his stand and get at him. Well, a parrot's a pretty good fighter when the fight's a fair one, and he gave her more than she bargained for. She retired from the fray with a piece bitten out of her ear.

"He gave her more than she bargained for."

"'Now will you believe me?' I said. 'And listen: she's going to get you yet—if there's any way to do it that she and the Devil can think up between them. Whatever you do, don't go to sleep while she is in the room. She's scared of you now, while you're facing her. But she won't be scared of you as soon as you're off your guard. One spring and a bite on the neck from her, and Polly won't want any more crackers. Remember—*don't go to sleep when she is in the room.*'"

The green canary paused a moment in her story to hop across the table and take a drink out of Gub-Gub's milk bowl—which greatly astonished the little pig. Then she cleaned her bill against the cruet stand and proceeded:

"She took a drink out of Gub-Gub's milk bowl."

"I couldn't tell you how many times I saved that foolish parrot's life. An easygoing bird, he loved regularity. He was a bachelor, making a great ceremony of all the little habits of his daily round. And he just couldn't bear to have anything interfere with them. He would be ruffled and sulky for days if the maid missed giving him his bath on Saturday afternoon or his piece of orange peel at Sunday breakfast. One of his little customs was to take a nap every day after lunch. I warned him over and over again that this was dangerous unless the doors and windows were shut and the cat outside. But the force of habit, years and years of bachelor regularity, were too strong for him. And I believe he would have taken that nap if the room had been full of cats."

The canary picked up another crumb, munched it thoughtfully and went on:

"I often think there was something fine about that parrot's independence. He had principles and nothing was allowed to change them. In the meantime, that horrible cat was waiting for her chance. Often when Pol was dozing off I'd see her come sneaking toward his stand, along the floor or creep across a table near enough to spring from. Then I'd give a terrific loud whistle and the parrot would wake up. And the cat would slink away, looking daggers at me for spoiling her game.

"As for the mistress we had, it never entered her empty head that the cat was a dangerous customer. One day a friend of hers asked if she wasn't afraid to leave the beast around when she had no cage over the parrot.

"'Oh, tut-tut!' said she. 'Pussums wouldn't hurt my nice Polly, would ums, Pussums?'

"And then that silky hypocrite would rub her neck against

the old lady's dress and purr as though butter wouldn't melt in her mouth.

"Well, I did my best. But the day came when even I was outwitted by the she-devil in white. The old lady had gone to visit friends in the country and let the maid take the day off while she was away. Both the parrot and I were given double rations of seed and water, the house was locked, and the keys put under the mat. The door of the parlor, where we were always kept, was closed, and I thanked my stars that for this day, anyhow, my friend should be safe.

"About noon a thunderstorm came up and the wind howled around the house dismally. And presently I saw the door of our room blow open. It had not been properly latched—just closed carelessly.

"'Don't go to sleep, Pol,' I said. 'That cat may come in any moment!'

"Well, for a long time she didn't. And after an hour I decided that the cat must have been shut in another room somewhere and that it was all right and I needn't worry. After his lunch Pol went sound asleep; and presently, feeling sort of drowsy myself, I too took a nap.

"I dreamed all sorts of awful things—monstrous cats leaping through the air, parrots defending themselves with swords and pitchforks—all manner of terrible stuff. At the most tragic moment in the worst dream I thought I heard a thud on the floor and suddenly woke up, wide awake, the way one does with nightmares. And there on the floor lay Pol, stone dead, and squatting on the carpet on the far side of him, staring up at me with a devilish smirk of glee on her horrible face, sat the white cat!"

The canary shivered a little and rubbed her bill with her right foot, as though to wipe away the memory of a bad dream.

"I was too horrified to say a word," she presently continued, "and I began to wonder whether the abominable wretch would eat my poor dead friend. But not a bit of it. She didn't want him for food at all. She got three square meals a day from the old lady, the daintiest morsels in the house. She just wanted to kill—to kill for the fun of killing. For three months she had watched and waited and calculated. And in the end she had won. With another grin of triumph in my direction, she slowly turned about, left the body where it lay and stalked toward the door.

"'Well,' I thought to myself, 'there's one thing: she can't escape the blame. At least the old lady will know her now for what she is, the murderess!'

"And then a curious thing happened. It reminded me of something my mother used to believe: that cats are helped by the devil. 'It would be impossible for them to be so fiendishly clever without,' she used to say. 'Never try to match your wits against a cat! They are helped by the devil.'

"I had never believed it, myself. But that afternoon I came very near believing it. Now, mark you, with that door blown open, anyone would know that it was the cat who had come in and killed the parrot, wouldn't they? But with that door shut—the way the old lady had thought she left it—and the cat outside of the room—no one could possibly suspect 'sweet pussums.' So then I felt quite certain that this time the cat was going to get in a good, stiff fight. Now comes the strange business; no sooner had she passed into the hall outside than the wind began again, howling and moaning about the house. And, to my horror, I saw the door slowly closing. Faster and faster it swung forward, and then with a bang that shook the house from cellar to garret, it slammed shut. The last glimpse I got of the hall outside showed me 'sweet pussums' squatting on the floor, still grinning at me in triumph. After that, I think you will admit, it was pardonable to believe that she was helped by the devil. For, mind you, if the wind had come two minutes earlier it would have shut her *inside* the room, instead of *out.*

"Of course, when the old lady came home she just couldn't understand it. There lay the parrot on the floor, his neck broken (the cat had done it very neatly and cleverly—just one spring, a bite, and a twist); the windows were shut; the door was shut.

"Finally that silly old woman said that perhaps boys had got in, probably down the chimney, wrung the parrot's neck and escaped, leaving no tracks. The mystery was never solved. She was frightfully upset, weeping all over the place—after it was too late.

"'Oh well,' she sobbed, 'anyhow, I have my canary left—and my sweet pussums.'

"And then that she-devil came up to her, purring, to be petted, and the old woman gave her a saucer of milk! No, never, never trust a cat."

"They're funny creatures," said the Doctor. "There's no gainsaying that. And their curious habit of killing even when they're not hungry is very hard to explain. Still, it's in their nature, I suppose, and one should never judge anyone without making allowances for the nature he was born with. You have been through some very interesting experiences, I see. When you were singing me the story of your life I was so busy getting the music down that I couldn't pay much attention to the words. After we have finished supper, would you mind telling it to me over again?"

"Why, certainly," said the canary. "I'll tell it to you conversationally—without music."

"Yes, I think that would be better," said the Doctor. "You can then put in all your adventures in detail, without bothering to make the lines scan and rhyme. Gub-Gub, as soon as you have finished that plateful of beechnuts, we will let Dab-Dab clear away."

"The old lady gave her a saucer of milk."

THE THIRD CHAPTER

An Animal Biography

IT WAS THUS THROUGH THE COMING OF THE little green canary that the Doctor wrote the first of his animal biographies. He had frequently considered doing this before. He claimed that in many instances the lives of animals were undoubtedly more interesting—if they were properly written—than the lives of some of our so-called great men. He had even thought of writing a series, or a set of books called *Great Animals of the Nineteenth Century*, or something like that. But so far he had not met many whose memories were good enough to remember all the things in their lives that make a biography interesting.

Gub-Gub, disappointed that no statue had been erected to him in Manchester, had often begged the Doctor to write his life for him, feeling certain that of course everybody would want to read it. But John Dolittle and his pets knew Gub-Gub's life by heart already. And while the Doctor felt that it would make good comic reading, Gub-Gub himself refused to have it written that way, now that he was a famous actor.

"I want a dignified biography," said he. "I may be funny on the stage—very funny. But in my biography I must be dignified."

"Pignified, you mean," growled Jip. "Your biography would be just one large meal after another—with stomachaches for adventures. Myself, I'd sooner read the life of a nice, round, smooth stone."

So this branch of the Doctor's natural history writing had remained untouched till the appearance of Pippinella, the canary who came to join his family circle under such curious circumstances. Pippinella, the Doctor often said, was a born biographer, for she had a marvelous memory for the little things that made a story interesting and real. And John Dolittle in the preface to this the first of his *Private Memoirs of Distinguished Animals* was careful to say that the entire book was Pippinella's own, he merely having translated it from Canary into English.

Those who read it declared it most interesting. But, like so many of the Doctor's works, it is now out of print and copies of it are almost impossible to obtain. One of the reasons for this was that the ordinary booksellers wouldn't keep it. "Pooh!" they said. "*The Life of a Canary*! What kind of life could that be—sitting in a cage all day!"

And as a consequence of their stupidity the book was only sold at the taxidermists' shops, naturalists' supply stores, and odd places like that. Probably that is why copies are so hard to find today. In its final completed form, under the title of *The Life of Coloratura Pippinella, Contralto Canary*, the story contained much of the bird's life that was lived after she joined the Dolittle household. Moreover, the Doctor went through the manuscript with the authoress several times and got her to tell him more about many little incidents and details which he thought would be of interest to the general public.

All this went to make it quite a long book. I have not space to set it down for you here just as the Doctor wrote it, but I will tell it to you in part, at all events, as Pippinella herself related it to John Dolittle and his family circle.

"People," Pippinella began, when Gub-Gub had finally ceased fidgeting, "might think that the biography of a cage canary would be a very dull monotonous story. But, as a matter of fact, the lives of cage birds are often far more varied and interesting than those of wild ones. I have heard the lives of several wild birds and they were most exceedingly dull and samey.

"Very well, then, I will begin at the beginning. I was born in an aviary, a private one, occupied by our family and a few others. My father was a bright lemon-yellow Harz Mountains canary and my mother was a greenfinch of very good family. My brothers and sisters—there were six of us altogether, three boys and three girls—were about the same as me to look at, sort of olive-green and yellow mixed up. Of course, until our eyes were open the thing that concerned us chiefly was getting enough food. Good parents—and ours were the most conscientious couple you ever saw—give their children when they are first hatched about fourteen meals a day."

"Huh!" muttered Gub-Gub. "That's more than I ever got."

"Sh!" said the Doctor. "Don't interrupt."

"Pardon me, Pippinella," said John Dolittle, "but that is a point that has often interested me: How do young birds know, before their eyes are open, when their parents are bringing food? I've noticed that they all open their mouths every time the old birds come back to the nest."

"We tell it, I imagine, by the vibration. Our parents stepping onto the edge of the nest is something that we get to recognize very early. And then, although our eyes are closed, we see the shadow that our parents make leaning over the nest coming in between us and the sunlight."

"Thank you," said the Doctor, making a note. "Please continue."

"As you may have observed," Pippinella went on, "young birds talk and peep and chirp almost as soon as they are out of the egg. That is one of the big differences between bird children and human children: you see before you talk, and we talk before we see."

"Huh!" Gub-Gub put in. "Your conversation can't have much sense to it, then. What on earth can you have to talk about if you haven't seen anything yet?"

"That," said the canary, turning upon Gub-Gub with rather a haughty manner, "is perhaps another important difference between bird babies and pig babies: we are born with a certain amount of sense, while pigs, from what I have observed, never get very much, even when they are grown up. No, this blind period with small birds is a very important thing in their education and development. You ask me what they talk about. Nothing very much. I and my brothers and sisters used to swap guesses with one another on what the world would look like when our eyes would open. But the value of that time lies in this: having to do without our eyes, we develop what we call our sixth sense. It is rather hard to explain. But Too-Too will tell you that it is something well known and recognized among all birds. When we talk of birds having sense, we always mean sixth sense."

"Excuse me," the Doctor put in, "but would you go into that a little further?"

"Certainly," said the canary. "But as I told you, it's frightfully hard to explain. You were speaking just now of the parents approaching the nest and the young ones opening their mouths. Well, even before they actually step on the nest we soon get to know that they are there without seeing or hearing them. And then birds are awfully busy with their ears during this time. They do a lot of listening. And, being unable to see, they get to be much better hearers than if they had the use of their eyes as well. We listened to everything with the greatest care, trying to learn from it what the world was going to look like—even to the mice scratching behind the panelings, and the boughs of the trees in the garden tapping the windowpane near our cage.

"'That's a strong wind, isn't it, Father?' we would say. 'There are many twigs scratching on the glass.'

"'Yes, children,' he would answer. 'It's a north wind. It is only the north and the northeast winds that press the jasmine up against the window. The others blow it away from the house.'

"Then, after that, you see, we could tell just by the tune the bough tips played upon the panes which way the wind was blowing and how strong it was. But much of our education we got without knowing the why or the wherefore at all. That is perhaps the best explanation of the sixth sense: just knowing a thing without knowing why or how you know it. Of course, in many matters the wild birds are much cleverer than we are. At geography, for instance: bird geography is all done by the sixth sense. But then, of course, we cage birds don't get much chance to study that. But at other things we are ahead of them a long way. Especially about people. You'd be surprised what a good judge of character most housebred canaries are. Altogether, as a grown-up bird, I've often astonished myself at what a lot I know—and how I know it I couldn't tell you to save my life. But I'm convinced that a great deal of the most important part of my education came to me, as it does to all of us, during that time when we lie in the nest with our eyes closed, trying to guess, by hearing and smelling and feeling, what the world is going to look like."

"Thank you," said the Doctor. "That is very interesting. Pray, pardon my interruption, but these things are important to me as a naturalist. Please continue with your story."

"It is quite an exciting moment," Pippinella continued, "for young birds when they first open their eyes. They usually stay awake most of the night before, lest they sleep past the time and their brothers and sisters crow over them that they saw the world first.

"Well, with us the day came in due course; and, myself, I was slightly disappointed. You must remember that for us cage birds the world was the inside of a room instead of an open meadow, hedgerow, or leafy forest. Of course, we had known something of what it was going to look like from asking our parents. But no matter how well a thing is described to you, you always form your own idea of it, more or less wrong. Very well, then. Our world, we discovered, was a long room, sort of parlor and conservatory combined—a pleasant enough place, containing flowerpots, palms, some furniture, and several cages of birds. By day a woman attended to us, supplying our parents with chopped egg and cracker crumbs, which they fed to us youngsters. At night a man, who apparently owned us, came in to inspect everything. He seemed a decent sort of fellow and evidently had our welfare at heart because he was forever scolding the woman for neglecting to clean cages, to change the water in the troughs, or to give the birds fresh lettuce.

"Raising prize singing birds was this man's hobby. He had

other cages in other rooms, because we could hear the birds singing. And when the doors were open, my father would sing back to them and carry on conversations with them about the woman, the quality of the new supply of seed, the temperature in the conservatory, and any odd gossip about the household.

"There was another family of young ones in a cage close to ours. And our parents used to chat with the other parents—my mother always boasting that we looked a much healthier brood than theirs.

"The man had two children of his own, and they would come into the conservatory occasionally to look at us and to play with toys on the floor. Their games provided us with entertainment and we were glad to have them, because most days the conservatory was rather quiet.

"My father was evidently quite a fine singer. And now and then, when he wasn't helping my mother shovel food into us hungry children, he'd sit on the edge of the nest and sing. He had a tremendous voice. But for my part, I can't say that I enjoyed it much. At that close range it was simply earsplitting, and we used to beg Mother to make him stop.

"Once he was taken away from us for a whole day. And Mother told us he had gone to a canary show, to see if he was a good enough singer to get a prize. And when the man brought him back to us in the evening there was great excitement throughout the house. All the family came in, talking. Father had won the first prize at the show! After that he used to sing louder than ever, and it was no use our asking Mother to stop him because she was even prouder of his success than he was. In between songs he told us all about the show and what the judges said and what sort of canaries he had had to sing against.

"It was a funny life—not nearly as dull as you'd think. As we got our feathers and grew bigger I used to look out of the window at the spring trees budding in the garden. Every once in a while I'd see a finch fly by and I'd get a sort of vague hankering to be out in the open, living a life of freedom. But one day I saw a hawk swoop down on a poor lame sparrow and carry him off. With a shudder I nestled down among my brothers and sisters and thanked my stars that I lived indoors. After all, I decided, there was a good deal to be said for this cage life, where we were protected from cats and birds of prey, given comfortable quarters and the best of food."

The Fourth Chapter

Pippinella Takes Her First Journey

"THE THING," PIPPINELLA CONTINUED, "THAT most interested every bird born at that house was whether he was going to be kept, sold, exchanged, or given away. For this man, while he did not run a regular shop, had many friends who were also interested in canaries. He seems to have been quite well known, for some of these people came long distances to see him and his birds. His place wasn't big enough to keep all the families that were born there. So when the young ones grew up and got their full feathers, he would pick out those that he wanted to keep himself. These were such as had good voices or who were prettily marked. The others he would sometimes exchange, sometimes give away, and sometimes sell. He never kept very many hens.

"One evening, about two weeks after we had left the nest and were hopping and pecking for ourselves, my parents were talking this matter over together. And of course we youngsters, since it was a subject that very deeply concerned us, were listening intently. Said my mother:

"'I'm afraid he will probably get rid of most of this brood. Nearly all his space is taken up and he seems to prefer those birds over in the next cage—though what he can see in the scrawny, long-necked little brats I don't know. I wouldn't exchange one of our babies for the whole batch.'

"'Well,' said my father, 'so far as the welfare of our own is concerned, it will be just as well if he does let them go—especially if they go separately.'

"'Why?' I asked.

"'Because you always get better cared for in houses where you are the only canary kept. In any place where they have an awful lot to look after, the treatment is usually slipshod and negligent. The worst of all are the animal shops. They are notoriously bad. You don't get your cage cleaned out more than once a week; you get put anyplace, sometimes in the hot sun, sometimes in an awful draft. And the noises and the smells are dreadful. No, I hope, for your sake, you don't get sent to an animal shop.'

"'But, Father,' I said, 'it's all right if you get bought right away, isn't it?'

"'Yes, but you seldom are, if you're a hen,' he said. 'People don't often come to an animal shop to buy hen canaries.'

"'Why?' I asked again.

"'Because they don't sing,' said he.

"You notice he said '*don't* sing,' not '*can't* sing.' I am afraid I've always been something of a rebel. Maybe I ought to have been born a boy. Anyway, that evening I felt particularly aggrieved at this stupid, unfair, old-fashioned custom.

"'Father, I think that's ridiculous,' I said. 'You know very well that hens are born with just as good voices as cocks. But merely because it isn't considered proper for them to sing they have to let their voices spoil for wont of practice when they're young. I think it's a crying shame.'

"Then my mother joined in.

"'How dare you speak to your father like that, you brazen hussy!' she cried. 'What are the girls coming to these days, I'd like to know? Go and stand down in the corner of the cage!'

"And she gave me a box on the ear with her wing that knocked me right off the perch.

"Well, although I had been reprimanded, I was by no means repentant. I saw that just because hens were not supposed to sing, I and my sisters stood a good chance of being packed off to some wretched crowded animal shop, instead of being bought by some private person who would treat us decently. And I determined to practice my singing secretly, so as to develop my voice and become just as valuable as my brothers.

"Well, in spite of frequent peckings, I continued to exercise my voice quietly when the others were busy eating or talking together. Finally the man who owned us noticed that I often got sat upon by the rest of my family and I was put in a separate cage. After that I could sing as long and as loud as I wanted to, and all that the others could do was to make rude remarks from across the room about the quality of my voice.

"And then one day the bird fancier, our owner, brought in a friend of his to see us. He wanted to make this friend a present of a canary, it seemed, and he offered him his choice out of the two new families of birds. I liked the man's face and I was determined he should pick me out, if I could make him. He was evidently rather taken with the coloring of the other family and he lingered around their cage quite a while. But I sang my loudest and my best and presently I saw I had caught his attention. He came over to my cage and asked the fancier if I, too, was part of the new broods. On hearing that I was, he said he would like to have me.

"Then, to my great delight, the fancier went and got a small traveling cage to lend his friend, until he could buy a bigger one for me. Into this I was changed and wrapping paper was put around and I couldn't see anything more after that.

"However, my parents and brothers and sisters could still hear me through the paper. They wished me good-bye and good luck. Then I felt my cage lifted up off the table and the first journey of my life began.

"Of course, I wondered, inside my paper-covered carriage, where I was being taken and what my new home would be like. From the motion, a curious jerky sort of swing, I guessed I was still being carried by someone walking. But soon I was put down again, just for a moment, and the suddenly cooling air told me I was outside the house. Next I heard the stamping of a horse's feet, and then I was lifted up again, high. After that a new kind of motion began and, from the swing of it and the regular beating of hooves, I knew I was being carried on horseback.

"I felt the wind blowing through my paper covering. Soon the scent of the ripe corn and poppies reached me and I knew that my owner was now beyond the town, out in the open country. I had never been in the country before, but my father had, when being taken to shows, and he had told me something about it.

"It was a cold ride, bumpy and uncomfortable. With the jolting motion of the saddle pommel on which my cage was held, every bit of the water and seed out of my troughs got spilled all over the cage—and me too.

"Presently the horse's pace slowed down and, hearing now the echoes of his hooves thrown back from near at hand, I guessed that we had entered the streets of another town. I wondered if this was the place where I was to live or if my owner would ride on through it. I heard sparrows chattering, pigeons cooing, dogs barking, people talking and calling. I hoped we would stay here. It seemed a nice, cheery place, from the sounds of it.

"And sure enough, to my great delight, that awful riding motion ceased. I felt my cage being handed down and taken by other hands. Somebody—a woman—was greeting my man on the horse. The air suddenly grew warm and a door slammed shut. I was inside a house—a house of many smells, most of them nice, comfortable, foody smells. My cage was set upon a table. Several voices were now chattering around me, some of them children's. Fingers began clawing at my wrapping paper to undo it. The string was cut with a *ponk* like the twang of a guitar. And then—at last—I could see."

THE FIFTH CHAPTER

The New Home

THE ROOM," PIPPINELLA CONTINUED, "IN which I found myself was quite different from any I had ever seen before. But then, of course, I had only seen one other, so far—the fancier's conservatory. This place was pretty large, with lots and lots of chairs in it, a ceiling of big smoked beams and funny pictures on the walls of men in scarlet jackets galloping across country on horseback. A pair of stag's horns were hung over the door. And above the fireplace there was an enormous dead fish in a glass box.

"Gathered about my cage stood four or five people, men, women, and children, all with fat, round faces and red cheeks. They were staring at me with great curiosity and—to judge from their smiles—with some admiration. I guessed them to be the family of my new owner. Presently another cage was brought and I was changed into it. It was quite roomy and decent inside and I was glad to get into it after the little crampy one which had been so messed up by the journey.

"Then there was evidently a good deal of discussion among the family about where I should be put. One pointed to one place and another to another. Finally it was decided to hang my cage in the big bay window that looked out on to a forecourt, or front yard.

"Of course, you must understand that up to this I had never seen very much of people. I was exceedingly young. At the fancier's all I ever saw, with very few exceptions, was one person at a time. But in this house it was entirely different. People in twos and threes were around, talking all the time. And, watching and listening to them the whole day, I soon began to understand many words of their language. Even that first day I guessed from signs and other things that the largest boy of the family was asking his mother if he could have the job of looking after me. Finally his mother consented—to my great sorrow later, because he was the most forgetful child that ever walked. Many was the time that he forgot to refill my water trough and I'd go thirsty for a whole day before he found it out. He was always dreadfully sorry when he discovered his mistake, but that didn't do me any good.

"At first I was very much puzzled by this house. The family seemed to be positively enormous. All day long new batches that I had never seen before, men, women, and children, kept arriving, some on horseback, some on foot, some in carriages. They would take meals in the dining room, and often sleep upstairs in the bedrooms overnight. Then they'd go away again and different ones would take their place. There was somebody arriving and somebody going away all the time.

"Then I decided these could not all belong to the family, and I supposed that my new owner was a man of many friends. Heaven only knows how long I would have gone on believing that if I had not one day had my youthful ignorance enlightened by a chaffinch. It was a warm afternoon and the bay window had been opened. I saw a chaffinch passing and repassing, with bits of horse hair in his mouth. He was busily building a nest in one of the poplars in the yard. I had not spoken to a bird since I had left my own family, so I hailed him, and he came over close to the window and chatted a while.

"'This seems an awfully funny house,' I said. 'Who's this man who has so many friends coming to visit him all day long?'

"'No one could mistake you for anything but a newborn cage bird,' said the chaffinch with a laugh. 'They aren't his friends. This isn't a private house. This is an inn, a hotel, where people pay to stop and eat. Haven't you noticed that big carriage that rattles into the yard every evening at five o'clock? Well, that's the coach from the north. And the one that comes early in the morning is the night coach from the south. Haven't you seen them changing horses? This is a regular coaching inn, one of the busiest spots in the country.'

"And very soon I decided that in my first venture away from the protection of my mother's wing I had been very lucky. Good fortune had given me a home that any cage bird could envy. I have often looked back with pleasure upon the nice, cheerful bustle of that inn. If you must be a cage bird—if you have to be deprived of the green forests and the open freedom of the skies—then it is good to be in close touch with the world. And there one was certainly that.

"Something new was happening all the time. Men went over this road not only to the capital but to foreign lands—for it was the highway to a great port from where ships sailed to the seven seas. Travelers coming and going brought news from everywhere. And the daily coaches always delivered the newspapers from the north, south, east, and west.

"All this I witnessed from my little cage. And when the summer weather came I used to be put outside every morning, high up on the wall beside the door. From there I could see down the road a long way. And the daily coaches were visible to me quite a while before they could be seen by anyone else. When the weather was dry I could tell them by the cloud of dust far, far off; and then I'd sing a special song that I made up. It began 'Maids, come out; the coach is here.' And though nobody understood the words of it, all the maids and the porters of the hotel soon got to know the tune. And whenever they heard me sing it they'd know the mail coach would arrive in a few minutes and they'd all get ready to receive the guests. The maids would take a last look at the dining room tables; the porters would come to the door for the valises and luggage; and the stable boys would open the yard gate and get ready the fresh horses to change for the tired ones coming in. It gave me quite a thrill on a quiet, drowsy afternoon to suddenly wake that inn up to a bustle and life, just by singing my song, 'Maids, Come Out; the Coach Is Here.' In that way, you see, I was not only in touch with the world but I was, in a manner, an active part of it. For though I lived in a cage, I felt myself a responsible member of the hotel staff.

"Another thing that is very important for a cage bird, if he is to lead a happy life, is that he shall like people. Most wild birds look upon people as just something to be afraid of and think they are all the same, like stones or beans. They're not. They're all different. There's just as much difference in people as there is in sparrows or canaries. But you can't make a wild bird believe that.

"I had not lived very long at that inn before I made a great number of very excellent friends—among the people. One I remember particularly: the old driver who drove the night coach from the north. He was what is called a very famous whip—that is, he could drive a four-in-hand with great skill. Every evening when he brought his great lumbering carriage into the yard he'd call to me from his box, 'Hulloa, there, Pip!' And he'd crack his long whip with a sound like a pistol shot. Then the hostlers would all come running out to change horses, polishing up the harness, washing the mud off the traces—as busy as bees putting everything in shipshape for the next stage of the journey. I made up another song for that nice, jolly-faced old driver—his name was Jack. And every evening when he cracked his whip I'd sing it to encourage the busy stable boys at their work around the coach. It was meant to sound like the jingle of harness and the *shish-shish-shish* of a currycomb. And it ended sudden and sharp—*'Jack!—Crack!'*

"Old Jack always brought me a lump of sugar in his pocket—never, never forgot. And on his way in to get his own supper he'd poke it into the bars of my cage and take out the old one that he had left there yesterday. He was one of the best friends I ever had was Jack, the driver of the night coach from the north."

THE SIXTH CHAPTER

An Adventurous Career

AS I HAVE ALREADY SAID, PIPPINELLA'S LIFE was quite a long story. And since this book is to be a history of the Doctor's adventures, I feel it would be wiser if I told the rest of the contralto canary's career in my own words, rather than in the longer form in which she narrated it herself to the Dolittle household in the caravan.

Certainly few cage birds, indeed few people, ever experienced so many thrills in the space of a short lifetime. From the inn where she had been so happy, she was bought and taken away by a nobleman who stopped there on his way to his country estate. Arriving at a very gorgeous castle, she was presented to the nobleman's wife and lived for some weeks in that lady's little boudoir at the top of a high tower.

Here she was introduced to an entirely different kind of life from what she had seen at the inn. From the grand silver cage into which she had been put, she saw trouble brewing all around her. The nobleman (a marquis) owned many square miles of land, whole towns, coal mines, factories, and whatnot. His wife, the kind marchioness in whose boudoir Pippinella lived, was unhappy. The canary sang songs to her to cheer her up—"The Harness Jingle," which she had composed for old Jack, the driver of the night coach from the north, and the merry call, "Maids, Come Out; the Coach Is Here."

She heard rumors of riots in the factory towns and the mines. The workers were discontented. One day when both the marquis and the marchioness were away, a mob attacked the castle, ransacked it, and set fire to it. The dogs and horses belonging to the estate were rescued by the workers themselves. But not so poor Pippinella. In her silver cage hung outside the tower window hundreds of feet above the ground, she was overlooked and left on the wall of the blazing building. Unable to escape, she saw the flames slowly but surely rising through the castle, floor by floor.

But just as all chance of rescue seemed most hopeless, she heard the sound of drums coming up the valley. A regiment of soldiers had been sent to put down the riot and save the estate. The workers fled. The fire was put out and Pippinella, the only living thing left in the gutted building, was rescued by the soldiers.

After this dramatic escape she was made the regimental mascot and traveled with the military wherever they went. She was treated extremely well, as an individual of great importance who would bring good luck so long as she survived. From place to place she went, always riding in her cage on top of the baggage wagon, while the Fusiliers (the regiment to which she had been attached) put down riots and disturbances in various small towns round about.

During this period she composed another song—a marching song for the soldiers of whom she had grown very fond; and it began

"Oh, I'm the midget mascot, I'm a feathered fusilier."

The day came when the soldiers were sent to a certain town to put down an uprising of the workers. They were commanded to fire on the crowd, which was unarmed. They did not openly rebel against orders. But being really in sympathy with the workers, they allowed themselves to be defeated. The baggage wagon on which the mascot Pippinella traveled was captured. And the contralto canary found herself suddenly transferred from the position of a pampered regimental pet to the possession of a laboring man who had won her in a raffle.

This man later attempted to escape from the town after it was besieged by fresh troops who had come to reinforce the defeated Fusiliers. With him he took a companion and Pippinella. On the way out through the sentry lines he was shot. And though he managed to escape and drag himself several miles into the country, he finally died of his injuries, and the canary passed into the possession of his companion.

Pippinella's new owner was apparently a coal miner and it was his intention to get to the next town and seek work in the coalpits. He begged a ride on a grocer's wagon and finally reached his destination.

The next chapter in Pippinella's story is a very strange and mournful one. It was apparently the custom in many mines to have canaries underground where the men worked. They were placed high up above the workers' heads on the walls of the galleries and tunnels. The idea was that the deadly gas, which is sometimes a source of great danger to the miners, would begin by gathering against the ceiling of the tunnels. Thus the behavior of these birds was supposed to give warning to the miners when they were in danger.

After some weeks of this dark and gloomy life, Pippinella saw an old lady coming through the mines on a visit. She was very interested in the presence of the canary here and asked if she could buy her. The price she offered was large and the miner who owned her jumped at the chance of making so much money. The old lady took Pippinella back to her home with her and a new and brighter life began.

It was springtime and Aunt Rosie (as Pippinella came to call her new owner) decided that her canary must have a mate and rear a brood. So a gentleman canary of very smart appearance was bought at the local livestock shop and introduced to Pippinella. She found him very stupid, she told the Doctor, but of a kind and thoughtful disposition. But the most remarkable thing about him was his voice. Pippinella considered herself (and rightly so, too) a good judge of bird voices. But she assured John Dolittle that among tenor canaries she had never heard, before or since, the equal of her first husband. His name was Twink.

Many quiet domestic weeks now followed during which Pippinella and Twink raised a lusty brood of young canaries to full growth. The youngsters were all given away, when they were old enough, to Aunt Rosie's friends. And finally Pippinella and her husband found themselves alone again.

It was at Aunt Rosie's home that Pippinella made the acquaintance of the man who had the greatest influence on her life. He was a window cleaner. Her cage had always hung in the window. And while this man polished the panes he would whistle to the canary and she would talk back to him. Pippinella said she knew at once that he had character—that he wasn't just an ordinary person, and that he probably only cleaned windows to make his bread and butter. Aunt Rosie, though she was kindhearted, Pippinella had found a rather tiresome woman. To the canary's great delight, she was eventually presented to the window cleaner as a gift.

It was no very terrible sorrow to her to leave Twink, who, while he was the greatest singer on earth, had proved a very dull mate. Pippinella went off with her window cleaner in high glee.

Her new home was a strange one. The window cleaner lived in an old broken-down windmill. He was away most of the day cleaning windows to earn his daily bread. But he used to work far into the night writing. He seemed to be very secretive about this writing, always hiding his manuscripts in a hole under the floor when he was finished.

One day he went off as usual to his work. By this time spring was coming again and he had set Pippinella's cage on a nail outside the window of the mill. It hung a good twenty feet from the ground. The hour came for his usual return, but he did not show up. Darkness came on—and still he had not come back. Two days went by, and still no window cleaner.

The canary's food was by this time of course long since exhausted. She felt something must have happened to her master and there was every chance, since he lived entirely alone, of her starving to death.

However on the third night, toward the morning hours, a great storm came up and her cage was finally blown off the nail in the mill tower and sent crashing to the ground. It broke in halves. The canary was unharmed; and suddenly, as the dawn showed in the east, she found herself, for the first time in her career, *free*!

The Seventh Chapter

Freedom

PIPPINELLA SPENT SOME TIME DESCRIBING TO the Doctor what that freedom meant. At first she rejoiced greatly: she could go where she wished, do as she liked. But, born and bred a cage bird, she soon found that life in the open held more dangers than comforts for one who was not experienced in it. When she attempted to make her way through the hedges like other birds, she got her wings all tangled up in the blackberry brambles. She was chased by a cat, weasels, and hawks. She did not know where to look for wild seed. Flights longer than a few yards tired her dreadfully. Much of her time was spent cowering in the holes of the mill tower to escape her enemies of the air and earth.

Then came along a greenfinch. Pippinella, you will remember, was a green canary, crossbred. The greenfinch had seen her escaping from a hawk and saved her life by drawing off that deadly enemy upon himself so she could escape. In the calm beauty of a spring evening he sang to her and offered to show her how the life of the wild should be lived. Pippinella was touched. This greenfinch had

"She got her wings all tangled up in the blackberry brambles."

saved her life. She went off with him. They were to build a nest and raise a brood.

Many leagues they traveled seeking the ideal spot for the nest that would be worthy of their romance. Often in those days she heard her lover sing that famous melody that later became well known, through her, to human audiences. She called it then "The Love Song of the Greenfinch in the Spring." Meanwhile her mate coached her in all the arts of the wild life, which she, as a cage bird, was ignorant of.

Those were idyllic days, as Pippinella described them to the

Doctor. But tragedy and sorrow lay ahead. One evening when she returned after seeking nesting materials (they had found the ideal place for their home in a little bay where the sea rolled in in gentle waves and the wild flowering bushes hung low down over the sandy shores) she discovered her mate in conversation with a full-bred greenfinch, a lady of his own kind. Pippinella knew at once, she told the Doctor, that the end of her romance had come. However, she tried to behave in a ladylike manner, and when introduced to the greenfinch damsel she was careful to be polite and courteous. The three birds roosted for the night on the limb of a flowering hawthorn bush. But Pippinella knew she wasn't wanted—after all, she was only a mongrel, a cage bird.

Very early, before the dawn had wakened her companions, she quietly left the hawthorn bush and betook herself to the shore. There on the sands she determined to fly to foreign lands, to forget—and start life anew.

By this time indeed she had already begun to weary of the wild life—of the freedom that has so many dangers for the cage bird. She wanted to find her old friend the window cleaner. It could not be that he was dead! And if he was alive, maybe he needed her. Her motherly instinct was aroused. Very well then, she would leave her faithless lover with his greenfinch hussy. And scouring foreign lands beyond the sea, maybe she'd meet her old friend. With him she would return to the life of captivity in which she had been born, and be useful and happy.

From this point on, her life story became one long series of adventures. Crossing the ocean without a wild bird's knowledge of geography and navigation was of course in itself a foolhardy thing to attempt. Moreover, she had as yet very little endurance for long-distance flying.

She was no sooner beyond the sight of land than she was lost and exhausted. She took refuge on some floating gulfweed till a passing curlew gave her directions as to how to reach the nearest land.

Following these instructions she finally came to Ebony Island, a jungle-covered mountainous piece of land only a few miles square. After she had recovered from her fatigue she examined the island and found it a pleasant-enough place. She was treated kindly by the native birds, many male finches vying for her affections. But she was still too brokenhearted over her lover's faithlessness and she encouraged none of them. She does not even tell them where she came from and she remains a sort of woman of mystery among the bird society of the island.

She fills in her time composing many new and beautiful songs. But after a few weeks she discovers that all her new songs are sad—none of them jolly, like "Maids, Come Out," or stirring, like "I'm the Midget Mascot." Wondering why this is, she decides that she is still mourning for her friend the window cleaner. She has an uncanny and unexplainable feeling all the time when she is flying about the island that he is near her, or that he has been here before her.

At length, just as she is about to leave, she discovers the window cleaner's dustrag tied to a pole at the summit of one of the island's hills. She is quite certain it is the towel that he dried the windows with because she knew every detail of it, and it has a mended tear in exactly the right place.

Hunting around in the neighborhood of this signal station (for the cloth had been clearly set up as a flag to attract the attention of passing ships), she finds a cave where her old friend had lived and other traces of his presence.

He must have been shipwrecked and cast away on this island, she thinks. What shall she do now? She sees a ship passing some miles away to westward. She fears her own ignorance of navigation; but following this ship she must surely be brought to land—possibly back to England where she had last seen her friend.

She sets off. But as soon as she is well out from the shores of the island a heavy rain squall drives her forward past the ship like a leaf in the wind. Her only hope of safety is to take refuge on the ship itself while there is yet time. This she does, and is immediately captured by one of the crew. She is put into a cage and placed in the ship's barbershop. There is another canary there who tells her all the gossip of the ship.

This new life was not a bad one. She was treated well and the business of the barbershop, where passengers came to be shaved and have their hair cut, provided a constant entertainment. During these days she taught the other canary to sing and she composed an amusing song that she called "The Razor Strop Duet." It imitated the *clip-clop* of a razor being sharpened and the tinkling of a shaving brush in a lather mug. Pippinella sang the contralto part of the duet and the other canary the soprano.

Still she was always hoping to escape, to get back to her friend the window cleaner.

One day a great excitement is started aboard ship by the sighting of a raft. The ship's course is changed and the castaway upon the raft (a strange, ragged individual with thick beard grown all over his face) is rescued and brought on board. He is in a state of extreme weakness and exhaustion and is at once put to bed by the ship's doctor. For several days neither Pippinella nor the passengers see any more of him.

But after a week he comes to the barbershop to have his dense beard shaved off. When this is done, Pippinella at once recognizes him as the window cleaner! She whistles familiar calls to him frantically as he goes to leave the shop, and he recognizes his own canary's voice.

After some argument and trial by test, his ownership of her is established and she is removed to his private cabin. There he sets to work writing his autobiography, and Pippinella herself gets the idea for the first time of composing her own life story in song. And it was that autobiography in music that she had sung to the Doctor when he first brought her home to his caravan.

"He sets to work writing his autobiography."

On the ship's arrival at the next port the window cleaner goes ashore to seek passage on another ship, which shall take him and Pippinella back to England.

And so at last they reached their home shores and the window cleaner at once proceeded to the windmill. He left the canary in her cage outside while he went around to the back to find a way into his old home. In his absence a tramp appeared and, hiding Pippinella's cage beneath his ragged coat, made off with her before the window cleaner returned.

Thus, after finding her old master again under most dramatic and extraordinary conditions, she was parted from him again at the very moment of their returning to the old place they had shared as home together for so many happy months.

After a few more changes of ownership Pippinella, the great contralto canary, was sold to the animal shop from which Matthew Mugg purchased her for the Doctor.

The Eighth Chapter

John Dolittle's Fame

AT THIS POINT GUB-GUB, WHO HAD BEEN fidgeting to say something for a long time, demanded to know what became of the window cleaner when he left the mill the first time and how he came to be floating about on a raft in the ocean. But Jip and Dab-Dab silenced him and bade him let Pippinella tell her story her own way.

"Well, that is practically all there is of it," said the canary. "The rest is in the animal shop."

"Humph! And quite enough, too, I should say—for one life," muttered the Doctor, stretching his cramped hand that had written steadily at high speed for over two hours. "But there are one or two more small things I'd like to get down, Pippinella. Would you sing us that song again? I want to get the words. I already have the music written out. I mean 'The Greenfinch's Love Song.'"

"Certainly," said Pippinella. "But my voice isn't what it used to be, you know."

As the canary threw back her head to sing, Matthew Mugg

entered the wagon, and at a sign from the Doctor for silence, took a place at the table and prepared to listen.

When the little contralto prima donna warbled in a whispering tremolo the opening notes of that short but thrilling melody, the whole company was instantly spellbound. At no point did the song, as Pippinella rendered it, reach full voice. Throughout it was subdued, caressing, almost like someone humming a lullaby a long way off beneath his breath. Then it seemed as though the singer were moving still farther away, hunting, searching, seeking through enchanted forests—now hopeful, now sad again; now distant, now near. It was all the mystery and beauty of the world packed into a little crooning tune. Quieter yet it grew, softer and farther away, and as it faded it rose in pitch and finally died out on a top note in a muffled but bell-like trill.

Then for a few moments there was complete silence in the wagon.

"Oh, my," gulped Gub-Gub at last. "Isn't it wonderful! It reminded me of dew-spangled cauliflowers glimmering palely in the moonlight."

Matthew Mugg, the cross-eyed Cat's-Meat-Man, who always said he did not care for music, turned to John Dolittle.

"Doctor," he said, "nobody ain't heard nothing like that never before. That bird's a marvel. And by Jiminy, why don't we make *this* the act for London?"

"That was what I planned to do, Matthew," said the Doctor. "*The Canary Opera*: I have a feeling it will be the best show we ever put on—the most artistic animal performance ever seen. It is all here. The story of the opera will be Pippinella's own life. You couldn't have a better libretto. The prima donna will be the lady herself. We will take London by storm."

"It reminded me of dew-spangled cauliflowers."

"Oh, not a doubt of it," said Matthew, blowing out his chest. "We'll bowl 'em right over. We'll put all the other opera-mongers out of business."

"Of course," the Doctor went on, "the details, such as choruses, orchestra, scenery, and costumes, we can work out later. But the main things are here: Pippinella's voice and Pippinella's story. In them we have the makings of a great performance."

"But look here," squealed Gub-Gub. "You're always blaming me for interrupting. Now you're all doing it. Pippinella hasn't finished yet. I want to know how she came to be in the animal shop where the Doctor bought her."

"You're quite right, Gub-Gub," said John Dolittle. "Pardon us, Pippinella. I was carried away. Matthew's remark about the London performance set me going. Please proceed with your autobiography."

And as he sharpened his pencil and turned over a new page in his notebook, Pippinella got back on to the tobacco box and prepared to continue the story of her life.

"It often seems sort of strange to me when I look back on it," she went on, "that I had never heard of you before, John Dolittle. Of course, if I had been a regular wild bird I could not have helped it. But you must remember that, while I had led a very eventful life, it had been spent more among people than among animals. Even when I had my liberty I did not, as I told you, mingle much with other wild birds. Still, it is curious, nonetheless, that I had not at least heard your name.

"Well, one day in the animal shop, while I sat dejectedly on the one dirty perch that our cage boasted of, thinking of the window cleaner—wondering, as usual, how he was getting on—I heard the other birds in our cage conversing.

"'Just look,' said one mangy hen to another, 'at that miserable thrush across the shop there. The little box they've put him in is so small he can scarcely turn around without crumpling his tail against the wall.'

"'Yes,' said another. 'And the poor blackbird next to him is worse off still. His place hasn't been decently cleaned out since he came here. He's ill, too.'

"'I wish,' said the first, 'that the Doctor would come. I'm so sick of this miserable place.'

"'And if he ever did,' said the other, 'why do you suppose he'd

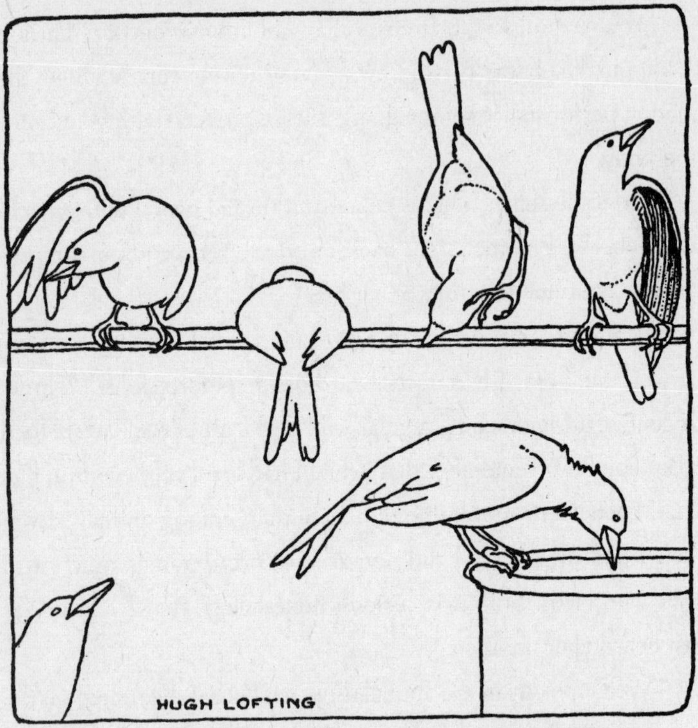

"'Yes,' said another, 'and the poor blackbird is worse off still.'"

pick you out of all the beasts, birds, and fishes gathered here? One can't expect him to buy the whole stock!'

"Then another scrubby runt who was eating at the seed trough joined in the conversation with her mouth full.

"'I'll tell you what we ought to do,' she piped. 'When John Dolittle comes, since he can't buy us all, we ought to ask him to set up a canary shop that's managed properly.'

"'And what kind of a shop would that be?' asked the others.

"'Well, for one thing,' said the little hen, 'it should only have the kind of cages that we approve of and proper, decent attendance for every bird in it. But, most important of all, the birds should be allowed to select their own buyer. If a customer came in whose face you didn't like, you wouldn't have to be sold to him.'

"'Oh, what's the use of talking,' said the first one. 'The Doctor won't come. I've been in this place for over a year and he's never shown up. They say he's afraid to come to animal shops—hardly ever goes near them.'

"'Why?' asked the little hen.

"'He can't bear to see the animals and birds badly cared for. They all yell at him as soon as he appears, imploring him to buy them. Of course, he can't. Hasn't got enough money—never has any money, apparently. And, understanding the language of animals as he does, he is merely made miserable by the visits without doing any good.'

"'Well,' said the little hen, 'you can't tell. He *might* come someday. And when he does, I'm going to ask him to buy me.'

"So far I had taken no part in the conversations. I had felt too unhappy for gossip, to tell you the truth. Hadn't opened my mouth, hardly, since I had been put in. But this talk interested me.

"'Who is this doctor?' I asked.

"They all looked at me in surprise.

"'*The* Doctor,' said one. 'Doctor Dolittle, of course.'

"'And who is he?' I asked.

"'Great heavens!' said the little hen. 'Can it be that you have never heard of him? Why, he is the only real animal doctor living. Talks all languages, from canary to elephant. I didn't know there was any creature left in the world who hadn't heard of him.'"

The Ninth Chapter

The Show for London

AND AFTER THAT I VERY SOON DISCOVERED from bits of odd conversation that drifted to me from all parts of the shop that every creature there, John Dolittle, had one hope always in his mind, and that was that someday you would walk in and buy him."

"Alas!" murmured the Doctor. "I wish I could. But what your neighbor told you was true: I just dread to go near an animal shop."

"Well," continued Pippinella, "my long story is nearly ended. After that I, too, joined the band of hope. Day after day and week after week I watched the door, like the rest, to see you come in. From the other birds I made inquiries to find out exactly what you looked like, so that I could recognize you at once, although I had never seen you before, if by chance you should someday come.

"Later I was given a separate cage and put in the window. And one day—I shall never forget it—I saw your high hat go past the shop. I made all kinds of signals, but you were not looking.

"I saw your high hat go past the shop."

You hurried on, afraid to be seen. But you had already been recognized by half the creatures in the place. I shared the general disappointment when you passed on without entering. Then the man with you came back. At once the news was shouted from cage to cage and pen to pen that he was your assistant and was making a purchase for you. But of course he didn't know bird talk and I couldn't make him understand the message I wanted carried to you. But at last you yourself reappeared and looked in the window. I shouted as loud as I could, but was unable to make you hear through the glass. You started to go away again. I fluttered and made signals. I saw that you noticed me. But still you went away.

A terrible feeling of despair came over me. And then your assistant reentered the shop. You can't imagine my delight when I saw that he was pointing to my cage and telling the proprietor that he wanted to buy *me*. The rest of the story you know. I was sorry for all those poor creatures I left behind—the ones whom you didn't buy. But oh goodness! I was glad to leave that smelly place and get back once more among people who treated me like a friend, instead of just as something to be sold."

There was a little silence after Pippinella stopped speaking—the only thing audible was the scribbling of the Doctor's pencil as he wrote the last words in his notebook of the contralto canary's autobiography.

"Well," said he at last. "It's a wonderful story, Pippinella. You have been through a great deal. Someday—who knows?—when we have made more money with the circus, I may yet set up the Canaries' Own Bird Shop along the lines suggested by your cage mates whom you had to leave behind. There is no reason why cage birds should not be allowed to pick their own buyers. I think your friend's idea is a very good one. We must see what can be done. And now I have a favor to ask of you. . . . Where did Matthew go, Jip? I didn't see him leave the wagon."

"I think he's over at the menagerie, Doctor," said Jip.

"All right," said the Doctor, turning to Pippinella again. "If you will wait here a minute till I go and fetch my assistant, Mr. Mugg, I would like to put a request before you for your consideration."

"Oh, dear!" Gub-Gub sighed as the Doctor left the wagon. "I'm so sorry the story's over."

"But it isn't over," said the white mouse. "Pippinella's story isn't finished while Pippinella is still alive. We've only heard the part that belongs to the past. There still remains that part that belongs to the future. After all, it's much better to feel that you are living a good story than that you are just telling one."

"Yes," said Gub-Gub. "I suppose so. Still—you can make it so much more exciting when you're only telling it. Myself, for instance, when I have daydreams about food—twenty-course meals, you know—they are so much better than the lunches and dinners I ever get in real life. Real life, I find, is not nearly so thrilling—seldom runs to more than boiled beef and cabbage and rice pudding."

"You have a romantic soul," growled Jip. "Food—always food!"

"'You have a romantic soul,' growled Jip."

"Well," said Gub-Gub, "there's lot of romance in food if you only knew it. Did you ever hear of Vermicelli Minestrone?"

"No," said the white mouse. "What is it—a soap?"

"Certainly not, "Gub-Gub retorted. "Vermicelli Minestrone was a poet—a famous food poet. He married Tabby Ochre. It was a runaway match. But she stuck to him through thick and thin. People said she was a colorless individual and would stick to anything. But he loved her dearly and they were very happy. They had two children—Pilaf and Macaroni. He was a great man, was Minestrone. His library consisted of nothing but cookbooks—cookbooks of every age and in every language. But he wrote some beautiful verses. His Spaghetti Sonnets, his Hominy Homilies, his Farina Fantasies—well, you should read them. You would never say again there was no romance in food."

"It's a sort of cereal story," groaned Jip, "mushy—ah, here comes the Doctor back, with Matthew."

A moment later Manager Dolittle, accompanied by his assistant, Matthew Mugg, reentered the wagon. With an air of business, they immediately closed the door and sat down at the table.

"Now, Pippinella," said the Doctor, "I want to talk something over with you that you have already heard Matthew and myself refer to. It is *The Canary Opera.* The story of your life, one of the most interesting accounts I have ever listened to, would make an excellent libretto for a musical production of an entirely new kind. We have, as you know, been invited to come to London and perform there. We want to give them something new and something good. *The Canary Opera* strikes us as just the thing. You will, of course, take the leading part—the heroine, the prima donna. We would have to have a cast of singing birds to support you—especially good voices for the principal roles and many others to form the choruses. Will you help us? Would you be willing to go into this?"

Pippinella put her head on one side and thought a moment.

"Why, of course," she said at last. "I'd be delighted."

"Splendid!" cried the Doctor, "splendid! Then in that case, Matthew, I think we will cancel the rest of our engagements with the small towns and get underway for London as soon as ever it can be managed."

The Tenth Chapter

On the Road

GREAT WAS THE EXCITEMENT AMONG THE animals of the Dolittle household when it became known that the circus was setting out for London earlier than had been planned. Even the thrilling weeks in Manchester (of which Gub-Gub, for one, never ceased to recall the details) took a second place when compared with this invitation to visit the capital.

"It's the biggest city in the world," the white mouse kept saying. "The Dolittle Circus is becoming a pretty important concern, you may be sure, when they send for us especially to come all this way. Maybe the queen and the people of the court will come and see the show."

Jip, who had been there before, could not help boasting of his knowledge. And the others would sit around him by the hour while he related the wonders of the great town and answered the hundreds of questions that were put to him.

Matthew Mugg left that same night. And, with a letter for the

London managers in his pocket, he set out to make arrangements for the coming of the Dolittle Circus. The Doctor felt it would be as well to put *The Puddleby Pantomime* in rehearsal again and to play that in London as well as *The Canary Opera.* And then, if at the last minute it should prove impossible to put on the opera, the pantomime could be made the principal act.

So Gub-Gub, Dab-Dab, Too-Too, and the three dogs—Jip, Toby, and Swizzle—filled up the few days of waiting by going over their parts and dances and making sure they remembered the pantomime without a hitch from beginning to end.

Much to Gub-Gub's dismay, he found that his figure had greatly altered since he was last on the stage. He had grown much fatter. He could hardly get into his clothes at all, and at the first rehearsal buttons kept flying off him in all directions and seams gave way with loud cracks. What was worse, he found that walking on his hind legs was now almost impossible. With all this weight in front, he was top-heavy.

"What shall I do, Doctor?" he asked, almost in tears.

"Well," said John Dolittle, "if you want to play in the pantomime, there's only one thing to be done: you'll have to diet."

"To *dye* it!—To dye what?"

"No, no. To *diet,*" the Doctor repeated. "That is, to eat only special things, things that don't make you fat."

Gub-Gub's face fell.

"What things?" he asked.

"You will have to give up vegetables," said the Doctor. "Stick to rice and that kind of thing."

"Give up all vegetables?" asked Gub-Gub: "Parsnips? Potatoes? Turnips? Beets?"

"What shall I do, Doctor?"

At each one the Doctor shook his head.

"What is life without vegetables?" asked Gub-Gub tragically.

"To beet or not to beet," Swizzle whispered into Jip's ear. "To diet—perchance to dream—"

Swizzle, the old circus dog, remembered a good deal of Shakespeare, which his master, Hop the clown, used to frequently misquote in the ring.

"Oh well," said Gub-Gub. "I suppose it has to be. The things we actors have to give up for our art! Maybe I can make up for it after the show is over."

Three days later Matthew Mugg rejoined the circus and told the Doctor that matters had been satisfactorily arranged in London. A camping ground had been booked and the managers, while impatient to have the Doctor's show as soon as possible, were quite willing to wait till he had got every detail the way he wanted it.

Then began the big business of packing up the circus. That, of course, was no extraordinary thing for them, whose life for so long had been one of continual shifting from town to town. But this occasion was a very special one, and on this trip they planned to do more miles per day than usual, so as to get to London as soon as possible.

The first real stop was to be Wendlemere. And the Doctor intended to get his own wagon there in one day, if it could be done with a change of horses. But, of course, sixty miles without a night's rest was too much for the others. Hercules, the strong man, was to bring on the remainder of the train the following day. Matthew was to travel in the Doctor's wagon.

So very early in the morning, before the rest of the circus was barely awake, Manager Dolittle's caravan, drawn by the fastest horses that the stables could provide, set out along the road to Wendlemere. About halfway they changed their horses at a village inn and took on fresh ones, which had been sent ahead of them the day before. The old ones were left behind, to get a good rest and be picked up by Hercules on the morrow. All these details had been arranged by Matthew Mugg, who at this part of the circus business, was as good as three men rolled into one.

With the fresh horses they reached Wendlemere easily a little after dark and pitched camp for the night just outside of it, on a strip of turf bordering the road.

"This town," said the Doctor, as Dab-Dab began to lay the table for supper and Jip to scurry around the hedges after sticks for the fire, "is famous for its buns. The Wendlemere buns are almost as well known as the Banbury cakes or the Melton Mowbray pies."

"Humph!" said Gub-Gub. "Did you say buns? How would it be if you should send Matthew in to get us a few, Doctor? It's only just dark and the shops will still be open."

"Buns," said the Doctor, "are very bad for the figure. If you want to play the part of Pantaloon, Gub-Gub, you will have to leave pastry alone for the present. It's dreadfully fattening."

"Oh, dear!" sighed the pig. "Vegetables and pastry and everything off the list! All I get is boiled rice and thin soup. Dear, dear! How I shall eat when the show is over! It's funny how some towns get well known for certain kinds of food, isn't it? You know, I heard of a place once which became famous for secondhand meats. Yes, they had a whole lot of hotels there which always wanted new, uncut joints on the sideboard. So as soon as a sirloin of beef or a saddle of mutton had been used for one meal, it was sent back to the secondhand meat merchant, to be sold over again. It's curious."

"Very skewerious, I should say," muttered Too-Too. "You're frightfully well informed—on food."

"Yes, indeed," said Gub-Gub proudly. "I intend to write a book on it some day—'The History of Eating.'"

The Eleventh Chapter

The Caravan Reaches London

IN TALKING OVER WITH PIPPINELLA WHERE good bird voices for the other principal parts in the opera could be obtained, the Doctor had agreed with her that if they could only get her husband, Twink, the leading tenor role would be very well filled. There was not much hope that he could be found. But the Doctor had before leaving made a special visit to Aunt Rosie to see if he could borrow Twink for the opera. He was told that the great tenor had been given away. Following the scent still further, he found the bird had next been sold to an animal shop in Wendlemere. It was for this reason that the caravan was proceeding to London by way of this route, which was not as short as the one usually followed by the stagecoaches.

The next day the Doctor, taking Matthew and Pippinella with him, set out for the animal shop in the town. John Dolittle himself did not venture inside, but sent Matthew, with Pippinella in her cage beneath his arm, to find out what they could about Twink.

The proprietor seemed a decent enough little man, anxious

to give any information he could. He was unable, however, to remember selling the bird that the Cat's-Meat-Man described. He said he'd sold a great number of singing birds in the course of six months and it was quite impossible for him to remember this one among so many. Then Matthew and Pippinella went around all the cages, to see if by chance Twink still remained in the shop. It had been arranged that Pippinella should give a loud whistle if she recognized her husband, so that Matthew should know which one to buy. But, as she had suspected, he had gone. Pippinella questioned several of the other birds, and they said they remembered him quite well. He had been sold, they thought, to a man who seemed to be a dealer from some other town—because he had bought up quite a number of good singers, Twink among them. But where he came from they did not know.

There seemed nothing further to be done. So they left the shop and rejoined the Doctor down the street, and Pippinella reported the results of their visit.

"Well," said John Dolittle, "it's too bad he's gone. But I do not give up hope. I shall have to send Matthew to several shops to get some of the birds we will require for the opera, and it is just possible that he may run across your husband in the course of making his purchases. I will have you go with him, so that you can help him."

Then they proceeded back to the wagon, where they found breakfast all cooked and laid out for them by the thoughtful Dab-Dab. After they had eaten they waited where they were for the rest of the circus to join them. And a little after noon the first caravan, in charge of Hercules the strong man, came in sight down the road.

The remainder of the day was spent in resting up the horses

for the next stage of the journey and in rehearsing *The Puddleby Pantomime.* Toward evening Gub-Gub suggested that the Doctor take him and the dogs for a walk. He was anxious to get his weight down as soon as possible, and he preferred doing it by exercise, he said, rather than by too much of this dieting, which was not at all to his liking.

So John Dolittle took them all for a brisk walk along the country roads. And Jip, Swizzle, and Toby put up a hare out of a hedge and gave him a fine cross-country run—pretending they didn't hear the Doctor calling to them to leave the poor thing in peace. Gub-Gub, bent on reducing his figure, joined in the chase. But he had a very hard time keeping up with the dogs and darting through the small holes in the hedges. And he hadn't gone across more than a couple of fields before an enormous sheepdog belonging to a farmer joined the hunting party and took the pig for the quarry instead of the hare. Poor Gub-Gub, who had set out hunting, was chased in a breathless state of exhaustion all the way home to the wagon, where he told the Doctor that, on the whole, he thought dieting had advantages over exercise as a means of reducing the figure.

Theodosia, Matthew Mugg's quiet but very useful wife, kept what she called the diary of the Dolittle Circus. Her ordinary duties were light: wardrobe woman, hostess at the regular afternoon tea, and general helper. In odd moments, when she wasn't sewing buttons on for Gub-Gub or wrapping up the packets of peppermints for the children, she took great pleasure in setting down the daily doings of the show. Her mastery of the arts of reading and writing were greatly and constantly admired by her husband, who was not, as you know, very well educated. And later, as a matter of fact, Theodosia's diary proved itself useful to John Dolittle himself on

"Poor Gub-Gub was chased all the way home."

more than one occasion, when he wanted to know on what date his circus had visited such and such a town or some other detail in his life as a showman.

Well, in due time the caravan reached the great town of London (amid terrific excitement among the Dolittle animal household). It was met by Matthew and was at once set up on the campground he had rented for it on Greenheath, just outside the city. And that day Theodosia entered in her journal as a red-letter date, marking the beginning of preparations for *The Canary Opera*, the work which John Dolittle considered the greatest achievement of his career as a showman.

"Sewing buttons on for Gub-Gub"

Without delay the Doctor turned his attention to the problem of getting chorus birds for his show. And the first thing he did was to consult Cheapside. He felt that that wise bird, so thoroughly familiar with all the resources of his native city, could give him the best advice on the birds available within the limits of London.

"What I need, Cheapside," said he, "is, firstly, some good canary voices for the principal parts, and secondly, a great number of birds for the choruses."

"What sort of birds?" asked the sparrow.

"Well, that's just the point," said the Doctor. "There are several choruses. I have not yet decided on what they shall be. I thought I would find out from you what would be possible here in London."

"Humph!" said Cheapside thoughtfully. "I reckon the first thing to do would be to go around the zoo and take a look at the collections. You won't be able to buy any there, of course. But, then, after you've picked out the kinds you think suitable, I'll see what can be done in the way of supply. O' course, for good singers we'd better try the bird shops."

"Well, that Matthew will have to do," said the Doctor. "But I think what you say sounds sensible. And if you are at liberty this afternoon I'll take a run up to the zoo with you and see if we can decide upon the best kinds of chorus birds for our show."

"Right you are, Doc," said Cheapside. "I ain't got nothing special to do today. The missus asked me to get 'er some greens for this evening, but I can pick them up in Regents Park. I'll be glad of the change. Ain't been to the zoo in weeks. You know, I used to live there once."

"What, inside the zoo?" asked the Doctor.

"Oh, not in the cages," said Cheapside. "But I was one of the Regents Park gang when I was a nipper. It's a good place for sparrows—quiet, except Sundays and bank holidays. I used to 'ang around the zoo enclosure a good deal. I know the place inside out, keepers and naturalists and bobbies and all. I'll be glad to take you over it."

"Good!" said the Doctor. "Let us have lunch and get on our way."

The Twelfth Chapter

Voice Trials

ON THEIR WAY TO REGENTS PARK JOHN Dolittle and Cheapside were joined by Becky, the cockney sparrow's wife. They all began by taking tea, when they had arrived within the zoological gardens, at one of the little teahouses that catered to visitors. Here the two birds, sitting on the table beside the Doctor's cup, stuffed themselves with cake crumbs and entertained him with many amusing stories of the days when they had lived here in the zoological gardens.

After their tea was finished they started out on their trip around the zoo. Although John Dolittle did not intend to visit more than the bird collections, he had in the course of his inspection to pass many cages and enclosures for animals. These so interested him that Cheapside had the hardest work to get him away from them. And Becky said more than once that it would surely be dark before the Doctor had seen all the birds.

"What is that little creature?" the Doctor asked as his guides tried to hurry him past a pen containing some slim, furred animal.

"Oh, that's the genet," said Cheapside. "Nifty-looking little cove, ain't 'e? See them smart stripes down 'is sides? 'E always reminds me of some trim old maid what wears 'er 'air just so. Can't abide 'avin' 'is cage untidy. 'E 'as tidiness on the brain. 'E's kept awful busy poking the peanuts back through the wire what the children push into 'im. 'E doesn't eat 'em. But that don't make no difference to the folks what comes to zoos. They think that everything in menageries eats peanuts. They're a bright lot, the public. They'd feed peanuts to a marble clock, they would. Yes, poor Mr. Genet spends 'alf 'is day tidying up 'is cage after the public 'as left, and the other 'alf brushing 'is 'air and cleaning 'is nails."

"Humph!" said the Doctor. "Not a very exciting life. Still, I suppose it's something to occupy the time. It must hang heavy in a zoo."

"A feller like the genet would find something to do in the Sahara Desert," said Cheapside, "probably tidying up the sand there. Now, the next cage, Doctor, is the laughing kingfishers. They're light'earted birds—guaranteed to liven up a funeral. 'Ow would they do for choruses, do you think? Fine, strong voices, they 'ave."

"Humph! They're not very musical, are they?" said the Doctor, as a dozen of the odd birds suddenly burst into hearty roars of merriment to show they appreciated the great man's visit.

"Yes, but they'd be fine for the comics," said Cheapside. "Was it a comic opera you was contemplatin'?"

"Er—not exactly," said the Doctor, "though, to be sure, there will be some comedy parts in it. But there the laughter ought to come from the audience, not from the stage. Let us go across to the big aviary over there."

This, when they reached it, proved to be a very beautiful place. It was a cage a good thirty feet high, fifty long, and forty wide. Within, quite large trees were growing, and it had a pond and rocks and plants and everything. A great number of different birds were flying around or dabbling in the water or settling in the boughs. There were flamingos, herons, gulls, ducks—birds of all sizes, shapes, and colors. It was a very pretty picture.

Picking out the ones whose appearance for stage purposes struck him as suitable, the Doctor called them over to him in turn and conversed with them through the wire. He got all of them to sing a few notes for him, so as to try out the pitch of their voices. And Mr. and Mrs. Cheapside had hard work concealing their laughter when huge birds that never sang a note in their lives opened their big bills and let out strange, deep grunts and gurgles.

"Lor' bless us, Becky!" tittered Cheapside, holding his wing over his face. "Seems to me as if the Doc would do better with Gub-Gub as a baritone. If it was me, I'd give some of these blokes a job as fog 'orn."

Before they left the aviaries and started back for Greenheath, the Doctor had practically decided on two choruses at all events: one of pelicans (bassos) and one of flamingos (altos). Cheapside said he knew of a rich man living on the other side of London who had a magnificent private park given over entirely to birds and waterfowl. The sparrow added that he would go there first thing tomorrow morning to see if there were any pelicans or flamingos in the collection.

The next day he came back to the caravan with the news that fifteen fine pelicans lived in the private park belonging to the rich man he had spoken of. And as soon as the Doctor had an opportunity to get away, he went and called upon their owner and asked permission to borrow them. It happened that this man, although he was very wealthy, was a naturalist himself. Rare birds and orchids were his two hobbies. Finding in John Dolittle a scientist after his own heart, he showed him over his whole estate. And the Doctor spent a most enjoyable afternoon inspecting acres of greenhouses filled with gorgeous orchids and touring through the immense private park where a great number of birds lived happily in a semiwild state. He was able to give the rich naturalist a great deal of information and advice on the proper preparation of thickets and ponds and nesting retreats for his different species of birds.

The Doctor was still full of all he had seen when he returned to his caravan in the evening.

"My goodness, Dab-Dab," said he as he sat down to supper, "that's my idea of a nice life—being able to spend all the money you want on your hobbies. Most rich men fritter their money away on theaters and cards and all manner of stupid stuff. Wealthy scientists are rare. That man deserves a great deal of credit for spending his time and his fortune on natural history. I've never wanted to be rich, but, by George, I came near to wishing it this afternoon when I saw the perfectly lovely place that man has up there."

"If you had been in his shoes you would have spent the fortune twenty-five years ago," said Dab-Dab sourly. "I sometimes think you should have been married—and had a strict, economical wife."

"But what would have been the good of that?" said John Dolittle. "Then I wouldn't have been able to do anything I want. Well now, cheer up, Dab-Dab. Maybe we'll make so much money with *The Canary Opera* that not even I will be able to spend it all."

"I used to hope for that—once," said Dab-Dab, gazing sadly out the window. "But you've made so many fortunes and lost them again. Puddleby and the dear old house and garden have grown to be just a dream—just a dream. Heigh-ho! What's the use? I suppose we'll be traveling circus folk now for the rest of our days."

"There were real tears in the housekeeper's eyes."

There were real tears in the housekeeper's eyes. For months and months now she had been hoping that the Doctor would turn his face homeward and get back to the little house with the big garden. But always something new turned up in this showman business that kept putting off his return.

"Oh, come, come!" said the Doctor, genuinely touched by the tone of bitter disappointment in his old friend's voice. "It's never too late to change. The sight of that man's place this afternoon set me thinking of my own garden—it was similar in many ways—a place where a man has tried to work out the chief interests of his life. It made me long for a sight of that old wall that overhangs the Oxenthorpe Road, Dab-Dab, really it did. And listen: I'm going to make a real effort this time. I think the opera's going to be a huge success. That naturalist will lend me the pelicans and flamingos I want. We'll make a fortune, Dab-Dab, and then—*then* we'll go back to Puddleby!"

The Thirteenth Chapter

The History of Bird Music

SHORTLY AFTER THAT, THE PELICANS AND THE flamingos from the rich man's park arrived at the Dolittle Circus. A special runway with a pond and thickets of bushes had been prepared for them, and although it was of course much more cramped for room than the spacious park they had left, they declared it was very comfortable and said they were quite content to put up with some inconvenience to oblige John Dolittle. There were a dozen birds of each kind. The public that visited the circus enclosure daily took them for part of the show. And, indeed, the strange appearance of the pelicans and the handsome figures and coloring of the flamingos, stalking about within the pen, presented quite a fine sight.

For the present the Doctor's intentions were only to get them used to seeing crowds of human faces, so that they should overcome their natural shyness, and to drill them in what they were expected to do on the stage. The singing rehearsals would have to wait till all the other birds had been collected and the musical score of the opera had been written out in every detail by Pippinella and Manager Dolittle.

The Doctor had a stage rigged up inside the birds' fence and every day he put them through their paces, showing them exactly how they were to walk on the stage, bow, and take their places.

In everything belonging to the opera, the inquisitive Cheapside took the greatest interest, and during these days he

"The pelican chorus"

followed the Doctor about wherever he went. This John Dolittle was very glad of, because the shrewd little sparrow often came in extremely handy. So quickly did he catch on to the idea of drilling a chorus that quite early in the proceedings the Doctor turned the entire duties of chorus master over to him. At four o'clock, the rehearsal hour, every afternoon the fence about the pelicans' enclosure was black with the crowds watching the small cockney sparrow drilling his enormous performers. The Doctor said it was a good thing that the public didn't understand bird language, otherwise Cheapside's dreadful swearing when any of the clumsy chorus birds made a false step or got out of place would surely have caused a great scandal.

Sitting upon the top of a bush, with his chest puffed out, the tiny chorus master looked like some angry sergeant drilling a squad of awkward recruits.

"Now, then!" he would yell. "Troop on, all in step, chins up and smiling at the haudience. No, no. That ain't a bit like it. Anyone would think this was Monday morning in the police court, instead of garlic night at the opera. This is *opera*, you understand, grand opera. Look 'appy, not guilty! Clear off again—all of yer! Lor' bless me! Look at Mrs. Bandylegs there, thinking over the gas bill! Cheer up! Smile! Come in, trippin'—light'earted, not 'eavy-footed. Now, then, once more: When the music strikes up, that's your cue to come on. Now—*lah, tah, tiddledy tah!*"

The next task for the Doctor was to gather together the rest of his cast for the opera. And as soon as he had turned over the training of the pelicans and flamingos to Cheapside, he took the first opportunity that presented itself in his busy life for a day in the country. On this expedition all of his animals accompanied him—even Gub-Gub, who so frequently of late had complained that he was let out of all parties. And, with the whole of his strange household following at his heels, John Dolittle betook him to the pleasant fields where, over an excellent picnic luncheon provided by Dab-Dab, the wild birds of the hedges and the woods gathered about him and sang him their songs.

On this expedition into the country Pippinella, of course, accompanied the Doctor to help in the judging of the voices. John Dolittle said afterward that he could not recall any outing that he had enjoyed more. It was one of those days late in the year when summer seems to try to come back again. The sun shone without being unpleasantly hot, and all the birds of the countryside that had not yet departed for the winter migration flocked around, anxious to be accepted for the Doctor's great experiment in bird music. Indeed, John Dolittle, experienced as he was, learned a great deal that day about the songs of birds and the history of their various melodies.

After trying out different birds for the treble chorus, both the Doctor and Pippinella were best of all impressed with the common thrush.

"Tell me," said the Doctor, as a fine cock finished off a wonderful melody, "that is what you call your 'Evening Song,' is it not? Now, has that song always been the same? I mean, have all thrushes sung it just that way always?"

"Oh, no," said the thrush. "But it has been sung pretty much that way for nearly seven hundred years. In medieval times it was quite different. Musically speaking, fashions were very much stricter then. For instance, in the song I've just sung you the middle crescendo passage was different. We ended on the major then, not the minor. Like this, *Toodledu—oo—too—tu!* instead of *Toodledu—du—tee—too!* About the thirteenth century a good many fine singers rebelled against several of the old musical rules, including the one forbidding consecutive fourths in the major scale and sevenths in the minor. That was around the time of the Magna Carta. Everybody was rebelling against

"That is what you call your 'Evening Song,' is it not?"

something then. They didn't allow accidentals in melodies before that either. Now we just throw them in regardless. But, in the main, the Evening Song of the Thrush is usually sung pretty much the same way now. It is in the little phrases, something between a call and a song, that you can tell whether a bird is a good composer or not. Because those are what he just makes up out of his head on the spur of the moment."

"You mean when he gets an idea which he thinks will sound pretty?" asked the Doctor.

"Yes," said the thrush. "For instance, when he sees a particularly fine sunrise and tries to describe it in a snatch of music, or when a thought comes into his head about the mate he spent last spring with."

"Good!" said the Doctor. "Now, I see that you yourself are quite a musician and I would greatly appreciate it if you would do me a favor. People's notions on music and birds' ideas are somewhat different. My plan in *The Canary Opera* is to show people what birds can do—musically. But in order to make the score understandable for people, I shall have to do certain things. I want you to compose the thrushes' chorus for me—the treble chorus that comes in the middle of the second act—when it is raining. I notice that thrushes always sing their best just when the rain is stopping. I will give you the words of the song later. I want you to get plenty of rain into your voices—it must describe the joys of rain from the thrushes' point of view. I would like you to get a choir of about twenty thrushes together and rehearse them yourself. And please be sure that the birds keep together—that they all sing the same parts of the song at the same time. I know this is not important in bird music, but it is very important in people's music. I will send you the words tonight and I'll come back here in a week's time to see how you are getting on. Can you do that for me?"

"Why, certainly," said the thrush. "I'll set about it right away."

THE FOURTEENTH CHAPTER

The Finding of Twink

A FEW DAYS LATER THE DOCTOR AGAIN went out into the country to see how the thrushes' choir was getting on. He heard the birds sing their "Rain Chorus" and was very well pleased with it.

"The next thing," he said to Matthew when he got back to the circus, "is to collect some good canaries for the principal parts. We shall need about five or six."

"Why, I thought there was only to be three altogether," said Matthew. "Pippinella, the tenor, and the baritone."

"No, you've forgotten her mother and father," said John Dolittle. "Besides, we shall need understudies as well."

"What's understudies?" asked Matthew.

"Understudies are extra actors," said the Doctor, "who learn the parts as well, so that in case any of the principals fall sick we have another to put in his place. But they won't all be canaries. We shall need four canaries and three greenfinches. But all must be the very best singers possible—no matter what they cost. I want you to do this purchasing for me, and I will send Pippinella with you in her traveling cage so that she can help you judge and try out the birds' voices properly. I will arrange with her to give you some kind of signal when you find any that she considers especially good."

"All right," said Matthew. "When shall I go?"

"I think you had better start off first thing tomorrow," said the Doctor. "Time is getting short. I have promised the theater owners to have everything in readiness to open by the second week of next month."

So on the morrow Matthew went off, bright and early, canary-hunting through the bird shops of London with Pippinella. And on his return in the evening the Doctor was delighted to see him carrying another cage under his arm beside the prima donna's little traveling cage.

"He was the best we could find, Doctor," said Pippinella as John Dolittle unwrapped the paper and discovered a neat little yellow-and-black canary within. "He has a fine voice and I think you will like him. But it's slow work. You'd be surprised how hard it is to find really good singers. And as for singing greenfinches, they seem to be scarcer than diamonds. We went to over a dozen shops. But we haven't covered half of London yet. We hope to do better tomorrow."

The Doctor was highly pleased with the new member of his opera company. And that night he began practicing the duets of the first act, which the two canaries would sing together.

On the morrow Matthew and Pippinella went forth again, and this time when they returned the Doctor could hear the prima donna calling to him even before the Cat's-Meat-Man reached the manager's wagon.

"He began practicing the duets of the first act."

"Doctor," she cried, "Doctor, listen!"

"What is it?" asked John Dolittle, jumping up from the table and coming to the door.

"What do you think?" said Pippinella. "You'd never guess. *We've found Twink*, my husband, after all! And we've got him with us."

"Well, well!" cried the Doctor. "This is a great piece of luck. Fancy your finding Twink after all this time! Uncover the cage, Matthew. I am most anxious to see him."

"Yes, and it was only by the merest chance we did it, Doctor," chattered Pippinella excitedly. "We came to the dirtiest little shop down in the East End of London. Matthew wasn't going to go in at all at first, it looked such a poor, mean place. But I thought to myself that if there *were* any good singers there, it would be a mercy to rescue them from such a disgusting home. So in spite of Matthew's not knowing any bird talk I did my best to make him see what I wanted. And finally, after I had fluttered all over the cage and squawked whenever he turned away from the shop, he saw what I meant and went in. With every shop that I had been taken into so far I began by asking in a loud voice, 'Are you here, Twink?' But in this one I was so appalled by the dirt and the misery of most of the creatures confined there that I had not uttered a word. But I was hardly within the door when I heard a canary crying from the back of the shop. 'Pippinella! Pippinella! It is I, Twink! Come over here and talk to me.'

"But it was no easy matter to come over there and talk to him. I don't know myself how I managed to steer Matthew and the shopkeeper to Twink's cage. It was poked away behind a lot of others, right at the back of the place. Then I gave the signal by scratching my left ear vigorously—and Matthew saw that this was one of the birds I wanted. Poor Twink! We bought him for a shilling—Twink, the finest tenor canary that ever sang! But it seems he had had a very sore throat when he came to the shop and had hardly attempted to peep the whole time he was there. So of course the proprietor had no idea of his value. Such is fame! Such is life!"

By this time John Dolittle had uncovered Twink's cage and placed it on the caravan table. The bird within, a bright lemon-yellow canary, slightly larger than Pippinella, looked very dejected and poorly. When he opened his bill to speak to the Doctor, instead of the golden voice of which Pippinella had so often spoken, a hoarse whisper was all that came forth.

"I have a terrible cold, Doctor," said he. "That fool of a

proprietor kept my cage in a draft and my throat got worse and worse the whole time I was there."

"Oh, well, just wait a minute," said John Dolittle, "till I get you some of my Canary Cough Mixture. It will relieve your throat almost at once, you will see."

Then the Doctor got out his little black medicine bag and from the bottom of it he produced a small bottle containing a pink liquid. He opened the door of Twink's cage and the bird hopped out onto his hand. Next he took a small quantity of the mixture on a glass rod and when Twink opened his bill, he let two drops fall into the bird's throat.

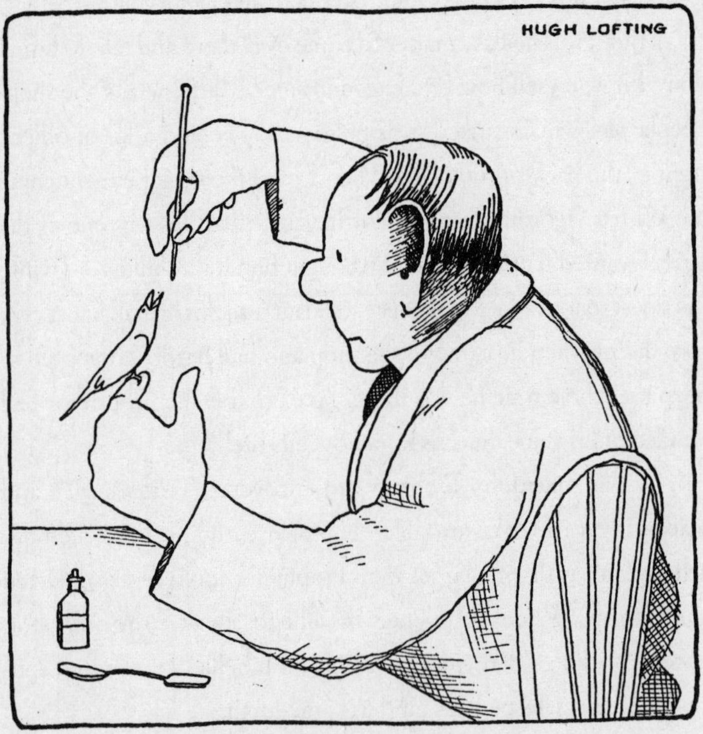

"He let two drops fall into the bird's throat."

"You will soon feel better now," said the Doctor, closing his bag and putting it away. "Remind me to give you two more drops tomorrow morning. In about twenty-four hours I think I can promise you you will be as well as ever."

For the present, although both he and Pippinella were most anxious to hear the story of Twink's adventures, the Doctor would not allow him to talk at all.

"Give your voice a complete rest until tomorrow," he said. "I'll cover your cage with a thick cloth and put it at the stove-end of the wagon so you will be warm and snug."

PART TWO

THE FIRST CHAPTER

The Doctor Is Disguised

THE NEXT DAY, EVEN BEFORE HE HAD HIS second dose of the famous Dolittle Canary Cough Mixture, Twink felt so much better that he was already warbling away softly within his cage when the Doctor got out of bed.

At breakfast he told the story of his adventures—everything since he had been parted from Pippinella right up to his coming to the shop where his clever wife had found him.

"And of all the awful places," he ended, "that shop is surely the worst. I have been in many animal shops in my time, but never in any quite so dreadful, quite so filthy, quite so wretched. There was hardly an animal or a bird in the place that was happy or in full health. The cages were dirty; the food was bad. Most of the birds were croupy, the dogs rickety. And do you know, John Dolittle, not half of the birds the man has there were born in cages. Most of his stock is bought from trappers. And, oh Lord, the sound of those poor thrushes and blackbirds and starlings fluttering, fluttering, fluttering all day long, trying to get out of their cages! Yesterday morning a man brought in a dozen blackbirds for sale, which he had caught in the fields. The proprietor bought them all for eighteen pence. This morning two of them were dead; had just battered themselves to death against the wires of the cage, trying to get out. It simply made me sick."

This recital greatly saddened the Doctor. His household had often heard him rail against the usual kind of bird shop. But Twink's story of the blackbirds was worse than anything he had ever listened to. For some moments he remained silent. Then he said: "How are the rest of the blackbirds getting on?"

"No more of them had died when I left," said Twink. "But hardly a one of them was eating any food. Goodness only knows how many will survive. But the blackbirds were not the only ones. Almost every other day some poacher or country lout would bring in a cage full of poor fluttering creatures—linnets, robins, tomtits—everything that he had caught in traps. All scared out of their wits. Some of them lived and some of them didn't, but all led a wretchedly unhappy existence there."

"Humph," muttered the Doctor. "If it was only the blackbirds, then I could send Matthew to buy them and let them go. But with all those other birds as well, it would require a lot of money to do that. It's horrible, horrible! I can't understand how any decent person can inflict such misery on living creatures."

All through supper the Doctor said hardly a word. In spite of his now having all three of his principal singers, he seemed to have forgotten all about *The Canary Opera* for the present. Twink's description of that bird shop had spoiled the evening for him. Both Jip and Dab-Dab tried several times during the meal to draw him into conversation, but he hardly seemed to hear what they said.

"Both Jip and Dab-Dab tried several times to draw him into conversation."

At last when supper was finished he thumped the table with his fist and muttered, "By Jove, I'll try it!"

"Try what?" asked Jip.

"Listen," said the Doctor, addressing the supper table in general. "Do you suppose it would be possible for me to disguise myself so that no animal or bird could recognize me?"

For a moment after the Doctor's question there was a complete silence in the caravan. Finally Gub-Gub said:

"But, Doctor, what on earth would you disguise yourself for? I should think you would be no end proud to have all the animals in the world know you."

John Dolittle did not answer.

"It would depend, Doctor, I should imagine," said Jip, "on how well those animals who saw you knew you. For what purpose did you mean to wear the disguise?"

"I want to go to that animal shop," said John Dolittle. "It's worrying me. As you know, I have made it a rule never to go into them because all the poor creatures clamor at me to buy them. And even if I were rich enough to buy out the entire stock of one shop, there would still be all the other animals in the other shops. But this place Twink has told us of seems to be so unusually awful that I thought I'd break my rule and go there."

"And do what?" asked Dab-Dab.

"Let every bird that is not cage-bred go free," said the Doctor.

"Ha-ha!" said Jip, getting interested. "I smell an adventure in this. How do you plan to go about it?"

"Well, first of all," said John Dolittle, "I must be disguised so that the creatures in the shop won't recognize me. Then I'll have to get into the place at night or at some time when I shan't be seen or interfered with."

"Good!" said Jip. "When will you go?"

"Tonight," said the Doctor firmly. "I shan't be able to sleep till I know that those blackbirds are returned to their freedom. As Twink says, heaven only knows how many will be living by the morning unless something is done."

The Doctor then explained his plan to Matthew, and he, like Jip, entered into the spirit of the idea with great relish—though the Doctor did not seem to care for the way he explained how easily he could pry open the door of the shop to let him in.

"Never mind about those details now, Matthew," said he.

"We'll attend to that matter when we come to it. If you accompany me you must understand that we are liable to be arrested and imprisoned for this. The law will probably call it burglary if we are caught."

"I ain't particular what name the law gives it," said Matthew with a chuckle, "because we ain't going to get caught. Nifty little party, I calls it. That man ain't got no right to keep them poor blackbirds in captivity, anyhow. And even if the cops did get us, the magistrate wouldn't be hard on us, you can bet. Look well in the papers, it would—good advertisement for the show: 'John Dolittle, the heminent naturalist, caught in humanitarian burglary!' 'Ow does that sound?"

"Nifty little party, I calls it."

"Well, let's set about working out a disguise," said the Doctor. "It's most essential that the animals don't recognize me. For not only would their requests be very embarrassing to me, but they would probably set up such a racket that the whole neighborhood would be awakened before we got halfway through our work."

Then, much to Gub-Gub's amusement, Matthew set to work to disguise the Doctor's appearance so that he should not be recognized by the animals among whom he had become so famous. The clown's makeup box was borrowed, also various suits of clothes from different members of the circus staff.

Matthew began by gumming a large red beard on the Doctor's chin, with bushy eyebrows to match. But this did not seem quite to satisfy his artistic judgment.

"Humph!" said he, drawing off and surveying the Doctor with his head to one side. "It don't seem to fill the bill. I reckon I could recognize you myself like that—on a dark night. Let's try a military mustache to cover that upper lip of yours."

"What, more hair on my face?" said the Doctor. "Are you trying to make a monkey of me?"

In response Matthew gummed a large, flowing red mustache over the Doctor's mouth.

"Good heavens!" said John Dolittle, gazing in the mirror. "I look like the butcher in Puddleby. Even if the animals don't recognize me like this, I shall certainly scare them to death."

"Well, you know," said Matthew, "a face like yours isn't easily disguised. No, I agree. It don't look quite natural. Well, we must try something else."

"Look here, Doctor," said Swizzle, the clown's dog, who

"Surveying the Doctor with this head to one side"

was watching the performance with a professional eye, "why don't you dress up like a woman? The animals in the shop would be much less likely to think it was you. And besides, as a man you'd never be able to hide that well-known figure of yours, even if you succeeded in disguising your face."

"Good idea!" cried John Dolittle. "Listen, Matthew, Swizzle suggests that I get myself up like a woman. Do you think Mrs. Mugg could lend me some things?"

"I'll go and ask her," said the Cat's-Meat-Man. "By Jingo, that's a notion worth two. I don't reckon we could ever do anything with you in trousers and a coat. Wait here a second."

Upon that, Matthew ran off and presently came back with not only some of his wife's things but with Theodosia herself.

"I brought the missus along," he said, "because she'll know how the things goes on and can make you look like a real lady. 'Old your face still, Doc, while I get this beard off."

Then while Gub-Gub and the white mouse squealed and tittered with delight, Mrs. Mugg put a skirt and bodice on the Doctor. Next, some sort of wig seemed to be necessary. But the able Matthew made bangs and curls out of the red beard. And after the back of the Doctor's head had been well covered with a poke bonnet and the bangs were tucked in the front around his temples, he looked like a very nice portly old lady.

"Fine!" cried Too-Too. "No one would ever recognize you, Doctor—not even your sister, Sarah."

"I feel frightfully silly," said the Doctor, tripping over the skirts as he walked toward the mirror.

"Good gracious!" cried Theodosia. "You mustn't walk that way, Doctor. No woman ever walked like that. Take little steps and don't swing your arms so. Now—that's more like it. Do you think you better have a veil over your face as well?"

"I do not," said the Doctor. "I'm uncomfortable enough as I am. Besides, I couldn't blow my nose with a veil on."

As soon as the Doctor could walk in a manner that satisfied Mrs. Mugg, he set out with Matthew and Jip on his extraordinary expedition.

It was quite a long way from Greenheath to the East End. But even when they finally reached the shop where Twink had been for sale, there were lights yet visible in the upper windows. This told them that although the store was closed, the proprietor or some of his household were still up. Across the front window of the shop was a sign reading, "Harris's Song Restorer for Canaries. Fourpence a Bottle."

"Good heavens!" whispered John Dolittle to his companion. "Sounds like a cure for baldness. I think, Matthew, we had better go somewhere to wait. We can't hang around here. We might arouse suspicion. Let's find a restaurant and have a cup of tea or something. It is now ten o'clock. We will come back in half an hour or so."

So they went off down the street. But it did not seem to be such an easy matter to find a restaurant open as late as this in that part of London. Moreover, the Doctor's skirts were causing him a great deal of inconvenience in walking. Finally, when they had reached a very quiet, practically deserted alley, Matthew said, "Listen, Doctor, suppose you wait here while I go hunting by myself? There must be places around here somewhere. I'm sure I can find one."

"All right," said the Doctor. "But hurry. I have had enough of walking in this getup."

Then while Matthew went off looking for a restaurant, the Doctor hung around the quiet street. Every time anyone appeared upon the scene he changed his pace to a brisk walk, so that he wouldn't appear to have no business there. He felt very uncomfortable and unhappy and hoped that Matthew wouldn't be long.

Finally a man and woman came down the street, and although the Doctor promptly broke into a smart and businesslike gait, he noticed that the couple were watching him for some reason or other. Presently he felt that his skirt was slipping off; and at his wit's end what to do, he sat down on a doorstep and tried to look as though he were a beggarwoman taking a rest.

Soon, to his horror, he saw out of the corner of his eye that the couple at the far end of the street were approaching him, apparently with the intention of speaking to him.

As they came near he kept his gaze upon the ground and sat as huddled up as he could so that his face would not be seen. A few minutes later he realized that they had stopped before him.

"Dear, dear!" said the man's voice. "This, Wife, is the kind of case one frequently meets with in the slums."

"Poor creature!" said the voice of the woman. "Listen, why do you sit here at this time of night?"

The huddled figure on the doorstep gave no answer.

"He sprang to his feet and ran."

"Have you no home to go to?" the woman asked.

The Doctor, afraid to remain silent any longer, looked up—and gazed into the faces of *his sister Sarah and her husband!*

Then, grasping his slipping skirt in both hands, he sprang to his feet and ran for all he was worth down the empty street. Sarah gave one shriek and fainted into her husband's arm.

At the first turning the Doctor ran into Matthew.

"What the matter?" asked the Cat's-Meat-Man.

"It's Sarah!" gasped John Dolittle. "And my beastly skirt is slipping off. Let's hide—quick!"

THE SECOND CHAPTER

The Release of the Blackbirds

SARAH!" SAID THE ASTONISHED MATTHEW AS he and the Doctor doubled around the corner and hastened away. "My, that woman has a real gift for turnin' up when she ain't wanted! But 'ow comes she to be 'ere? I thought she was married to the Reverend Dangle, up in Wendlemere."

"Dingle, Matthew, *Dingle*," the Doctor corrected as he panted along the pavement. "Yes, he's one of the canons of the cathedral there. But I suppose they are on a visit to London. Seem to be out on a slumming expedition, or something of the kind. It's just my luck that they should run into me. Are they following us, Matthew?"

"No," said the Cat's-Meat-Man, looking back. "I don't see no one."

"Well, I must get somewhere where I can fasten up this wretched skirt," gasped the Doctor. "Can't you find me a dark passage or a doorway or something?"

A little farther on they came to the vaulted entrance to a stable yard, which seemed to offer the sort of seclusion that they wanted. Making sure that no one should see them go in, they retired into its welcome darkness, and the Doctor did his best to recover his breath while Matthew fastened up his skirt securely. But without any light to see by, he got the hem of it so high that the ends of the Doctor's trousers were visible beneath it. This was not discovered till they had ventured out upon the street again. So once more they had to retire to their makeshift dressing room and put the gown right.

"I found a restaurant, Doctor," said Matthew. "Shall we go to there now?"

"No," said the Doctor, getting out his watch with great difficulty from under Theodosia's bodice. "It's already eleven, and I am sort of anxious about Sarah. I think we had better go back to the shop and leave this neighborhood alone."

So they set off in the direction of the shop. And after about five minutes of walking they came in sight of it, only to find that, although no light now showed in the windows, there was a policeman standing beneath the lamppost opposite.

"Luck seems to be against us tonight, Matthew," said the Doctor, as they drew back around the corner. "Of all the places on his beat, of course, the policeman *would* have to stop there!"

"'Ow would it be, Doctor," said Matthew, "if I went up behind him from the other end of the street and tapped him on the head with a screwdriver?"

"Good heavens, no!" whispered the Doctor. "Besides, where would you get a screwdriver from?"

"I got one in my pocket," said Matthew.

"What for?" asked John Dolittle.

"To pry the door open with," said the Cat's-Meat-Man. "I

always carry a screwdriver at night—in self-defense, as you might say. But it comes in handy for all sorts of things. Some folks carries a cane or an umbrella; I always carry a screwdriver."

"Well, don't use it on the police," said the Doctor. "That fellow will probably move away if we wait a little while. They have to go around their whole beat every so often. What's the back of the shop like?"

"It opens onto a small yard," said the Cat's-Meat-Man. "But there's no way of getting to it from the street. We'll have to tackle the house from the front."

"At last, with a yawn, the constable stretched his arms above his head."

Then followed a wearisome fifteen minutes while the two, with their noses around the corner, watched the figure of the policeman near the shop.

At last, with a yawn, the constable stretched his arms above his head and moved off.

"Now's our chance," whispered Matthew, getting out his screwdriver. "Come along."

"And don't forget, Doctor," Matthew added, as they walked down the street toward the shop, "if we get interfered with, begin by talking like a lady, see? We may be able to pass it off as though we found the door open and was just going to tell the owner. But if they get nasty and it looks as though we were going to be grabbed, chuck your skirt away and run for it. Here we are. Now you keep an eye open both ways, up and down the street, while I hinvestigate this lock."

"Try not to break the latch or spoil the door, Matthew," said the Doctor. "We mustn't do the man's property any damage. All we want is to liberate those birds."

"Trust me, Doc," chuckled Matthew, setting to work. "I could open this lock with me eyes shut and no one know that I bin near it. There you are! Walk right in and make yourself at home. It's a shame to take the money."

The Doctor turned from watching the street and, to his astonishment, found the door already open. Matthew was putting his mysterious screwdriver back in his pocket as he bowed upon the threshold.

"Good heavens! That was quick work," said John Dolittle, stepping within.

"Sh!" whispered Matthew as he closed the door noiselessly behind him. "This is where the hartistic work begins. Tie these here

"Keep an eye open up and down the street."

dusters over your boots while I get the bull's-eye lantern lit—No, I reckon we can see enough with the streetlamp 'cross the way. But watch how you tread, for the love of Henry!"

"Get the window into the yard open," said the Doctor. "And as I hand the cages over to you open them and let the birds go into the open air—*Phew!* Isn't the horrible place stuffy?"

John Dolittle's eyes were now beginning to get used to what dim light filtered into the shop from the lamppost on the other side of the street. It was not a large place, but it was packed and crowded with cages and pens from the ceiling to the floor. In what clear space there was in the middle of the room stood a line of more cages on stands and little tables covered with dirty cloths of different colors.

The Doctor had been careful to learn from Twink the exact position in the shop of the unfortunate blackbirds' cages and of some of the others that contained starlings and thrushes lately caught and brought here. And as soon as he had his big boots swathed in the dusters that Matthew had provided, he made his way cautiously through piles of pens and boxes till he reached the cages where the blackbirds were kept.

These were pretty large and there were quite a number of them, not more than two or three birds being kept in each. By this time Matthew had the window at the back end of the shop open and a grateful draft of cool air blew into the stuffy room. One by one the cages were handed across to the Cat's-Meat-Man, who deftly opened the little doors and shook the astonished birds out into the night. Of just what was happening they had no idea. But they did not linger to find out. Thanking their lucky stars, they soared upward out of the grimy backyard and winged their way across the chimneypots of London for freedom and the open country.

"Are they all alive, Matthew?" asked John Dolittle as he handed up the last blackbird cage.

"Not a dead one so far," whispered Matthew.

"Good," said the Doctor. "I'm glad we were in time to save what was left of the poor fellows. Now we'll set to work on the starlings and thrushes."

John Dolittle next proceeded to find the cages of the other birds who had been caught in the wild and brought here for sale. This was not so easy because many of the cages were covered; and in the poor light it was hard enough to tell even what kind of bird they contained, let alone whether their occupants were from the country or not.

Moreover, the Doctor had to work with the greatest care lest he wake up other birds in the shop and cause some outcry that might bring down the proprietor or his family.

Most luckily the dogs here were very few—only one retriever and a mongrel bulldog. Both had so far remained fast asleep in their little pens beneath a stack of boxes on the left-hand side of the room.

After a good deal of climbing and searching, John Dolittle found a large cage full of starlings and managed to get them across to Matthew and so into the open air without mishap—though one or two of them did chirp a little and were answered sleepily by some bird in the other corner of the room. Two big wooden cages of thrushes were also discovered and emptied in like manner.

Every once in a while Matthew would make the Doctor stop and remain motionless while he listened for any sound or sign from upstairs. But on each occasion the Cat's-Meat-Man was convinced that as yet the proprietor and his household were sleeping soundly, quite unconscious of what was going on below them.

Even after he had set free all the blackbirds, starlings, and thrushes he could find, the Doctor still went on wandering quietly around the room, peering under cage cloths to see if he could discover any other poor unfortunates who were pining for their native fields and woods.

While he was engaged in this he heard two parrots, whose cages were covered, talking in low tones to each other at the far end of the shop.

"He opened the little doors and shook the birds into the night."

"Listen," said one. "There seems to be something moving around the room. Don't you hear it?"

"Yes," said the other. "I thought I heard something, too. It must have been that which woke me up. What is it? Has some animal got out?"

"I've no idea," said the first bird. "I hope it isn't one of the cats. There are two gray Manx cats in the pen near the door. If either of them got loose, none of us would be safe."

The Doctor, listening intently, made a sign to Matthew to keep still.

"I'll bet that's what it is," the other parrot answered. "Only cats could make so little noise. And the two of them are loose, I'm sure, because a minute ago I distinctly heard a sound in two corners of the room at once. What'll we do about it?"

"Better screech for the proprietor," said the other. "Because—"

"No, no," whispered the Doctor quickly in parrot language. "Don't do that. You'll—"

"Good gracious!" said the first parrot. "Did you hear that? Someone talking in parrot language! But it's no parrot. The accent isn't right. Odd!"

By this time the Doctor realized that the parrots' conversation had disturbed other bird sleepers around the room. For from all sides came the gentle rustling of wings and scratching of perches. He hastily signaled to Matthew that he wanted to leave in a hurry. But just at that moment he was overcome with a desire to sneeze. He suppressed it as best he could, but the noise he made, muffled though it was, could not be mistaken for anything else.

"For goodness' sake!" said one of the parrots. "Why, there's a man in the shop somewhere!"

As the Doctor once more made frantic signs to Matthew that he wanted to get out and away, he wondered whether he should take the parrots into his confidence or try to get out before the birds guessed who he was. As the second parrot did not answer immediately, but still seemed to be puzzling over the problem, he decided to try and beat a retreat while the coast was clear.

But the parrots within the covered cages did not take very long to realize that there *was* only one being in the world who could sneeze like a man and talk like a bird—even if he did it with an accent. And suddenly one of them cried out loud: "Why, it must be John Dolittle!"

"Sh!" said the Doctor.

But he was too late. The second parrot was too overjoyed and excited to pay any attention.

"Why, of course!" he squawked. "It's the Doctor. Birds, wake up! The Doctor's come! Wake up! Wake up!"

In a moment every bird in the place was cackling and chattering and screeching and whistling away at the top of its voice. The Doctor made a jump for the door. But in the half-light he did not notice a box on the floor. He stumbled over it, came down with a crash, and brought a pile of empty cages clattering on top of his head.

"Look out!" hissed Matthew. "I hear steps overhead. We've woken the whole house. Let's get out!"

"I can't get out," said the Doctor. "Take some of these cages off my chest."

By this time, of course, the two dogs were awake and yelping away for all they were worth. As Matthew struggled to get the Doctor's legs and skirt disentangled from the pile of fallen cages, he saw the glimmer of a light up the stairs that led to the room above.

"Is it really you, Doctor?" yelped the bulldog from his pen.

"Of course it is," snapped John Dolittle, still floundering around on his back, trying to get up. "For heaven's sake, keep quiet about it! I've got to get away. I'll be put in prison for this if I'm caught."

"Undo the latches of our pens, then," said the bulldog, "and *we'll* see you get away all right."

"Never mind me. Let the dogs out, Matthew," said the Doctor. "Quick!"

Matthew, experienced adventurer though he was, never

stopped to argue when the Doctor spoke in a voice like that. In spite of the fact that the proprietor was already standing at the head of the stairs with a poker in his hand, he delayed his flight long enough to let the bulldog and the retriever out of their pens.

"Police! Police! Murder! Thieves!" yelled the proprietor, rushing down the stairs.

"Get out, Matthew! I'll manage," shouted the Doctor.

He had not yet quite regained his feet and the proprietor was halfway down the stairs, but again Matthew did not question the Doctor's orders. Leaving his manager to his own devices, he leapt through the front door and disappeared.

Raising his poker above his head, the shopkeeper prepared to jump the last three steps onto his victim's prostrate body. But suddenly two snarling dogs appeared at the foot of the staircase on either side of John Dolittle and dared him to come down. Stiffly the Doctor rose to his feet and arranged his skirt becomingly over his trousers, which had been very evident beneath.

"You ought to be ashamed of yourself," he said severely to the proprietor, as one of his false bangs fluttered from his bonnet to the floor, "for keeping such a disgusting animal shop. If he beats you for this," he added to the dogs, "I'll give you a home. My circus is on Greenheath."

Then he strode out through the open door and set off on the run to follow Matthew, whose figure could just be seen beckoning to him at the corner of the street.

The Third Chapter

The Doctor's Return

ALTHOUGH THE TWO DOGS SUCCESSFULLY kept the proprietor of the animal shop (his name was Harris) from following the Doctor and Matthew, they could not prevent his running upstairs and opening his bedroom window. From there he continued to bawl lustily for the police, till the constable, whom John Dolittle had seen earlier in the evening, appeared upon the scene.

Stuttering with rage, Mr. Harris told him that his store had been broken into and gave him a very minute description of the Doctor. Matthew he had not seen so clearly, but he described him too as best he could.

Then the constable blew a long blast upon his whistle and very soon he was joined by two other members of the police force. Following the direction pointed out by the excited proprietor, they set out on the run to overtake the culprits.

But in the meantime the experienced and intelligent Cat's-Meat-Man was piloting the Doctor through a regular maze of narrow back

"He continued to bawl lustily for the police."

streets that bordered the river. Presently he stopped and listened.

"I think we've shook 'em for the present, Doctor," said he. "Now let's dodge behind this old warehouse and get them togs off you."

Within the shadow of the shed the Doctor was then divested of his skirt, bodice, and bonnet.

"Theodosia will 'ave to do without them," said the Cat's-Meat-Man as he threw them into the swirling river. "They're no great loss. Next thing, Doc, we must separate and go back to Greenheath different ways. Would never do if the cops saw us together—even though you have changed your clothes."

"But what shall I wear for a hat?" asked John Dolittle, watching Theodosia's bonnet drift downstream. "I can't be seen bareheaded."

"I thought of that," said Matthew, bringing a cap out of his pocket. "I brought a spare headpiece along with me, see? With this—and your coat and trousers underneath—I reckoned I could transform you at a moment's notice if we got into a tight place. There's nothing like being prepared."

"Good heavens, it's awfully small!" said the Doctor, trying it on.

"Never mind. Stick it on the back of your 'ead," said Matthew. "Now you look all right. And remember, after I've left you, if any cop comes up and asks you questions, remember, you're a greengrocer's assistant on his way to Covent Garden Market. There ain't many jobs, you see, what gets a man up so early as this. So remember: *a greengrocer's assistant.*"

"Do I really look like one?" asked the Doctor, trying to keep the small cap from slipping off the back of his head.

"Well—you'll do," said Matthew. "Turn your coat collar up and don't talk too grammatic—no fancy lingo—see?"

"Very good," said the Doctor. "Which way are you going home?"

"I'm going back through Wapping," said Matthew. "You find some other way and use back streets all you can. I heard that big-footed cop a' blowing on 'is whistle like mad a while ago. So he's likely got all the metropolitan police force on the lookout for us. So long, Doc, I'll see you at breakfast."

Then Matthew disappeared around a corner and melted away into the night, while the Doctor, after looking vaguely about him for a moment, chose a narrow passage that seemed to run parallel with the river in a southeasterly direction.

"I'm a greengrocer's assistant," he muttered as he started off.

He had not gone very far along the passage before a voice suddenly hailed him from behind.

"Hi! What are you doing down there?"

He turned around and saw a policeman, with bull's-eye lantern shining at his belt, not more than ten paces away. To run for it seemed hopeless. He retraced his steps.

"Pardon," said he to the constable. "Were you addressing me?"

"I was," said the policeman. "I want to know what you're doing nosing around the backs of houses at this time of night?"

"I was going to Covent Garden," said the Doctor. "I'm a gardener's assistant."

The policeman turned the light of his lantern on the Doctor's figure and slowly scanned him from his ill-fitting cap to his large boots.

"Covent Garden ain't down that way," said he. "And if you had anything to do with it you'd know better where it was. Come on. Out with it. What's your game?"

There was an uncomfortable silence, during which the Doctor noticed over the constable's shoulder that more people were approaching from the end of the passage.

In the meantime Matthew, experienced in the ways of cities and city police, was gradually approaching Greenheath by roundabout and quiet streets. The gray light of the dawn was just beginning to show when he clambered over the gate of the circus enclosure. In his own caravan he found his wife still sitting up for him, for she was anxious about the results of the expedition.

"It is all right, Theodosia," said he. "The Doctor ought to be along any minute now. I'll just lie down and take forty winks, and then I must get around to my jobs. Wake me up if the Doc gets here before breakfast time."

Breakfast time came, but the Doctor did not. And when, halfway through the morning, he still had not appeared, Matthew and his wife began to get uneasy.

However, about eleven o'clock, just when the Cat's-Meat-Man was preparing to go out and hunt for him, he turned up, looking very tired, disheveled, and soaking wet.

"Why, Doctor," said Matthew, "what happened to you? I expected you'd be here pretty near as soon as I was."

"A policeman stopped me," said the Doctor, "and asked me a whole lot of questions. He had evidently been warned to be on the lookout for us, but my clothes didn't fit the description, and if I had only been able to answer his questions properly he would have let me go, I'm sure. However, right in the middle of his cross-examination that wretched Harris, the proprietor, appeared on the scene—with another policeman. So—er—I had to employ other methods to get away."

"Well," said the other, "what did you do?"

"I'm afraid I had to use violence," said the Doctor, looking embarrassed and ashamed. "You see, the policeman, when the others came down the passage, got on the far side of me, so I couldn't get out of it at either end. I knew Harris would recognize me, even without my makeup. So—er—I knocked the policeman down with a punch on the jaw, jumped over him, and ran for it. At the end of the passage I saw two more constables, cutting me off. There was only the river left. I dived into it, swam under a barge, and came up on the other side. They then decided, I imagine, that I had been drowned. Anyway, I heard no further sound of pursuit. And presently I let myself drift downstream a mile or two, crept ashore on the other bank and made my way back here. I was sorry to have to punch the policeman. But what else could I do?"

"Don't apologize, Doc," giggled Matthew, "don't apologize. The only thing I'm regretting is that I wasn't there to see it. But listen, 'ow did you get 'ere like that, drippin' wet, without havin' people looking at you suspiciouslike?"

"I didn't," said the Doctor. "They followed me in crowds, but no one stopped me."

"I dived into it."

"Humph!" muttered Matthew with a frown. "That don't sound so good. I don't reckon them cops would give a man up for drowned so easy as you think, specially after getting a poke in the face like what you describe. And if you've left a wet trail behind you all the way from Billingsgate 'ere—with the folks talking—I think you'd better pack yourself away for a while—as soon as you've had a change of togs. 'Cause something tells me we can count on a call or two from the police department during the afternoon—Hulloa! What dog's that?"

The Doctor looked out of his wagon and saw the mongrel bulldog of Mr. Harris's establishment trotting toward him across the enclosure accompanied by Jip, Swizzle, and Toby.

"Good morning," said John Dolittle when the canine committee had arrived at the steps. "Did that wretched man punish you for your part in last night's adventures?"

"He wanted to," said the bulldog. "But I and the retriever had agreed to put up a fight together and defend each other if he attempted it. He couldn't lick the two of us at once. Then he tried to separate us and was going to call in help. So I gave the retriever—Blackie's his name—the wink, and we ran off together. Harris came after us, hotfoot, bellowing to everybody in the street to stop us because we were running away. I saw we'd stand no chance of getting to you if we stayed together. So as we pelted down the street, I whispered to Blackie, 'At the next corner you go one way and I'll go the other. We may reach the Doctor's singly, but we'll never do it together!'

"'All right,' says he. And that's what we did. How he fared I have no idea. But the chances are Harris will succeed in following one or the other of us here."

"I see," said the Doctor. "Well, there's no use in borrowing trouble. He hasn't followed you yet. What's your name?"

"Grab," said the bulldog.

"If Harris does come we'll give him a fine welcome," growled Jip, showing his teeth.

"You bet," said Swizzle. "Listen, Doctor, Grab says he wants to stay here with us. He can, can't he?"

"Certainly," said the Doctor—"and Blackie too, if he comes—provided of course we can manage things with Harris. He may not want to sell them to me, just out of spite."

"Don't worry, Doctor," said Matthew, "even if old Harris does come here and we get hauled up for it, they'll only give us a few days in jail. And the advertisement will be fine for the show."

"Yes, that would be all very well, Matthew," said John Dolittle, "if I hadn't knocked the policeman down. The law might treat us lightly for our burglary, seeing we were doing it for the sake of animals not properly cared for. But no judge is going to let me off lightly for punching a policeman on the jaw to escape arrest."

"Doctor," said Grab, "let me come inside your wagon and shut the door a moment. I've got something I'd like to tell you. It's about Harris and it may be useful to you."

John Dolittle then took Grab inside the wagon. None of the other dogs, Jip, Toby, or Swizzle—although they were crazy to hear what the bulldog had to tell the Doctor—were allowed in.

The door was closed for about ten minutes, and when it opened again Jip heard the Doctor say as he came out, "And what was the man's name, Grab?"

"Jennings," said the dog, "Jeremiah Jennings. And he lived in Whitechapel."

"All right," said the Doctor. "I'll remember that."

As John Dolittle descended the steps, a flight of blackbirds suddenly arrived from somewhere out of the sky and settled all over the roof of his wagon.

"We wanted to thank you," said one of them, perching on the Doctor's shoulder. "We didn't know last night who it was that had let us out. We were only too glad to get away and did not stop to inquire. But this morning a thrush out in the fields, who is doing some choir work for you, told us that two of his friends had been caught and sold to the same shop. You let them out, too, it seems. And then, of course, we knew who must have done it. So we thought we'd like to come and tell you that we appreciate your kindness very much."

"Don't mention it," said the Doctor. "Good heavens, why here's Blackie—and Harris running after him. This is where the trouble begins."

They had turned, and there, sure enough, was the retriever coming in at the gate at full speed, followed by Harris, the proprietor of the animal store. Jip and Swizzle went for him, snarling like tigers, but the Doctor called them off.

"Leave him alone," said he. "We'll accomplish nothing by that now. Well, Mr. Harris, good morning!"

"Don't you wish me any good mornings," squeaked the little man. "You're a thief. And now that I've found you, I'm going to get you locked up. My wife can identify you in the police court as well as I can. She saw you in the shop stealing blackbirds."

"Mind your tongue—calling people thieves around here," said Matthew. "I'm liable to hit you over the crust with a broom handle if you get sassy."

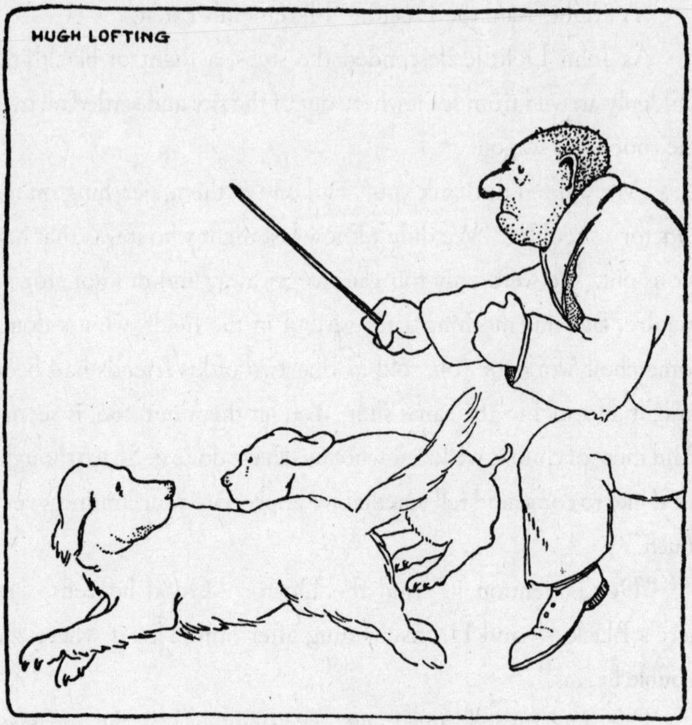

"Harris running after them"

"And you were the other one," said Harris, turning and leveling an accusing finger at the Cat's-Meat-Man. "Good! Now I've got you both, and I'm going off to get the police and land you both in jail. I've got the evidence right here: all them blackbirds on the roof there what you stole and these two dogs that you enticed away. I've caught you red-handed."

"I didn't steal these blackbirds," said the Doctor quietly. "They are at liberty, as they ought to be. You can see I'm not holding them. And as for the dogs, they came to me of their own free will. They want to stay with me. I am quite willing to buy them from you."

"They're coming back to my shop to be sold to honest

"And you were the other one,' said Harris."

customers," said Harris. "The blackbirds you stole. I found the cages in the shop, with the doors opened, after you'd left. I'm going to get the police."

His ugly face purple with fury, the little man turned on his heel and started for the gate.

"Er—just a minute, Mr. Harris," the Doctor called.

"What is it now?" snarled the proprietor, pausing a moment. "I ain't got no time for foolishness. I'm going to get you locked up before tonight."

"I have something I'd like to tell you privately," said the Doctor. "Will you come into my van a moment, please?"

"Anything you've got to say to me you can say in court," snarled Harris, starting for the gate once more.

"I don't think you'd like me to say it in court," John Dolittle called after him. "It's about Jennings—Jeremiah Jennings, of Whitechapel."

The hurrying figure of the proprietor suddenly halted. He turned a scowling face upon the Doctor. Then he came slowly back and walked up the steps into the wagon.

THE FOURTH CHAPTER

Mr. Harris's Past

WIDE-EYED WITH CURIOSITY OVER Harris's sudden change of mood, Matthew and the three dogs watched the Doctor follow the man into the wagon and close the door after him.

"I wonder what it is," said Toby in a busybody whisper. "Did you ever see a man suddenly calm down so?"

"The Doctor's got wind of something," said Jip. "That's why Mr. Harris is singing a different tune."

"What was it you told the Doctor, Grab?" asked Swizzle. But the bulldog wouldn't tell them.

"That's my business—and the Doctor's," he said. And that was all they could get out of him.

Meanwhile, within the van, John Dolittle had offered his guest a chair.

"Let us sit down and talk this over calmly," he said.

"No, I don't want to sit," said Harris in a surly tone. "Tell me, what do you know about Jeremiah Jennings?"

"'I wonder what it is,' said Toby."

"Well," said the Doctor, getting out his pipe and reaching for the tobacco jar on the shelf, "I don't believe in raking up a man's past or poking my nose into other people's business. But you have threatened to have me arrested for something that I didn't do. I did not steal those blackbirds, but I did let them go out of your back window because they were wild birds, and you had no business to buy them from the trappers. Incidentally, your animal shop is a disgrace to humanity. But in spite of all that, if I were arrested, in the eyes of the law I should be convicted of burglary and probably sentenced to imprisonment. If, on the other hand, you don't bring any charge against me, nothing will likely be done about it."

"Well?" said Harris as the Doctor paused.

"It has been brought to my attention by a very reliable authority," John Dolittle went on, "that besides your trade of selling animals you have, or had, another one, that of—er—receiving stolen goods, Mr. Harris. Isn't that so?"

The ugly little man who had been fidgeting around the van sprang forward and thumped the table.

"It is a lie!" he hissed.

"I think not," said the Doctor quietly. "Mr. Jennings, of Whitechapel, who has been in jail for burglary more than once, was one of your best customers. I have enough evidence to put both you and him in prison for a much longer term than you could get me condemned for. I know all about the little—er—'job,' I think you call it, at Number 70 Cavendish Square. I know that you knew the silverware was stolen when it was brought to your cellar for sale. And I know a good deal about Squinty Ted, who had only three fingers on one hand but was remarkably clever at opening safes. And Jeff Bottomley and—"

"Stop!" stuttered Harris. "Where did you get all this? Did Jennings tell you?"

"He did not," said the Doctor. "None of your shady friends told me. I got it from a much more reliable source; and I can prove every word I say. I can even take you to the hole in your cellar wall where you hid the gold candlesticks that came from Lord Weatherby's mansion."

In silent wonder, his ugly face twisted with fear and hate, the little man glared at the Doctor for a moment.

"I believe you're the Devil himself, in disguise," he whispered at last. "Well, what do you mean to do about it?"

The Doctor relit his pipe, which had gone out.

"Nothing at all, Mr. Harris," the Doctor said at length, "*provided* you will agree to a few conditions that I shall lay down."

"Humph!" grunted Harris doubtfully. "And if I don't agree?"

"Then," said the Doctor, "I shall, much against my will, be compelled to hand this information over to the police, to act upon as they see fit."

Mr. Harris thought a moment. Then he jerked his head upward and said:

"Well, what's the conditions?"

"First of all," the Doctor began, "you must agree, of course, not to proceed with this charge you bring against me. After that, you must give me your solemn oath that you will receive no more stolen goods or aid in any way burglars or people of similar character. Next, you will have to hand over to me the two dogs, Blackie and Grab—for which, of course, I will pay you. Finally, you must give up the animal shop business altogether. You don't understand it and should never have gone into it."

Harris threw up his hands in despair.

"Do you want to ruin me?" he wailed. "How am I to earn an honest living?"

"Not by selling poor wild birds who have been caught in traps," the Doctor answered. "Nor, certainly, by receiving property that has been obtained dishonestly. You were an iron founder once, I understand—which trade you found very useful in melting down precious metal that was brought to your store. Go back to that work—in the foundries."

Harris made a wry face.

"Yes, I know," added John Dolittle, "it isn't nearly such a

comfortable profession as sitting in a shop, selling defenseless animals. But you can likely change it for some other work later."

"Now, look here," began the other in a whine, "you've got a kind face. You wouldn't be 'ard on a poor man like me. I've got children to support, I 'ave. And—"

"No," the Doctor interrupted firmly, bringing his fist down with a bang upon the table, which rattled the china and made Jip outside cock his ears, frowning. "So have the poor birds got children to support—which are just as important to them as yours are to you. My mind is made up. I give you one week to dispose of your stock and close up the animal shop. You're a healthy man. You can

"'Do you want to ruin me?' he wailed."

earn a living some other way. If the conditions I lay down are not fulfilled within seven days, I hand over a written statement to the police, giving your complete record as a receiver of stolen goods. Now, what is your answer?"

Slowly the ugly little man took his hat up off the table. Something in the set of the Doctor's chin told him that further arguments or prayers would be of no avail.

"All right," he said sullenly. "In a week, then."

"Here is half a sovereign," said John Dolittle, taking a coin out of his pocket. "I am paying you five shillings apiece for these two dogs, Grab and Blackie. They will remain here with me. I will come and take a look at your place in a week's time. And as for the receiving game, remember, I have ways of finding out things—those same ways through which I got my other information."

The Doctor held open the door of his van while Harris shuffled down the steps and set off toward the gate.

"Lor' bless me, Doctor!" murmured Matthew, gazing after him. "'E don't seem so uppish as 'e did. Is 'e on 'is way to the police station again?"

"No," said John Dolittle, patting Grab the bulldog on the head. "I think he'll leave the police alone for good—and the animal business, too."

The Fifth Chapter

Scenery, Costumes, and Orchestra

WHILE MATTHEW AND THE FIVE DOGS were congratulating John Dolittle over his successful dismissal of Harris, the Doctor noticed that the blackbirds were still perched around the roof of his wagon, evidently anxious to tell him something.

"Why," said he, addressing one of the cocks who seemed to be the leader of the party, "I had forgotten all about you during this excitement. I consider it very thoughtful of you to come and visit me. What do you think of my circus?"

"We like it immensely," said the blackbird. "The animals are all so cheerful and clearly enjoying their work. Too-Too has just been telling us about your bird opera. And we were wondering if you would like us to help you with it in any way. We are pretty good singers, you know."

"Thank you," said the Doctor. "That's an excellent idea. For, to tell you the truth, I find that I am really in need of another chorus, and your sleek black plumage would look very well against the colored scenery. But time is so short, now. I have promised to have the show in readiness in a week or so. Could you prepare a chorus in so short a time as that?"

"Oh yes, I think so," said the blackbird.

"Good," said the Doctor. "Then if you'll get about a dozen cocks together, I'll read over the score with you and we can decide upon the wording of the lyric for you. By the way, I want a few small birds, as well—very small, to take the parts of a family of youngsters in the nest. What would you recommend?"

"Wrens," said the blackbird. "They're about as small a species as we have in this country. And they're very intelligent. You could teach them anything."

"Do you think you could get me some—four or five?" asked the Doctor.

"Yes, I imagine so," said the blackbird. "I'll go off right away, while it's still light, and see if I can hunt up a few in the woods and farms beyond Highgate."

It was only now, in spite of his having started long before, that the Doctor was able to give his entire time to the opera. So many interruptions had claimed his attention. But from that morning on until the opening night, he worked like a Trojan all day long. Indeed, there was a tremendous number of things that had to be looked after. For, although the opera, when it was finally performed, was put on within the limits of a very tiny stage—not much larger than an ordinary room—yet John Dolittle insisted on the smallest details of the production being made as perfect as possible.

He got the theater owners to supply him with quite a famous artist to paint the scenery for him. And he would spend hours talking over and trying out different arrangements, just to get

"He would spend hours trying out different arrangements."

one little thing right, such as the moonlight glinting on floating seaweed or the evening shadows beneath the hawthorns. In everything he consulted Pippinella's opinion, and if the scenery artist's work did not please her, the Doctor would change it, and go on changing it, till she was satisfied.

In the rehearsing, whenever it was possible, he kept the different scenes and passages separate. For instance, with the wrens, when they finally arrived, he practiced the nest scene—where they were to act like a hungry brood being fed by a mother bird—in an old tent quite apart from the other members of the opera cast.

He had found that when all the bird actors were together, they gossiped and chattered so much that no work was done. And it was his intention to rehearse the different groups by themselves until all were quite at home in their parts, and only to bring them together for the complete performance when they were so sure of what they had to do and sing that there could be no fear of their getting distracted.

The costuming for the opera was not very extensive, but it was difficult. The Doctor decided that only the biggest birds would wear clothes. The pelicans were to be dressed as sailors. The flamingos would appear as ladies, passengers on a ship. A set of little parasols, light red to match the color of their legs, were specially made by a West End umbrella firm, and these were carried under their right wings, which were covered with loose-fitting chiffon sleeves.

For dressmaking, of course, the useful Theodosia was called in. Mrs. Mugg, a handy woman with her needle, had always looked after the costumes for the whole circus. For the pelicans she made a set of very natty white sailor suits with little hats to match. And when they were completed, chorus master Cheapside had to put his troupe through several dress rehearsals of the "Sailor's Chorus" because, of course, it was highly necessary that they should learn to walk and behave naturally in clothes they had never worn before.

"Now," said the Doctor to Pippinella, Twink, and the other principals one day, "we must take up the question of the orchestral instruments. What do you like best for an accompaniment?"

"Well, of course," Pippinella answered, "it depends somewhat on the song we're singing. Nothing like fiddles or flutes.

"She made them a set of very natty white sailor suits."

That's not an accompaniment—it's a competition. The instrument that canaries like best to sing to is the sewing machine. But any quiet, buzzy, humming noise will do."

"Wouldn't you like a piano?" asked the white mouse, who was listening at the other end of the van. "In Puddleby I lived inside the Doctor's piano. I know a good deal about that instrument. I liked best the old one that the Doctor had before he went to Africa. That was a German piano, very solidly made—a Steinmetz. It was so warm in winter. After the Steinmetz I like a Wilkinson—an English make. The felt on the hammer is so thick. It's fine for lining the nests for the young ones."

"No," said Pippinella, "a piano's too loud for a canary to sing to."

"Yes, that's true," agreed the white mouse. "I remember one of the Doctor's old patients used to play on the Steinmetz while he was waiting for John Dolittle to come in from the garden. It kept my children awake—until I complained to the Doctor and asked him to lock up the keyboard cover so the patients couldn't disturb us."

"We shall want a razor strop in the orchestra, Doctor," Pippinella went on, "for the duet in the barbershop aboard ship. That's in the third act, isn't it? It should be an easy instrument to play."

"Very good," said John Dolittle, making a note. "We'll have a razor strop. One of the Pinto Brothers can play on it, and Matthew can perform on the sewing machine. Now, what else?"

"We will need a chain," said the prima donna, "for the 'Jingling Harness Song'—a nice light chain with a clear, silvery clink to it. Tie one end to a music stand and get a boy to shake it like this at regular intervals: *"JING—jingle-jing; JING—jingle-jing; JING—jingle-jing.* I begin singing on the fourth *JING."*

"All right," said the Doctor, making another note. "Anything else? What about the 'Greenfinch's Love Song'?"

"That will be done without accompaniment," said the greenfinch, who was playing the part of the prima donna's faithless lover. "Most of the passages are so soft and whispering that any other noise would completely drown them. But please ask the audience, Doctor, to keep perfect silence during the whole of it; otherwise it will be spoiled entirely."

"I'll attend to that," said John Dolittle, jotting in his notebook again. "I'll have a special request notice printed in the programs. Now, what other instruments will we want?"

"Nothing further besides a cobbler's last and hammer," said Pippinella. "But that instrument will have to be played with a good deal of skill because we'll use it to keep time in several of the solos—also in the trio at the end of the second act, where my mate goes off with the greenfinch and leaves me mourning on the seashore—also to imitate the raindrops, played very lightly, in the 'Thrushes' Rain Chorus.'"

"Very good," said the Doctor, closing his notebook. "Then our orchestra will consist of a sewing machine, a razor strop, a chain, and a cobbler's last. I will get them all tomorrow, and we will run through the score with music."

THE SIXTH CHAPTER

The Prima Donna Disappears

EVERYTHING WENT SMOOTHLY WITH *THE Canary Opera* up to within three days of the opening date. Then troubles seemed to descend on Manager Dolittle's head thick and fast. First a serious epidemic of laryngitis and sore throats broke out among the blackbirds; and in spite of the famous cough mixture, it ran through the ranks like wildfire. This necessitated not only keeping the rehearsals back (because of course the Doctor could not allow the whole cast on the stage at once for fear the sickness spread to the other birds), but last-minute changes had to be made in the score of the opera when it became clear that the blackbirds would not be cured in time for the first performance.

However, the Doctor packed the birds off into the country (he put the sickness down to using their throats too much in the bad air of the city); and Cheapside suggested that he bring forward a gang of his sparrows to take the blackbirds' place. This was done. And in spite of the fact that the city birds did not have nearly such good voices and nothing like the elegant appearance of the others, the chorus was changed into a sort of comic song and went very well.

As a matter of fact, the Doctor had been thinking that he had not quite enough comedy in the opera; and in the end the "Sparrows' Chorus" in the fourth act (where the cheeky birds make fun of the pelican sailors newly arrived from foreign parts) turned out to be one of the most successful numbers in the whole show.

The next trouble was the sudden and mysterious disappearance of the prima donna herself two days before the opera was advertised to open. No one knew what had become of her, and the Doctor was beside himself with anxiety lest harm had befallen his star performer. He had another canary trained as an understudy, it is true. But the posters and all the advertisements laid special stress on the facts that this was the great contralto's first personal appearance in London and that the opera itself was the story of her own life. Jip had disappeared too.

Finally, after the Doctor had put all of Cheapside's city sparrow gangs to hunting for her and called in the help of most of the wild birds around London as well, she was found with Jip over on the east side of London and brought back.

On their return to the circus it came out that on a Saturday morning Pippinella had seen someone in the circus enclosure whom she had thought might be her beloved master, the window cleaner. Calling on Jip to help her, she had gone off to follow him and the two had tracked the man right across the city, and finally, in the smelly quarters of the docks, Jip had lost the trail and been compelled to give up the hunt. John Dolittle implored his leading lady not to disappear again and said that later, when the opera was in running order, he would see what he could do to help her find her friend. At that, Pippinella promised not to go off again and rehearsals proceeded.

That same day the Doctor moved his operatic troupe into the city proper, so as to be nearer the theater where the last full dress rehearsals were taking place. A big empty town house was put at his disposal, and for fear of further epidemics and mishaps he kept the different kinds of birds in separate rooms. The pelicans had the drawing room, the canaries the dining room, the flamingos the big double bedroom on the first floor, the sparrows the kitchen, while Pippinella the star had a room to herself, which had been the

"A crowd of small boys was constantly outside."

late owner's study. The Doctor slept in the basement and Mr. and Mrs. Mugg in the attic.

By this time the birds were all very excited over the nearness of the first performance. And the noise they made running over their songs all day long was so great, even with the front windows closed, that a crowd of small boys was constantly to be seen outside, listening and wondering what was happening within.

As it happened, the week in which the opera was to have its first performance was Christmas week. And when Gub-Gub, Jip, and the others of the Doctor's household made a tour through the city they were delighted with the festive holiday appearance of the shops, where good things to eat and elegant presents were set out in windows decorated with holly and mistletoe.

They saw many posters and highly colored announcements of various pantomimes and Christmas shows for children. And conspicuous among these were several large advertisements that read:

PIPPINELLA:
THE CANARY OPERA
In which Madame Coloratura Pippinella,
the unique contralto canary, will appear
for the first time in London, supported
by the well-known Dolittle
Company of Performing Birds.
At THE REGENT'S THEATER
in the Strand
to be followed by the one and only
PUDDLEBY PANTOMIME
(Straight from its smashing success in Manchester!)

Great was their thrill on reading these announcements of their first appearance in the capital. But Jip was almost as much interested in the posters of the other shows. And the Doctor was pestered until he promised to take his whole household to see Dick Whittington (which was being given at the Frivolity Theater) or some other entertainment.

The night before the opera's opening date a grand dinner was arranged at Patti's, a very popular Italian restaurant in the Strand. The theater managers were the hosts and the banquet was especially given for John Dolittle and his staff to celebrate the opera's first appearance in London. The Doctor wore his old dress suit, which he hadn't had on since the days of his regular practice as a physician in Puddleby. Mr. and Mrs. Matthew Mugg came, Hop the clown, Hercules the strong man, Henry Crockett the Punch-and-Judy man, the Pinto Brothers and their wives, and Fred the menagerie-keeper.

It was a very jolly meal in spite of the fact that during the second course the Doctor's dress coat (which had become too tight for him) suddenly gave way when he was leaning across the table to converse with one of the guests and split up the back with a loud report. Matthew and Theodosia, who up till then had been uncomfortably overawed by the elegance of the table and the fine dresses of the managers' wives, were by this amusing accident to the Doctor's coat put entirely at their ease, and they enjoyed the rest of the meal with great zest.

At the end, over the port wine, speeches were made by the managers, by the Doctor, by Matthew, and by Hercules. The managers said how glad they were to welcome John Dolittle and his opera at their theater.

"Matthew Mugg made quite a long speech."

The Doctor spoke entirely about music and what he hoped to do for musicians and composers by thus bringing forward the musical ideas of the animal kingdom.

Matthew Mugg made quite a long speech. In a hired dress suit his bosom swelled with pride as he spoke of his early ambition to become a showman. He told the managers ("my fellow showmen," he called them) that this was the proudest moment of his life, when he and his partner, the famous John Dolittle, were welcomed to London to exhibit their greatest creation, *The Canary Opera.* Such honors, he claimed he had himself foretold long ago, when he helped persuade the great naturalist to go into the show business. Much more he said—and still more he would have said if

Theodosia hadn't kept twitching his coattail and telling him in loud whispers not to talk all night.

Hercules made quite a short speech, mostly about the Doctor's system of running a cooperative circus, in which all profits were shared by the staff. This, he declared, had made him a moderately rich man in a short time, and he hoped soon to retire from the road, for it was his life's ambition to settle down in a seaside cottage with a nice garden where he could grow chrysanthemums and roses.

The Pinto Brothers, when called upon, said they had no speech to make, but offered to give the company a trapeze performance on the restaurant's chandeliers. However, it was feared that these would not be strong enough and the idea was abandoned. Then after some newspaper reporters, who were also guests, had welcomed the Doctor to London in the name of the press, the party broke up at one o'clock in the morning, and everyone went home very happy.

THE SEVENTH CHAPTER

The First Performance of The Canary Opera

DAB-DAB WAS VERY WORRIED ABOUT THE Doctor's health these days. He entered into the excitement of the whole thing with a boyish enthusiasm even greater than that of the performers themselves. He never stopped running about and seemed to be actually in two or three places at once. And the thoughtful old housekeeper shook her head gravely over the possible results.

"I know he's a man of iron," she said, "but for the last three days he has been on the go without rest and has hardly slept at all. Thank goodness the opening night is here at last! For human flesh and blood couldn't stand the pace he's been going much longer."

The Regent's was by no means a small or unimportant theater. There many great actors had produced Shakespeare's plays. It was accustomed to have only the highest and best kind of entertainments; the managers enjoyed a good reputation with the public; and the first nights were well attended by critics from the newspapers. The Regent's could hold nearly two thousand people. And its stage was very large and furnished with all the most up-to-date inventions for lighting, scenery moving, etc.

However, for *The Canary Opera* the Doctor had had the big stage opening considerably reduced by enormous great curtains of canary-yellow silk, which cost the managers a large sum of money. The programs were printed on canary-yellow paper, and the ushers who showed the people to their places were dressed in canary-yellow plush uniforms.

Up to the last minute of course John Dolittle was busy behind the scenes looking after the thousand small matters which always get left unattended to up to the opening night, even in the best-run shows. He was being ably assisted by Matthew, Theodosia, and Cheapside—who did more swearing on that important night than on any other in the whole of his profane career. The two partners who owned the theater were also doing all they could to help, but it was not much that the Doctor could let them do. Altogether "behind the scenes" was a very busy and excited place.

Jip did not have to dress for his part in the pantomime until much later, and during the first part of the evening he ran in and out, bringing the Doctor news of the audience and how the tickets were being sold at the box office.

"Listen, Doctor!" he whispered, appearing for the fourth time and interrupting John Dolittle in the makeup of one of the sailor pelicans: "It's like a mob outside! There are three policemen keeping the people in order around the ticket office—the line stretches the whole way down the street. And just now a frightfully swell carriage drew up at the door and two ladies and a gentleman got out with diamonds all over them. Maybe one of them was the queen, for all I know—certainly the carriage must have been a duke's at least."

A few minutes later Jip's report was confirmed by one of the managers who had been around to the front on a tour of inspection.

"My friend," he said, grasping the Doctor firmly by the hand, "this is going to be the greatest first night the Regent's ever saw. The seats have all gone; we are selling standing room already, and it's still twenty minutes before the curtain goes up."

"What kind of an audience does it look like," asked the Doctor, "intelligent?"

"The best people in town," said the manager. "Come and take a look at them through the peephole. We've especially tried to get the musical folk here, the highbrows and the gentry."

The Doctor, followed by the manager, Jip, and Gub-Gub, went to the side of the curtain where there was a little eyehole through which the actors could see the audience without being visible themselves.

"Well, what do you think of 'em?" asked the manager after the Doctor had looked through a moment.

"Great heavens!" cried the Doctor, his eye still to the hole. "Why, there's Paganini himself!"

"Piggy-ninny!" squeaked Gub-Gub. "Who's he?"

"No—Paganini," the Doctor repeated. "The greatest violinist in the world. That's he in the fifth row, talking to an old gray-haired lady behind him. I've always wanted to meet him. Good! There's one, I think, at least, who will understand the music of our show."

The opera's unusual orchestra consisted of Matthew Mugg (sewing machine), George Pinto (razor and strop), Hercules (chain), and a member of the theater's regular orchestra (cobbler's

"A little eyehole through which the actors could see the audience"

last and hammer). When the musicians trooped in carrying their strange instruments, a general titter ran through the audience, who did not know quite what to make of it.

And they were still snickering when the conductor (John Dolittle himself) walked to the desk, carrying the usual little white baton. At precisely eight o'clock the Doctor turned to the audience and at once everybody became silent, seeing that some kind of a speech or announcement was going to be made.

The Doctor then told the people in a few words how and why he had devised *The Canary Opera.* He said that, while the work was intended to amuse and entertain, it must not be taken merely as a farce or burlesque, such as was *The Puddleby Pantomime*, which would follow the opera. Musically speaking, this production was put forward seriously and its producers felt that it was entitled to the study and consideration of composers and musicians as being the first attempt ever made to bring together the musical ideas of both man and beast. And it was hoped that those serious musicians in the audience would not criticize too early much that was apparently harsh to the ordinary ear, but would wait before giving judgment till the whole four acts had been heard.

Then with a little bow the Doctor turned around and, facing his orchestra, tapped his desk with the stick to command their attention. The audience gave one final fidget (as it always does when the music is about to begin) and settled down to listen in comfortable silence. John Dolittle raised the little white stick, gazed around at his musicians, and the overture began.

The orchestra, heard by itself, certainly provided a strange and new kind of music. But, in spite of the odd character of the instruments, the effect was musical without a doubt. The overture was very short, but in a few moments it ran through all the accompaniments and tempos of the main songs of the opera. And the silvery jingle of the chain, the constant droning of the sewing machine, the *rap-a-tap-tap* of the hammer and last, and the soft *zip-zip-ping* of the razor strop provided a mixture of sounds surprisingly pleasing to the ear.

Some of the audience tittered again, but some were clearly not at all inclined to ridicule. One old lady with glasses, in the front row, leaned over and told her neighbor it reminded her of a sleigh ride she had taken in Russia years ago, on the shores of the Black Sea.

"The horses," the Doctor heard her whisper, "galloped right along the snow-laden beach, so near the water that the spray of the

"And the overture began."

surf sometimes showered right over us. That sounds exactly like it—the thumping of the hooves, the jingle of the harness, the droning of the wind, and the whispering of the sea. I remember telling my niece, who was with me at the time, what a wonderful motif it would have made for an opera, if only a composer could have heard it. I'm glad I came tonight."

In five minutes the overture was already dwindling away to a finish, and once more the audience moved expectantly in their seats as they saw from the changing of the lights around the stage that the curtain was about to go up.

The Doctor, as a matter of fact, was now listening with one

ear for people going out. Because he had expected that, with anything as new and strange to average audiences as this, there would be some who would go before the overture was finished. But no one left his seat. If the people were not yet enthusiastic, at all events they were interested. And when at last the curtain slid slowly and silently up, a general half-suppressed gasp ran through the house at the beauty and novelty of the scene displayed upon the stage.

The Eighth Chapter

The Drama of Pippinella's Life

THE ENTIRE STAGE AT FIRST APPEARED TO BE occupied by an enormous birdcage. But on closer investigation the audience found that one could see through this into a room that lay behind. The setting had been so designed that you got the impression that you were yourself inside the cage, looking outward upon the world. Beyond the large bars, the perches and the water and seed pots, a parlor-maid (Mrs. Mugg) was dusting a mantelpiece and bustling silently to and fro over other housework. From a window at the back of the stage a shaft of golden sunlight flooded the cage and the room in which it was supposed to be hanging. High up in the front part of the cage nearest the audience was a nest with the head of a sitting mother bird just visible. And in spite of the enormous size of the cage and the small size of the nest and the birds, it did not seem odd or out of proportion at all. You just felt that you yourself had been made very small and put inside a cage with some canaries.

When the parlormaid came forward and pushed a piece of

lettuce into the bars of the cage it could be seen that her big figure had been increased by padding and special boots so that she should look the right size when compared with the cage.

There also seemed to be other devices of specially arranged lights and even of magnifying glass screens that made the tiny bird performers clearly visible to the audience at the longest range of the theater.

Presently a second bird who had been down and out of sight near the water pot hopped upon a perch and stood right in the center of the bar of sunlight. Seen thus from the darkened theater, his bright plumage fairly shimmered with yellow brilliance. This bird

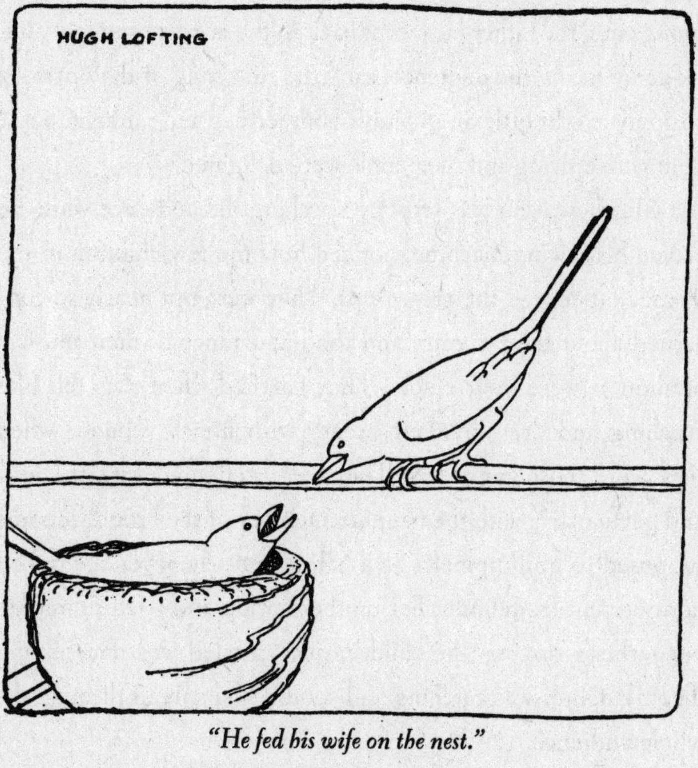

"He fed his wife on the nest."

was taking the part of Pippinella's father, for the first act was to represent the great prima donna's childhood, and these were supposed to be the nest and the cage where she was born.

After a moment the father bird went and took some of the lettuce and, carrying it up to the upper perches, fed his wife on the nest. Then the mother bird got off and the youngsters were fed. The wrens played their parts extremely well. The one who was taking the part of Pippinella as a baby was particularly good. She was the cheeky member of the family and was always reaching up and grabbing the food intended for the others and nearly falling out of the nest half the time.

After the mother bird had settled down again to sitting on her young ones, the father bird went back to the beam of sunlight and, suddenly facing the audience, sang the first song of the opera. It was only a light little air, mainly about lettuce and sunlight, but it went with a swing and the people were delighted.

Matthew, who was secretly watching the audience while he played his sewing machine, noticed how the few children in the theater influenced the grown-ups. They were not nearly so concerned about their dignity and the importance of their musical opinion as were their elders. They laughed when they felt like laughing and drew in their breath with honest wonder when they were most impressed. They were delighted with the nest and particularly with the naughty member of the brood who was supposed to be Pippinella as a baby. And whenever she poked her nose out from under her mother's wing and tried to imitate her father's singing, the children just gurgled with merriment. Their laughter was catching and soon it had spread through the whole audience.

And as he silenced his sewing machine at the end of the first solo, Matthew decided that it looked like a good reception for the opera. For the crowd was already in excellent humor, while none of the best voices had been heard yet, none of the choruses had come on, and the finest scenery and settings were still to be shown.

At the end of the first act, anxious though he was to hear the comments of the audience, the Doctor had to leave his conductor's desk and hurry behind the scenes. There were a hundred and one things in preparation for the next act that he wanted to attend to personally.

"The Doctor left the conductor's desk and hurried behind the scenes."

Here he was soon joined by one of the managers, who had been scouting out front.

"Well," asked the Doctor, "how do they like it?"

"It's hard to say," said the other. "You've got 'em interested. There's no doubt about that. I never saw an audience fidget less or pay better attention. But as for the music, I'm not sure they quite understand it—even the highbrows. I'm not sure I understand it myself. Still, it's going to cause a lot of talk, this, unless I'm a bad guesser. And that's sometimes better than having the audience love you. Anything that promotes discussion and argument gets the public curious and they want to come and hear for themselves. And say, talk about argument! I wish you could step out in front a minute. You never saw so many wrangles going on to the square inch in all your life."

"How did Paganini seem to take it?" asked the Doctor, tying a sailor's hat on a pelican's head.

"He isn't saying much," answered the manager. "But he's thinking awful hard. Sits there wrapped up as always in his usual diabolic calm. But he's interested, too. He'd have left long before this if he hadn't been, you can bet on that. The whole thing will depend on how the critics treat us. So long as we get plenty of space in the papers tomorrow we'll be all right. It's my experience with musical shows that it doesn't matter if the critics say hard things about you so long as they say plenty. Discussion is what we want. And I think we're going to get it."

In the second act Pippinella appeared in person for the first time. The Doctor had especially arranged this in order to save the voice of the prima donna, who was almost continuously on the stage throughout the last three acts. There were several scenes to this act, the curtain being lowered, and the ordinary Regent's Theater orchestra playing, during the intervals between them. The first scene was the inn. Contralto canaries are rare and a voice of Pippinella's quality did not need a musical ear to appreciate it. The first song that the prima donna sang was "Maids, Come Out; the Coach Is Here!" It was a great hit. And when she sang the "Jingling Harness" song, to the accompaniment of the strong man's chain, some people were so carried away that they stood up in their seats at the end of it and called for an encore. The conductor nodded to his orchestra and the song was repeated.

The second scene was with the fusiliers. And in this the jolly marching song—"I'm the midget mascot; I'm a feathered fusilier"—literally brought down the house. The Doctor had arranged to have several of his tent riggers behind the scene tramping to the music. And the audience this time demanded two encores. And even after the second one several people called for more repetitions, until Conductor Dolittle hurried on with the opera, fearing to overtax the leading lady's voice.

Of course, all the incidents in Pippinella's adventurous life could not be crowded into one opera. Yet the main parts were all there: her childhood; her days at the inn; her travels with the soldiers; her underground life in the coal mine (this was a very impressive scene, all dark save a little miner's lamp showing a wooden bird cage on a black wall, with the clinking sound of picks and shovels heard constantly from behind the scenes). Then followed her stay with Aunt Rosie, still another part played by the clever Mrs. Mugg; her restful time at the mill; the storm, beautifully staged, when her cage was blown down; her escape from the cat—for this the Doctor had borrowed the theater cat, who played his part with villainous skill; her meeting with her second husband, the greenfinch, and his heartless desertion of her on the seashore; her flight over the sea and landing on the island.

That brought the opera to the end of the third act. Throughout the whole story it was wonderful to see how John Dolittle contrived to tell Pippinella's life in stage pictures, so that people who did not understand the language of the actors could yet see clearly what was taking place. This he had often said, while writing the libretto with Pippinella, was the proper way to construct a play, whether musical or unmusical—to have the audience able to see what was happening almost without hearing the words. And in *The Canary Opera* he certainly succeeded. The people in the theater—and the children, too—never missed anything of what was going on, even the general meaning of the songs was clear to them without their understanding the tongue in which they were sung.

But without any doubt the part of the opera that both musically and poetically most delighted the audience was the scene on the seashore. It was in this that that wonderful mysterious melody, the "Greenfinch's Love Song," was sung while Pippinella and her husband are hunting for a nesting place. The lights on the stage were dimmed to a pale evening dusk and a little glow of sunset flushed the sky and sea. You could have heard a pin drop in the big crowded theater while the greenfinch warbled and whispered through his trembling serenade, occasionally answered by his mate, Pippinella, from behind the scenes.

The same old lady in the front row got out her handkerchief and began to weep. And when Pippinella, on finding herself deserted by her faithless lover, took wing across the sea to foreign shores, the old lady broke down altogether and sobbed loudly.

"The chorus of pelican sailors"

The scenes aboard the passenger boat, however, with the chorus of boisterous pelican sailors, who came bellowing into the ship's barbershop to be shaved to the tune of "The Razor Strop Duet," cheered the old lady up no end. And her tears of sympathy quickly changed to giggles of amusement at the comic antics of the hoarse-voiced bassos.

As soon as the curtain had come down at the end of the last act the Doctor, ignoring the clapping and applause, hurried behind the scenes again to look after the company. But he had hardly reached the dressing room before one of the managers grabbed him by the arm.

"Half the audience wants to kill you and the other half wants to kiss you," said he breathlessly. "Some say you're a humbug and the others call you a genius. But you'll have to make a speech, anyhow. Listen to them yelling for you. And I've brought a special message from Paganini himself. He wants to be allowed to meet you before the pantomime goes on."

THE NINTH CHAPTER

A Triumph and a Success

THAT STRANGE FIGURE OF GENIUS, PAGANINI, had, at the time John Dolittle first met him, for years enjoyed a worldwide fame that has never quite been equaled. He had done things with a violin that were never done before nor since. The Doctor, as he had said, had always wanted to meet him, ever since he had first heard him play, as a much younger man, in Vienna.

On receiving the message from the manager he called at once for Matthew Mugg, and, giving him a few hasty instructions for the pantomime, he followed his guide out into the front part of the theater.

Niccolo Paganini was a tall, gaunt man, with a thin face surrounded by straggly hair. Many people who saw him said he reminded them of the Devil himself. He was standing up as the Doctor came down the aisle. And when, after shaking hands with a quaint foreign bow, he invited John Dolittle to take the vacant seat beside him, many people in the audience put their heads together, pointing and whispering. The manager, returning behind the scenes, was very pleased to notice this. Because of course the striking figure of the great violinist was known to everyone, and the fact that he had especially sent for the producer of the opera meant that he, in any event, approved of the strange new music that the Doctor had put before the public. This would make a great impression upon the critics.

"This that you have given us is most interesting, sir," said Paganini gravely. "Do you play any instrument yourself?"

"The flute," the Doctor replied. "But only very amateurishly."

"He was standing up as the Doctor came down the aisle."

"Humph! And have you written much music before this?"

"No," said John Dolittle. "And this, you know, is not my own. This has been composed by the birds themselves. I just did the arranging, the orchestration, such as it is—and that under their direction."

"Indeed?" said Paganini. "But how did you find out what sort of arrangement they wanted?"

"Oh—er—I—er—talk bird language," said the Doctor awkwardly. "But I don't, as a rule, speak of that."

"Why?"

"Because people usually laugh at me."

To the Doctor's surprise Paganini showed no sign of doubt or disbelief.

"How absurd of them!" he said quietly, an odd, dreamy light coming into his gleaming eyes. "No one but a fool could listen to your opera without seeing at once that you must have talked with birds and beasts for years to be able so wonderfully to express their ideas in music. What I like about it particularly is that you have not played down to vulgar tastes. And yet it is all so simple, native, natural. You have even included notes in your arias that are so high that the ordinary human ear does not catch them. But my ear is unusual. I could hear them quite distinctly, while most of the audience was asking why the bird kept his mouth still open after the sound had ceased."

"Yes, Pippinella spoke to me of that," said the Doctor. "There is a passage in the 'Jingling Harness Song' and another in the 'Greenfinch's Love Song' where some of the notes go right up beyond the pitch where the human ear can follow."

"You have given us a great treat, sir," said Paganini. "I trust and hope there will be enough really musical folk in London to appreciate what you have done."

By this time the pantomime had begun—to the music of the Regent's ordinary orchestra. And the Doctor, after he had been thanked again by the great musician, made his way back behind the scenes, feeling that he could consider himself repaid for his labors, even if no others understood the work he had put before the world.

As a matter of fact, neither the Doctor nor the theater manager had any idea on that first night what a tremendous sensation they had started. For it was one of those successes that begin more or less gently, but grow and grow as time goes on. In the end *The Canary Opera*, the Doctor's last big achievement as a showman, turned out to be not only the greatest thing in the history of the Dolittle Circus but the outstanding event of the London musical season.

This no one would have suspected at the outset, successful though it was. The Doctor had ordered copies of all the leading London newspapers to be delivered to his wagon on the morning following the first night. In these, the opinions varied a great deal, some spoke well of the opera, others badly. But all devoted a good deal of space to it. One or two of them called it the greatest artistic achievement of the century—"a musical revolution." Some couldn't call it enough hard names.

"The most monstrous piece of humbug" (said one paper) "ever set before an intelligent audience was perpetrated last night at the Regent's Theater, when a menagerie owner by the name of Dolittle placed a collection of squawking birds upon the stage and had them accompanied by an *orchestra* of tin pans, hammers, razor strops, and rattles."

By far the majority of newspapers were too cautious to give a downright opinion before they found out how the musical public was going to take it. These called the opera "strange but interesting," "bizarre," "humorous," "quaint," "novel," and so forth. Paganini's presence and apparent approval of the work had made a big difference to many opinions.

The result of all this criticism—good, bad, and indifferent—was to make the general public extremely curious. Anything which could call forth such different verdicts must be worth looking into. The second night the Regent was more crowded even than the first. Furthermore, in those circles of society where music and the other arts are discussed, *The Canary Opera* was for weeks the main topic of conversation. Signor Paganini was called upon by newspaper reporters and asked to publish an opinion. Well-known composers who flocked to the Regent's in the first week were also asked to write what they thought for the newspapers. They did—and some continued to condemn it as humbug in no undecided terms. But still the discussion went on, and still the theater was packed tighter and tighter every night.

Soon another problem arose, for yet more talk appeared in the press: Who was the mysterious Doctor Dolittle? And could he, as Paganini said he could, really talk with birds in their own tongue? Then the Doctor's empty house in the West End and his circus caravan on Greenheath were stormed all day long by newspaper men, demanding to see him, clamoring to know if this incredible thing could be true.

By no means anxious to be interviewed, sketched, and talked at all day long, the Doctor disguised and hid himself and kept out of the way as best he could. But in this he was not very successful. Then Hercules came to his rescue with an idea. He offered to wear the Doctor's high hat and sit in a chair all through the day with a pillow under his waistcoat, and be sketched and interviewed in his stead.

And that accounts for the many strange portraits of "John Dolittle" that appeared in the London papers about this time—also for many of the extraordinary musical opinions given by him in answer to the questions asked by experts for publication. For, while poor Hercules could wear the Doctor's hat (after padding it to make it fit), he could not wear the Doctor's brain inside it.

"Hercules is interviewed as John Dolittle."

Indeed, so far as music was concerned, the strong man did not know one note from another.

The managers of the Regent's Theater were of course delighted at all this discussion and advertisement. For they knew that if it kept up it would be only a question of time before the general public—as well as the "highbrow" or musical—would want to hear the opera.

And, sure enough, by the end of the first week the demand for tickets was so great that they were already seriously considering taking the opera out of their own theater and leasing a still larger one that could better accommodate the crowds that every night had to be denied admission.

But no one was more pleased with the Doctor's London success than were his own animals. Every evening after the Puddleby Pantomimics had taken their last bow before the curtain, they would gather in the dressing rooms to remove their makeup and chat over the night's performance.

"If," Dab-Dab said a dozen times, "we can only keep the Doctor *this* time from spending all the money he is going to make, everything will be all right. I've no idea what arrangement he made with the theater owners. But whatever it was, he just can't help, with audiences as big as these, making a small fortune at least."

"Yes, but you must remember," said Jip, tugging his Pierrot suit over his head with his front paws, "that whatever the profits are, the rest of the circus staff has got to share them. There's Hercules, Hop the clown, Toby's boss, the Punch-and-Judy man, the Muggses, and the Pinto Brothers. A lot of money doesn't look so big when you've got to split it up among eight."

"I don't care," said Dab-Dab, polishing up the mirror with her

"'But remember,' said Jip, tugging his Pierrot suit over his head."

ballet skirt, which she had just taken off. "Even so, it must be a large amount. Oh, I do hope the Doctor doesn't go off setting up any more homes for aged horses or sick cats and things, and spending all the money that should take us back to Puddleby."

"Good old Puddleby," murmured Jip, slipping his head into his famous gold collar, which was still his everyday walking-out suit. "My, but it will be good to see the old garden again! And the marketplace, and the bridge, and the river!"

"And the house," sighed Dab-Dab. "The poor place must be falling to pieces for want of paint."

"It seems a whole lifetime since we were there," grunted Gub-Gub. "Bother this spirit gum!" How it does stick! I wish Theodosia would find some other way to keep my wig on. Heigh-ho! I suppose the kitchen garden will be all overgrown and the rhubarb beds smothered in weeds."

"Myself," said Swizzle rather sadly, "I don't share you fellows' rejoicing at the idea of going back. It leaves me and Toby out. When the Doctor leaves show business, I don't suppose we'll see him anymore. You can't expect us to be glad he's got rich. It'll be terrible to have him go. He made the circus game into a different life for us. Hop, my man, is a decent fellow in a way. So is old Crockett, Toby's boss. But the world won't seem the same for us after John Dolittle has gone."

"Humph!" said Jip. "I hadn't thought of that before. Well, cheer up! Maybe we can arrange something. The Doctor has got a whole bunch of dogs now, with Grab and Blackie. Perhaps if Hop and Crockett get rich over this, they'll let you fellows come with us and the Doctor to Puddleby. It would be a shame to break up the family."

The Tenth Chapter

Animal Advertising

THE SUCCESS AT THE THEATER IN THE WEST End affected the business of the circus also. The newspapers in their frequent references to the opera, in their almost daily reports of the notable people who were among the audience last night, spoke of a peculiar and novel kind of circus that this extraordinary man was also running outside the city. And before long, as had happened in other towns, crowds of society folk who ordinarily never went to circuses at all were flocking out to Greenheath. Many important people who had the welfare of animals at heart did a lot of private advertising for the Doctor by talking about the happy condition of his performers, and quite a number of entire schools were taken out there and given peppermints and tea and a perfectly wonderful time by the Doctor, Matthew and Theodosia, and the animal hosts and hostesses.

Early in the second week another matter came up, something which had never before arisen out of the Doctor's other

"Society folk came flocking out to Greenheath."

successes. This was the subject of animal advertising. The papers and the public were still very much exercised over the question of whether John Dolittle (or the Wizard of Puddleby, as some journalists called him) could or could not communicate with birds and beasts in their own language. That he could do all manner of new things, such as making bird choirs sing in unison, had been proved beyond doubt. Also, there was no question about his having a very mysterious power for getting these animals to perform their strange feats without training, happily and naturally. But whether he could really talk with them was still much debated.

Throughout all this argument and publicity the Doctor maintained the same modesty that he had always done. He refused to discuss the subject. His work with the animals, he said, was all accomplished by the animals themselves, of their own free will. And whether in that work he actually talked with them or not, people must decide themselves from the results.

Well, it began by his receiving quite a number of letters from business firms, asking if he would lend his animals for advertising. The work would be very well paid, the letters said. One manufacturer of birdcages wrote that he would pay twenty guineas a day to have Coloratura Pippinella, the famous contralto canary, demonstrate in his shop window in Jermyn Street the superior virtues of his birdcages. She would be wanted for only three hours a day—in other words, the prima donna's time would be paid for at the rate of £7 an hour. All she would be required to do while on duty would be to hop in and out of the cages in the window, to show that even while she was free, she preferred this manufacturer's cages to freedom because they were so comfortable and so excellently made.

Then there was another letter that came to the Doctor from a sausage manufacturer. This gentleman offered a similarly large salary to have Gub-Gub do his Pantaloon antics in another shop window. All the pig would be asked to do was to go through his skipping dance out of *The Puddleby Pantomime*, using a string of the firm's well known Cambridgeshire pork sausages as a skipping rope.

Still another letter, intended to interest the Doctor in animal advertising, contained a request for the Pushmi-Pullyu. This was from a large restaurant that wanted to employ the two-headed animal as a sandwich man. He would only be required, the letter said, to walk through a few of the main streets near the restaurant with signboards draped over his back reading: "Whether You're Coming or Going, Take Your Meals at Merriman's Chophouse. Table d'Hôte Luncheon, One Shilling and Sixpence."

"Good gracious!" cried the Doctor, after he had read a few of these letters aloud to Matthew Mugg. "What do these people think we are, I'd like to know? I never heard of anything so vulgar or inconsiderate of animals."

"Well," said the Cat's-Meat-Man, rubbing his chin thoughtfully, "I'm not so sure, Doctor."

"'I'm not sure, Doctor,' said the Cat's-Meat-Man."

"Not sure of what, Matthew?" asked John Dolittle indignantly.

"I ain't so sure you ought to set your face against the idea flat," said Matthew. "Listen, there's this to be said: Suppose this feller's birdcages *are* better than anybody else's; there's no harm in Pippinella's advertising the fact, is there? It seems to me that if, instead of snubbing these firms outright, you was to offer to do *your* kind of animal advertising, a lot of good could be done *and* a lot of money made."

"I don't quite follow you, Matthew," said the Doctor. "The whole idea is very distasteful to me, and I'm sure it would be to my animals. What do you mean, my kind of advertising?"

"Any kind of advertising that would make people think and act more considerate to animals," said the Cat's-Meat-Man, rising from his chair in enthusiastic eloquence. "All your life you've been trying to make folks more thoughtful of the hanimal kingdom, 'aven't you? Very well, then, 'ere's your chance. Write to all these here blokes and say, *not* 'Dear Sir: I think you're a low-down hound,' but say 'Dear Sir: I and my animals will be interested in any kind of advertising what spreads the doctrine of the humanitarian treatment of dumb creatures.'"

"Not *dumb*, Matthew," the Doctor put in. "I've never met a creature yet that was dumb. But I know what you mean. Excuse the interruption. Go on."

"Then," the Cat's-Meat-Man continued, "if they come forward with any scheme that will advertise what *you* want as well as what *they* want, why not go into it?"

"But how about the animals themselves?" asked John Dolittle. "I don't imagine the idea will appeal to them at all."

"Not to old Push," said Matthew. "I reckon he'd die of hembarrassment as a sandwich man. But the others, so long as the work improved conditions for their fellow critters, why, they'd be no end pleased. Take this offer from the cage makers, for instance: Pippinella wouldn't mind that, I'm sure. And if the cages this man makes are not the kind you approve of, tell him to make the kind you *do* approve of, and that then you'll advertise them for him. See what I mean?"

"Humph!" said the Doctor when the Cat's-Meat-Man finally ended his lecture on the virtues of honest advertisement. "I suppose there may be something in what you say, Matthew. But I fear the opportunities for popularizing the right kind of goods will not be as frequent as those for the wrong."

"Oh, I don't know," said Matthew. "This end of the business ain't hardly begun yet. You haven't even gone through all the letters you got this morning. Didn't you say there was one from the cattle committee of the agricultural show?"

"Hum—er—yes, I believe there was," said John Dolittle, turning to a pile at his elbow. Out of this, after some rummaging, he took a long, important-looking blue envelope and read the letter it contained to Matthew.

"There you are," said the Cat's-Meat-Man when the Doctor had finished. "What could you have better than that? A general hinvitation to cohoperate with the Royal Hagricultural Society for the himprovement of farm animals. Asking you to send in any ideas for the show—for novel exhibits—what occur to you. I calls that a pretty big honor, myself. The Royal Hagricultural Society is no small potatoes. The biggest of its kind in the country. The queen 'erself is one of the patrons. You see, you're getting a big name now as an animal expert. Well, there's your chance."

"By Jove, Matthew!" said the Doctor, rising, "I believe you're right. Do you remember those drinking cups for cattle that I invented once?"

"You bet I do!" said the Cat's-Meat-Man. "The Dolittle Sanitary Drinking Cups for Cattle—they was designed to prevent the spread of hoof-and-mouth disease. But you could never get the farmers interested in 'em. The what-was-good-enough-for-Father brigade wouldn't let you put 'em on the market. Well, there's something, you see. If you bring them cups forward under the patronage of the Society and gets 'em demonstrated at the hagricultural show, you'll find the farmers will treat your ideas very different."

While the Doctor was still thinking over Matthew's words, a knock sounded on the door of the room. (This was at the big house in the West End.) And in answer to his "Come in!" Theodosia entered leading a small, thick man whose face seemed vaguely familiar to John Dolittle.

"This man wants to see you, Doctor," said Mrs. Mugg.

"My name's Brown," said the visitor. "Last time I saw you you had me run out of the circus because you didn't approve of the medicines I was selling."

"Oh—ah—yes," said John Dolittle. "Now I remember. Well, it wasn't my fault you were turned out. It was your own. The people wouldn't listen to you as soon as they knew you were selling quack concoctions. What have you come back for?"

"That's the point, Doctor," said the other. "I don't bear no

"Theodosia entered leading a small, thick man."

ill feelings for what you did—though I was pretty mad about it at the time. I admit the stuff I sold wasn't much good, but it was harmless anyway. Now I've come back with some good stuff. I have here" (the little man took a bottle with a printed label on it from his pocket) "a real good horse lotion, an embrocation. And I ain't going to ask you to take my word that it's good. I'm going to leave it with you so you can test it and try it out. And maybe if you approve of it, you'll help me sell it. I've had a hard time making ends meet since you downed me on the platform that evening.

Just the same, I have faith in this lotion, and I'd like to get your opinion on it."

"Well," said the Doctor in a kindly tone, "you have perseverance anyway. I will certainly have your embrocation analyzed and if I think it contributes anything to animal medicine, I will do my best to help you make it known."

The Eleventh Chapter

Gub-Gub's Eating Palace

THE OFFICIAL LIVING QUARTERS OF THE Doctor's animal household had by this time also been moved to the big empty house in the West End. This was done so that the cast of *The Puddleby Pantomime* would be nearer to the theater. They still, however, spend part of almost every day at the circus. And very grand they felt, traveling back and forth between their city residences and Greenheath, now that John Dolittle could afford to take them in a cab.

The great big five-story house had given them a lot of fun, exploring it from cellar to attic when they first went to live there. Dab-Dab told the Doctor right away that the opera birds living in the kitchen must be kept somewhere else if *she* was to do the housekeeping. Some pots and pans had to be bought, too, and a few pieces of furniture.

One of the features of the new house that caught Gub-Gub's immediate attention was a dumbwaiter, a small elevator intended for carrying the food from the kitchen in the basement to the dining room and the other floors above. He was so fascinated by it that Dab-Dab could scarcely make him stop playing with it for a moment.

"Why, with this thing," said he, just as they were about to sit down to supper the first evening they were there, "I could invent a wonderful new game. Look, it runs up to all the floors of the house. D'you know what the new game would be?"

"Hunt-the-onion!" suggested Jip, "or some kind of indoor food sport, I'll bet."

"No, listen," said Gub-Gub. "This is a great idea—one of my best. I would build a palace, an Eating Palace. It would have a

"Gub-Gub and the dumbwaiter"

great number of floors, and one of these little food elevators running from the bottom of the house to the top. All the floors above would be dining rooms, but they'd all be different. There would be the Ice Cream Nursery, in the attic. Of course, I'd have to have a good food architect to design the house. Then would come the Pastry Parlor, on, say, the fifth floor. Below that I'd have the Soup Saloon—so the ice creamers above couldn't hear the soup drinkers below. In the Soup Saloon at least a dozen different kinds of soups would be set out on the wide table all day long. On the third floor there would be the Stew Studio—Irish stew, goulashes, curries, etc. Next would come—"

"Oh, stop!" Dab-Dab interrupted. "We know the rest of your silly game: after you had put a different kind of restaurant on each floor, then you'd get into the dumbwaiter and ride up and down, giving yourself a new stomachache at every floor where you stopped. Come and sit down at the table, for pity's sake! You're keeping the supper back."

"Good ideas are thrown away on some people," said Gub-Gub, seating himself sadly before a plate of porridge. "Just the same, that would a house worth calling a home."

"But where would you sleep, Gub-Gub," asked the Doctor, "if all your floors were dining rooms?"

"In the dumbwaiter, of course," said Gub-Gub, "so as to be ready for breakfast. But you wouldn't have to sleep very much, because by the time you had stopped at all the floors coming down you'd be hungry again, and you'd go back and begin all over from the top."

The pig's delight with this new contrivance and the great possibilities it suggested for the art of eating, occupied all his spare time in the new home. He was forever giving himself free rides up and down the dumbwaiter, deciding where he would have the tomato cupboard and the apple closet and a hundred other new additions to his imaginary Eating Palace. Till one day he got stuck halfway between two floors and missed lunch. Because, although Dab-Dab knew where he was and plainly heard his cries for help, she refused to go to his assistance until after the meal was over, in order to teach him a lesson.

THE TWELFTH CHAPTER

The Animals' Treat

THESE, AS YOU CAN WELL IMAGINE, WERE very thrilling times for the Doctor's household—accustomed though it was to a busy life. Something new seemed to happen every day. And then London at the Christmas holiday season seemed so happy and bustling; just to go through the busy, crowded streets was in itself quite an event for anyone unused to big cities.

The animals, as I have already mentioned, had frequently pestered John Dolittle to take them to one of the many shows that were going on in town. This he fully intended to do, but had not yet managed it on account of work and also because, of course, most theaters would not allow animals (especially a pig and a duck) in their ordinary seats as audience. But one day, early in the third week of the opera's run, the Doctor for the first time felt that he could afford to give himself a little rest and recreation. So, remembering that he had promised to take his family to a show, he spoke to Matthew about the possibility of getting seats. The willing Mr. Mugg, always on the lookout for anything that would get into the papers and be good advertisement for the circus or the opera, saw a great chance here—though he did not speak of it to the Doctor at the time. All he said was: "Right you are, Doc. I'll get you seats. What show do the animals want to see?"

"Gub-Gub," said the Doctor, "wants to go to *Dick Whittington*, the pantomime at the Frivolity Theater. But the dogs want to see the vaudeville show at the Westminster Music Hall. There are several trained animal acts on the program there. And Jip and Swizzle and Toby are professionally interested. I think we'd better take them to the music hall—that is, of course, if the management will admit them."

The Doctor had been long accustomed to go through the streets with his strange animal family following at his heels—though of late, since he had money, he had more frequently taken them by cab for convenience. But he had his doubts about Matthew's getting any theater to consent to his taking them in.

However, the Cat's-Meat-Man did not go to the ordinary booking office to buy his tickets. He put on his best suit of clothes, had a shave, and went to call on the proprietor of the Westminster Music Hall. To him he introduced himself in a very lordly manner as John Dolittle's partner. He said that the great composer and impresario was desirous of buying a box for next Wednesday's matinee performance. His party would consist of none other than the original cast of the far-famed *Puddleby Pantomime*, now playing at the Regent's with *The Canary Opera*. This party would be made up of three dogs, a pig, a duck, an owl, and a white mouse. The appearance of this distinguished theatrical company in the audience would, Matthew reminded the proprietor, be excellent advertisement for the Westminster—particularly since the great

John Dolittle, of whom all London was talking, would himself be present. And as the party would occupy a box to themselves, the rest of the audience could not possibly object.

The proprietor of the Westminster saw at once that this would indeed be a good thing for his theater. And not only did he consent to let Matthew have the box, but he gave it to him for the Doctor free of charge with the compliments of the management. Then the Cat's-Meat-Man, feeling surer than ever that he was born to be a great showman, proceeded (still in his best suit and manner) to call at most of the newspaper offices in London. There

"The Cat's-Meat-Man went to call on the proprietor of the Westminster Music Hall."

he informed the editors that John Dolittle was taking his company to the Westminster next Wednesday and they must be sure to have a reporter present to write it up for the papers and to make sketches of the famous animals seeing the show.

Great was the rejoicing among the Puddleby Pantomimics when they learned that their seats had been secured and they were really going to have the theater party for which they had been asking so long. Although he had selected *Dick Whittington*, Gub-Gub was just as well pleased when the Doctor explained to him that the Westminster's was a variety show—that is, several different acts—animal acts among them. His enthusiasm was not even dampened when Theodosia insisted on washing his face for him (a performance he usually made a terrible fuss about) before he started.

The party was taken there in a cab. At the doors of the theater several newspaper reporters (whom Matthew had arranged for) attempted to interview the Doctor. He objected to this, saying that he was out for a day's holiday. But Matthew persuaded him to stop and say a word to them before he went in.

The ushers, who had been warned, of course, by the manager that this extraordinary theater party was expected, conducted them to their box with all gravity and politeness. On the way there the Doctor remembered that he had meant to bring chocolates for his family, and he was about to send Matthew out to get some, as he felt that no theater party could be considered complete without chocolates. But on entering the box he found that the proprietor had, with rare hospitality, thought of their comfort even in this. On every chair there was an edible souvenir for each of the members of the party. There was a bunch of carrots for Gub-Gub, a piece of cheese for the white mouse, a sardine for Dab-Dab, a small meat pie for

Too-Too, a box of chocolates for the Doctor and Matthew, and a lamb cutlet for each of the three dogs.

"Very thoughtful!" said the Doctor, biting into a caramel. "Very thoughtful. My! Just look at the audience! The house is quite full."

The animals gazed down over the sea of heads below and around them with a thrill of anticipation. But very soon they noticed that they themselves were the center of considerable attention. In all parts of the house people were whispering and pointing in their direction.

"Dear me! I've been recognized," said Gub-Gub. "Do you think I ought to get up and bow, Doctor?"

"'Dear me, I've been recognized!' said Gub-Gub."

"No," said John Dolittle. "It isn't necessary. And look, the show is just going to begin."

The first act was a comic tramp with three dogs. This interested Jip, Toby, and Swizzle to no end. They kept whispering to one another what they thought of the act and at one point in the middle of a ticklish balancing feat, they got so excited that they started barking down directions to the dogs upon the stage. This caused a still greater sensation, because the performing dogs, hearing them bark, looked up and, recognizing John Dolittle, they let their performance go to pieces and started jumping out into the audience to reach the box and greet the Doctor's party. Order was restored after a little, however, and the dogs were caught and taken back to their owner on the stage.

Between the second and the third turn on the program, Dab-Dab said to Gub-Gub: "What are you keeping so still for, with that silly smile on your face all the time?"

"Sh!" said Gub-Gub. "One of the newspapermen is making a sketch of me. He's down in the second row. I want to look my best."

"He's not sketching you," said Jip. "He's making a picture of the Doctor."

At that moment a knock sounded on the door of the box and the proprietor himself appeared to pay his compliments.

"It would be nice," he said, after chatting a moment or two, "if at the end of the next act, when the intermission comes, you and your party would go out for a walk in the promenade. There have been many requests from the audience to get a closer view of you and your company—that is, of course, if you have no objection."

"I shall be very pleased," said Gub-Gub in his grandest manner.

PART THREE

The First Chapter

The Princess's Dinner Party

WHEN, DURING THE INTERMISSION, they appeared in that part of the Westminster Music Hall that was called the promenade, the Doctor's party caused quite a sensation. It was a wide space this, behind the seats on the ground floor, where little tables were set for people to sit and take refreshments. Also, for those of the audience who were tired of sitting down, there was room to stretch the legs and walk about.

As the pig with the dogs and the duck (Too-Too and the white mouse stayed on the Doctor's shoulder to avoid the crush) walked back and forth, they were followed by a train of children who giggled and tittered with delight; while the grown-ups fell back on either side and made a lane for them to walk in, like a street crowd at a royal wedding. Whispers ran in all directions.

"That's John Dolittle himself in the high hat—t'other one, the cross-eyed feller, is his assistant. They say the Doctor talks every animal language there is," said a thick fat man to his wife.

"I don't believe it," answered the woman. "But he's got a kind face."

"It's true, Mother," said a small boy (also very round and fat) who was holding the woman's hand. "I have a friend at school who was taken to see the Puddleby Pantomime. He said it was the most wonderful show he ever saw. The pig is simply marvelous; the duck dances in a ballet skirt; and that dog—the middle one, right behind the Doctor now—he takes the part of a Pierrot."

"Yes, Willie, but all that doesn't say the man can talk to 'em in their own language," said the woman. "Wonderful things can be done by a good trainer."

"But my friend *saw* him doing it," said the boy. "In the middle of the show the pig's wig began to slip off and the Doctor called to him out of the wings, something in pig language. Because as soon as he heard it, the pig put up his front foot and fixed his wig tight."

Gub-Gub of course put on more airs of greatness than ever here, where all the children—many of whom had seen him performing at his own theater—pointed him out as the great comedian, the first animal actor to interpret the historic part of Pantaloon. Before the bell rang to show that the intermission was over, a schoolgirl had come up and asked the Doctor to sign her autograph album; and numerous other people had interrupted his promenade with congratulations, interviews, and whatnot.

Among these was the man who had written him about advertising the birdcages with Pippinella. He was delighted, he said, at this opportunity of meeting the naturalist-composer in person. He had heard *The Canary Opera* four times already and was going again the day after tomorrow to take an aunt of his who was coming to visit him from the country. Before leaving, he asked had the Doctor decided yet whether he would allow the canary prima donna to advertise for him. John Dolittle said he would first have to consult Pippinella and would let him know in the course of a day or two.

Then another, who seemed to have been half listening to this conversation, came up and introduced himself (with a strong French accent) as M. Jules Poulain, of Paris. He was a manufacturer of perfumes, he said. He had been reading a great deal about Doctor Dolittle of late and also about his now quite famous dog Jip. The stories told in the newspapers (provided for reporters by Matthew, of course) of Jip's marvelous skill in smells, had led M. Poulain to believe that the dog could possibly add a great deal of useful information to the art and science of perfume manufacture. Would the Doctor be willing to let the firm consult him as an expert, and himself act as interpreter for the interview?

Now that the Doctor's household had become theatrical folk, many changes became necessary in the routine of their daily habits. In the old days, when they were only part of a circus, their duties were over regularly by eight o'clock every evening, and the Doctor had always insisted on their being in bed by nine. But now that their work did not end before eleven o'clock at night, early bed was out of the question and late supper had to be instituted. This was something they all greatly enjoyed, when after the show was done they returned to the big city house and Dab-Dab prepared omelettes and salad and cocoa, over which they chatted and made merry.

Another change that, besides the late extra meal, greatly appealed to Gub-Gub was the late hour for getting up in the morning. He had appropriated the dumbwaiter as his bedroom and had it lined with straw cushions. Here the great comedian snored peacefully up to ten or eleven in the morning, at which hour Dab-Dab, preparing breakfast for the company, usually threw a saucepan lid into the dumbwaiter to wake him up.

Often the hour of retiring was made still later by invitations to supper after the show was over. On one occasion they were all asked to a terribly elegant town house owned by a beautiful Russian princess who delighted in giving unusual parties of any kind. The idea of having the Puddleby Pantomimics, with the far-famed Contralto Canary, as guests appealed to her immensely. Feeling that probably the princess wanted his company only as something to be laughed at, the Doctor had made up his mind to refuse the invitation. But before he had time to send an answer, it was repeated—this time by word of mouth. And, as the messenger who brought it was none other than the great Paganini himself (who had suggested the idea to the princess in all seriousness), the Doctor was very glad to accept on behalf of his company and himself.

Pippinella and Twink were included in the invitation, and the princess sent a private coach with two footmen to fetch them. The supper was a most gorgeous and splendid affair. All the prominent people in town were there—famous continental opera stars, great composers, writers, painters, sculptors, as well as ambassadors, dukes, earls, and a large gathering of lesser nobility.

In spite of this notable assembly, the Puddleby Pantomimics were clearly the guests of honor. Everybody was astonished at the wonderful table manners of the animals and how well they conducted themselves in society. To be sure, one or two little accidents occurred, but nothing of serious importance. For instance, when they first arrived in the gorgeously furnished mansion, Jip opened the evening by chasing the princess's white Angora cat up the chimney—from which she had to be rescued and had to be taken away to be washed. Then during dinner Gub-Gub (he was seated between a marchioness and the conductor of the symphony orchestra) caused a little sensation when a footman brought around the celery. Instead of taking one stick of celery, Gub-Gub emptied the dish, thinking its entire contents were intended for him. He also somewhat astonished the guests at the dessert by putting his apples and oranges whole into his mouth, instead of peeling them or cutting them.

But otherwise the evening went off extremely well. And after the meal was over, Pippinella and Twink delighted the company by singing a duet out of the third act of their opera, accompanied by the Doctor on the sewing machine.

THE SECOND CHAPTER

Jip and the Perfume Manufacturer

AS MATTHEW HAD PROPHESIED, IT TURNED out that the animals were not only willing to help, but quite keen about the idea when the subject of advertising was put before them.

This John Dolittle did at their after-the-show supper on the same day that he took them to the matinee.

"Why, Doctor," cried the white mouse, "of course the Cat's-Meat-Man is right! You could do no end of good with the proper kind of advertising. And it would be lots of fun for us. Just think of Gub-Gub waltzing with a skipping rope in a pork butcher's window!"

"I will *not* advertise sausages for anybody," said Gub-Gub firmly. "I don't mind working for a skipping rope manufacturer—dancing in a toy shop or something like that. But sausages? Certainly not!"

"No, I think you're quite right," said John Dolittle.

"But just look at all the other things you could advertise, Doctor," said Jip, "things specially for animals. There's that mange cure you experimented with on me. Remember?—when you were working out a special winter-coat thickener for the Eskimo dogs who wrote to you—that was wonderful stuff. My coat grew so fast for two months afterward, though it was stiflingly hot in that African climate."

"And how about the famous Dolittle Canary Cough Mixture?" said Twink. "Every old animal shop has a song restorer of its own brand, but none as good as yours. Why not give the birds the best?"

"Then there's your system of exercises for flat-footed ducklings," Dab-Dab put in. "If you got every mother duck to raise her children on your system, you would do no end of good to the whole race."

"And your hair restorer for mice," squeaked the white mouse, "that you used on me when I got dyed blue by that stupid old rat. That was a tremendously important invention."

"It seems to me," said Swizzle, "that if the Doctor wrote a book on animal surgery and medicine and got it popular with some of those fool vets, a great deal of good would be done. No one realizes except the animals that have been cured by him, what wonderful things John Dolittle has added to the science of doctoring."

Well, the discussion went on lively and late over the supper table, all the animals making suggestions to the Doctor on how he could advertise and make known to the world the marvelous inventions and discoveries that he had made in the course of his long and unusual experience with the animal kingdom.

The result of it was that before the Doctor packed his family off to bed (about two in the morning), he was made to promise that he would enter the field of advertising and let them help.

"All right," said the Doctor, as he took down a candle from the mantelpiece and lit it. "I shall be answering some of the letters from these firms in the morning. And I will see what can be done. In any event, it would do no harm to talk it over with them. If they won't agree to advertise in the way I want them to, we can always drop it. To begin with, I think, Jip, I'll see that French perfume manufacturer from Paris. I fancy that your skill in smelling might really add quite a bit to science when investigated by technical folk such as M. Poulain and his staff."

The next day the Doctor went with Jip to see M. Poulain of Paris. That well-known manufacturer of perfumes had lately set up in London a branch with experts and workmen brought over from France.

He was delighted when the Doctor appeared with his dog. He had begun to fear that John Dolittle had decided not to act upon the suggestion he had made, nor even to answer his letter. In spite of the visitor's shabby appearance, the Frenchman treated him with great courtesy and at once led the way into an inner office. There, after a little polite conversation, he sent for various chemists and foremen and managers.

When these arrived, about five in all, M. Poulain closed the door and addressed the meeting in French, for all his firm were of that nationality, and he had discovered that the Doctor spoke this language with considerable ease.

"Gentlemen," he said, "I take great pleasure in introducing to you Doctor John Dolittle, the eminent scientist. He is the first person in history who has successfully got in touch with the animal kingdom. And though many people have cast doubts upon his being able to talk the language of beasts, I for one believe he can. And *if* he can, certainly much will be added to science by his discoveries. He has with him, as you see, a dog. Our business, gentlemen, is the business of scents, of smells. But no man can smell as well as a dog can. Besides, this particular dog is no ordinary one. The gold collar that you see him wearing was presented to him for saving a life at sea, which he accomplished solely by his sense of smell. That is correct, Doctor, is it not?"

"Yes," the Doctor replied (also in French). "I did not know that the story had been made public. Jip does not like to boast of it. I suppose my assistant, Mr. Mugg, must have given it to the papers. But since it is known, it cannot be denied. Yes, it is true."

"Very good," said M. Poulain. "So I think, gentlemen, we can consider ourselves very fortunate in being able to consult this remarkable dog—through the Doctor's interpretation—on the science of scents. And I propose that you now put any questions to him you wish."

Thereupon a sample of perfume was brought forward for the criticism of Jip, the great expert in smells. His first opinion (which was of course translated by the Doctor from dog language into French) somewhat surprised M. Poulain and his staff.

"Why," said Jip, sniffing at a bottle of the firm's very choicest and most expensive perfume, "this smells of cheese!"

"Of *cheese*!" cried the chief chemist, springing forward and smelling the bottle himself. "There must be some mistake. No, I don't smell cheese there—only jasmine and honeysuckle. It is a blend we are very proud of."

"I can't help that," said Jip. "I smell the flowers you speak of, of course. But I also detect the aroma of cheese—Camembert, at that."

There was great consternation among the experts seated around the board.

"This is terrible," said M. Poulain, wringing his hands. "Just to think that our famous *Reverie d'Amour* should be confused with cheese! I cannot smell it myself, but if the dog can detect the odor, maybe there are others—customers—who can. M. Dalbert, who is the last workman who would have touched this bottle?"

"The man who put the label on," said M. Dalbert, the manager.

"Then send for the chief labeler immediately," said M. Poulain. "And if he or any of his men is in the habit of eating cheese, we must change his diet at once. Never, *never* shall it be said that our exquisite *Reverie d'Amour* reminded anyone—even distantly—of Camembert!"

Then the manager, M. Dalbert, hurriedly left the council room and presently reappeared with a weedy-looking little Frenchman who seemed to be scared to death at this sudden summons before the heads of the firm. He was the foreman of the labelers.

"Do you eat cheese?" thundered M. Poulain, leveling a finger at him. "Answer me!"

With tears in his eyes the little man confessed that he was accustomed to take cheese sandwiches for lunch (Camembert cheese), which his wife put up for him in the morning to bring to the factory. But he had always been most careful not to let his lunch get mixed up with the scents. Indeed, he kept his sandwiches in another room, far removed from the bottling and labeling rooms.

"It does not matter," said M. Poulain severely. "It has got into the perfume—or the labels—somehow. You must not bring it to my factory. If you must eat cheese, do so when you are on holiday."

So, on the little man's promising solemnly that he would only indulge in Camembert when he was taking his vacation by the seaside, he was dismissed from the council.

Some of the men who had been brought in to question Jip

had been inclined at the outset to ridicule the whole performance. Either they did not believe that a mere dog could teach them anything about their business, or they doubted, like most of the public, that the Doctor really was able to understand and translate animal ideas. But after this remarkable detection of the guilty, cheese-eating labeler, they began to feel that there was something in this of scientific value. Thereupon the consultation of the great expert proceeded in all seriousness, and samples of toilet waters, sachet powders, and scented soaps were brought forward for him to test.

But it seemed as though a dog's nose was entirely too subtle, too refined, for a human scent factory. With almost every product put before him (excepting only one or two where the chemical smell was very powerful), Jip's opinion was most unflattering. For he kept detecting some entirely different odor that had been allowed to creep into the prescription.

"I don't think anything of that hair oil," he said, pushing a bottle aside. "You can smell lard in it a mile off. And as for this soap, the man who made it wore a homespun suit. I can distinctly smell the odor of homespun wool. And the fat used was very rank."

"Try this," said M. Poulain, pushing forward a dainty satin box of face powder. "We always thought this delicious."

"Tobacco," said Jip after one sniff. "It just reeks of tobacco—French cigarettes."

M. Poulain was in despair.

"Well, tell me," he said after a moment, "what is your own favorite perfume?"

"Roast beef," said Jip. "Why don't you have a roast beef perfume?"

"Oh, la la!" cried the Frenchman, throwing up his hands. "But the ladies do not wish to smell of roast beef!"

"I don't see why not," said Jip. "It's a good, healthy smell."

But finally, after Jip had thrown the whole firm into deep gloom by his uncomplimentary remarks about their wares, the Doctor himself turned the proceedings of the meeting in a more profitable direction by remarking, "It seems to me, gentlemen, that we would derive more benefit from this dog's skill if we allowed him to deliver a lecture on scents in general or if you consulted him on where, in his own experience, the most delicate and delightful perfumes are to be found."

"You're right," cried M. Poulain, springing to his feet. "Subtlety is what we want in our perfumes, delicacy, finesse, refinement. And that the dog has, heaven knows. But *roast beef*, his own favorite perfume!—Oh, la la!"

"That," said the Doctor, "is only a question of taste. A dog's taste in smells is naturally different from yours. But if I try to explain to him the kind of thing you and your public like, I think he will be able to help you."

Upon that, after the Doctor had done a little explaining to Jip, the great expert got up at the head of the table and delivered a lecture on the general subject of smells. That morning was written down in Theodosia's diary of the Dolittle Circus as the first time in history that a dog ever delivered a lecture (even with an interpreter) to a human audience.

It was a great success and was listened to by M. Poulain and his staff (in spite of Jip's former unflattering remarks about their skill) with great attention. The first part of it was devoted to what Jip called "the isolation of smells." For over half an hour the lecturer dwelt on the great difficulty of separating a single smell absolutely by itself—so that you got it quite pure. This, he said, was what was wrong with most of the wares of the firm of Poulain & Co. It was also what was wrong with most humans as good smellers. When a person went down to the seashore, he told them, he would sniff long and loud and say, "How delicious is the smell of the sea!" and let it go at that. While all the time he wasn't smelling the sea *alone* at all. He was smelling a dozen different scents that often come together and that he had grown to call "the salt smell of the sea." The dog professor then gave many learned example of what he called "group smells"—that is, combinations of different odors frequently encountered in daily life. Until a person had learned to analyze these, to break them up into their different single scents, he could never hope to be a good smeller.

The latter part of his lecture was given over to describing where his audience could find certain subtle scents, which, from what the Doctor told him, he supposed would be the kind of thing they were seeking for the perfume market. Many of these were very curious and surprised his hearers not a little. For instance, he told them that down at the bottom of old holes made by a certain kind of field mouse they would find a bed of leaves that were always gathered in the same way and according to the same mixture. These leaves, many of which were aromatic, formed a potpourri more delicate than any he had ever smelled in the finest flower garden. He told them also of a certain swamp bird, a relative of the heron family, that lined its nest with other birds' feathers and with special kinds of moss. This, too, provided a wonderfully delicate faint bouquet that, in his opinion (and in that particular department of smells), had no equal. Much more he told them—of roots that he had come across, when delving after rats and rabbits, that had wonderful fragrance when bitten or bruised.

All of Jip's information was taken down, when the Doctor had translated it, by M. Poulain's secretary. And that same week the Paris perfumer hired botanists and naturalists to go out in pursuit of the ingredients that the famous expert had described. The result was that a few months later several new perfumes and powders were put on the market whose delicate fragrance wafted the fame of Poulain, of Paris, to every corner of the earth where refined noses were to be found.

The Third Chapter

The Ways of Advertisement

THE DOCTOR, IN HIS USUAL UNBUSINESSLIKE way, had made no money arrangements with M. Poulain for Jip's services as an expert in smells. Nevertheless, the Frenchman behaved very handsomely. And a check for a considerable sum of money arrived by mail not long after the interview I have just described.

"Humph!" said the Doctor, taking it out of the envelope and noting the amount. "Well, this money should belong to you, Jip, by rights. *I* certainly did not earn it."

"Oh, what would I do with money, Doctor?" said Jip, poking his nose out of the window to sniff for rats in the backyard. "You keep it. You're always in need of money. And besides, don't I owe you a whole lot for the good home you've given me all these years?"

"There you go, Doctor," said Dab-Dab, in a flutter. "Always, when money comes in, you want to disclaim owning it. I never saw anyone like you."

"But Dab-Dab," said the Doctor, "we're making so much

from the opera now. It isn't as though I were poor anymore. Last week I paid off every single debt the circus owed. And still my bank account shows a bigger balance than I ever had in my life."

"No bank balance is too big for you to spend," said Dab-Dab. "My only worry now is to get you back to Puddleby before you're penniless again."

"Just the same," said the Doctor, fingering the check, "I feel I ought to put this money in the bank in Jip's name. Who knows? The day may come when he will need money. Suppose anything should happen to me . . . I wonder if a bank would accept a savings account in a dog's name. A very interesting point. I must look into that."

Jip's performance with Poulain & Co. led a few days later to another offer from a firm of dog-collar makers that had a small but smart shop in St. James Street. This was a company who specialized in all sorts of things for pets. Here society women came to buy silk sweaters for their Pomeranians, porcelain drinking bowls for lap dogs, and expensively upholstered sleeping baskets for prize Persian cats. It was a prosperous, well-to-do house. And in the letter they wrote the Doctor they said that as for the way in which the advertising was done, they would gladly leave that entirely to him and his animals.

Jip when he was told about it was not very enthusiastic.

"I know that kind of shop," he said. "They sell all sorts of absurd, faddy things for overfed pugs: satin-ribbon collars; rubber pacifiers for puppies, shaped like bones; and all sorts of other rubbish. I'd sooner not have anything to do with a shop like that. Why should these pampered pets of society dames have silk sweaters around their silly, fat stomachs, when there are hundreds of good dogs—real dogs, even if they are called mongrels—slinking round the East End of London trying to pick up a square meal?"

The Doctor agreed with Jip and the matter was dropped. But Dab-Dab, who had overheard the conversation, took Jip aside later and explained to him that if money could be made for the Doctor in this way it would be a good thing.

"Because listen, Jip," she said, "the more money we have, the surer—and the sooner—we'll get the Doctor back to Puddleby. And most of it will be spent on deserving animals, in the end, anyway."

"All right," said Jip. "I'll see if I can't arrange something. But I *won't* advertise satin collars or cat's cradles."

Jip then set to work, and with the help of the Doctor he got up quite an interesting show, to be given in the window of the dog collar shop. He called in as assistant actors all the other dogs attached to the Dolittle caravan: Swizzle, Toby, Grab, and Blackie. They were a well-mixed company. Swizzle was, of course, as usual, the comedy dog, making a joke of everything and everybody. Toby was the self-important, cheeky, small dog who just *has* to boss anything that's going on. Grab looked the picture of a ferocious fighter (though he was really quite a good-natured animal); while Blackie, the retriever, was a good sample of the larger, more serious type of dog.

The little play that they arranged was quite simple; and a good deal of it was not planned ahead but contrived on the spur of the moment. They just sat or stood around in the window as though it were a sort of dogs' club. And Jip, pretending he was a peddler of wares, brought to them collars and winter coats and dog soap and whatnot for sale. Toby acted with great skill the part of the fussy sort of spoiled pet who was pleased with nothing. Blackie played the more dignified role of the large dog on whom were tried all the big collars and coats and things. Swizzle, as the buffoon, pretended he didn't know how any of the things were worn. He put the collars on inside out, the coats on upside down, and generally tripped over, or bungled, everything.

Live animals in a shop window will always attract the attention of the passerby. But such a gathering as this, of dogs actually doing things, brought a crowd around the shop such as had never been seen before. Policemen came to see what the matter was. And of course their presence brought still more people, who thought something serious was taking place. It was quite the best advertisement this shop had ever obtained.

Matthew Mugg, with his usual business cleverness, had insisted on the shopkeepers putting a sign in the window telling the public that these dogs were part of the far-famed Dolittle Animal Theatrical and Operatic Company. And of course this was very good advertisement for *The Canary Opera*, *The Puddleby Pantomime*, and the circus on Greenheath.

Gub-Gub, who had refused to enter the field of advertisement to help sausage manufacturers, did so later with great success in a West End toy shop. Here, amid delighted children who romped around him all day long, the pig comedian jumped a skipping rope, played with mechanical toys, and generally amused himself as well as his audience.

Pippinella, too (after she had privately inspected the cages made by the manufacturer who had written for her services), fulfilled her contract. Hers was the very simple task of hopping in and out of cages, showing by her lively and sprightly manner that she approved of their design. But the fame of her wonderful voice had now spread so far that her mere presence in the shop more than repaid the firm that had employed her at the enormously large salary of seven pounds an hour.

THE FOURTH CHAPTER

The Pocket Horse

BUT BY FAR THE MOST USEFUL VENTURE INTO advertising undertaken by the Doctor of his household was with the Royal Agricultural Society. This large and important association was accustomed to hold its annual show in one of the biggest halls to be found in London. And not only did it occupy the hall itself, but its sideshows and smaller exhibits spread over into adjoining grounds and other buildings. It was a yearly event of long standing with the public. It ran for a fortnight and it was well patronized, not only by the citizens, but by great numbers of farmers and others interested in agriculture and stock raising who came from every corner of England to attend it.

Each day in the fortnight was devoted to some special department, though of course there was much that was on show continually throughout the two weeks. One day there would be cattle-judging, when prizes were given for the best-bred cows or the fattest sheep. Other days a parade of Shire horses—to which would be sent the finest stallions and champion plowing teams from all over the country—would take place. Still another day would be given over to butter-churning competitions, dairy demonstrations, fancy poultry, and so on.

Now as soon as Matthew Mugg had learned that the Doctor had been written to by the Royal Agricultural Society he had, without consulting his manager, made a call upon the Exhibition Committee. The show had not yet opened, but was due to do so the following week. To this committee Matthew had introduced himself in his usual manner, as the partner of the great John Dolittle, M. D. He congratulated the committee on their wisdom and foresight in inviting the renowned naturalist to work with them for the success of the Royal Agricultural Show. Then having once broken loose on his favorite subject, he went on for over an hour telling the committee of the astonishing discoveries, inventions, and scientific achievements of his partner. Much of it was even more astonishing than anything the Doctor had ever done. But it was convincing enough to greatly impress the committee.

The result of this little advance expedition of Mr. Mugg's was that the Doctor was called upon two days later by the chairman and secretary in person. This, even for the famous Doctor , was no small honor. And he took great pride (he was at Greenheath when they called upon him) in conducting his distinguished guests round his circus.

They were delighted at the wonderful condition of all the animals kept there. Fred took them through his model menagerie and showed them elephant stalls and lions' dens such as they had never seen before.

But it was with the Doctor's circus stables that they were most impressed. These were John Dolittle's pride. The enameled iron hay managers, the white earthenware drinking troughs, the washable cotton tether ropes and blankets, the ventilators that the horses could open and close themselves, the marvelous cleanliness, the atmosphere of health and good cheer, fairly took their breath away. They asked the Doctor how had he accomplished all this, where had he gotten these ideas from? He giggled and changed the subject. The chairman of the committee insisted, however.

"Come! Don't you want to tell us?" he asked.

"Oh yes," said the Doctor. "I'm quite willing to tell you. But you probably won't believe me—most people don't. You see, practically every detail and device in these stables has been invented by the horses themselves. These ideas are their own—this is their conception of a well-run stable. I have merely carried out their wishes. I—er—talk their language, you understand."

Well, the outcome of the chairman's and secretary's visit to Greenheath was that the committee was keener than ever to have the Doctor take part in the Agricultural Show. And he was sent a special invitation to visit the hall and grounds two days before they were thrown open to the public, to help with his advice on the livestock housing and to give the committee the benefit of his ideas in any other departments.

On this trip Matthew, of course, accompanied him. And likewise did Dab-Dab, whose opinions he wanted on the Aylesbury Duck Exhibit. Jip also came, because he was very interested in a special demonstration of trained sheep dogs that the society was giving, and Gub-Gub, too, joined the party, as he wanted to see the prize potatoes.

They found the premises of the show even greater than they had expected. Some of the stands and tents had not been put up yet and many were still in the course of building. But even so, the extent of the whole affair was enormous. There was something of everything that has, or ever has had, to do with farming: plows, harrows, harvesting machinery, incubators, chicken houses, traveling boxes for eggs, sheep wool clippers, sheep fencing, prize vegetables, tomato hothouses, chemical apparatus for testing soils, magnificent horses of all breeds, from the heavy Shire horses to little Shetland ponies. Altogether, indoors and outdoors, there were literally acres of things to be seen.

Matthew, of course, as usual, was very much on the lookout for opportunities to get the Doctor to show off his knowledge. And as John Dolittle stopped on his way round to admire some Shetland ponies that were being shown, the man who was exhibiting them came up and spoke to him.

"I hear, Doctor," said he, "that you have done some quite interesting work in pony breeding yourself."

"Oh, dear!" laughed the Doctor. "Has Matthew been bragging about that, too? Yes, I have done a certain amount—not very much."

"Why," cried Matthew, "what about that dwarf horse you produced? Smaller than any of these Shetlands here, wasn't it?"

"Oh yes," said John Dolittle. "It was certainly that."

"Well, smallness is what we want in Shetlands now," said the breeder. "You can get any price for good teams if they're well matched and small enough. We'll be glad to learn anything you can teach us."

"The occasion Matthew speaks of," said the Doctor, "was some years ago in Burma, when I was on a voyage. I learned of a special kind of rice which, when cattle were fed on it from birth, kept their size down in a remarkable way. They had a craze there, too, for small animals at that time, and I thought I'd like to see what I could do. After some experimental work I produced a pony that I could put inside my hat. A very intelligent little creature. But I did not repeat the breed at all. I found that he was not happy when brought down to such an unnatural size. Of course, he got petted to death by all the Burmese ladies and had an excellent time that way. But one day a dog mistook him for a rabbit and ran off with my horse in his mouth and I had quite a time overtaking him. I then realized that I would have to restrict his liberty a great deal if he was to be safe from a whole lot of enemies who, were he of ordinary size, wouldn't have dared to attack him. And that didn't seem quite fair. I finally gave him to the king of Siam, who had a special little garden made for him, with a big wall around and a grating on top to protect him from the hawks. But I made up my mind that I would breed no more pocket horses."

The part that the Doctor finally played in the Royal Agricultural Show turned out to be very useful. For one thing, he got the committee to give him a special stand with half a dozen fine horses and cows to demonstrate his Sanitary Drinking Cups for Cattle. These he had invented some years before to prevent the spread of hoof-and-mouth disease and other animal complaints. The cups were self-draining contrivances which, when the horse pushed his nose into them, turned the water on and filled themselves automatically. They also drained and rinsed themselves when not in use. The cattle were thus always provided with fresh, clean water.

The horses and cows who gave the demonstration very soon got on to the workings of the Dolittle sanitary cups and throughout the show there was always quite a crowd gathered about their stand watching them.

Then another thing that the Doctor introduced was an animal drugstore. Here were displayed all the medicines and embrocations and soaps and hair restorers and other things that he had found in his long experience as an animal doctor to be good, reliable products. Among them was Brown's horse liniment, which John Dolittle had analyzed and found to be very good. Also his own Canary Cough Mixture (which worked equally well with poultry) and his mange cure and many more.

Further, in this stand he also demonstrated every afternoon in person many discoveries he had made in animal surgery. Most of the patients who flocked to Greenheath were directed by Jip and Dab-Dab to come here instead. And the Doctor set bones and cured all sorts of ailments publicly in dogs and calves and horses so that those who were interested in the science of animal surgery could get the benefit of his experience.

This animal drugstore and surgery was frowned on by many of the vets who came to the show and tried to discredit the Doctor as a quack. But so extraordinary were many of his cures, that finally there was no doubt in the minds of the public about the genuineness of his remarkable skill. Also the fact that he held a degree as a graduated Doctor of Medicine made it difficult for the envious ones to arouse feeling against him. And very soon the veterinary surgeons became convinced themselves that he knew more than they and they were only too glad to learn from him.

During the last week of the show the Doctor's consulting hours became a sort of class in veterinary surgery and medicine. You could hardly see his stand at all for the crowds of vets and students who watched and listened while he set the broken shoulder of a sheep; relieved a limping horse; put gold fillings in cows' teeth; and performed delicate and wondrous feats of surgery that had never been seen before.

The committee said at the end of the show that this year the general admission at the gate had been twice as large as it have ever been before, and they put this extraordinary interest of the public down to the fact that Dr. John Dolittle had taken part in their annual exhibition.

The Fifth Chapter

The Dolittle Circus Staff Holds a Meeting

THE RUN OF *THE CANARY OPERA* AT THE Regent's Theater broke all records in successful theatrical productions. Week after week went by and instead of the attendance falling off, the house seemed packed a little tighter—and the crowd turned away a little bigger—every night.

The one hundredth performance was celebrated with another dinner at Patti's in the Strand. But on this occasion some of the faces that surrounded the table at the first celebration were absent. The reason for this was that many of the original staff of the Dolittle Circus had made enough money to retire. Hercules had gone to his peaceful cottage and rose garden by the sea; the Pinto Brothers had departed; and so had Henry Crockett, the Punch-and-Judy man.

Furthermore, when the meal was over and speeches came to be made, Hop the clown arose and told the company that this was his farewell appearance in public. He too, he said, had made enough money to retire, and much as he disliked the idea of parting from his excellent friend and manager, John Dolittle (cries of "Hear! Hear!"), he had wanted all his life to travel abroad. And now at last he had the means to do it. His dog Swizzle, however, had chosen to remain with the Doctor, so that he did not feel he was altogether deserting the show, since his best friend, the companion of many years of circus life, would remain in the ring to keep his memory green.

At this dinner the dress of the company was noticeably different from that worn at the first. Mrs. Mugg, the Mistress of the Wardrobe and chronicler of the Dolittle Circus, fairly shimmered with jewelry. Matthew, too, when he arose and launched into a long and eloquent speech, was seen to be wearing three enormous diamonds in the bosom of his shirt and another, even larger, in a ring upon his finger. The Doctor himself wore a brand-new dress suit made by a Bond Street tailor; but he said it did not feel nearly as comfortable as the one that had split up the back at the dinner given to welcome his operatic company to London.

The Doctor, in his own address, spoke of the disappearance of familiar faces from the dinner table. He said he was glad that his remaining so long in show business had given opportunities for many to realize their ambitions and to do those things they wanted most to do. Money itself he always regarded as a terrible curse, he said, as it too often prevented people from doing the things they most wished for, instead of helping them. They had now been in London three months. And the budding of spring on the park trees reminded him of his own home in Puddleby, of his garden and his plans that he had so long neglected. Before another three months had passed, he said, he hoped that he himself would be able to retire from the theatrical world, and that the other members of the company who had made *The Canary Opera* the success it was would be sufficiently well off to do likewise, if they wished.

The departure of Hop the clown from the Dolittle Circus was an event of importance. Both Swizzle and he wept on each other's necks when they came to say good-bye. Swizzle was torn between two loves. He wanted to stay with Hop, but he also wanted to stay with John Dolittle and his jolly, crazy household. He could not do both. And it was only after Hop had promised, through the Doctor, that he would keep him posted by letter on how he got on, that the circus dog was consoled. Even then, all that night he kept Jip and Toby awake, having qualms and scruples about deserting his old master.

"You know," he'd say suddenly when the others were just feel-

"'Oh, forget about it and go to sleep!' said Toby."

ing sure and glad that he'd gone to sleep, "it isn't as if I *had* to let him go alone. They say a dog's place is by his master's side. He was always an awfully kind, considerate sort of boss, was Hop. I feel a terrible pig deserting him after all these years."

"Oh, forget about it and go to sleep!" said Toby irritably. "I don't see what you're blaming yourself for. You worked for your living. You helped his act in the ring—in fact, you were the better clown of the two. The audiences always laughed more at your antics than they did at his. Now he's going out of show business with plenty of money—which you helped him make. If you prefer to stay with Doctor Dolittle while Hop travels around the world enjoying himself, that's your business."

"Yes, I suppose so," said Swizzle thoughtfully. "Still, he was such a decent fellow, was Hop."

"And so was Henry Crockett, my man," said Toby. "But I left him, or rather he left me, in the same way. I wanted to stay with the Doctor, too. I helped him make the Punch-and-Judy show a success. I don't feel guilty. My goodness! After all, our lives are our own even if we are dogs."

Well, finally Swizzle was persuaded that he need not let his conscience bother him about Hop; and Jip and Toby got a little undisturbed sleep somewhere between two in the morning and getting-up time. As it happened, the Doctor himself was wakeful, too, that night, thinking over various problems connected with the opera; and as the dogs' quarters were situated in the passage outside his room, he had heard the whole conversation.

What Toby (who, as you will remember, always insisted upon his rights) had said about their lives being their own, even if they were dogs, set John Dolittle thinking. And the next day, after he had spent more than an hour talking over money matters with Too-Too the accountant, he called a meeting of the circus staff.

For this he went out to Greenheath, taking his household with him. It was an odd gathering. The animals present outnumbered the humans by far. The Doctor himself had not fully realized up to this point how the ranks of his performers had thinned. In one of the larger sideshow tents where they were all collected, Manager Dolittle rose and made an address, first in English to the people and then in animal language to the rest.

"The cooperative system," he said, "which we have followed has proved, I think I can say, a great success. But I feel that it is only fair that now when we have a big balance in the bank, due largely to *The Canary Opera*, the animals who have taken so important a part in all our shows should share in the profits. And in any case, it is desirable that all our performers should be provided for when we disband. I therefore propose that the animal members of the staff share with the rest of us on the same basis and that bank accounts should be opened in their own names. I have looked into this matter and find that it is quite possible for animals to have bank accounts and checkbooks—with certain banks—provided that someone is authorized to make out the checks for them. It is to discuss this matter that I have called you together, and I now propose that this measure be put to the vote."

Then followed a short discussion. Of course, the animals were all in favor of the Doctor's idea, with one or two exceptions; and the only active objections came from a tent rigger and the clerk that sold the tickets at the circus box office. They said that they couldn't see what animals wanted money for, and they opposed the idea.

However, the other three human members present—the

Doctor, Matthew, and Fred—were in favor, and the motion was carried, on the human side, three votes to two.

In talking over this matter that same night at their after-the-show supper in the town house, the Doctor further explained his reasons for proposing such an idea.

"You see," said he, pouring himself a second cup of cocoa, "I am not only thinking of providing for the animals in their old age, when perhaps I shall no longer be here for them to come to. But I hope by this to improve the standing of animals in general. There is an old saying: Money talks, and—"

"'Monkey talks,' did you say?" asked Gub-Gub.

"No. *Money* talks," the Doctor repeated. "It is a horrible thing, money. But it is also horrible to be the only one who hasn't got any. One of my chief complaints against people has always been that they had no respect for animals. But many people have a great respect for money. Animals with bank accounts of their own will be in a position to insist upon respect. If anyone does anything unjust or unfair to them, they will be able to hire lawyers of their own and prosecute the offenders in the usual manner."

"But how about their making out checks, Doctor?" asked Too-Too the accountant.

"I have already gone into that matter," said John Dolittle, "with lawyers and several bank managers. Most of them thought I was crazy and wouldn't listen to me at all. But two banks, the Eastminster and Chelsea, and the Middlesex Joint Stock Bank, agreed that if some person were given what is called power of attorney—and did the writing of the checks, the depositing and the drawing—those banks would have no objection to putting accounts in their books under the names of animals. Of course, about the lawyer part of it, if any prosecution should be necessary, it remains to be seen what the courts will do. It would be something entirely new—and very interesting. I rather hope we do have a lawsuit come along soon so that we can see how it turns out. But in any event it will improve the standing of animals in the community, this having bank accounts of their own and lawyers of their own."

Shortly after this, arrangements were made for the animals' sharing in the profits of the Dolittle cooperative circus, and bank accounts were actually opened in the names of the animal members of the staff.

Gub-Gub, when he was handed a checkbook of his own, was

"He used to bother Too-Too four or five times a day."

highly delighted. He used to bother Too-Too four or five times a day to know how much money he had in the Eastminster and Chelsea. And he boasted to every pig he met that they had better be careful how they talked to him or he would write a letter to his lawyer and have him hauled into court.

Jip had an account opened at the Middlesex Joint Stock—and a very substantial balance he had when the Doctor had placed the money from M. Poulain to the dog's credit.

Dab-Dab said she had no preference where she banked. At first she hadn't approved of the idea at all. But on consideration she decided it was an excellent thing because she could thus keep part of the money safe from the Doctor's spending—to be used later, if need be, to get him back to Puddleby and a peaceful life.

THE SIXTH CHAPTER

Ways of Spending Money

IT WAS THE DOCTOR'S INTENTION, ONCE HE HAD banked the money in the animals' names, to allow them to do what they liked with it, to give them complete control. To tell the truth, he was vastly interested to see what they would do with it. It was a new experiment.

It is most likely if the animals had been left to work out, each one by himself, how they should spend their new riches that there would have been a good deal of squandering. But although the Doctor did not influence them at all in the matter, they did influence one another quite a good deal.

On the evening of the day when they first came into their fortunes, the Doctor was kept late at the theater talking with the managers; and the animal household sat down to supper in the kitchen of the town house without him.

"What are you going to do with *your* money, Jip?" asked the white mouse.

"I'm not quite sure yet," said Jip. "I've often had a notion that

"The animal household sat down to supper."

I'd like to set up a dogs' soup kitchen in the East End—a sort of free hotel for dogs. You've no idea what a lot of them are starving around the streets. A place where the waifs and strays could come and get a bone or a square meal and perhaps a bed for the night—and no questions asked—would be a good thing. I spoke of it once to the Doctor, and he said he would see what could be done about it."

"Oh no you don't!" snapped Dab-Dab. "No more homes for broken-down horses or stray dogs, thank you! I know what that means. You remember the Retired Cab Horses' Association? That's the very thing we want to keep the Doctor away from. I'm going to leave my money where it is, in the bank. John Dolittle may be rich now: if what

Too-Too says is true, he's as rich as the Lord Mayor of London—but nobody can get through money the way he can once he gets started. The day will come when he's poor again, never fear. Then, if we've still got the money that he put in the bank for us, we'll be able to help him. He can say all he likes about our having earned it. But you know very well if it wasn't for him, we wouldn't have a penny."

"With my money," said Gub-Gub, blowing out his chest, "I'm going to set myself up in a business as a greengrocer."

"Oh, for heaven's sake, listen to that!" groaned Dab-Dab, rolling her eyes.

"Well, why not?" said Gub-Gub. "I'm rich enough now to buy all the cabbages in England. I'm one of the wealthiest animals in London."

"You're the stupidest pig in the world," snorted the housekeeper. "And you'd probably eat all your vegetables instead of selling them. If you must go into the greengrocery business, for pity's sake wait till we've got the family back to Puddleby."

And so, in spite of the fact that they were the first animals to obtain the independence that comes with money, in the end, after they had talked things over among themselves, they did not show any disposition toward reckless or foolish spending. What new comforts they did provide for themselves were all of a reasonable kind. And the Doctor felt that this was a great triumph for his theory that animals, if treated properly, could behave quite as sensibly as people could.

But, of course, it would be unnatural to expect that the animals would not wish to buy something with their new wealth. And each in his own way (after he had questioned Too-Too about his balance) did a little shopping—just to celebrate, as Gub-Gub put it.

The white mouse's first purchase was a selection of foreign

cheeses. He went with the Doctor to a very expensive West End grocery and bought a quarter of a pound of every kind of cheese that had ever been invented. The Doctor had never heard the names of half of them; and even to Gub-Gub, the great expert in foods, several were quite unknown. However, the pig made a note of their names and a description of their taste to be put in his new book, *The Encyclopedia of Food* (ten volumes), which he said he was now writing.

Gub-Gub's own investment was a selection of hothouse vegetables and fruits. He bought some of everything that was out of season, from artichokes to grapes. A lady customer who happened to be in the shop was very shocked at the idea of these delicacies being bought for a pig (Gub-Gub sampled most of them right away). And being a busybody, she remonstrated with the Doctor for giving such dainties to him.

"Tell her I've bought them with my own money," said Gub-Gub, sauntering out on to the street with his nose in the air and his mouth full of asparagus.

Another of Gub-Gub's new luxuries was having his trotters shined every day. An arrangement was made with a shoeblack, a small boy who lived not very far from the Doctor's town house. And every morning Gub-Gub stood very elegantly on the steps while his hooves were polished till he could see his face in them. Dab-Dab was furious at this. She called it a vain, nonsensical waste of money. But the Doctor said it was not a very extravagant matter (it only cost a penny a day); and, after all, what was the use of Gub-Gub's having money of his own if he wasn't allowed to spend at least a little of it on frivolities?

"But why should he?" said Dab-Dab, her feathers bristling

with indignation. "It doesn't do him any good to have his silly feet polished, and it certainly doesn't do us any good."

"What an idea!" said Gub-Gub. "Why, I'm the best dressed pig in town."

"Best *dressed*!" snorted Dab-Dab, "when you don't wear any clothes."

"Well, I'm the best groomed, anyhow," said Gub-Gub. "And it's right that I should be. I have my reputation to keep up. Everywhere I go children point at me and say, 'Look, there's Gub-Gub, the famous comedian!'"

"The famous nincompoop, more likely," muttered Dab-Dab, turning back to her cooking. "I suppose I can work myself to death

"Gub-Gub gets his trotters shined."

over the kitchen sink, while that overfed clown goes mincing around the streets, cutting a dash."

"Well, but Dab-Dab," said the Doctor, "you don't *have* to do the housekeeping, you know—not now anymore—if you would sooner not. We can afford to engage a woman housekeeper or a butler."

"No," said Dab-Dab, "I'm not complaining about that. Nobody else could take care of you the way I can. This is my job. I wouldn't want to let anyone else take it over. The thing I object to is that stupid pig standing on the front steps every morning so the people passing on the street will see him having his hooves shined. He doesn't really enjoy being clean. He just thinks it's smart."

But some of the animals' first use of money was not that of buying in shops. Dab-Dab finally decided that she *would* hire a scullery maid to help her with the washing up. The housekeeper insisted that the new servant's wages should be paid for out of her bank account and not the Doctor's.

"After all, she is my assistant, and I ought to pay her," said she. "The Doctor's money will be needed for enough things without scullery maids' wages. Of course, she'll have to sleep out; I haven't room for her in the house unless I put her in with the pelicans. And they might object to that—a scullery maid. As soon as animals go on the stage, they start putting on airs. Well, as the Doctor says, we shall see."

The scullery maid was engaged, and after she had been instructed in her duties by Housekeeper Dab-Dab (the Doctor acting as interpreter, of course), she fitted into the strange household extremely well. The effect on her of becoming a part of this theatrical family was that she became crazy to go on the stage herself. She wanted to sing in opera. Dab-Dab said she did all right for singing over the kitchen sink, but for opera she was hopeless. Nevertheless, she pestered the Doctor whenever she saw him to get her onto the operatic stage, until finally he arranged never to get home until after she had left, and in the mornings he would get Dab-Dab to inform him whereabouts in the house she was, so that he could escape from his room (where he took his breakfast in bed) and out into the street without meeting her in the hall or on the stairs.

Swizzle's first use of his bank account was rather peculiar and opened up still another new possibility for moneyed animals. He discovered, while in the city (through some of the sick dogs who visited the Doctor's surgery on Greenheath), that he had a sister living in a suburb on the south bank of the Thames. Swizzle went to visit her when he learned of her whereabouts and took the Doctor along for a walk. He found that his sister had been married (it was seven years since he had seen her last) and now had a family of five very jolly little puppies. Two of them, however, were somewhat ailing, and Swizzle's sister (her name was Maggie) was very glad that the Doctor had accompanied her brother on the visit because she could now get the benefit of his professional advice.

"Well," said John Dolittle, "there's nothing seriously wrong with any of your children, Maggie. What they need is fresh air, all of them. London air isn't much to boast of, at best. But, you see, this shed here where you have your kennel is very close and airless. You must get the puppies out more."

"But how can I, Doctor?" said Maggie. "They're scarcely able to walk yet. And even if they were, I'd never dare to take them on the streets till they have more sense—for fear they'd get run over."

"Humph!" said John Dolittle thoughtfully. "Yes, that's so."

"I tell you what, Doctor," said Swizzle suddenly. "Let's hire a nursemaid for my sister's family. Now I've got money of my own, I can pay for one."

And that was what was finally done. A day or so later, the citizens of London were provided with still another Dolittle surprise. A smart nursemaid was seen walking through the streets pushing a perambulator with five puppies in it, each wearing a warm knitted coat of white wool. Sometimes they were accompanied by their proud uncle, Swizzle, the clown dog from the Dolittle Circus.

The nursemaid was discharged, however, after her second week of employment and another engaged in her place. The puppies had complained that she would clean their ears in public, and they demanded a nursemaid who would be more considerate of their dignity.

"A smart nursemaid pushing a perambulator with five puppies in it"

The Seventh Chapter

The Opening of the Animals' Bank

ONE MORE THING THAT CAME ABOUT through the idea of the Doctor's that animals should have money of their own was "The Animals' Bank." This institution did not enjoy a very long life but it deserves to be recorded in the memoirs of Doctor Dolittle as something well worthy of notices—as a remarkable event in the social history of animal life.

Jip, who was always interested in the welfare of his fellow dogs of less fortunate circumstances than his own, first got the Doctor thinking over the plan. He had been speaking of his own experience (a story which you have already heard) when he first tired his hand at making money for the lame pavement artist.

"You know, Doctor," said he, "if I could earn money with that secondhand bone shop of mine, I don't see why other dogs couldn't do the same thing. But one of the reasons they never try it is that they'd have no means of keeping their money even if they made any. That's why I say, why not set up a regular

Animals' Bank? Once it became established that animals had a right to hold property the same as people—well, there's no knowing how far the idea might go. You could have animals in all sort of professions, earning salaries in jobs, making profits in private businesses and everything. But the first thing you need is an Animals' Bank."

"I see your point, Jip," said the Doctor. "I've always felt that horses, for example, had a perfect right to charge for their services in pulling carts—so much a load, you know. And there is no reason why watchdogs should not receive the same pay as watchmen. They do the same work, and usually do it better. Well, what would you

"'Yes, I think you're right,' said the Doctor."

suggest that it be called, the 'Working Beasts' Savings Banks,' the 'Cat and Dog Trust Company,' eh?"

"No, I wouldn't have it the 'Cat and Dog' anything," said Jip. That sounds like a fight to start with. Besides, cats wouldn't go into it. They have no use for money. They'd never earn any. Cats are not public-spirited. They are naturally lazy. All they want is a soft place in the sun or a fire to sleep by. No, I'd just make it a general Animals' Bank, a place where any kind of creature, who wanted to, could bring his money—or goods to be turned into money—and know that it would be looked after and that he wouldn't be cheated."

"Yes, I think you're right," said the Doctor. "Well, we must see what can be done. It will be difficult probably to get a banking staff who will be willing to take over the duties of such an institution. Bank clerks are very particular, you know. The idea of cashing checks for horses and dogs may not appeal to them as in keeping with their dignity. And then it will likely be quite a job to get the financiers interested. You see, the animals' savings will have to be invested from them by the bank—otherwise they get no interest and the bank won't pay. However, we shall see. I'll begin by going to that wealthy naturalist who lent me the pelicans and flamingos from his private park. He has banking interests all over the city. He ought to be interested in the idea."

In what spare time he could give to it, John Dolittle now set about the establishment of the Animals' Bank. He found the wealthy naturalist anxious to do anything he could to help.

"The advertisement alone, Doctor Dolittle," said he, after the scheme had been explained to him, "will be worthwhile for the furtherance of humanitarian treatment of animals. The idea sounds like a pretty wild one. But even if it proves impossible to keep up, it will be a good thing to have got it started. It will likely lead to other efforts from other quarters that may be more successful.

Thereupon he got in touch with some of his banking associates and persuaded them to give the plan a trial. A building in a good part of the city was rented and strong safes were set into the walls.

"THE ANIMALS' BANK, INCORPORATED" was placed above the doors on a large signboard and in white enamel letters on the windows. Clerks and cashiers were engaged, and desks

"A large signboard was placed over the door."

and counters and money drawers were built for them. Ledgers and big account books were printed and bound with the name of the bank in gold on the backs—also checkbooks were gotten ready in large numbers, especially made of strong rag paper so they would be able to stand the wear and tear of animals' use.

In addition to this, booklets, called prospectuses, were printed and sent out by mail in hundreds to tell the public that the bank had been organized, what it was for, and all about it. Notices were also printed in the newspapers that the bank would be opened to customers on a certain day.

This caused quite a bit of attention, criticism, and comment. Jokes were made about the institution in all the funny papers, and editorials were written in a frivolous spirit in many of the biggest London dailies. But the staff of the Animal Bank, backed by the wealthy naturalist, took no notice of this ridicule and kept right on with their preparations.

One of the results of the newspaper discussion was that the public became very curious to see how this extraordinary institution would succeed and how the difficulties of banking for animals would be overcome. To make sure that the affair should not be a failure, the Doctor had made careful plans. All his own animals had been given their share of the circus and opera profits the night before. And in spite of some of them already having bank accounts in other, older banks in London, they lined up before the doors were open, with their money for deposit, to show that the Animal Bank was an institution in which they trusted.

In addition to his own animals, the Doctor had provided all the blackbirds with money to deposit and all the other birds of the opera cast, as well as tremendous number of animals from London and the suburbs. Further, he had sent out word to all wild creatures in the country around about (by Too-Too and the white mouse) that the bank would start business at a certain hour and any wishing to make deposits in goods or money should try to be there at the first opening so as to make as good an impression on the public as possible.

Well, so far as the opening of the bank was concerned, the event surpassed even the Doctor's and Jip's wildest hopes. Long before the hour announced for the commencement of business, the street in which the back was situated was thronged with people anxious to see the strange ceremony. Moreover, the name of the mysterious John Dolittle, who had figured so prominently in the papers of late, added a considerable attraction to the occasion.

One old woman in the crowd who had evidently come in from the country was heard to declare that she did not care anything about the bank. But she had taken the coach at five o'clock in the morning in order to get a glimpse of that "Wizard of Puddleby" who, the papers said, was at the bottom of this.

Besides the crowd of sightseers marshalled along the pavements by police constables, there was a long line of animal depositors waiting for admission to the bank. The Doctor's own animals formed only a small part of these. There were horses, cows, dogs, sheep, hedgehogs, badgers, weasels, otters, hens, geese, and many other kinds.

The Doctor remarked to Matthew and the wealthy naturalist that already their plan was working—even before the bank opened—because none of the animals were being molested by the people. Ordinarily, he said, the boys and idlers on the street would have teased or tried to catch some of these wild creatures who were strangers to city eyes. But the fact that they were here to deposit money in the bank like ordinary citizens already made the people treat them with respect. And although the crowd cracked many a joke as some timid hare or cheeky jackdaw came to join the waiting line, nobody attempted to annoy them or interfere with their business rights.

Finally, as a neighboring church bell struck the hour of nine, a little wave of excitement passed through the crowd. The big doors of the bank were seen to be swinging open. The throng

"He received a checkbook from the manager himself."

surged forward to get a glimpse through the windows of what would happen. Policemen had to form a line to keep them back. Reporters from the newspapers clamored for permission to get nearer so that they could make pictures of the first animal going into the Animals' Bank.

It was one of the rules of the bank that every animal wishing to deposit money must be accompanied by a person having power of attorney. And as each depositor came up to the door, the Doctor or Matthew went in with him and gave his name at the cashier's desk.

There were several thrills during the course of the morning's work that made the crowd feel that the show had been worth waiting for. One was when a badger came forward with over a hundred ancient gold coins (old buried treasure) that he had dug up while making his hole in the side of a hill. The gold was weighed and its value deposited to the badger's credit. Another stir was caused when a closed van drove up to the door through the dense crowds and a live African lion got out, accompanied by Fred (it was the Dolittle Circus lion). With great dignity, the King of Beasts strode into the Animals' Bank, deposited ten pounds, and received a special gilt-edged checkbook from the bank manager himself—who also made a short speech. It was the star turn of the day's business and was reported (with pictures) in all the evening papers throughout the city.

The Eighth Chapter

News of Puddleby

BUT OF COURSE FOR THE UPKEEP OF A regular bank a tremendous lot of constant business is a necessary thing. And although the number of depositors appearing on the opening day was very considerable, the amount of money they put in did not, even when it was added together, make a big sum.

Further, many of the animal customers were so delighted to have checkbooks of their own that they immediately began writing out checks to see how it worked; and with those whose balance was only a small amount to begin with, this soon brought them back to where they were before.

And then after the excitement of the opening day was over, the number of daily customers doing business at the bank fell off noticeably. It was a difficult thing for out-of-town depositors to get into the city. The general manager of the Animals' Bank, Inc., told the Doctor at the end of the first week that if the institution were to pay the ordinary interest on the customers' money, a much larger amount of business would be necessary.

However, the wealthy naturalist was determined to keep the institution open for the animals and the Doctor a fortnight at least. And he promised to make good any loss that the bank might suffer and to see that the clerks and staff were paid their salaries—even if the bank made no profits at all.

Dab-Dab was very anxious over the Doctor's part in the business. She repeatedly told Jip and Too-Too that she wouldn't feel safe and happy until she got him back to Puddleby.

"Of course even then," she said, "I can't make him sensible

"'Of course,' said Dab-Dab, 'I can't make him sensible in money matters.'"

in money matters. But he will have less temptation for spending. Here in London, with so much going on, you can't tell from day to day what he may do next. It was only by the greatest stroke of luck that I heard he was going to the rescue of the Animals' Bank with his entire fortune when he heard they were close to failing. He said he would be the one human depositor there and he did not want his naturalist friend to lose any more money when he had already been so helpful. It took me over an hour to dissuade him from the crazy notion."

But while the comic papers had a good deal of fun over the closing of the Animals' Bank, neither the animals themselves nor anyone who had helped with the starting of it felt that it had been by any means a failure. Matthew Mugg, who was always on the lookout for chances for advertisement, kept the last week of the bank's career full of interesting incidents. Many societies whose purpose was the prevention of cruelty to animals and similar aims were invited to inspect the bank and meet the Doctor. These occasions were all reported in the newspapers and served to keep the name of *The Canary Opera* and Dolittle Circus before the public.

Matthew also announced at the Doctor's orders that the circus and opera would probably go out of business before very long. This, the Cat's-Meat-Man did in such a way that the public, feeling this was their last chance to see these wonderful shows, thronged to the Regent's Theater and the Greenheath circus grounds in larger numbers than ever.

It was shortly after the events just described that Gub-Gub started another new thing and nearly drove Dab-Dab crazy. One evening after supper the now wealthy pig comedian suddenly said, "Doctor, I have an idea."

"One of your best?" asked Jip, who was warming himself by the fire.

"Yes. One of my very best," said Gub-Gub, carefully choosing an apple to take away from the table for eating in bed. "Listen, we have had *The Canary Opera*, which was a more or less serious affair—very successful—but now about to be closed. Why not let us have a *Food Opera*—a comic opera?"

A chorus of laughs came from the household. But Dab-Dab seemed in no mood for nonsense. She approached the great comedian and pushed her bill close up to his nose.

"Carefully choosing an apple for eating in bed"

"If you dare," said she, "to start any new foolishness to keep the Doctor away from Puddleby any longer, you won't get a thing more to eat while I'm in charge of the housekeeping."

"Well, but wait a minute," said the Doctor, laughing. "There's no harm in hearing what Gub-Gub has to suggest, even if we don't produce his *Food Opera*. What kind of a show did you mean it to be, Gub-Gub?"

"Quite light," said the pig. "In fact comic throughout, with the exception of one poetic little scene where food fairies dance around the spring lettuces in the moonlight."

"But I don't see how you could write an opera entirely around food," said the Doctor. "Describe some of it for us."

"Well," said Gub-Gub, "for instance, there was one number called the 'Knife and Fork Quartet.' You know what a lot of noise some people make with their knives and forks at table—and then they always lay them together on the plate, to show that the meal is over. Well, I thought if one had four people and trained them to eat in time, all together—it's a pleasant noise after all, the noise of a knife and fork—you could work out a very interesting quartet."

"I see," said the Doctor. "And what else?"

"Then there was a soup chorus that I had in mind," Gub-Gub went on. "I've noticed everybody drinks soup in a different key—some very musically. The treble parts could be drunk by small dogs like Toby here. And the bass parts by—"

"Pigs," put in Jip.

"How unspeakably vulgar!" muttered Dab-Dab. "For heaven's sake, Doctor, send that pig to bed before I forget I'm a lady!"

"Any dances in your show, Gubby?" asked Swizzle. "Nothing but guzzling?"

"Certainly there are dances," said Gub-Gub. "There is a napkin ballet in the first act, and a very grand 'Waiters' March' in the second—besides the 'Caper Sauce Caper' at the finale. Oh, there are lots of good turns in the *Food Opera.* One of the arias is called, 'Songs My Kettle Used to Sing.' Another is entitled, 'Poor Little Broken Pie Crust'—very light—sung by a comic character called Popper Popover. Then there's a love ballad that begins, 'Meet Me in the Moonlight by the Garbage Heap.'"

"Your opera sounds very indigestible to me," said Jip.

"Well," Gub-Gub explained, "it isn't meant to be grand opera. It's light opera—not a heavy meal. Mine would be the kind of show they call in French *opéra bouffe.*"

"Opera beef, I should call it," growled Jip.

"You know, Dab-Dab," said the Doctor, "there's something in it. Gub-Gub has ideas."

"I always thought I could write," muttered the pig beneath his breath.

"And, you see," the Doctor went on, "now that Gub-Gub has a name, the fact that the opera was written by him would have a good deal of weight with the public."

"Lord deliver us!" cried Dab-Dab. "Haven't we had enough of the stage for a while? Haven't we had enough success—made enough money? The London playgoer isn't going to come to crazy animal shows forever. To me, this looks like a fine thing for you to lose all your money on, Doctor. Why can't you let well enough alone? You want to go back to Puddleby—we all want to go back. Very well, then, let's go while we've still got money enough. This pig's vanity is running away with him. And you're letting it run away with you too."

"We could have a splendid orchestra," Gub-Gub went on

thoughtfully, "with all the kitchen utensils—dish covers and tinkling wineglasses."

Happily for poor Dab-Dab, who was almost in tears at the prospect of the Doctor's launching into a new theatrical enterprise on the eve of his leaving show business altogether, Cheapside, the London sparrow, suddenly turned up while the discussion was still going on.

That excellent chorus master had a week before taken a run down to Puddleby with his wife, Becky. The pelicans and flamingos had, of course, become perfect in their parts after more than a hundred performances, and Cheapside had decided that a few days' change in the country would do both him and his wife good. Now, as soon as the two sparrows appeared, the entire party, including the Doctor himself, forgot all about the *Food Opera* and clamored for news.

"Well," said Cheapside in answer to the general chorus of questions, "the country looks lovely—just lovely—though, of course, there ain't no flowers to be seen yet 'cept a few sprigs of hawthorn here and there. But the trees is budding green all over, and spring is started, all right. The garden? Well, the less said about that the better. There was a half dozen crocuses pushing themselves up through the lawn, but it's 'ard work for the poor things. Break anybody's 'eart it would, to push 'is 'ead up through *that* lawn and see the mess. Hay—old dead hay from last year, a foot thick, is all that's left of your lawn, John Dolittle. If you don't go back soon and put that garden straight, you won't be able to find the house for weeds."

Dab-Dab, saddened though she was at Cheapside's description of the beloved home, drew a good deal of satisfaction from noticing that the Doctor, too, seemed deeply impressed by Cheapside's words.

"How about the apple trees, Cheapside?" asked John Dolittle presently, after a moment's silence.

"Pretty far gone, Doc," said the sparrow. "A good gardener might be able to save 'em, if he got after 'em right away. They ain't been pruned in so long they look more like old men with beards on than apple trees. But the blackbirds and thrushes are building in 'em just the same."

"Humph!" muttered the Doctor. "And the old lame horse, he's all right of course?"

"Yes," said Cheapside. "He's all right, in a way, but he gave me a message for you. Told me to be very particular how I gave it, too, because he didn't want you to be offended. It seems he's lonely. Gets all the food he wants, of course—goes out on the back lawn whenever he wants grass, and since you wrote to the hay-and-feed merchant in Puddleby he's had oats and all sorts of grain, as much as he could eat. 'But,' 'e says to me, 'e says, 'tell the Doctor I ain't complaining, but I've heard about this Retired Cab and Wagon Horses' Association what he started on a farm of their own up Kettleby way. An old friend of mine, a fire horse, what used to pull the fire engine in Great Culmington, has joined. And, well, I ain't complaining, but it's awful lonely here all by myself with nobody to talk to. And if the Doctor's going to be away much longer I'd like to be sent up to the Association's farm. I'm getting kind of tired of talkin' to meself.'"

"Well now," said Dab-Dab, bustling forward as Cheapside ended, "there you are, Doctor! We're going to lose one of our oldest friends if you don't get back—besides having the finest garden in the west country go to ruin and the house fall to pieces. I tell you, if you don't go back soon you never will be able to make that place into what it was. It will just get beyond repair."

"Yes, I suppose you're right," said the Doctor. "And goodness knows, I'm dying to see the dear old place again. Well, Gub-Gub's opera will have to wait. Maybe even when we've gone out of show business we may try it out sometime in Puddleby, a private performance, perhaps to celebrate the author's birthday. Now listen, Cheapside, I wish you'd fly down to Puddleby again tomorrow and tell the old lame horse that I'm coming back just the earliest moment I can. We have some clearing up matters to attend to here before we can leave. I must see that the menagerie animals are properly provided for, of course. But just as soon as ever we can get away, we're all coming back to Puddleby."

"'Well now,' said Dab-Dab, bustling forward."

THE NINTH CHAPTER

The Legend of the Jobberjee Ghosts

CLOSING UP A CIRCUS IS NO SMALL MATTER. There are a terrible lot of things to be thought of and provided for. Poor Dab-Dab grew more and more anxious, as the preparations proceeded, lest at the last minute something should crop up to alter or put off the Doctor's intention of retiring from show business.

But it did really look as though this time John Dolittle himself were determined that nothing should interfere.

Still, it was more than anyone could hope for, of course, that the Doctor could get through such an enormous undertaking without extravagance (as Dab-Dab called it) of some kind. And the most costly item on the list of his expenditures was caused by the wild animals of the menagerie. Of these now remaining there were only three: the elephant, the leopard, and the lion—all Africans. You should have heard the rejoicing in the menagerie when the Doctor announced to them that he intended sending them back to freedom and their native land! The leopard sprang around his cage yelping for joy; the lion roared so that folks on Greenheath thought that the end of the world was at hand; and the elephant, trumpeting at the top of his voice, executed his stage dance with such abandoned enthusiasm that he nearly wrecked his stable. Gub-Gub said it reminded him of the night when the menagerie animals helped Sophie to escape by kicking up a prearranged rumpus.

But it was not merely the sending of the animals back to Africa that was so expensive—though, to be sure, even that would have cost a lot of money. But John Dolittle was determined that these performers, in return for their faithful services in his circus, should travel in luxury. He very strongly disapproved of the usual manner in which animals were made to travel—he said there wasn't one of them that was given decent quarters, from chickens to elephants. And his animals were going to have a ship of their own!

Poor Dab-Dab! She did not know exactly how much a ship big enough to carry an elephant, a lion, and a leopard would cost, but she knew it would be expensive. She threw up her wings in horror.

"Why on earth can't they go by the ordinary liners that sail between London and Africa?" she squawked.

"Because, Dab-Dab," said the Doctor, "no ordinary ship can possibly give room enough to animals of that size if they carry other freight or passengers. And besides, these ordinary packet boats and liners only go to the big ports, where my animals would probably be captured or shot as soon as they were landed. I want them, after their years of service, to be accommodated properly on the voyage and set ashore exactly where they want to land."

And so in spite of all protest from his housekeeper the Doctor advertised in the London papers for a ship. He received dozens of answers by mail. But in choosing the craft, the captain, and crew he was very particular. Many of those who answered the advertisement refused when they found out what freight they were to carry and what were the conditions under which they were to sail, to take on the job at all. The Doctor insisted that the animals were to be given the run of the ship and that they would be confined belowdecks only when the weather was stormy. Their comfort in everything was to be the chief consideration throughout.

But a few captains when they learned that Fred, the menagerie-keeper, was going to accompany the animals (the Doctor was sending him to make sure that his friends were properly treated) were willing to consider the proposition. Then came the task of finding out

"The elephant makes the acquaintance of the captain."

whether the animals themselves approved of the ship and the crew.

This John Dolittle did by first visiting several of the crafts himself, and after he had picked out two or three of the best of them, he made arrangements to have the elephant, the lion, and the leopard go down to the docks in their circus traveling wagons to look over their quarters and make the acquaintance of the captain and the sailors who were to take them.

The second ship that the animals looked over they declared themselves very pleased with. It was the one that the Doctor himself thought the best, too. The captain was a good-hearted old salt, and after he had been introduced to the animals and been shown that they had no intention of molesting anyone on board, he said that he would personally see to it that they were treated like first-class passengers and given the best of everything.

The Doctor arranged with Fred and the animals a system of signals whereby they could make their wants known to him and he would convey them to the captain and the crew.

It was a good thing that the Doctor had made so much money with the opera and circus. Because although he had expected that this chartering of a special vessel would be a very expensive matter, the actual sum required turned out to be a good deal more even than he had anticipated. For one thing, for carrying such large animals as elephants and lions, almost the whole ship had to be refitted and altered. Carpenters were busy on her for weeks before she sailed.

A most luxurious stall was made for the elephant amidships, with specially strong padded sides, in order that he would not be banged about if the weather got rough. In the forecastle an enormous shower bath was put in for him, so he could keep cool in the hottest weather. The quarters for the lion and the leopard were simi-

"The Doctor arranged between Fred and the animals a system of signals."

larly provided with the most up-to-date kind of traveling luxuries.

Then the provisioning for such a long voyage was another considerable matter, especially as the Doctor wanted the animals to have every delicacy they wished for on this last journey they would make in human care.

However, the Dolittle bank account was now, for a while anyhow, big enough to withstand even this with ease. And although Dab-Dab kept pestering Too-Too the accountant for statements, the Doctor and he were able to show her that there would still be lots of money left.

The voyage, as Fred described it to the Doctor on his return, was quite pleasant and successful. Good weather favored the travelers nearly all the way, with the exception of a few rough days crossing the Bay of Biscay, when the elephant kept to his bunk in his luxurious cabin and the lion lolled on a specially constructed couch in the saloon, sipping chicken broth. For the rest of the voyage the animals were able to stay on deck all day long. Their appetites from the sea air grew enormous, and the provisions were only just enough to last them comfortably, although a very large stock had been laid in.

As to their exact destination, even the animals themselves were unable to instruct the Doctor very definitely, although he had done his best to get from their descriptions of their homes some idea of what point on the African coast the captain should make for. Because, of course, their knowledge of geography, outside of their own particular country, was very small. So the best that could be done was to make landings at various parts of the coast of Africa and let the animals go ashore to see if they recognized it as their own home district. The Doctor knew that the leopard probably had been captured somewhere in West Africa, and he told the captain to stop in at Sierra Leone first and see if that was not his home. And sure enough, the leopard at the first port of call sped off into the jungle with a yowl of delight and was not heard from again.

The finding of the homes of the elephant and the lion was not, however, so easy. The lion had described his home as a mountainous part of Africa, where the woods were broken up with open stretches of parkland and many nice small streams of good water. The elephant said that the thing he best remembered about his particular section was that the grass grew very high (up to his shoulders and higher), and that generally it was flat or gently rolling. From this the Doctor concluded that both of them came from somewhere between the Zambesi and the Djuba rivers. But, as this was a very long stretch of coast, many landings had to be made before the animals were sure that they had reached the country of their birth.

Putting an elephant ashore when you have no proper wharf to moor your ship to is quite an undertaking. So a good deal of time was spent in making the various stops.

On his return Fred told the Doctor that during several of these halts, when they were engaged in hoisting the elephant's huge bulk over the side with a sling and a derrick, government officials and coastguardsmen came up and wanted to know what they were doing. When it was explained that a wealthy circus owner had sent a special ship down to put his performing animals back on their native soil, the government officials said he must be very rich and very crazy and went on.

At each of these landings, of course, Fred went ashore with the animals to see if they had come to the right place. And finally, about a hundred miles south of the mouth of the Zambesi River, both the lion and the elephant sniffed the wind as soon as they landed and generally behaved in such a way that Fred decided they had come to the right place at last. But, he told the Doctor, he was somewhat surprised at this, because from their description, it would appear that the two had come from different parts of Africa. After climbing a small hill, where they could get a good view of the surrounding country, they seemed to be quite certain that this was the land they were seeking. They evidently wanted to show Fred before they left him that they were grateful for his kind treatment of them, and he gathered that they were also trying to give him some farewell message to carry to the Doctor. But his knowledge of their language and signs was so poor that he could not get the meaning of what they were trying to say. At last, frisking and frolicking like kittens at play, they plunged down the hillside together and disappeared into the thick bush.

Fred said that he felt sure that they had only reached the lion's country, but not the elephant's, though of course the two species of animals often inhabit the same areas. And he decided that the elephant, after his long friendship with the lion, had determined to stay with him for company.

And this may very likely account for the strange legends and

"Standing on a tree stump, waving his trunk"

tales that the Doctor later heard from natives of that part of Africa. Many hunters and trackers declared that they had often seen a lion and an elephant going through the jungle together as though they were inseparable companions. And that at nighttime they frequently came down together to the salt licks, where many wild creatures were gathered, attracted by that particular delicacy. Here in the African moonlight they would give a strange performance, which seemed greatly to entertain the other denizens of the jungle—the elephant doing a curious dance, standing on a tree stump, waving his trunk from side to side as though music were being played for him; while the lion gave jumping exhibitions, springing up on to the elephant's back and down the other side. This extraordinary team of jungle performers came to be called by the Africans the "Jobberjee Ghosts."

The sportsmen who came there after big game paid very little attention to these stories of the mysterious Jobberjees, considering them merely to be tall tales. But the Doctor knew that they were probably quite true—that his circus animals, who in the Dolittle show ring ran their own performance without the aid of whips or human orders, had carried their tricks into the heart of the African jungle.

The Tenth Chapter

The Dolittle Circus Folds Its Tents for the Last Time

During his stay in London and Greenheath the Doctor had, as I have told you, attended to a very large number of animal patients, who began and continued to come to him as soon as the news of his arrival had spread. These were, of course, mostly city animals, such as dogs and cats and rats and those birds who make their homes near the haunts of man.

For the Doctor the dogs were the most interesting. Jip used to love to go off by himself, wandering around the back streets and the slums of London; and whenever he met a sickly-looking mongrel or a stray that seemed to have no home, he would get into conversation with him and always ended by giving him the Doctor's address. Jip was thoroughly democratic and very charitable. And he believed in giving his fellow creatures whose fortunes had fallen low a helping paw.

This, of course, was very commendable, but it was not approved of by Dab-Dab at all. Every time the Doctor got back to his circus wagon at Greenheath he found it simply surrounded by the tramps and outcasts of dogdom. Some were sick or lame and needed medical attention. But the greater part of them had just come hoping to get a glimpse of the great man, a square meal, or a bone. But all brought with them a secret hope in their hearts that the Doctor would adopt them and take them into his famous household.

In spite of the work and the time it took up, the Doctor was always glad to see them. His only regret was that he could not take every one of them as part of his animal family—as Jip hoped he would. Jip was never jealous of his famous master's attention. It was his belief that the Doctor could not have too many dogs.

"After all," he used to say, "dogs *are* the most intelligent animals to keep. Why not have plenty of them?"

It was while the Doctor was still in the midst of his preparations to leave the circus life and return to Puddleby that Jip once more suggested his idea for a dog's free food kitchen in the East End of London. He wanted to spend his own money on it, he said. But the Doctor explained to him that the cost of keeping a free kitchen open continually would be much more than he expected.

"Why, Jip," said John Dolittle, "you would have to have at least one cook on duty all the time, and his wages alone, without counting anything for provisions, would run into a considerable amount of money per year!"

"Well, perhaps we could do without a cook, then," said Jip. "Many dogs would just as soon have their meat raw. Bones are always better uncooked."

"Humph!" said the Doctor. "Possibly, if you brought the idea down to just a bone distribution station and got a boy to run it for you, it would not be so expensive—that is, for a while, anyhow.

But your bank account would not be big enough to keep it open forever, that's certain."

Jip was very disappointed. However, after making inquiries through the Doctor as to the wages that boys got, he went over estimates and costs with Too-Too the accountant and found that he could run a free bone counter for a week without beggaring himself.

So he set to work and hired a healthy, strong boy. Then he rented a cellar in Whitechapel and opened an account with a butcher who was to supply the bones fresh every day. These business transactions, of course, he did through the Doctor, but he was very particular that all expenses came out of his own money.

"So he hired a healthy, strong boy."

Thus came into existence—even though a brief existence only—*Jip's East End Free Bone Counter for Indigent Dogs.* It was a great success while it lasted. Jip himself was in attendance at the cellar door almost continually. And night and day a constant procession of half-starved mongrels traipsed up and down the steps, carrying away bones with them, ranging in size from a lamb cutlet to a shoulder of mutton. Jip was careful to inspect all the dogs as they came in, to make sure that they were deserving cases. If the dogs wore smart collars or had well-brushed coats he knew that they were owned by rich folks and were merely coming out of curiosity. These he chased away. But to the ragtag and bobtail of dog society he was most hospitable and kind, often waiting on the poorest of them himself.

When it became known at Jip's bone kitchen that the Dolittle household was shortly leaving London for Puddleby, the Doctor was besieged with applications from dogs who wanted to come with him. What made poor Dab-Dab particularly angry was that Matthew Mugg, who had a great love for dogs of every kind, aided and abetted Jip in trying to get the Doctor to take every mongrel that applied.

"I'd like to know, Jip," said she, "where in heaven we would put all those disreputable creatures if the Doctor only took half of them. I should have thought you would have more sense. The Puddleby house is crowded as it is. Yet for every mongrel that asks to be taken in you put in a good word, and that stupid Matthew, too, just as though the house were as big as a hotel."

"Oh, well," said Jip, "the garden's large enough—even if the house is small. They could camp outside in kennels, or something."

"He was besieged with applications."

"Yes," snorted Dab-Dab angrily, "and a fine garden it would be—with hundreds of half-breeds rooting around in it! A garden is for flowers, not for the riffraff of London streets."

Well, finally the Doctor said that perhaps later, when they were properly settled back at Puddleby, he might take a piece of land and start a home for crossbred dogs similar to the rest farm for retired cab and wagon horses. And with this Jip had to be content.

Getting the rest of his circus animals properly disposed of was not so hard for the Doctor as had been the case with the large menagerie animals. Through his rich naturalist friend who had lent him the pelicans and flamingos he heard of a certain Mr. Wilson, a reliable person, who was shortly sailing for America. With him the Doctor made arrangements for the opossum (whom Blossom had styled "the famous Hurri-Gurri") and the six American black-snakes, which Fatima had called king cobras. These, while they were not exactly the easiest kinds of pets to travel with, could, after all, be made comfortable in properly constructed boxes that would be small enough to go as personal baggage.

Mr. Wilson was not a naturalist in any sense of the word. But he promised the Doctor as a special favor that he would see to it that the opossum and the snakes were properly cared for on the voyage.

John Dolittle did not realize that he was giving Mr. Wilson anything but a very simple commission to carry out. But, as a matter of fact, these creatures caused quite a little sensation of a harmless kind before they were returned to their native soil. On the voyage while the opossum was being given an airing on the deck in charge of one of the stewards, he decided that the ship's mast was a new kind of tree. And suddenly he scaled up it at tremendous speed and began hanging from the ropes by his tail. The steward, who was not good at climbing, called him, but he refused to come down. A crowd of passengers gathered on the deck to watch the show. Finally, a sailor was summoned by the captain and sent aloft to capture the opossum. But he was not easily caught. He liked the view from his new quarters in the rigging and he meant to stay there for the rest of the voyage.

Seeing that the sailor was trying to take him prisoner, he kept swinging from mast to mast, running around the rigging as though he were on dry land. The sailor, good climber though he was, stood no earthly chance of catching him single-handed, and he called down for more assistance. Then another deckhand was sent up. But still the agile little animal kept out of their grasp.

Finally, all the crew that could be spared were sent off for the hunt. But even with six sailors trying to capture him, the opossum continued to give his pursuers the slip and to enjoy the view.

Night came on and still Mr. Opossum was in the rigging and the six sailors had grown very tired of climbing about on ropes. All they had succeeded in doing was to give the passengers a very amusing show to watch. With the coming of darkness, the hunt had to be given up.

However, during the night a cold wind sprang up, and the opossum found that his lofty quarters were a trifle chilly. So he came down of his own accord. He was found by his steward shivering behind a ventilator and put back in his box in Mr. Wilson's cabin—to which warm comfort he was very glad to return.

But Mr. Wilson's troubles were not over yet. When the ship docked at New York and his luggage was opened and examined by the customs officials, the six blacksnakes got out and started wriggling all over the dock, delighted at the chance to stretch themselves after the confinement of the voyage. Everybody was scared to touch them. And a special man from the zoo was sent to get them back into captivity.

When he arrived and the snakes realized that they were being chased, they too got scared, and, diving among the passengers' baggage, they tried to hide behind trunks and handbags as best they could. One of them got into an old lady's valise which was opened for inspection and its owner went into a faint when she saw a four-foot-long blacksnake squirming around among her laces and shawls.

But finally they were all captured and Mr. Wilson commissioned the man from the zoo to take them and the opossum into the country and set them free.

The Canary Opera had, sometime before this, of course, given its last performance and disbanded. The thrushes, the wrens, and the rest of the birds who had helped had taken wing back to their natural haunts. The Dolittle town house had been given up and charwomen were cleaning it, after its five months' duty as an operatic aviary. On Greenheath the Dolittle Circus enclosure looked very empty and deserted. Most of the tents and wagons and caravans had been sold at auction and hauled away. The mechanical merry-go-round and the Punch-and-Judy theater had been presented by the Doctor to a school for foundlings. John Dolittle's own wagon (the original one that Blossom had made and painted specially for him) and the wagon occupied by Mr. and Mrs. Mugg were, with the Pushmi-Pullyu's stand, about all that was left of a once colorful and elaborate circus.

Matthew said he just couldn't bear to look at the scene, it saddened him so. But his wife, Theodosia, said she didn't see what he had to complain of—even if the days of the Dolittle Circus were over—now that he was better off than he had ever been in his life.

Many hundreds of children living in the neighborhood of Greenheath (who had frequently visited the circus which the Doctor had designed particularly for young folk) were, even more than Matthew, saddened at the prospect of its closing up for good. On the day before the Doctor announced he would leave, a vast throng of youngsters came with an enormous bouquet of flowers to bid him good-bye. And this, when he walked down the steps of

"A throng of youngsters came with an enormous bouquet."

his wagon and for the last time distributed the free peppermints to the children, was (he told Matthew afterward when they were on the road for Puddleby) the only thing that made him feel sorry at leaving the life of the circus behind.

The End

DOCTOR DOLITTLE

AND THE GREEN CANARY

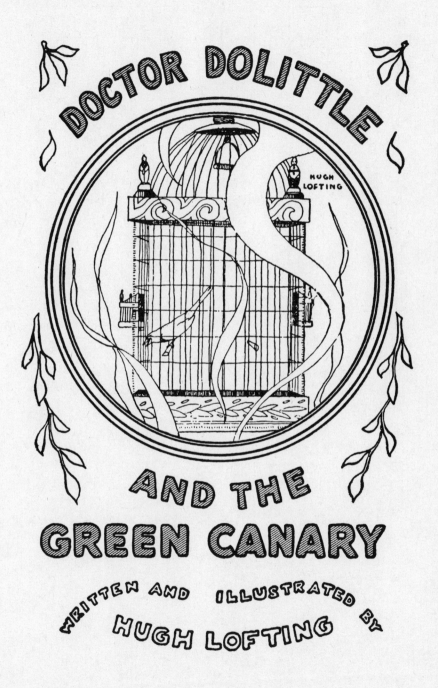

WRITTEN AND ILLUSTRATED BY
HUGH LOFTING

Contents

PART ONE

THE FIRST CHAPTER

The Doctor Meets the Green Canary

THIS STORY OF THE FURTHER ADVENTURES OF Pippinella, the green canary, begins during the time of the Dolittle Circus. It will tell—in much greater detail—the strange events that took place in the life of the little bird before she came to live with John Dolittle.

Pippinella was a rare kind of canary that the Doctor had found in an animal shop while taking a walk with Matthew Mugg, the Cat's-Meat-Man. Thinking he had made a bad bargain because—as he thought—hen canaries couldn't sing, he had been greatly astonished, on getting her back to the caravan, to find she had a most unusual mezzo-contralto voice.

And what was more unusual still, she had traveled many thousands of miles and lived a most varied and interesting life. When she had told the Doctor some of the dramatic happenings that led up to her being sold to the animal shop, he interrupted her to say:

"You know, Pippinella, for many years now, I have wanted to do a series of animal biographies. But because most birds and animals have such poor memories for details, I have never been able to get onto paper a complete record of any one animal. However, you seem to be different—to have the knack for remembering the proper things. You're a born storyteller. Would you be willing to help me write your biography?"

"Why, certainly, Doctor," replied Pippinella. "When would you like to begin?"

"Anytime you feel rested enough," said the Doctor. "I'll have Too-Too fetch some extra notebooks from the storage tent. How about tomorrow evening after the circus is closed up for the night?"

"All right," said the canary. "I'll be happy to begin tomorrow. I *am* rather tired tonight; this has been a most trying day. You know, Doctor Dolittle, for a few moments this afternoon I was afraid you were going to pass right by that dreadful shop and leave me there."

"Indeed, I might have," said John Dolittle, "if your cage hadn't been hanging in the window where I could see how disappointed you looked as I began to move away."

"Thank heaven you came back!" sighed Pippinella. "I don't know how I could have borne another moment in that dirty shop."

"Well," said the Doctor, "that's all over now. I hope you'll be very happy with us. We live quite simply here—as you can see. These animals and birds I call my family, and—for the time being—this wagon is our home. One day when we have had enough of circus life, you shall return to Puddleby with us. There you will find life a great deal quieter—but pleasant just the same."

This conversation, which the Doctor had with the green canary, was all carried on in the bird's own language. You will remember—from previous stories about John Dolittle and his animal family—

that he had learned, many years before, to speak the language of animals and birds. This unique ability had earned for him the friendship and loyalty of all living creatures and had influenced him to change his doctoring of humans to a busy life of caring for the illnesses and injuries of animals, fish, and birds.

While the Doctor was talking with Pippinella about writing her biography, the members of his household had withdrawn to a corner of the wagon and were carrying on a lively discussion. Gub-Gub the pig, as well as Dab-Dab the duck, Jip the dog, and Too-Too the owl, were quite indignant that the Doctor should choose a newcomer to the group for this great honor. Whitey, the white mouse, being more timid than the others, just listened and thought about the idea. But Gub-Gub, the most conceited of the lot, said that he was going to speak to the Doctor about it.

So the next evening, when the family had gathered in the wagon to hear the continuation of the canary's story, Gub-Gub cleared his throat nervously and spoke up.

"I don't see why anyone would want to read the biography of a mere canary," he grumbled. "My life is much more interesting. Why, the places I've been! Africa, Asia, and the Fiji Islands. Not to mention the food I've eaten. I'm a celebrity for that if for nothing else. Now, what can a canary know about food—eating nothing but dried-up seeds and bread crumbs? And where could she go—cooped up in a cage most of her life?"

"Food! Food! That's all you think about," snapped Too-Too. "I think it's more important to be a good mathematician. Take me, for instance; I know to the penny how much gold there is in the Bank of England!"

"I have a gold collar from a king," said Jip. "That's something!"

"'I think it's more important to be a good mathematician,' snapped Too-Too."

"I suppose it's nothing that I can make a bed so it's fit for decent folk to sleep in!" snapped Dab-Dab. "And who, I'd like to know, keeps you all healthy and well fed. I think that's more important!"

Whitey just sat there and didn't say a word; he didn't really think his life was interesting enough for a biography. When the Doctor looked at him with a questioning expression on his face, Whitey dropped his eyelids and pretended to be asleep.

"Haven't *you* anything to say, Whitey?" asked the Doctor.

"No, sir—I mean, yes!" said the white mouse timidly. "I think the biography of Pippinella will be very nice."

"Well, let's get on with it, then," said the Doctor. "Please—if you're ready—we are, Pippinella."

The canary then told them how she was born in an aviary—a small one where the man who bred canaries gave her special attention because of her unusual voice; how she came to be such a rare shade of green because her father was a lemon-yellow Harz Mountain canary and her mother a greenfinch of very good family; and how she shared a nest with three brothers and two sisters—until it was discovered that she was that rare thing: a hen bird who sang as beautifully as a cock.

Pippinella explained that it was not true that females could not sing as well as males. It was only that males did not encourage them to sing.

It was because of her beautiful voice that Pippinella finally acquired a master who bought her and carried her off to a new home; an inn where travelers from all over the world stopped on their way to the seaport to eat and sleep the night.

After the canary had described the inn more fully, the Doctor interrupted her to ask:

"Pardon me, Pippinella. Could that have been the inn on the road from London to Liverpool? I believe it is called the Inn of the Seven Seas."

"That's the one, Doctor," answered the little bird. "Have you been there?"

"Indeed we have," replied John Dolittle, "several times."

Gub-Gub jumped up so suddenly from his chair that he crashed into the table where Pippinella sat telling her story and sent the water out of the canary's drinking dish, sloshing over the sides.

"I remember!" he cried. "That's where the turnips were

especially good—done with a parsley sauce and a little dash of nutmeg."

"If I'm not mistaken," said Jip. "I left a perfectly good knucklebone buried there. Cook gave it to me right after dinner and I planned to eat it later. But the Doctor was in such a hurry to move on, I hadn't a moment to dig it up before we left."

"I'll bet you wished many times that you had it, eh, Jip?" said Too-Too. "But then, you must have had plenty of bones buried back at Puddleby."

"Not more than three or four," Jip replied. "Those were lean days."

"They would have been leaner if I'd not found that gold sovereign just as we were leaving," piped up Whitey.

"Gold sovereign?" asked the Doctor. "You didn't tell me about it. Whatever did you do with it, Whitey?"

Whitey looked confused and kept glancing from Dab-Dab back to the Doctor. He wished he'd kept quiet about the sovereign.

Dab-Dab ruffled her feathers and made a clucking noise.

"He gave it to me, John Dolittle!" she said crossly. "How do you think we would have eaten at all after that scoundrel, Blossom, departed with all the circus funds? You know our larder was empty, Doctor. Except for about a teaspoonful of tea and some moldy tapioca."

"But the sovereign didn't belong to you," said the Doctor.

"It did—just as much as to anyone else," said Whitey. "It was lying in the dust right smack between the hind feet of one of the coach horses. And he was trampling and kicking up the dirt so that I could hardly keep my eyes on it—good as they are."

"No one but Whitey—with his microscopic eyes—would

ever have seen it," said Dab-Dab. "There was no point in running around asking stable boys and kitchen maids if it belonged to them. Who could recognize a gold sovereign as his? Anyway, it's spent now—that was almost a year ago."

"Well, well," sighed the doctor. "I suppose it was all right. Shall we get on with the story, Pippinella?"

"I was treated with great respect and admiration by the owner of the inn and his wife and children," continued the canary. "And I made many friends there. Everybody stopped to speak to me and listen to my songs—it was very gratifying.

"The coming and going of coaches from all directions, and the busy, cheerful people who worked for my master, inspired me with no end of ideas for new songs. It was a wonderful place for composing!

"On nice days my master would hang my cage on a hook high up beside the entrance to the inn. There I would greet the incoming guests with my very best songs. One little verse I made up and set to music became very popular with everyone who heard it. I called it 'Maids, Come Out; the Coach Is Here,' and whenever I heard the sound of approaching horses I'd sing it at the top of my lungs to announce to the stable boys and porters that another coach-load of travelers was nearing the inn.

"Among the people who came to be my friends was one named Jack, who drove the night coach from the north. For him I composed a merry tune called 'The Harness Jingle Song.' Old Jack would call out to me as he rolled his coach into the noisy courtyard, "Hulloa there, Pip! Hulloa!" and I'd answer him by singing another verse of his song."

THE SECOND CHAPTER

The Inn of the Seven Seas

AFTER A SHORT PAUSE IN WHICH THE GREEN canary seemed to be lost in thought, she continued her story.

"Besides the many friends that I made among the people in that place, I made lots more among the animals. I knew all the coach horses and I would hail them by name as they came trotting into the yard. And dog friends I had too: the watchdog who lived in a kennel by the gate and several terriers who hung about the stables. They knew all the local gossip of the town. There was a dovecote above the loft where they kept the hay for the horses. And here carrier pigeons lived who were trained to fly long distances with messages. And many were the interesting tales that they could tell of an evening, when they sat on the gutters of the roof or strutted about the yard beneath my cage, picking up the bits of corn that had fallen from the horses' nosebags.

"Yes, as I look back over all the places I have been, that nice, busy old inn seems as good a home as any cage bird could wish to find.

"I had been there, I suppose, about five months when, just as the poplars were beginning to turn yellow, I noticed a peculiar thing: knots of people used to gather in the yard of an evening and talk with serious, worried faces. I listened to such conversations as were near enough for me to hear. But although I knew by this time the meaning of a great number of human words, I couldn't make anything out of this talk. It seemed to be mostly about what you call politics. There was an air of restlessness. Everybody seemed to be expecting or fearing something.

"And then one day for the first time I saw soldiers. They came tramping into the inn yard in the morning. They had heavy packs on their backs. Evidently they had been marching all night, because many of them were so weary that they sat down against the stable wall with their boots covered with dust, and slept. They stayed with us till the following day, eating their meals in the yard out of little tin dishes that they took from the packs they had carried.

"Some of them had friends among the maids of the inn. And when they left I noticed that two of the maids who waved to them from the dining room window were weeping. There was quite a crowd to see them go off. And very smart they looked in their red coats, marching out of the gate in rows of four with their guns on their shoulders and their packs on their backs, stepping in time to the drummer's *rap—rap, rappatap, tap, tap!*

"Not many days after they had gone we had another new kind of excitement, another army. But this one did not wear smart uniforms or march to the beat of a drum. It was composed of ragged people, wild eyed, untidy, and disorderly! They came scrambling into the inn yard, shouting and waving sticks. A leader

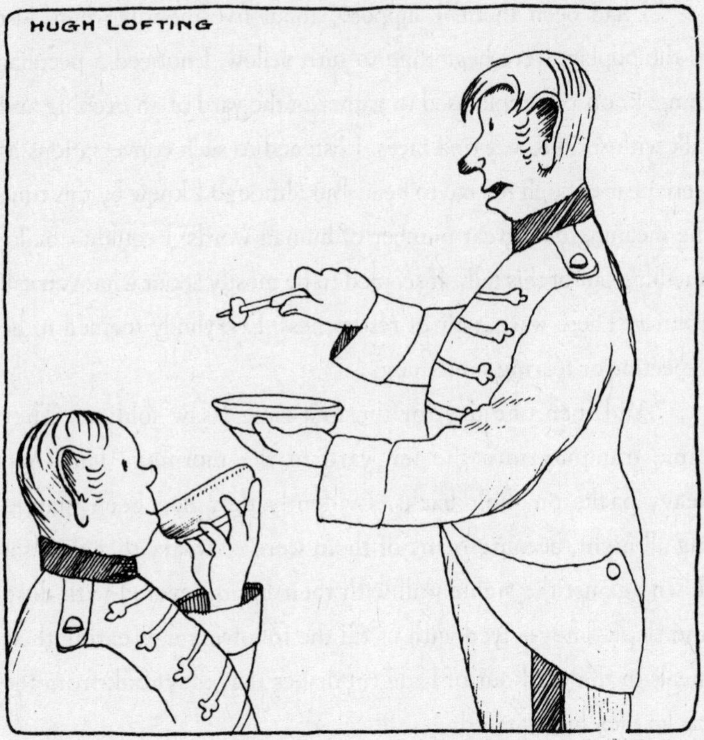

"Eating their meals in the yard out of little tin dishes"

among them stood on an upturned bucket and made a speech. The owner of the inn begged the leader to take them away. He was evidently very worried about having them in his yard. But the leader wouldn't listen. When one speech was finished, another would begin. But what any of them was about I couldn't make out.

"Finally the ragged mob drifted away of its own accord. And as soon as the yard was clear, the innkeeper shut and locked the gate so they couldn't come back.

"I asked one of my pigeon friends what it all meant. He shook his head seriously:

"'I don't quite know,' he said. 'Something's been going on for weeks now. I hope it isn't war. Two of the carriers, the best flyers in the dovecote, were taken away last Monday. We don't know where they went to. But those two pigeons were used for carrying war messages before.'

"'What is war?' I asked.

"'Oh, it's a messy, stupid business,' he said. 'Two sides wave flags and beat drums and shoot one another dead. It always begins this way—making speeches, talking about rights, and all that sort of thing.'

"'But what is it for? What do they get out of it?'

"'I don't know,' he said. 'To tell you the truth, I don't think they know themselves. When I was young I carried war messages myself once. But it never seemed to me that anyone, not even the generals, knew any more of what it was all about than I did.'"

Pippinella stopped in her story long enough to take a sip of water and then went on again.

"That same week that the ragged people came to the inn to make speeches we had still another unusual arrival. This was a frightfully elegant private coach. It had a wonderful picture painted on the door, handles and mountings of silver, outriders on fine horses to guard it, and altogether it was the grandest equipage I had ever seen.

"On its first appearance way down the road I had started singing my usual song, 'Maids, Come Out,' and so forth. And I was still singing when it came to a halt in the yard and a tall superior sort of gentleman got out of it. The innkeeper was already on the steps, bowing low, and porters were standing around to help the guest out and to attend to his luggage. But strangely enough, the first thing that the elegant person took any notice of was myself.

"'By Jove!' he said, putting a quizzing glass to his eye and sauntering toward my cage. 'What a marvelous singer! Is it a canary?'

"'Yes, my lord,' said the host, coming forward, 'a green canary.'

"'I'll buy it from you,' said the elegant gentleman. 'Buckley, my secretary, will pay you whatever the price is. Have it ready to travel with me in the morning, please.'

"I saw the innkeeper's face fall at this. For he was very much attached to me and the idea of selling me, even for a big price, evidently did not appeal to him. But this grand person was clearly someone whom he was afraid to displease by refusing.

"'Very good, my lord,' said he in a low voice, and he followed the guest into the hotel.

"For my part I was greatly disturbed. Life here was very pleasant. I did not wish to exchange it for something I knew nothing of. However, I had been sold. There was nothing I could do about it. That is perhaps the biggest disadvantage in being a cage bird: you're not allowed to choose your own owner or home.

"Well, after they had gone inside the inn I was sitting on my perch pondering rather miserably over this new turn of affairs, when along came my chaffinch friend who nested in the yard.

"'Listen,' I said. 'Who is this haughty person who drove up in the coach just now?'

"'Oh, that's the marquis,' said he. 'A very big swell. He owns half the country around here—mills, mines, farms, and everything. He's frightfully rich and powerful. Why do you ask?'

"'He has bought me,' I said. 'Just told the innkeeper to wrap me up, like a pound of cheese or something—without even asking first if he wanted to sell me.'

"'Yes,' said the chaffinch, nodding his head, 'the marquis is like that. He takes it for granted that everybody will do what he wants—and most people do, for that manner. He's awfully powerful. However, there are some who think things are going to change. That meeting, you remember, when the workmen and ragged people came here making speeches? Well, that was mostly over him. He has put a whole lot of machinery into the mills and mines, it seems. There has been a terrible lot of grumbling and bad feeling over it. It is even widespread that the marquis's life is in danger all the time now.'

"'Well,' I said, 'he won't get me to do what he wants. If he takes me away from here I won't sing another note. So there!'

"'I don't see why you should grumble,' he said. 'You will have the most elegant home. Why, he lives in a castle with over a hundred servants, they say. I know he has a tremendous lot of gardeners myself, because I've built my nest in his garden and I've seen them. If you ask me, I should say you are very lucky.'

"'I don't care anything about his hundred servants,' I said. 'I don't like his face. I want to live here with the host and his family and old Jack and the other coach drivers. They are my friends. If the marquis takes me away I'll stop singing.'

"'That's rather a joke,' chuckled the chaffinch thoughtfully. 'The all-powerful marquis getting defied by a cage bird. He got his way with everybody till he met a canary who didn't like his face! Splendid! I must go to tell that to the wife.'

"Well, the next morning my cage was wrapped up while the children of the family stood around weeping. I was ready to weep

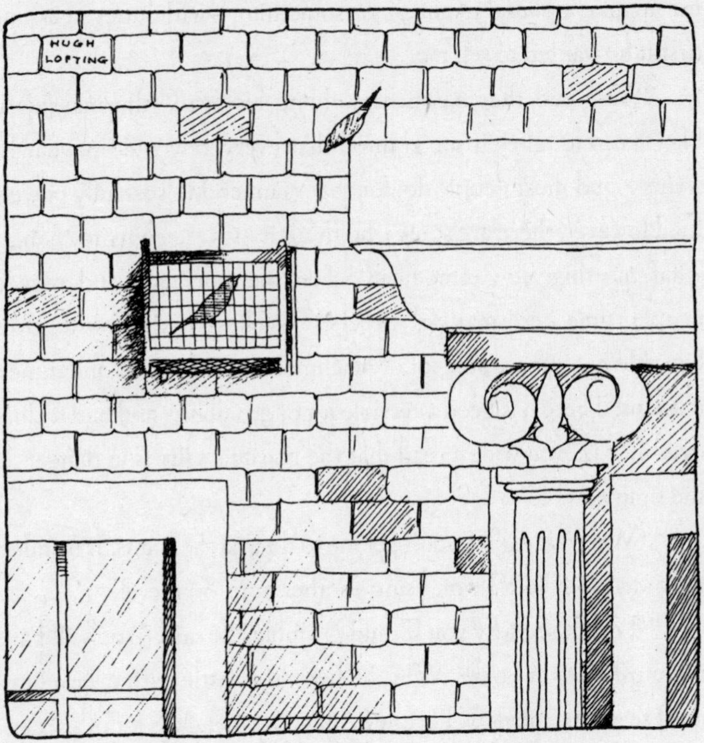

"'That's rather a joke,' chuckled the chaffinch."

myself, to tell the truth. After I was all covered up, the youngest one broke a hole in the top of my paper to say a last farewell to me. She dropped a couple of large tears on my head, too. Then I felt myself being carried out into the yard.

"And so, after weeks and months of watching people arrive and depart from my inn, I too was to set forth by coach along the white road that led away to the horizon. Whither was I going? What adventures were in store for me? I fell to thinking of good old Jack. I wondered how his cheery face would look as he swung into the gate this evening to find my cage gone from the wall and no Pip to whistle 'Thank you' for his lump of sugar. Would he care very much? I asked myself. After all, to him I was only a canary—not even his canary at that. Oh well, I thought, as the horses started forward with a jerk, it was no use being sentimental over it, I would face the future with a stout heart."

THE THIRD CHAPTER

At the Marquis's Castle

IT WAS A LONG JOURNEY. SOMETIMES I FELT THE coach going uphill, the horses panting, slowed to a walk. At other times we descended into valleys with the brakes creaking and groaning on the wheels. At last, after about seven hours of driving, we came to a halt and I heard the patter of hurrying feet. By the echoes I gathered that we had passed into some kind of a courtyard or the stone portico to a big building. My cage was taken out and carried up a long, long winding flight of stairs.

"At length, on the wrapping paper being taken off, I found myself in a small, very beautifully furnished round room. There were two people in it—the marquis and a woman. The woman had a very nice face. She seemed sort of scared of the marquis.

"'Marjorie,' said he, 'I've brought you a present. This canary is a magnificent singer.'

"'Thank you, Henry,' said she. 'It was very thoughtful of you.'

"And that was all, I could see there was something wrong. Marjorie was evidently the marquis's wife. But after his being away from her for several days that was all she said: 'Thank you. It was very thoughtful of you.'

"After he had gone, a cage was produced by the servants; the most elegant thing in cages you ever saw. It was made of solid silver. It had perches of carved ivory, food troughs of enameled gold, and a swing made of mother-of-pearl. As I was changed into it I wondered what other birds had lived in this gorgeous home and whether they had led happy lives.

"Well, after a few days at the castle I decided that I had not made such a bad move after all. Fortune had again been kind. I was certainly treated royally. My cage was cleaned out scrupulously every day. A piece of apple was given me in the morning and a leaf of lettuce in the evening. The quality of the seed was of the very best. I was given a silver pannikin of warm water to bathe in every other day. And altogether the care and service given me left nothing to be wished for.

"To all this, Marjorie, the marquis's kind and gentle wife, herself attended—although she evidently had any number of servants to wait on her if she only rang the bell. I became very much attached to her. A thing that bothered me a good deal was that she did a lot of secret weeping. She was clearly very unhappy about something and I wondered what it was. You remember I had sworn I wouldn't sing a note if I was taken from the inn. And I didn't for over a week—much to the marquis's disgust. He was all for sending me back to the inn when he found out that I hadn't sung since I had been in the castle. But his wife begged him to let her keep me, and he consented. That night—later, I saw her weeping again. And I felt so sorry for her that I suddenly started singing at the top of my voice to see if I could cheer her up. And sure enough she raised her head and smiled and came and talked to me. After that I often sang to drive her tears away—all the happy songs I knew, like 'Maids, Come Out, the Coach Is Here,' and the jingling harness, currycomb song. But I wouldn't sing for the marquis—not a note. And whenever he came into the room, if I was in the middle of a song, I'd stop at once.

"In that same small, round room I lived all the time I was at the castle. It was apparently a special, letter-writing room, part of the private apartments of the marquis's wife—or the marchioness, as she was called. On warm days she would hang my cage on a nail outside the window, and from there I had a wonderfully fine view of the grounds and all the country for miles and miles around.

"One evening I got some idea of the thing—or one of the things—that was wrong between the marquis and his wife. They had a long argument. It was all about the workmen in the mines and the mills. She wanted him to be kinder to them and to keep more of them working. But he said that with the new machinery he did not need even as many as he had. She told him that a lot of workmen's wives and children were starving. He said that wasn't his fault.

"Further, I gathered from this discussion that in one mine some distance away the workmen who had been dismissed had come back in a crowd and smashed the machines and wrecked the mine. Then soldiers had been called in and many workers were shot and women left widows and children orphans. The marchioness begged her husband on her knees to stop this kind of thing. He only laughed. The machines were bound to come, he said, to take men's places and do more work. In all the mills and mines throughout the country machinery was being put in and idle men were opposing it. It was the march of time, he told her.

"After the marquis had gone, a letter came for the marchioness. I could see her getting terribly agitated as she read it. She called in a trusted companion, a sort of secretary she had, and told her all about it. It was from a woman in one of the mill towns within the marquis's lands. It told of the awful distress in the homes of idle workmen—starving children and what not. And that night the marchioness dressed herself like a working woman and stole out of the castle grounds by the little orchard gate. I saw her from my window in the tower. With loaves of bread and foodstuffs in a basket she went miles and miles on foot to find the woman who had written the letter. When she came back it was after two in the morning. And I, who had been left on my peg outside the window all that time, was nearly frozen in the chill morning air. She brought me in and wept over me when she discovered her forgetfulness. But I quite understood—and anyway, it was the only time she had ever neglected me.

"Two days after that, news came in that another factory had had its machinery smashed. The marquis was furious, though. As usual, he was very quiet and dignified and cold even in his fury. He sent word for more soldiers to protect the mines and factories. And it seems that the same day that the soldiers arrived, one of the sergeants got into a quarrel with a workman. Before anybody knew what was happening a general battle had begun between the troops and the workers. When it was over it was found that one hundred and fifty workers had been killed.

"This caused a tremendous sensation and everybody was talking about it. I heard the servants who swept the room saying that this was war—that the marquis had better look out. Powerful though he was, he couldn't shoot people down in crowds like

"She brought me in and wept over me."

dogs, they said. One maid there was who used to bring trays up from the kitchen to the marchioness's little tower room. She had a brother among the workmen who had been killed. I remember her going off in tears to help her sister-in-law, who now had no husband. Many of the castle servants were for going with her, they were so indignant. They were talking angrily around the weeping maid on the front steps when suddenly the marquis appeared from the garden. He asked them what all the noise was about. And so great was the respect and fear in which he was held that the group without a word melted away, leaving the maid all alone. The marquis gave her several guineas and turned to go into the house. But the maid flung the money after him and screamed:

"'I want my brother back, not your dirty money!'

"Then she fled, weeping, through the garden. It was the first time I had seen the marquis openly defied.

"After that," Pippinella continued, "feeling began to run high. From all quarters came word that workmen were saying what they thought about the big fight—or slaughter, as they called it. Nearly all those who were employed to run machines went on strike out of sympathy for the relatives of those who had been killed. That, of course, made matters worse, because even more wives and families went hungry than before.

"One morning I was sitting in my cage beside the tower window, looking out at the peaceful woods down below, when I saw a man urging a panting horse up the hill toward the castle as fast as he could go. The marchioness saw him also from the window and sent a maid down at once to find out what news the man brought. The maid returned in a few minutes in a great state of excitement and told her mistress that the whole countryside was up in arms. Thousands of workers, some from towns miles away, were marching toward the castle. The messenger had come to warn the marquis that his life was in danger. Word had been sent to the soldiers, but no regiments were near enough to come to the rescue for some hours yet. The workers had been joined by many farmers on the marquis's lands and now an army, thousands strong, was on its way here bent on mischief and destruction.

"Hearing this the marchioness ran downstairs at once to find her husband. When she was gone I heard a very peculiar noise from beyond the woods. It was a dull, low roar, coming nearer all the time, growing louder and louder. Presently I saw the marquis and his wife in the garden at the foot of the tower. She was trying to persuade him to fly. At first he refused. But soon, as the howling army of workmen drew nearer, he consented and led the way toward the stables to get horses. The marchioness had not gone many steps before she evidently remembered me. Because she stopped, pointed up at my cage and said something to her husband. But he only took her by the wrist and dragged her on toward the stables. She looked back several times but the marquis wouldn't let her linger. Presently they disappeared from view around the hedge and that was the last I ever saw of either of them.

"When finally the workmen came in sight they were certainly a strange army to behold. You never saw such a ragged, half-starved, wild-looking lot. At first they were afraid they might be fired on from the battlements and windows. And they approached cautiously, keeping within the cover of the woods.

"When the workmen saw there was no danger, they gathered in hundreds and thousands in front of the castle, howling and swearing and singing songs, waving hammers and pitchforks. Some of the servants came out to join them. But the butler, an old, old man who had the keys, was determined to defend his master's property to the last. He locked the doors and barred the windows and would let no one in.

"But the leader of the workmen sent for a heavy beam. And with this as a battering-ram they soon beat in the main door, drove the old butler out, and had the place to themselves.

"Then a crazy feast of destruction began. Bottles and barrels of wine were hauled up from the cellar, opened on the lawn and drunk by the workmen. Costly silks, hangings, clocks, and furniture were thrown from the windows. Anything of value that wasn't smashed was stolen. They didn't come up the tower stairs as high as my room, but I could hear them in the rooms below me, laughing and roaring and breaking things with hammers.

"Looking down into the castle forecourt again I saw the leader calling to everyone to leave the buildings. I heard the men in the rooms below mine go clattering down the stairs. Soon I was the only one left in the castle. I wondered what this new move meant. When they were all gathered about him outside I saw the leader raise his hand for silence. He was going to tell them something. As the crazy mob grew quiet, I strained my ears to catch his words. I heard them. And they almost made my heart stand still. For he was ordering them to bring straw from the stables and oil from the cellars. They were going to set the castle on fire!"

It was now quite late—long after midnight—and Pippinella's story still seemed far from being finished. The Doctor was by this time so thoroughly absorbed and interested that it is not likely he would have thought of the time at all had not the sudden neighing of one of the horses from the nearby stables reminded him that the circus must open to the public at ten o'clock, as usual, tomorrow morning, and that he must be up to see it upon. So, in spite of the protests of Gub-Gub (who dearly loved, you will remember, any excuse for staying up late), the green canary was put in her cage and the Dolittle family circle was packed off to bed. But this was not done before a promise had been obtained from the Doctor that, without fail, the story should be continued the following evening.

The Fourth Chapter

The Rescue

THE FOLLOWING EVENING, AFTER THE CROWDS had left the circus enclosure and the sideshows had been closed up and everything put in shipshape for the night, Too-Too went over the accounts with the Doctor before supper, instead of after, so as to leave the evening free for the continuation of Pippinella's story. And as soon as Dab-Dab had cleared away the supper things the door of the little green canary's cage was opened and she flew down onto the table and took her seat on the Doctor's tobacco box.

"All right," said John Dolittle, opening his notebook and taking a pencil from his pocket. "As soon as you are ready—"

"Just a minute," said Gub-Gub. "My chair's too low, I must get a cushion. I don't listen well when I'm not sitting high."

"Fussbox!" snorted Dab-Dab.

"Well," Pippinella began, "you can imagine how I felt—or rather, you can't imagine it. No one could without being in my shoes. I really thought my last hour had come. I watched the crowd

"'I don't listen well when I'm not sitting high,' said Gub-Gub."

below in fascinated horror. I saw groups of men running between the front entrance of the castle and the stable, bearing bales of straw. These they piled against the great oak door, and some more inside the main hall. Then they brought up from the cellar jugs of oil, cans of oil, barrels of oil. They soaked the straw with this and threw more of it over the long curtains that were floating from the open windows in front of the castle.

"Then I saw the leader going around, getting all his men out of the building before he set fire to it. He sent some off singly down into the woods—to be on the lookout for anyone's approach, I suppose. He was probably afraid of the soldier's coming. For a moment there was a strange awed silence while the match was being put to the straw. It was clear that they all realized the seriousness of the crime they were committing. But as the bonfire flared up, sudden and bright, within the hall, a fiendish roar of delight broke from the ragged crew. And, joining hands in a great ring, they danced a wild jig around the burning home of the man they hated.

"What horses were left in the stables had been taken out and tethered in safety among the trees some distance away. Even the marquis's dogs, a Russian wolfhound and a King Charles spaniel, had been rescued and led out before the straw was lit. I alone had been overlooked. After the flame had taken hold of the great oak doors and fire and smoke barred all admittance, some of the men at last caught sight of me, high up on the tower wall. For I saw several pointing up. But if they had wanted to save me then it was too late. The paneling, the doors, the floors, the stairs, everything of wood in the lower part of the building was now a seething, roaring mass of flame.

"Waves of hot air, clouds of choking smoke, flurries of burning sparks swirled upward around my silver cage. The smoke was the worst. At first I thought I would surely be suffocated long before I was burned.

"But luckily, soon after the fire started, a fitful breeze began. And every once in a while, when I thought I had reached my last gasp, the wind would sweep the rising smoke away to the side and give me a chance to breathe again.

"I pecked and tugged at the bars of my cage. Although I knew there wasn't the least possibility of my getting out, like a drowning man I still hoped that a lucky chance would show me something loose or weak enough to bend or break. But soon I saw I was merely wasting my strength in struggling. Then I started calling to whatever wild birds I saw flying in the neighborhood. But the swirling smoke terrified them so they were afraid to venture close. And, even if they had, I doubt if there would have been anything they could have done to help me.

"From my position I could see inside the tower through the open window, as well as down onto the woods and all around outside. And presently, as I peered into the room, wondering if any help could come from that quarter, I saw a mouse run out into the middle of the floor in a great state of excitement.

"'Where's the smoke coming from?' she cried. 'What's burning?'

"'The castle's on fire,' I said. 'Come up here and see if you can gnaw a hole through this cage of mine. I'm going to be roasted if somebody doesn't let me out.'

"'What do you think I am,' she said, 'a pair of pliers or a file? I can't eat through silver. Besides I've got a family of five children down in my hole under the floor. I must look after them.'

"She ran to the door, muttering to herself, and disappeared down the winding stair. In a minute she was back again.

"'I can't take them that way,' she said. 'Below the third landing the whole staircase is burning.'

"She sprang up onto the windowsill. It's funny how little details, in moments of great distress, stick in your mind. I remember exactly how she looked, not six inches from the wall of my cage, this tiny creature gazing over the lip of the stone windowsill, down from that tremendous height into the garden and the treetops far below. Her whiskers trembled and her nose twitched at the end. She wasn't concerned about me, shut up and powerless to escape—though goodness knows she had stolen my food often enough. All she was thinking of was those wretched little brats of hers in the nest beneath the floor.

"'Bother it!' the mouse muttered. 'What a distance. Well, it's the only chance. I might as well begin.'

"And she turned around, sprang down into the room, shot across the floor and disappeared into her hole. She wasn't gone more than a moment. When she showed up again she had a scrubby little pink baby in her mouth, without any fur on it yet and eyes still closed. It looked like a pig the size of a bean. She came to the edge of the sill and without the least hesitation started out on the face of the wall, scrambling her way along the mortar cracks between the stones. You'd think it would be impossible even for a mouse to make its way down the outside of a high tower like that. But the weather and rain had worn the joints deep in most places; and mice have a wonderful way of clinging.

"I watched her get two-thirds of the way down, and then the heat and smoke of the fire below were too much for her. I saw her looking across at the tree, whose topmost boughs came close to the tower. She measured the distance with her eye. And, still clutching her scrubby youngster in her teeth, she leapt. She just caught the endmost leaves with her claws. And the slender limb swayed gently downward with her weight. Then she scuttled along the bough, reached the trunk, dumped her child in some crack or crevice and started back to fetch the rest.

"That mouse, to get her five children singly over that long trip, had a terrible lot of hard work ahead of her. As I watched her

"Still clutching her scrubby youngster in her teeth, she leapt."

scrambling laboriously up the tower again, disappearing in and out of the mortar cracks, an idea came to me. And when she regained the windowsill, I said to her:

"'You've got four more to carry down. And the fire is creeping higher up the stairs every minute. If I was out of my cage, I could fly down with them in a tenth of the time you'd take. Why don't you try to set me free?'

"I saw her glance up at me shrewdly with her little beady eyes.

"'I don't trust canaries,' she said after a moment. 'And in any case, there's no place in that cage that I could bite through.'

"And she ran off to her hole for another load.

"She was back even quicker than the first time.

"'It's getting hot under the floor,' she said. 'And the smoke is already drifting through the joints. I think I'll bring all the children out on to the sill so that they won't suffocate.'

"And she went and fetched the remainder of her precious family and laid them side by side on the stone beside my cage. Then, taking one at a time, she started off to carry them to safety. Four times I saw her descend that giddy zigzag trail of hers into the welter of smoke and sparks that seethed, denser and blacker every minute, about the base of the tower. And four more times she made that leap from the sheer face of the stonework, with a baby in her mouth, across the tips of the tree boughs. The leaves of these were now blackened and scorched with the high-reaching fire. On the third trip I saw that mouse actually jump through tongues of flames. But still she came back for the fourth. As she reached the still for the last load she was staggering and weak and I could see that her fur and whiskers had been singed.

"It was not many minutes after she had gone for good that I heard a tremendous crash inside the tower and a shower of sparks came up into the little round room. The long spiral staircase, or part of it, had fallen down. Its lower supports had been burned away below. I sometimes think that that was the thing that saved me as much as anything else. Because it cut off my little room at the top from the burning woodwork lower down. If the fire had ever reached that room I would have been gone for sure. For, although my cage was in the open air outside, it was much too close to the edge of the window to be safe. Below me I could now see flames pouring out of the windows, just as though they were furnace chimneys.

"I saw the leader of the workmen shout to his men to keep well back from the walls. They evidently expected the whole tower soon to crumble and fall down. That would mean the end for me, of course, because I would almost certainly fall right into the middle of the fire raging on the lower floors.

"In answer to their leader's orders the men were moving off among the trees, when I noticed that some new excitement had caught their attention. They began talking and calling to one another and pointing down the hill toward the foot of the woods. With the noise of the roaring fire I could hear neither what they said nor what it was they were so concerned about. Soon a sort of general panic broke out among them. For, gathering up what stolen goods they could carry, they scattered away from the castle, looking backward over their shoulders toward the woods as they ran. In two minutes there wasn't one of them left in sight. The mouse had gone. The men had gone. I was alone with the fire.

"And then suddenly, in a lull in the roaring of the flames, I heard a sound that brought hope back into my despairing heart. It was the *rap-rap-rap, rap-a-tap, tap, tap* of a drum.

"I sprang to my perch and craned my neck to look out over the woods. And there, winding toward me, up the road, far, far off, like a thin red ribbon, were soldiers marching in fours!

"By the time the soldiers reached the castle the smoke coming up from below was so bad that I could see only occasionally with any clearness at all. I was now gasping and choking for breath and felt very dizzy in the head. I managed to make out, however, that the officer in charge was dividing his men into two parties. One, which he took command of himself, went off in pursuit of the workmen. The other was left behind to put out the fire. But the castle, of course, was entirely ruined. Shortly after they arrived, one of the side walls of the main hall fell in with a crash and a large part of the roof came down with it. Yet my tower still stood.

"There was a large fish pond not far from the front door. And the soldiers got a lot of buckets from the stables and formed a chain, handing the water up to some of their companions, who threw it on the fire.

"Almost immediately the heat and smoke rising around my cage began to lessen. But, of course, it took hours of this bucket work to get the fire really under control.

"The officer with the other party returned. He had caught no one. Some of his men held the horses that they had found tied among the trees. These and some provisions in the cellars and a few small outhouses were all of that magnificent property to be saved. And it had been one of the finest castles in the country, famous for its beauty the world over.

"The officer, seeing there was nothing more he could do, now left a sergeant in charge and, taking one of the soldiers with him, went back down the road leading through the woods. The rest continued with the work of fighting the fire and making sure that it did not break out again.

"As soon as my ears had caught the cheerful beating of that drum I had started singing. But on account of the smoke, my song had been little more than coughs and splutters. Now, however, with the air cleared, I opened my throat and let go for all I was worth, 'Maids, Come Out, the Coach Is Here.' And the old sergeant, who was superintending the soldiers' work, lifted his head and listened. He couldn't make out where the sound was coming from. But presently he caught sight of my cage way, way up at the top of the blackened tower.

"'By Jove, boys!' I heard him cry. 'A canary! The sole survivor of the garrison. Let's get him for good luck.'

"But getting me was no easy matter. Piles of fallen stonework now covered every entrance. Then they searched the stables for a ladder. They found one long enough to reach the lowest of the tower windows. But the soldier who scaled up it called down to his companions that the staircase inside was gone and he could get no higher. Nevertheless, the old sergeant was determined to get me.

"The sergeant was convinced that I, who had come through such a fire and could still sing songs, would bring luck to any regiment. And he swore a tremendous oath that he would get me down or break his neck. Then he went back to the stable and got some ropes and himself ascended the ladder to the bottom window of the tower. By throwing the rope over broken beams and other bits of ruined woodwork that still remained within, he hauled himself upward little by little. And finally I saw his funny face appear through the hole in the floor of my room where the staircase had been. He had a terrible scar across his cheek from an old wound, I suppose. But it was a nice face, for all that.

"'Hulloa, my lad!' said he, hoisting himself into the room and coming to the window. 'So you're the only one who stood by the castle, eh? By the hinges of hell, you're a real soldier, you are! You come and join the Fusiliers, Dick. And we'll make you the mascot of the regiment.'

"As my rescuer stuck his head out of the window to lift my cage off its nail, his companions down below sent up a cheer. He fastened his rope to the silver ring of the cage and started to lower me down the outside of the tower. I descended slowly, swinging like the pendulum of some great clock from that enormous height. And finally I landed safe on solid earth in the midst of a crowd of cheering soldiers.

"And that is how another chapter in my life ended—and still another began."

THE FIFTH CHAPTER

The Midget Mascot

AND THUS I BECAME A SOLDIER—THE MASCOT of the Fusiliers. There are not many canaries who can boast of that—that they have traveled with the troops, taken part in battles and skirmishes, and led a regular military life."

"Well, I've led a sailor's life," said Gub-Gub. "Sailed all around the world, and without getting seasick, too."

"Never mind that now," said the Doctor. "Let Pippinella get on with her story."

"Those soldiers," the canary continued, "had no love for the marquis. They had been ordered to come to the rescue of his home and they had obeyed. But their hearts were more with the workers in this struggle. And I think they must have known that he was already dead when they arrived at the castle, or they would never have dared to take me just the way they did. As a matter of fact, he had been killed outside the next town. The marchioness, who had always been so kind to the poor, was not molested. But the whole thing saddened her dreadfully and she went abroad immediately and remained there the rest of her days.

"My beautiful silver cage was sold by one of the soldiers (they were afraid to keep it, of course, lest it be recognized as the marquis's property) and I was changed into a plain one of wood. That old sergeant with the funny scarred face took me under his own particular care and protection. He had my new wooden cage enameled red, white, and blue. The crest of the regiment was painted on the side and ribbons were hung on the corners to make it even happier.

"Well—it's funny—those men were convinced that I bore a charmed life. The story of how they found me singing in the burning castle was told over and over and over again. And each time it was retold, an extra bit was added on to it to make it just a little more wonderful. I came to be regarded with an almost sacred importance. It was believed that nothing could kill me, and that so long as I was with the Fusiliers, the regiment must have good luck. I remember once, when I was ill—just an ordinary case of colic, you know, nothing serious—those soldiers stood around my cage in droves for hours on end, with the most woebegone expression in their faces you ever saw. They were terrified, terrified that I was going to die. And when I finally got well and started to sing again they cheered and bellowed songs the whole night through to celebrate my recovery.

"Once, in a skirmish, two bullets went right through my cage, one smashing my water pot, the other carrying away the very perch I was standing on. When the fight was over and this was discovered, my cage was handed round the whole regiment, to show everybody the proof (as they thought it) that I did indeed have a charmed life and could not be killed. Those funny, funny men spoke in whispers, almost as though they were in church, as they took my cage in their hands and gazed with reverent wonder at the smashed perch, the broken water pot, and me hopping around unharmed.

"That night they went through the ceremony of giving me a medal for distinguished conduct under fire. A whole platoon of them lined up and presented arms while my old sergeant hung the decoration on the corner of my cage. The next day the commanding officer got to hear of it and I was sent for and carried to the officer's mess, where everything was very grand and elegant. The colonel and the major and the adjutant listened while the old sergeant recited the record of my military career. But when they asked him where he had gotten me from, he suddenly blushed and became all embarrassed. Finally he blurted out the truth and told them of my rescue from the fire. The colonel frowned and said something about looting. But finally he agreed to let the man keep me till he had written to the marchioness and got her consent—which later she willingly gave. Then the adjutant pointed to the medal hanging on my cage and they all laughed. The major said that even if I'd begun by being stolen, I was surely the only canary who ever had been decorated for distinguished conduct under fire and that any regiment ought to be proud to claim me as a mascot.

"Well, it was a funny life, the army. I had always thought that if you were a soldier, of course you spent most of your time fighting. I was astonished to find that you don't. You spend the greater part of it polishing buttons. Polishing with the military is a perfect passion. If it isn't buttons, it's belt buckles or bayonets or gun barrels or shoes. Even on my cage they found something to polish. A small drummer boy was given the job of shining up the little brass feet

"My old sergeant hung the decoration on the corner of my cage."

on the bottom of it every morning—and a great nuisance he was, shaking and jostling me all over the place when I wanted to get my breakfast in peace.

"I used to love the marching and I always had a real thrill when I heard the bugler blowing the fall-in, for it often meant that we were moving off to new scenes and new adventures. I used to travel with the baggage cart that carried the cooking implements and other paraphernalia in the rear. And as they always put my cage on the top of everything, I was quite high up and in a splendid position to see all there was to be seen.

"The men used to sing songs to cheer themselves upon long, tiresome marches. And I, too, made up a marching song of my own and sang it always when I saw them getting tired and hot and weary.

"'Oh, I'm the Midget Mascot, I'm a feathered Fusilier,' it began. And then I put a lot of twiddly bits, trills, cadenzas, and runs to imitate the piping of the drum and fife band. It was one of the best musical compositions I ever did. There was a real military swing to it and it had four hundred and twenty-five verses, so as to last through a good, long march. The men loved it. And as I watched them trudging down the road ahead of me, I again felt that I was taking an active part, even though a small one, in the lives of men.

"War at its best is a silly, stupid business. And this form of soldiering that my companions were engaged in was a particularly disagreeable one. For at this time they were not fighting with a foreign enemy. The machinery riots of which I have already spoken had spread all over that part of the country. And the Fusiliers, and several other regiments, too, were kept busy these days going from town to town to suppress lawlessness and the mob violence of striking workmen.

"Shortly after I joined the Fusiliers our regiment was ordered to proceed at once to an outbreak in a region to the north and we started off. At inns and villages along the road we were told that one of the factory towns at which we would shortly arrive was entirely in the hands of the rioting workers. They had heard of our coming and were preparing to give us a hot reception. But it was lucky for us that the town was not a walled or fortified one. Weak places were found where our soldiers could slip in among the houses. And immediately they had gained the streets, doubling around and coming back upon the gunners unaware from the inside. In less than an hour after the fight began more than half of the guns had been captured in this way, and the rest were still shooting cannonballs harmlessly across the fields at cows and dogs and bushes that they mistook for skirmishing infantry in the distance. The crews of these captured guns usually escaped. For the soldiers, who were doing their work with as little slaughter as possible, let them go without firing at them whenever they did not actually stand and fight.

"When the battle was over it was discovered that nearly all the fighting workmen had retired to a big mine in the western half of the town. In the buildings of this and in a large factory alongside it they were going to make a last stand against the soldiers and die rather than be captured. But it didn't work out that way. When my Fusiliers were ordered to fire on the buildings, they deliberately aimed the guns so that the cannonballs whistled harmlessly over the roofs. Again and again this was repeated until the general was livid with rage.

"By this time the workers inside the buildings, watching through loopholes, had realized that the soldier were inclined to side with them. And while the general broke out into another tirade and confusion reigned, the workers suddenly opened the doors of the buildings and rushed forward toward the square at top speed.

"Well, in the end my gallant Fusiliers were defeated by a crowd of ragged workmen, half of them without arms of any kind. But of course they wanted to be defeated. Rather than be compelled to fire canons on unfortified buildings full of their fellow countrymen, they were quite willing for once in their lives to be taken prisoners. I heard afterward that they were sent abroad to more regular warlike fighting, where there would be no danger of their sympathizing with the enemy.

"In the meantime the baggage wagon on which my cage was tied was treated as the booty of war. And I suddenly found myself taken over by a couple of very dirty men and trundled out of the square, down some winding streets that seemed to be leading into the workmen's quarters of the town.

"My short but brilliant military career was over."

As Pippinella came to the end of this part of her story Dab-Dab began to bustle around busily, making preparations for bed. Although she enjoyed every word of the canary's account of her life, Dab-Dab was the practical one. She had to keep an eye on the Doctor and his family else they would sit up the whole night.

"Time for bed!" she said firmly. "Tomorrow's another day—and a busy one."

Then the Doctor and his family began tucking themselves away for the night. Too-Too perched high on a shelf in a dark corner of the caravan, Whitey curled up in the pocket of an old jacket that belonged to the Doctor, and Jip lay on a mat folded under the Doctor's bed.

Pippinella, of course, returned to her cage, which hung on a hook near the window of the wagon; and Dab-Dab, after seeing that everyone was comfortable and that the lights were out, waddled off to a small nestlike bed the Doctor had made out of an empty wooden crate.

"I'm hungry!" wailed Gub-Gub from his place beside the vegetable bin. "These turnips smell so good it keeps me awake."

"Sh-sh-sh!" whispered Dab-Dab. "There'll be no eating here until morning!"

THE SIXTH CHAPTER

The Fortunes of War

"MY CAPTORS WERE EVIDENTLY IN A HURRY," began Pippinella the next evening when the Doctor and his animals had settled themselves to hear the continuation of her story. "The baggage wagon was pushed over the jolting, cobbly streets on the run. It was growing dark, and I could not see whither I was being carried. The horses had been removed from the shafts and taken somewhere else.

"I think that these men who ran off with the regimental cart must have thought that it contained food. Because when they came to a quiet corner of the street they stopped and felt through the inside of it. I heard them cursing in the dark when their groping hands touched nothing but pots and pans and spare harnesses. And after they had put me back and hurried on, I saw their faces in the glimmer of a streetlamp, and the poor fellows looked dreadfully pinched and thin.

"I then supposed that their intention was to sell me and the wagon to get money to buy food with. And I was right. After they

"The baggage wagon was pushed over the jolting, cobbly streets on the run."

had gone a little farther, we turned into a narrow alley, passed under an archway, and came into a big, big hall. It seemed to be some kind of factory workshop and the place was jammed with workers. It was dimly lighted with only a few candles and sputtering torches. The men were gathered in groups, talking in low voices with their heads together. When my fellows pushed open the doors and entered, all the whispering ceased. The crowd turned and glared at us.

"As soon as we were admitted the door was carefully locked and barred. And then I noticed that all the windows were covered with wooden shutters so that the lights could not be seen from outside. And all of a sudden its dawned on me that I had been brought to the mine, or the big factory alongside of it, and that this was one of the buildings that the general had commanded the Fusiliers to bombard. I began to wonder how long it would be before he would have other troops brought to the town that would not hesitate to fire cannonballs into crowded factories.

"As soon as the barring of the door had been attended to, the men thronged around my little cart and started to claw through it to see what it contained. Suddenly a big man, who seemed to be a leader, ordered them in a rough voice to leave it alone. They fell back, evidently much afraid of him. Something in the man's face struck me as familiar and I began to cudgel my brain to think where I had seen him before. And then in a flash I remembered: it was the same man who had led the workers in their attack on the marquis's castle.

"He went through the cart himself and told the disappointed crowd that it contained no food.

"'Then let's sell it and buy some,' cried the men.

"But as it clearly would not bring enough to buy food for all of them, it was finally agreed that lots should be drawn and that the winner should get the cart.

"'And what about the canary?' called one. 'Likely a man could get as much for him as for the old truck and all the pans put together.'

"'All right,' said the leader. 'Then draw lots for the bird separate. We'll put two marked papers in the hat—one for the cart and one for the canary. The first winner gets his choice; the second gets what's left, and the rest get nothing.'

"'Aye, Aye!' called the crowd. 'That's fair enough.'

"'Sh!' hissed the leader. 'Not so loud! How do we know who's sneaking around outside? I don't trust them bloomin' Fusiliers—even though they did give in so easy. Talk low, talk low!'

"So my next experience was to have a lot of ragged workers draw lots for me. As I saw them crowding around the hat that contained bits of paper I wondered which of them I would fall to. Some of them looked hungry and wild enough to cook me and eat me. The prospects for the future were not pleasing.

"One by one they began picking out their bits of paper. Five, ten, fifteen opened them—and with a grunt of disgust flung them on the floor. It seemed to be taking hours, but of course it was really only minutes.

"At length a cry announced that a lucky ticket had been drawn. The owner brought it, smiling, to the leader and showed a rough cross in pencil on it.

"'Well, that gives you the first choice,' said the big man. 'Which are you going to take, the cart or the canary?'

"The man, a thin fellow with a limp, looked from the wagon to me and back to the wagon again. I didn't like his face.

"'The cart,' he said at last, to my great delight.

"Another cry. A second lucky ticket had been drawn. I craned my neck to peer over the crowd and get a glimpse of the man's face. I finally saw him and my heart lifted. Although his cheeks were lined and gaunt with hunger, it was a kind face.

"'The canary's yours,' said the big man, handing him my cage. 'And that's the end of the show.'

"The winner took my cage in his hands and left the building. The question of food interested us both at this point more than anything else. Heaven only knows how long he had been going on half rations or less, and I had had no seed or water all day. As we went along I saw lots of autumn seed on weeds and wild flowers that would have made good eating for me—if only I could get at it. He, of course, not knowing what wild seeds are edible for canaries, couldn't help me. He did, however, stop by a stream and fill my water bowl for me, which I was very glad of. And later he found some groundsel growing among the standing corn, and that, too, he gave me. I still felt hungry, but far less so than I had been.

"After he had come near to a farmhouse he hid my cage under a hedge and went forward to the door to ask for food for himself. Evidently the farmer's wife took pity on his haggard and hungry looks and gave him a good, square meal of bread and cold meat. He brought back a small crust when he came to fetch me and stuck it into the bars of my cage. It was good homemade bread and I could have eaten two more of the same size.

"So, both of us fortified with food, we set out to do the ten miles to the mining town that we eventually reached. It was a pleasant, sunny morning. And something of the sadness with which the grim night had weighed me down left my spirits as the man strode forward in the fresh early air, with my cage beneath his arm. He, too, seemed in a cheerier mood. We were now upon a main highway running north and south. Wagons and carriages passed us occasionally, going either way. I hoped that one of these would offer us a lift, because traveling in a cage under a man's arm is not the most comfortable kind of journeying by a great deal. And sure enough, after we had tramped along for about half an hour, the driver of a covered cart—a sort of general grocer's wagon—stopped and asked if we would like a lift. He was evidently going to the town we were bound for and I was delighted when my man put me in the back among the groceries and got up himself beside the driver.

"As it happened, my cage had been placed right next to a picket of oatmeal. I smelled it through the paper bag. It didn't take more than a moment for me to peck a hole through the covering, and I helped myself to a thimbleful of the grocer's wares. I felt rather mean doing it to the man who was giving us a free ride. But it was only a very little I took—not enough for anyone to miss—and I hadn't tasted food except for the crumb of bread for over twenty-four hours.

"It didn't take more than a minute for me to peck a hole through the covering."

"My man chatted with the grocer as we drove. I gathered from the conversation that he had a brother, who was also a miner at this town we were coming to. Apparently it was his intention to stay at his house, if there was room, till he got a job in the mines.

"If I had known," Pippinella continued in rather a sadly reminiscent voice, "what sort of life I was heading to I wouldn't have been half as cheerful over that journey in spite of the nice, fresh morning. I had for some time now been among miners. But I didn't yet know anything about their homes, their lives, or their work."

The Seventh Chapter

The Coal Mine

THE FIRST IMPRESSION THAT I GOT OF THE town as we approached it was anything but encouraging. As I have said, there had been no rioting here and work was proceeding as usual. For more than a mile outside, all the grass and trees seemed sick and dirty. The sky over the town was murky with smoke from the tall chimneys and foundries and factories. In every spare piece of ground, instead of a statue or a fountain or a garden, there was a messy pile of cinders, scrap iron, or furnace slag. I wondered why men did this; it did not seem to me that all the coal and all the steel in the world was worth it—ruining the landscape in this way.

"And they didn't seem any happier for it. I looked at their faces as we passed them, trudging down the streets to work in the early morning. Their clothes were all black and sooty, their faces pale and cheerless. They carried little tin boxes that contained their lunches, to be eaten in the mines or at the factory benches.

"In the middle of the town my man got down from the cart,

took me out and thanked the driver for his ride. Then he went off through some narrow streets, where all the houses seemed alike—plain, ugly redbrick—and finally knocked on a door.

"A pale-faced untidy woman answered it, with three dirty children clinging to her skirts. She greeted him and invited him to come in. We passed to the back of the house into a small kitchen. The whole place smelled terribly of stale cooking. The woman went on with washing some clothes, at which she had evidently been interrupted, and the man sat down and talked with her. In the meantime the children poked their jammy fingers through the bars of my cage, which had been placed upon the table among a lot of dirty dishes. I was afraid they were going to upset it while the man was busy talking, so I pecked one on the hand, just slightly, to warm him to be careful. He immediately burst into howls. Then my cage was taken and hung up in the window, where I got an elegant view of two dustbins and a brick wall.

"'Good Lord,' I thought to myself, 'is this what I've come to? Such a home! What a life!'

"In the evening the brother returned from work, covered with coal grit, tired and weary. He washed his face in the kitchen sink while the newcomer told him how he had left his own town and journeyed hither, seeking work. The brother said he would speak to the foreman and try to get him a job in the same mine he worked in.

"Then they had supper. Ordinarily the cheerful noise of knives and forks and dishes would have made me sing. It always did in the castle, when the marchioness took her meals with me in the little tower room. And so it did with the soldiers when they all sat around my baggage cart and rattled their dishes and ate stew with a hissing noise like horses. But somehow, here in this squalid, smelly room,

"She greeted him and invited him to come in."

among these tired, dirty people, I just couldn't sing. I felt almost as though I'd never be able to sing again.

"And after the woman had put some broken rice and bread crumbs into my seed-trough I ate a little, put my head under my wing to shut out the picture of that wretched room, and miserably went to sleep.

"Well, my man got his job. And two days later he started out with his brother to go to work in the morning, and he returned with him in the evening. And, supposing that I was going to be here for some time, I tried to settle down and take an interest in the household and in the family. But I found it very hard work. Their conversation was so dull, what there was of it. In the morning the men got up, leaving only time enough to gobble their breakfast and rush off to work. In the evening the poor fellows were so tired that they went to bed almost immediately after supper was over. And in between all I had to listen to was the children bawling and the woman scolding them.

"Many a time I'd say to myself: 'Look here, my girl, this won't do. You must cheer up. Laugh at your troubles and sing a song.'

"And then I'd throw my head back and try to fool myself that I was out in the green woods, all merry and bright. But before I'd sing more than two notes one of the brats would start crying or the harassed mother would interrupt with some complaint. It was no use. I just couldn't sing in that house.

"After I'd been there a week I gathered from the conversation of the men one evening that I was going to be taken somewhere the following day. I was delighted. For I thought to myself that, no matter where it was, the change couldn't be for the worse.

"But I was wrong. Where do you suppose I was taken? You could never guess. I was taken down into the coal mine. I didn't know at the time that it was customary to keep canaries in coal mines. It seems that there is a very dangerous kind of gas, called coal damp, that sometimes comes out underground and kills the men working there if they are not warned in time to escape. The idea of having canaries down there is, apparently, that the birds being higher up than the men—hung on the walls of the passages—will get the gas first. Then if the birds start to suffocate the men are warned that it is time to get out of the mine. While the canaries are lively and hopping about, they know it's all right.

"Well, I had never seen the inside of a coal mine before. And I hope I never will again. Of all the dreadful places to work and live, I think that must be the worst. My cage was taken by my owner and his brother the next morning, and he walked a good mile before we came to the mouth of the pit. Then we got into a sort of big box with a rope to it. And wheels began to turn and we went down and down and down and down. The sun could not be seen. For light the men had little lamps fastened to their hats. The box stopped and we got out and went along a long, narrow passage that had little rails with wagons on them, running the length of it. Into these little wagons the coal was put, a long way back in the inside of the mine. Then it was trundled along till it came to the big shaft, where the sliding box, or lift, took it up to the top.

"After we had gone a good distance underground, the men stopped and my owner hung my cage on a nail high up on a wall of the passage. There they left me and went to their work. And all day long men passed and repassed with little wagons of coal, while others picked with pick-axes and loaded the trucks with shovels. Again I was taking an active part in the lives of men. Such lives, poor wretches! My job was to wait for gas—to give warning, by coughing or choking or dying, that the deadly coal damp was stealing down the corridors to poison them.

"At first I feared I was going to be left there all night after the men went home. But I wasn't. When a whistle blew at the end of the day I was taken down from the wall, back to the sliding box and up into the open air—and home to the kitchen and the squalling children. It was now late in the autumn and the daylight was short. It was barely dawn when we went to work in the morning, and dark again before we came up at night. The only sunlight we saw was on Saturday afternoon and Sunday. I had been an inn coach announcer; I had been a marchioness's pet in a silver cage; I had been a crack regiment's mascot. Now I was a miner, working nine hours a day—sniffing for gas! . . . It's a funny world.

"This was, I think, the unhappiest part of my life. My fortunes had fallen very low—they couldn't get much lower than the bottom of a coal mine, could they? So I had that consolation, anyhow; whatever change fate brought along it was bound to be an improvement. And, curious though it may seem, I preferred the working hours in the mine to the so-called resting time in the miner's home. Down in the pit there was at all events a spirit of work. I felt something was being done, accomplished, as each loaded wagon rattled past my cage on its way to the hoisting shaft. And I was helping, doing my share. While the dingy, squalid home—well, it was nothing. One wondered why it had to be, that's all."

"But in the mine," Dab-Dab put in, "weren't you always in continued dread of this horrible gas poisoning you?"

"At the beginning, yes I was," said Pippinella. "But after I had my first experience of it, I was not so scared. I had supposed that if the gas ever did come while I was there, that of course would be the end of me. But I was wrong. We had several goes of it in my mine, but no fatal accidents. I remember the first one especially. It was a little after noon and the men had only been working about half an hour since lunch. I noticed a peculiar smell. Not knowing what gas smelled like, I didn't at first suspect what it was. It got stronger and stronger. Then suddenly my head began to swim and I thought, "Gosh! This is it, sure enough!" And I started to squawk and flutter about the cage and carry on. There were men working not more than seven or eight feet from my cage. But with the noise of their own shovels and picks they did not hear me. And their heads, of course, being lower than mine, they had not yet smelled the gas, which always floats to the top of a room first.

"After a couple of minutes had gone by and still they hadn't taken any notice of me, things began to look pretty bad. The beastly stuff was all in my nose and throat now, choking me, so I could hardly squeak at all. But still I kept on fluttering madly about the cage, even though I couldn't see where I was going. And just at the last minute, when everything was getting all dreamy in my head, the men put down their shovels and picks to take a rest. And in a voice that sounded all sort of funny and far away I heard one of them cry:

"'Bill—look at the bird!—Gas!'

"Then that signal word 'Gas!' was shouted up and down the passages of the whole mine. Tools were dropped with a clatter on the ground; and the men, bending down to keep their heads low, started running for the hoist shaft. My man Bill leapt up and snatched my cage from the wall and fled after them.

"At the shaft we found hundreds of workers gathered, waiting their turn to go up in the sliding box. The whistle up at the top was blowing away like mad to warn any stray men who might still be lingering in the passages.

"When everyone had reached the open air, big suction fans were set to work to draw the gas out of the mine before the men would go to work again. It took hours to get all the passages cleared and safe. And we did not go down again that day.

"And then I realized that these men were taking the same risk as I was. After that first time, when we nearly got caught and suffocated, they were more careful. And at least one of the workers always kept an eye on my cage. If I showed the least sign of choking or feeling ill, they would give the alarm and clear out of the mine.

"The winter wore on. Sadly I wondered how long I was to be a miner. For the first time since I had been a fledgling in the nest I fell to envying the wild birds again. What did it matter how many enemies you had—hawks, shrikes, cats and what not—as long as you had liberty? The wild birds were free to sweep the skies: I lived under the ground—in a cage. I often thought of what my mother had told me of foreign birds—birds of paradise and bright-plumed macaws that flitted through jungles hung with orchids, in far-off tropic lands. Then I'd look around at the black coal walls of this underground burrow, at the lights on the men's caps glimmering in the gloom; and it seemed to me that one day of freedom in India, Africa, or Venezuela would be a good exchange for a whole life such as mine. Was I here for the rest of my days? Nine hours of work; home; to bed; and back to work again. Would the end never come?

"And at last it did. You know a canary is a somewhat smaller creature than a human being, but his life and what happens in it are just as important for him. Only that, of the two, the canary is the better philosopher. I've often thought that if a man or woman had had my job in that mine he would probably have pined away and died from sheer boredom and misery. The way I endured it was by just refusing to think too much. I kept saying to myself: 'Something must happen some day. And whatever it is it'll be something new.'

"One morning at eleven o'clock a party of visitors came to look over the mine. You wouldn't think if you had ever worked in a coal mine that anybody would want to go and look at one. But folks will do all sorts of things out of curiosity. And these people came to inspect us and our mine in rather the way they'd go to a zoo.

"The manager himself came down first to announce their coming. He asked the foreman of the gang in which my owner worked to see that the visitors were shown everything and were treated politely. And a little later the party itself arrived. There were about six of them altogether, ladies and gentlemen. They all wore long coats that the manager had lent them to protect their fine clothes from the coal dust and dirt. They were greatly impressed by things which to us miners were ordinary, everyday matters. And many were the sarcastic remarks the workers made beneath their breath as their fastidious folks poked around and asked stupid questions.

"Among them was an old lady, a funny, fussy old thing, with a plain but very kind face. She was the first in the party to notice me.

"She was the first in the party to notice me."

"'Good gracious!' she cried. 'A canary! What's he doing here?'

"'He's for the gas, ma'am,' said the foreman.

"And then, of course, she wanted to know what that meant, and the foreman told her all about it.

"'Good gracious!' she kept saying. 'I had no idea they had canaries in coal mines. How very interesting! But how dreadful for the poor birds! Can I buy this one? I'd just love to have a canary who have lived in a coal mine.'

"My heart jumped. The chance had come at last, a chance to get back into the open air—to a decent life!

"A long talk began between the old lady and the foreman and my owner. My owner said I was an especially good bird for gas, very sensitive and gave warning at the first traces. But the old lady seemed very determined. She really wanted to help me, I think, to give me a better kind of life. But she was also greatly attracted by the idea of having a bird who had lived in a real coal mine—as a sort of souvenir, perhaps. Also, she seemed to have a good deal of money. Because every time my owner shook his head, she would offer him a higher price, till finally she got to ten guineas. Still he refused, and still the old lady went higher. The workmen stood around listening, gaping with interest. But they weren't half so interested as I was. For on the result of this bargaining my life, or at least my happiness, depended.

"At last, when the bidding had gone to twelve guineas, my owner gave in. I suppose I ought to have felt very proud, for it was a tremendous sum for a canary to cost. But I was much too busy feeling glad to have time for any other kind of sentiment.

"My cage was taken down from the wall and handed to the old lady. She gave the man her address—where he was to come the following day to get his money.

"'Is it a male?' she asked.

"'I don't know, ma'am,' said the man. 'I understand it was a cock. But he hasn't sung a single note since he's been with me.'

"'I'd like to know who would—here,' growled one of the miners.

"'Well, I'll take him anyway,' said the woman. 'I dare say he'll sing when he gets into the air and sunlight.'

"And so ended another chapter in the story of my adventures. For when the old lady, with the rest of the party, took me up in the sliding box, I left the lift of a miner behind me for good. I often thought afterward of those poor wretches toiling away underground and wondered how the other canary got along who took my place. But, oh my, I was glad that for me it was all over and some new kind of a life was in sight!"

"I should think so!" declared the Doctor. "I've always felt terribly sorry for canaries that were forced to do such disagreeable work."

"Why must they use birds?" asked Whitey. "Wouldn't cats do just as well? I'm sure it would be a great relief to know that some of them were shut up in the coal mines."

The Doctor laughed at the mouse's remark.

"Yes, Whitey," he said. "For a mouse or a bird that *would* be a comfort. But, you see, birds—especially canaries—have a very sensitive respiratory system. They can detect the faintest odor of gas while any other animal would be unconscious of its presence."

Then the Doctor closed his notebook for the night.

"Dab-Dab," he said. "Could we have some cocoa and toast before we go to bed. I feel a bit hungry. How about the rest of you?"

"Hurray!" cried Gub-Gub. "There's nothing I like better than cocoa and toast—unless it's cauliflower."

"Cauliflower!" howled Jip. "That horrible stuff! I'd rather eat horseradish root!"

"That's good, too!" said Gub-Gub, smacking his lips.

"Well, there's not going to be any cauliflower—or horse-radish root," snapped Dab-Dab. "It will be cocoa and toast—as the Doctor ordered—OR NOTHING!"

So they all sat down to steaming cups of cocoa and heaps of hot buttered toast, which they finished to the last drop and crumb. Pippinella, remembering the happy days that followed her miserable sojourn in the mines, sang them a tender lullaby that she had composed while living at Aunt Rosie's house.

The Eighth Chapter

Aunt Rosie's House

"AT THE MOUTH OF THE PIT," PIPPINELLA BEGAN the next evening, "there was a sort of cab or hired coach waiting for the old lady. And into this she put me and got in herself. And then we drove a long, long way through the country. I saw at once that she was a kind person, but dreadfully fussy and particular. She kept moving my cage from one part of the cab to another.

"'Little birdie mustn't be in a draft,' she would say. And she'd take me off the seat and put me on the floor. But two minutes later she'd lift me up onto her lap.

"'Little birdie getting enough air down there?' she'd ask. 'Tweet-tweet! Like to sit on Aunt Rosie's lap and look out the window? See the corn sprouting in the pretty fields? Doesn't that look nice after living in a coal mine, little birdie?'

"And it did look nice, even though Aunt Rosie's chatter was tiresome and silly. She meant well. And nothing could have spoiled the beauty of the country for me that morning. Spring was in the

"She'd lift me onto her lap."

air. I had lived through the winter underground, and now when my release had come, the hedges were budding and the crops showing green in the plowed furrows. Out of the carriage window I saw birds hurrying here and there, in pairs, looking for places to build their nests. I hadn't talked to another bird for months and months. Somehow, for almost the first time since I had left my parents, I felt lonely for company of my own kind. I started to figure out exactly how long it was since I had spoken to another bird. But I was interrupted by Aunt Rosie speaking again.

"'Little birdie sing a song?—Tweet-tweet!'

"And then it flashed upon me that I had been practically dumb ever since I left the Fusiliers. I had sung them my marching song as they tramped to the town where all the fighting had been. I wondered if without practice for so long my voice was still any good at all.

"'Little birdie sing a song?' Aunt Rosie repeated.

"With a flourish of wings I sprang to the top perch and threw back my head to begin 'The Midget Mascot,' but just at that moment two more birds, a thrush and his wife, sped by the carriage window with bits of dried grass hanging from their mouths.

"I've never built a nest," I thought to myself. "It's spring, and I'm tired of being alone. It must be lots of fun to have a whole family of young ones to bring up. Aunt Rosie doesn't know whether I'm a cock or a hen. If I sing, then I'm a male, so far as she's concerned. But if I don't, perhaps she'll decide I'm a hen and get me a mate. Then I'll build a nest the way mother and father used to do. It's worth trying anyway. All right; I'll stay dumb for a while longer."

"The town to which the old lady brought me in her cab was very different from the one we had left. It was what is called a cathedral town. Here no factories blackened the air with smoke or poisoned the trees with bad air. Here no droves of pale-faced workers hurried underground in the early morning and dragged their weary bodies up again at night. In this town all was peace and leisured, comfortable life. The old, old cathedral rose in the center of it, gray against the sky, and choughs and crows circled around it and built their nests in the belfry tower. Soft-toned, deep-voiced bells rolled out the hours through the day, chiming a pleasant little tune at all the quarters. There were lots of nice gardens and old houses, substantial and well built—and all different styles.

"The front of Aunt Rosie's house was right on a street, but

it had a fine garden at the back. It was the kind of house and the kind of street that she would live in. When my cage was first hung in the window I noticed two peculiar things. One was that the other window to the same room had a small mirror fixed outside of it on a little bracket. I wondered what this was for at first. But later on, when the old lady sat in her armchair and did her knitting, I saw that it was for watching the neighbors. From where she sat she could, in the mirror, see who was coming down the street. And I noticed that several houses across the way had similar arrangements fixed outside the windows. Apparently watching the neighbors pass while you did your needlework was a favorite

"My cage was hung in the window."

occupation in this town. It was the kind of town where people had time to sit at their windows.

"The other thing that I observed was a streetlamp outside, close to the wall of Aunt Rosie's house. It was not more than a few feet from the bottom of my cage. And every evening an old lamplighter would hobble round with a ladder and climb up and light this lamp, and in the very early morning he'd come and put it out. The light used to shine right into the room—even through the blind. It kept me awake the first few nights—until the old lady noticed that it disturbed me. Then she always put the cover over my cage as soon as the streetlamp was lit. She embroidered a special one herself, made of heavy dark stuff, so that the light wouldn't shine through.

"I made a number of quite interesting friends while I stayed at Aunt Rosie's house. And the hobbling lamplighter was one of them. I never talked to him. But his arrival every night and morning was a regular and pleasant thing to make a note of. Here life generally moved along regular and pleasant lines.

"The old lady had lots of friends, all women. Several times a week they would come in to take tea with her, and they always brought their sewing with them. And to every new lot that came, Aunt Rosie told the story over again of how she had bought me out of a coal mine, way down under the earth. Then they'd gather round my cage and gaze at me.

"All through this I still kept mum and never a note did I sing, though often enough I felt like it, with the trees in the street growing greener every day and spring coming on in leaps and bounds. It was a nice place I had come to. But I wanted company of my own kind. And I was determined I wouldn't sing till the old lady got me a mate.

"It was on one of these sewing-circle occasions that a very

peculiar incident occurred. Aunt Rosie was telling my story to a new group of women friends, when one of them stepped forward and peered closely at me through the bars of my cage. Although her face seemed familiar I couldn't, at first, remember where I'd seen her before. But suddenly, because of a strange way she had of squinting one eye when she looked at me, it came to me.

"She was the wife of one of my gallant Fusiliers!

"I forgot all about my determination not to sing and burst out with 'The Midget Mascot' song.

"Aunt Rosie was so astonished to hear me sing that all she could say was:

"'Why, good gracious! My birdie is singing!'

"'Of course she's singing!' declared the woman. 'She's one of the finest songstresses in the country!'

"'How do you know that?' asked Aunt Rosie, looking very puzzled indeed.

"'Because this is the same bird that belonged to my husband's regiment,' replied the woman. 'He told me before he went off to India that she'd disappeared during the mine riots and that no one had seen her again. Naturally the whole regiment assumed she'd been killed. . . . I do declare!' she muttered. 'This is the strangest thing I've ever seen.'

"By this time Aunt Rosie was as excited as the woman was.

"'Are you sure it's the same one?' she asked. 'You know, I found him working in a miserable coal mine. It cost me twelve guineas to get that miner fellow to give him up.'

"'He's not a he,' the woman said, laughing. 'He's a she! And her name is Pippinella.'

"'Pippinella!' cried Aunt Rosie. 'What a beautiful name.

But if it's a hen, how is it that she sings? I always understood hens couldn't sing.'

"'Nonsense!' declared the woman. 'Hens sing just as well as males. Especially this one.'

"Well," Pippinella continued, "I was glad at last to be identified. For a long time now I had been called Dick or Birdie—or just simply 'it.' But, of course, now I had to worry about Aunt Rosie discovering I could sing. How would I ever make her understand that I wanted a companion of my own kind?

"But it came about quite simply. I suppose I must have gotten to look rather sad and mopey after a while. It wasn't intentional, but the old lady noticed it. For one day, when she took the cover off my cage and gave me seed and water, I was delighted to hear her say:

"'Dear, dear, tut-tut-tut! How sad we look this morning. Maybe my little Pippinella wants a mate. Yes? All right. Aunt Rosie will go and get her another little birdie to talk to!'

"Then she put on her bonnet and went off to the animal shop to get me a husband. Well, I wish you could have seen the husband she brought back."

Pippinella closed her eyes and shrugged up the shoulders of her wings.

"He was a fool—a perfect fool! I've never seen such a stupid bird in my life. The old lady supplied us with cotton wool and other stuffs to build a nest with. Now, building a nest in a cage is a very simple matter, provided the cage is big enough. And ours was amply large. My new husband—his name was Twink—said he knew all about it. We set to work. He didn't agree with anything I did; and I didn't agree with anything he did. And then he'd argue with me—my goodness, how he argued! Just as though he knew, you know! First it was about the position of the nest. I'd get it half done in one corner of the cage, and then he'd put his empty head on one side and say:

"'No, my dear, I don't think that's a good place. The light will shine too much in the children's eyes. Let's put it over in this corner.'

"And he'd want to pull it all down and rebuild it on the other side of the cage. And the next time it would be the way the inside was lined. Even when I was sitting in the nest he'd come fussing around, pulling bits out here and there—right from under me.

"Finally I saw that if I was ever going to get a brood raised at all that year I had better just rule him out of the building altogether. Then we had a violent row, during which he pecked me on the head and I knocked him off the perch. But I won my point. I told him that if he touched the nest again I wouldn't lay a single egg.

"But one thing must be said for Twink. And that was that he had a marvelous voice."

"Better than your own?" asked the Doctor.

"Oh, by far," said Pippinella. "In the upper register—well, it almost seemed at times as if there wasn't any note he couldn't reach. And even in the bass his tones were wonderfully clear and full. Of course, like all husbands, he didn't care to have his wife sing. But as a matter of fact, I never attempted to compete with him, because when eggs and youngsters have to be looked after, we women don't get much time for it.

"And Aunt Rosie may not have known a great deal about canaries, but she knew enough to see that I got peace and quiet during setting time. She kept the cover on, half over the cage, even during the day, so that I shouldn't be disturbed by what was going on in the room. The only direction I could see in was outward, through the window. It was an ideal town anyway for hatching eggs—so restful.

Nothing ever happened in the street more exciting than the regular visits of the old hobbling lamplighter, the arrival of the muffin-seller, with his bell and tray, or an occasional organ-grinder, who stopped before the house and ground out wheezy tunes till Twink sang songs to drown out his sour music.

"So, while Aunt Rosie sat at her window and over her needlework watched the neighbors pass, I sat at mine and over the hatching of the eggs and watched the leaves on the shady trees grow greener and denser—watched the spring turning into the summer. And every time the old lamplighter put the lamp out in the morning I'd say to myself: 'Well, that's another day gone. I have only so many left now before the children will break open their shells.'

"There was great excitement the day when our family at last appeared. They were five strong, healthy birds. Aunt Rosie was even more thrilled and worked up than we were. Ten times a day she would come to the nest and peer in; and every group of her friends who visited her would also be brought to have a look. And they all said the same things: 'Oh my, aren't they ugly!' Goodness! I don't know what they expected newborn birds to look like, I'm sure. Maybe they thought they ought to be hatched out with bonnets and capes on.

"It was now that the real work began for me and my husband. Feeding five hungry children is a big job—even when there are two of you at it. Aunt Rosie used to bring us chopped eggs and biscuit crumbs six times a day. Each lot only lasted about an hour and a quarter, for we had to shovel it into those hungry mouths every thirty minutes. And then there was the lettuce and apple and other green stuff that had to be given them as well.

"But it was lots of fun, even if it was hard work. Twink, I found,

"Ten times a day she would come and peer in."

after the nest-building problems were over, was not nearly so irritating. We got along very well together. He used to sit on the edge of the nest and sing to me when I was keeping the children warm between meals, and many were the beautiful lullabies he made up.

"When the brood was strong enough to leave the nest we both felt awfully proud with the five hulking youngsters crowding on the perch, all in a row beside us. Of course, they quarreled, the way children will, and the two biggest tried to bully it over the rest. Twink and I had our hands full keeping them in order, I can tell you. With seven full-grown birds in it, the cage was now none too big.

"Well, the day came when Aunt Rosie decided she would have to part with some of the family. Many of her friends wanted canaries, and one by one my children went off to new homes, till finally only Twink and I were left. And then, because one of her friends had told the old lady that males sing better if they are alone (which is perfectly true), she gave Twink a separate cage and put him in another room.

"So toward the end of the summer I found myself alone again, now watching the leaves turn brown on the shade trees in the street. The old lamplighter used to come earlier in the evenings now and later in the mornings, because the days were shorter and the nights longer. A swallow had built her nest under the eaves of the roof, just above my window. During the course of the summer I had watched her hatch out two broods and teach them to fly. Now I saw her with many of her friends, gathering and chattering and skimming around the house. They were getting ready to fly south to avoid the cold of the coming winter. I wondered what adventures and strange things they would see on their long trip. And once more I had a vague sort of hankering for a free life that would let me wander where I would.

"For a whole day the swallows kept gathering, more and more arriving all the time. I could not see them sitting on the gutters of the roof, because it was out of sight from my window, but I could hear them twittering, making no end of noise. And the top of the streetlamp was covered with them. In tight-packed rows, their white breasts framed the edges of it, presenting a very pretty picture. Seeing them made me feel like traveling, the way people going off always does.

"At last, with a great farewell fluttering and whistling, they took to the air and set off on their journey. I felt rather sad in the silence that they left behind. But presently through the window I saw Aunt Rosie's white Persian cat slinking along the street with a bird in her mouth. And once more I was reminded of the security and comfort I enjoyed as a cage bird; once more I consoled myself, as the old man came and lit the lamp, that a quiet, stay-at-home, regular life had its compensations. Who knows whether, if Twink and I had built our nest in some forest or hedgerow, instead of raising our brood to fine healthy growth, we would not have seen our children carried off before our very eyes by some prowling cat?"

THE NINTH CHAPTER

The Old Windmill

"I HAVE TOLD YOU THAT I MADE SEVERAL RATHER odd friends while I was at Aunt Rosie's house," Pippinella continued. "Among them was a window-cleaner. The old lady was frightfully particular about having her windows cleaned—so, I supposed, would anybody be who spent so much time looking out of them. And, instead of having the maids of the house do it, she had a regular come, a man who made a business of cleaning windows.

"He was the funniest person to look at I have ever seen—one of those faces that makes you smile the moment you catch sight of it. He whistled cheerful tunes all the time while he was working. He had a very big mouth and when he breathed on the glass to put an extra shine on it, I always had to laugh outright. I used to look forward to his coming. And he took a great liking to me. He always spent an especially long time over my window, getting it immaculately clean with his red-and-white polishing cloth. And he'd whistle and make faces at me through the glass, and I'd whistle back to him. I often thought it would be lots of fun to have him for an owner. I was sure he'd be much more interesting than Aunt Rosie.

"I always felt dreadfully sorry when he was gone. And I would spatter my bathwater all over the window with my wings, so as to make it nice and dirty. I knew that Aunt Rosie had lots of money to pay for cleaning windows. And it seemed to me quite proper that I should help my friend's trade in his way. I could see from his clothes that he was very poor. And so I made it necessary for him to come once a week, instead of once a month.

"He'd whistle and make faces at me through the glass."

"One day Aunt Rosie was speaking to him in my room while he was doing the inside of the window, and their conversation turned to the subject of canaries. He had made some very flattering remarks about me and, to my great joy, she asked him if he would like to have me. Now that she had another bird who sang all day, the novelty had worn off and she did not mind giving me away.

"Then my dirtying up of the windows every week may have had something to do with her willingness to part with me—she was one of those frightfully particular housekeepers. But so long as I was to go to the window-cleaner, I was just as well pleased.

"Well, my friend was quite overcome with joy when the old lady told him he could have me. And that night he wrapped me up and took me to his home.

"It was the strangest place. He lived in an old windmill. It had not worked for many years and was nearly a ruin. I imagine he got it very cheap—if, indeed, he paid any rent at all for it. But inside he had made it very comfortable. It was just a round tower, like most windmills, but of good, solid stonework. He lived in a little room at the bottom, which he had furnished with homemade chairs and tables and shelves. It had a little stove, whose pipe ran up the tower and out at the top. He had no family—lived all by himself and cooked his own meals. He had lots and lots of secondhand books, which he bought after the covers had fallen off them—very cheaply, I suppose.

"He spent all his evenings reading and writing. I believe he was secretly writing a book himself, because he carefully kept all the sheets of paper he wrote on in a tin box in a hole in the floor. He was quite a character, but one of the nicest man I ever knew. He cleaned windows only because he needed money to live on. Of that

I am sure. Because the windows of his own home were in a shocking state, so he evidently didn't polish glass for the love of it.

"And so I settled down to live with my funny new master. He was indeed an odd fellow. I believe if he had been able he would have spent all his time reading and writing. But he had to go to work in the morning and he was gone until teatime. I used to look forward to Sunday, because then he was home all day. The rest of the week I felt rather lonely. When he left in the morning he locked up his old windmill with a homemade lock, and all day long I had nothing to do but watch the rats chase one another over his homemade furniture or look at the view through the window-cleaner's dirty window. And although the view was quite remarkable—the mill was on a hill on the outskirts of the town—you soon got used to it. And as for the rats, I always considered them vulgar creatures and their conversation and low games did not interest me.

"But the evenings were great fun. When he came home, my friend would talk to me the whole time he was cooking his dinner. Of course, he had no idea I understood him. But I think he was glad of anyone to converse with. For he, too, led a very lonely life—and, what is more, he was not used to it, like me. Yes, he'd tell me the whole day's doings while he fried his eggs or stirred his soup—what houses he had been in, what sort of people he had seen, whether their windows were extra dirty, and if they had bird cages hanging in them or not. In this way he often brought me news of Aunt Rosie and my husband, Twink, and even of my children, who had gone to other houses whose windows he was accustomed to cleaning.

"I was puzzled about my strange friend a good deal—about what had been in his life before he took to this profession. If he had any relatives at all they did not live in these parts. He never got any

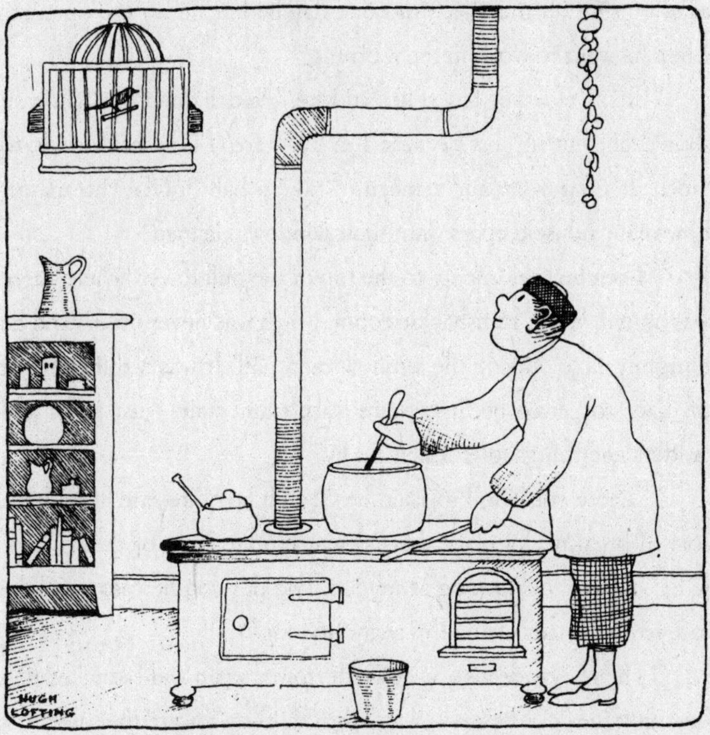

"He would tell me the day's doings while he stirred his soup."

letters, nor wrote any. He was a man cut off, as it were, from all his fellows. I often wondered whether he had brought this about himself in order to keep his life undisturbed for studying and writing, or whether he had some secret that made it necessary for him to live thus—almost in hiding, as you might say.

"Well, the writer wore pleasantly on, and soon the spring was at hand once more. This was a time when my master was particularly busy, for everyone was doing spring-cleaning—which always means a lot of extra window washing. Some nights he did not get home till quite late. When the days got warmer he would put my cage outside on the wall. And one day he left me in the open air when he went to work in the morning.

"'It's a pleasant day, Pip,' said he. 'And I don't see why you should be shut up just because I'm not here. I'll be back early to lunch. It's Saturday and I mean to take a half holiday, no matter how many housekeepers want their windows cleaned.'

"Then he took me up to the top of the mill tower, where there was an old, leaky, ramshackle room, which was never used. And he hung my cage outside the window on a nail. It was a difficult sort of place to get to because there wasn't any stair—just poles and ladders and things to scramble up by.

"'There you are, Pip,' said he. 'You'll be quite safe here. It's a sort of breaknecky place, but no worse than some of the window ledges I have to stand on at my job. I've put you here so you'll be safe from the cats, while I'm away. So long.'

"Then he made his way down the tower again and I watched him go out of the door below and walk briskly away toward the town.

"It was very nice to be in the open. It was the first time my cage had been set out this year. The mild spring sunshine was invigorating and refreshing. From my lofty lookout I watched wild birds of various kinds flying here and there and everywhere.

"Lunchtime came, but my friend did not return.

"'Oh well,' I thought, 'he has been delayed. He can't afford to disappoint his customers. Some old lady has asked him to stay on and do a few extra windows. He'll turn up soon.'"

"And even when teatime came, and still he hadn't appeared, I continued to make excuses for him. But when the sun had set and the evening star was twinkling in the dusky sky and my cage had not yet been taken in, I began to get really anxious.

"As the darkness settled down about my cage I began to shiver with the cold. It was still, you see, quite early in the year, and even indoors I was accustomed to have a cover over me.

"I got no sleep at all. All night I kept wondering what could have become of my friend. Had he fallen from some high place while cleaning windows? Had he been run over? Something must have happened to him, that was certain. Because he was always very thoughtful of me and he couldn't have forgotten that he had left me out in the open. And, even supposing that that had slipped his memory, he could never have forgotten that I would need food and fresh water by the end of the day.

"Well, the dawn came at last—after a night that seemed a whole eternity in length. As the sun gradually rose in the heavens and the warmth of it glowed upon my shivering wings, my spirits revived somewhat. There was still a little seed left in my trough and some water in the pot. I was about to take breakfast—which I always did at sunrise—when it suddenly occurred to me that I had better economize and make my supply last as long as possible. Because the more I thought of it the more certain I became that I had seen the last of my good friend the window-cleaner.

"You see, with an ordinary person who had a family living with him or friends calling at his house or tradesmen delivering daily goods, I would sooner or later have received assistance. But this man never had a soul come near him from one end of the year to the other. So I made up my mind to two things: first, something serious had happened to my owner; the second, that I couldn't expect any help or food except by some chance accident. It was a bad outlook all around.

"Still, where there's life there's hope. I ate a very tiny breakfast—just enough to keep me going. Lunchtime came and I did the same—and the same again at dusk. Another cold, miserable night. Another shivering dawn. By now I had only a few grains of food left. My spirits were dreadfully low. I ate the last of my supply and, utterly worn out, fell asleep as the sun began to rise.

"Just how long I slept I don't know—till an hour or so beyond noon, I imagine. I was awakened by a great racket, and, opening my eyes, found the sky dark with rain clouds. A storm was brewing. Every few seconds great tongues of lightning flashed across the face of the gloomy heavens, followed by deafening crashes of thunder.

"Great tongues of lightning flashed across the face of the gloomy heavens."

"As the first big drops of rain came plopping onto the floor of my cage, I saw I was in for a good soaking in addition to my other troubles. But that storm was a blessing in disguise. Such a storm! I have never seen anything like it. My mill tower, placed where all the winds of heaven could reach it, got the full benefit of its fury. Five minutes after I woke up I was drenched and chilled to the marrow of my bones. I tried to crouch down under my water-pot and get some shelter that way. But it was no use. The gale blew the rain in every direction and there was no escaping it. The floor of my cage was just swimming in water.

"Suddenly I heard a rending crackling sound and saw a piece of mill roof hurtle earthward, through the air, just wrenched off the tower by the strength of the wind. In between the claps of thunder I heard other crashes below me. All sorts of things were being blown down or smashed by the tempest.

"And then, zip! I felt my cage struck upward, as though someone had hit the bottom with the palm of his hand. And the next minute I, too, was sailing earthward. My cage had been blown off its nail.

"After my cage jumped off its nail and started sailing through the air, I haven't a very clear recollection of things. I remember feeling it turn over and over till I was giddy, and on its way down I think it struck a roof or something and bounced off. I clung to the perch with my claws—more out of fright than anything else—and just turned over with it as it spun.

"Then there was a crash. Suddenly I found myself sitting in a puddle on the ground, quite unharmed but very wet. The two halves of my cage, neatly broken in the center, lay on either side of me. The rain was still beating down in torrents. I had landed on a cobble pavement, right in front of the mill. Under the steps there was a hole between the stones. I crept into the shelter of it and tried to collect my scattered wits while I waited for the rain to stop.

"'So,' I thought to myself, 'I am a free bird at last! If this storm hadn't come along and blown my cage down, I would have starved to death up there in two or three more days, at most. Well, well! And now, after wondering so often what it would feel like to be uncaged, here I am—free! But oh, so hungry, so cold and so wet!'

"And thus—"

"But what happened to the window-cleaner?" Gub-Gub interrupted. "Why hadn't he come back?"

"Wait and you will see," said Pippinella severely.

"And thus began still another chapter of my story—when, after being born and brought up a cage bird I was suddenly made by Fate into a wild one. For the present, sad and unhappy though I was about my good friend the window cleaner, I only had two ideas in my mind—to get dry and to find food. I was literally starving."

PART TWO

THE FIRST CHAPTER

The Green Canary Learns to Fly

AFTER ABOUT HALF AN HOUR THE STORM abated, the rain stopped and the sun come out. I at once left my rat hole and started to fly around in the open to get the wet shaken out of my feathers.

"I was astonished to discover that I could hardly fly at all, I decided that this was due to the soaking I had had—and to exhaustion from want of food. But even when, by constant fluttering, I got perfectly dry, I found that the best I could do was just tiny, short distances; and that the effort of these was frightfully tiring. As a cage bird I had learned to keep up a flight only from one perch to another—hardly flying at all, you might say. Before I could take to the air like a regular free bird I had to learn—just as though I were a baby leaving the nest for the first time.

"Well, there was no food here. And if I was to go foraging for any I had better get busy. So I set to work practicing my flight. There was an old packing-case close to the door of the mill and I began by flying up onto it and down again. Presently, while I was doing this, I noticed a lean, hungry-looking cat watching me. "'Ha, ha, my beauty,' I thought. 'I may be a very green cage bird, but I know you and your kind.'

"And by short stages I flew up on the roofs of some old tumble-down outhouses that stood near. She followed me up there. Then I returned to the yard. In spite of my poor flying I could keep out of her claws so long as I knew where she was. And I never lingered anywhere in the neighborhood of an ambushing place, where she could pounce out on me unawares.

"In the meantime I kept on practicing. And although it was very

"Presently I noticed a cat watching me."

exhausting work, I felt I was improving hourly and would soon be able to make the top of the mill tower in one flight. From there I hoped I would be able to get inside the building through a hole in the roof and make my way down to the kitchen, where I could find some food.

"Seeing what a poor flyer I was, Madam Pussy, in the mean-souled way that cats have, had made up her mind that I was injured or a weakling and would be easy prey. And she stayed around and watched and waited. She was determined to get me. But I was equally determined that she wouldn't.

"Most people would think, I suppose, that it is a very simple matter for a cage bird to change herself in a moment into a wild one. But it isn't easy—not by a great deal. You see, wild birds are taught when they are very young to take care of themselves. They learn from their parents and from watching and imitating other birds: where to search for water, at what seasons seed is to be found, where and when to look for certain kinds of berries, what places to roost in at night so they'll be protected from winds and safe from pouncing weasels, and—well, a million and a half other things. All this education I had missed. And for me my freedom at its beginning was just about the same as it would be for Gub-Gub there suddenly to find himself in the jungle with wild boars and tigers and snakes, after spending his life in a nice, comfortable sty."

"Pardon me," said Gub-Gub, turning up his nose. "But I have already been in the jungle and enjoyed it greatly."

"Yes, and got lost there," growled Jip. "Dry up!"

"Well," Pippinella continued, "I realized this at once. I saw that if I was to escape the dangers that threatened me and to survive in the open I would have to be very careful, to depend on common sense and take no risks. That was the chief reason why I began by making my way into the inside of the building. Within its walls I should be safe. I knew that owls and hawks and shrikes swept around this hill every once in a while on the lookout for anything small enough to kill. And until my flying was a great deal better, I would stand no earthly chance of escape, once a bird of prey started out to get me.

"I found a hole in the top of the tower and I made my way downward through all sorts of funny dark flues and passages till I came to the kitchen door. This was locked. But luckily the old things was all warped and it didn't fit very well. There was a space over the top big enough for me to slip through.

"There was a space over the top big enough for me to slip through."

"I lived in that kitchen for a week. I found my seed where I knew the window-cleaner always kept it, in a paper bag on the mantelshelf. In the corner by the stove there was a bucket of water. So I was well stocked with provisions, besides being snugly protected behind solid stone walls from my natural enemies and the cold of the nights. There I went on practicing my flying. Round and round that kitchen I flew, counting the number of laps. And after I had got as high as a thousand I thought, 'Well, I don't know just how far that would be in a straight line, but it must be a good long way.'

"Still I wasn't satisfied. I knew that often in the open I would have to fly miles and miles at high speed. And I kept on circling the kitchen by the hour. One morning, when I rested on the mantelpiece after two hours of steady flying, I suddenly spied that wretched cat, squatting behind the stove, watching me. How she had got in I don't know—certainly not the way I had come. But cats are mysterious creatures and can slip through unbelievably small spaces when they want to.

"Well, anyway, there she was. My comfortable kitchen wasn't safe anymore. However, I found a place to rest at night—the funniest roosting-place you ever saw; on a string of dried onions that hung from the ceiling. I knew she couldn't reach me there and I could go to sleep in safety.

"But, as a matter of fact, I got very little rest. The cat was on my mind all the time. And although I knew perfectly well that she couldn't jump as high as that string, somehow—they're such horribly clever things—every time she moved I woke up, thinking that perhaps she'd discovered some devilish trick to reach me after all.

"Finally I said to myself: 'Tomorrow I will leave the mill and take to the open. It's a little earlier than I had planned to go, but

I'll get no peace, now she has found her way here. Tomorrow I will journey forth to seek my fortune.'

"Back I traveled through the little space above the door, up the dark, dusty, dilapidated mill tower, until I came to the hole in the stonework at the top. It was a beautiful morning. A lovely scene lay before me as I—"

"But when's the window-cleaner coming back?" whined Gub-Gub. "I want to know what happened to that window-cleaner."

"Be patient," said the Doctor. "Pippinella has told you to wait and see."

"A lovely scene," the canary repeated, "lay before me as I gazed out over the countryside. For a moment I felt almost scared to launch myself down upon the bosom of the air from that height. I picked out a little copse over to the east. 'That can't be more than a quarter of a mile away,' I said to myself. 'I can surely fly that far. All right—here goes!'

"And I shot off the tower top in the direction of the little wood. Once more I found myself faced with the problems of my own inexperience. I had never before flown high up in the open air. I had no idea of how to tackle the winds and the air currents that pushed me and turned me this way and that. Any ordinary bird would have reached that copse with hardly a flutter—just sailed down to it with motionless, outstretched wings. But I—well, I was like some badly loaded boat without a rudder in a gale. I pitched and tossed and wobbled and staggered. I heard some crows who passed laughing at me in their hoarse, cracky voices.

"'Haw, haw!' they crackled. 'Look at the feather-duster the wind blew up! Put your tail down, chicken! Stick to it! Mind you don't fall!—Whoa!'

"They're vulgar, low birds, crows. But I suppose I must have looked comical enough, fluttering and flapping around at the mercy of the fitful wind. I got down to the woods somehow and made a sort of wild spread-eagle landing in the top boughs of an oak. I was all exhausted. But I felt encouraged, anyway. I had proved that I could get where I wanted to, even with a moderate wind against me.

"I rested awhile to regain my breath and then started hopping around through the woods. I found it much easier to get my wings all caught up in the blackberry brambles than to shoot in and out of the thickets like the other birds did. But I took the crows' advice and stuck to it, knowing that the only way to learn even this was by practice.

"While I was hopping about, making discoveries and collecting experience, I became aware that once more I was being watched by enemies. This time it was a large sparrow hawk. Whenever I came out into a clearing I'd see the same round-shouldered bird, sitting motionless at the top of small tall tree. He pretended to be dozing in the sun. But I felt quite certain that he had noticed my awkward, clumsy flight and was only waiting for a chance to swoop on me. I knew that so long as I stayed near the bramble thickets I was safe. For with his wide wings he couldn't possibly follow me into the little tiny spaces of the thorny blackberry tangles.

"After a while I supposed he had given me up as a bad job. For he flew off with easy, gliding flight and made away over the treetops as though leaving the woods for good. Then, feeling safe once more I proceeded with further explorations and after a little I decided to venture out in the open again.

"This time I thought I'd try traveling downwind. And I set out flying back in the general direction from which I had approached the wood. It was much easier work, but required quite a lot of skill to keep a straight line with the wind at my back.

"About halfway across the fields that lay beneath the copse and the windmill hill I noticed a flock of sparrows rise out of a hedge below me in a great state of alarm. They were looking upward at the sky as they scattered, chattering, in all directions. They were evidently in a panic about something. And suddenly I guessed what it was—I had forgotten all about the hawk. I turned my head, and there he was, not more than a hundred and fifty yards behind, speeding after me like a bullet. I never had such a fright in my life. There was no place in the fields where I could hide.

"'The hole in the tower,' I thought to myself. 'If I can reach that I am safe. He isn't small enough to follow me into that hole in the roof.'

"And putting on the best speed I could, I shut my beak tight and made for the old mill.

"It was a terrible race," Pippinella went on, shaking her head. "That hawk had the speed of the wind itself and there were times when I thought I'd never get away from him. I was afraid to look back, lest even the turning of my head delay my flight. I could hear the swish, swish, swish of his great wings beating the air behind me.

"But fortunately the rising sparrows had warned me in time, so I had a pretty fair start on him. And in so short a flight, even he was not swift enough to overtake me. He came awfully close to it, though. As I shot into the mill roof and tumbled down gasping for breath among the cobwebs, I saw his great shadow sweep over the hole not more than a foot behind me.

"'You wait!' I heard him hiss as he tilted upward and veered away over the mill roof. 'I'll get you yet!'"

"You haven't forgotten about the window-cleaner, have you?" asked Gub-Gub. "What's happening to him all this time?"

"Oh, be quiet," snapped Jip.

"I spent the night in the tower," Pippinella continued. "The cat did not know I was there yet, so I wasn't bothered by her. But I felt very miserable as I settled down to sleep. An ordinary free bird, I suppose, would have not been greatly disturbed by being chased by a hawk—so long as he got away. But it was my first experience in the wild. And it seemed to me as though the whole world was full of enemies, of creatures that wanted to kill me. I felt dreadfully friendless and lonely.

"After a fitful, nightmary sort of sleep I was awakened in the morning by a very agreeable sound, the love song of a greenfinch. Somewhere on a ledge just outside the hole a bird was singing. And he was singing to me. I was, as it were, being serenaded at my window. I got up, brushed the cobwebs out of my tail, spruced up my feathers, and prepared to go out and take a look at my caller.

"I peeped out cautiously through the hole and there he was—the handsomest little male you ever saw in your life. His head was thrown back, his wings slightly raised, and his throat puffed out. He was singing away with all his might. I do not know any song, myself, that I like better than the love song of the greenfinch in the spring. There's a peculiar dreamy, poetic sort of quality to it that no other bird melody possesses. You have no idea what it did for me that morning. In a moment I had forgotten about the hawk and the cat and all my troubles. The whole world seemed changed, friendly, full of pleasant adventures. I waited there, listening in the dark, till he had finished. Then I stepped out of the hole on to the roof.

"'Good morning,' he said, smiling in an embarrassed sort of way. 'I hope I didn't wake you too early.'

"'Oh, not at all,' I answered. 'It was very good of you to come!'

"'Well,' he said, 'I saw you being chased by that beastly sparrow hawk last night. I had noticed you in the copse earlier. From your sort of stiff way of flying I guessed you were a cage bird just newly freed. I'm glad you got away from the old brute. I was awfully afraid you wouldn't. You are partly a greenfinch yourself, are you not?'

"'Yes,' I replied. 'My mother was a greenfinch and my father a canary.'

"'I guessed that, too, from your feathers,' said he. 'I think you're very pretty—with those fine yellow bars on your wings.'

"'Would you care to take a fly around the woods?' my new acquaintance asked me. 'It's a pleasant morning.'

"'Thank you,' I said. 'I certainly would. I'm very hungry and I don't know very much as yet about foraging for food in the open.'

"'Well, let's be off, then,' he said. 'Wait till I take a look around to make sure the squint-eyed old hawk isn't snooping about. Then we'll go across to Eastdale Farm. I know a granary there where there are whole sacks of millet seed kept. And some of it is always lying around loose near the door where the men load it in. Ha, the coast is clear! Come along.'

"So off we went, as happy as you please—for all the world like two children out for a romp. On the way my friend, whose name I found was Nippit, gave me no end of new tips about flying—how to set the wings against a twisting air current, what effect had the spreading of the tail fanlike when the wind was behind me, dodges for raising myself without the work of flapping, how to drop or dive without turning over.

"We reached the farm he had spoken of. A fine, substantial, old-fashioned place, it looked just charming in early morning sunlight.

"'I don't think the men are up yet,' he said. 'Not that they would bother us even if they were. But it's more comfortable getting your breakfast without disturbances. There's the granary, that big brick building with the elms hanging over it.'

"He led me to the door at the back, and there, as he had said, was quite a lot of millet seed scattered around loose, where it had fallen from the sacks on their way into the storerooms.

"While we were gobbling away he suddenly shouted, 'Look out!' at the top of his voice. And we both leapt into the air in the nick of time. The farm dog, one of those spaniels they use for shooting, had made a rush at us from behind. I hadn't seen him coming at all. But my friend's eyes were twice as sharp as mine and he never ate near the ground without keeping one eye constantly on the lookout all around. His vigilance had saved my life."

The Second Chapter

Nippit the Greenfinch

NIPPIT AND I BECAME CLOSER FRIENDS THAN ever, and I often think that if it had not been for him I would never have survived the life of the open or be here now to tell the tale. His experience not only protected me from my enemies, but his wisdom provided me with food. He took me under his care, as it were, and with great patience he taught me the things a wild bird needs to know."

To the animals' great surprise, Pippinella, who had always seemed a very practical sort of bird, at this point sniffed slightly, as though for the moment overcome with emotion.

"You must excuse me," she gulped. "I know it's very silly of me, but whenever I think of Nippit I nearly always get sentimental and wobbly in the voice—I mean, when I think about the part I am now going to tell you . . . I was terribly fond of him—more fond than I have ever been of anyone or anything. And he was most frightfully in love with me. One moonlight night we swore to be true to one another till death, to go off and find a place to build a nest and raise a family of young ones. We described to each other what the place should look like. We were terribly particular about the details. It was a real romance.

"The next day we started off. We journeyed a great distance. The spot we had determined for our home was very hard to find. And finally we came to the seashore. We explored a little bay—the very loveliest thing you could wish to see. Big drooping willows hung down off rocks and dabbled their wands in the blue water. Beautiful wildflowers and colored mosses carpeted the shore. It was a secluded little cove where people never came. The peace and the beauty of it were just ideal. And there at the bottom of the bay, where a little sparkly mountain stream fell laughing into the sea, we found the spot we had come so far to seek—exact in every detail."

"Maybe the window-cleaner sprained his ankle," murmured Gub-Gub, "or ate something that disagreed with him and had to go to a hospital. But I would like to know why he didn't send someone to take his canary in."

"For heaven sakes, will you wait?" growled Jip. "Keep quiet! Wait and see what happened!"

"But I don't like waiting," said Gub-Gub. "I never was a good waiter. Why doesn't she come right out with it? She knows what happened to her friend."

"Gub-Gub," said the Doctor wearily, "if you don't keep quiet you will have to leave the wagon."

"Right away," Pippinella continued, "we set to work hunting for materials to build a nest. You know, each kind of bird has fads and fancies about nest building—each one uses materials of his own special kind. The greenfinch's nest is not more extraordinary in this than any others; but some of the stuffs used are not always easily found. In these parts they were exceptionally scarce. So we went off hunting in different directions, agreeing that either should come and let the other know as soon as the stuff we were after was discovered.

"I went a long way down the shore and after about an hour's search I came upon the material we sought. It was a special kind of grass. I marked the spot in my mind and set off back to tell my mate. I had some difficulty in finding him, but eventually I did—and" (again Pippinella's voice grew tearful) "he was talking to a greenfinch hen. She was very handsome, slightly younger than either Nippit or myself. The instant I saw them talking together something told me the end of our romance had come.

"He introduced me to her—rather awkwardly. And she smirked and smiled like the brazan hussy that she was. It was now too late in the evening to go on with the nest building; and anyway, I had no heart for it. After we had had something to eat and taken a drink in the little sparkling stream, we all three roosted on a flowering hawthorn bush.

"I cannot believe that it was all Nippit's fault. But by morning I knew what I must do. Quietly, while my faithless mate and that hypocritical minx still slept, I dropped to a lower branch of the hawthorn bush and made my way down to the edge of the sea."

The sadness in Pippinella's silvery voice reminded John Dolittle of that first evening when he had brought her home. You will remember how, after her covered cage had been put up on a shelf, she had sung for him for the first time through the wrapping paper.

Now, as she paused a moment in her story, evidently very close to the verge of tears, the Doctor was glad of an interruption that arrived just at the right moment to cover her embarrassment. It was the chief tent rigger, who wished to consult Manager Dolittle about

"We all three roosted on a flowering hawthorn bush."

buying a new tent for the snakes. The old one, he said, was so full of mends and patches that he felt it would be better economy to throw it away and buy a new one—especially in view of the circus's going visit to London, where they would want everything to be as smart and up-to-date as possible.

When the discussion was over and the tent rigger had departed, Pippinella took a sip of water and presently went on with her story.

"The day was rising in the east. The calm water reflected the mingled gray and pink of the dawn sky and way out on the horizon little flashes of gold here and there showed where the sun would soon come up.

"It was a lovely scene. But I didn't care. I hated everything about this place now—the snug bay, the weeping willows, the murmuring mountain brook—everything.

"Some birds nearby started their morning song. A finch flew past and twittered a greeting to me on the wing. But still I sat there gazing out from the sands toward the wide-stretching sea. It seemed to yawn and roll lazily, rubbing the sleep out of its eyes as the night retired from the face of the water and the rising sun glowed around its rim. Its mystery, its vastness, called to me, sympathizing with my mood.

"'The sea!' I murmured. 'I've never crossed the salt water.

"'What country,' I asked, 'lies beyond this ocean?'"

I've never looked on foreign lands, as all the other wild birds have. Those jungles my mother told me of, where blue and yellow macaws climb on crimson flowering vines, they must be nice, they would be new. There surely, among fresh scenes and different company, I shall be able to forget. Everything around me here I hate, for it reminds me of my mate who was false, of my love that was spurned.'

"You see, it was my first romance, so I felt especially sentimental. 'Very well,' I said, 'I will leave this land and cross the sea.'

"I went down closer to the breaking surf and stood upon the firm, smooth, hard-packed sand of the beach. I noticed a small bird, a goldfinch, coming inland. He looked as though he had flown a long way. I hailed him.

"'What country,' I asked, 'lies beyond this ocean?'

"With a neat curve he landed on the sand beside me, I noticed him eyeing my crossbred feathers with curiosity.

"'Many lands,' he answered. 'Where do you want to go?'

"'Anywhere,' I answered. 'Anywhere, so long as I get away from here.'

"'That's odd,' said he. 'Most birds are coming this way now. Spring and summer are the seasons here. I came over with the goldfinches. The main flock arrived last night. But I was delayed and followed on behind. Did you ever cross the ocean before? Do you know the way?'

"'No,' I said, bursting into tears. 'I know no geography nor navigation. I'm a cage bird. My heart is broken. I want to reach the land where the blue and yellow macaws climb ropes of crimson orchids.'

"'Well,' said he, 'that could be almost anywhere in the tropics. But it's pretty dangerous, you know, ocean travel, if you're not experienced at it.'

"'I don't care anything about the danger,' I cried. 'I'm desperate. I want to go to a new land and begin life all over again. Good-bye!'

"And springing into the air I headed out over the sea just as the full glory of the rising sun flooded the blue waters in dazzling light."

The Third Chapter

Ebony Island

JOHN DOLITTLE STARED AT PIPPINELLA IN amazement.

"That was an extremely dangerous thing for you to have undertaken," he said. "I'm surprised you are here at all to tell the story."

Pippinella smiled sadly, nodding her head in agreement. "Yes, Doctor," she replied. "But I had no thought for the dangers I was facing. All I wanted to do was get away—as far away as my wings would carry me.

"Had I been a regular wild bird I would have known some of the geography of the land. Then such a journey would not have been so hazardous. From time beyond remembrance the goldfinch or swallow, or any one of the migrating birds, has made his two yearly journeys from one land to another—one way in the spring, the other in the fall. They would no more dream of getting lost than they would of forgetting how to fly. After they have made the first trip with the flock it becomes a perfectly simple matter for them, and I really believe most of them could do it with their eyes shut.

"But for me? Well, if I hadn't been desperate with grief, I would never have embarked upon such a mad adventure. It was only after I had flown steadily for two hours, and then on looking behind me found I had passed beyond sight of land, that I fully realized what I had done. On all sides—north, east, south, and west—the sky met the sea in a flat ring. No clouds marred the even color of the heavens, nothing broke the smoothness of the blue-green sea. In turning my head to look back I had changed my direction without thinking. Now I didn't even know if I was going the same way or not. I tried to remember from what quarter the wind had been blowing when I started. But I couldn't recollect. And anyway, there was no wind blowing now. So I could get no guidance from that.

"A terrible feeling of helplessness came over me as I gazed down. I was flying at a great height—at the wide-stretching water below me. Where was I? Whither was I going?

"And then it occurred to me that in this, as in my other first difficulties of freedom, I had to learn—to learn or perish. 'Well,' I thought, 'I'll go and take a closer look at the surface of the water. I'm too high up to see anything here. Perhaps I can learn something from that.'

"So I shut my wings and dropped a couple of thousand feet. As I came nearer to the water I noticed many little patches of brown on it, thousands of them. They were evidently some kind of seaweed or grass. They floated in straggly chains, like long processions of tortoises or crabs. But these chains all lay in the same direction.

"'Ah, hah!' I said. 'That's a current.' I had seen something of the same kind before, grasses and leaves pushed across a lake by a river that flowed into it. And I knew there was a force in that water down below me that drove all those weed clumps the same way.

"'I'll follow the drift of that weed,' I thought. 'It will keep me in a straight line, anyhow, and maybe bring me to the mouth of the river from which the current flows.'

"Well, my idea would have been all right if my strength had held out. You must remember that it wasn't many months since I had flown at all in the open. And suddenly as I skimmed over the weed chains I got an awful cramp in my left wing muscle. I just felt I had to stop and rest. But where? I couldn't sit on the water like a duck. There was nothing for it but to keep on. I had been going three hours at seventy miles an hour, some two hundred miles—by far the longest flight I had ever made. The wonder was that I hadn't given out before.

"Things looked bad. In spite of all my efforts to keep at the same level, I was coming down nearer the water all the time. Finally I was skimming along only a few feet above the swells. I was so near now I could see the tiny sea beetles clinging to the weed tufts. In between, in the clear spaces, I saw my own reflection looking up at me, a tiny fool of a land bird with wildly flapping outstretched wings, trying to make her way across a never-ending ocean, lost, giving out, coming nearer to a watery grave second by second.

"The thing that saved me was the little sea beetles that crawled upon the floating weed. They gave me an idea. If the shred of weed could carry them, I thought, why wouldn't larger clumps of it carry me? I looked along the straggling chains that wound over the sea ahead of me. About a hundred years farther on I spied a bigger bunch of the stuff. Making a tremendous effort, I spurted along and just gained it in time. I dropped on it as lightly as I could in the exhausted condition I had reached. To my great delight it bore me up—for the moment. The relief of being able to relax my weary muscles and rest was wonderful. For the present I didn't bother about anything else, but just stood there on my little seaweed boat and rose and fell on the heaving bosom of the sea.

"But soon I noticed that my feet were getting wet. The water had risen right over my ankles. My odd craft would carry my small weight for a few moments only; then it had gone slowly under. It was of the utmost importance that I should not, in my exhausted state, get my feathers waterlogged. I looked around. Not more than six feet away another clump of weed about the size of a tea tray was floating. With a spring and a flip, I leapt from my old raft to the new one. Being a little larger, it carried me a moment or two longer than the one I had left. But it, too, sank in time and the warning water rising around my feet drove me on to yet another refuge.

"It wasn't the most comfortable way in the world to take a rest—hopping from one sinking island to another. Still, it was better than nothing. In the short jumps I did not have to use my wings much and I already felt the cramp in my left shoulder improving. I decided that I could keep this up as long as I liked. It was the steady drive of constant flying that tired me. So long as there were enough large weed clumps and no storms came, I was safe.

"But that was all. I wasn't going ahead. The current was moving very slowly—and that in the wrong direction for me. I was hungry and thirsty. There was no food here, and no prospect of getting any. There were, it is true, the tiny sea creatures that crawled upon the weeds. But I was afraid to eat them, saturated in salt water, lest the thirst I had already should grow worse. The only thing to do for the present was to be thankful for this assistance, to rest up, and then go on again.

"Presently I began to notice the sun. It had been getting higher and higher all the time since I had left land, but soon it seemed to be standing still and then to descend. That meant that midday had been passed. I began to wonder if I could get much farther before night fell. There was no moon, I knew, till early morning, and in the darkness flying for me would be impossible if I could not see my guiding current.

"While I was wondering, I suddenly spied a flock of birds coming toward me from the opposite direction. They were evidently land birds, and when they got nearer I saw that they were finches, though of a kind that I had never seen before. They were slamming along at a great pace and their freshness and speed made me feel very foolish and weak, squatting on my lump of seaweed like a turtle. It occurred to me that this was a chance to get some advice that might not come again in a long while. So, putting my best foot forward, as you might say, I flew up to meet them in mid-air. The leaders were very decent fellows and pulled up as soon as I called to them.

"'Where will I get to if I keep going straight along this current?' I asked.

"'Oh, great heavens!' they said. 'That currents meanders all the way down into the Antarctic. Where do you want to get to?'

"'The nearest land—now, I suppose,' said I. 'I'm dead beat and can't go many more hours without something to eat and a real rest.'

"'Well, turn and cut right across the current, then,' said they. 'To your left as you're flying now. That'll bring you to Ebony Island.

"Squatting on my lump of seaweed like a turtle"

Keep high up and you can't miss it. It's got mountains. That's the nearest land. About a two-hour fly. So long!'

"Without wasting further daylight—for it was now getting late in the afternoon—I took the finches' advice and headed away to the left of the current in search of Ebony Island. This time I kept direction by flying square across the drifting chains of seaweed instead of following their course.

"Well, it may have been only a two-hour trip for those finches, but it was a very different thing for me. After three hours of steady going my wing began to trouble me again. The big setting sun was already standing on the skyline like an enormous plate. It would be dark in twenty minutes more. Here the seaweed was no longer visible. I had passed beyond the path of the current. And still no land had come in sight. I took a sort of bearing by the position of the sun and plugged along.

"Darkness came, but with it came a star. It twinkled out of the gloomy sky right ahead of me as the sun disappeared beneath the sea's edge. And although I knew that the stars do not stand still, I reckoned that this one hadn't moved very much in a couple of hours, and that was certainly as long as I would be able to keep going with a groggy wing. So, heading straight for that guiding silver point in a world of blackness, I plowed on and on.

"Another hour went by. Weary and winded, I now began to wonder if the finch leader could have made a mistake. He had said there were mountains on the island. As more and more stars had come twinkling out into the gloomy bowl of the sky, the night had grown lighter. And although there was no moon, the air was clear of mist and I could see the horizon all around me. And still no land!

"'Maybe I wasn't high enough,' I thought. With a tremendous effort I tilted my head upward, and still plowing forward on the line of my big star, I raised my level a thousand feet or so. And suddenly, slightly to the left of my direction, I spied something white and woolly-looking, apparently floating between sky and sea.

"'That surely can't be land!' I thought. 'White in color! It looks more like clouds.'

"Presently as I flapped along like a machine, just overwhelmed with weariness, exhaustion and thirst, strange new smells began to reach me—vaguely and dimly—sort of spicy odours, things that I hadn't smelled before, but which I knew did not belong to the sea. My floating clouds grew bigger as I approached. As I realized how high up in the sky they hung, I became surer than ever that they were just white clouds or mist. Then the air seemed to change its temperature fitfully. Little drafts and breezes, now warm, now freezing cold, beat gently in my face.

"And then! At last I saw that my clouds were not floating at all. They were connected with the sea, but that which they stood on, being darker in color, had been invisible until I got close. The white, snowcapped tops of mountains, glistening in the dim starlight, had beckoned to me across the sea. From the icy wastes of the upper levels had come the chilly winds; but down lower, now

"The white, snowcapped tops of mountains had beckoned to me."

visible right under me, tangled sleeping jungles of dark green sent forth the fragrance of spices and tropic fruits. I was hovering over Ebony Island.

"With a cry of joy I shut my aching wings and dropped like a stone through the eight thousand feet of air, which grew warmer and warmer as I came down.

"I landed beside a little purling stream that carried the melting snows of the peaks down through the woodlands to the sea. And, wading knee-deep in the cold, fresh water, I bathed my tired wings and drank and drank and drank!

"In the morning, after a good sleep, I went forth to hunt for food and explore my new home. Nuts and seeds and fruit I found in abundance. The climate was delightful, hot down by the sea—quite hot—but you could get almost any temperature you fancied just by moving to the higher levels up the mountains. It was uninhabited by people and almost entirely free from birds of prey. What there were were fish eagles—who would not bother me—and one or two kinds of owls, who preferred mice to small birds. I decided that it was an ideal place that I had come to.

"'So!' I said. 'Here I will settle down and live as an old maid. No more will I bother my head about fickle mates. I'm a mongrel, anyway. Never again will I risk being deserted for a thoroughbred minx. I'll be like Aunt Rosie—live alone and watch the world pass by and the year go round in peace. Poof! What do I care for all the males in the world! This beautiful island belongs to me. Here will I live and die, a crossbred but dignified hermit.'

"My island was large and its scenery varied. There were always new parts to explore—mountains, valleys, hillsides, meadows, jungles, sedgy swamps, golden-sand, laughing shores, and little inland lakes. Later, as I came to the shore on the far side, I could see, in the distance, another piece of land. I decided it must be another island such as the one on which I had landed.

"Later I explored this island, too, and found it only one of many more that lay in a sort of chain. There was no end of variety in the scenery and of beautiful flowers, and I began to think of the whole string of islands as belonging to me. I composed some wonderful poetry and many excellent songs and kept my voice in good form practicing scales three hours a day.

"But all my verses had a melancholy ring. I couldn't seem to convince myself that living alone like this was the happiest way to exist. That was the first sign I had that something funny was happening to me.

"'Look here,' I said. 'This won't do. Even if you're going to be an old maid you needn't be a sour old maid. This is a beautiful and cheerful island. Why be sad?'

"And I set out deliberately to work to make up a cheerful song. It went all right for the first two or three verses, but it ended mournfully, like the rest.

"Then I tried to get to know the other finches and small birds that lived on the island. They were very hospitable and nice to me. And the males vied with one another to be seen in my company. To them, of course, I was a foreigner. I never said anything about my romance or where I had come from. And I aroused considerable interest among them as a bird with a mysterious past. But, after all, it was only a sort of idle curiosity on their part, and I found them intensely dull and somewhat stupid. I tried hard to overcome it and take part in their society chatter and community life, but I just couldn't.

"And then another curious thing happened: the window-cleaner kept coming to my mind."

"Ah!" said Gub-Gub. But Jip promptly put a large paw over Gub-Gub's mouth, and Pippinella went on.

"In some mysterious way, my good friend of the windmill—well, I can't quite explain it—but it almost seemed at times as though I felt him near me somewhere. I spent hours and hours working out all the things that could have happened to him—that might have prevented him from coming back that night when he left me hanging on the wall, exposed to the storms of heaven.

"And then it suddenly occurred to me that I should never have left the neighborhood of the mill. Something told me that he wasn't dead. And if he was still alive he would certainly return someday—the first moment that he could. And I should have been there to welcome him back—as I always had done when he returned from work. I started to blame myself.

"'If you had been a dog,' I said, 'you would never have come away. You would have stayed on and on, knowing that you could trust him—knowing that if he still lived, in the end he would come back.'"

The Fourth Chapter

Pippinella Finds a Clue

THE NEXT EVENING, AS THE DOLITTLE HOUSEhold took their places at the little table in the wagon to hear the continuation of the canary's story, Gub-Gub appeared to be in a great state of excitement. He was the first to sit down. He provided himself with an extra-high cushion and he kept whispering to his neighbors.

"The window-cleaner's coming back this time. I know it. Goodness! He has taken an age, hasn't he? But it's all right. He wasn't killed. He's coming back into the story tonight, sure as you're alive."

"Sh!" said the Doctor, tapping his notebook with a pencil.

When everyone was settled, Pippinella hopped up onto a box and began:

"One day, about a week after I had left the company of the other birds and returned to my solitary life, I decided to fly over to the small island that lay south of Ebony Island. Perhaps it would help to take my mind off my loneliness; for my friend, the window-cleaner, was still very much in my thoughts. It was the first clear day we had

had for weeks and I was able to see again the shore of the smaller island. I came to a place where big shoulders of rocks jutted right down into the sea. In such places as this, little berry bushes often grew. I flew up onto the rocks to hunt for fruit. On the top I found a flat, level place from which you could get a fine view of the sea in front. Behind one the mountains rose straight, like a wall. And in the face of this wall of rock there was an opening to a cave.

"Out of idle curiosity, I went into the cave to explore it. It wasn't very deep. I hopped around the floor awhile and then started to come out. Suddenly I stood still, my attention held spellbound by a stick that leaned against the wall of the cave near the entrance. The stick, about six feet long, had a square piece of rag tied to its top, like a flag. There was nothing very extraordinary in that. Even though I felt sure the island wasn't inhabited now, there was no reason why it shouldn't have been in times past—by some shipwrecked seamen who had taken refuge in this cave. But it was the rag that held me there, gazing motionless with open bill and staring eyes. For I knew that rag as well as I know my own feathers. It was the cloth my friend the window-cleaner used to clean windows with!

"How often had I studied it as he rubbed it over the glass not more than six inches from my nose at Aunt Rosie's! How many times had I watched him wash it out in the kitchen sink at the windmill when he returned from work and then hang it up to dry, close to my cage over the stove! I remembered that it had a rip close to one corner, which had been stitched up clumsily with heavy thread. I sprang up onto the top of the stick and pulled its hanging folds out with my bill. And there was the mended tear. There could be no mistake. It was my window-cleaner's rag.

"Suddenly I found myself weeping. Just why I didn't know.

"I pulled its hanging folds out with my bill."

But one thing was made clear to me at last! I knew now why I couldn't settle down a happy old maid; I knew why all my songs were sad; I knew why I couldn't content myself with the company of other island birds. I was lonely for people. It was natural. I had been born and bred a cage bird. I had grown to love the haunts of men. And all this time I had been longing to get back to them. I thought of all the good people—friends that I had known—old Jack, the merry driver of the night coach from the north; the kindly marchioness who lived in the castle; the scarred-faced old sergeant and my comrades of the Fusiliers, and finally, the one I had loved the best of all, the odd, studious window-cleaner who wrote books in a windmill. What had I to do with the blue and yellow macaws that climbed the orchid vines in gorgeous jungle land? People was what I wanted. And him whom I wanted most, he had been here, lived in this cave! Yet I was certain, after my thorough exploration of the island, that he was here no longer. Where—where was he now?

"After that I thought of nothing else but getting away—or getting back to civilization and the haunts of men. I would return, I was determined, to the windmill, and there I would wait till my friend the window-cleaner made his way back to his old home.

"I returned to the main island and prepared to set out for home. But getting away was no easy matter. The autumnal equinox was just beginning. For days on end strong winds blew across my island and whipped the sea into a continuous state of unrest. Such birds of passage as passed over were all going the wrong way for me. It was now the Season of Return. Once again I, the exile, the cage bird, was trying to make my way against the current of traffic, instead of with it.

"I was afraid, alone and inexperienced, to pit my feeble strength against tempestuous weather. This time I was not desperate or in any such foolhardy state of mind as when I launched out after I left Nippit. Now life meant much; the future held promise. And if I was to get back to my window-cleaner philosopher, I must not take any crazy chances.

"For days I watched the sea, waiting for calmer weather. But the blustering winds continued, and when I tried my strength against them over the land, to see if I could make any headway, I found that I was like a feather and they could drive me where they would.

"One afternoon when I was sitting on the rocks looking out to sea, I saw a big ship come over the horizon. The wind had changed its direction earlier in the day, and now, with a powerful breeze behind it, this boat was traveling along at quite a good speed. It seemed to be going pretty much the way I wanted. And it occurred to me that if I followed this boat I might easily come to the land I had left. At the worst, if I got exhausted, I would have something to land on.

"The ship came nearer and nearer. At one time I thought it was actually going to call at the islands. But I was wrong. When it had come within less than half a mile of a steep mountainous cape at one corner, it changed its course slightly, rounded the angle of the coast, and passed on. At that close range I could see men mov-

"The ship came nearer and nearer."

ing on the deck. The sight of them made me more homesick than ever for human company. As the boat grew smaller, moving away from me now, I made up my mind. I leapt off the rocks and shot out over the sea to follow it.

"Well, I was still an inexperienced navigator. I very soon found out that my little plan, which had seemed perfectly simple, just didn't work. For one thing, on the side of the island where I had been standing one was protected from the weather. And it was only after I had got well out away from the shore that the full strength of the wind hit me. When it had changed, it had changed for the worse—growing stronger with its new direction. Across the sky rain clouds gathered. Rumbles of thunder warned me that I should never have attempted this mad excursion.

"Further, on getting close to the ship, I found that its pace was dreadfully slow, in spite of the wind behind it. It was pitching clumsily in the swell and seemed heavy laden. If it had taken me a whole day to make the voyage at seventy miles an hour, it would take this vessel a week at least. During that week I would be starved to death twice over. I realized in a moment that my plan was no good. I must head back for the island and reach it before that drenching shower reached me.

"I returned. And, oh my! I thought I had known how strong that wind was. But I hadn't any idea of it until I swung around and faced it. It was a veritable gale. I flapped my wings as fast as I could, and the only result I got was to stand still. Even that I couldn't keep up. And soon, slowly, I found I was moving backward while working to go forward like mad.

"And then, slish! The rain squall hit me in the face and in a moment I was drenched to the skin.

"So there I was, fairly caught, a good three miles offshore, unable to regain the land in the teeth of that terrible wind. What a fool I had been to leave my snug, safe harbor before calm weather came!

"The soaking of the rain squall made flying doubly hard. After a few moments of it I decided not to try to beat into the wind at all. That was hopeless. I must wait till the fury of the gale let up. In the meantime I was compelled to give all my attention to keeping up above the level of the sea, for with my drenched and soggy feathers I found myself descending all the time nearer and nearer to the tossing surface of the water.

"But far from weakening, the force of the wind got suddenly stronger. I felt myself now being swept along like a leaf. The curtain of the rain had shut out all view of the island. You couldn't see more than a few yards in any direction. Above and below and around, all was gray—just gray wetness.

"As the wind hurled me along over the sea, I caught sight of the ship. The gale was driving me right past it—beyond, into the hopeless waste of the angry ocean. I remember the picture of it very clearly as it rose up in the dim veil of rain. It looked like a great gray horse mired and floundering in a field of gray mud. I suddenly realized that this vessel was my last and only chance. If I got driven beyond it, it was over for me.

"Frantically I flapped at the wet air to change the angle of my flight—to descend sideways and strike the vessel's deck.

"Well, somehow I managed it. As the squall drove me through the rigging, I clutched at a rope ladder stretched between the rail and the masthead. I grabbed it with my claws and threw my wings around it, rather like a monkey climbing on a pole. For the present I didn't attempt to move up or down. I decided to let well enough alone. I was on the ship. That was the main thing. I would stay where I was until the rain shower passed on.

"By that time I was numbed with the cold and the wet. The air cleared and the sun came out, as it does, suddenly, after those squalls at sea. But still the wind held very strong. I set about making my way down to some more sheltered place. For the first time I had a chance to look around me and take in the details of the ship I had boarded. I was about seven feet above the level of the deck. Not far away from me there was a little house with round windows and a door in it. If I could get close up against the wall of this, I thought I would be protected from the wind and would still have the sunshine to dry my feathers in. I was afraid to fly the short distance, lest the wind catch me up and carry me overboard. So, like a sailor, I started climbing down my rope ladder hand over hand.

"In my hurry to get to some warmer, safer place I had not noticed much about the ship beyond just a glimpse, which told me it was a vessel of considerable size. And on my way down the rope I was much too busy clinging tight and battling with the wind—which seemed determined to tear me loose and hurl me into the sea—to notice anything around me.

"Anyway, suddenly I felt a large hand close around my whole body and lift me off the rope like a fly. I looked up and found myself staring into the brown face of an enormous sailor dressed in a tarpaulin coat and hat. A wild bird, I suppose, would have been scared to death. But I had often been held in people's hands before and that in itself did not greatly alarm me. The sailor had kind eyes and I knew he would do me no harm. But I also knew that this probably meant the end of my freedom for the present, because sailors are fond of pets and most ships have at least one cage of canaries aboard them.

"'Hulloa, hulloa!' said the big man. 'What'cher climbing in the rigging for? Don't you know no better than that? You ain't been to sea long, I'll warrant. Why, if we was to ship water with you tight-rope walking like that you'd go overboard before you could blink! I reckon you signed on as we passed the island, eh? Well, well! Bless me, ain't you wet! You come below, mate, and get dried out where it's snug and warm.'

"Then the man moved forward across the pitching, rolling deck to the little house and opened the door. Inside there was a flight of steps and down this he carried me. We entered a small, low room, with beds set in the wall all around, like shelves. A lamp hung

"Bless me, ain't you wet!"

from the center of the ceiling and swung from side to side with the motion of the ship. On the tables and chairs coats and capes had been thrown. There was a warm smell of tar and wet clothes. In two of the bunks men were snoring with their mouths open.

"My captor, still holding me firmly in his hand, opened a heavy wooden locker and brought forth a small cage. Into this he put me, and then filled the drawer with seed and the pot with water.

"'There you are, mate,' says he. 'Now you're all fixed up. Get your feathers dry and then you'll feel better.'

"And so I entered on still another chapter in my varied career. After the dead quiet of the island, the cheerful bustle of that ship was most invigorating. It was, as I have told you, quite a large vessel, and it carried both cargo and passengers. To begin with, my cage was kept in that little cabin to which I had first been taken. It was the bunkroom for the crew. There was nearly always somebody sleeping there, because the men took turns in watches to work the ship.

"Later, when the weather got fair again, I was put outside on the wall of the little deckhouse. This was much nicer. Lots and lots of people came to talk to me—especially the passengers, who seemed to have nothing to do to occupy their time beyond walking up and down the deck in smart clothes.

"And, although I was terribly annoyed at being caged up again before I had gotten back to my window-cleaner, I counted myself lucky on the whole. I had escaped the dangers of the sea when escape seemed impossible. There was always a good chance that I might still get away and reach the windmill—after we got to land—if I kept my eye open for the opportunity. In the meantime, I was back again among pleasant people and agreeable scenes.

"There was another canary aboard the ship. I heard him singing the first day that I was put outside on the deck. Singing is hardly the word for it, for the poor fellow had only a few squeaky calls without any melody to them. But he was very persevering and seemed determined to work up a song of some kind. Just whereabouts on the vessel he was I couldn't make out—nearer amidships than I was, by the sound if it. His unmusical efforts sort of annoyed me after a while and presently I gave a performance myself—more to drown out his racket in self-defense than anything else.

"But my singing caused something of a sensation. Passengers, sailors, stewards and officers, gathered around to listen to me. Inquiries were made as to whom I belonged. And finally I was bought from the big sailor who had caught me and taken to quite a different part of the ship.

"The man who bought me turned out to be the ship's barber. I was carried to a little cabin on the main deck, in the center of the passenger's quarters. This was the barber's shop, all fitted up with shaving chairs and basins, like a regular hairdressing establishment on land.

"And there I discovered the other canary, hanging in a cage from the ceiling. It was the barber's idea, apparently, that I should teach this other bird how to sing.

"I was now in a very much better position to keep in touch with the life of the ship than I was before. For nearly everyone on board came, sooner or later, to the barber's shop. My new master was patronized not only by the passengers but the officers and even the crew, who came to be shaved or to have their hair cut in the early hours of the morning before the shop was supposed to be open.

"And while the customers were being attended to or waiting their turn, the barber would chat and gossip with them. And from their conversation I learned a good deal. And then the other canary, the funny little squeaker to whom I was supposed to give singing lessons, he had been on the ship quite a number of voyages, and he, too, gave me a lot of information.

"He was really a decent sort of bird—even if he couldn't sing. And he explained many things to me about the life of the sea and the running of a ship that I had never known before. As for teaching him to sing, that was a pretty hopeless task, for he had no voice to speak of at all. Still, he improved a good deal, and after about a week, his gratey squeaks and shrill whistles were not nearly so harsh to the ear.

"One song that I composed at this time I was rather proud of. I called it 'The Razor Strop Duet.' Listening to the barber stropping this razor gave me the idea, the motif, for it. You know the clip-clop, clip-clop, clip-clop that a razor makes when it is sharpened on leather? Well, I imitated that and mixed it up with the sound of a shaving brush lathering in a mug. But it was a little difficult to do the two with one voice. So I did the razor and I made the other canary do the shaving brush. As a song it could not compare with some of my other compositions—with 'The Midget Mascot,' for instance, or 'The Harness Jingle.' It was a sort of comic song, 'The Razor Strop Duet.' But it was a great success and the barber was forever showing us off to his customers by giving his razor an extra stropping, for he knew that that would always set us going.

"I questioned the other canary very minutely as to the places we would touch and about our port of destination. For all this time, you must understand, I had one idea very much in mind, and that was to escape from my cage and the ship as soon as we dropped anchor in a convenient harbor. I gathered from what he told me that our next port of call was the land that I had left—the land of the windmill and the window-cleaner.

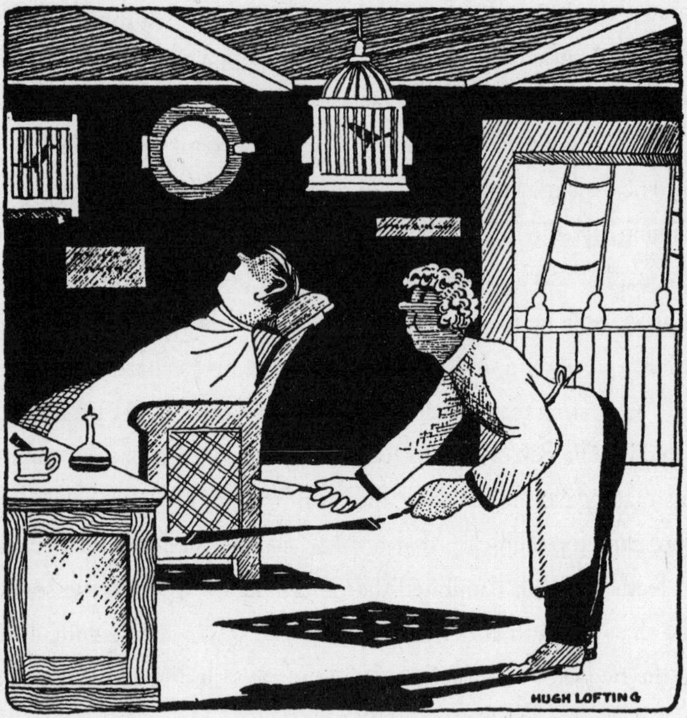

"The Razor Strop Duet"

"Continually now I was trying my utmost to show the barber how tame I was. When he cleaned out the cage I would hop onto his finger. And after a little he would sometimes close the doors and windows and allow me to go free in the room. I would fly from the floor to the table, then onto his hand. And finally he would let me out even with the doors open. This was what I wanted. I did not attempt to escape yet, of course, because we were still at sea. And whenever he wished me to return into the cage, I would go back as good as gold.

"But I was only biding my time. When we were in port he would, if all went well, let me out of my cage once too often."

The Fifth Chapter

The Window-Cleaner at Last!

ONE DAY TOWARD EVENING THERE WAS A great commotion on the deck. Passengers were running forward with spyglasses and pointing over the sea. Land had been sighted. We were now only half an hour or so from the port where I hoped to escape.

"It was very amusing to me to see how carefully and with what a lot of trouble and fuss a ship is brought to the land. On the sea, with their sails all billowing in the wind, they are such graceful things; but at the docks they become great, clumsy masses of wood and canvas: difficult to handle and always in danger of being rammed on the pilings by the waves washing toward the shore.

"As we neared the land, men came out in boats to guide us into the harbor; there was no end of signaling and shouting between the ship and the shore and finally, when we did creep in at a snail's pace, they tied the vessel down from every angle. I could not help comparing all this with the carefree, simple manner in which birds make their landing in a new country after a voyage of many thousands of miles.

"From my position hanging inside the barber's shop I could not see a great deal of the port in which we had landed, beyond little glimpses through the door and porthole. But from them I recognized the place. It was a town not more than fifty miles from the hill on which the windmill stood. Shortly after we were moved up to a wharf, some friends of the barber came aboard to see him. They sat around laughing and chatting and presently one of them said to him:

"'I see you've got another canary, Bill?'

"'Yes,' said the barber. 'A good singer, too. And he's that tame he'll come right out onto my hand. Wait a minute and I'll show you.'

"'Ah, ha!' I thought to myself. 'Now my chance is coming.'

"Then the barber opened my cage door and, standing a few paces off, he held out his hand and called to me to fly out onto it. Through the open door of the shop I could see part of the town, steep streets straggling up toward hills and pleasant rolling pasture land. I hopped onto the sill of my cage and stood a moment, half in and half out.

"'Now, watch him,' called the barber to his friends. 'He'll fly right onto my finger. He's done it lots of times. Come on, Dick! Here I am. Come on!'

"And then I flew—but not onto his finger. Taking a line on those steep streets that I could see in the distance straggling up the hill, I made for the open door.

"But, alas! Such off chances can upset the best plans! Just as I was about to skim through the doorway it was suddenly blocked by an enormous figure. It was my big sailor. Of course it would be—pretty nearly the largest man that ever walked, coming through the

"I stood half in, half out."

smallest doorway ever built. There were just two narrow little places at either side of his head through which I might get by him. I tilted upward and made for one of them.

"'Look out!' yelled the barber. 'The bird's getting away. Grab him!'

"But the big sailor had already seen me. As I tried to slip out over his shoulder, he clapped his two big hands together and caught me just like a ball that had been thrown to him.

"And that was the end of my great hopes and careful scheming! Because of course, after that the barber never trusted me out with the door or windows open again. I was put back into the cage and there I stayed.

"Well, after six or seven hours the ship began to make ready to set sail again.

"'What's the next port of call at which we stop?' I asked the other canary.

"'Oh, a long ways on,' said he. 'We go pretty nearly the whole length of the sea we're in now and touch at a group of islands at the mouth of a narrow straight. It takes nine days. But the islands are very pretty and worth seeing.'

"But what did I care for the beauty of the islands! As the ropes were untied and the vessel moved out away form the wharf I saw the steep streets growing smaller. Beside myself with disappointment and annoyance, I beat the bars of my cage in senseless fury. I was sailing away from my friend, from the land of the windmill. And now, with my owner suspicious, heaven only knew when I'd ever have a chance to get back to it again!

"For the next three days our voyage was uneventful. Calm, sunny weather prevailed. And the barber's shop was kept quite busy, because passengers aboard ship don't seem to bother very much about shaving or having their hair cut when the sea is rough, but in calmer weather it serves as a pastime to break the monotony of the voyage.

"On the fourth day we had a little excitement. A wreck was sighted. Unfortunately, my cage was not hung outside that day and I could see practically nothing of the show. But from conversation and a little guesswork on my part, I managed to piece most of the story together.

"About noon, some kind of craft was seen by the man in the

crow's nest—as the lookout on the mast is called. It was evidently in distress. There was a lot of signaling and a good deal of running about and looking through telescopes. Our ship's course was changed and we headed in the direction of the stranger.

"On closer inspection it was found not to be a wreck but a raft with one man on it. The man was either unconscious or dead. He lay face downward and gave no answer when he was hailed. A boat was lowered and he was brought aboard. There was much cheering among the passengers when it was announced that he was still breathing. He was, nevertheless, in a terrible state of exhaustion from hunger and exposure. He was handed over into the care of the ship's doctor, and, still unconscious, was taken below and put to bed. Then our boat was set back upon her course and on we went.

"I thought no more about the incident after the customers who came to the barber's had ceased to talk about it. The weather continued fair. And, for want of something better to do—also to keep my mind off my own troubles—I went on giving the other canary singing lessons.

"One day about a week later, when we were supposed to be getting near our next port of call, a most extraordinary-looking man entered the barber's shop. His strange appearance seemed to cause him a good deal of embarrassment. Without looking around at all, he sat down in the barber's chair. The barber must have expected him, for he set to work at once without asking any questions, shaving off his beard and cutting his hair. The man's back was turned to me as he sat in the chair, and all I could see of him after the white apron was tied about his chin, was the top of his wild-looking head of tangled, matted hair.

"In the middle of the clipping and shaving the barber went to the door to speak to someone. And I gathered from the conversation that the man in the chair was he who had been saved from the raft. He was only now recovered enough to leave his bed for the first time. This made me more interested in him than ever. And, fascinated, I watched in silence as the barber clipped away at that enormous shock of hair. I fell to wondering what he would look like when that beard had been removed.

"At last the barber finished, and with a flick and a flourish removed the apron from around his customer's neck. Weakly the man got out of the chair and stood up. He turned around and I saw his face.

"You could never guess who it was."

"The window-cleaner!" yelled Gub-Gub, slipping off his cushion and disappearing under the table in his excitement.

"Yes," said Pippinella quietly, "it was the window-cleaner."

Gub-Gub's sudden disappearance caused a short interruption and some two or three minutes were spent fishing him out from under the table and putting him and his cushion back on the stool. There, slightly bruised but otherwise none the worse for his accident, he continued to show intense interest in the canary's story while occasionally rubbing the side of his head, which he had bumped on the leg of the table.

"Well," Pippinella continued, "I was greatly shocked at my friend's appearance. I recognized him, beyond all doubt, instantly, of course. But, oh so thin he looked—pale, weary, and weak! As yet he had not noticed me. Standing by the barber's chair, embarrassed, staring awkwardly at the floor, he started to put his hand in his pocket. Then, seeming to remember halfway that he had no

"'The window-cleaner!' yelled Gub-Gub."

money, he murmured something to the barber in explanation and hurried to leave the shop.

"There was a certain call that I used to give—a kind of greeting whistle—whenever he returned in days gone by to the windmill of an evening after his work was over. As he took hold of the door handle to go out onto the deck, I repeated it twice. Then he turned around and saw me.

"Never have I seen anyone's face so light up with joy and gladness.

"'Oh, Pip!' he cried, coming close up to my cage and peering in. 'Is it really you? Yes. There could be no doubt about those markings. I could pick you out from a million!'

"'Pardon me,' said the barber. 'Do you know my canary?'

"'*Your* canary!' said the window-cleaner. 'There is some mistake here. The bird is mine. I am quite sure of it.'

"And then began a long argument. Of course, quite naturally, the barber wasn't going to give me up just on the other man's saying so. The sailor who had first caught me was called in. Then various stewards and other members of the crew joined the discussion. My friend, the window-cleaner, was a very polite through it all, but very firm. He was asked how long ago it was that I had been in his possession. And when he said it was many months since he had seen me last, the others all laughed at him, saying that his claim was simply ridiculous. Never have I wished harder that I could talk the language of people, so that I might explain to them beyond all doubt which one was my real owner.

"Finally the matter was taken to the captain. Already many of the passengers were interested in the argument, and when he came down to the barber's shop the place was crowded with people who were all giving advice and taking sides.

"The captain began by telling everybody to keep quiet while he heard both versions of the story. Then the barber and the window-cleaner in turn put forward their claims, giving reasons and particulars and all the rest. Next, the big sailor stated how he had found me in the rigging during a rain squall and had taken me below and later sold me to the barber.

"When they were all done the captain turned to the window-cleaner and said:

"'I don't see how you can claim ownership of the bird on such evidence. There could easily be many birds marked the same as this one. The chances are that this was a wild bird that took refuge on this ship during bad weather. In the circumstances, I feel that the barber has every right to keep it.'

"Well, that seemed to be the end of the matter. The question had been referred to the captain, the highest authority on the ship, and he had decided in favor of the barber. It look as though I was going to remain in his possession.

"But the window-cleaner and his romantic rescue from the sea had greatly interested the passengers. His face was the kind of face that everyone would instinctively trust as honest. Many people felt that he would not have laid claim to me with such sureness and determination if he was not really my owner. And as the captain stepped out onto the deck, one of the passengers—a funny, fussy old gentleman with side-whiskers—followed him and touched him on the arm.

"'Pardon me, Captain,' said he. 'I have a feeling that our castaway is an upright and honorable person. If his claim to the canary should be just, possibly the bird will know him. Perhaps he can even do tricks with it. Would it not be as well to try some test of that kind before dismissing the case?'

"The captain turned back and all the other passengers who had been leaving now reentered the barber's shop, their interest reviving at the prospect of a new trial.

"'Listen,' said the captain, addressing the window-cleaner: 'You say you know the canary well. Does the bird know you at all? Is there anything you can do to prove that what you say is true?'

"'Yes, the bird knows me, sir,' said the barber. 'He'll hop right out of the cage onto my hand when I call him. If you'll shut the door I'll show you.'

"'Very good,' said the captain. 'Close the door.'

"Then, with the little cabin crowded with people, the barber opened my cage, held up his hand, and called to me to come out. I did—and of course flew straight to the window-cleaner's shoulder.

"A whisper of astonishment ran around among the passengers. Then I climbed off my friend's shoulder and clawed my way down his waistcoat. I wanted to remind him of an old trick he used to do with me at the mill. At supper he would sometimes put a lump of sugar in his waistcoat pocket and I would fish it out and drop it in his teacup. As soon as I started to walk down off his shoulder he remembered it and asked for a lump of sugar and a cup. They were

"I flew straight to the window-cleaner's shoulder."

brought forward by a steward. Then he explained to the captain what he was going to do, put the sugar in his pocket and the teacup on the barber's washstand.

"Well, I wish you could have seen the barber's face when I pulled that sugar out, flew to the cup, and dropped it in.

"'Why, Captain,' cried the old gentleman with the side-whiskers, 'there can be no question now, surely, as to who is the owner. The bird will do anything for this man. I thought he wouldn't have claimed it if it wasn't his own.'

"'Yes,' said the captain, 'the canary is his. There can be no doubt of that.'

"And amid much talking and congratulations from the passengers, the window-cleaner prepared to take me away. Then came the question of the ownership of the cage. That belonged to the barber, of course. But as there was no other empty one to be had aboard the ship, my friend couldn't very well take me without it. However, the old gentleman with the side-whiskers, who seemed genuinely interested in the strange story of my funny owner and myself, came forward and volunteered to pay the barber the value of the cage.

"The window-cleaner thanked him and asked him for his name and address. He hadn't any money now, he said, but he wanted to send it to him after he got to land. Then I and my friend from whom I had been separated so long left the barber's shop and proceeded to the forward part of the ship, where he had his quarters.

"'Well, Pip,' said he, shaking up the mattress of his bed, 'here we are again! The captains's been pretty generous. Gave me a first-class cabin for nothing. Of course, I can't expect to have the services of a steward as well. So I make my own bed—where the dickens did that pillow get to? Oh, there it is, on the floor. . . . Poor old Pip! What ages it is since we talked to each other. And then to find you aboard the ship that rescued me, living in the barber's shop! Dear, dear, what a strange world it is, to be sure! There goes five bells. That means half-past six. It'll soon be dinnertime. Are you hungry, Pip? Let's see. Oh no, you've got plenty of seed. And I'll bring you a piece of apple from the dining saloon. What a decent chap that be-whiskered old fellow was, wasn't he—paying for your cage and all like that? Heaven only knows when he'll get his money back. I haven't a penny in the world. But I must see that he gets it somehow.'

"While he finished making the bed he went vaguely about this and that, gradually coming to the part I wanted to hear the most.

"'Pip,' he said finally in a more confidential tone. 'I sometimes believe you understand every word I say. Do you know why? Whenever I talk, you keep silent. Is it possible you *do* know what I am saying?'

"I tried to make a sound similar to the human word for yes but it just came out a peep, which surprised him a little for he looked at me sharply and smiled.

"'Never mind, Pip,' he said. 'Whether you understand or not, I still get great comfort from talking to you. Oh, goodness, I feel weak!' he said, dropping down onto the bunk. 'I better sit down awhile. The least exertion tires me out now. I haven't got over that starving and the sun. Listen, Pip, would you like to know the real reason why I never came back to the mill that night? Just a minute—'

"He went over to the door, opened it and looked outside.

"'It's all right,' he said, coming back to his seat on the bunk. 'There's no one eavesdropping.'

"His voice sank to a whisper as he leaned forward toward my cage, which stood on a table near this bunk. He seemed to be suddenly overcome with a spell of dizziness, for he closed his eye a moment. I felt that he really ought to be in bed, recovering from his terrible trip. But I also felt very proud, because I realized that what he was about to tell me had most likely never been told to a living soul."

THE SIXTH CHAPTER

The Window-Cleaner's Adventures

YOU REMEMBER THOSE BOOKS I USED TO write, Pip?' the window-cleaner began. 'Well, they were books about governments—foreign governments. Before you knew me—before I was a window-cleaner—I had traveled the world a great deal. And in many countries I found that the people were not treated well. I tried to speak about it, but I wasn't allowed to. So I decided that I would go back to my own land and write about it. And that is what I did. I wrote in newspapers and magazines. But the government there didn't like the sort of thing I wrote—although it had not been written against them exactly. They sent to the editors of these magazines and newspapers and asked them not to allow me to write for them anymore.

"'In those days I had a great many friends—and a good deal of money, too, for I was born of quite wealthy parents. But when my friends found out that I was getting into hot water with the government, many of them wouldn't be seen with me anymore. Some of them thought I was just a harmless crank, sort of crazy, you know—

the way people always do regard you if you do anything different from the herd.

"'And so,' he went on, 'I set out to disappear. One day I took a boat and went for a row on the sea. When there was no one around I upset the boat and swam to shore. Then I made my way secretly on foot a long distance from those parts and was never seen again by any of my friends or relatives. Of course, when the upturned boat was found, people decided that I had been drowned. Most of my money and houses and property went to my younger brother as the next of kin and very soon I was forgotten.

"'In the meantime, I had become a window-cleaner in the town where you met me. I rented that old ramshackle mill from a farmer for five shillings a month. And there I settled down to write the books with which I hoped to change the world. I have never been so happy in my life as I was there, Pip. I had never been so free before. And the first book that I wrote did change things—even more than I expected. It was printed in a foreign country and read by a great number of people. They decided that what I wrote was true and they began to make a whole lot of fuss and to try to change their government.

"'But they were not quite strong enough and their attempt failed. In the meantime, the government men of that particular country got very busy trying to find out who had written the book that caused so much trouble and that nearly lost them their jobs.'

"At that point," Pippinella continued, "the window-cleaner was interrupted by the ringing of six bells and the bugle for dinner. He excused himself and left the cabin.

"In about half an hour he returned, bringing with him a piece of apple, a stump of celery, and some other titbits from the table for me. While he was putting them in my cage the ship's doctor came to see him. He was still, of course, more or less under his care. The doctor examined my friend and seemed satisfied with his progress. But on leaving he ordered him to go to bed early and to avoid all serious exertion for the present.

"After the doctor had gone my friend started to undress and I supposed that I should hear no more of the story for the present. But after he had gotten into the bed he continued talking to me. I have since thought that this was perhaps a sign that he was still very weak from all he had gone through. It seemed as though he just had to talk—but he was afraid to do it when there were any people around to hear him. So I, the canary, was his audience.

"'How that foreign government,' he went on, 'found out that it was I who wrote the books I do not know to this day. But I suppose they must have traced my letters because, after calling at the post office that Saturday when I left you outside on the wall, I was followed by three men as I left. I did not see them until it was too late. At a lonely part of the road leading back toward the mill I was struck to the ground with a blow on the head.

"'When I woke up I was aboard a ship far out at sea. I demanded to know why I had been kidnapped. I was told that the ship was short of crew and they had to get an extra man somehow. This, of course, is—or was—often done by ships that were short-handed. But from the start I was suspicious. The town they had taken me from was a long way from the sea. And no ship would send so far inland to shanghai sailors. Besides, nobody would ever take me for a seaman. Further, I soon noticed that there were a group of foreigners on board; and later I learned that the port we were bound for was in that country about which I had written my book.

"'I knew what would happen to me if I ever landed there; I would be arrested and thrown into prison on some false charge. So far as my relatives and friends were concerned, was I not dead long ago? No one in my own land would make inquiries. Once in the clutches of the government I had made an enemy of, I would never be heard of again.'

"The window-cleaner lay back on his pillow as though exhausted from the effort of talking. He remained motionless so long that I began to think he had fallen asleep. And I was glad, because I did not want him to over tire himself. But presently he sat up again and drew my cage nearer to him across the table. With his feverish eyes burning more brightly than ever, he went on.

"'As the ship carried me away, one thing, Pip, besides my own plight worried me dreadfully. And that was you—you, my companion, my only friend. I had left your cage outside hanging on the wall. Would you be frozen to death by the cold night? Who would feed you? I remembered what a lonely place that old mill was. What chance was there that any passerby would see you? And even if he did, there would be nothing to show him, unless he broke in and found the kitchen empty, that you had been deserted. I imagined what you must be thinking of me as the hours and days went by—starving days and freezing nights—waiting, waiting for me to return, while all the time that accursed ship carried me farther and farther away! . . . Poor Pip! Even now I can't believe it's you. Still, there you are, sure enough, with the yellow bars on your wings and the funny black patch across your throat and that cheeky trick of cocking your head to one side when you're listening—and—and everything."

"And then, still murmuring fitfully, at last the window-cleaner fell asleep. From my cage I looked at his haggard, pinched face on the pillow. I felt stupidly useless. I wished I were a person so I could take care of him and nurse him back to full health. For I realized now that he was still dreadfully ill. However, it was a great deal to be with him again. I put my head under my wing and prepared to settle down myself. But I didn't get much rest. For all night long he kept jumping and murmuring in his sleep."

"But how did the window-cleaner come to be on the raft?" whined Gub-Gub. "You've let him go to sleep now without telling us."

"At last the window-cleaner fell asleep."

"Well, he hasn't gone to sleep forever," said the white mouse. "Give him a chance, can't you?"

"Oh, that pig," sighed Dab-Dab. "I don't know why we always have him in the party."

"Myself," growled Jip, "I'd sooner have a nice, smooth round stone for company."

"Quiet, please!" said the Doctor. "Let Pippinella go on."

"Well," said the canary, "in the morning while he was dressing, the window-cleaner told me the rest of his story. Realizing that if he had remained on that ship till the end of its journey he would be cast into prison—probably for the rest of his days—he determined to escape from it at any cost before it reached port. He had been given work to do about the ship like the other sailors; so fortunately he was still free—in appearance, at all events. He bided his time and pretended not to be suspicious concerning his captor's intentions.

"After some days of sailing they passed an island at nighttime. The land was some three miles away at least, but its high mountain tops were visible in the moonlight. On account of the distance, the men never dreamed that he would attempt to swim ashore. It was very late and no one was on deck. Taking a life vest from the rail, my friend slipped quietly into the sea near the stern of the boat and struck out for the island.

"It was a tremendous, long swim. And if it had not been for the vest, he told me, he could never have done it. But finally, more dead than alive from exhaustion, he staggered up onto the beach in the moonlight and lay down to rest and sleep."

Pippinella paused a moment while the whole Dolittle family waited eagerly for the rest of her story.

"I know!" shouted Gub-Gub. "Don't tell me. Let me guess. He landed on Ebony Island—the same as you did!"

"No," said the canary, shaking her head. "It would have been simpler had he done that. No, the island on which he landed was one of the same group—but it lay two or three miles to the south of my island. I only found that out later as he described his further adventures."

"Incredible!" exclaimed John Dolittle. "Why, he must have been there at the same time you were living on the larger one. I know that group of islands well; they're close enough together to make visibility very good. Strange you didn't see him."

"Well, no, Doctor," replied the canary. "You see, it was the time of the autumn rains and the sky was overcast and gray from one day to the next. I could never have seen him from my island. But you will remember that I told you I occasionally visited the other islands just to relieve the monotony. I must have been on his while he was on mine. You'll see, as my story progresses, how that could have happened."

"Quite so," said the Doctor. "Do go on, Pippinella. I've never heard a more astonishing example of sheer coincidence."

"When the window-cleaner awoke," continued the canary, "it was daylight and the first thing he saw was the ship about six or seven miles off, coming back to look for him.

"Fortunately he had lain down in the shadow of some bushes and had not yet been seen through the telescopes from the ship. Like a rabbit he made his way inland, keeping always in the cover of the underbrush. Reaching the far side of the island he crept up into the higher mountain levels, where from certain vantage points he could see without being seen.

"He watched the vessel draw near and send boats ashore with

search parties. Then began a long game of hide-and-seek. About two dozen men in all were brought onto the island. And from these twenty-four he had to remain hidden.

"All day long my friend watched like a hunted fox, peering out from the bushes and rocks at his pursuers. Darkness began to fall and he supposed that the men would now return to their ship. But to his horror he saw that they were settling down for the night, putting up bivouacs of boughs and lighting camp fires.

"For two days this continued. You might wonder why I didn't see the ship and the fires and the boats going back and forth from the ship to the shore. But it all must have taken place on the other side of the island—out of sight of where I stayed most of the time. And then, too, the fog was so thick that seeing more than a few feet in any direction was impossible.

"Finally, when it began to look as though his pursuers were never going to leave the island, my friend hit upon a plan. At nighttime he went down to the beach on that side of the island where the ship had come to anchor. You remember the life vest that he used to come ashore with?"

"Yes," said Gub-Gub, sneezing heartily.

"Well, he took that life vest, which had the ship's name written on it, and he flung it out beyond the surf. He watched it for a little to make sure that it was not washed back onshore, and then he made his way up again to his mountain retreats.

"Now at least once a day, sometimes more, boats passed between the island and the ship to get news of how the hunt was progressing or to bring supplies to the search parties. The following morning one of these boats sighted the life vest floating in the sea. It was captured and taken aboard the ship. When news of its

"He flung it out beyond the surf."

discovery was brought to the captain he decided that my friend had been drowned in his attempt to reach the island, and he signaled to the search parties to rejoin the ship.

"About half an hour later the window-cleaner, watching from his mountain hiding places, saw the vessel weigh anchor and sail away. He described to me his great joy when he first realized that his plan had worked, that his enemies had at last departed and left him in peace. The first thing he did was to have a good sleep. Anxiety about the movements of his hunters had prevented his getting any real rest since he had seen the ship return.

"But after a while he found that his situation was by no means good. Immediate danger from the men who had kidnapped him was over, to be sure. But he was now marooned on an uninhabited island, with every prospect of staying there indefinitely. As week after week went by and he never even sighted the sail of a passing ship, he came to the conclusion that this island was far out of the paths of ocean traffic.

"All this time, anxiety about the safety of his book added to his other troubles. He begrudged every day—every hour—spent here in useless idleness when his enemies might be busy behind his back, ransacking his home for the work on which he had labored so long.

"For food he subsisted on nuts, fish, and fruit mostly. He took his quarters in that cave that I had described. On the peak just above this he erected a flag made out of the cleaning rag that I found tied to the stick. This, he hoped, might catch the attention of some passing vessels. But none ever came.

"At last, when he had given up all hope of rescue from chance visitors, he decided that his only way of escape was to set out on a raft and try to get into the path of ships. So, somehow, with great patience, he fastened together a number of dry logs upon the beach. He fashioned a mast out of a pole and wove a sail by plaiting vines and leaves. Big seashells and other strange vessels were prepared to carry a supply of fresh water. He laid in a large store of nuts and bananas. When everything was ready, he thrust his raft out into the surf and prepared to sail away.

"But everything was against him. The weather, which had been fairly decent for some days, suddenly worsened just as he put out to sea. A violent wind blew the small, ill-fitted raft in a wide circle and flung it—all battered and broken—onto the beach of Ebony Island.

Of course, he didn't realize at first that he wasn't back on his own island; he only found it out after he had dragged himself to shelter and waited out the storm.

"It must have been during this same storm that I foolishly tried to follow the vessel that later was the means of saving my life. I suppose the reason he didn't see the ship was that he was lying exhausted in a small cove, waiting for the storm to subside.

"He told me how he began all over again to rebuild the raft; how he waited each day for some vessel to show up; and how finally in desperation, he set out.

"I don't know when I have ever heard," said Pippinella, "anything more terrible than the window-cleaner's description of his voyage on that raft. With all his careful and thoughtful preparations, and because of the overcast sky, I suppose, he had neglected one important thing: some protection from the fierce rays of the sun. The first two days he had not realized his oversight, for a continual drift of light clouds across the sky shaded him even better than a parasol. But when on the third day the full glare of the tropical sun beat down on him, his little sailing boat had made such good progress before the wind, that he calculated he was three hundred miles from the island and going back was out of the question.

"For five days the window-cleaner drifted. By that time his fresh water was all gone and most of his food. He kept seeing imaginary ships appear on the skyline, he told me. He would get up and wave to them frantically, like a madman, then fall down in a state of utter collapse.

"Luckily he had not taken down his basketwork sail to use as a sunshade—sorely though he needed it. He was always hoping that

"He kept seeing imaginary ships."

a wind would come along, and he feared that if he unlashed it from the mast he would not have strength to get it up again. It was this that saved him. Long after he had fallen unconscious for the last time it was sighted by the ship in which I was traveling. The captain told him afterward that it was very doubtful if the raft would have been seen at all if it had not been for that strange sail—which stood up high above the water—especially as the ship's course was by no means heading in that direction, but would have carried us by him at a distance of over twelve miles.

"'However,' the window-cleaner said to me, 'all is well that ends well, Pip. Somehow my coming through this, my escape from the kidnappers, my rescue from the sea, make me feel I'm going to win after all—so that the work I have begun will go forward to a successful end. It was a terrible experience. But I'm getting over it. And it has given me faith, Pip, faith in my star. I will yet upset that thieving government. I will yet live to see those people freed and happy.'

"That morning it was announced that we would most likely reach our next port the day after tomorrow. The kind old passenger with the side-whiskers still stuck to my friend, the window-cleaner. He had gathered at the time of the discussion about the cage that my friend had no money. He came to our cabin later in the day and asked him what he proposed to do when he landed. The window-cleaner shrugged his shoulders and, with a smile, said:

"'Thank you, I don't just know exactly. But I'll manage somehow—get a job, I suppose, till I've made enough to buy a passage home.'

"'But look here,' said the old gentleman, 'this port we're coming to is inhabited by natives. You'll have great difficulty, I fear, in securing employment. Besides, you're still far from well.'

"Nevertheless, my friend insisted, while thanking the other for his kind interest, that he would be able to get along somehow. But the old gentleman shook his head. And as he left the cabin he murmured:

"'You're not strong enough yet. I must see if something can't be arranged.'

"That old gentleman reminded me a good deal of Aunt Rosie. He was one of those unfortunate elderly person who, while apparently leading rather carefree lives, spend much time and thought doing good to others. He did arrange something, and that was a concert among the passengers. And the money they collected was presented to us. The window-cleaner for a long time refused to take it. But in the end they made him.

"And it was a good thing they did, too, for heaven only knows how we would have gotten along without it. Because when we finally reached the port, we found it little more than a collection of huts. It was hard enough to get a bed and a decent meal there, let alone a job. None of the other passengers was landing here and our ship had only stopped to unload part of her cargo. The window-cleaner, after thanking everybody aboard for his kindness, was given a great send-off as he walked down the gangplank, his only baggage a bird cage beneath his arm. Both he and I were, I think, a little sorry to see the good ship weigh anchor and sail away. Certainly if it had not been for her hospitality both of us would have succumbed to the perils of the sea. He had paid the barber for his hair cut and shave out of the money he had received from the concert. In this way the barber suffered no loss. And I was glad of that. Because he was a real decent fellow, that man, and his hair-dressing parlor had been quite a pleasant place to live in."

THE SEVENTH CHAPTER

The Ragged Tramp

AFTER THAT WE SETTLED DOWN IN SUCH quarters as the port afforded, to wait for a vessel homeward bound. Boats' arrivals and departures were not so certain then as they are now—particularly in that outlandish spot. We were told that a ship was expected in a fortnight, but that it might be three weeks before it came.

"This was a great disappointment to my friend, who was still itching to get back and find out about the fate of his book. And it seemed as though the nearer he got to his goal, the harder it became for him to wait.

"'You see, the trouble is, Pip,' he kept on saying as he walked the seawall with my cage beneath his arm, scanning the horizon for an approaching sail, 'the trouble is that mill is so unprotected. Those fellows could take up their quarters there and stay as long as they liked and no one would know the difference. And you can be sure, once they're certain they have found the house where I lived and wrote, they won't rest till they've discovered my papers.'

"Well, at last a ship came—not a very fine craft, far smaller and less elegant than the one that had brought us here. This was a cargo vessel, pure and simple. My friend made arrangements with the captain to take us as far as a certain port in his own country. Some hours were spent in unloading freight and taking on supplies—and one or two more in signing papers and talking about manifests, port dues, customs, quarantines, and all the other things that a ship has to fuss with when she enters or leaves a harbor.

"Finally, near nightfall, we got away. The window-cleaner now appeared to throw care aside and regain something of his old habitual jolliness. It was the feeling of motion, action at last, after all the waiting that buoyed him up. As the vessel plowed merrily forward through the water, he paced up and down the deck with a firmer, more vigorous manner than I had seen in him since we had rejoined each other.

"We had at least a two weeks' voyage ahead of us. My friend procured pens and ink and reams of paper. And hour after hour he would sit in his cabin, writing, writing, writing. He was describing his adventures with the agents or spies of the enemy government, he told me. He was going to add it to his book—if it still existed. Watching him scribbling away at his desk, stopping every once in a while to try to remember some detail of his life on the islands or whatnot, gave me the idea to record in some way the story of my own life. For it was then for the first time that it occurred to me that perhaps my days had been adventurous enough to be worth telling.

"Now I'm happy that I did. For if I had not composed those verses and songs, it would not be so easy for me to recall all the details so that you could put them down in a regular book."

"Indeed," said the Doctor. "I'm glad you did, too. This, I'm sure, will be a most unique book—a real animal biography—such as I've wanted to do for so long. Shall we go on or are you too tired?"

"Not at all," replied Pippinella, "I want to finish tonight, if possible.

"While the window-cleaner scribbled away at his desk over the story of his kidnapping and escape at sea, I warbled away in my cage, trying out phrases and melodies till I had put together the whole song of my life in a manner that seemed musically fitting. Occasionally he would look up from his work and smile. He liked it. He always liked to hear me sing. But he seemed particularly struck by the love song of the greenfinch in the spring. It's funny how everyone seems to like that best. You remember yourself, John Dolittle, how when I sang for you that first time through the wrapping paper of my cage, it was the greenfinch's spring song?"

"Yes, I recollect," said the Doctor. "Sing it for us again, will you please?"

"Certainly," said Pippinella. "I'll be glad to."

While the canary sang the beautiful and sad love story of the greenfinch, with the Doctor writing it all down in his notebook, the idea for a Canary Opera came to John Dolittle. It would be the most unusual dramatic production the world had ever seen, with Pippinella as the heroine and a cast of singing birds in the supporting roles. He determined to talk it over with her the moment her life story was finished.

The awful silence that greeted Pippinella at the end of her song convinced the Doctor more than ever that she was just the star he needed to take London by storm. Gub-Gub was sitting—silently, for a change—on his stool with a big tear standing on the end of his nose. Dab-Dab was trying self-consciously to hide the emotion she was feeling at the conclusion of the song. And the other animals—Too-Too, Whitey, and Jip—were openly wiping their eyes and snuffling their noses.

After a moment or two, while everyone composed himself again, the Doctor asked the canary to continue her story. Pippinella took another small sip of water and went on:

"At last our journey came to its end, as all journeys do, and we went ashore one fine morning and set about finding some means of transportation to get us to the town of the windmill.

"My friend's money was not yet exhausted, so happily we were able to pay for the journey by coach. The window-cleaner's anxiety and excitement about the fate of his book continued to grow as we drew nearer to his home. As we rumbled along over the country roads he kept muttering about the slowness of the horses and wondering aloud if the old mill had been burned to the ground or been struck by lightning or pulled down to make room for another building, and a hundred and one other possibilities that might prevent him from regaining his papers, if his enemies had not stolen them.

"And when finally the coach set us down at an inn in the town where Aunt Rosie lived, he took my cage beneath his arm and fairly ran along the road that led toward the mill. At the corner of the street he gave a cry:

"'Thank goodness, Pip! It's still there. Look, the mill is all right. The next thing is to see whether the kitchen has been broken into.'

"And he ran stumbling on. The road up the hill was quite steep, and he was all out of breath by the time he reached the little tumble-down fence that surrounded the bit of ground in which the mill tower stood. The place looked even more decayed and dilapidated than when we had seen it last. Long, lanky weeds grew in the chinks between the stones of the front walk. The little gate by which we entered hung by a single hinge.

"But the thing that struck us both was the fact that the front door of the mill had boards nailed across it.

"'Humph!' I heard him mutter. 'The old farmer's been around and found the door letting the weather in.'

"Then he went to the side of the tower where the kitchen window was. And that, too, had been nailed up.

"'Looks as though we're going to have a job to get in, Pip,' said he. 'I think I'll set you down here while I run over to the outhouse and find a ladder. That second-story window seems about the only entrance—unless I break in. You wait here. I won't be a minute.'

"And he set my cage down on an old packing-case near the front door and ran off toward the outhouse."

Pippinella paused.

"It's funny," she said presently, "what odd things happen at odd places. At that moment I was just as excited as he to know the fate of his papers. But when he disappeared into that outhouse that was the last I ever saw of him."

"Why, what happened?" asked Gub-Gub. "Was he kidnapped again?"

"No," said Pippinella, "but I was. While I listened to him rummaging around in that old shed, searching for a ladder, I saw a ragged person, very evidently a tramp, creep out from behind the tower. His appearance at once made me suspicious. And I started to call for the window-cleaner at the top of my voice. But I suppose the noise that he was making himself prevented him from hearing anything else. The tramp, with a glance over his shoulder, drew nearer. I hoped my friend would show up again any minute, for I knew at once what was going to happen. But he didn't. He was evidently entirely absorbed in his hunt for the ladder. As I gave an extra loud scream the tramp whipped my cage up, thrust it under his coat to muffle the sound of my voice, tiptoed out of the gate, and set off quickly down the hill.

"It would be impossible to describe to you how I felt. After all my striving, after all my traveling, there on the very doorstep of the mill, within a few moments of knowing what had happened to the book, within earshot of my beloved friend to whom I had only just been reunited, to be stolen by a tramp while his back was

"The tramp, with a glance over his shoulder, drew nearer."

turned! Fortune has dealt me some bitter blows, but none quite as bad as that.

"I think he was some kind of a wanderer. He looked like one. And later he fell in with a caravan of travelers, who seemed to know him, and traveled part of the way with them.

"I guessed at once that he had not stolen me because he was fond of birds. His idea was to sell me. He had lifted me up and taken me along just as he would a knife or any other bit of movable property, when the owner wasn't looking. And now he just awaited opportunity to dispose of me for money.

"He was a strange individual. His hand seemed to be set, his heart hardened, against everyone in the world except the other members of this mysterious group to which he belonged. He begged and stole his way across the country, sleeping in barns, under hayricks, or in some caravan whose owners offered him hospitality.

"And for two weeks I shared this wandering, hand-to-mouth existence. Often I was hungry; often I was cold; often I was wet. Still, I saw a tremendous lot of the countryside, and when the weather was fair I felt that I might easily be worse off, so far as the mere comforts of life were concerned.

"I tried to mark the way, to notice the road we followed, so that in case an opportunity to escape should occur I would know how to get back. But the course of his journeys was too meandering to keep track of for long. I calculated at the end of ten days that we had covered a hundred and fifty miles or so. But how much of it was in a straight line I had no idea.

"At one place my tramp nearly got caught picking a farmer's pocket at a cattle show. And I thought perhaps my chance to escape was at hand when the crowd started to come after him. But he was a wily rascal. He gave them the slip and got away.

"The tramp had tried several times to sell me at fairs and at wayside houses that he had passed. And for my part, I hoped he would succeed. But somehow he didn't. Perhaps people had an uncomfortable feeling that he may have stolen me—for he looked like a very suspicious sort of character.

"Anyway, after a while I saw that what I feared most would probably come to pass—he would sell me at a bird shop. One early morning he made his way into a small town and, with my cage under his arm, presented himself at an animal store just as the doors were being opened and the place swept out. My heart sank as we entered. The smell and the noise and the crowding! Oh my! They are still a sort of nightmare to me. I clung to the hope as we went in that the proprietor wouldn't buy me, or would offer a price so low that the tramp would keep me, for naturally, rascal though he was, his open, wandering life through the countryside was better by far than the close quarters of that noisome establishment.

"But, alas! He was apparently desperately in need of a little money, and while he struck as good a bargain as he could, he was evidently determined to sell me this time for anything he could get. And, after a little haggling, he left me on the counter, took the money, and went away.

"And then began what was, I think—after my experience of the coal mine—the unhappiest chapter in my life's story. Why should I tell you all the drab details of that miserable existence? You probably know them already, and for my part, I hate to recall them. An animal shop! Heaven preserve all animals from sinking to that dreary state. There's no reason, of course, why these places shouldn't be run properly—so far as the cage birds are concerned, at all events. But the fact remains that they very seldom are. I found that all my parents had told me about them was true—and a good deal more in this case.

"The main trouble is the crowding. No one person—nor two people—can look after a couple of hundred birds, several dozen rabbits, six pairs of guinea pigs, four tanks of goldfish, a score of dogs, cases upon cases of pigeons, ten parrots, a monkey or two, white mice, squirrels, ferrets and heaven knows what more, and give proper attention to them all. Yet this is what they try to do. It isn't

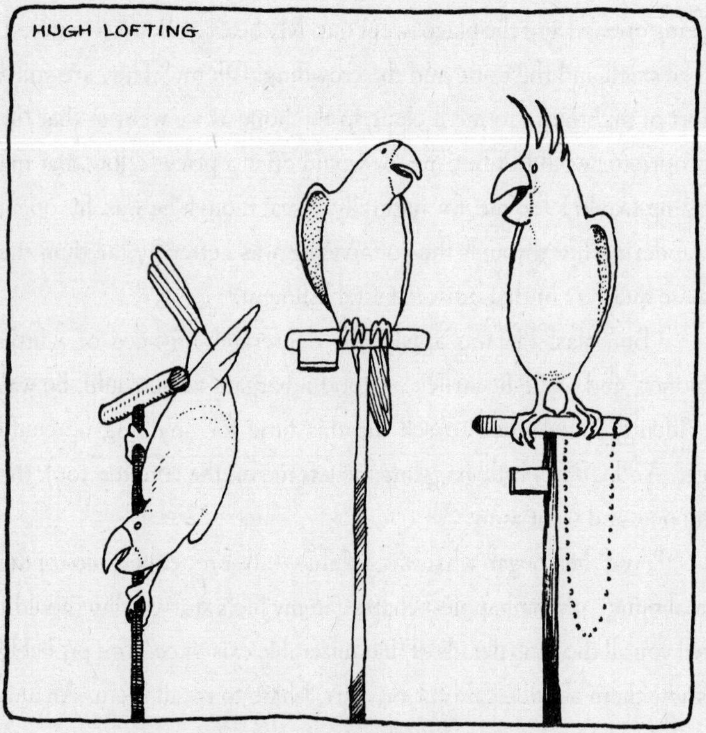

"In the middle of the room parrots on stands screeched and squawked all day long."

that they want to be unkind. They are just careless—horribly careless. They want to make money. That's the main idea.

"Right from the start I was taken out of my little wooden cage where I had lived since I'd been aboard ship and pushed into a larger one that was crowded with other crossbred canaries. We stood on a shelf, one in a long line of cages, and over us and under us and all around us there were more cages still. My partners who shared my miserable box were a motley crew of half-moulted hens, some of them with sore feet, others with colds in the head—hardly one of them a decent, full-blooded member of society. In the middle of the room parrots on stands screeched and squawked all day long. Twice a day—but why go on? There is only one good thing that I can say about that animal shop, John Dolittle. And it is that there I first heard about you from the other poor creatures who shared my miserable fate; and it was there you found me and rescued me from existence too horrible to describe further."

"My, my!" said the Doctor. "A most dramatic turn of events! Just right for an opera."

"Opera?" screamed Gub-Gub. "You mean we're going to do an opera? How elegant. I shall sing the baritone's role—Figaro! Figaro! Figaro-Figaro-*Figaro*!"

"Oh, be quiet!" scolded Dab-Dab. "Nobody said we were going to do an opera. You're always jumping to conclusions."

"The Doctor said Pip's life was just right for an opera," said Gub-Gub crossly. "That's what you said, John Dolittle, didn't you?"

"Yes, I did," replied the Doctor. "But the opera I have in mind is for birds only. You—and the rest of the family—may help with the production. That is, if Pippinella is willing."

Then the Doctor outlined his plan to the canary and asked her if she would be willing to assume the leading role. He explained that he would use the exact story of her life for the plot and hire other birds to play the supporting roles. It was just the idea he had been hunting for, he told her, and he felt sure London audiences would be charmed by such a production.

"Thank you, John Dolittle," Pippinella said. "It is a very great compliment. I hope you won't be disappointed in me. I shall need a great deal of coaching—opera is another thing again from singing just for the pleasure of it. But I have a small favour to ask of you. Doctor."

"Anything, Pippinella," said the Doctor. "What is it?"

"John Dolittle," replied the canary. "I want you to find my friend the window-cleaner. If we go up to London, as you planned, we may just find some trace of him there."

"It is little enough to ask," said the Doctor. "And London will be a good place to start. We have many friends there. Cheapside, the London sparrow who makes his home on St. Paul's Cathedral, can give us some valuable help, I'm sure."

Gub-Gub bounced down off his stool and, grabbing Dab-Dab around the middle, began to waltz her round and round, singing:

"We're off to London to see the queen! Tra-la-la-la, la-la-la, la-la!"

"Oh, stop it!" cried Dab-Dab. "You're making me dizzy!" But she was smiling just the same, and joined in the jubilation with the others.

PART THREE

THE FIRST CHAPTER

The Canary Opera

THE DOLITTLE CARAVAN AND CIRCUS STARTED immediately for London and set up camp on Greenheath well outside the city. Cheapside was found, and helped the Doctor and Matthew Mugg, the Cat's-Meat-Man, with the gathering together of birds from private aviaries, the zoo, and from the open fields. Theodosia, Matthew's wife, took over the making of all the costumes for the opera while the doctor and the Cat's-Meat-Man attended to the details of production.

When it came time for rehearsals to begin, they still had not found a suitable bird to play opposite Pippinella—to sing the tenor role.

"We need a voice that will blend perfectly with hers," said John Dolittle to Matthew. "It's important that he be of good appearance, too."

Before Matthew could reply, Pippinella, who was listening from her cage nearby, called out:

"Why don't we try to find Twink—the mate I had when I was with Aunt Rosie?"

"Oh, Lor' bless us, Pip!" cried Matthew Mugg. "It'd be like tryin' to find a needle in an 'aystack."

"Let's not give up until we've had a look around," said the Doctor. "It may be possible to find Twink."

With Pippinella going along to help, Matthew visited every animal shop in the vicinity of London. Strangely enough, one day in a dirty shop in the East End, who should turn up but Twink. He was desperately ill with a cold and a sore throat, but the Doctor soon cured that with his Canary Cough Mixture and Twink's voice came back stronger and more beautiful than it had been before. Pippinella was delighted to see him again and, for the time being, stopped fretting about her friend, the window-cleaner.

Twink's account of the miserable conditions under which the birds and animals existed in the shop in the East End so disturbed the Doctor that he and Matthew took time out from rehearsals to stage one of the greatest mass rescues in the Doctor's career—the release of Twink's former associates from their imprisonment in the shop.

In spite of the fact that the Doctor often neglected the business of the opera to follow up some clue that seemed to be leading to the window-cleaner, Pippinella's beloved master was still not found. One day, when the Doctor had called a final dress rehearsal, it was discovered that the green canary and Jip were missing. Cheapside, who was assisting the Doctor by drilling the chorus and dance numbers, was all for finding a new prima donna.

"Tempermental hartists!" sniffed the cockney sparrow. "I bet them two is off 'untin' for 'er window polisher. Say, Doc, what's the matter with me singin' her part? We could dye my feathers green and nobody'd know the difference."

"Hah!" snorted Dab-Dab. "If you so much as opened your cockney mouth you would empty the house in two minutes!"

"I like that!" replied Cheapside in a huff. "I'm considered the most musical bird in these 'ere parts, I am!"

"Now, now," admonished the Doctor. "Pippinella must be found. We can hold up opening for a day or two. I'm sure she can't be far away."

And Pippinella *was* found. She explained that she had seen a man in the circus enclosure who looked like her window-cleaner friend. Jip had gone with her to follow him across London. But in the smelly quarters of the docks, even Jip's sensitive nose could not keep track of the scent.

The Doctor was most understanding.

"I know how much you miss him, Pippinella," he said. "But do be patient. As soon as the opera is over we will devote every minute to make a thorough search for him. Please promise me you won't run off again."

"All right, Doctor," replied the canary. "I'll wait."

The Canary Opera was a smashing success. Pippinella's solos, "Maids, Come Out, the Coach Is Here," "The Harness Jingle," and "The Midget Mascot" were tremendous hits. She was so taken up with the excitement of being the toast of London that, for the time being, thoughts of her friend, the window-cleaner, were completely driven from her mind.

Many honors, too, came to the green canary because of the opera. She was wined and dined at the most famous restaurants in London. Admirers sent her baskets and bouquets of flowers; and a famous manufacturer of bird cages paid her a large salary to hop in and out of one of his cages in a store window, showing by her presence and sprightly manner that she approved of the design.

The successful opera season came to a close. Twink went off to live with Hop, the clown from the circus, who had decided to retire. The pelicans and flamingos had been returned to the naturalist from whom the Doctor had borrowed them for the chorus; and the thrushes and wrens had left for their native haunts. All that was left to do now, before the family could return to Puddleby while the Doctor and Pippinella went to look for the canary's friends, was for the circus animals and personnel to be placed in proper homes for their comfort and well-being.

This the Doctor did with great care. He chartered a special ship to send the lion, the leopard, and the elephant back to Africa. The snakes went, too, and caused great consternation when they got out of the basket on the dock and started diving and wiggling among the passenger's baggage just for the fun of a good stretch. One old lady fainted dead away when she opened her bag and found one of them squirming among her shawls and laces.

However, they were captured and made the trip safely and happily back to their native soil where they became the talk of all snakedom with the fandango dance that they had learned for the circus and now performed for their newfound friends.

The day finally came when all the business of the circus had been completed. The enclosure was cleared of its equipment; nothing remained now except the Doctor's caravan—in which members of his household lived—and the smaller covered wagon that served Theodosia and Matthew Mugg as a home.

A vast throng of children—after presenting the Doctor with

a huge bouquet of flowers—were departing tearfully, sucking peppermint drops John Dolittle had given them as a farewell gift. The Doctor turned to face the members of his family who were gathered around him.

"I—a—er, have something to tell you," he said. He paused, at a loss for the proper words.

Dab-Dab, quick to sense what was on the Doctor's mind, pushed forward to stand in front of him.

"Now, John Dolittle," she said crossly. "Don't tell me we are not going home. I simply cannot stand another minute of this existence! My nerves are at breaking point!"

"There, there," said John Dolittle, leaning forward to comfort her. "I know it's been difficult. But you've done wonderfully. And I wouldn't even consider keeping you here. How soon will you be able to leave?"

"Why, within the hour!" said Dab-Dab, brightening. "I have one or two little things still to do." She spreads her wings and, calling to the others to come and pick up their rubbish, flew right through the doorway of the wagon. Matthew and Theodosia also hustled off to complete their preparations, while the Doctor just stood in the empty lot staring off into space.

Barely a moment elapsed before Dab-Dab thrust her head out of the wagon and looked at the Doctor with a worried expression on her kindly face.

"I just remembered something, Doctor," said the duck. "You didn't say what it was you had to tell us."

"Why, I—er—a—you see, Dab-Dab," he began.

"Don't tell me—I know," she said, coming slowly down the wagon steps. "You're not going to Puddleby with us. I might have guessed it. You have some notion of finding that window-cleaner fellow, haven't you, John Dolittle?"

"Yes," said the Doctor. "I made a promise and it must be fulfilled before I can return to Puddleby."

"All right!" declared Dab-Dab. "If that's the way you feel, then nobody goes to Puddleby until you do."

"Oh, that isn't necessary, Dab-Dab," remonstrated the Doctor. "Perhaps the others *want* to go home."

With that there was a chorus of denials; nobody wanted to go home without the Doctor.

"We can all help find Pip's friend!" shouted Gub-Gub. "I'm a first class rooter!"

"Where do you think he's hiding?" asked the duck, all thoughts of Puddleby driven from her head. "Under a cauliflower plant?"

"Jip will be better at hunting him out than any of us," said the white mouse. "He can track a person by sniffing the grass along the roadside."

"Whitey would be valuable wherever doors are locked," offered Jip. "He can squeeze through a hole the size of a farthing."

"How about me?" asked Too-Too the owl. "We may need to do some night work. And you know how well I see in the dark."

Pippinella, perched on a discarded orange crate, listened to all this with a lifting heart. During the earlier proceedings she had become terribly downcast, for she too had mistaken the Doctor's intentions. But when she heard with what enthusiasm the family accepted the change in plans, she flew to the group and lit on the Doctor's high hat.

"I want you to know how much I appreciate this," she said in a most gracious manner. "Someday, perhaps I can do something for you besides upsetting your plans."

"Tut-tut," said Dab-Dab, who was secretly a great admirer of the little prima donna. "We frequently change our plans, don't we, Doctor?"

"Yes, indeed," said John Dolittle. "Now let's work out the beginning of our campaign. Pippinella, do you know the name of the town where the windmill stood? That seems the best place for us to start."

"Yes," replied the canary. "It's called Wendlemere; a little town with a cathedral right in the middle and a river that makes a sort of loop around three sides of it."

"The cathedral stands at one end of a large market square, doesn't it?" asked the Doctor.

"Yes," said Pippinella. "That's the town."

"Fine," said the Doctor. "Now we're on the trail. Did you ever hear your friend's name?"

"Never once," said the canary. "He was careful always to avoid giving any names. And, as I told you, so far as his life at the mill was concerned, no one was ever there to ask it."

"Humph!" said the Doctor. "It isn't much to go on, just the name of the town. Still, people have been found before today with no more information than that. I will do my best. Now, let's all go back to the caravan for supper. Dab-Dab, have we something extra nice? Some kippers and tea would taste good after this busy day."

"Kippers!" squealed Gub-Gub. "I'd rather have a kipper than a dozen truffles!"

During supper a lively discussion went on; everybody wanted to go along to hunt for the window-cleaner. But it was finally decided that only Jip and Pippinella should accompany the Doctor.

Matthew and Theodosia were commissioned to see that Dab-Dab had sufficient food for the larder at all times; and the family all joined with Pippinella in making plans for the trip to the windmill.

In the morning the Doctor, Pippinella, and Jip were up and away early. It took them the whole day to complete the journey to Wendlemere, and by the time they got there darkness had fallen.

"I'm going to have a look around," said the Doctor. "One can tell better at night if a place is occupied—by the lights in the windows, you know."

"Smells are good at night, too," said Jip. "The dampness makes them hang close to the ground. I'll go with you, if you don't mind, Doctor?"

"Certainly, Jip," said the Doctor. "Pippinella, you come onto my shoulder. We'll stroll around and see what we can see."

The little party set out for the mill while the rest of the town slept. They went immediately to the foot of the hill on which the windmill stood, to see if any light was visible in the tower. But all was in darkness.

"Perhaps he's gone to bed," said the canary hopefully. "It's long after midnight. And he used to turn in early when we lived here before."

"Yes," said the Doctor, "and I think that's what we better do, too. We'll find a room at the inn and wait until morning to investigate further."

On the morrow they returned after a hasty breakfast to the home of the solitary philosopher. Their first glance at the mill from below the hill was quite discouraging. No smoke rose from the stove pipe that stuck out of the roof. Yet it was the hour when breakfast, if the mill was occupied, should be cooking. With a sinking feeling of failure, the Doctor, with Pippinella on his shoulder and Jip at his heels, hurried up the hill till finally he stood before the little gate in the ramshackle fence. The stone walk leading to the tower door showed no footprints of habitation.

Heavy at heart, the Doctor turned his head to speak to Pippinella.

"We've come on a wild goose chase, Pippinella," he said. "Your friend has evidently been gone from here a long time."

"I'm afraid you're right, Doctor," said the canary. "What do we do now?"

"He stood before the little gate in the ramshackle fence."

Jip jumped up and put his front paws on the Doctor's leg.

"There's a man over there in the field," said he. "Why don't you ask him if he's seen the window-cleaner?"

"That's a good idea, Jip," said the Doctor. "Perhaps he owns this place. He'd be sure to know something about his tenant if he did."

The man, a weather-beaten, gray-haired countryman of about fifty years of age, turned out to be a civil fellow—only too willing to rest his plow and gossip, if he got the chance.

"No," he said. "I ain't seen nowt of that loon for—let me see—not for over a year. He used to pay me a few shillings a month for the use of the old mill. He'd bring me the money regular, himself, while he was here. Didn't like to have me come up and collect it. It seemed he hadn't no wish for human company around him. I never even heard what his business was."

Suddenly the man peered sharply at Pippinella sitting on the Doctor's shoulder.

"That's odd, sir," he said. "That fellow you're lookin' for had a bird that the spittin' image of that one. Used to hang his cage on a hook outside the tower window—when the weather was good. But of course it couldn't be the same one. Yours seems sorta tame like—the way he sits there—not moving or nothing."

The Doctor was relieved that the man did not pursue the subject further; it would be awkward to try to explain his relationship with birds and animals to this simple countryman.

"He wur surely a strange, strange man," the farmer went on. "I used to say to the wife, I'd say, 'Maybe he's a hanarchist, a mixing dynamite and bombs up there in my mill—never did see a soul live so secret and solitary.' 'Oh, go along,' she'd say, 'no man with a

"'He wur surely a strange, strange man,' the farmer said."

face like his'n never mixed bombs to blow folks up with. He looks more to me like a minister—and not any of your simpering, psalm-singing kind neither, but just a plain, honest man who thinks more of others than himself.' That wur the wife's opinion. Howsomever, hanarchist or minister, he wur a strange duck, all right."

"Do you remember exactly," the Doctor asked, "what day it was you saw him last?"

The farmer called to his team to stand, and he scratched his head.

"Aye," he said after a moment. "I mind it wur the day I took the potatoes in off the north field. It rained about noon and I had to stop 'cause potatoes don't store good when they're wet. I hadn't even seen him go away. But his not coming with the rent told me that he'd gone off and I'd like as not ever see him again. Then, when I were starting for home I saw a man a crossin' down from the mill to the gate. It wur him. He wur running, crazy like. 'So,' I thinks to myself, 'he's come back, 'as he?' Minding he never like to have me come to see him, I thinks to meself: 'He'll be round to my place afore long with his rent and I'll not bother.' And I goes off home in the rain. But he never comed and I never seen him from the fields here while I was plowing. And at the end of the week I goes up to the mill anyhow. But he wasn't there."

"Yes, but what day was that?" asked the Doctor.

"It wur the day I took the potatoes off the north field," the farmer repeated, "end of the first week in September. That'll be twelve months ago come Friday."

"And have you seen anyone else around the mill, either before or since?"

"Not a soul. Nobody ever comes up here."

"Thank you," said the Doctor. And bidding the farmer good-bye, he set off to return to the town.

THE SECOND CHAPTER

The Green Parrot Has a Clue

WHEN JOHN DOLITTLE GOT BACK TO the inn he put Pippinella back in the small traveling cage he had made for her.

"There's plenty of seed and fresh water, I believe," he said. "You must be very hungry."

"No, Doctor," said the canary. "I'm too discouraged to eat."

"You mustn't feel that way," said the Doctor. "We've only begun to look for your friend. I feel sure he'll turn up. Have some food—and rest awhile. I'm going out to ask around the town whether a stranger has been seen lately. Jip, you stay here to keep Pippinella company. Try to cheer her up while I'm gone."

Jip wagged his tail and said he would.

At a corner of a long street of stately old-fashioned mansions the Doctor paused a moment, looking upward at a curious lamppost that stood close to one of the houses. Two fine shady trees spread their branches overhead. Outside the corner window of the house a mirror was fastened on a bracket. A plump, white-haired lady sat knitting at the window, and the Doctor noticed that she was looking at him in the mirror. Something about the spot struck John Dolittle as familiar. And while he paused, an old lame man came along, put a ladder against the lamppost, and climbed up to clean the lamp.

A smile of recognition suddenly spread over the Doctor's face.

"Aunt Rosie's house!" he whispered. "Of course. I wonder if she's heard anything of the window-cleaner. There she is, still knitting, still watching the neighbors pass. I'll go and call on her."

Aunt Rosie, while knitting at her window, had noticed a small, round man pause at the corner of the street.

"Hah! A stranger!" she muttered, dropping a stitch. "Distinguished-looking man. A scientist or a barrister—possibly a diplomat. I wonder what house he's bound for. Doesn't look like a relative of anyone in this street. Goodness gracious, I believe he's coming here! Yes, he's walking up my steps. Well, did you ever! Emily, Emily!"

A maid, neatly dressed with white cap and apron, entered from the next room in answer to her mistress's cry.

"Emily," said Aunt Rosie. "There's a caller at the door—a gentleman caller. I'm not dressed or anything. Get me my cashmere shawl quickly. It's on the top of my bureau. And take this old woolen one away. There's the bell. Hurry! I've no idea who it is, but it looks like someone very important. He's got a black bag. Come from out of town, that's clear. Are the tea things ready? Answer the door, girl. Don't stand there! No, get the shawl first. And don't forget the buttered toast. Hurry, I tell you! Here, come back. Put this old woolen thing out of sight."

In a great state of flutter and excitement, Aunt Rosie threw off the white knitted shawl from her shoulders—nearly upsetting a green parrot that perched on a stand at her elbow. The maid, bewildered at receiving half a dozen orders at once, took it from her and left the room. In the hall she set it down upon a chair and went to open the front door.

Outside she found a small, round man, with a very kind face.

"Er—er—hum—er—a. Is Aunt Rosie in?" asked the Doctor.

The maid stared at him in astonishment.

"She is, I know," the Doctor went on, answering his own question. "Because I saw her at the window."

Emily, though still somewhat surprised, finally found her voice.

"Won't you come in, sir?" she murmured.

"Thank you," said the Doctor, stepping across the threshold.

In the hall on his way to the parlor the Doctor was met by the hostess herself, who came forward, fluttering, to greet him.

"Ah, how do you do, Aunt Rosie?" said he, holding out his hand.

Now "Aunt Rosie" was a nickname for this lady, used only by herself when talking with her pets and some of her relatives. Imagine, then, her astonishment to be greeted in this fashion by an entire stranger. However, her guest seemed such an amiable, disarming person, she supposed he must be someone whom she ought to know and whose face she had forgotten.

"Good afternoon," she murmured feebly. "Emily, take this gentleman's hat and bag."

Then she led the way into the room where she always sat and the first thing the Doctor noticed was the green parrot perched on the stand.

"Ah!" said he. "I see you've got a new parrot. The other one was a gray one, wasn't he?"

"Er—yes. Quite so," muttered Aunt Rosie, feeling surer than

ever that this man, if not one of her own relatives greatly altered, must at least be someone she ought to know extremely well. Afraid to offend him by asking him his name, she proceeded to putter around with the tea things while she watched the doctor out of the corner of her eye and sought wildly to remember who he was.

Before the Doctor had a chance to explain the object of his visit he was offered, to his great delight, a cup of tea by his fluttering hostess.

"I hope you will pardon my dropping in unexpectedly like this," he began, taking the teacup from her.

"Oh, don't mention it," said she, returning to the tray. "Let me see, I've forgotten whether you take sugar?"

"Two lumps, please," said the Doctor.

"Yes, of course," murmured Aunt Rosie.

"Well, now," said John Dolittle, "I wanted to ask you about your window-cleaner. You remember the odd fellow that you used to employ, the one you gave the canary to?"

"Oh, perfectly," the hostess answered, still cudgeling her brains for the name of this man who apparently knew her private affairs so well. "A quite extraordinary individual—most peculiar."

"Have you seen him recently?" asked the Doctor. "I mean, since you gave up having your windows done regularly by him—that was somewhat over a year ago, wasn't it?"

"Yes," said Aunt Rosie, "I have."

For the quiet old lady of the sleepy cathedral town that odd character, the window-cleaner, had always held the spice of mystery. Many a time she had tried by questioning him and inquiring among the neighbors to find out more about him. But she had met with nothing but baffling failure. The object of the Doctor's visit, therefore, threw Aunt Rosie into a greater state of excitement than ever. She stopped rattling the teacups and leaned forward in her chair as though about to impart some terrible secret.

"I had not seen that man," she whispered, "for fifteen months. I supposed that he had left the town, and I'm quite certain that he had, for several of my neighbors used to employ him, and if he had been working in the town I would surely have seen him. Well, then, one day, as I was feeding the parrot, I saw him come up the steps. I noticed at a glance that he was greatly changed, much thinner—he used to be quite plump, you know. And when the maid let him in, he asked for work. I didn't really need him

"She leaned forward in her chair."

to do the windows, because I have them done by the maids now. But he looked so down-at-heel and poverty-stricken that I hadn't the heart to say no. So I told him to do all the windows on the top floor. On the way upstairs he suddenly swayed weakly against the wall. I guessed at once what was the matter. I whispered to the maid to take him to the kitchen and give him a good meal. And do you know, the poor man was actually starving. The cook told me he ate nearly everything in the larder. Then I questioned him while he was at work, to see if I could find out what had befallen him. But he would tell me hardly anything. Just murmured something about having run into bad luck."

As Aunt Rosie finished her long speech the green parrot on the stand moved restlessly, jingling the chain about his leg.

"And did you, madam," asked the Doctor, "see him again after that?"

"Only once," said the old lady, handing her guest the buttered toast. "Seeing what sad straits he was in, I told him I wanted the rest of the windows done the following day. He came back early on the morrow—very early—and the maids told me they had seen him hanging around the house in the small hours. I believe he never went to bed at all; perhaps he had no place to go, but just waited through the night to do the rest of his work the following day. When all the windows were done and there was nothing further to keep him I asked him, as I paid him his money, whether he intended staying in the town for some time. He glanced at me suspiciously, as though I were trying to incriminate him, and then said no, he was only remaining long enough to earn his coach fare to go on farther."

"Did he say where he was going?" the Doctor asked.

"No," said the old lady. "But I'm pretty sure he left the town that night. Because he finished his work here in the morning, and I never saw him again."

At this moment Emily, the maid, entered and whispered something in her mistress's ear.

"Excuse me," said Aunt Rosie, rising. "I have to see the butcher about his bill. I'll be back in a moment."

And she left the room, accompanied by the maid.

John Dolittle put down his teacup and leaned back in his chair, staring in a puzzled manner at the ceiling.

"Confound the luck!" he said aloud. "It looks as though the trail leads no farther. For heaven only knows where he went when he left the town."

Suddenly the Doctor heard a rattle behind him. Thinking it was perhaps his host returning, he sprang to his feet politely and turned about. But he found that he was still alone, except for the green parrot, whom he had forgotten. That wise-looking bird now seemed very wide awake. He stepped gravely to the end of his short perch and craned his neck out toward the Doctor.

"Oh, how do you do?" said John Dolittle in parrot language. "You had been so quiet behind me there I had forgotten all about you. I suppose you can't help me in this problem?"

The parrot glanced over his shoulder at the door still ajar and listened a moment. Then he motioned with his head to the Doctor to come a little nearer. John Dolittle at once stepped up to his stand.

"He went to London, Doctor," the parrot whispered. "You know, as the old lady told you, he used to mutter a lot—talk aloud to himself—but only when there were no people about. While he was doing the window of this room, standing on the sill outside, with the window half-open, he looked in and saw me on my perch here.

Seemed sort of mesmerized at first. Then he laughed kind of childish-like and went on polishing the window. There was no one in the room but me. 'Good old Pip,' he kept saying. 'There you are, still, sitting in the window. Watching me polish up the glass. So you came back to the old lady, did you, Pip? Well, she's a good sort. She'll take better care of you than I did. Poor old Pip! But you're looking well—you've grown bigger. Shan't see you again after today—not for a long time. I'm just making enough money to get after them, Pip. Curse them! Curse them! I'm just making enough money to buy a coach ride. Then I'm off. I know where they've gone, Pip. They've gone to London. And I'm going after them—tonight!'"

As the green parrot finished speaking, the Doctor heard Aunt Rosie's footsteps in the distance, coming up the kitchen stairs.

"Listen," he whispered quickly, "did you get any idea of where he was going in London—any names of people he meant to see, eh?"

"No," said the parrot, "nothing more. I don't think he had a very clear idea himself. He seemed very vague and hazy. Tell me, Doctor, how is Polynesia getting on?"

"Oh, did you know my Polynesia?" asked John Dolittle.

"Why, certainly!" said the parrot. "She was a distant relative of mine. I heard that she was living at your house in Puddleby."

"I left Polynesia in Africa," sighed the Doctor. "Last time I was there. I have missed her terribly."

"She's lucky," said the parrot. "She always was a lucky bird, was Polynesia. Look out, here's the old lady coming back!"

When Aunt Rosie reentered the room she found her caller scratching the parrot's head.

"I'm sorry to have been so long," she said. "But you know how these tradesmen are. That dreadful man insisted that I had a pound of steak last Tuesday, when that is my meatless day. I haven't eaten meat on a Tuesday for three years—not since Doctor Matthews put me on a diet. Then he discovers that he sent the steak to somebody else in the street—someone who really had ordered it—and he had charged it to me by mistake."

"Very trying," said the Doctor. "Very trying."

Aunt Rosie now settled down again to her tea, hoping to find out from her caller something of the private history of her mysterious window-cleaner. But before she had a chance to ask a single question, the Doctor began asking questions himself.

"Perhaps your maid—the one who opened the door for me—could remember something that would help me find the window-cleaner," said the Doctor.

"Oh, Emily!" said Aunt Rosie, wrinkling up her nose. "She never notices really important things. But we'll ask her anyway."

Then Emily was summoned and questioned by her mistress. She said all she knew was that he hadn't done a very good job on the windows the last time he'd washed them. As she was retiring, the front doorbell rang.

"Pardon me," said Aunt Rosie, rising. "This is my at-home day. Some friends drop in regularly and bring their needlework with them."

"Oh—er," said the Doctor, getting up out of his chair. "I think I ought to be going—really."

"Oh no, don't run away," said Aunt Rosie. "I'll just see who it is. I'll be back in a moment."

And before the Doctor had a chance to protest, his hostess had left the room again and closed the door behind her.

"Then Emily was summoned and questioned by her mistress."

In the hall Aunt Rosie greeted a sour-faced lady who had just been admitted by the maid.

"My dear," she said, fluttering forward, "I'm so glad you've come. Listen: there's a man in the parlor whom I can't make out at all. He seems to know all about me and my private affairs. And I suppose it's someone whom I ought to know extremely well. Perhaps you can help me. If you recognize him, whisper his name to me when he's not looking, will you?"

"Is that his?" asked the sour-faced lady, sternly pointing to the Doctor's high hat hanging on the stand in the hall.

"Yes," said Aunt Rosie.

"Then I know already," said the other.

Now, as soon as Aunt Rosie had left the parlor the Doctor was summoned by a sharp "Pst!" from the corner of the room. He slipped across to the parrot's side and leaned down to listen.

"It's your sister, Sarah," whispered the bird. "She's always the first to arrive at these sewing circles. They're all a dreadful lot of old gossips. But she's the worst of them all. A sparrow told me that she was your sister."

"Good heavens!" said the Doctor. "Sarah! How can I get out of here, I wonder?"

"Push the window up and drop down onto the street," said the parrot.

"But my hat and bag are in the hall," whispered the Doctor. "I can't go without them. Oh, Lord! And she'll start in about the circus again, I suppose, as soon as she meets me."

"Listen," whispered the parrot. "You see that other door over there? That leads around through the pantry. Go through it and wait just on the other side. As soon as they come in here and the hall is clear I'll give a loud squawk. Then hurry along the passage and it will bring you out into the hall. Take your hat and bag and let yourself out the front door. Hurry up! I hear them coming."

The Doctor only just closed the door behind him as Sarah and Aunt Rosie entered the room. He waited a moment in the narrow, dark passage till a hearty screech from the parrot told him that the coast was clear. Then he groped his way along till he found the door at the end, passed into the hall, grabbed his hat and bag, and let himself out into the street.

"Dear me!" he muttered as he hurried around the corner and

set off toward the inn. "A lucky escape, a merciful escape! I don't know what poor Aunt Rosie will think of me—running off like that—after she had given me a cup of tea and everything. Good tea it was, too. . . . Oh well, I'll write her a letter and tell her I was afraid I'd miss the coach. Fancy that old fellow being a relative of Polynesia's—good old Polynesia! I wonder how she's getting on. What a small world it is, to be sure. Well, well! I haven't found out an awful lot about the window-cleaner. Still, it's a good deal to know that he's in London. And the search lies in our direction, too. It's an awfully big city, though. But you can't tell. I have a feeling that we'll find him."

The Third Chapter

Cheapside Helps the Doctor

THE DOCTOR WENT IMMEDIATELY TO HIS room at the inn and told Pippinella the result of his expedition. When he had finished, the canary shook her head.

"It looks bad," she said, "very bad, Doctor. From what both the farmer and Aunt Rosie told you, there is no doubt in my mind that the window-cleaner found his kitchen ransacked and his papers gone. Oh, dear! Poor man. I suppose he was just distracted with grief. What can we do, Doctor? What can we do?"

"Well, now," said John Dolittle, "be patient. After all, it's something that we know he went to London. I have a notion that we're going to succeed in finding him."

"Oh, I hope so," sighed Pippinella. "I hope so. I'm so worried about him."

"I hope we don't end up down at the East End docks again," said Jip. "I simply can't get the smells untangled. What with tar smells mixing with the scents from boxes of spices the ships from India unload on the docks, and the fish smells so strong one can barely breathe, I find it impossible to pick out the man smell."

"Yes," said the Doctor. "It must be very difficult. Let's hope we don't have to go there."

That evening the little party took the London coach from the town square. As there were no other passengers for that journey, the Doctor was able to stretch out on one seat and sleep most of the way. When they reached the city it was early morning and everything was bustling with activity. The Doctor tucked Pippinella's little traveling cage under his arm so that in case they should meet the window-cleaner among the crowds on the streets, the canary could recognize him. Jip trotted along at John Dolittle's heels, ready for action.

As they walked along the thronged pavements, Pippinella, with her keen eyes, searched the faces of every passerby, hoping to find her friend. After about two hours of this they all began to be a bit tired. On his way across a bridge that spanned the river, the Doctor sat down on one of the public seats to take a rest.

"Dear me, Doctor," said the canary. "I'm afraid there isn't much chance of our running into him haphazardly. Look at those crowds across the bridge! Their faces all swim together when I try to pick out one at a time."

The Doctor, who was beginning to be depressed about the prospect himself, did not answer. Presently he got up and moved off, with the intention of finding Cheapside, the London sparrow who had promised to help them find the window-cleaner.

Passing by St. Paul's Cathedral he looked up at the statue of St. Edmund, which stood against the sky. The Doctor knew that Cheapside and Becky, his wife, made their nest in the ear of the great statue. And although he couldn't see it from that distance, he hoped it was there and that Cheapside would be at home and would see him.

Suddenly he saw a small speck shoot out of the statue's ear. It dropped to earth with the speed of a bullet, and, with a fluttering of wings, landed on his shoulder.

"Lor' bless me, Doc!" said Cheapside. "I 'ad no idear you was in town. When I looked down off St. Edmund's ear just now and see'd your old stovepipe 'at, you could 'ave knocked me over with a feather!"

"Well, well, Cheapside," said the Doctor. "I'm glad I found you so easily."

"'Lor' bless me, Doc!' said Cheapside."

"But what are you doin' 'ere, Doctor?" asked the sparrow. "When I went out to Greenheath yesterday they told me you was in Wendlemere—'untin' for Pip's friend."

"We were," replied the Doctor. "But we had no luck. Nobody there has seen him for months and months. However, I did hear that he'd come up to London. Then I remembered that you had promised to help us and we came to find you."

"So I did," said Cheapside. "So I did. And I ain't one to go back on my word. I'll do my best. London's a big place. Still, there ain't no one knows it better than what I do. Hullo, Pip," he said, peering into the cage under the Doctor's arm. 'Ow's the primer donner this morning?"

"Very well, thank you," said Pippinella. "But I'm terribly worried about my friend."

"Don't you fret now, Pip," said the sparrow. "We'll find the bloke if we 'ave to 'unt the whole of England over. Just you leave it to old Cheapside. I'm the champion 'unter of the British Hempire, I am! You and the Doc—and Jip—Hullo, Jip," he said. "I was so busy talkin' I forgot to say hullo."

The sparrow hopped over onto the Doctor's other shoulder.

"As I was sayin'," continued the sparrow, "you three go back 'ome and wait to hear from me. I'll bring you word as soon as I 'ave something to tell you."

"I'm awfully glad we found him," said John Dolittle as they made their way homeward toward Greenheath. "He'll be much better at tracing your friend than I could ever hope to be. You see, he's lived in London all his life—knows every street and house in the whole city."

"I do hope he finds him," sighed Pippinella. "But I'm very fearful. Suppose those spies have found him again and taken him off on that dreadful ship."

"Now, now, Pippinella," said the Doctor. "We mustn't look on the dark side. I still feel confident he's around somewhere. Let's leave it to Cheapside for a while. If it's possible to find him he'll do it. He'll do anything for me."

Reaching Greenheath, the Doctor was met by Gub-Gub and the rest of the family clamoring for news of the window-cleaner. They were tremendously interested to hear of the Doctor's visit to Wendlemere and of his meeting with Cheapside in London, and they began at once to look forward to the visit of the little cockney sparrow. For they always found the worldly little city bird excellent company and never tired of his comic chatter and amusing anecdotes.

And they had not long to wait, as a matter of fact. About noon the next day, when the Dolittle household was sitting down to lunch in the wagon, two sparrows suddenly flew in at the open door and settled in the middle of the table—Mr. and Mrs. Cheapside.

As soon as the greetings were over, Dab-Dab provided them with a place beside the white mouse (next to the salt cellar) and gave them a supply of crumbs and millet seed.

"Bless me, Doctor," said Cheapside with his mouth full. "It's nice to sit down to dinner with you again. Becky and me 'ave been lonely for you since the opera closed."

"It's nice of you to say so," replied the Doctor. "We've missed you too."

"Ah, Doc," said Cheapside. But he was secretly very pleased.

"By the way, Cheapside," said the Doctor. "I don't want to seem impatient, but have you started your search for Pippinella's friend yet?"

"Mr. and Mrs. Cheapside"

"Who's that?" asked the sparrow.

"The window-cleaner—you know," said the Doctor, "the man I spoke to you about yesterday."

"Oh, 'im!" said the sparrow. "Yes, we found him, all right."

"You found him!" cried the Doctor, springing to his feet. "Already? Good heavens!"

"Yes," said Cheapside. "We ran him down this morning—about eleven o'clock."

A regular chorus of exclamations broke out around the Doctor's luncheon table after Cheapside's extraordinary statement.

"When will he come here?" asked Gub-Gub, climbing up on to his chair to make himself heard. "I'm so anxious to see that window-cleaner."

"How was he looking?" asked Pippinella.

"Whereabouts did you find him?" Dab-Dab wanted to know.

"But, Cheapside," said the Doctor. "How on earth did you do it in so short a time?"

"Well," said the sparrow when the general noise and clatter had quieted down, "the first thing I did was to go around to the gangs."

"What do you mean, the gangs?" squeaked the white mouse.

"The sparrow gangs, of course," said Cheapside. "The city sparrows are divided into gangs. Very exclusive, some of them, too. For instance, the West-Enders; oh my! They're lah-di-dah, they are! Live in Berkeley Square, Park Lane, and Belgravia. Call 'emselves the Four Thousand—gentry, you know. They wouldn't be seen speakin' to a Whitechapel sparrow or any of the Wapping gang, Mile-Enders, Houndsditchers, and low bird-life like that. Ho no, indeed. Then there's the sort of betwixt-and-betweeners—the Chelsea push, live among the artists; the Highgate and Hampstead lot, 'ang around among the writers, they do. They're kind of half-and-half, sort of dingy—you know, down-at-heel genteel—look glum on Sundays, never do their fightin' in the street, all for keepin' up appearances. But they're all the same to me, see? Whitechapel, Highgate or Belgravia, I don't take no lip from none of them.

"Well, when you says you wants to find this window-washer of yours, I says to the missus, I says: 'Becky, the Doc wants this bloke found. It's up to us to run 'im down. You go 'round the high-life gangs—you see, she uses better class talk than what I do—and I'll go 'round the East-Enders and the middle-class 'ippocrites. I'll meet you on the top of Cleopatra's Needle at ten o'clock sharp. Tell the gang leaders the job is for the Doctor and I'll want to know the reason why it ain't done right. If that bloomin' window-swabber ain't found by noon, the feathers'll begin to fly—and they won't be mine, neither.'

"So Becky goes off one way and I goes off another. The first bunch I hinvestigates is the Greenwich squad. They 'ang 'round the docks, all the way from the Tower to the Isle of Dogs. I looks up the leader right away, One-Eyed Alf, they calls 'im—the Wapping Terror. Thinks 'imself a fighter. I 'ad to push 'is 'ead in the gutter before I could make him listen to reason. 'Hark at me, you crumb-snatchin' Stevedore,' I says, ''ave there been any strangers come 'round your district lately?'

"''Ow should I know?' 'e says, 'I ain't the Lord Mayor!'

"'Well, look 'ere,' I says, 'you get busy with your boys and bloomin' well find out, see? There's a window-cleaner missin' and the Doctor wants 'im found. Your gang of pickpockets will know if any new faces have settled in the Greenwich District. I'll be back this way in half an hour. And I'll hexcept reports, see! Now, hop about it, you moth-eaten son of a dishrag!'

"It's no use mincin' words with that Greenwich lot. A kick behind the ear is the only hargument they understand. Well, then, I goes off up the river for Chelsea, to set the next gang to work.

"Inside of half an hour," Cheapside continued, "I'd got around all the gangs in my half of London. And I felt pretty sure that if your friend had settled anywhere within their boundaries I'd get to hear of it, all right, because, you'd be surprised, there's nothing that escapes the eye of a city sparrow. Other birds what visit towns casual, as you might say, like the thrushes and starlings, that come into the parks and gardens—well, they don't bother much with the human side of city life. They're only visitors, anyway. But we London sparrows, we are citizens, part of the town. You could ask any bird in the Piccadilly circus gang at what hour any of the theaters close up and they could tell you to a minute. You see, they get their living picking up the scraps of cake that the ushers sweep out when the audiences go home. The Westminster lot could tell you the name of any member of Parliament that you might see going or coming out of the House of Commons. The Pall Mall set could spell off the membership list of the Athenaeum Club for you—with the family history of the waiters and all. The St. James Park lot could tell you what the queen had for breakfast and whether the royal babies slept well last night. We go everywhere. We see everything. Yes, when it comes to city news there ain't nothing we don't know. Ah, many's the 'air-raisin' yarn I could spin yer of outlandish goin's-on in 'igh places—Jiminy!

"Well, to return to where we was on my way back to Cleopatra's Needle to keep my appointment with Becky 'ere. I drops in again on One-Eyed Alf, to see what news 'e 'ad for me. 'E told me as 'ow he tracked down three or four window-washers, new arrivals, in his district. But not one of them answered the description I'd given 'im. You remember Pippinella had told me that 'er man had a scar across the side of 'is 'ead where the 'air didn't grow no more. And, although several of Alf's gang had spent hours 'angin' 'round sundry window-cleaners at work, waiting for them to take their 'ats off to scratch their 'eads, they 'adn't seen one with a scar like what you canary 'ad described."

"But he might not be working at window-cleaning at all now," said Pippinella. "That wasn't his real profession."

"Yes, I know. But we found him, anyway," said Cheapside, "as you will hear. And it came about through that scar you told me of, too. I questioned Alf for a few minutes and I come to the conclusion as 'ow 'e 'ad covered the ground thorough. So I scratches Greenwich and the Lower River off the list and goes on to meet Becky."

"Yes, and you didn't get there by ten, as you said you would," chirped Mrs. Cheapside, bringing her sharp little nose out of a saucer of milk she was drinking.

"Of all the—" cried Cheapside. "'Ow could I, with all that ground to cover? And I suppose you ain't never kept me waitin', Mrs. Quick Tongue? I suppose you don't remember that time last winter when I sat shivering in the—"

"Come, come," said the Doctor quietly, "don't quarrel. Get on and tell us about the window-cleaner."

"Becky told me," Cheapside went on, "that she hadn't been able to find out nothing. 'It's strange, Beck,' I says. 'Very strange.' Then she says to me, she says, 'Maybe the man's sick'—you know you'd spoken of his being unwell—'and if 'e is sick,' says Becky, 'he'd not be seen by the ordinary sparrows. Better get the hospital birds on the job.'

"Right you are," I says. And off we both go to look up the hospitals. There's quite a lot of them in London, you know. But with the 'elp of some gang leaders we goes around them all. When we'd come to the last of 'em and still 'adn't 'eard nothing, I say to the missus, I says: 'Becky, it looks as though we'd got to go back to the Doctor with empty 'ands.'

"'It's a shame,' she says. 'And 'im trustin' us and all.'

"And then, just as we was movin' off to come 'ere, up flies One-Eyed Alf, the Wapping Terror.

"'We've found 'im,' 'e says, short like.

"'You 'ave?' I says. 'Where is 'e?'

"''E's in the Workhouse Infirmary,' 'e says, 'over in Billingsgate.'

"'You're sure it's 'im,' says Becky.

"'Yes,' says 'e. 'Not a doubt of it. Come over and take a look at 'im, if you don't believe me.'

"Then we flies off with Alf and he takes us to a dingy sort of place in Billingsgate, next to a glue factory. It's a sort of an institution for the destitute. Old men and women and folks that ain't got no 'ome is took in there. And those what are able-bodied 'as to work, and those what ain't walks around in a yard with 'igh walls. Kind of a cheerless place.

"'Come over 'ere,' says Alf, leading us off to the north end of the yard. 'This is the infirmary, where they keeps the sick ones, that yellow brick building with all the windows in it.'

"We follows 'im and he flies along a line of windows, lookin' in as he passes, and at the fifth one he stops and we lights beside 'im on the sill. Inside we sees a bed and a man's 'ead a-lyin' on the pillow. Across the side of 'is 'ead was a scar. I goes close up to the glass, and presently the man rolls 'is 'ead from side to side and starts talking to 'isself. 'Pippinella,' he cries. 'Where are you? They've opened the hole in the floor and the papers are gone.'

"What he meant I don't know. But as soon as I 'eard 'im call the canary's name I knew we'd run the right man down at last.

"'Come on,' says Becky. 'That's 'im, all right. Let's go and tell the Doctor, quick.' And 'ere we are."

"'Can't I come with you, Doctor?' asked Gub-Gub."

The sparrow had hardly finished speaking before the Doctor had risen from his chair and was reaching for his hat.

"Thank you, Cheapside," said he. "We are both ever so grateful to you. If you and your wife have finished lunch we will go down there at once, and you can show us the way. Did you mark the room so I can inquire for the right bed? We don't even know the man's name."

"I couldn't tell you what the inside of the infirmary is like, Doc," said Cheapside. "But you can find him, all right, because I saw a card hung upon the foot of his bed and on it was written a number—No. 17."

"Can't I come with you, Doctor?" asked Gub-Gub, as John Dolittle hurried toward the door of the wagon.

"I'm sorry, Gub-Gub," said the Doctor. "But I'm afraid it won't be possible. You see, I'm going to a hospital."

"But I don't mind going to a hospital," said Gub-Gub.

"No, quite so," said John Dolittle. "But—er—I'm a little afraid they may not let me in if I brought too many pets. They're sometimes rather fussy in hospitals."

Gub-Gub was very disappointed, but the Doctor had to be quite firm because he was really afraid that he might not be admitted himself if he took the pig with him. Jip, too, had to be left at home for the same reason. Finally John Dolittle set out with Pippinella and Mr. and Mrs. Cheapside for London.

The Fourth Chapter

John Dolittle, M. D.

JOHN DOLITTLE HADN'T BEEN IN LONDON more than five minutes before he discovered news of his arrival had already spread among the animal life of the city. This, of course, was due to the gossip of Cheapside and his fellow sparrows of the streets. While the Doctor and his party were still at the inn yard where they had just stepped down from the Greenheath coach, a funny, scrubby little bird flew up and whispered something to Cheapside who was traveling with the Doctor. Cheapside brought him forward and introduced him.

"This is One-Eyed Alf, Doctor," said Cheapside, "the feller I was telling you about. "'E's got something 'e wants to say to you."

"Oh, how do you do?" said John Dolittle. "I'm very glad to make your acquaintance. I learn that it was largely through you that we have been able to trace our man. We are very grateful to you."

The newcomer was indeed a strange-looking bird. The first thing the Doctor noticed about him was that, in spite of his having only one eye, he seemed very alert and wide-awake. He had several feathers missing form his tail and altogether looked like a very rough customer.

"Don't mention it, Doc," said he. "Only too glad to be of any help. O' course, I'd heard a whole lot about you, and we city folks are always 'appy when you pays us a visit. I got a sister over in Wapping what got herself tangled up in a clothesline. I'd be glad if you could come and take a look at her. She's broke a wing, I think. Ain't been able to fly for over a month. We've had to bring 'er crumbs to 'er and feed 'er like a baby."

"I'll certainly do anything I can," said the Doctor. "Take us to where she is and I'll see what can be done."

"Look here, Cheapside," whispered Pippinella as the party set off in a new direction under the guidance of One-Eyed Alf, "you'll have to protect the Doctor. Once it gets round that he is doctoring animals, he will be swamped with patients of all kinds. Dab-Dab told me it always happens this way. He'll never get to my window-cleaner if you let him be side-tracked by every sparrow who wants to see him."

And it turned out that Pippinella was right in her fears. For when John Dolittle arrived at the place where One-Eyed Alf was leading them, he found plenty of work for him. In the backyard of an empty house in one of London's slummiest quarters there was awaiting him not one sparrow but over fifty. Birds with broken legs, birds that had been bitten by dogs, birds that had fallen into paint pots—even birds that had their tails injured under carriage wheels were there. All the accidents, all the casualties of London's sparrowdom were gathered to await the arrival of the famous Doctor.

"I'm sorry, Doc," said One-Eyed Alf as he gazed over the collection of patients waiting in the grimy yard. "I didn't mean to let you in for nothing like this."

"Lor' bless us!" murmured Cheapside, scratching the top of his head with a thoughtful claw. "Like Puddleby days, ain't it, Doctor? I don't know what you better do. I s'pose the dogs and cats will 'ear of it next and you'll have another bunch of hinvalids waitin' for you tomorrow. P'raps you better disguise yourself and let me give it out that you've left town."

"No, Cheapside," said the Doctor. "That would never do. I must patch these birds up, now I'm here. But I think you had better let it be known that I will see animal patients between seven and ten every morning out at Greenheath. That's what I've had to do in other towns—regular dispensary hours. Now, which is your sister, Alf?"

"That's Maria across there, in the corner," said the gang leader. "Hey, Maria! Come over 'ere. The Doctor wants you."

A very dejected little bird, trailing a stiff wing behind her on the ground, shuffled her way through the throng of sparrows and approached the Doctor.

In a moment John Dolittle had his little black bag open, and then his fat but nimble fingers got busy with the tiny wing joints of the patient.

"Yes," he said, "it's broken—in the upper bone. But we can mend it. You'll have to wear a cast for a week or two and carry your wing in a sling. Find a dry sheltered spot, a place where cats can't reach you, and keep perfectly still for ten days at least. Have your brother, Alf, bring your meals to you as before. Don't peck this plaster off till I have seen you again. There you are, now! A strip of this handkerchief will make a sling for you—just so—round your neck. Now you're all fixed up. Next, please."

The second patient to come forward was a very woeful sight—a young, inexperienced bird who had been fighting on a new building. In his excitement he had fallen into a paint pot and all his feathers were caked stiff with white lead, making it, of course, impossible for him to fly. The Doctor's task here was to take the paint out of the plumage without injuring the bird's skin.

Then came a bad case of dog bite. A sparrow who lived around a cabstand, feeding on the oats that fell from the nose-bags, had been caught off his guard and severely mauled by a fox terrier.

"One of the cab horses moved and trod on the dog's tail just in the nick of time," said the patient, telling the story of his adventures as the Doctor's swift hands felt for the injured rib. "If he hadn't 'a done that I'd be a goner for sure. I was halfway down his throat when he gave an awful yelp and coughed me up again. Then I scurried under the cab-man's shelter while he nursed his tail."

"The horse must have been a friend of yours," said the Doctor. "Lucky escape. No serious harm done. Some sprains. You'll be all over it in a week. Next, please!"

The afternoon was more than half gone before the Doctor had attended to all his patients and was able to continue his way to the workhouse.

Reaching that gloomy building at last, he knocked upon the door marked "Visitors" and was admitted by a porter. He had asked Cheapside and Becky to wait for him outside. He was conducted to a large waiting room and presently the superintendent appeared and inquired whom it was he wished to see. When he said it was someone in the infirmary, the doctor in charge was brought forward. Not knowing the window-cleaner's name, John Dolittle had to describe him as best he could, and at length he succeeded in making the authorities understand who its was.

"Oh, you mean the man in bed No. 17," said the doctor in charge. "Humph! You can't see him. He's very sick."

"What's the matter with him?" asked John Dolittle.

"Memory gone," said the other, shaking his head gravely. "A very bad case."

Finally, after explaining that he himself was a doctor of medicine, the visitor was told that he might see the sick man, but must not remain with him long.

"He gets so easily excited," the workhouse doctor explained as he led the way down a long passage and up a flight of stairs. "We

"You can't see him."

moved him into a private room last week. It's a very mysterious case altogether. He seems to have forgotten even his name. Gets dreadfully worked up when anyone asks him. I'm afraid we have very little hope of his recovery."

Upstairs they proceeded to a small room at the end of another corridor. And by the light of a candle, for it was now growing dark, the Doctor saw a man lying in a bed.

"He seems to be sleeping," John Dolittle whispered to the doctor in charge. "Would you please leave me with him till he wakes up?"

"All right," said the other. "But don't stay long, and *please* don't get him excited."

As soon as the door was closed the Doctor brought Pippinella's cage out of his pocket and stood it on the table beside the bed.

"It's he, Doctor," whispered the canary. And she chirruped gently with joy. Instantly the man on the bed opened his eyes and tried weakly to sit up. For a moment he stared stupidly at the bird in the cage.

"Pip-Pippin—" he began hesitatingly. "No, I can't remember. It's all hazy."

"Pippinella—your canary. Don't you recognize her?" said the Doctor quietly from the chair beside the bed.

The sick man had not realized there was another person in the room. He turned suddenly and glared at the Doctor in a funny, frightened sort of way.

"Who are you?" he asked suspiciously.

"My name is Dolittle," said the Doctor. "John Dolittle. I'm a physician. Don't be afraid of me. I've brought you your canary—Pippinella."

"I don't know you," said the window-cleaner in a hoarse gasp. "This is some plot—a trick. But it's no good now. You can't worm any secrets out of me. I haven't any. Don't even know my own name. Hah! It's a good joke. Everything a blank. Memory gone. And no one can get it back for me. I was so successful keeping my life a secret from the world that now no one can tell me even who I am!"

As the window-cleaner finished speaking, he sank back on the bed and closed his eyes.

"Oh, dear!" whispered Pippinella. "What shall we do, Doctor? What shall we do?"

The Doctor thought a moment in silence. Then he leaned forward and touched the patient gently on the shoulder.

"Listen," he said. "Please believe that I am your friend. I don't want to trick you into telling me your secrets. I know a great deal of your life already. In fact, I am the only man in the world who does know. You have been very ill. But you are going to get all right again. You are going to get your memory back. Let us see if we can't recall things. You remember the windmill on the hill?"

Very quietly and soothingly John Dolittle then told the window-cleaner the story of his own life, which he had learned through his knowledge of bird language from Pippinella. At first the man on the bed listened without a great deal of attention. On and on the Doctor went, telling of the old cathedral town, of Aunt Rosie's house, of the secret writings, of the kidnapping, the escape from the ship, of Ebony Island, the raft, the rescue. Gradually the window-cleaner's haggard face showed interest. At length, when the Doctor was describing his return to the mill and his finding the place deserted, the patient suddenly gave a cry and clutched John Dolittle by the arm.

"Stop!" he cried. "I remember now. The old windmill—the hole in the floor where I kept my papers. Did you steal them?"

"No," said the Doctor quietly. "I have told you I am your friend."

"But how do you know all this?" cried the other. "It's all true—every word. It's coming back to me. Tell me what you are?"

"I'm just a doctor," said John Dolittle. "A doctor who has spent most of his life learning the ways and the speech of animals. Most people think I'm crazy when I tell them that. But it's true. You see the canary on the table there?"

"'I'm just a doctor,' said John Dolittle."

"Yes," said the window-cleaner. "That's Pippinella. She was stolen from me when I got back to the mill."

"Exactly," said the Doctor. "Well, it was she who told me the story of your life. If you don't believe me, give me some question now to ask her and I'll show you that I can do as I say."

The sick man gazed at the Doctor a moment, still with something of suspicion in his eyes.

"Either you are crazy or I am," he said at last.

"I know," said the Doctor, smiling. "That's what everybody says. But give me a question to ask and I'll prove it."

"Ask her," said the window-cleaner, "where I kept the ink."

And then he chuckled to himself quietly.

The Doctor turned and exchanged a few words with the canary at his elbow.

"She tells me," said he, facing the bed again, "that you never used ink at all. You wrote in indelible pencil—everything. Is that right? She says you kept a box of them on the kitchen mantelpiece."

The window-cleaner's eyes grew wide with wonder.

"It's uncanny," he murmured, "absolutely uncanny. And yet—what you say *must* be true. The things you've told me, about the journey back to the mill—and all the rest—there was no one there but her, Pippinella. Funny, I always thought she was listening and watching. So you speak her language, eh? It sounds impossible. But it must be true. I—I am sorry if I mistrusted you."

When the infirmary doctor reentered the room, John Dolittle at once broached the subject of the patient's being moved as soon as possible. This apparently meant a great deal of filling out of papers and signing of documents. The Doctor had to guarantee that he would care for the sick man for a certain length of time.

That of course he was quite willing to do. And after a day had been agreed upon for his next visit, he and Pippinella left and set off on their way home.

The canary's joy knew no bounds. She was a different bird. She sang all the way home. The night air was cold; so the Doctor put her little traveling cage in his pocket. But even there, so great was her relief to know that her friend the window-cleaner was safe, she went on warbling away at the top of her voice. And people passing the Doctor in the street were greatly puzzled to know where the sound was coming from.

"The whole family gathered about him."

When the Doctor and Pippinella arrived at Greenheath, the whole family gathered about him as soon as he entered the wagon, clamoring for news.

"When is he coming?" cried Gub-Gub.

"Next Thursday," said the Doctor, "if he is well enough to make the journey. I think he will recover more quickly here than at the infirmary. Theodosia, do you think you could fix up a bed in your wagon for Pippinella's friend? He'll need a great deal of rest at first."

"Certainly, Doctor," said Theodosia. "I'll be happy to."

That night Pippinella entertained the whole company with her happiest songs. She was in splendid voice because the window-cleaner was found and would have gone on all night if Dab-Dab hadn't brought the celebration to an end by reminding them that it was past twelve o'clock and time they were all asleep.

The Fifth Chapter

The Window-Cleaner Tells His Name

THURSDAY CAME, THE DAY WHEN THE Doctor had said he would bring Pippinella's friend away from the hospital if he was well enough to travel. And the devoted canary had the poor Doctor out of his bed very early that morning, you may be sure. Indeed, it was barely light when John Dolittle, driving a hired wagon so as to have plenty of space to carry Pippinella's friend comfortably, set out with Matthew Mugg for Billingsgate.

On their arrival Matthew took charge of the horses at the door while the Doctor went in to see the patient.

He found the window-cleaner greatly improved and most anxious to leave and come with him. And as soon as some more forms had been filled out and signed, the sick man was helped into the wagon and they started back for Greenheath.

On the way the Doctor discovered that now that the window-cleaner had recovered his memory, he was most anxious to get on the trail of his lost papers again. It was quite clear, too, that whatever

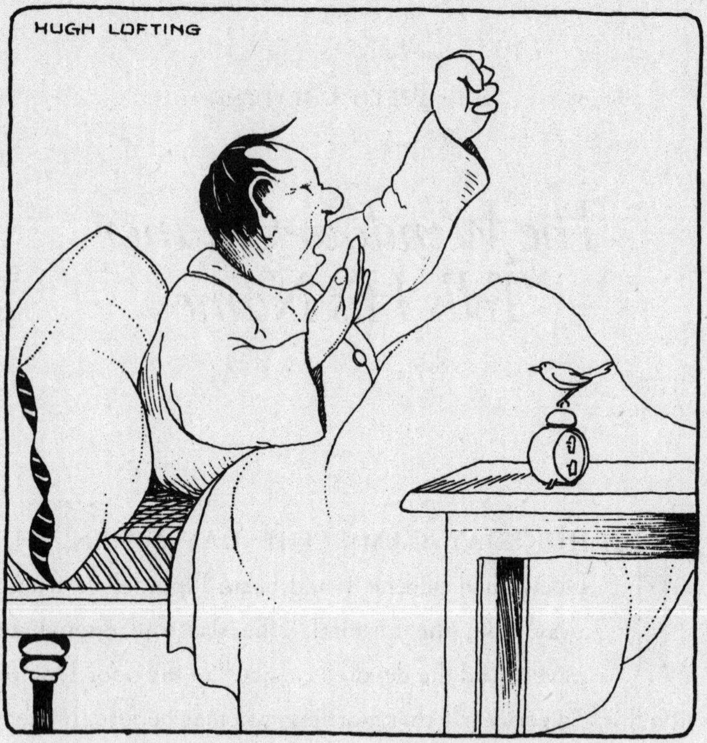

"The canary had the Doctor out of his bed very early."

suspicions he had had about John Dolittle's honesty, he now trusted him completely.

"And is it your intention," the doctor asked, "to go on with your writing as soon as you are able?"

"Why, certainly," said the other. "But I must first get some sort of a job by which I can earn enough money for living expenses."

The window-cleaner was half sitting, half lying, in the covered wagon. The Doctor was seated beside him. Matthew was up in front driving.

"Humph!" murmured the Doctor. "Er—by the way, I never

learned your name. Of course, if you don't want to tell me, it is your business and you have a perfect right to keep it to yourself. But while you are with us it would be more convenient if we have some name to call you by."

The sick man sat forward slightly to see if Matthew was listening. Then he turned to the Doctor again.

"I trust you," he said. "I am—or was—the Duke of Loughborough."

"Great heavens!" said the Doctor. "But who then is this man who now holds the title? The day we arrived in London I noticed in the papers that he was leaving town for the north."

"That is my younger brother," said the window-cleaner. "When I disappeared, he came into the estate and the title. They supposed I was dead—as I intended they should."

"Well, well!" murmured the Doctor. "Tell me, why did you do it?"

"It was impossible for me to write what I wanted to write, freely, while I was still a duke. I would have gotten my friends into trouble."

"I see," said John Dolittle. "And have you never regretted disappearing? Have you never wished to go back to your dukedom?"

"No," said the other firmly, "never! I may often have been sorry that I had no money to do the things I wished. But I've never regretted the step I took."

"I understand," said the Doctor. "Well, now listen: we must have some sort of a name to call you by while you are with us. Have you any preferences?"

"Call me Stephen," said the window-cleaner.

"Very good," said the Doctor. "Ah, look, we're coming to Greenheath now. Matthew and Mrs. Mugg have made room for you in their wagon; and you are to make yourself entirely at home. And please, ask for anything you want."

On their arrival at the now-deserted circus enclosure, the Doctor insisted on the window-cleaner going to bed at once and remaining there until he gave him permission to get up. His meals were given to him by Theodosia, and he was treated like one of the family.

So great was Gub-Gub's interest in the window-cleaner that the pig sneaked around secretly to get a glimpse of him from behind Mrs. Mugg's skirts when she brought his lunch to him. And after he had

"He sneaked around secretly to get a glimpse of him from behind Mrs. Mugg's skirts."

learned that the window-cleaner was a real duke, Gub-Gub could scarcely be kept away from the neighborhood of the Muggs' wagon.

"You know, I always suspected," he said at supper that evening, "that he was some great person in disguise. I suppose he used to ride in a carriage and drink out of gold basins before he became a window-cleaner. Fancy giving up all that just to be able to write!"

"He gave it up for the sake of other people he would help by his writing," said Too-Too.

"It's a good thing, Doctor," Dab-Dab put in, "that you are the only one who can understand animals' language. Otherwise the man's secret would be all over the country now that pig knows it."

"How long is he going to stay with us, Doctor?" asked Jip.

"I'm not sure yet," said John Dolittle. "Certainly till he is well enough to get about by himself. For the present, he needs constant medical attention. He has not taken care of himself at all. That's one reason why his condition is so low."

"But after he gets well," asked Jip, "is he going back to the mill?"

"I haven't discussed that with him," said the Doctor. "He says he will need some kind of a job—just to make enough money to carry on with."

Pippinella, who had been listening to the Doctor's family discuss her friend, came forward and said:

"I won't hear of him going to work, Doctor. I have plenty of money saved up from the opera. He took care of me, now I'm going to take care of him."

"Well, Pippinella," said the Doctor. "You can put it to no better use, I'm sure. In the meantime, he shall stay with us as long as he wishes."

Within a day or two after Steve joined the Doctor's family, John Dolittle noticed that he did not seem as contented as he might be. Not that he said anything or complained. On the contrary, he frequently spoke gratefully of how fortunate it had been for him that he made the Doctor's acquaintance. But he so often seemed moody and wrapped in thought.

"He's thinking of those papers he lost, Doctor," said the canary one evening after supper when they were discussing Steve. "His health is much better and he's getting stronger all the time. But that is what is making him unhappy. In the evenings he lies in bed with a pad on his knees and tries to write, but always it ends the same way. "What's the use," he mutters. "Even if I could remember the book and rewrite it word for word—which I couldn't—even then I wouldn't have the documents to prove what I say." Then he falls to mumbling and cursing the men who robbed him."

"Humph, too bad! Too bad!" murmured the Doctor. "I wonder if there's anything I could do. Let me see, I might go back to the mill with him. But I doubt even then if I could do much."

"Well, try it anyway, Doctor," Pippinella pleaded. "You never can tell."

"All right," said John Dolittle. "If he wants me to go with him, we'll take a run up one day soon. I'm sure he's well enough now. We'll take Jip with us."

Dab-Dab, who had been listening to the Doctor and Pippinella, fluttered her wings with annoyance.

"John Dolittle!" she demanded noisily. "You said that as soon as you found Pippinella's friend we would go back to Puddleby. Well, now he's found. Why must we wait in this deserted old mud-hole?"

"Dab-Dab," said the Doctor. "I'm just as anxious as you to get home. But neither Pippinella nor Steve will be really happy until we at least make an effort to find the missing papers. I'm sorry, Puddleby will have to wait."

"Oh, bother!" snapped the duck. "The trouble with you, John Dolittle, is that you never think of yourself."

Whitey, who was curled up half-asleep in the Doctor's pocket, stuck his head out and said:

"Listen to who's talking, Doctor. Why, Dab-Dab spends every minute of every day doing something for others."

"Quite so, Whitey," said John Dolittle, smiling. "Quite so."

The following morning, after the Doctor had examined Steve thoroughly, he told him that he could get up now and spend part of each day in the sunshine. But the good news didn't raise the window-cleaner's spirits as it should have. He obeyed the Doctor but sat dejectedly on the wagon steps staring into space. Then the Doctor asked him if he would like to take a run up to Wendlemere in a day or so and have a look around the old mill. Steve jumped at the offer with such enthusiasm that even Dab-Dab was glad they were going to have a try at finding the lost papers.

And that is how John Dolittle came to make still another trip to Aunt Rosie's town—this time accompanied by the window-cleaner himself. Dab-Dab packed a lunch for the two men—with a bone for Jip and seed for Pippinella. They took the morning coach from Greenheath with the canary in her traveling cage and Jip under the seat at the Doctor's feet.

THE SIXTH CHAPTER

The Search for the Missing Papers

THE PARTY REACHED ITS DESTINATION LATE in the evening and, after spending the night at the inn, proceeded the next morning to the mill. Things here were, of course, in a more dilapidated condition than before. But it surprised the Doctor somewhat to find the door to the kitchen unlocked and a great litter of nut shells and fruit stalks and other rubbish about the floors and windowsills. This he at first supposed must have been left by rats or squirrels. But of these creatures themselves—or, indeed, of any animal life—nothing could be seen. Hanging from a beam on the ceiling were two bats fast asleep.

In the center of the kitchen floor was the hole where Steve had kept his papers. Beside it lay the big stone that had covered it, just as he had left it when, after discovering that his property had gone, he had departed, determined to proceed to London.

In bringing Jip, the Doctor had hoped that his keen sense of smell and his eye for tracks might help in the search. And they were hardly inside the door when Jip put his nose down in the hole and sniffed long and noisily.

"Well," asked the Doctor, "what about it, Jip?"

For a moment Jip did not answer but continued sniffing and snuffling at the hole in the floor. Then he smelled the stone that had been the lid, or cover, to the hole. Finally, he looked up at the Doctor and said:

"The scents are mostly quite old ones and therefore very faint. It's curious the strongest of them is a badger—but not in the room here, only in the hole."

"Jip put his nose down in the hole."

"How odd!" said the Doctor. "Badgers don't usually have much to do with buildings. But how about the scent of men? That's there, too, isn't it?"

"Yes," said Jip, "surely. But it is very dim. Of course I can plainly smell your friend the window-cleaner. The scent of his hands on the stone is fairly distinct still. But other men have been in the room around the hole quite a while before, and some again since Steve was here, I should judge. That's what puzzles me so. It would seem as though there had been two lots of men here—at different times. And then on top of it all, the smell of this old badger is so strong that I'm surprised the other scents are not drowned out entirely. It is a very difficult problem in smelling altogether."

"Humph!" muttered Steve gloomily, though of course he had not understood what Jip said. "I'm afraid I've brought you on a fool's errand, Doctor. Everything is pretty much as I left it. You can see for yourself that the hole is empty."

"What did he say, Doctor?" asked Jip. "I didn't quite get that."

"He is discouraged," said John Dolittle. "He fears that there isn't much chance of your doing anything."

"Well, don't let him go away yet," said Jip. "I haven't finished by any means."

"There's some sort of mystery here," Jip continued. "It's funny how different those two lots of men smelled. The first lot had a sort of office smell—parchment, sealing wax and ink, and all that sort of thing. Probably there were two in the party. And the other was an open-air man, smelled of wood fires, stables, the mud of roads, and rank tobacco. Oh, look out! Don't disturb that hole, Doctor!"

John Dolittle had knelt down and was feeling around in the loose earth that lay at the bottom of the hole.

"Why, Jip?" he asked, rising.

"You'll get the smells all mixed," said the dog. "Let's just leave it exactly as we found it. It'll be much easier to pick up a scent. The first thing we've got to do is to try and run down that old badger. While you're going over the mill on the inside to see if you can find out anything, I'll make a circle outside round the hill and try to pick up that badger's trail. I have a kind of notion that if we can only get hold of him he'll be able to tell us a whole lot."

"Why?" asked the Doctor.

"Well—I've a notion," said the dog.

Jip, who as you know was quite a wonder at the fine arts of smelling and tracking, dearly loved to wrap a certain amount of mystery around his doings when employed on work of this kind. The Doctor was always willing to humor him in this and never insisted on an answer if the great expert seemed unwilling to give one. So this morning he just drew Steve away and set about examining the house and left Jip to his own devices.

All this time Pippinella was tucked away in her little traveling cage in the Doctor's pocket. She had kept absolutely quiet as she didn't want to be a bother to them. But she was relieved when John Dolittle put his hand in his pocket and drew her out.

"My goodness, Pippinella," said the Doctor anxiously. "I'd forgotten all about you. I *am* sorry."

"That's all right. Doctor," said the canary, blinking at the unaccustomed light. "Perhaps if you let me out I could be of some help to you and Jip."

"Certainly," said John Dolittle, releasing the catch on the cage door. "But don't go too far away from us. We may have to run for it and we don't want to leave you behind."

"I'll be careful," said Pippinella. "I'll just ride around on Steve's shoulder—if you don't mind."

"Not at all," said the Doctor. "Your place is with him."

Of course the window-cleaner could not understand the conversation between the Doctor and Pippinella, but he smiled and stroked her head when she flew onto his shoulder.

"Good old Pip," said he. "It's like old times to see you there."

The Doctor with Steve then made a thorough examination of the premises both inside and out. They discovered very little, beyond what appeared to be signs that the mill had been occupied not so very long ago. There were still bits of candle ends here and there, some moldy apple peel, a needle and thread that the window-cleaner was quite sure he had not left behind.

These, of course, might have showed nothing more than that the farmer had rented the mill again to some other person since Steve had left. But both the Doctor and Steve thought it wiser not to go and ask him.

In the meantime the hour for lunch arrived, and the Doctor sat down with his companion to enjoy the meal Dab-Dab had prepared for them. And still Jip had not returned. Indeed, it was four o'clock in the afternoon before he showed up. And when he did he looked anything but satisfied with the results of his expedition.

"It does beat everything," he sighed as he flopped down wearily on the kitchen floor, "how far a badger can travel when he makes up his mind to move his quarters. Holy smoke! Since I last saw you, Doctor, I've covered a circle a good twenty miles across, but not a vestige of that long-snouted old vagabond could I find. I struck many a trail, dozens—none of them very fresh—but I followed each one to the bitter end, just to make sure. They all wound up the same—at the old hole that Mr. Badger had rented out to some beetles a month or so before I got there. Then I consulted all the farm dogs within miles. Most of them knew him—and said he was a funny, cunning dodger. They'd never been able to catch him, though every one of them had tried many times. They reckoned it was about two or three months since he had disappeared. And that's all I got for one of the heaviest days of work I've ever put in."

"Perhaps some of the dogs killed him—ones whom you didn't talk with," said the Doctor. "Or possibly he may have died of old age. Badgers don't live terribly long, you know."

"No," said Jip patiently. "I hardly think that's worth taking into account. This fellow was not an old badger, and from what I hear he should have been easily able to take care of himself against dogs. And as for traps, well, you know how farm dogs get around. They nose into every corner of the countryside and find out everything; they say there aren't any traps set in these parts. And there you are."

"Humph!" said the Doctor. "And you couldn't find any other badgers?"

"Not one," muttered Jip.

The Doctor gazed through the dirty, cobwebby kitchen window for a moment, thoughtfully watching the setting sun that reddened the sky in the west.

"How about the rats and the mice in this place?" Pippinella asked. "There used to be plenty of them when we lived there. Perhaps they could tell us something."

"That's what I was thinking as I came back across the fields," said Jip. "But I don't suppose the fools will know. They never know anything useful. But we might try. You'll have to do it, of course. They're scared to death of me. I'd better get outside so they won't smell me so strong."

"All right," said the Doctor. "I'll see what I can do."

And then, as soon as Jip had disappeared, the duke of Loughborough, otherwise known as Steve, was treated to the spectacle of John Dolittle summoning his friends the rats. Standing in the center of the kitchen floor, the great naturalist suddenly screwed up his face and squeaked in an extraordinarily high voice, at the same time gently scratching the wood of the tabletop with his fingernails. Then he sat down in the chair and waited.

After five minutes had passed and nothing had happened, the Doctor went to another part of the room and repeated his peculiar summons. But still neither rats nor mice appeared.

"That's very extraordinary," said John Dolittle. "I wonder why they don't come. A place like this, unoccupied, must be simply riddled with rats."

Just as he was about to go through his performance, for a third time Jip scratched at the door and the Doctor let him in.

"It's no use," the dog said. "You can save yourself the trouble, Doctor. There are no rats here."

"None here!" cried the Doctor. "Why, that's hardly possible. I should have said this was an ideal home for rats and mice."

"No," said Jip. "There isn't a one. I've been around the outside examining the place where the holes come up into the open air. I know the looks of a hole that's occupied. Even without smelling it I can tell whether it's in use or not. And I didn't find a single one that rats had passed through in weeks."

"Well," said the Doctor, "I'm not going to doubt the opinion

"The Doctor let him in."

of an old ratter like you, Jip. But it's most extraordinary. I wonder what's the reason for it."

"Poison," said Jip shortly, "rat poison. Lucky for me they used a kind I know the smell of. I picked up a bone round the back of the mill, and I was just going to start chewing it up when I caught a sniff that made me drop it like a red-hot poker. I've been laid up once by eating meat that had been poisoned and set out for rats to nibble. And I'll never get caught again. For two weeks I was so sick I could scarcely move. Well, to go back: after I'd dropped the bone I started to nose around the outhouses, and I came across some bits of stale bread that had more poison smeared on them. Then I found one or two dead rats in the ditch a little distance away. That's the reason that there are none in the house. Someone poisoned them all off. And, if you ask me, I should say it was a pretty experienced rat-catcher."

"Well, but they'd come back," said the Doctor, "if this work was done some time ago—as it surely must have been. Other rats would have come to live here even if all the old ones had been killed off. There's no one living in the place now to keep it clear of them."

Jip came up close to the Doctor and whispered in a mysterious manner. "I'm not so sure."

"What do you mean?" asked John Dolittle.

"I'm not so sure there isn't someone living here—right now," Jip whispered. "I told you there was something mighty odd about this place. I saw signs around the doors of those outhouses that makes me almost believe that someone is making his home here."

"Great heavens!" muttered the Doctor. "This is uncanny. But if someone was living here, even in hiding, you'd have smelled him surely, wouldn't you? Your nose would have led you right to the place where he's concealed."

"It would," growled Jip, "if it wasn't for that blessed old badger. The trails are so crossed and the scents so mixed up, no dog could follow a smell there without getting led off it after two or three yards. Wait! Did you hear that sound?"

"No," said the Doctor. "Where was it coming from? My goodness, how dark it's getting. The sun has dropped below the hill. I had no idea it was so late."

"No, I didn't hear any sound," the Doctor repeated.

"I thought I did," said Jip, "a sort of fluttering noise. But perhaps I was mistaken."

"Listen, Jip," said John Dolittle. "If what you suspect is true, and there is someone living here, we had better set to work to find him. I don't think it's possible, myself. But your suspicions are so often correct. Now, let's see, what places are there where a man could hide? There's that old attic over our heads; there are the outhouses. And that's about all, isn't it? Oh, what about a cellar? No, there can't be any cellar, because that hole in the floor has earth in it, and if there was a cellar beneath we could see right down into it. No, the attic in the tower and the outhouses are the only places we need bother with. All right? Let's set to work."

"They got an old ramshackle ladder and climbed into the attic."

And after the Doctor had explained Jip's suspicions to Steve, they got an old ramshackle ladder and climbed into the attic. Jip stayed below to watch and help, should they discover anyone there, and Pippinella went along with the Doctor and Steve.

"Hang on tightly to Steve's shoulder, Pippinella," said the Doctor. "We mustn't get separated in the dark."

THE SEVENTH CHAPTER

The Secret Hiding Place

THE ATTIC OF THE OLD MILL WAS FILLED WITH every conceivable kind of rubbish. Bundles of old newspapers were piled on top of broken furniture; cobwebs had gathered on dilapidated trunks and boxes; and discarded clothing lay in heaps of dust and dirt, their threads chewed and crumbled by a hundred generations of moths and beetles.

"It's obvious no one has been up here for a long time," said the Doctor, lighting another match. "This dust hasn't been disturbed since these things were put here."

However, the Doctor crawled around on his hands and knees and peered into every corner. When they came down and after the Doctor had taken a candle out of his little black bag (for now they could barely see a foot ahead of them, the night was so black), they went round to the back of the mill to examine the outhouses.

Here they had no better success. The ruined buildings contained nothing more than junk, lumber, and odd parts of mill machinery.

"Humph!" muttered the Doctor as they started back for the kitchen. "I think you must be mistaken, Jip, although, goodness knows, you very seldom are in these funny notions of yours. If we could find some life in the place, rats, mice, squirrels—any kind of animals—I could question them and get some information. Listen, Steve, you are sure there is no cellar to the place?

"There was none when I was here," said Steve. "Of that I'm sure."

On reaching the kitchen they found it quite dark inside. For more light the Doctor was about to open his bag and get a second candle, when he discovered to his astonishment that it was no longer on the table.

"That's curious!" he muttered. "I could have sworn I left the bag on the table."

"So could I," said Jip. "But look, there it is on the chair."

"And it has been opened," said the Doctor, going toward it. "I'm certain that I latched it when I left the kitchen."

The Doctor opened the bag and looked inside.

"Why, somebody's been through it!" he whispered in astonishment. "Everything's here, all right. But it's all topsy-turvy inside. *It has been searched while we were out!*"

For a moment the Doctor and the dog gazed at one another in silence. Finally John Dolittle whispered:

"You're right, Jip. There's someone in the house. But where?"

Slowly the Doctor looked around the walls.

"If only I could find some animal life," he murmured.

"Sh!" said Jip. "Listen!"

All four of them kept still. And presently, faintly but quite plainly, they heard a curious little fluttering, rustling sound.

"Look!" said Jip, pointing his sharp nose up at the ceiling. "The bats! They're just waking up with the coming of dark."

The Doctor looked up. And there, from a beam across the ceiling, hung two little bats. Fitfully and sleepily they stirred their wings, making ready to start out on their night rounds. They were the only living things that John Dolittle had seen since he had entered the mill.

"Dear me!" he said. "Why didn't I think of that before? Bats—of course! Nobody could poison them off without first poisoning the flies. Well, I must see what they can tell us."

The odd, furry creatures were now circling around the room,

"The odd, furry creatures were now circling around the room."

their strange shapes throwing strange shadows on the wall in the dim light of the candle.

"Listen," said the Doctor in bat language (it was a very strange language and consisted mostly of high needlelike squeaks, so faint that they could scarcely be heard by the ordinary ear). "I have several things I would like to ask you. First of all, is this house occupied?"

"Oh yes," said the bats, still flying around in endless circles. "Someone has been living here off and on for ever so long."

"Is there anyone here now?" asked the Doctor.

"Most likely," said they. "He was here last night. But during the daytime we sleep. He may have gone away."

"What can you tell me about this hole?" asked the Doctor, pointing to the floor.

"That was where the man beside you kept his papers," said the bats.

"Yes, I know that," said John Dolittle. "But the papers were stolen or something during his absence. Did you see anything of that?"

"It was a very complicated, mixed-up business," squeaked the bats. "But as it happened, we saw it all, because, although the papers changed hands three times, it all took place in the evening or night, and we were awake and watching."

"The papers changed hands three times!" cried the Doctor. "Good heaven! Go on, go on! Who took them first?"

"The badger," said the bats. "He used to live outside, but he thought he'd like to come inside for the winter. So he started making a tunnel from the outside. We watched him. He bored right down and came up in the middle of the floor. But the flagging stones were too heavy for him to lift and he could get no farther. However, one evening a man came and made his home here. Then about a week afterward, two more men came. The man who was living here hid himself. The two newcomers hunted and hunted as though they were looking for something. At last they started taking up the stones of the floor and they found that hole and got the cover of it pried halfway up. But just at that moment the farmer who owns this place came to the mill with one of his helpers. The men in the kitchen only just had time to scuttle away, leaving the hole as it was. It was the funniest thing. You'd think it was some new kind of hide-and-seek game. The farmer did some bolting and hammering up—he didn't come inside the kitchen—and then he left. Very soon we saw the badger's nose appear at the half-opened stone, trying to get up into the kitchen and scratching away like everything. But soon *he* was disturbed, because the first man—the one who had been living here all the time—appeared again and pulled the stone right up and laid it down as you see it now. But the badger, who had been working underneath, had thrown earth all over the papers and you couldn't see anything inside but dirt. So the man just left the hole the way it was and set about preparing his supper. And all the time the papers were still lying underneath.

"There the paper would have stayed awhile," the bats went on, "if the badger hadn't, late that night when the man was sleeping, again started poking about in the hole. He had made up his mind, it seemed, to have that hole for a home, and the first thing he did was throw the papers out onto the floor of the kitchen. And there the papers lay for anyone to pick up. We supposed," said the bat, "the man who was staying here would find them in the morning and keep them, but the other two fellows came back about an hour after he had gone to sleep. However, he heard them coming and woke up. Then he hid himself and watched. The other two did not, of course, know there was anyone staying at the mill.

"And as soon as they felt sure the farmer had gone for the night, they entered the kitchen, lit candles, and made themselves at home. And there, the first thing they saw, were the papers they had been looking for, lying on the floor, as large as life. They put them on the table and started going through them. After a while one of them went out to investigate a noise they heard, and while he was gone, he must have fallen and hurt himself, for he suddenly called

"The first thing he did was throw the papers out onto the floor."

to his partner, who left the papers and hurriedly ran out to join him. Then, while they were both gone, the man who was living here sneaked out, took the papers, and hid himself again.

"When the two came back they didn't know what to make of it. Finally they decided the mill must be occupied. And, drawing pistols out of their pockets, they went hunting around the place, looking for the man who had taken the papers. But they never found him, and finally, about dawn, when we were thinking of going to bed, they departed in disgust and never showed up again."

"And they left the papers in the hands of the man who still occupies the mill?" the Doctor asked.

"Yes," said the bats, "so far as we know, he has them still."

"Good heavens!" muttered the Doctor. "What an extraordinary story."

And, turning, he translated what the bats had told him to Steve. Meanwhile the odd creatures went on wheeling in silent circles about the dimly lit room, as though playing a game of touch with their shadows on the walls.

"Splendid!" whispered Steve, when the Doctor finished. "Then we may rescue them yet."

John Dolittle turned back to the bats.

"And you never found out where the man hides himself?" he asked.

"Why, certainly," said the bats. "He hides himself in the cellar. He's probably there now."

"But I understood there was no cellar," said the Doctor, gazing down into the hole in the floor. "This gentleman with me lived here for years, and he says he never found one."

"No," said the bats, "no one would find it except by chance.

There's a secret passage to it. The man who lives there blundered on it by accident. It isn't under the part of the floor where the hole is at all. It's under the other half of the kitchen. Listen; you see that big white stone in the wall over there at about the height of a man's head? Well, you push it at the lower left-hand corner and it will swing inward, showing a passage. Then if you stand on a chair and crawl into a hole, you'll find a stairway leading downward on your left, built inside the wall."

Again the Doctor translated to Steve. And the window-cleaner got so excited he was all for getting a chair and starting right away. But the Doctor held up his hand.

"We've got to go slowly," he whispered. "We don't know yet whether this man has the papers on him. Wait, now. This needs to be thought through."

In whispers, then, the Doctor and Steve worked out a plan of action while the bats went on circling around the guttering candles. Under the table Jip, with ears cocked, sat tense and still, listening for sounds from beneath the floor.

"It is most important," said the Doctor, "not to alarm the man before we are certain where he has those papers. Because once he knows what we're after, you may be sure he'll never let us get a glimpse of them."

"Quite right," whispered Steve. "Certainly he realizes their value. I imagine his idea is to blackmail the agents of the government who came here for them and sell the papers to them, if he gets a chance. I have no notion who he can be; just some chance shady character, I fancy, who has blundered into this by accident and hopes to make some money out of it. What plan would you suggest?"

"Let us pretend that we are leaving the mill altogether," said the Doctor. "I don't think he can have any idea yet what we're after. Then we'll come back and watch. If we are lucky, he may go to the place where he has hidden the papers and give the show away. Then we'll have to rush him and hope to overpower him before he destroys them."

"Your idea is good," said Steve seriously. "Could we overlook the kitchen from the window, do you think?"

"Quite easily," said the Doctor. "But we must be terribly careful that he does not see us or get suspicious. We will begin by noisily making preparation for our departure. When we are outside we can settle other details."

The Eighth Chapter

The Thief Escapes

THEN SUDDENLY TALKING OUT LOUD, THE Doctor closed his bag with a snap. And with much tramping of feet, the two of them, followed by Jip, left the mill.

After they had gone about a hundred yards along the path that led down the hill into the town, the Doctor said to Jip:

"Now you run on ahead and do a little barking—just like a dog setting out on a walk would do. Don't bother about us; we're going to stay here awhile and then go back to the mill. But I want you to continue barking, moving slowly farther away all the time, so the man will think we're going on into the town."

"All right," said Jip. "I understand. But don't forget to whistle for me if there's a fight."

The Doctor assured Jip that he would. Then, taking Pippinella's small cage out of his pocket, he put the green canary in it and returned it to its hiding place.

"If we should have some trouble," he said to her, "you'll be safer there. Most birds—except bats and owls—don't see too well in the dark."

"Yes," said Pippinella. "That's why we hide ourselves in the trees when the sun goes down. With cats on the prowl at night, that's the only way we can hope to be safe."

"Quite so," said John Dolittle. "Please be very quiet, Pippinella."

By now Jip was off down the hill and Steve and the Doctor could hear him bark out every once in a while, each time a little farther away. After waiting a few minutes they turned and made their way slowly and carefully back.

"They hid themselves behind some bushes."

When they were within about fifty yards of the mill the Doctor motioned to Steve, and they hid themselves behind some bushes.

"I ought to have told those bats to keep me informed," whispered the Doctor. "Silly of me not to have thought of it. Listen! There's somebody opening the kitchen door."

Presently Steve and the Doctor saw the door of the mill open slowly. A man came out and stood motionless, listening. In the distance Jip, still cheerfully yapping for an imaginary man to throw sticks, could be plainly heard from below the hill.

After a while the man seemed satisfied that his visitors had really departed, for he reentered cautiously and closed the door behind him.

"Look!" said the Doctor. "He's lighting candles. He has hung something over the window, but you can just see a glimmer through the cracks of the door."

The Doctor and Steve were about to move forward from their hiding places when they heard the faint fluttering of wings near their heads. Against the sky they saw funny little shapes dancing. It was the bats.

"He turned us out," they said to the Doctor. "We wanted to stay and see if we could get you any information, but he flapped us out of the kitchen with a towel. You know some people think we bring bad luck."

"Did you see anything of the papers?" asked the Doctor.

"Yes," said they. "He went and brought them up from the cellar, after he had closed the door and lit the candles. He's examining them on the table. He doesn't seem to be able to read very well, because he spends an awful long time over one line. We couldn't find out any more, because shortly after he started reading, he saw us and drove us out."

"Thank you," said the Doctor. "What you have told us is very valuable." And he translated the bats' information for the benefit of Steve.

"We're going to have a job," the Doctor added, "because that door is probably securely fastened from the inside. And the window is too small to get through in a hurry."

"I should think," said Steve, "the best way would be to watch him and wait till he goes out for a minute. The chances are that he'll leave them on the table if he does."

"Well," said the Doctor, "let's sneak up and get a look at him, if we can, through the cracks of the door. Then we may be able to know better what to do."

Taking the utmost care to make no noise, the two crept forward to the hill till they stood beneath the great towering shadow of the mill. On the left-hand side of the door the woodwork had warped away from the frame, leaving a narrow crack. Through this the Doctor peered.

Inside he saw a ragged, rough-looking man with a stubby growth of beard on his chin, seated at the table. The table was littered deep in papers. Underneath the table was a piece of sacking spread out flat, in which they had evidently been wrapped and carried.

"Tweet! Tweet!" whistled the canary from the Doctor's pocket.

"What is it, Pippinella?" asked John Dolittle, bringing her tiny cage in the open.

"Do you mind if I have a peek at that fellow?" she asked. "I may need to recognize him later."

"Certainly," said the Doctor. And he placed the cage at the opening through which they had been peering.

When she had memorized his features thoroughly, the

Doctor returned her to his pocket and said to Steve:

"If only I knew," he said, "what kind of a fastening this door had on the inside, I could tell what chance we'd have in rushing it. If it gave way to one good heave we might grab the fellow and secure your papers before he had time to do anything."

"No. Better wait," whispered Steve. "If the door should not break down easily he'd be warned and have lots of time to destroy the papers in the fireplace or anything else. Better wait to see if he comes out. Can't you think of a way to entice him out?"

"'If I only knew,' he said, 'what kind of a fastening this door had on the inside.'"

"Humph!" said the Doctor. "Not without grave risk of arousing his suspicions and making matters worse than they are. Well, let's wait a while, then, and see what he does."

So, despite the cold night wind, which had now begun to blow freshly from the east, the Doctor and Steve kept guard at the door, watching through the cracks, hoping the man would get up and come out. John Dolittle had it all planned exactly how they should jump on him, one from each side, and secure him before he had a chance to resist.

But hour after hour went by, and still old Jip kept cheerfully yapping away below the hill and never a sign or a move did the man make.

Finally the Doctor thought he had better go down the hill and relieve poor Jip, who was still performing the part given him and barking cheerily at regular intervals. So, leaving Steve to continue watching, John Dolittle set off down the hill, and finally found Jip—by this time well within the streets of the town—and told him how things were.

"Bother the luck!" muttered Jip. "Well, what are you going to do, Doctor?"

"I don't know, Jip," said John Dolittle. "But we are determined we're going to get those papers, if we have to wait all night."

"How would it be, Doctor," asked the dog, "if I were to moan and whine around the mill? Maybe that would entice him out and you could jump on him at the door."

"No," said the Doctor, "I think not. We're so afraid of scaring him, you see."

"You couldn't get up on top of the tower and drop down on him from the inside?" asked Jip.

"Not without making enough noise to wake the dead," said the Doctor. "You better stop barking now. You may get the townsfolk aroused and do more harm than good. Come on up the hill, nearer the mill, but, for heaven's sake, don't make a sound!"

So once more they proceeded cautiously up the hill, and, after the Doctor had stowed Jip away beneath a hedge and repeated his instructions about keeping quiet, he rejoined Steve at the door.

"Has he moved yet?" he asked.

"Not an inch," whispered the window-cleaner. "I believe he's reading my book from beginning to end."

"Tut-tut!" muttered the Doctor. "Luck seems against us tonight. What's that? Oh, the bats again."

Once more the little hovering shadows circled around John Dolittle's head.

"Listen!" the Doctor whispered. "Do you think you could get inside from the top and tell me what kind of a fastening he has on this door?"

"Oh, we know already," said the bats. "He has hardly anything at all—just a small, crazy bolt that you could easily force.

"Good," said John Dolittle.

"Then he explained to Steve how they were both to draw back and rush the door together.

"With the weight of the two of us it should surely give," he whispered. "But we must be sure to hit it together. Now, are you ready? Go!"

Together they charged. And together their shoulders hit the panels with a crash. The door gave way to the splintering sound of wood and fell inward. But unfortunately, the Doctor fell on top of it and tripped Steve up, too. With a sweep of his hand the man at the table put out the candle. The Doctor scrambled to his feet and jumped for where he thought the table was. He found the table, but no man and no papers. The thief had lifted the piece of sacking cloth bodily and rolled it up.

"Guard the door, Steve!" yelled the doctor. "Don't let him out!"

But he was too late. Steve, anxious to recover his papers, had already plunged into the dark room and was feeling and stumbling around wildly. Against the patch of sky framed in the doorway the Doctor saw a man's figure, with a bundle under his arm, bound outward into the night.

"Jip!" he yelled. "Jip! Look out, Jip! He's getting away. *And he's got the papers with him!*"

Still calling for Jip, the Doctor jumped over the fallen door and ran out into the open. The wind had now increased and was blowing strongly from the east. John Dolittle, knowing that the man had doubled away to the right, realized at once that the weather was again him. Jip, who he had left a little below the crest of the hill, was to the windward. But the Doctor's voice and the man's scent would be carried in the opposite direction.

Thus it was at least two minutes elapsed before John Dolittle could get Jip's attention at all. And by that time the man had got a good start, downwind. However, Jip shot away on the trail at once, and the Doctor and Steve blundered after him through the windy night as best they could.

"Even with the weather against him," the Doctor panted as he stumbled over the uneven ground, "Jip may yet keep in touch with the scamp. He's a wonder, that dog, when it comes to tracking."

"I only hope that fellow doesn't destroy the papers," muttered Steve.

"No, I don't think that's likely," said John Dolittle. "After all, why should he? He certainly could not make anything out of them if he did that."

"He might want to get rid of evidence that he had stolen them," said Steve.

After about a twenty-minute run, during which the two men entirely lost touch with the dog, they ran into Jip returning from the hunt. His miserable, dejected appearance told them at once that he had met with nothing but failure.

"It's no good Doctor," said he. "He got away, confound him! As soon as I heard you call I dashed off to try to get ahead of him, where the wind would blow the smell of him toward me instead of away. But what with the start he had and the crossed trails that wretched old badger had left behind, it couldn't be done. He must have gone into the woods below the second field—of course he'd know the country like his own hand, having lived here. And, although my speed is better than his, the lay of the land is new to me. I hunted right through the woods and along every ditch where he might have hidden. The forest was quite large, and beyond it I came out on a road. I followed it a way, thinking he'd likely have stuck to it because it gave him a chance for clear running in the dark.

"This road led round, in a wandering sort of zigzag, back into the town on the far side," continued Jip. "There, the wind was against me again. And to find him by myself among the houses would be pretty nearly impossible, even if he did not go on through the town—which he probably did. I'm sorry to have failed you, Doctor. But you see how things were, don't you?"

"Oh, quite, Jip, quite." said the Doctor. "Too bad, too bad! Have you anything to suggest that we might do?"

"We could go into the town," said Jip gloomily. "The three of us, by hunting through it thoroughly, *might* run him down. But I have my doubts. I've a notion that customer had been chased before and knows a good deal about the game of lying low."

The Doctor explained to Steve what the dog had said and the three of them, after the door had been put back in its place to keep the rain out, made their way down into the town. By the time they got there it was three o'clock in the morning. As yet, except for a sleepy watchman in the market square, there was no one abroad.

"The three of them made their way down into the town."

The Doctor had very little hope of accomplishing anything, but he proceeded with the help of his companions to make a thorough search of all the streets. Each one took a section of the town, and it was agreed that they should meet again in the square after an hour had passed.

But quite early in the hunt John Dolittle realized that it would be perfectly easy for a man to hide, when hunted at such a time as this with all the townsfolk abed, to find some shrubbery in a garden, or a stable, or other place of refuge, from which he could not be routed without waking up the whole town. And as the nature of their business was something that Steve did not wish to have made public, it would not be possible to arrest him in the ordinary way.

When the Doctor returned to the square, the first of the market gardeners were beginning to arrive with their wagons of vegetables. While he waited for the return of Steve and Jip, John Dolittle reviewed the events of the night; he tried to imagine what he would do, were he the hunted man. The only idea that came to him was that he would most likely try to make his way to London where it would be easy to lose oneself in the crowds. With this in mind he made inquiries of the farmers who were arriving from that direction, hoping to hear that one of them had seen the tramp with the sacking bundle under his arm. But they all gave him the same reply. Nobody had seen the stranger the Doctor described.

Neither Steve nor Jip, when they finally turned up, had any better report to give than his own. It was decided then to have breakfast and talk over what they would do next.

THE NINTH CHAPTER

The Runaway Coach

BREAKFAST WAS A SAD AFFAIR. STEVE'S dejection over the loss of his papers affected all the members of the party. The Doctor sat in silence, eating his boiled egg, with little relish, while Steve just pushed the bacon on his plate from one spot to the other.

"You know, Doctor," he began, "I don't believe I was ever meant to finish my book. I think I had better drop the whole thing."

"I wouldn't do that," replied the Doctor. "Men like you are needed in this topsy-turvy world. If someone doesn't do something about the unfortunate people in other countries, they may start another war—and then, sooner or later we'd get mixed up in it too. Cheer up, Steve. We're not giving up yet. That fellow may still be lurking about round here—waiting for a chance to get a ride up to London."

"And if he does," said Steve, "how on earth are we ever going to find him there?"

"We found you, didn't we?" said the Doctor. "Cheapside and

his sparrow gangs spent less than a day doing it, too." The Doctor smiled. "I wish we had had him here; that thief wouldn't have got very far with your papers." And turning to Jip, the Doctor went on:

"I don't blame you, Jip. Not even a pack of bloodhounds could have held his scent in that wind. But birds—with their wonderful ability to dart in and out of trees—could have kept him in sight when he went into the woods."

Jip looked a little crestfallen.

"But, Doctor," he said, "you forget, it was pitch dark in that woods and—"

"So it was," said the doctor thoughtfully. "So it was, Jip—I had forgotten. Well now, don't worry. I still think you're the best tracker I ever knew."

With that Jip brightened up. "The crowds are gathering in the market square," he said. "Couldn't we just walk round and see if I can pick up his scent?"

"A splendid idea, Jip," said John Dolittle. "I'll pay the innkeeper for our breakfast and lodging and we'll get started."

While explaining the new plan to Steve, the Doctor finished his tea and called for his bill. Pippinella had breakfasted handsomely on toast crumbs and bits of Steve's neglected bacon and was ready to start off on the hunt again. She took her place on her friend's shoulder and said to the Doctor:

"Please tell Steve that I can look out for myself. He might waste time trying to protect me when he should be concentrating on catching the rascal who has his papers."

"Yes, Pippinella," said the Doctor. "I'll explain to him what you said."

Then they walked among the fruit and vegetable stalls, peering into the faces of those who came to buy. Jip kept sniffing at the heels of each passerby until someone accidentally bumped him on the nose with a heavy boot. Jip let out a squeal of pain and rubbed his paw over his aching nose.

"Serves me right," he mumbled. "I'm acting like an amateur. If he's anywhere around here I'll get his scent without having to put my nose on every pair of heels in the marketplace."

The Doctor and Pippinella laughed at Jip's remark. But Steve, not understanding dog language, looked more put out at the heartlessness of their laughter until the Doctor explained.

"Jip is right," John Dolittle said, after he'd repeated the dog's remark. "We're all too tense. I think we had better go and sit down for a while. We can watch people coming and going from the bench over there."

The sun was warm and the Doctor and Steve were very tired, not having slept at all the night before. Fully intending to keep a sharp look out for the thief, they soon found themselves dozing off into a deep slumber. Jip was curled up at the Doctor's feet, his head on his paws, watching with one eye open and the other snatching a moment of sleep now and then, the people milling about the square. It wasn't long before he, too, gave up and went to sleep.

But Pippinella was wide awake. Something about the night's adventures had fired her imagination. She felt as if she were living part of her life over again—just which part she couldn't decide. But there was an excitement in the air—a kind of anticipation—as she sat on Steve's sleeping shoulder, watching the activity all around her.

Suddenly, as the crowd parted in front of her, Pippinella saw a familiar figure in a cashmere shawl with a market basket on her arm, walk briskly along the path in front of a group of vegetable stalls.

"Aunt Rosie!" whispered Pippinella. "I'd forgotten she lived near here."

Without waking her three companions, the canary flew over the heads of the villages and landed on Aunt Rosie's shoulder.

"E-e-eh!" squealed the little old lady, dropping her basket and throwing her arms into the air. "What's that? What's that?"

As she turned her head to see what had frightened her, she gasped with astonishment.

"Pippinella!" she cried. "I do declare! What a start you gave me. Where did you come from? Why, I thought you were up in London. I saw you in the opera. Quite a celebrity you are these days. And just imagine—you lived in my very own parlor!"

While she chattered on, a gentleman, who had stopped to watch the funny behavior of the little old lady, picked up Aunt Rosie's basket, and with a bow, handed it to her.

"Are you ill, madam?" he asked.

"Certainly not!" she snapped. "I was startled by this bird. She's the prima donna of that famous opera a doctor by the name of Dolittle presented in London a few months ago. You must have read about it in the papers, sir. It made quite a sensation."

"Indeed," said the man, raising his eyebrows quizzically "But if this is the same bird, what is she doing here? And how does it happen she picked you out to land on?"

"Nincompoop!" muttered Aunt Rosie under her breath. And then, smiling very smugly, she answered the stranger.

"Some time ago she used to belong to me. I gave her away to a fellow who washed windows for me. He must have given her to that opera fellow—sold her, most likely; he was very poor. I can't imagine what she is doing here, but she must have recognized me. I wonder if she's lost."

"Perhaps the doctor you speak of is somewhere about here," said the man, glancing over his shoulder. "That might account for the bird's presence."

The idea so surprised Aunt Rosie that she walked abruptly away from the man without so much as a nod. She began peering into the faces of the people around her, searching for the famous impresario of the opera, Doctor Dolittle. Suddenly she stopped.

"Why, my goodness, Pippinella!" she said. "I don't even know what he looks like. Everybody in London was talking about him. And the papers were full of his pictures, but each one was so different from the others I couldn't make up my mind what he *did* look like. I know he wore a high silk hat and—and—"

Aunt Rosie was staring across the square with her head thrust forward. When Pippinella realized that the old lady had spotted the Doctor, she spread her wings and took off for the bench.

"Doctor Dolittle! Wake up!" the canary cried. "Aunt Rosie is coming this way!"

John Dolittle opened his eyes with a start and pushed his hat to the back of his head.

"A—um," he said sleepily. "What did you say, Pippinella?"

"Aunt Rosie is here," Pippinella said. "You remember, Doctor, the little old lady who took me out of the coal mine."

By the time the Doctor was fully awake and had straightened his tie, Aunt Rosie was standing before him. John Dolittle quickly arose and bowed to her.

"Doctor John Dolittle!" she cried. "Why—my gracious me!

You're the same man who came to tea that afternoon—and left in such a hurry to catch the coach. Your sister said something about your being a doctor and all that. But I was so disappointed at your sudden departure I didn't pay much attention. Imagine me having entertained the great John Dolittle. And didn't know it. I declare! I must tell the ladies of my sewing circle about this."

Doctor Dolittle just stood there—hat in hand. It always confused the modest little man to be treated like a celebrity. He much preferred to allow others to take the bows and receive the praise.

"Good morning, madam," he said, bowing to cover up his shyness. "I'm very happy to see you again."

With that, Aunt Rosie let loose a flood of questions. How had the Doctor come by Pippinella? Did he know his sister, Sarah, had moved to Liverpool? Was he planning any more operas to be presented in London? Did he ever find that fellow, the window-cleaner? Wouldn't he please come to tea someday soon and meet the ladies of the sewing circle?

The Doctor kept opening and closing his mouth in an effort to answer each question as it tumbled forth. But Aunt Rosie didn't give him a chance; she wasn't really concerned with the answers—all she wanted to do was to engage the Doctor's attention long enough so that her friends around the marketplace should see her talking to the famous John Dolittle.

Suddenly, in the middle of another question, she caught sight of Steve, who had awakened and shoved his hat off his face where it had served as a shield against the bright sun. Pointing her finger at him, she cried:

"Why, there he is now—the window-cleaner! Whatever happened to *you*, my good man? I thought surely you'd be back to do my windows again. That maid of mine, Emily, is simply no good at it. Are you still cleaning windows?"

While Aunt Rosie was chattering on, Steve had risen from the bench, removed his hat, and was waiting for the flood of questions to cease so that he could answer one of them, at least.

"No, madam," he finally managed to say. "I'm living with the Doctor now. You see, the window-washing was just a means to an end. A way to earn some money so that I could get back to London."

"Well, I'm not surprised," said the old lady. "I knew there was something different about you. I suppose you're in one of the arts—as the Doctor is?"

"In a way," Steve replied.

The Doctor, realizing that Aunt Rosie would not stop probing until she discovered something she could take to her sewing circle friends, decided to bring the interview to an end. He took his gold watch out of his pocket and consulted it.

"We really must be going, Aunt Rosie," he said. "It's ten minutes to eight and we—"

"Oh, my gracious!" interrupted the woman. "The coach for London will be here any moment. I came up to market to get some eggs for my sister—she lives in Knightsbridge, you know. Has six children and uses a tremendous quantity of food. And they get the most abominable eggs in the city—not fit to feed to a pig! It gives me a good excuse to pay her a visit every fortnight or so. Today I'm taking her some cheese as well. Did you ever taste our local cheese, Doctor? It's made right here in Wendlemere. There's none better, I tell you—finer than imported."

"Indeed!" said the Doctor. "I must try it sometime."

He glanced at Steve, who was waiting uncomfortably for Aunt Rosie to stop talking. The window-cleaner stepped to the old lady's side and offered her his arm.

"May I escort you to your coach, madam?" he asked politely, knowing that John Dolittle was having a difficult time getting rid of Aunt Rosie.

"I must get my eggs and cheese first," she said, taking his arm. "We can chat on the way. Good-bye, Doctor. Don't forget your promise to come to tea one day."

John Dolittle nodded as they hurried way. Pippinella, who had been on Steve's shoulder all during the conversation, called out as they left the Doctor and Jip.

"I'll just go along with Steve, if you don't mind, Doctor. I may catch a glimpse of that fellow in the crowd. If I do, I'll be back in a hurry."

The Doctor and Jip watched Steve piloting Aunt Rosie among the stalls as she made her purchases. Finally they saw them heading toward the coach stop at the north end of the square. In the distance could be heard the clippity-clop of horses's hooves and the jingle of harness as the London coach approached the town. Over the various sounds that accompanied a market gathering, the Doctor heard the clear sweet voice of the canary as she gaily sang "The Harness Jingle Song."

"Pippinella is happy again with her master," he said to Jip. "I suppose the jingle of the harness recalls the song she composed when she lived at the Inn of the Seven Seas."

"Yes," said Jip. "It's good to hear her singing again. I hope nothing happens to part her from her friend—now that he's found."

As they listened, the sound of the approaching coach grew

louder. In the distance, the Doctor could see Aunt Rosie with her arm upraised as a signal to the driver to stop. Business around the marketplace momentarily suspended while merchants and townspeople turned their heads to watch the coach from the north arrive.

Suddenly, with a thundering of hooves and a rumble of carriage wheels, the coach tore past the stop and continued right on through the marketplace. People scattered in fright, chickens and ducks ran for their lives—their feathers flying—and the dust threw a screen over the whole town.

"What do you make of that?" asked Jip, looking puzzled. "The driver certainly could see that Aunt Rosie wanted to get on."

"It's very odd," said the Doctor. "Wendlemere is a regular stop on this coach route. It didn't look as though the horses were running away, either. Oh look, Jip! Here comes Pippinella."

The green canary landed with a fluttering of wings on the Doctor's outstretched hand. Her eyes were watering from the dust cloud through which she'd flown. She was gasping for breath.

"Dear me!" exclaimed the Doctor. "You might have crashed into a tree—flying blind like that. Now, rest a moment before you try to talk."

He held her gently in his hand until she was able to speak.

"You saw what happened, Doctor?" she finally managed to gasp between breaths.

"Yes," replied John Dolittle. "And it was most puzzling. Didn't the driver see Aunt Rosie?"

"Oh, he saw her, all right!" answered the canary. "But he drove by anyway. There's something very strange about it. I know that man. He's the most reliable driver on this road."

"What do you mean, Pippinella," said the Doctor. "I don't understand. Did you say you recognized the coachman?"

"Yes, Doctor," replied the canary. "I saw his face very clearly. He's my old friend, Jack—the one who used to bring me a lump of sugar when he stopped at the Inn of the Seven Seas."

"Then something surely is amiss!" said the Doctor. "Pippinella, do you think you could catch up to that coach?"

"Certainly!" she said. "I can outfly him by fifty times his speed."

"Well, go quickly then!" said the Doctor, raising his hand so that she could take off. "And find out why he didn't stop. I'll be busy here getting help, should we need it. Report back to me as soon as you can."

THE TENTH CHAPTER

The Papers Recovered—and Puddleby Again

WHEN THE GREEN CANARY LEFT THE Doctor's hand she darted through the leafy oaks that circled the market square. As she reached the outskirts of town she could see, in the distance, a cloud of dust that marked the swiftly disappearing coach. Cutting across a field to where the road swerved to the right, she overtook the galloping horses and lit on the driver's shoulder.

"Jingle! Jingle! Crack and tingle. Coachman hold your horses!" she sang at the top of her lungs so as to be heard above the racket of the rumbling wheels. This song, she felt sure, Jack would remember, as she had sung it to him every time his coach had entered the courtyard of the Inn of the Seven Seas.

"Pippinella!" he cried. "My old friend, Pippinella."

But instead of smiling at her he drew his brows together and, grasping the reins more tightly in his hands, urged the panting horses on.

"Go away, Pip!" he yelled. "Go away! There's danger here!"

But Pippinella clung more tightly than ever to the cloth of

Jack's coat. Sensing that something was seriously wrong, she dug her claws more firmly into the fabric and leaned way out to see who rode in the body of the carriage. A face with a stubbly beard and piercing black eyes hung out of the window. In his hand the man held a big black pistol that he was aiming at Jack's head.

It was the thief who had stolen the window-cleaner's papers!

"Go away, I say!" shouted Jack again. "You'll get hurt if that rascal decides to pull the trigger!"

An evil gleam came into the eyes of the thief. He brandished the pistol. "Who are y' callin' a rascal?" he screamed. "I'll blow yer into kingdom come if yer gets sassy with me!"

Pippinella hopped to Jack's other shoulder so as not to further antagonize the dangerous passenger. For a moment or two she wondered what she had better do. Then, remembering the Doctor's orders to report back to him as soon as she could, the canary flew into the air and headed back to town.

Meanwhile the Doctor had not been idle. With the help of Jip he had rounded up a half dozen mongrel dogs who were noted for their bravery and fighting ability.

"Listen," said the Doctor in dog language when they had ceased barking their pleasure at meeting the famous animal physician. "Can I count on you for some help—if I need it?"

"Why, sur-r-re, sur-r-re!" said Mac, a Scottish terrier of mixed origin. "We're verra happy to assist ye, Doctor Dolittle. What is it ye want done?"

"I don't know yet," replied the Doctor. "But it may be very dangerous." And glancing from one to the other of the eager faces watching him, he went on:

"Are you all agreed on Mac's decision?"

The dogs answered the Doctor with a perfect avalanche of tail-waggings, ear-scratchings, and nose-twitchings.

"Come with me, then!" ordered John Dolittle. And he started down the London road at a fast pace, with Steve at his side and Jip and the pack of mongrel dogs at his heels.

As he scanned the sky for some sight of Pippinella, the Doctor heard the thud of a small object on his high silk hat. Reaching up to investigate, he felt a pair of tiny claws clutching his finger.

"It's you, Pippinella," he said, lowering his hand as he continued running.

"No, it ain't 'you, Pip,'" said the bird. "It's me, Cheapside! And I'd like to-know where *yer* goin'—and in such a hurry. It ain't good for your heart, Doc."

"Never mind that now," said the Doctor. "I'm delighted to see you again, Cheapside. How does it happen you are down this way?"

"I didn't 'appen—as you say, Doc," said the London sparrow. "I were lookin' for you. Becky went off to visit her maw who's building a new 'ome in Hyde Park—snooty, the old girl's got since she landed on the queen's bonnet during a parade least week. Says Piccadilly ain't no fit place for a bird what's sat on the queen's new bonnet. Well, as I was sayin': Becky went off for the day and I thought I'd 'ave a run down to Puddleby to see 'ow you was gettin' on. When I found you wasn't there I 'ad a quick look around—Lor' bless me, Doc, things is in a mess. Then I went to Greenheath and 'eard how you was off on another 'unt—for some missin' papers. Say, Doc, slow up a bit, will you? I 'ave to shout me lungs out to make myself 'eard. And what's the 'ounds doing at yer heels? Say the word, and I'll peck out their eyes!"

"No, no, Cheapside!" cried the Doctor. "We're on our way to help Pippinella's friend, Jack, the coachman."

As the Doctor was about to continue, he saw a tiny speck in the sky coming closer and closer.

"Here comes Pippinella now!" he said, slowing to a walk. "She'll tell you the rest."

The little party stood in the road and waited for the canary to arrive.

"She flies good—for a primer donner—don't she?" said the sparrow.

When the little canary landed on the Doctor's hand, she had to sit gasping for a moment before she could speak. Then she described the predicament Jack was in.

"And the man with the pistol," gasped Pippinella, "is *the fellow who stole Steve's papers!*"

"Are you sure?" asked the Doctor.

"Yes!" replied the canary. "One never forgets a face as ugly as his."

"What about Steve's papers?" John Dolittle asked, anxiously. "Did he have them with him?"

"I don't know," replied Pippinella. "But in any case we must help Jack."

"Yes, indeed!" said the Doctor. "We must carry out our plan quickly now," he continued. He translated the canary's story to Steve in as few words as possible. Then turning to Jip, he said:

"Jip, take Mac and the others and follow Pippinella as fast as you can. Catch up to that coach and tell the horses I want them to stop. Mac, while Jip is explaining to the horses, you get into the carriage and see that that rascal doesn't use his pistol!"

"We're on our way!" cried Jip. "That thief isn't going to get away this time!"

"Wait for me," cried Cheapside. "What makes you think I ain't goin' along to 'ave some fun too?"

The two birds shot into the air as the pack of dogs, led by Jip, raced down the road. By now the coach was no more than a tiny speck on the horizon and it took the strange group of pursuers a good ten minutes at their best speed to close the ever increasing distance between them. When they began to near the speeding carriage the dust became so thick they could barely see one another, nor could they breathe with comfort.

"Cut across this hayfield!" called Pippinella from above. "The road makes a sharp turn just before those elms. We can reach the place ahead of the coach and cut them off."

With Pippinella and Cheapside flying lower over the standing grain, the dogs followed through the hay leaving a path behind them like the wake of a ship at sea. When they broke into the open the canary was ahead of them, pointing the way with her bill.

"That's the spot—over there!" she cried. "Follow me!"

They reached the shelter of the big elms as the coach rounded the bend. It was lurching from side to side as the horses pounded on in panic. Jack continued to urge them on while the man in the back hung out of the window shouting orders and waving his pistol in the air.

Jip dashed into the road and raced beside the galloping horses.

"Stop!" he cried. "Doctor Dolittle orders you to stop!"

"We can't," whined the horse on Jip's side. "If we do, Jack will be killed!"

"Do what I tell you!" Jip commanded, nipping at the horse's foreleg. "The other dogs will take care of that fellow with the pistol!"

Cheapside, sitting on the horse's ear, leaned over and shouted into it:

"Do like he tells you, Milly! Else I'll peck out yer eyes!"

"Oh, hello, Cheapside," said Milly. "I'm happy to see you again."

"Never mind the pink tea chatter, you dumb wagon-puller!" screamed the sparrow. "The Doc says stop! And I'm 'ere to see his horders is carried out!"

Milly turned her head nervously and looked back over her shoulder while she raced on. She saw that what Jip had said was true; the dogs, led by Mac, the Scottish terrier, were jumping and clawing their way through the open window of the speeding carriage. The thief had disappeared from the window and the sound of scuffling could be heard from within. The exhausted mare turned to her teammate and, puffing and panting, said:

"Stop, Josephine! It's all right. Those dogs have taken care of that fellow. Thank goodness, Jack is safe and we can stop this senseless running."

Gradually the two mares brought the lumbering coach to a halt. With relief from the nervous strain, they became quite hysterical and wept openly.

"Brace up, me 'earties!" said Cheapside. "There ain't no cause fer weepin'. You only did what you 'ad to!"

Milly shook the tears from her eyes and nudged Josephine with her nose.

"Cheapside's right," she said. "It wasn't our fault."

With the stopping of the coach, the thief managed to turn the handle on the door and man and dogs tumbled out onto the dusty road. He tried to get onto his feet to make a break for freedom but the dogs piled on him and knocked him to the ground again. Pippinella and Cheapside kept making short dives at his head, pecking him on the ears and generally worrying him into complete confusion.

"'Elp! 'Elp!" yelled the frightened man. "Call off your dogs! I'll come quiet like!"

Jack, with carriage whip in hand, stood over the milling mass of dogs and man.

"You're not so brave now," he said, "without your pistol."

Jip, seeing that Mac and his gang had the situation well in hand, was hunting frantically for the bundle of missing papers. With a yelp of joy he found them under the seat of the coach, where the thief had hoped to conceal them.

"Pip! Pip!" he yelled. "Come here! I've found Steve's papers!"

Meanwhile, down the winding road could be seen the rapidly approaching figures of the Doctor and Steve, their jackets billowing out behind them. Pippinella flew to meet them with the good news that the papers had been recovered. The Doctor told Steve what Pippinella had said.

"Good old Pip!" said Steve. "You're the best friend a man ever had."

"Oh, I didn't do anything," replied the canary. "Jip was the one. He's guarding them until you get there."

Again the Doctor interpreted.

When they reached the coach they found Jack trying to persuade Jip to let him have the bundle of papers. Knowing nothing of their history, he naturally supposed they belonged to the man the dogs were holding and that they would disclose his identity.

"Good doggy," Jack was saying as he poked his head into the carriage and tried to remove the bundle. "I won't harm them."

But Jip was adamant. He didn't know Jack—except through

Pippinella—and he wasn't going to take any chances. He growled and bared his teeth at the coachman. But when he saw the Doctor framed in the open carriage doorway he let out a yelp of welcome.

"Thank goodness, you've come!" he said. "I didn't want to have to bite Pip's friend. But I was determined to do it if he insisted on removing Steve's papers."

The Doctor then took the bundle and handed it to Steve.

"Excellent work!" he said to Jip. "I'm proud you. Come—we'll take a look at this rascal who has given us so much trouble."

John Dolittle—with a smile at the comical positions of the dogs

"The dogs all piled helter-skelter on top of the cringing man."

all piled helter-skelter on top of the cringing man—said to Mac:

"You may release him now. I want a word with him."

The dogs untangled themselves, shook their rumpled coats, and came to stand beside the Doctor. As the man got to his feet, the Doctor turned again to Mac.

"You and your friends are excellent hunters," he said. "Not a scratch on your quarry. I want to commend you very highly."

"Thank you, Doctor Dolittle," said the Scottish terrier. "It was a bit difficult—when he got rambunctious—not t'nip his ears. But we remembered what ye said t'us.—Aboot not drawin' blood."

The man, puzzled by the strange maneuvers of the Doctor and Mac—for, of course, they spoke in dog language—turned his head frantically from left to right, looking for a means of escape.

"I wouldn't make any attempts to get way if I were you," said the Doctor. "My friends here would overtake you in a matter of moments. And I'm not so sure I'd caution them against tearing you to pieces this time."

"I didn't mean no 'arm, governor!" whined the man. "I were just lookin' for a place t' get out of the weather when I seen those fellows a'sneakin' around the old mill and a'diggin' under the floor. 'Well,' I says to myself, 'there must be something mighty important in this 'ere mill. I'll stick around and see what it is.'"

By this time everyone—Steve, Jack, Pippinella, and Cheapside—had joined the Doctor and the pack of dogs and were listening to the stranger's story.

"Like I said," continued the man. "I ain't no regular thief. I thought if those papers were so important to somebody else, they might fetch a quid or two if I could find the right person. They weren't no good to me, goodness knows, I couldn't make 'ead nor tail of 'em. All full of political talk—and about foreigners, at that. Please, governor, let me go. I ain't done no 'arm. If I'd 'a knowed this bloke were the rightful owner I'd 'a been 'appy to turn them over to 'im."

Steve and the Doctor exchanged a glance and the window-cleaner, smiling, nodded.

"All right," said the Doctor, to the relief of all the party who were feeling sorry for the man and didn't want to see him punished after all. "You may go. But try and stay out of trouble from now on. The police might not be so lenient with you."

While the man started back up the road toward Wendlemere the Doctor thanked Mac and his friends for their assistance and dismissed them with a promise to return someday and pay them a visit.

Cheapside, perched on top of the coach, spoke to the Doctor.

"Is it 'ome to Puddleby now, Doc?" he asked.

"Yes, Cheapside," replied the Doctor. "It's home to Puddleby at last! I'm ready for a good long rest by the fireside."

"Hoh! Hoh!" laughed the sparrow. "If it's rest you want, Doc, better not go 'ome. The 'ouse looks like a bloomin' 'ospital, it does—since some gossipin' blue jays passed the word around that you might be comin' back. Rabbits with busted paws sleepin' all over the place, 'orses with 'eaves lodgin' two to a stall in the stable, and a sneakin' weasel with her 'ole brood a' nasty little brats coughin' their 'eads off under the 'ouse."

"Oh, dear," sighed the Doctor. "Then I must get there quickly. I'd feel terrible if one of them should die because it hadn't had the proper care."

Jack would listen to nothing else but that he should drive the whole party home to Puddleby.

"Oh, I couldn't let you do that," said John Dolittle. "You see, we must go to Greenheath first and collect the rest of my family."

"Well, that's all right," the coachman said. "Greenheath is on the way to Puddleby."

"But there must be other passengers on the road waiting for you at this very moment," said the Doctor.

"Probably," said Jack. "But I'm so late now it doesn't matter. The twelve o'clock coach will be along shortly and can pick up anyone bound for London. Besides," Jack continued, "you saved my life and I'd like to show my gratitude in some small way. Hop in, and we'll get started."

"Well," said the Doctor, hesitating. "If you're sure it will be all right, we'd be delighted to go home in such splendor. My, my! Our own private coach! Won't Gub-Gub be surprised? Come along, Steve and Pippinella."

"We don't want to be a bother, Doctor," said the window-cleaner. "Pip and I can go up to London and—"

"Nonsense!" declared the Doctor. "There's plenty of room at Puddleby. You can finish your book and enjoy some of Dab-Dab's excellent cooking at the same time. There is nothing she likes better than to have a company of hungry people around her table. Now, now," he continued as Steve began to protest further. "I won't hear of anything else. Get aboard everybody. We're off for Greenheath and home—home to Puddleby at last!"

The End